WAR AND PEACE

BARNES
& NOBLE
CLASSICS

WAR AND PEACE

Leo Tolstoy

BARNES
&NOBLE
BOOKS
NEW YORK

This edition of *War & Peace* has been translated and abridged by
Princess Alexandra Kropotkin.

This edition published by Barnes & Noble, Inc.

1993 Barnes & Noble Books

ISBN 1-56619-027-4 *casebound*
ISBN 1-56619-307-9 *paperback*

Printed and bound in the United States of America

MC 11 10 9 8 7 6 5 4 3
MP 9 8 7 6 5 4 3 2 1

Contents

1805

For thirteen years, off and on, there has been war in Europe; but now, in 1805, there is an uneasy peace. The European monarchs, who took arms in fright against the revolution that overthrew the Bourbon king of France, have had no success against the military genius of Napoleon Bonaparte. Only Britain, supreme by sea, remains at war with France; Russia, Austria, the other powers have withdrawn. Napoleon has illegally seized and summarily executed the young Duc d'Enghien, Bourbon heir, and has crowned himself Emperor of the French. While the royal courts of Europe scoff at his pretensions (and call him Buonaparte to imply that he is neither royal nor even a Frenchman), Napoleon expands his empire. He prepares to invade England. He annexes the republics of Liguria (Genoa) and Lucca on the Italian peninsula. The European powers, fearful of losing their own territories, think once more of war.

Part First

"WELL, prince, Genoa and Lucca are now nothing more than estates of the Bonaparte family. I warn you that if you do not tell me we are going to have war, if you still allow yourself to condone all the infamies, all the atrocities, of this Antichrist—on my word I believe he is Antichrist—I will not recognize you; that is the end of our friendship; you shall no longer be my faithful slave, as you call yourself. There now, cheer up, cheer up, I see I frighten you. Come, sit down and tell me about it."

Thus on a July evening in 1805 the well-known Anna Pavlovna Scherer, maid of honor and confidential friend of the Empress Maria Feodorovna, greeted the influential statesman Prince Vasili Kuragin, who was the first to arrive at her reception.

Anna Pavlovna had been coughing for several days; she had the grippe, as she called it—grippe being then a new word used only by a few.

Her notes of invitation, distributed that morning by a footman in red livery, had been written all alike to all:

Count (or prince), if you have nothing better to do, and if the prospect of an evening with a poor invalid is not too frightful, I shall be very glad to see you tonight at my house between seven and ten.

ANNA SCHERER.

"Oh! what a cruel attack!" exclaimed the prince, as he came forward in his embroidered court uniform, stockings, and diamond-buckled shoes, and with an expression of serenity on his fleshy face: he was not in the least disturbed by this reception.

He spoke that elegant French in which Russians formerly not only talked but also thought. He went up to Anna Pavlovna, kissed her hand, bending down to it his perfumed and polished bald head, and then he seated himself comfortably on the divan.

"First tell me how you are feeling; calm your friend's anxiety," said he, not altering the tone of his voice, which, in spite of the gallant and sympathetic nature of his remark, still betrayed indifference and even raillery.

"How can one be well—when one's moral sensibilities are so tormented? How in these days can anyone with feelings remain calm?" exclaimed Anna Pavlovna. "You will spend the evening with me, I hope?"

"But the English ambassador's reception? I must show myself there," said the prince. "My daughter is coming for me, to take me there."

"I thought that reception had been postponed. I confess all these fêtes and fireworks are beginning to grow tiresome!"

"If they had known you wished it, they would have postponed the reception."

Prince Vasili always spoke indolently, like an actor rehearsing an old part. Anna Pavlovna, on the contrary, in spite of her forty years, was full of vivacity and impulses. In fact, her peculiar social position depended upon her unfailing enthusiasm.

"À propos," she said, "this evening two very interesting men will be here: the Viscount de Montemart, connected with the Montmorencys through the Rohans, one of the best families in France. He is one of the decent emigrants of the genuine sort. And then the Abbé Morio; do you know that profound mind? He has been received by the sovereign."

"Ah! I shall be most happy," said the prince. "But tell me," he went on to say, as if something occurred to him for the first time, whereas in reality the matter was the chief object of his visit, "is it true that the dowager empress wishes Baron Funke to be named as first secretary at Vienna? It seems to me that this baron is a wretched creature."

Prince Vasili was anxious for his son to get this appointment, which others were trying to secure for the baron through the influence of the Empress Maria Feodorovna.

Anna Pavlovna almost closed her eyes, to signify that neither she nor anyone else could tell what would satisfy or please the empress.

"Baron Funke was recommended to the dowager empress by her sister," said she in a dry, melancholy tone. Whenever Anna Pavlovna spoke of the empress, her face suddenly assumed a deep and genuine expression of devotion and deference tinged with melancholy, and this was characteristic of her at all times when she was reminded of her august patroness.

The prince said nothing and looked indifferent. Anna Pavlovna, with feminine quickness and a courtly dexterity characteristic of her, wished to give the prince a rap because he had dared to speak in dispraise of a person recommended to the empress, and at the same time to console him. "But speaking of your family," she added, "do you know that your daughter, since she came out, has roused the enthusiasm of our best society? She is considered to be as lovely as the day."

The prince bowed in token of his respect and gratitude.

"I often think," pursued Anna Pavlovna after a moment's silence, drawing a little closer to the prince and giving him a flattering smile, as if to imply that nothing more was to be said about politics and society, but that now they might have a confidential chat: "I often think how unfairly the good things of life are distributed. Why should fate have given you two such splendid children? I don't count Anatol, your youngest, I don't like him," she said decisively, and raising her brows. "Between you and me [here her face assumed its melancholy expression], they have been talking about him at her majesty's, and they feel sorry for you."

The prince made no reply, but she paused and looked at him significantly while waiting for his answer. He frowned.

"What do you wish me to do!" he exclaimed at last. "You know I have done everything for their education that a father can do, and both have turned out imbeciles. Ippolit is at least only an inoffensive idiot, but Anatol is a nuisance. There is that difference between them," said he, with a smile more natural and animated than usual, and at the same time very distinctly displaying an unexpectedly coarse and disagreeable expression in the wrinkles around his mouth.

Anna Pavlovna was lost in thought.

"Has it never occurred to you to find a wife for your prodigal son? They say old maids have a mania for matchmaking; I am not as yet conscious of this weakness, but I know a young girl who is very unhappy with her father; she is a relative of ours, Princess Bolkonsky."

Prince Vasili made no reply, but the motion of his head showed that, with the swiftness of calculation and memory characteristic of men of the world, he was taking her suggestion into consideration.

"Did you know that this Anatol costs me forty thousand a year?" said he, evidently unable to restrain the painful current of his thoughts. He hesitated: "What will it be five years hence, if it goes at this rate? That is the advantage of being a father. Is she rich, this princess of yours?"

"Her father is very rich and stingy. He lives in the country. You know, he is that famous Prince Bolkonsky, who retired during the lifetime of the late emperor. He was nicknamed 'The King of Prussia.' He is a man of genius, but full of whims and very trying. The poor little girl is as unhappy as she can be. She has a brother who recently married Lisa Meinen. He is on Kutuzof's staff. He will be here this evening."

"Listen, my dear Annette," said the prince, suddenly taking his companion's hand and bending it down for some reason. "Arrange this business for me, and I will be your most faithful slave forever and ever. She is of good family and rich—that is all I require."

And with that easy and natural grace for which he was distinguished, he raised her hand, kissed it, and having kissed it, still retained it in his, while he settled back in his armchair and looked to one side.

"Just wait!" said Anna Pavlovna, after a moment of consideration. "I will speak about it this evening to Lisa (young Bolkonsky's wife), and perhaps it can be arranged. I shall begin my old maid's apprenticeship in your family."

II

ANNA PAVLOVNA's drawing-room gradually began to be filled. The highest aristocracy of Petersburg came; people most widely differing in age and in character, but alike in that they all belonged to the same class of society. Prince Vasili's daughter, the beautiful Helene, came, in order to go with her father to the ambassador's reception. She was in ball dress and wore the imperial decoration. There came also the little, young Princess Bolkonsky, known as "the most fascinating woman in Petersburg." She had been married during the winter before, and now, owing to her condition, had ceased to appear at large entertainments, but still went to small receptions. Prince Ippolit, Prince Vasili's son, came with Montemart, whom he was introducing. The Abbé Morio and many others also came.

The young Princess Bolkonsky had brought some work in a gold-embroidered velvet bag. Her pretty little upper lip, just shaded by an almost imperceptible down, was rather short, but all the more fascinating when it displayed her teeth, and more fascinating still when she drew it down a little and closed it against the underlip. As is always the case with perfectly charming women, her defect of a short lip and a half-open mouth seemed like a distinction, her peculiar beauty.

"I have brought my work," she said, opening her reticule, and addressing the whole company in French. "Now see here, Annette, don't play a naughty trick on me," she went on, turning to the hostess. "You wrote me that it was to be a little informal soirée; see how unsuitably I am dressed!"

And she spread out her arms so as to display her elegant gray gown trimmed with lace and belted high with a wide ribbon.

"Do not be disturbed, Lisa," replied Anna Pavlovna, "you will always be the most beautiful of all."

"You know my husband is deserting me," continued the young princess,

4

still in French, and addressing a general. "He is going to meet his death. Tell me, why this wretched war?" she added, this time speaking to Prince Vasili; and without waiting for his rejoinder, she made some remark to Prince Vasili's daughter, the handsome Helene.

"What a charming creature that little princess is!" whispered Prince Vasili to Anna Pavlovna.

Shortly after the young princess' arrival, a huge, stout young man came in. His head was close-cropped, he had on eyeglasses, and he wore stylish light trousers, an immense frill, and a cinnamon-colored coat. This stout young man was the illegitimate son of Count Bezukhof, a famous grandee of Catherine's time, now lying at the point of death in Moscow. He had not as yet entered any branch of the service, having just returned from abroad, where he had been educated, and this was his first appearance in society. Anna Pavlovna welcomed him with a nod reserved for men of the very least importance in the hierarchy of her salon. But notwithstanding this greeting, almost contemptuous in its way, Anna Pavlovna's face, as Pierre came toward her, expressed anxiety and dismay such as one experiences at the sight of anything too huge and out of place. Pierre was indeed rather taller than anyone else in the room, but her dismay may have been caused only by the young man's intelligent, and at the same time diffident, glance, so honest and keen that it distinguished him from everyone else in the room.

"It is very kind of you, Monsieur Pierre, to come and see a poor invalid," said Anna Pavlovna.

Pierre blurted out some incoherent reply, and continued to let his eyes wander around the assembly. He smiled with pleasure and bowed to the little princess as if she were an intimate friend.

Anna Pavlovna walked up and down her drawing-room, and as she came to some group that was silent, or that was talking too excitedly, by a single word or a slight transposition set the talking machine in regular decorous running order again. But while she was occupied with these labors, it could be seen that she was in especial dread of Pierre. She watched him anxiously while he went to listen to what was said in the circle around Montemart, and then joined another group where the abbé was discoursing.

Pierre knew that all the intellect of Petersburg was gathered here, and like a child in a toy show he kept his eyes open. He was all the time afraid of missing some clever conversation that might interest him. As he saw the assured and refined expressions on the faces of those gathered here, he was ever on the lookout for something especially intellectual. He stood waiting a chance to air his opinions, as young men are fond of doing.

In Montemart's circle they had immediately begun to discuss the murder of Duc d'Enghien. The viscount maintained that the duke had fallen a victim of his own magnanimity, and that there had been personal reasons for Bonaparte's ill will.

"Ah! there now, tell us about it, viscount," said Anna Pavlovna eagerly. The viscount bowed in token of submission, and smiled urbanely. Anna

5

Pavlovna made her circle close in around the viscount, and invited all to hear his account.

"Come over here, dear Helene," she said to the lovely young princess, who was seated at some little distance, the center of a second group.

Princess Elena stood up, smiling that unchanging smile with which she first came into the room—the smile of a perfectly beautiful woman. With the rustle of her white ball dress, ornamented with smilax and moss, with shoulders gleaming white, with glossy hair and flashing gems, she made her way through the ranks of men, who stood aside to let her pass; and not looking at anyone in particular, but smiling on all as though amiably granting each one the privilege of admiring the beauty of her form, of her plump shoulders, of her beautiful bosom and back, exposed by the low cut of dress then in vogue, seeming to personify the radiance of festivity, she crossed straight over to Anna Pavlovna. Helene was so lovely that not only did she display no shade of coquetry but even seemed to be conscience-stricken at her indubitable and all-conquering maidenly beauty. She seemed to have the will but not the power to diminish the effect of her loveliness.

"What a beautiful girl!" was remarked by all who saw her.

The viscount, as if overwhelmed by something extraordinary, shrugged his shoulders and dropped his eyes as she took her seat in front of him and turned upon him the radiance of that perpetual smile.

"Madame, I fear my ability is not on a par with such an audience," he said, inclining his head with a smile.

The young princess rested her bare round arm on the table, and did not think she needed to reply. She smiled and waited.

The viscount gave a very clever rendering of an anecdote at that time going the rounds, to the effect that the Duc d'Enghien had gone secretly to Paris to see Mlle. George, and there met Bonaparte, who also enjoyed the favors of the famous actress; and that Napoleon on meeting the duke there happened to fall into one of the epileptic fits to which he was subject, and thus came into the duke's power; but the duke refrained from taking advantage of it, while Bonaparte revenged himself for such magnanimity by compassing the duke's death. The story was very nice and interesting, especially at the place where the rivals suddenly recognize each other, and the ladies, it appeared, were moved.

"Charming!" exclaimed Anna Pavlovna.

"Charming," whispered the little princess, looking for her needle in her work, as if to signify that the interest and fascination of the story had prevented her from going on with her sewing.

A new personage appeared in the drawing-room. This new personage was young Prince Andrei Bolkonsky, the husband of the little princess. Prince Bolkonsky was a very handsome young man of medium height, with strongly marked and stern features. Everything about him, from the dull and weary expression of his eyes to the measured deliberation of his step, presented a striking contrast to his lively little wife. He was not only acquainted, it seemed, with *everyone* in the room, but found *them* so tedious that even to look at them and hear their voices was a great bore. Of all the tiresome faces, the face of his lovely little wife apparently bored him most. With a grimace that disfigured his handsome face, he turned away from her. He kissed Anna Pavlovna's hand, and with half-closed eyes looked around at the assembly.

"So you are getting ready for war, prince?" asked Anna Pavlovna.

"General Kutuzof has been kind enough to desire me as his aide-de-camp."

He spoke in French and, like a Frenchman, accented the last syllable of Kutuzof's name.

"And Lisa, your wife?"

"She will go into the country."

"Isn't it a sin for you to deprive us of your charming wife?"

"Andrei," exclaimed the little princess, addressing her husband in the same coquettish tone that she employed toward strangers, "such a fascinating story the viscount has been telling us about Mlle. George and Bonaparte!"

Prince Andrei frowned and turned away. Pierre, who from the moment when Prince Andrei entered the room had not taken his merry kindly eyes from him, now came up and took him by the arm. Prince Andrei, without looking round, again contracted his face into a grimace expressing annoyance that anyone should touch his arm; but when he saw Pierre's smiling face, he smiled with an unexpectedly kind and pleasant smile.

"What is this! You also in gay society?" said he to Pierre.

"I knew that you would be here," replied Pierre. "I will go home to supper with you," he added in a whisper, so as not to disturb the viscount, who was proceeding with his story; "may I?"

"No, it's impossible!" said Prince Andrei, laughing, and by a pressure of the hand giving Pierre to understand that he had no need of asking such a question.

He had something more on the tip of his tongue, but at this moment Prince Vasili and his daughter arose and the two young men stood aside to give them room to pass. Princess Elena, gracefully holding the folds of her dress, made her way among the chairs, and the smile on her lovely face was more radiant than ever. Pierre looked with almost startled, enthusiastic eyes at the beauty as she passed by him.

"Very handsome," said Prince Andrei.

"Very," said Pierre.

As he went by, Prince Vasili seized Pierre by the hand and turned to Anna Pavlovna.

"Train this bear for me," said he. "Here he has been living a month at my house, and this is the first time that I have seen him in society. Nothing is so advantageous for a young man as the society of clever women."

III

An ELDERLY lady jumped up hastily and followed Prince Vasili into the entry. Her face lost all its former pretense of interest. Her kind, tear-worn face expressed only anxiety and alarm.

"What can you tell me, prince, about my Boris?" she said, as she followed him. "I cannot stay any longer in Petersburg. Tell me what tidings I can take to my poor boy."

Although Prince Vasili's manner in listening to the old lady was reluctant and almost uncivil, and even showed impatience, still she gave him a flattering and affectionate smile and took his arm to keep him from going.

"What would it cost you to say a word to the emperor; and then he would be at once admitted to the Guards!" she added.

"Be assured that I will do all I can, princess," replied Prince Vasili; "but it is hard for me to ask his majesty: I would advise you to appeal to Rumyantsof through Prince Galitsin. That would be wiser."

The elderly lady was Princess Anna Mikhailovna Drubetskoy, and belonged to one of the best families in Russia, but she was poor, had long been out of society, and had lost her former connections. She had now come to town to secure the admittance of her only son into the Imperial Guards. Merely for the sake of meeting Prince Vasili, she had accepted Anna Pavlovna's invitation and come to the reception. Her once handsome face expressed vexation, but this lasted only an instant. She smiled again and clasped Prince Vasili's arm more firmly.

"Listen, prince," she said, "I have never asked anything of you, and I never shall ask anything of you again and I have never reminded you of the friendship that my father had for you. But now I beg of you, in God's name, do this for my son—and I will look upon you as our benefactor," she added hastily. "No, don't be angry, but promise me this. I have asked Galitsin; he refused. Be kind as you used to be!" she said, trying to smile, though the tears were in her eyes.

"Papa, we shall be late," said Princess Elena, turning her lovely head on her classic shoulders as she stood waiting at the door.

Now influence in society is a capital which has to be economized lest it be exhausted. Prince Vasili understood this, and having once come to the conclusion that if he asked favors for everybody who applied to him, it would soon be impossible to ask anything for himself, he rarely exerted his influence. Princess Drubetskoy's last appeal, however, caused him to feel something like a pang of conscience. She reminded him of the fact that he owed to her father his first advancement in his career. Moreover, he saw by her manner that she was one of those women, notably mothers, who, having once got a notion into their heads, do not desist until their desires are gratified, and in case they fail are ready every day, every moment, with fresh urgencies and even scenes. This last consideration turned the scale with him.

"Dear princess," said he, with his usual familiarity and with ill-humor in his voice; "it is almost impossible for me to do what you wish; but to show you how fond I am of you, and how much I honor your father's memory, I will do the impossible; your son shall be admitted to the Guards, here is my hand on it. Are you satisfied?"

"My dear, you are our benefactor. I expected nothing less from you—I knew how kind you were." He started to go. "Wait, two words more. When once he is admitted . . ." she hesitated. "You and Mikhail Ilarionovitch Kutuzof are good friends, do recommend Boris to him as aide-de-camp. Then I should be content, and then—"

Prince Vasili smiled.

"That I will not promise. You have no idea how Kutuzof has been besieged since he was appointed commander-in-chief. He himself told me that all the ladies of Moscow had offered him all their sons as adjutants."

"No, promise me; I will not let you go, my dear friend, my benefactor—"

"Papa," again insisted the beautiful Helene, in the same tone, "we shall be late."

"Well, au revoir, good-by. Do you see?"

"Then tomorrow you will speak to the emperor?"

"Without fail, but I cannot promise about Kutuzof."

"No, but promise, promise, Vasili," insisted Anna Mikhailovna, with a coquettish smile which perhaps in days long gone might have been becoming to her, but now ill suited her haggard face. She returned to the group where the viscount was still telling stories, and again she pretended to listen, though she was anxiously waiting for the time to go, now that her purpose was accomplished.

"If Bonaparte remains a year longer on the throne of France, things will have gone quite too far," the viscount was saying, like a man who, without listening to others, and considering himself the best informed on any subject, insists on following the lead of his own thoughts. "By intrigue, violence, proscriptions and capital punishment, society, I mean good society, French society, will be utterly destroyed, and then—"

"I have recently heard," remarked Pierre, with a flushed face venturing to take part in the conversation, "that almost all the nobility have gone over to Bonaparte."

"Not at all," said the viscount. "After the murder of the duke, even the most partial ceased to look on him as a hero."

"The punishment of the Duc d'Enghien," said Pierre, "was an imperial necessity, and I for one regard it as magnanimous of Napoleon not to hesitate to assume the sole responsibility for this act."

"*Dieu! mon Dieu!*" exclaimed Anna Pavlovna, in a whisper of dismay.

"What, Monsieur Pierre! you see magnanimity in assassination?" exclaimed the little princess, smiling and moving her work nearer to her.

"Ah! . . . Oh!" said different voices.

9

The viscount merely shrugged his shoulders.

Pierre looked triumphantly at the company over his spectacles.

"I say this," he went on to explain, in a sort of desperation, "because the Bourbons fled from the revolution, leaving their people a prey to anarchy. And Napoleon was the only man able to understand the revolution, to conquer it; and consequently, for the sake of the general good, he could not hesitate over the life of an individual."

"Don't you want to come over to this table?" suggested Anna Pavlovna.

But Pierre, without heeding her, went on with his discourse.

"No," said he, growing more and more excited, "Napoleon is great because he stands superior to the revolution, because he has stamped out its abuses, preserving all that was good—the equality of citizens, and freedom of speech and of the press, and only thus he gained power."

"Yes, if, when he gained the power, instead of using it for assassination, he had restored it to the legitimate king," said the viscount, "then I would have called him a great man."

"But he could not do that. The power was granted him by the people solely that he might deliver them from the Bourbons, and because they saw that he was a great man. The revolution was a mighty fact," continued Monsieur Pierre, betraying by this desperate and forced proposition his extreme youth and his propensity to speak out whatever was in his mind.

"Revolution and regicide are mighty facts! . . . After this . . . but will you not come over to this table?" insisted Anna Pavlovna.

"I am not talking about regicide, I am talking about ideas."

"Yes, ideas of pillage, murder, and regicide," suggested an ironical voice.

"Those are the extremes, of course, and the real significance is not in such things, but in the rights of man, in emancipation from prejudices, in equality of the citizens; and all these principles Napoleon has preserved in all their integrity."

"Liberty and equality!" exclaimed the viscount scornfully, as if he had at last made up his mind seriously to prove to this young man all the foolishness of his arguments. "All high-sounding words which long ago were shown to be dangerous. Who does not love liberty and equality? Our Saviour himself preached liberty and equality. But after the revolution were men any happier? On the contrary! We wanted freedom, and Bonaparte has destroyed it."

Prince Andrei with a smile looked now at Pierre, now at the viscount, now at the hostess. During the first instant of Pierre's outbreak, Anna Pavlovna was appalled, notwithstanding her experience in society; but when she saw that Pierre's sacrilegious utterances did not make the viscount lose his temper, and when she became convinced that it was impossible to check them, she collected her forces, and taking the viscount's side, she attacked the young orator.

"But, my dear Monsieur Pierre," said Anna Pavlovna, "how can you call

a man great who can put to death a duke—simply a man, when you come to analyze it—without trial and without cause?"

"And the prisoners in Africa, whom he killed?" suggested the little princess. "That was horrible!" and she shrugged her shoulders.

"He is a low fellow, whatever you may say."

Monsieur Pierre did not know which one to answer; he looked at them all and smiled. His smile was unlike other men's, falsely compounded of seriousness. Whenever a smile came on his face, the serious and even stern expression suddenly vanished and in its place came another, genial, frank, and like that of a child asking forgiveness.

Suddenly Prince Ippolit arose, and with a gesture of his hand detaining the company, and begging them to be seated, he went on to say:

"Oh, I was told today such a charming Russian story. I must give you the benefit of it. You will excuse me, viscount, I must tell it in Russian. Otherwise, the flavor of the story will be lost."

And Prince Ippolit began to speak in Russian, with much the same fluency as Frenchmen who have spent a year in Russia usually attain. All stopped to listen, because Prince Ippolit had been so strenuously urgent in attracting their attention to his story.

"In Moscow there is a lady, *une dame,* and she is very miserly. She has to have two footmen behind her carriage. And very tall ones. That was her hobby. And she had a chambermaid, who was also very tall. She said—" Here Prince Ippolit paused to think, evidently at a loss to collect his wits.

"She said—yes, she said, 'Girl (to her *femme de chambre*), put on a livery and go with me, behind the carriage, and make some calls.'"

Here Prince Ippolit snickered and laughed long before his hearers, and their silence produced a very disheartening effect upon the narrator. However, a few, including the elderly lady and Anna Pavlovna, smiled.

"She drove off. Suddenly a strong wind blew up. The girl lost her hat and her long hair came down."

Here he could not hold in any longer, but through his bursts of broken laughter he managed to say these words: "And everyone knew about it."

That was the end of the anecdote. Although it was incomprehensible why he told it, and why he felt called on to tell it in Russian rather than French, still Anna Pavlovna and the others appreciated Prince Ippolit's cleverness in so agreeably putting an end to Monsieur Pierre's disagreeable and stupid outburst.

After the anecdote, the company broke up into little groups, busily engaged in insignificant small talk about some ball that had been or some ball that was to be, or the theater, or when and where they should meet again.

IV

CONGRATULATING Anna Pavlovna on what they called her charming soirée, the guests began to take their departure.

Pierre, as we have already said, was awkward. Stout, of more than average height, broad-shouldered, with huge red hands, he had no idea of the proper way to enter a drawing-room, and still less the proper way of making his exit; in other words, he did not know how to make some especially agreeable remark to his hostess before taking his leave. Moreover, he was absentminded. He got up, and instead of taking his own hat he seized the plumed three-cornered hat of some general and held it, pulling at the feathers until the general came and asked him to surrender it. But all his absent-mindedness and clumsiness about entering a drawing-room and about suitable subjects of conversation were redeemed by his expression of genuine goodness, simplicity, and modesty.

Anna Pavlovna turned to him, and with Christian sweetness expressing her forgiveness for his behavior, nodded to him, and said, "I hope I shall see you again, but I hope also that you will change your opinions, my dear Monsieur Pierre."

He could find no words to answer her; he only bowed, and let everyone again see his smile, which really said nothing except this: "Opinions are opinions, and you can see what a good and noble young man I am." And all, Anna Pavlovna included, could not help feeling this.

Prince Andrei went into the anteroom, allowed the lackey to throw his mantle over his shoulders, and with cool indifference listened to the chatter of his wife and Prince Ippolit, who had also come into the anteroom.

Prince Ippolit stood near the pretty little princess, and stared straight at her through his lorgnette.

"Go back, Annette, you will take cold," said the little princess, by way of farewell to Anna Pavlovna. "It is all understood," she added, in an undertone.

Anna Pavlovna had already had a chance to speak a word with Lisa about the suggested match between Anatol and the little princess' sister-in-law.

"I shall depend upon you, my dear," said Anna Pavlovna, also in an undertone. "You write to her and tell me how her father will look at it. Au revoir." And she went back from the anteroom.

"I am very glad that I did not go to the ambassador's," said Prince Ippolit. "A bore—we've had a lovely evening, haven't we? Lovely."

"They say it will be a very fine ball," replied the princess, curling her downy lip. "All the pretty women in society will be there."

"Not all, because you are not there, certainly not all," said Prince Ippolit, gaily laughing; and taking the shawl from the servant, he pushed him away and began to wrap it around the princess. Either through awkwardness or

intentionally (no one could tell which), it was a long time before he took his arms away from her, even after the shawl was well wrapped round her, and he seemed to be embracing the young woman.

Prince Andrei's eyes were closed; he seemed so tired and sleepy!

"Excuse me, sir," he said in a cold, disagreeable tone, addressing Prince Ippolit, who stood in his way.

"I shall expect you, Pierre," said the same voice, but warmly and affectionately.

The postilion whipped up the horses and the carriage rolled noisily away. Prince Ippolit laughed nervously, as he stood on the steps, waiting for the viscount, whom he had promised to take home.

"Well, my dear fellow, your little princess is charming, very charming," said the viscount, as he took his seat in the carriage with Ippolit; "yes, indeed, she's charming." He kissed the tips of his fingers. "And really quite Frenchy." Ippolit roared with laughter.

"And do you know, you are terrible with your little innocent ways," continued the viscount. "I pity the poor husband—that little officer who puts on the airs of a reigning prince."

Ippolit again went off into a burst of laughter, through which he managed to articulate:

"And yet you said that the Russian ladies were not anywhere equal to the French ladies! One must know how to manage them."

Pierre, being the first to reach the house, went into Prince Andrei's own room like one thoroughly at home, and immediately stretched himself out on the divan, as his habit was, took up the first book that he found on the shelf—it was *Cæsar's Commentaries*—and leaning on his elbow began to read in the middle of the volume.

"What have you been doing to Mlle. Scherer? She will be quite sick now," said Prince Andrei, coming into the room and rubbing his small white hands together.

Pierre turned over with his whole body, making the divan creak, looked up at Prince Andrei with an eager face, smiled and waved his hand.

"It is not good form, my dear fellow, always and everywhere to say what you think. But have you come to any final decision yet as to your career? Will you be a horse-guardsman or a diplomat?" asked Prince Andrei after a moment's silence.

Pierre sat up on the divan, doubling his legs under him.

"Imagine, I have not the slightest idea yet. Neither one pleases me."

Pierre at the age of ten had been sent abroad with an abbé for a tutor, and had remained there till he was twenty. On his return to Moscow, his father dismissed the abbé and said to the young man:

"Now go to Petersburg, look about, and take your choice. I give my consent to anything. Here is a letter to Prince Vasili, and here is money for you. Write me about everything, and I will help you."

Pierre had been trying for three months to choose a career, and had not succeeded.

"That is all nonsense," said Prince Andrei, stopping him short; "let's talk about your affairs. Have you been to the Horse Guards?"

"No, not yet, but here is an idea that occurred to me and I wanted to tell you; now there is war against Napoleon. If it had been a war for freedom, I would have taken part, I would have been the first to enter the military service; but to help England and Austria against the greatest man in the world, that is not good."

Prince Andrei merely shrugged his shoulders at Pierre's childish talk. He pretended that it was impossible to reply to such stupidities, but in reality it was difficult to treat this naive statement in any other way.

"If all men made war only for their convictions, there would be no war," said he.

"That would be splendid," said Pierre.

Prince Andrei laughed.

"Very likely it would be splendid, but it will never be."

"Now, why are you going to war?" asked Pierre.

"Why? I don't know. It must be so. Besides, I'm going—" he paused. "I am going because the life I lead here, my life, is not to my taste."

V

THE RUSTLE of a woman's gown was heard in the adjoining room. As if caught napping, Prince Andrei shook himself, and his face assumed the same expression it had worn in Anna Pavlovna's drawing-room. Pierre put his feet down from the sofa. The princess came in. She had already changed her gown for another, a house dress, but equally fresh and elegant. Prince Andrei got up and courteously pushed forward an easy-chair.

"Why is it, I often wonder," she remarked, speaking as always in French, and at the same time briskly and spryly sitting down in the easy-chair, "why Annette never married? How stupid you all are, messieurs, that you never married her. You will excuse me for saying so, but you have not the slightest notion how to talk with women. What an arguer you are, Monsieur Pierre."

"Your husband and I were just this moment arguing. I cannot understand why he wants to go to war," said Pierre, addressing the princess without any of the embarrassment so commonly shown in the relations of a young man toward a young woman.

The princess gave a start. Evidently Pierre's words touched her to the quick.

"Ah, that is exactly what I say!" said she. "I do not understand, really I do not understand why men cannot live without war. Why is it that we women do not want it and do not need it at all? Everybody knows him.

Everybody esteems him. He might very easily be even one of his majesty's aides. You know the emperor spoke very cordially with him. Annette and I have talked it all over; it might be very easily arranged. What do you think?"

Pierre glanced at Prince Andrei, and seeing that this conversation did not please his friend, made no reply to her.

"When are you going?" he asked.

"Ah! don't speak of going, don't speak of it. I do not wish to hear a word of it!" exclaimed the princess, in the same capriciously vivacious tone in which she had spoken to Ippolit. It was obviously out of place in the family circle, in which Pierre was an adopted member.

"Today when it came over me that I had to break off from all these pleasant relations—and then, you know, Andrei"—she blinked her eyes significantly at her husband. "I dread it, I dread it," she whispered, making a shiver run down her back.

Her husband looked at her with a surprised expression, as if for the first time he had noticed that anyone besides himself and Pierre had come into the room. Then with a cool politeness he addressed his wife, inquiringly: "What is it that you dread, Lisa? I cannot understand," said he.

"Now how selfish all you men are, all, all selfish. Simply from his own whim, God knows why, he deserts me, shuts me up in the country alone."

"With my father and sister, don't forget that," said Prince Andrei, gently.

"All alone, just the same, away from my friends—and he expects me not to be afraid."

Her tone grew querulous; her lip was lifted, so that her face looked not mirthful, but repulsive and like a squirrel's. She paused, as if she regarded it as indecorous to speak of her condition before Pierre, though this was the real secret of her fear.

"And still I do not understand what you dread," said Prince Andrei deliberately, not taking his eyes from his wife.

The princess blushed and spread open her hands with a gesture of despair.

"No, Andrei, I insist upon it, you have changed so!"

"Your doctor bids you go to bed earlier," said Prince Andrei. "You had better retire."

The princess made no answer, and suddenly her short downy lip trembled; Prince Andrei, shrugging his shoulders, began to walk up and down the room.

Pierre gazed through his glasses with naive curiosity, first at him, then at the princess, and made a motion as if he also would get up, but then changed his mind.

"What difference does it make to me if Monsieur Pierre is here!" suddenly exclaimed the little princess, and her pretty face at the same time was contracted into a tearful grimace. "I have been wanting for a long time to ask you, Andrei, why you have changed toward me so? What have I done to you? You are going to the army, you do not pity me at all. Why is it?"

"Lisa!" exclaimed Prince Andrei, but this one word carried an entreaty,

15

a threat, and above all a conviction that she herself would regret what she had said; but she went on hurriedly:

"You treat me as if I were ill or a child. I see it all. You were not so six months ago."

"Lisa, I beg of you to stop," said Prince Andrei, still more earnestly.

Pierre, growing more and more agitated as this conversation proceeded, arose and went to the princess. He evidently could not endure the sight of tears, and he himself was ready to weep.

"Calm yourself, princess. This is only your fancy, because, I assure you, I myself have experienced . . . and so . . . because . . . No, excuse me, a stranger is in the way . . . No, calm yourself . . . good-by."

Prince Andrei detained him, taking him by the arm:

"No, stay, Pierre. The princess is so kind that she will not have the heart to deprive me of the pleasure of spending the rest of the evening with you."

"Yes, he only thinks about his own pleasure!" exclaimed the princess, not restraining her angry tears.

"Lisa," said Prince Andrei, dryly, raising his voice sufficiently to show that his patience was exhausted.

Suddenly the angry, squirrel-like expression on the princess' pretty little face changed to one of alarm, both fascinating and provocative of sympathy; her beautiful eyes looked from under her long lashes at her husband, and there came into her face that timid look of subjection a dog has when it wags its drooping tail quickly but doubtfully.

"*Mon Dieu! Mon Dieu!*" muttered the princess, and gathering up the skirt of her dress with one hand, she went to her husband and kissed him on the forehead.

"Good night, Lisa," said Prince Andrei, getting up and courteously kissing her hand as if she were a stranger.

The friends were silent. Neither felt like being the first to speak. Pierre looked at Prince Andrei; Prince Andrei rubbed his forehead with his slender hand.

"Let's have some supper," said he with a sigh, getting up and going to the door.

They went into the dining room, elegantly, newly and richly furnished in the latest style. Everything, from the napkins to the silver, the china, and the glassware, had that peculiar imprint of newness characteristic of the establishment of a young couple. In the midst of supper Prince Andrei leaned forward on his elbows, and, like a man who has for a long time had something on his heart and suddenly determines to confess it, he began to talk with an expression of nervous exasperation such as Pierre had never before beheld in his friend:

"Never, never get married, my friend! This is my advice to you. Do not marry until you have come to the conclusion that you have done all it is in your power to do, and until you have ceased to love the woman whom you have chosen, until you have seen clearly what she is; otherwise you will make a sad and irreparable mistake. When you are old and good for nothing, then get married. . . . Otherwise, all that is good and noble in you will be thrown away. All will be wasted in trifles. Yes, yes, yes! Don't look at me in such amazement. If ever you have any hope of anything ahead of you, you will be made to feel at every step that, as far as you are concerned, all is at an end, all closed to you, except the drawing-room, where you will rank with court lackeys and idiots. That's a fact!"

He waved his hand energetically.

Pierre took off his spectacles, and this made his face, as he gazed in amazement at his friend, even more expressive than usual of his goodness of heart.

"My wife," continued Prince Andrei, "is a lovely woman. She is one of those few women to whom a man can feel that his honor is safely intrusted; but, my God! what would I not give at this moment if I were not married! You are the first and only person to whom I have said this, and it is because I love you."

Prince Andrei, in saying this, was still less like the Bolkonsky who, that same evening, had been sitting in Anna Pavlovna's easy-chairs, murmuring French phrases as he blinked his eyes. Every muscle in his spare face was quivering with nervous strain; his eyes, in which the fire of life had seemed to be extinguished, now gleamed with a fierce and intense brilliancy. It was evident, that, however apathetic he might appear in ordinary circumstances, he more than made up for it by his energy at moments of almost morbid excitability.

"You cannot understand why I say this to you," he went on. "Why, it is the whole history of a life. You talk about Bonaparte and his career," said he, although Pierre had not said a word about Bonaparte. "You talk about Bonaparte, but Bonaparte, when he was toiling, went step by step straight for his goal; he was free; he let nothing stand between him and his goal, and he reached it. But tie yourself to a woman and you are like a prisoner in chains, your whole freedom is destroyed. And in proportion as you feel that you have hope and powers, the more you will be weighed down and tormented with regrets. Drawing-rooms, tittle-tattle, balls, vulgar show, meanness—such is the charmed circle from which I cannot escape. I am now getting ready for the war, the greatest war that ever was, and yet I know nothing and am fit for nothing. I am very, very likable and very keen," continued Prince Andrei, "and at Anna Pavlovna's they like to hear me talk. And this stupid society, without which my wife cannot live, and these women . . . If you could only know what all these distinguished women and women in general amount to! My father is right. Egotism, ostentations, stupidity, meanness in every respect—such are women when they show themselves as they are. You see them in society and think they amount to something, but they are nothing, nothing, nothing! No, don't marry, old fellow, don't marry," said Prince Andrei in conclusion.

"It seems ridiculous to me," said Pierre, "that you should regard yourself as incompetent and your life as spoiled. Everything is before you—everything. And you . . ."

He did not finish his sentence, but his very tone made it evident how highly he prized his friend and how much he expected from him in the future.

How can he speak so! thought Pierre, who considered Prince Andrei the model of all accomplishments, for the very reason that Prince Andrei united in himself, to the highest degree, all those qualities that were lacking in Pierre and that more nearly than anything else express the concept, will power. Pierre always admired Prince Andrei's ability to meet, with perfect ease, all sorts of people; his extraordinary memory, his breadth of knowledge —he had read everything, he knew about everything, he had ideas on every subject—and, above all, his powers of work and study. And if Pierre was often struck by Andrei's lack of aptitude for speculative philosophy—which was his own specialty—he at least regarded it not as a fault but as a sign of strength.

In all the best relations, however friendly and simple, flattery or praise is indispensable, just as grease is indispensable for making wheels move easily.

"I have reached the end of things," said Prince Andrei. "What is there to say about me? Let us talk about yourself," said he, after a short silence, and smiled at his consoling thoughts. This smile was instantly reflected on Pierre's face.

"But what is there to say about me?" asked Pierre, his lips parting in a gay, careless smile. "What am I, anyway? I am a bastard!"

And suddenly his face grew red. It was evident that he had exerted great effort to say that. "Without name, without fortune! . . . And yet it is true . . ." He did not say what was true.

"I am free for the present, and I like it. Only I don't know what to take up. I would like to have a serious talk with you on the subject."

Prince Andrei looked at him with kindly eyes. But his glance, friendly and affectionate as it was, betrayed the consciousness of his superiority.

"I am fond of you for the special reason that you are the only live man in all our circle. It is well with you. Choose whatever you like, it is all the same. It will be well with you anywhere; but there's one thing. Stop going to those Kuragins' and leading their kind of life. That sort of thing does not become you: all those revels, that wild life, and all—"

"What do you care, my dear fellow?" exclaimed Pierre, shrugging his shoulders. "Women, my dear, women!"

"I don't understand it," replied Andrei. "Respectable women, that is another thing, but Kuragin's women, women and wine, I don't understand it."

Pierre had been living at Prince Vasili Kuragin's, and had been taking part in the dissipated life of his son Anatol, the young man it had been proposed to reform by marrying him to Prince Andrei's sister.

"Do you know," said Pierre, as if a happy thought had come unexpectedly

18

into his mind, "seriously, I have been thinking about it for some time. Since I have been leading this sort of life, I have not been able to think or to come to any decision. My head aches; I have no money. This evening he invited me, but I am not going."

"Give me your word of honor that you will not go again."

"Here's my word on it!"

VI

IT WAS already two o'clock when Pierre left his friend. It was a luminous June night, characteristic of Petersburg. Pierre took his seat in the hired carriage with the intention of going home, but the farther he rode the more impossible he found it to think of sleeping on such a night, which was more like twilight or early morning. He could see far down through the empty streets. On the way it occurred to him that the gambling club was to meet as usual that evening at Anatol Kuragin's, after which they were accustomed to have a drinking bout, topping off with one of Pierre's favorite entertainments.

"It would be good fun to go to Kuragin's," said he to himself, but instantly he remembered that he had given Prince Andrei his word of honor not to go there again.

But, as happens to men of no strength of character, he immediately felt such a violent desire to have one more last taste of this dissipated life, so well known to him, that he determined to go. And, in excuse for it, the thought entered his mind that his promise was not binding, because, before he had given it to Prince Andrei, he had also promised Anatol to be present at his house; moreover, he reasoned that all such pledges were merely conditional and had no definite meaning, especially if it were taken into consideration that perhaps by the next day he might be dead, or something might happen to him so extraordinary that the distinctions of honorable and dishonorable would entirely vanish. Arguments of this nature often occurred to Pierre, entirely nullifying his plans and purposes. He went to Kuragin's.

Driving up to the great house at the Horse-Guard barracks where Anatol lived, he sprang onto the lighted porch, ran up the steps, and entered the open door. There was no one in the anteroom; empty bottles, cloaks and overshoes were scattered about; there was an odor of wine; farther on he heard loud talking and shouts.

Play and supper were over, but the guests had not yet dispersed. Pierre threw off his cloak and went into the first room, where were the remains of the supper; a single waiter, thinking that no one could see him, was stealthily drinking up the wine in the half-empty glasses. In a third room were heard the sounds of scuffling, laughter, the shouts of well-known voices, and the growl of a bear. Eight young men were eagerly crowding around an open window. Three were having sport with a young bear, which one of their number was dragging by a chain and trying to frighten the others with.

"I bet a hundred on Stevens," cried one.

"See, he can't hold him," cried a second.

"I bet on Dolokhof," cried a third. "Get those fellows away, Kuragin."

"There, let Mishka go! This is the wager."

"Without stopping to breathe, or he loses," cried a fourth.

"Yakof, bring the bottle, Yakof!" cried the host of the evening, a tall, handsome fellow, standing in the midst of the crowd, in a single thin shirt thrown open at the chest. "Hold on, gentlemen! Here he is, here is our dear friend, good old Pierre," he cried.

A short man with clear blue eyes, whose voice, among all those drunken voices, was noticeable for its tone of sobriety, shouted from the window:

"Come here and hear about the wagers."

This was Dolokhof, an officer of the Semeonovsky regiment, a well-known gambler and duelist, whose home was with Anatol. Pierre smiled, as he gaily looked around him.

"I don't understand at all. What's up?"

"Hold on! He's not drunk. Bring a bottle," cried Anatol, and taking a glass from the table, went up to Pierre.

"First of all, drink."

Pierre proceeded to drain glass after glass, at the same time closely observing and listening to the drunken guests, who had again crowded around the window. Anatol kept his glass filled with wine, and told him how Dolokhof had laid a wager with Stevens, an English naval man who happened to be there, that he, Dolokhof, was to drink a bottle of rum, sitting in the fourth-story window with his legs hanging out.

"There, now, drink it all," said Anatol, handing the last glass to Pierre, "I won't let you off."

"No, I don't want any more," replied Pierre, and pushing Anatol aside, he went to the window. Dolokhof was holding the Englishman by the arm, and was clearly and explicitly laying down the conditions of the wager, turning more particularly to Anatol and Pierre as they approached.

Dolokhof was a man of medium height, with curly hair and bright blue eyes. He was twenty-five years old. Like all infantry officers, he wore no mustache, so that his mouth, which was the most striking feature of his face, was wholly revealed. The lines of the mouth were drawn with remarkable delicacy. The upper lip closed firmly over the strong lower one in a sharp curve at the center, and in the corners hovered constantly something in the nature of two smiles—one in each corner! and all taken together, and especially in conjunction with a straightforward, bold, intelligent look, made it impossible not to take notice of his face. Dolokhof was not a rich man, and he had no influential connections. But although Anatol spent ten thousand rubles a year and it was known that Dolokhof lived with him, nevertheless he had succeeded in winning such a position that

Anatol and all who were acquainted with the two men had a higher regard for him than for Anatol. Dolokhof played nearly every kind of game and almost always won. However much he drank, he never was known to lose his head. Both Kuragin and Dolokhof were at this time notorious among the rakes and spendthrifts of Petersburg.

The bottle of rum was brought. Two lackeys, evidently made timid and nervous by the orders and shouts of the boon companions, tried to pull away the sash that hindered anyone from sitting on the outer slope of the window ledge.

Anatol, with his swaggering way, came up to the window. He wanted to smash something. He pushed the lackeys away and tugged at the sash, but the sash would not yield. He broke the windowpanes.

"Now you try it, you man of muscle," said he, calling Pierre.

Pierre seized hold of the crossbar and pulled, and the oaken framework gave way with a crash.

"Take it all out, or they'll think I clung to it," said Dolokhof.

"The Englishman accepts it, does he? All right?" asked Anatol.

"All right," said Pierre, glancing at Dolokhof, who took the bottle of rum and went to the window, through which could be seen the sky where the evening and morning light were beginning to mingle.

He leaped on the window sill with the bottle in his hand.

"Listen!" he cried, as he stood there and looked back into the room.

All were silent.

"I wager"—he spoke French so that the Englishman might understand him, and spoke it none too well either—"I wager fifty sovereigns; or perhaps you prefer a hundred?" he added, addressing the Englishman.

"No, fifty," replied the Englishman.

"Very well, then, fifty it is—that I will drink this whole bottle of rum without taking it once from my mouth; drink it sitting in this window, in that place there"—he bent over and pointed to the sloping projection of the wall outside the window—"and not holding on to anything. Is that understood?"

"Very good," said the Englishman.

Anatol turned to the Englishman and holding him by the button of his coat and looking down on him—for the Englishman was short—began to repeat the terms of the wager in English.

"Wait!" cried Dolokhof, thumping on the window with the bottle in order to attract attention. "Wait, Kuragin, listen! If anyone else does the same thing, then I will pay down a hundred sovereigns. Do you understand?"

The Englishman nodded his head, though he did not make it apparent whether or not he was prepared to accept this new wager. Anatol still held him by the button and, in spite of his nods to signify that he understood all that was said, Anatol insisted on translating Dolokhof's words into English.

A lean young life-guardsman, who had been playing a losing game all evening, climbed on the window, leaned over, and gazed down.

"Oo! Oo! Oo!" he exclaimed, as he looked down from the window to the flagstones below.

"Hush!" cried Dolokhof, and he pulled the officer back from the window. Getting his feet entangled in his spurs, the lad awkwardly leaped down into the room.

Placing the bottle on the window sill so as to be within reach of it, Dolokhof warily and coolly climbed into the window. Letting down his legs and spreading out both hands, he measured the width of the window, sat down, let go his hands, moved to the right, then to the left, and took up the bottle. Anatol brought two candles and set them on the window seat, although it was now quite light. Dolokhof's back in the white shirt, and his curly head, were illuminated on both sides. All gathered around the window. The Englishman stood in the front row. Pierre smiled and said nothing. One of the older men present suddenly stepped forward with a stern and frightened face, and attempted to seize Dolokhof by the shirt.

"Gentlemen, this is folly; he will kill himself," said this man, who was less foolhardy than the rest.

Anatol restrained him.

"Don't touch him; you will startle him, and then he might fall. What if he should? Hey?"

Dolokhof turned around, straightening himself up and again stretching out his hands.

"If anyone touches me again," said he, hissing the words through his thin compressed lips, "I will send him flying down there! So now!"

Thus having spoken, he resumed his former position, dropped his hands, and seizing the bottle he put it to his lips, bent his head back, and raised his free arm as a balance. One of the lackeys, who had begun to clear away the broken glass, paused in his work, and, still bending down, fixed his eyes on the window and Dolokhof's back. Anatol stood straight with staring eyes. The Englishman, thrusting out his lips, looked askance. The man who had tried to stop the proceedings repaired to one corner of the room and threw himself on the divan with his face to the wall. Pierre covered his eyes, and though the feeble smile still hovered over his lips, his face now expressed horror and apprehension. All were silent. Pierre took his hand from his eyes. Dolokhof was still sitting in the same position, only his head was thrown farther back, so that the curly hair in the nape of his neck touched his shirt collar, and the hand holding the bottle was lifted higher and higher, trembling under the effort. The bottle was evidently nearly empty and consequently had to be held almost perpendicularly over his head.

"Why should it take so long?" thought Pierre. It seemed to him as if more than a half-hour had elapsed. Suddenly Dolokhof's body made a backward motion and his hand trembled nervously; this tremor was sufficient to make him slip as he sat on the sloping ledge. In fact, he slipped, and his arm and head wavered more violently as he struggled to regain his balance. He stretched out one hand to clutch the window seat, but refrained from touching it. Pierre again covered his eyes and declared to himself that he would not open them again. Suddenly he was conscious that there was a commotion around him. He looked up. Dolokhof was standing on the window seat; his face was pale but radiant. "Empty!"

He flung the bottle at the Englishman, who cleverly caught it. Dolokhof sprang down from the window. He exhaled a powerful odor of rum.

"Capital!" . . . "Bravo!" . . . "That's a wager worth while!" . . . "The devil take you!" were the shouts that rang from all sides.

The Englishman, taking out his purse, was counting out his money. Dolokhof was scowling and had nothing to say. Pierre started for the window.

"Gentlemen! Who wants to make the bet with me? I will do the same thing," he cried. "But there's no need of any wager. Give me a bottle. I will do it anyway. Bring a bottle."

"Let him! Let him!" said Dolokhof, smiling.

"What is the matter with you?" . . . "Are you crazy?" . . . "We won't let you!" . . . "It makes you dizzy even on a staircase!" were shouted from various sides.

"I will drink it; give me a bottle of rum," cried Pierre, pounding on the table with a drunken and resolute gesture and climbing into the window. He was seized by the arm, but his strength was so great that whoever approached him was sent flying across the room.

"No, you will never dissuade him that way," said Anatol. "Hold on; I will deceive him. Listen, I will make the wager with you, but tomorrow; but now we are all going to . . ."

"Come on," cried Pierre, "come on! And we will take Mishka with us." And seizing the bear, he began to gallop around the room with him.

VII

PRINCE VASILI fulfilled the promise he had made to Princess Drubetskoy. The request had been preferred to the emperor, and Boris was allowed to enter the Semeonovsky regiment of the Guard as ensign. But in spite of all Anna Mikhailovna's efforts and intrigues, he was not made aide to Kutuzof.

Shortly after Anna Pavlovna's reception, Princess Drubetskoy returned to Moscow and went straight to her rich relatives, the Rostofs. The Rostofs were celebrating the saint's-day of the mother and the youngest daughter, both of whom were named Natalya [Natasha]. Since morning there had been an unceasing stream of carriages coming and going with guests who brought their congratulations to the countess' great mansion on the Povarskaya, so well known to all Moscow.

The Countess Rostof was a woman of forty-five, of a thin Oriental type of countenance, and evidently worn out by her cares as mother of a dozen children. Her languid gestures and monotonous speech, the result of her delicate health, gave her a certain dignity which commanded respect.

Princess Anna Mikhailovna Drubetskoy, in her capacity of friend of the family, was also in the drawing-room, helping to receive the company and join in the conversation. The young people were in the rear rooms, not considering it incumbent upon them to take part in receiving the visitors. The count met the guests, and escorted them to the door again, urging them all to dine with him.

"Very, very much obliged to you, my dear" (he called everyone "my dear," without the slightest shadow of difference whether the guest stood high or low in the social scale), "much obliged to you for myself and for my dear ones whose saint's-day we are celebrating. Now, come to dinner. You will affront me if you do not, my dear. Cordially I invite you, and my whole family join with me, my dear." These words he repeated to all, without exception or variation, with an unchanging expression on his round, jolly, clean-shaven countenance. He accompanied his words with a monotonously firm grip of the hand, and with repeated short bows. Having escorted a guest to his carriage, the count would return to this, that or the other visitor still remaining in the drawing-room, and dropping down on a chair with the expression of a man who understands and enjoys the secret of life, he would cross his legs in boyish fashion, lay his hands on his knees, and shaking his head significantly, would set forth his conjectures concerning the weather, or exchange confidences about health, sometimes speaking in Russian, sometimes in very execrable but self-confident French; and then again with the air of a weary man who is nevertheless bound to fulfil all obligations, he would go to the door with still another departing guest, straightening the thin, gray hairs on his bald head and dutifully proffering the invitations to dinner.

Sometimes, returning through the entry to the drawing-room, he would pass through the conservatory and butler's room to the great marble hall where covers were laid for eighty guests, and glancing at the butlers who were bringing the silver and china, setting the tables and unfolding the damask table linen, he would summon Dmitri Vasilyevitch, a man of noble family, who had charge of all his affairs, and would say:

"Well, well, Mitenka, see that everything is all right. That's good, that's good," he would say, glancing with satisfaction on the huge extension table. "The principal thing is the service. Very good, very good."

Then, with a deep sigh of satisfaction, he would go back to the drawing-room once more.

"Marya Lvovna Karagina and her daughter," announced the countess' footman in a thundering bass voice, coming to the door. The countess was thoughtful for a moment, and took a pinch of snuff from a gold snuffbox ornamented with a miniature of her husband.

"These callers have tired me out," said she. "Well, she is the last one I shall receive. She is very affected. . . . Ask her to come in," said she to the footman in a mournful voice, as if her words had been: "Kill me and have done with it."

A tall, portly, haughty-looking lady in a rustling gown came into the drawing-room, followed by her round-faced, smiling young daughter.

"Dear countess, it has been such a long time . . . she has been ill in bed, poor girl." . . . "At the Razumovsky ball . . ." "*Et la Comtesse Apraksine* . . ." "I have had such an enjoyable time . . ." Such were the phrases, spoken by lively feminine voices interrupting one another and mingling with the rustle of silks and the moving of chairs. The conversation was turned to the chief item of city news at that time, namely, the illness of the well-known old Count Bezukhof, one of the richest and handsomest men of Catherine's time, and also to his illegitimate son, Pierre.

"I am very sorry for the old count," said one of the ladies. "His health is so wretched, and now the mortification his son causes him—it will be the death of him."

"What is that?" asked the countess, as if she were not aware of what the visitor was talking about, although she had heard fifty times already the cause of Count Bezukhof's mortification.

"It all comes from the present system of education. Sending them abroad!" pursued the lady. "This young man has been left to himself, and now they say that he has been carrying on so outrageously in Petersburg that the police had to send him out of the city."

"Please, tell us about it," urged the countess.

"He made a bad choice of friends," remarked Princess Anna Mikhailovna. "Prince Vasili's son, this Pierre, and a man named Dolokhof, they say, have been doing—heaven only knows what. But all of them have had to suffer for it. Dolokhof has been reduced to the ranks, and Bezukhof's son has been sent to Moscow, and Anatol Kuragin has been taken in charge by his father. At all events, he has been sent away from Petersburg."

"Yes, but what have they been doing?" asked the countess.

"They acted like perfect cutthroats, especially Dolokhof," said the visitor. "He is a son of Marya Ivanovna Dolokhof—such an excellent woman, just think of it! Can you imagine it? The three of them, somehow, got hold of a bear, took it with them into a carriage, and carried it to the house of some actresses. The police hastened to apprehend them. The young ruffians seized the police officer and tied him back-to-back to the bear, and then threw the bear into the Moika; the bear floated off with the police officer on his back!"

"Wonderful, my dear, what a figure the policeman must have cut!" cried the count, shaking with laughter.

"Oh, how terrible! how can you laugh, count?" But the ladies had to laugh in spite of themselves.

"It was with difficulty that they rescued the unfortunate man," pursued the visitor. "And to think that a son of Count Bezukhof should find amusement in such pursuits," she added. "I hope that no one in Moscow will receive him, though he is so rich."

"Why did you say that this young man is so rich?" asked the countess, leaning away from the younger ladies, who immediately pretended not to hear what she was saying. "You know, he has only illegitimate children. It seems—Pierre is also illegitimate."

The guest waved her hand: "I imagine he has a score of them."

Princess Anna Mikhailovna took part in the conversation, with the evident desire of showing off her powerful connections and her acquaintance with all the details of high life.

"This is the truth of the matter," said she, significantly and also in a half-whisper. "Count Bezukhof's reputation is notorious; as for his children, he has lost count of them, but this Pierre has been his favorite."

"How handsome the old man was," said the countess, "even last year! I never saw a handsomer man!"

"Now he is very much changed," said Anna Mikhailovna. "As I was going to say, on his wife's side, Prince Vasili is the direct heir to all his property, but the old man is very fond of Pierre, has taken great pains with his education, and has written to the emperor about him; so that no one knows, if he should die—he is so weak that it may happen any moment, and Dr. Lorrain has come up from Petersburg—no one knows, I say, who will get his colossal fortune, Pierre or Prince Vasili. He has forty thousand serfs, and millions! I know all about this, because Prince Vasili himself told me. Yes, and besides, Count Bazukhof is my great-uncle on my mother's side. And he is also Boris' godfather," she added, pretending that she attributed no significance to this circumstance.

"Prince Vasili came to Moscow yesterday. He is on some official business, I was told," said the guest.

"Yes, but *entre nous*," said the princess, "that's a pretext; he has come principally on account of Count Bezukhof, because he knew he was so sick."

"At all events, my dear, that was a splendid joke," said the count; and perceiving that the elderly visitor did not hear him, he turned his attention to the young ladies. "Charming figure, that cut by the police officer—I can imagine it!"

And imitating the way the unfortunate police officer would have waved his arms, he again burst out into a ringing bass laugh that made his portly form fairly shake, as men laugh who always live well, and indulge in generous wines. "So glad to have you dine with us," said he.

Silence ensued. The countess looked at the caller, smiling pleasantly, but nevertheless making no attempt to hide her lack of regret should the caller depart. Suddenly from the next room came the noise of several persons running toward the door, then the sound of a falling chair, and into the drawing-room darted a girl of thirteen, concealing something in her short muslin skirt. She halted in the middle of the room, and it was evident that her wild frolic had carried her farther than she had intended. At the same instant

26

there appeared in the door a student with a crimson collar, a young officer of the Guard, a young lady of fifteen, and a plump rosy-faced little boy in a smock.

The count jumped up, and, opening his arms, threw them around the little girl who had come running in.

"Ah! here she is," he cried, with a jolly laugh. "Her saint's-day, my dear, her saint's-day!"

"My dear child, there is a time for all things," said the countess, feigning severity. "You are always spoiling her, Ilya," she added, addressing her husband.

"How do you do, my dear; I congratulate you," said the visitor. "What a fascinating girl!" she added, turning to the mother.

The little girl was at that charming age when she is no longer a child nor yet a young lady. She was full of life, but not pretty. Her eyes were black and her mouth was large; her bare childish shoulders were rising and falling in her bodice from the excitement of her race; her dark locks were tossed back; her thin arms were bare; she wore lace-trimmed pantalets and her low shoes displayed her slender little ankles.

Tearing herself away from her father, she ran to her mother, and giving no heed to her stern reproof, hid her blushing face in the lace folds of her mother's mantilla and went into a fit of laughter. The cause of her laughter was the doll which she took out from under her skirt, trying to tell some fragmentary story about it.

"Do you see? . . . my doll . . . Mimi . . . You see . . ."

And Natasha was unable to say any more, it all seemed to her so ludicrous. She leaned on her mother and laughed so merrily and infectiously that all, even the conceited visitor, in spite of herself, joined in her amusement.

"Now, run away, run away with your monster," admonished the mother, pushing away her daughter with pretended sternness. "She is my youngest daughter," she added, turning to the visitor.

Natasha, for a moment raising her face from her mother's lace mantilla, glanced up at the stranger through her tears of laughter, and again hid her face.

The visitor, compelled to admire this family scene, felt it incumbent upon her to take some part in it.

"Tell me, my dear," said she, addressing Natasha, "what relation is this Mimi to you? She is your daughter, I suppose."

Natasha was displeased by the condescending tone in which the lady addressed her. She made no reply and looked solemnly at her.

Meantime, all the young people—the officer, Boris, the son of Princess Anna Mikhailovna; Nikolai the student, the count's oldest son; Sonya, the count's fifteen-year-old niece; and little Petrusha, his youngest boy—crowded into the drawing-room, evidently doing their utmost to restrain within the bounds of propriety the excitement and merriment that convulsed their faces. Occasionally they would glance at one another and find it hard to refrain from bursting into laughter again.

The two young men, the student and the officer, who had been friends from childhood, were of the same age and were both good-looking, but totally unlike each other. Boris was tall and fair, with regular, delicate features and a placid expression. Nikolai was a short, curly-haired young man with a frank, open countenance. On his upper lip the first dark down had already begun to appear, and his whole face expressed impetuosity and enthusiasm. Nikolai's face had flushed crimson the moment he entered the drawing-room. It was plain to see that he strove in vain to find something to say; Boris, on the contrary, immediately regained his self-possession, and began to relate, calmly and humorously, how he had been acquainted with this Mimi-doll when she was a fine young lady, before her nose had lost its beauty; how since their acquaintance began five years before, she had grown aged and the whole top of her head had cracked.

As he said this he looked at Natasha, but she turned away from him and looked at her little brother, who was squeezing his eyes together and shaking with suppressed laughter, and finding that she could no longer control herself, snickered out loud and darted from the room as fast as her nimble little feet would carry her. Boris managed to preserve his composure.

"Mama, do you not want to go for a drive? Shall I order the carriage?" he asked, turning to his mother with a smile.

"Yes, yes, go and order it, please," said she, returning his smile.

Boris quietly left the room and went in pursuit of Natasha; the plump little boy trotted sturdily after them.

VIII

OF THE YOUNG people, not reckoning the young lady caller and the count's oldest daughter, who was four years older than her sister and regarded herself as already grown up, only Nikolai and the niece Sonya remained in the drawing-room.

Sonya was a slender miniature little brunette, with a tawny-tinted complexion especially noticeable on her neck and bare arms, which were slender, but graceful and muscular. She had soft eyes shaded by long lashes, and she wore her thick black hair in a braid twined twice about her head. By the easy grace of her movements, by the suppleness and softness of her slender limbs, and by a certain cunning and coyness of manner, she reminded one of a beautiful kitten which promises soon to grow into a lovely cat.

"Yes, my dear," said the old count, turning to their caller and pointing to Nikolai, "his friend Boris, here, has been appointed an officer in the Guard, and they are such good friends they cannot be separated; so he gives up the University and deserts his old father, and is going into the military service, my dear. And yet there was a place all ready for him in the Department of the Archives. That's what friendship is," concluded the count, with a dubious shake of the head.

"Yes, there's going to be war, they say," said the visitor.

"They have been saying so for a long time," replied the count, "and they will say so again, and keep saying so, and that will be the end of it. My dear, that's what friendship is," he repeated, "he is going to join the hussars."

The visitor, not knowing what reply to make, shook her head.

"It is not out of friendship at all," declared Nikolai, flushing and spurning the accusation as if it were a shameful aspersion on his character. "It is not from friendship at all, but simply because I feel drawn to a military life."

He glanced at his cousin and at the young lady visitor; both were looking at him with a smile of approbation.

"Colonel Schubert of the Pavlograd regiment of hussars is going to dine with us tonight. He is home on leave of absence, and is going to take Nikolai back with him. What's to be done about it?" asked the count, shrugging his shoulders and affecting to treat as a jest what had evidently occasioned him much pain.

"I have already told you, dear papa," said the lad, "that if you do not wish me to go, I will stay at home. But I know that I am not good for anything except the army; I cannot be a diplomat or a goverment official, I can't hide what I feel," and as he said this he glanced, with a handsome young fellow's coquetry, at Sonya and the young lady visitor.

The kitten feasted her eyes on him and seemed ready at a second's notice to play and show all her kittenish nature.

"Well, well, let it go," said the old count. "He's burning with enthusiasm! This Bonaparte has turned all their heads; they all think what an example he gave them in rising from a lieutenant to be an emperor. Well, good luck to them," he added, not noticing his visitor's sarcastic smile.

They began to talk about Napoleon. Julie Karagina turned to young Rostof.

"How sorry I was that you didn't come last Thursday to the Arkharofs'. It was a bore to be there without you," said she, giving him an affectionate smile.

The young man, much flattered, drew his chair nearer to her and engaged the smiling Julie in a confidential conversation, entirely oblivious that this coquettish smile cut as with a knife the jealous heart of poor Sonya, who flushed and tried to force a smile.

In the midst of this conversation he happened to glance at her. She gave him a look of passionate anger, and scarcely able to hold back her tears, but with the fixed smile still on her lips, got up and left the room. All Nikolai's animation deserted him. He availed himself of the first break in the conversation, and with a disturbed countenance left the room in search of Sonya.

"How the secrets of these young folks are sewed with white threads!" exclaimed Anna Mikhailovna, nodding in the direction of the vanishing Nikolai. "Cousinship's a risky relationship," she added.

"Yes," replied the countess, when, as it were, the very light of the sun had departed from the room with these young people; and then, as if she were answering a question which no one had asked, but which was constantly in her mind: "How much suffering, how much trouble, we must experience before we can have some joy in them! And even now! truly there's more sorrow than joy. One is always filled with anxiety, always on the alert! This is the age when there are so many perils both for young girls and for boys."

"It all depends upon the education," said the visitor.

"Yes, you are right," continued the countess. "So far I have been, thank God, the friend of my children, and enjoy their complete confidence," she declared, repeating the error of many parents who cherish the illusion that their children have no secrets in which they do not share. "I know that I shall always be my daughter's chief confidante, and that Nikolai, though with his impetuous nature he may play some pranks, as all boys, will not be like those Petersburg young men!"

"Yes, they're splendid, splendid children," emphatically affirmed the count, who always settled every question too complicated for him by finding everything splendid. "But what's to be done! He wanted to go into the hussars! What would you have, my love?"

"What a charming creature your youngest girl is!" said the visitor. "So spontaneous!"

"Yes, spontaneous," said the count. "She resembles me! And what a voice she has! Although she is my daughter, yet I am not afraid to say that she is going to be a singer, a second Salomoni. We have engaged an Italian master to teach her."

"Isn't she too young yet? They say it is bad for the voice to study at her age."

"Oh, no! why do you consider it too early?" exclaimed the count. "Didn't our mothers get married when they were twelve or thirteen?"

"And she's already in love with Boris! Just think of it!" said the countess, looking at the princess with a sweet smile; then apparently answering a thought which constantly occupied her, she went on to say:

"Well, now, you see if I were too strict with her, if I were to forbid her . . . God knows what they might be doing on the sly!" (She meant, they might exchange kisses.) "But now I know everything they say. She comes to me herself every evening, and tells me all about it. Maybe I spoil her, but indeed this seems to be the best plan. I was far too strict with my eldest daughter."

"Yes, I was brought up in an entirely different way," said the oldest daughter, the handsome Countess Vera, smiling. But the smile did not add to the beauty of her face, as often happens; on the contrary, it lost its natural expression and therefore became unpleasant. She was handsome, intelligent, well-bred, well educated, her voice was pleasant, what she said was right and proper enough, and yet, strange to say, her mother and all the others looked at her as if surprised at her saying such a thing, and regarded it as one of the things that had better have been left unsaid.

"People always try to be very wise with their eldest children—try to accomplish something extraordinary," said the visitor.

"How naughty to prevaricate, my love! The dear countess tried to be very wise with Vera," said the count. "Well, on the whole, she has succeeded splendidly," he added, winking approvingly at his daughter.

The visitors got up and took their departure, promising to return to dinner. "What manners! they kept staying and staying," remarked the countess, after she had seen her visitors to the door.

I X

WHEN Natasha left the drawing-room, she ran only as far as the conservatory. There she paused, listening to the chatter in the drawing-room and expecting Boris to follow her. She was already beginning to grow impatient, and stamped her foot, on the very verge of crying because he did not follow her instantly, when she heard the young man's noisy, deliberate steps. Natasha hastily placed herself behind some tubs full of flowers and concealed herself.

Boris paused in the center of the room, looked around him, brushed some specks of dust from the sleeve of his uniform, and then, going to a mirror, contemplated his handsome face. Natasha, holding her breath, peered out from her hiding place and waited to see what he would do. He stood for some moments in front of the mirror, smiled with satisfaction, and went toward the entrance door.

Natasha was just about to call to him, but then she thought better of it. "Let him find me," she said to herself.

As soon as Boris had left the conservatory, Sonya came in from the other door, all flushed, and angrily muttering to herself. Natasha restrained her first impulse to run to her and remained in her hiding place, as if under an invisible cap, looking at what was going on in the world. She was experiencing a new and peculiar enjoyment.

Sonya was still muttering something, and looked expectantly toward the drawing-room. Then Nikolai made his appearance.

"Sonya! what is the matter? How can you behave so?" he asked, going up to her.

"No, no, leave me alone!" and Sonya began to sob.

"Well, I know what the trouble is."

"If you know, so much the better; go back to her, then."

"So-o-nya! How can you torment me, and torment yourself, for a mere fancy!" asked Nikolai, taking her hand.

Sonya did not withdraw her hand and ceased weeping.

Natasha, not moving and hardly breathing, with sparkling eyes peered from her concealment. "What will they do now, I wonder?" she said to herself.

"Sonya! The whole world is nothing to me! You alone mean everything to me," said Nikolai. "I will prove it to you!"

"I don't like it when you talk so with . . ."

"Well, I won't do so any more, only forgive me, Sonya!"

He drew her to him and kissed her.

"Ah! how nice!" thought Natasha, and when Sonya and Nikolai had left the room, she followed them and called Boris to her.

"Boris! Come here," said she, with her face full of mischievous cunning. "I want to tell you something. Here, come here!" she said, and drew him into the conservatory, to the very place among the tubs where she had been in hiding. Boris, smiling, followed her.

"What may this something be?" he inquired.

She grew confused, glanced around her, and espying the doll which she had thrown on one of the tubs, she took it up.

"Kiss the doll," said she. Boris looked down into her eager face with an attentive gentle look, and made no reply.

"Don't you want to? Well, then, come here," said she, and made her way deeper among the flowers, at the same time throwing away the doll. "Nearer, nearer," she whispered. She seized the lapels of his coat and her flushed face expressed eagerness and fear. "Then, will you kiss me?" she whispered, so low as hardly to be heard, looking up at him and smiling, and almost crying with emotion.

Boris reddened. "How absurd you are!" he exclaimed, but he bent over to her, reddening still more violently, but not quite able to make up his mind whether to kiss her or not.

Natasha suddenly sprang on a tub, so that she was taller than he, threw both slender bare arms around his neck, and by a motion of her head tossing back her curls, kissed him full on the lips. Then she slipped away between the flowerpots, and hanging her head, stood still on the other side.

"Natasha," said he, "you know that I love you, but . . ."

"Are you in love with me?" asked Natasha, interrupting him.

"Yes, I am, but please let's not do this again . . . In four years—then I will ask for your hand." Natasha pondered.

"Thirteen, fourteen, fifteen, sixteen," said she, reckoning on her delicate fingers. "Good! Then it is decided?" And a smile of joy and satisfaction lighted up her animated face.

"Yes, it is decided," said Boris.

"Forever and ever," said the girl. "Till death itself!" And taking his arm, she went with a happy face into the sitting room with him.

The countess was now so tired of receiving that she gave orders not to admit any more visitors, and the doorman was told to invite anyone else who came to return to dinner.

The countess was anxious to have a confidential talk with the friend of her childhood, Princess Anna Mikhailovna, whom she had scarcely seen since her return from Petersburg. Anna Mikhailovna, with her sad but pleasant face, drew her armchair nearer to the countess.

"I will be perfectly frank with you," said she. "We have very few of our old friends left. And that's why I prize your friendship so highly!"

She glanced at Vera, and paused.

The countess pressed her hand; then she said, addressing her eldest daughter, who was evidently not her favorite:

"Vera, haven't you any perception at all? Cannot you see that you are in the way? Go to your sisters, or . . ."

The handsome Vera smiled scornfully, evidently not feeling the least offended.

"If you had only told me sooner, dear mama, I would have gone immediately," said she, as she left the room. But as she was going past the sitting room, she saw that two couples were snugly settled in the embrasures of the two windows. She paused and smiled satirically. Sonya was sitting close by Nikolai, who was copying some verses in her honor—the first he had ever written. Boris and Natasha were sitting in the other window, and stopped talking as Vera passed. Both of the girls looked up at her with guilty and yet happy faces. It was both amusing and touching to see these two girls, so head over ears in love, but the sight of them evidently did not rouse pleasant thoughts in Vera's mind.

"How many times have I asked you not to take my things?" said she. "You have your own room."

And she snatched the inkstand away from her brother.

"Wait a minute, wait a minute," said he, dipping his pen.

"You always succeed in doing things at just the wrong time," exclaimed Vera. "There you came running into the drawing-room, so that everyone was mortified on your account."

In spite of the fact, or perhaps because what she said was perfectly true, no one made any reply, and all four only exchanged glances among themselves. Vera lingered in the room, holding the inkstand in her hand.

"And how can such young things as Natasha and Boris and you two have 'secrets'?—it's all nonsense!"

"Well, what concern is it of yours, Vera?" asked Natasha in a gentle voice, defending herself. She was evidently more than ordinarily sweet and well disposed to everyone on that day.

"It's very stupid," said Vera; "I blush for you. What sort of 'secrets' . . ."

"Everyone has his own. We don't meddle with you and Berg," said Natasha hotly.

"I suppose you don't," said Vera, "and because you can't find anything improper in my behavior. But I am going to tell mama how you and Boris behave."

"Natasha behaves very well to me," said Boris; "I cannot complain of it."

"Stop, Boris, you are such a diplomat"—the word "diplomat" was in great vogue among the young people, who gave it a special meaning—"it's very annoying," said Natasha, in an offended, trembling voice. "Why should she worry me so? You will never understand such things," she added, turning to Vera, "because you never were in love with anyone, you have no heart, you are only Madame de Genlis"—this was a nickname considered very insulting, which had been first applied to Vera by Nikolai—"and your chief pleasure is to cause other people annoyance. You may flirt with Berg as much as you please," she said spitefully.

"Well, at all events, you don't find me running after a young man in the presence of visitors."

"There, now, you have done what you wanted," interrupted Nikolai, "you have said all sorts of unpleasant things, and disturbed us all. Let's go to the nursery."

All four, like a frightened bevy of birds, jumped up and flew out of the room.

"You are the ones who have been saying unpleasant things, but I haven't said anything to anyone," cried Vera.

"Madame de Genlis! Madame de Genlis!" shouted the merry voices from the other room through the open door.

The handsome Vera, who found a perverted pleasure in doing unpleasant and irritating things, smiled, evidently undisturbed by what was said of her, went to the mirror, and rearranged her sash and hair. As she caught a glimpse of her pretty face she became, to all appearances, cooler and more self-satisfied.

Meantime, the ladies in the drawing-room continued their talk:

"Ah, dear one," said the countess, "in my life it is not all rose-color. I cannot help seeing that at the rate we are going our property will not hold out much longer. And then his club, and his easy ways. Even if we live in the country, how much rest do we get? Theatricals, hunting, and heaven knows what. But what's the use of talking! . . . Now tell me how you manage to get along. I often marvel at you, Annette; how it is that you, at your time of life, fly about so in your carriage alone, in Moscow, in Petersburg, to all the ministers, to all the notables, and succeed in getting around them all, I marvel at it! Now tell me how you do it. I cannot understand it at all."

"Ah! my dearest," replied Princess Anna Mikhailovna, "may God forbid that you ever learn by experience what it is to be left a widow, and without any protector, with a son whom you adore. You get accustomed to everything," she went on to say, with some pride. "My lawsuit has given me a great experience. If I need to see any 'bigwig,' I write a note: 'Princess so and so desires to see such and such a person,' and I myself go in a hired carriage, twice, three times, four times, until I get what I need. It is a matter of indifference to me what they think of me."

"Well now, how was it, whom did you apply to for Boris?" asked the countess. "There he is already an officer of the Guard, and my young Nikolai is merely a cadet. There was no one to work for him. Whom did you ask?"

"Prince Vasili. He was very kind. He immediately consented to do all in his power, and he laid the matter before the emperor," said Princess Anna Mikhailovna, entirely forgetting in her enthusiasm all the humiliation through which she had passed for the attainment of her ends.

"Prince Vasili must have aged somewhat?" queried the countess. "I have not seen him since our theatricals at the Rumyantsofs'. I suppose he has entirely forgotten me. He was very assiduous in his attention to me," she added, with a smile.

"He is just the same as ever," replied Anna Mikhailovna, "polite and full of compliments. His head hasn't been turned at all by all his promotion. 'I am grieved that I can do so little for you, my dear princess,' said he. 'You have only to command me.' Yes, he's a splendid man and a lovely relative to have. But you know, Natalya, my love for my boy. I don't know what I would not do for his happiness. But my means are so small for doing anything," she continued, in a melancholy tone, lowering her voice. "They are so small that I am really in a most terrible position. My unlucky lawsuit eats up all that I have, and is no nearer an end. I have nothing, you can imagine it, literally I haven't a penny, and I don't know how I shall get Boris his uniform."

She drew out her handkerchief and began to weep.

"I must have five hundred rubles, and all I have is a twenty-five ruble bill. I am in such a position! I have only one hope now—in Count Bezukhof. If he will not help out his godson—for you see he stood sponsor to Boris—and grant him something for his support, then all my pains will have been lost. I shall not have enough to pay for his uniform."

The countess shed some sympathetic tears, and sat silently pondering.

"Maybe it's a sin," said the princess, "but I often think: There is Count Kirill Bezukhof, living alone . . . that enormous fortune . . . and why does he live on? Life is a burden for him, while Boris is only just beginning to live."

"He will probably leave something to Boris," said the countess.

"God only knows, dear friend! These rich men and grandees are so selfish! But nevertheless, I am going right away to see him with Boris, and I am going to tell him plainly how things are. Let them think what they please of me, it is all the same to me when my son's fate depends upon it." The princess got up. "It is now two o'clock and you dine at four. I shall have plenty of time to go there."

And with the decision of the true Petersburg lady of business, who knows how to make the best use of her time, she called her son and went with him into the anteroom.

"Good-by, dear," said she to the countess, who accompanied her to the door. "Wish me good luck," she added in a whisper, so that her son might not hear.

"So you are going to Count Kirill, my dear," said the count, coming out from the dining room into the anteroom. "If he is better, ask Pierre to come and dine with me. You see he used to be here a great deal, and danced with the children. Be sure to bring him, my dear!"

X

"My dear Boris," said Princess Anna Mikhailovna to her son, as Countess Rostof's carriage, in which they were riding, rolled along the straw-covered street and entered the wide court of Count Bezukhof's residence. "My dear Boris," said the mother, stretching out her hand from under her old mantle and laying it on her son's with a timid and affectionate gesture, "be amiable and considerate. Count Bezukhof is your godfather, and your prospects depend upon him. Remember this, my dear; be nice as you can be."

"If I knew that anything would come from this except humiliation," replied the son, coldly. "But I have given you my promise, and I do it for your sake."

Though it was a respectable carriage which drove up to the steps, the doorman, noticing the lady's well-worn mantle, looked askance at mother and son (who without sending the footman to announce them had walked straight into the mirror-lined vestibule between two rows of statues standing in the niches) and asked them whom they wished to see, the young princesses or the count; and when they said the count, he told them that his excellency was worse and could not receive anyone today. "Then let us go," said the son, in French.

"My love!" exclaimed the mother, in a supplicating voice, again laying her hand on his arm, as if her touch had the effect of calming or encouraging him. Boris said no more, but without removing his cloak looked dubiously at his mother.

"My good fellow," said the princess in a wheedling tone turning to the doorman, "I know that the count is very ill . . . that's why I came. I am a relative of his. I do not wish to disturb him, my good man . . . I only wanted to see Prince Vasili Kuragin; I understand he is here. Be so good as to announce us."

The doorman gave a hard pull at the bell cord and turned away.

"Princess Drubetskoy for Prince Kuragin," he called to the footman in knee breeches, pumps, and dress coat, who ran to the head of the stairs and looked over from above.

The princess straightened the folds of her dyed silk dress, glanced at the massive Venetian mirror on the wall, and firmly mounted the carpeted staircase in her old worn shoes.

"My dear, you have given me your promise!" said she, turning round to her son and encouraging him with a touch of her hand. The young man, dropping his eyes, silently followed her.

They went into a hall which led into the suite of rooms occupied by Prince Vasili. Just as the mother and son started to walk through this room and were about to ask the way of an elderly footman, who on their approach had sprung to his feet, the bronze doorknob of one of the heavy doors turned and Prince Vasili himself, dressed in a velvet housecoat with a single star, came in, escorting a handsome, black-bearded man. This man was the celebrated Petersburg doctor, Lorrain.

"So then it is certain?" the prince was saying.

"Prince, *'errare humanum est'*; but . . ." replied the doctor, who swallowed his *r's* and spoke the Latin words "To err is human" with a strong French accent.

"Very good, very good . . ."

Perceiving Anna Mikhailovna and her son, Prince Vasili dismissed the doctor with a bow and advanced in silence and with an inquiring look toward them. The son noticed that his mother's eyes suddenly took on an expression of deep concern and grief, and he smiled a little.

"Under what melancholy circumstances we meet again, prince. . . , Well, how is our dear invalid?" said she, pretending not to notice the cold, insolent glance he gave her. Prince Vasili, as if he were surprised to see them there, looked questioningly at her and then at Boris.

Boris bowed civilly. Prince Vasili, entirely ignoring him, replied to Anna Mikhailovna's question by a significant motion of his head and lips, giving her to understand that there was very slim hope for the sick man.

"Is it possible?" cried Anna Mikhailovna. "Ah! this is terrible! Fearful to think . . . This is my son," she added, indicating Boris. "He was anxious to thank you in person." Boris again bowed politely.

"Be assured, prince, that a mother's heart will never forget what you have done for us."

"I am glad if I have been able to be of service to you, my dear Anna Mikhailovna," said Prince Vasili, adjusting his frill and manifesting, both in tone and manner, here in Moscow before Anna Mikhailovna, whom he had put under deep obligation, a far more consequential air than at Petersburg at Anna Scherer's reception.

"Do your best to serve with credit and prove yourself deserving," he added, turning to Boris. "I am glad . . . Are you here on leave of absence?" he asked, in his coldest tone.

"I am waiting for orders, your excellency, before setting out for my new position," replied Boris, manifesting not the slightest resentment of the prince's peremptory manner, nor any inclination to pursue the conversation, but bearing himself with such dignity and deference that the prince gave him an attentive glance.

"Do you live with your mother?"

"I live at the Countess Rostof's," said Boris, again taking pains to add, "your excellency."

"It is that Ilya Rostof who married Natalya Shinshin," said Anna Mikhailovna.

"I know, I know," returned Prince Vasili, in his monotonous voice. "I never could understand how Natalya made up her mind to marry that uncouth bear. Such a stupid and absurd creature, and a gambler besides, they say."

"But an excellent man, prince," remarked Anna Mikhailovna, smiling with a touching smile, as if she, too, knew very well that Count Rostof deserved such a reputation, but did her best to say a good word for the poor old man.

"What do the doctors say?" asked the princess after a short silence, and again allowing an expression of deep grief to settle upon her careworn face.

"Very little hope," said the prince.

"I wanted so much to thank my uncle once more, for all his kindnesses to me and Boris—he's his godson," she added in French, in such a tone as if this piece of information must be highly delightful to the prince.

Prince Vasili thought this over and frowned. Anna Mikhailovna realized that he was apprehensive lest she were a rival for the count's inheritance. She hastened to reassure him.

"If it were not for my true love and devotion to my uncle," said she, uttering the words "my uncle" with special firmness and unconcern—"I know his noble, straightforward character; but you see, he has only the young princesses with him: they are all so inexperienced." She inclined her head and added, in a whisper: "It's indispensable that I should see him, however hard it may be for me; but then, I am accustomed to sorrow."

The prince evidently knew only too well, just as he had known at Anna Scherer's, that he would have difficulty in getting rid of Anna Mikhailovna.

"This interview might be very injurious for him, my dear Anna Mikhailovna; better wait till evening; the doctors have been expecting a crisis."

"But it is impossible to wait, prince, at such moments. Ah, it is terrible, the duties of a Christian."

A door opened and from an inner chamber appeared one of the count's nieces, a young lady with a sour, cold face, and with a waist disproportionately long for her stature. Prince Vasili went toward her.

"Well, how is he?"

"Just about the same; but what could you expect—this noise," said the princess, staring at Anna Mikhailovna as if she were a stranger.

"Ah, my dear, I did not recognize you," exclaimed Anna Mikhailovna with a beaming smile and moving lightly forward toward the count's niece. "I have just come, and I am at your service to help you take care of my uncle. I can imagine how much you have suffered," she added, sympathetically turning up her eyes.

The count's niece made no reply, nor did she even smile, but immediately left the room. Anna Mikhailovna took off her gloves and established herself in an armchair in a victorious attitude, and motioned the prince to sit down near her.

"Boris," said she to her son, with a smile, "I am going to see the count, my uncle; in the meantime, you go and find Pierre, and don't forget to give him the invitation from the Rostofs. They ask him to dinner. I think very likely he may not wish to come," she suggested, turning to the prince.

"On the contrary," returned the prince, evidently very much annoyed, "I should be very glad to have him taken off my hands. He is staying here. The count has not asked for him once."

He shrugged his shoulders. A footman conducted the young man downstairs and then up, by another flight, to Pierre's quarters.

XI

PIERRE HAD arrived in Moscow a few days earlier and had taken up his abode as usual in his father's house. Although he foresaw that the story would be noised abroad in Moscow, and that the ladies who formed his father's household and who were always hostile to him would take advantage of this occurrence to influence the count against him, nevertheless, on the very day of his arrival, he started to go to his father's apartments. As he went into the drawing-room, where the princesses usually sat, he stopped to pay his respects to the ladies, who were busy with their embroidery frames while listening to a book which one of them was reading aloud. There were three of them. The oldest, a severely prim old maid with a long waist—the one who had tried to snub Anna Mikhailovna—was the reader; the younger ones, both pink-cheeked and rather pretty, and exactly alike, except that one of them had a little mole on her lip, decidedly adding to her beauty, were busy with their embroidery.

Pierre was received like a ghost or a leper. The oldest princess ceased reading and silently looked at him with frightened eyes. The one without the mole did the same. The third, who had the mole and some sense of humor, bent over the embroidery to conceal a smile caused by what she thought promised to be an amusing scene. She drew the thread down and bent over, as if studying the pattern, but could hardly keep from laughing.

"Good morning, cousin," said Pierre, "don't you know who I am?"

"I know you very well, altogether too well."

"How is the count? May I see him?" asked Pierre, awkwardly as usual, but still not disconcerted.

"The count is suffering, both in body and in spirit, and it seems you have taken pains to cause him the greater part of his moral suffering."

"May I see the count?" repeated Pierre.

"Hm! If you desire to kill him, to kill him out and out, then you may see him. Olga, go and see if the bouillon is ready for dear uncle, it is high time," she added, making Pierre see by this that they were wholly absorbed in caring for his father, while he, on the contrary, was palpably bent on annoying him.

Olga left the room. Pierre stood still, looking at the sisters, and then said with a bow: "Well, I will go back to my room. As soon as it is possible, you will please tell me."

He went out, and behind his back was heard the clear but subdued laughter of the sister with the mole.

On the next day Prince Vasili had come and put up at the count's. He called Pierre to him, and said: "My dear fellow, if you carry on here as you have in Petersburg, you will fare very badly; that's all I have to say to you. The count is very, very ill; it is imperative that you should not see him."

From that time Pierre had been left severely alone, and spent his days in solitude, upstairs in his own rooms.

When Boris appeared at the door, Pierre was walking up and down his room, occasionally pausing in the corners and making threatening gestures at the walls, as if trying to thrust his sword through some unknown enemy, and looking savagely over his spectacles and then again beginning his restless walking, muttering indistinct words, shrugging his shoulders and spreading out his hands.

"England has outlived its glory," he was declaiming, with a frown and pointing at some imaginary person with his finger. "Pitt, as a traitor to the nation and to the law of nations, is condemned to . . ."

He was imagining that he was at that instant Napoleon himself, and he pictured how his hero would make the perilous passage across from Calais and take London by storm, but he had not completed his denunciation of Pitt when he caught sight of a handsome, graceful young officer coming toward him. He stopped short.

Boris had been a lad of fourteen when he last saw him, and he did not recognize him at all; but nevertheless he seized him by the hand in his impulsive, cordial way, and smiled affectionately.

"Do you remember me?" asked Boris, calmly, with a pleasant smile. "I came with my mother to see the count, but it seems he is very ill."

"Yes, he is very ill. They keep him worried all the time," returned Pierre, striving to recollect who this young man was.

Boris was certain that Pierre did not recognize him, but he did not think it necessary to tell his name, and without manifesting the slightest awkwardness he looked him full in the face.

"Count Rostof invites you to dine with him this afternoon," said he, after a rather long silence which made Pierre feel uncomfortable.

"Ah! Count Rostof," exclaimed Pierre, joyfully. "Then you are his son Ilya. At the first instant I did not recognize you, as you can easily imagine. Do you remember how you and I and Madame Jaquot used to go out walking on the Sparrow Hills—years ago?"

"You are mistaken," said Boris deliberately, and with a bold and rather derisive smile; "I am Boris, the son of Princess Anna Mikhailovna Drubetskoy. Rostof's father is named Ilya, and his name is Nikolai. And I never knew Madame Jaquot."

Pierre made a gesture with his hands and head, as if mosquitoes or bees were attacking him.

"Ah! is that so indeed? I have mixed everything up. I have so many relatives in Moscow! So you are Boris—yes. Well, you and I seem to have begun with a misunderstanding. Well, what do you think of the Boulogne expedition? It will go pretty hard with the English if Napoleon crosses the Channel, won't it? I think the expedition is very feasible!"

Boris knew nothing about the Boulogne expedition; he had not read the newspapers.

"We here in Moscow are more taken up with dinners and gossip than with politics," said he, in his calm, satirical tone. "Now you and the count are the talk."

Pierre smiled his good-natured smile, as if fearing lest his companion might say something that he would regret. But Boris spoke with circumspection, clearly and dryly, looking straight into Pierre's eyes.

"Moscow likes to do nothing better than gossip," he repeated. "All are speculating to whom the count is going to leave his property; and yet, very possibly, he will outlive all of us. I hope so with all my heart." . . .

"Yes, this is all very trying," interrupted Pierre—"very trying."

Pierre was apprehensive lest this young officer should unexpectedly turn the conversation into some awkward channel.

"But it must seem to you," said Boris, flushing slightly, but not allowing his voice or his manner to vary, "it must seem to you that everyone takes an interest in this simply because they hope to get something from the estate."

"That's just it," thought Pierre.

"I expressly wish to tell you, lest any misunderstanding should arise, that you are entirely mistaken if you reckon me and my mother among these people. We are very poor, but I at least say this on my own account for the very reason that your father is rich, that I do not consider myself a relative of his, and neither I nor my mother would ask or even be willing to receive anything from him."

Pierre for some time failed to comprehend, but when the idea dawned upon him, he jumped up from the sofa, seized Boris by the arm with characteristic impetuosity and clumsiness, and while he grew even redder than the other, he began to speak with a mixed feeling of vexation and shame:

"Now, this is strange! I then . . . indeed and who would have ever thought . . . I know very well . . ." But Boris again interrupted him.

"I am glad I have told you all. Perhaps it was disagreeable to you; you will pardon me," said he, soothing Pierre instead of letting himself be soothed by him. "I hope I have not offended you. It is a principle with me to speak frankly. What answer am I to give? Will you come to dinner at the Rostofs'?"

And Boris, having acquitted himself of a difficult explanation, and got himself out of an awkward position by putting another into it, again became perfectly agreeable.

"Now, look here, listen," said Pierre, calming down. "You are a remarkable man. What you have just said is very fine, very fine. Of course, you don't know me. I would not have done such a thing, I would not have had the courage, but it is excellent. Strange," he added, after a short silence and smiling, "strange that you should have had such an idea of me." He laughed. "Well, who knows? We will become better acquainted, I hope." He pressed Boris' hand.

"And do you think Napoleon will succeed in getting his army across?" asked Boris, with a smile.

Pierre understood that Boris wanted to change the conversation, and taking his cue he began to expound the advantages and disadvantages of the Boulogne expedition.

A footman came to summon Boris to his mother. The princess was ready to start. Pierre promised to come and dine with the Rostofs so as to get better acquainted with Boris, and he warmly pressed his hand, looking through his spectacles straight into his eyes.

⚫ XII

AFTER Anna Mikhailovna had gone, the Countess Rostof sat for some time alone, applying her handkerchief to her eyes. At last she rang the bell.

"What is the matter with you, my dear?" she demanded severely of the maid, who had kept her waiting several minutes. "Don't you care to serve me? If not, I can find another place for you."

The countess was greatly affected by her old friend's grief and humiliation, and therefore she was out of sorts, as could be seen by her manner in addressing the maid.

"Beg pardon," said the maid.

"Ask the count to come to me."

The count came waddling to his wife with a rather guilty look, as usual.

"Well, my little countess, what a *sauté au madère* of woodcock we are going to have, my love. I have been sampling it. Taras is well worth the thousand rubles I gave for him. It was well spent."

He took a seat near his wife, with a gesture of bravado, leaning one hand on his knee, and with the other rumpling up his gray hair: "What do you wish, little countess?"

"Look, my love; how did you get that spot on you?" said she, pointing to his waistcoat. "It is evidently some of your sauté," she added, with a smile. "Listen, count, I need some money."

His face grew mournful. "Ah, my dear!" . . .

And the count made a great ado in getting out his pocketbook.

"I want a good deal, count; I want five hundred rubles." And she took her handkerchief and began to rub her husband's waistcoat.

"You shall have it at once. Hey, there!" cried the count, in a tone used only by men who are certain that those whom they command will rush headlong at their call. "Send Mitenka to me!"

Mitenka, the nobleman's son whom the count had brought up and had now put in charge of all his affairs, came with soft noiseless steps into the room.

"See here, my boy," said the count to the deferential young man as he entered the door. "Bring me"—he hesitated—"yes, bring me seven hundred rubles, yes. And don't bring such torn and filthy ones as you do sometimes, but clean ones; they are for the countess."

"Yes, Mitenka, please see that they are clean," said the countess, sighing deeply.

"Your excellency, when do you wish them?" asked Mitenka. "You will deign to know that . . . however, don't allow yourself to be uneasy," he added, perceiving that the count was already beginning to breathe heavily and rapidly, which was always a sign of a burst of rage. "I had forgotten. Will you have them this instant?"

"Yes, yes, instantly; bring them. Give them to the countess."

"What a treasure that Mitenka is!" he added with a smile, as the young man left the room. "He never finds anything impossible. That is a thing I cannot endure. All things are possible."

"Ah! money, count, money; how much sorrow it causes in the world!" exclaimed the countess. "But this money is very important for me."

"Little countess, you are a terrible spendthrift," declared the count, and kissing his wife's hand he disappeared again into his own apartment.

When Anna Mikhailovna returned from her visit to Bezukhof, the money, all in new clean bank notes, was lying on a stand under a handkerchief in the countess' room. Anna Mikhailovna noticed that the countess was excited over something.

"Well, my dear?" asked the countess.

"Ah! he's in a terrible state! you would never know him, he is so ill, so ill! I stayed only a short minute and didn't say two words."

"Annette, for heaven's sake don't refuse me," suddenly exclaimed the countess, taking out the money from under the handkerchief, while her old, thin, grave face flushed in a way that was strange to see.

Anna Mikhailovna instantly understood what she meant, and was already bending over so as to embrace the countess, gracefully at the right moment. "It is from me to Boris, for his outfit."

Anna Mikhailovna interrupted her by throwing her arms around her and bursting into tears. The countess wept with her. They wept because they were friends and because they were kind-hearted, and because, having been friends from childhood, they were now occupied with such a sordid matter as money, and because their youth had passed. But theirs were pleasant tears.

XIII

The Countess Rostof, with her daughters and a large number of guests, sat in the drawing-room. The count had taken the men into his study and was showing them his favorite collection of Turkish pipes. Occasionally he would go out and ask: "Hasn't she come yet?"

Everyone was waiting for Marya Dmitrievna Akhrosimova, called in society "the terrible dragon"; a lady who was distinguished not for her wealth or her titles, but for the honesty of her character, and her frank, simple ways. The imperial family knew her, all Moscow knew her, and all Petersburg; and both cities, while they laughed at her brusque manners on the sly and repeated anecdotes about her, all nevertheless, without exception, respected and feared her.

The conversation in the study, which was full of smoke, turned on the war which had just been declared through a manifesto, and on the recruiting. No one had as yet read the manifesto, but all were aware that it had appeared. The count sat on a low ottoman between two of his friends, who were talking and smoking. He himself was neither talking nor smoking, but with his head now to one side, now to the other, he looked with obvious satisfaction at those who did, and listened to the conversation of the two friends.

One of the men was a civilian, with a wrinkled, sallow, clean-shaven lean face; though he was approaching old age, he was dressed in the height of style, like a young man. This was the old bachelor Shinshin, the countess' own cousin, a "venomous tongue," as it was said of him in Moscow drawing-rooms. He seemed to be condescending to his opponent. The other, a fresh, ruddy young officer of the Guard, irreproachably belted, buttoned, and barbered, held an amber mouthpiece in his mouth, gently sucking the smoke through his rosy lips, expelling it in rings from his handsome mouth. This was Lieutenant Berg, about whom Natasha had teased Vera by calling him her suitor.

Berg always spoke very accurately, calmly, and politely. His conversation invariably had himself as its central point; he always preserved a discreet silence when people were talking about anything that did not directly concern himself, and he could sit that way silently for hours without feeling or causing others to feel the slightest sense of awkwardness. But as soon as the conversation touched any subject in which he was personally interested, he would begin to talk at length and with evident satisfaction.

"Consider my position, count: If I were in the cavalry, I would not receive more than two hundred a quarter, even with the rank of lieutenant, but now I get two hundred and thirty," said he, with a pleasant, happy smile, glancing at Shinshin and the count, as if it were plain to him that his success would always be a subject of interest to everybody.

"Moreover, count," continued Berg, "by being transferred to the Guard, I am not forgotten; vacancies in the Guards occur far more often. So, you can see for yourself, on two hundred and thirty rubles a quarter, how well I can live. I can save some money and send some to my father too," he went on to say, puffing out a ring of smoke.

"A German can grind corn on the butt of his hatchet, as the proverb puts it," said Shinshin, shifting the mouthpiece of his pipe to the other side of his mouth and winking at the count.

The count laughed heartily. Berg smiled with self-satisfaction. The count, followed by his guests, went into the drawing-room.

It was the time just before dinner is announced when the assembled guests, in expectation of being summoned to partake of the hors d'oeuvres, are disinclined to embark on lengthy conversations and, at the same time, feel they should move about and say something to show that they are in no haste to sit down at table. The host and hostess keep watch of the door and exchange glances from time to time. The guests try to read in those glances for whom or for what their hosts are waiting—some belated influential guest, or some dish that is not yet ready.

Pierre came in just before the dinner hour and awkwardly sat down in the first chair he saw, right in the middle of the drawing-room, so that he was in everyone's way. The countess tried to engage him in conversation, but he merely answered her questions in monosyllables and kept looking naively around him through his spectacles, as if in search of someone. It was exceedingly annoying, but he was the only person who did not notice it. The majority of the guests, aware of his adventure with the bear, looked curiously at this big, tall, quiet-looking man, and found it difficult to believe that one so burly and unassuming could have played such a trick on a police officer.

"Have you only just come?" asked the countess.

"Yes, madame," replied he, glancing around.

"You have not seen my husband?"

"No, madame."

And he smiled at the wrong moment.

"You were in Paris lately, I believe. I think it is very interesting."

"Very interesting."

The countess exchanged glances with Anna Mikhailovna, who perceived that she was required to take charge of this young man. She took a seat by his side and began to talk to him about his father, but he answered her just as he had the countess, merely in monosyllables. The countess got up and went into the hall.

"Is that you, Marya Dmitrievna?" rang her voice through the hall.

"My own self," was the answer in a harsh voice, and Marya Dmitrievna entered the room. All the young ladies and even the married women, except those who were quite old, rose. Marya Dmitrievna paused in the doorway, and from the height of her imposing stature, with her head held high and its ringlets showing the gray of fifty years, she took a deliberate survey of the guests and adjusted the wide sleeves of her gown as if they were disarranged. Marya Dmitrievna always spoke in Russian.

"Congratulations to the dear one and her children on this happy day," said she, in her loud, deep voice, which drowned all other sounds. "Well, you old sinner, how are you?" she said, addressing the count, who kissed her hand. "I suppose you are bored to death in Moscow? Hey? Nowhere to give the dogs a run. Well, what's to be done, old boy, when you have these grown-up chickens?" She waved her hand toward the young ladies. "Whether you wish it or not, you have to find husbands for them. Well, my Cossack," said she (Marya Dmitrievna always called Natasha the Cossack), patting Natasha as she came running up to kiss her hand gaily and without any fear. "I know this little girl is a madcap, and I am fond of her all the same."

She took out of a monstrous reticule a pair of pear-shaped amethyst earrings, and gave them to the blushing Natasha in honor of her name day; then she turned immediately from her and addressed Pierre.

"He! he! my dear! come here, right here!" she cried in an insincerely gentle voice. "Come here, my dear fellow." And she threateningly hitched up her sleeves.

Pierre went to her, ingenuously looking at her through his spectacles.

"Come here, come, my dear fellow. I was the only one who dared tell your father the whole truth when he was fit to hear it, and now I shall do the same with you. It's God's will."

She paused. All held their breath, waiting for what was to come, and feeling that this was but the prologue.

"He's a fine lad, I must say, a fine lad! His father lying on his deathbed, and this young man amuses himself by tying a policeman on a bear's back! For shame, my boy, for shame. You would better have gone to the war."

She turned away from him and gave her hand to the count, who found it difficult to keep from laughing outright.

"Well, then, let us go in to dinner; it's ready, I believe," said Marya Dmitrievna.

The count led the way with Marya Dmitrievna, followed by the countess escorted by a colonel of hussars, a man of influence whose regiment Nikolai was to join. Anna Mikhailovna went with Shinshin. Berg gave his arm to Vera. The smiling Julie Karagina went with Nikolai to the table. Behind them followed the rest in couples, making a long line through the hall, and the rear was brought up by the tutors and governesses, each leading one of the children. The waiters bustled about, chairs were noisily pushed back, an orchestra played in the gallery, and the guests took their places. The sounds of the count's private band were soon drowned in the clatter of knives and forks, the voices of the guests, and the hurrying steps of the waiters.

At the head of the table sat the countess, Marya Dmitrievna at her right, Anna Mikhailovna at her left; then the other ladies. At the other end of the table sat the count, with the colonel of hussars at his left, and Shinshin and the other men at his right. At one side of the long table were the young gentlemen and ladies; Vera next to Berg, Pierre next to Boris; on the other side the children and their tutors and governesses.

The count, from behind the barricade of crystal bottles and comports laden with fruit, looked across to his wife and her towering headdress with its blue ribbons, and zealously helped his neighbors to wine, not forgetting himself. The countess also, not neglecting the duties as a hostess, cast significant glances at her husband over the tops of the pineapples, and it seemed to her that his bald forehead and face were all the more conspicuously rubicund from the contrast of his gray hair.

On the ladies' side there was an unceasing buzz of conversation. On the side of the men the voices grew louder and louder; and loudest of all talked the colonel of hussars, who ate and drank all he could, his face growing more and more flushed, so that the count felt called upon to hold him up to the other guests as an example. Berg, with an affectionate smile, talked with Vera, arguing that love was not an earthly but a heavenly feeling. Boris was enlightening his new friend Pierre as to the guests who were at the table, and occasionally exchanging glances with Natasha, who sat on the opposite side.

Pierre said little but ate much, while he scanned the faces of the guests. Having been offered two soups, he had chosen turtle, and from the fish baked in puff pastry to the hazel hens, he did not refuse a single dish or any of the wines which the butler offered him, thrusting the bottle, mysteriously wrapped in a white napkin, over his neighbor's shoulder, murmuring: "Dry Madeira," or "Hungarian," or "Rhine wine." Pierre raised the first glass that he happened to lay his hand on, of the four wine glasses, engraved with the count's arms, that stood before each guest; and drank rapturously, and the face that he turned upon the guests grew constantly more and more friendly.

Natasha, sitting opposite, gazed at Boris, as only young girls of thirteen can, on the lad with whom they have just exchanged kisses and are very much in love. Occasionally she let her eyes rest on Pierre, and this silly little girl, so exuberantly gay and animated, made him feel like laughing; though he could not tell why.

Nikolai was seated at some distance from Sonya, next to Julie Karagina, talking with Julie with the same automatic smile. Sonya also had a smile on her lips, but it was not natural, and she was evidently tortured by jealousy; first she turned pale, then red, while she did her best to imagine what Nikolai and Julie were talking about.

The governess was looking around nervously, as if prepared for combat should anyone presume to injure her young charges. The German tutor was endeavoring to fix in his memory all the different courses, desserts, and wines, so as to give a full description of it when he wrote home to Germany; he felt sorely grieved because the butler who had the bottle wrapped in the napkin passed him by. He frowned, and tried to make believe that he had no wish to taste that wine and was only affronted because no one was willing to see that he needed the wine, not for allaying his thirst, or from greediness, but from motives of curiosity.

At the men's end of the table, the conversation grew more and more animated. The colonel recounted that the manifesto dealing with the declaration of war had already appeared in Petersburg, and that he had seen a copy which had been brought that day by a courier to the commander-in-chief.

"Why the devil do we have to fight Bonaparte?" exclaimed Shinshin. "He has already smacked down Austria. I fear that now it will be our turn."

The colonel was a stout, tall German of sanguine temperament, but a thorough soldier and a patriot, nevertheless. He felt affronted at what Shinshin said.

"But why, my dear sir," said he, mispronouncing every word, "inasmuch as de emperor knows dat? In his mahnifest, he says dat he cahnnot looke with indeeference on de danjers treetening Russia, and dat de safety of de empire and de sanctity of de allies . . ." and he put a special emphasis on the word allies, as if it were the whole crux of the matter.

"What are you making such a noise about there?" suddenly spoke up Marya Dmitrievna, her deep voice booming across the table. "Why are you pounding on the table?" she demanded of the hussar. "What are you getting so excited about? You must imagine that the French are right here before you!"

"I am delling the druth," said the hussar, smiling.

"Always talking about the war," cried the count, across the table. "You must remember that I have a son who is going. Marya Dmitrievna, my son is going."

"Well, I have four sons in the army, but I don't mourn over it. It is all God's will. You may die at home lying on your bed, or God may bring you safe out of battle," rang Marya Dmitrievna's loud voice, without any effort, from the farther end of the table.

"That is so."

And again the conversation was confined among the ladies at their end of the table and among the men at theirs.

Before the sherbets were brought in, champagne was handed around. Again the orchestra played, the count exchanged kisses with his "little countess," and the guests stood up to drink a health to the hostess, clinking their glasses across the table with the count, with the children, and with each other. Again the waiters bustled about, there was the noise of moving chairs, and in the same order but with more flushed faces the guests returned to the drawing-room and to the count's study.

XIV

THE CARD tables were brought out, and the count's guests scattered through the sitting room, the two drawing-rooms, and the library. The young people at the countess' prompting gathered around the clavichord and the harp. Julie, first, by general request, played a piece with variations on the harp; and then she joined with the rest of the girls in urging Natasha and Nikolai, whose musical talent was known to all, to sing something. Natasha was evidently very much flattered by this request and at the same time filled with anxiety.

"What shall we sing?" she asked.

" 'The Fountain,' " suggested Nikolai.

"Well, give me the music, quick; Boris, come here," said Natasha. "But where is Sonya?"

She looked around, and seeing that her cousin was nowhere in the room, she set out to find her.

She ran into Sonya's room and not seeing her there, hastened to the nursery, but Sonya was not there. Natasha then decided that Sonya might be in the corridor sitting on the great chest. The great chest in the corridor was the place of sorrows for all the young women of the house of Rostof. There she found Sonya with her frilled pink frock all crumpled, lying flat on her face on a dirty striped pillow which belonged to the nurse, hiding her face in her hands, and crying as if her heart would break, while her bare shoulders shook with sobs.

Natasha's face, which had been so radiant all through her saint's-day, was suddenly transformed; her eyes grew fixed, then her throat contracted, and the corners of her mouth drew down.

"Sonya! What is the matter? Tell me, what is it; what is the matter with you? Oo-oo-oo!"

And Natasha, opening her large mouth and becoming quite ugly, cried like a child, without knowing any reason for it except that Sonya was crying. Sonya tried to lift up her head, tried to answer, but found it impossible and hid her face again. Natasha sat down on the blue cushion and threw her arms around her dear cousin. At length Sonya made an effort, sat up, and began to wipe away her tears, saying:

"Nikolai is going away in a week . . . his papers . . . have come . . . he himself told me so. But I should not have wept." . . . She held out a piece of paper she had been reading; it contained the verses that Nikolai had written for her. . . . "I should not have wept for that . . . but you cannot understand . . . no one can understand . . . what a noble heart he has."

And once more her tears began to flow at the thought of what a noble heart he had.

"You are happy . . . I do not envy you . . . I love you and Boris too," said she, composing herself with an effort. "He is good . . . for you there are no obstacles. But Nikolai is my cousin . . . we should have to . . . the archbishop himself would have to give us a dispensation . . . otherwise it would be impossible. And then if dear mama"—Sonya always regarded the countess as her mother and called her so—"she will say that I am spoiling Nikolai's career, that I am heartless and ungrateful, and she would be right too; but God is my witness"—she crossed herself—"I love her so and all of you, except only Vera . . . and why is it? What have I done to her? . . . I am so grateful to you that I would gladly make any sacrifice for you . . . but it's no use . . ." Sonya could say no more, and again she buried her face in the cushion and her hands. Natasha tried to calm her, but it was obvious by her face that she understood all the depth of Sonya's woe.

"Sonya!" she exclaimed suddenly, as if surmising the actual reason of her cousin's grief, "truly, didn't Vera say something to you after dinner? Tell me!"

"Nikolai wrote these verses himself, and I copied off some other ones; and she found them on my table and said that she was going to show them to dear mama, and she said, too, that I was ungrateful, that dear mama would never let him marry me, and that he was going to marry Julie. You saw how he behaved with her all the time . . . Natasha! why should such things happen?"

And again she began to sob, more bitterly than before. Natasha tried to raise her, threw her arms around her, and smiling through her tears, began to console her.

"Sonya, don't you believe her, dear heart; don't believe her. Don't you remember we three and Nikolai talked together in the sitting room, after lunch? Why, we thought it all out, how everything would be. I don't exactly remember how it was, but you know it will be all right and everything can be arranged. There was Uncle Shinshin's brother married his own cousin, and we are only second cousins. And Boris said that that was perfectly possible. You know I tell him everything. For he is so clever and so kind," said Natasha. "Now, Sonya, don't cry any more, darling, sweetheart, Sonya," and she kissed her, and laughed happily; "Vera is spiteful, I'm sorry for her! But all will be well, and she won't say anything to dear mama; Nikolai himself will tell her, and he doesn't care anything about Julie," and she kissed Sonya on her hair.

Sonya jumped up and again the kitten became lively, its eyes danced, and it was ready, waving its tail, to spring down on its soft little paws and to play with the ball again, as was perfectly natural for it to do.

"Do you think so? Truly? Do you swear it?" said she quickly, smoothing out her crumpled dress and hair.

"Truly! I swear it!" replied Natasha, tucking an unruly tuft of curly hair back under her cousin's braid. "Now, let us go and sing 'The Fountain.'"

XV

AT THE very time when in the Rostofs' ballroom they were dancing the sixth *Anglaise*, and the musicians from weariness were beginning to play out of tune, and the tired servants and cooks were preparing the late supper, Count Bezukhof had his sixth stroke of apoplexy. The doctors declared there was not the slightest hope that he would rally from it. Confession and Communion were administered to the dying man, and preparations were being made for extreme unction, while the mansion was filled with the bustle and expectation usual in such circumstances. Outside the house, around the doors, hidden by the throngs of carriages, gathered the undertakers, hoping to reap a rich harvest from the count's obsequies. The military governor of Moscow, who had sent his adjutant constantly to inquire about the count, this evening came himself to bid farewell to the famous grandee of Catherine's time.

The magnificent reception room was crowded. All rose deferentially when the governor, who had been closeted for half an hour with the sick man, came out, bowing slightly in reply to the salutations and endeavoring to pass as rapidly as possible by the doctors, priests and relatives who fixed their eyes upon him. Prince Vasili, grown a trifle thinner and paler during these last days, accompanied the military governor, repeating something in an undertone.

Having seen the military governor to the door, Prince Vasili sat down alone in the salon, threw one leg over the other, rested his elbow on his knee and covered his eyes with his hand. Having sat that way for some little time, he got up and with hasty irregular steps, looking around with startled eyes, he passed through the long corridor that led to the rear portion of the house, to the room occupied by the oldest of the three princesses. It was almost dark in the room; two votary lamps flickered before the holy images and there was a pleasant odor of incense and flowers. The whole room was furnished with small pieces of furniture, chiffoniers, cabinets, and little tables. Behind a screen could be seen the white curtain of a high-posted bedstead. A little dog came running out and barking.

"Ah, is it you, cousin?"

She got up and smoothed her hair, which, as always, was so extraordinarily smooth that one would have thought it made of one piece with her head and then covered with varnish.

"What is it? What has happened?" she asked. "You startled me so!"

"Nothing! There is no change, I only came to have a talk with you, Catherine—about business," said the prince, wearily sitting down in the chair

51

from which she had just risen. "How warm it is here," he exclaimed. "However, sit down; let us talk."

"I thought something must have happened," said the princess, and she took a seat in front of him, with her face hard and stony as usual and prepared to hear what he had to say. "I was trying to get a nap, cousin, and I could not."

"Well, my dear," said Prince Vasili, taking the princess' hand and bending it over in a way peculiar to himself.

It was evident that this "well, my dear," referred to a number of things, which, though unspoken, were understood by both of them.

The princess, having picked up the little dog, held it in her dry, thin hands on her lap and scrutinized the prince sharply, but it was plain to see that she did not intend to break the silence by asking any question, even though she sat till morning.

"Do you not see, my dear princess and cousin," continued Prince Vasili, evidently bringing himself, not without an inward struggle, to attack the subject; "at such moments as this, we must think about all contingencies. We must think about the future, about ourselves. . . . I love all of you as if you were my own children; you know that."

The princess gazed at him stonily, betraying no sign of her feelings.

"Finally, it is necessary, also, to think of my family," continued Prince Vasili, averting his eyes from her and irritably giving a small table a push. "You know, Catherine, that you three Mamontof sisters and my wife are the count's only direct heirs. I know, I know how hard it is for you to speak and think about such things. And it is no easier for me; but, my dear, I am sixty years old, I must be ready for anything. Do you know that I had to send for Pierre? The count pointed directly at his portrait, signifying that he wanted to see him."

Prince Vasili looked questioningly at the princess, but he could not make out whether she comprehended what he had said to her or was simply looking at him.

"Cousin, I do not cease to pray God for him," she replied, "that He will pardon him and grant his noble soul a peaceful passage from this . . ."

"Yes, of course," hastily interposed Prince Vasili, rubbing his bald forehead and again angrily drawing toward him the table that he had just pushed away. "But—but—to make a long story short, this is what I mean: You yourself know that last winter the count signed a will by which all his property was left to Pierre, and all the rest of us were left out in the cold."

"But think how many wills he has made!" replied the princess, calmly. "Besides, he can't leave his property to Pierre. Pierre is illegitimate."

"My dear girl," said Prince Vasili, suddenly clutching the table in his excitement, and speaking more rapidly, "but supposing a letter has been written to the emperor, in which the count begs to have Pierre legitimatized? Don't you understand that in view of the count's services his petition would be granted?"

The princess smiled that smile of superiority peculiar to people who think they know more about any matter than those with whom they are talking.

"I will tell you, moreover," pursued Prince Vasili, seizing her by the hand, "the letter has been written, but it has not been sent yet, and the emperor knows about it. The question is this: has it been destroyed or not? If not, then, as soon as all is over"—Prince Vasili sighed, giving to understand what he meant to convey by the words "all is over"—"then the count's papers will be opened, the will and the letter will be handed to the emperor, and the petition will undoubtedly be granted. Pierre, as the legitimate son, will inherit all!"

"But our share?" demanded the princess, smiling ironically, as if all things except this were possible.

"But, my poor Catherine, it is as clear as day. Then he will be the only legal heir and will have everything, and you will simply get nothing. You ought to know, my dear, whether the will and the letter have been written, or whether they have been destroyed. And if they have been forgotten, then you ought to know where they are and how to find them, so that . . ."

"That's the last straw!" interrupted the princess, smiling sardonically without changing the expression of her eyes. "I am a woman, and according to your idea all of us women are stupid, but I know well enough that an illegitimate son cannot inherit . . . *un bâtard!*" she added, with the intention of showing the prince, by this French term, conclusively how inconsistent he was.

"Why can't you understand, Catherine! You are so clever! Why can't you understand that if the count has written a letter to the emperor begging him to legitimatize his son, of course, Pierre will not be Pierre any longer, but Count Bezukhof, and then he will inherit the whole according to the will? And if the will and the letter are not destroyed, then you will get nothing except the consolation of knowing that you were dutiful and brought these consequences on us all! That is one sure thing!"

"I know that the will has been signed, but I know also that it not good for anything, and it seems to me, cousin, that you take me for a perfect fool," said the princess, with that expression that women assume when they think they have said something pointed and insulting.

"My dear Princess Catherine," impatiently reiterated Prince Vasili, "I did not come with the intention of having an argument with you, but to talk with you about your own interests as with a relative—a kind, good, true relative. I tell you for the tenth time that if this letter to the emperor and the will in Pierre's favor are among the count's papers, then you, my dear little pigeon, will not inherit anything, nor your sisters either. If you don't believe me, then ask somebody who does know. I have just been talking with Dmitri Onufriyitch (the count's lawyer), and he says the same thing."

A change came over the princess' thoughts; her thin lips grew white (her eyes remained the same), and her voice when she spoke evidently surprised even herself by the violence of its gusty outburst.

53

"That would be fine!" said she. "I have never desired anything, and I don't now." She pushed the dog from her lap and straightened the folds of her dress. "Here is gratitude, here's recognition for all the sacrifices that people have made for him!" cried she. "Excellent! Admirable! I don't need anything, prince."

"Yes, but it is not you alone: you have sisters," replied Prince Vasili. The princess, however, did not heed him.

"Yes, I have known for a long time, but I had forgotten it, that I had nothing to expect in this house except baseness, deception, envy, intrigue; nothing except ingratitude, the blackest ingratitude."

"Do you know or do you not know where that will is?" asked Prince Vasili, his cheeks twitching even more than before.

"Yes, I was stupid; I have always had faith in people, and loved them, and sacrificed myself. But only those are successful who are base and low. I know through whose intrigues this came about."

The princess wanted to rise, but the prince detained her by the arm. The princess' face suddenly took on the expression of one who has become soured against the whole human race; she looked angrily at her relative.

"There is still time enough, my pet. You must know, my dear Catherine, that all this may have been done hastily, in a moment of pique, of illness, and then forgotten. Our duty, my dear, is to correct his mistake, to soothe his last moments, so that he cannot in decency commit this injustice; we must let him die with the idea that he was making unhappy those who—"

"Those who have sacrificed everything for him," interrupted the princess, taking the words out of his mouth. Again she tried to get up, but still the prince would not allow her. "And he has never had the sense to perceive it. No, cousin," she added, with a sigh, "I shall yet live to learn that it is idle to expect one's reward in this world; that in this world there is no such thing as honor or justice; in this world one must be shrewd and wicked."

"Well, well, now calm yourself; I know your good heart."

"No; I have a wicked heart."

"I know your heart," repeated the prince. "I prize your friendship, and I could wish that you had as high an opinion of me. Calm yourself and let us talk sensibly. Now is the time . . . perhaps we have a few hours, perhaps a few moments . . . now tell me all you know about this will, and above all where it is; you must know. He has probably forgotten all about it. Now we must take it and show it to the count. Probably he has forgotten all about it, and would wish it to be destroyed. You understand that my sole desire is to religiously carry out his wishes, and that is why I came here. I am here only to help him and you."

"Now I understand all. I know whose intrigues are to blame. I know," said the princess.

"That is not to the point, my dear."

"It is your protégée, your dear Princess Drubetskoy, Anna Mikhailovna, whom I would not hire as my chambermaid—that filthy, low woman!"

"Let us not lose time," said the prince, in French.

"Oh! don't speak to me. Last winter she sneaked in here, and she told the count such vile things, such foul things, about all of us, especially about Sophie—I cannot repeat them—so that the count was taken ill, and for two weeks would not see any of us. It was at that time, I know, that he wrote that nasty, vile paper, but I supposed that it was not important."

"That is just the point; why didn't you tell me before?"

"In the hand-painted portfolio which he keeps under his pillow. Now I know," continued the princess. "Yes, if I have any sins on my soul, my greatest sin is my hatred of that horrid woman," she almost cried, her face all convulsed. "And why did she sneak in here? But I will tell her what I think of her, that I will. The time will come!"

XVI

WHILE THIS conversation went on in the princess' apartment, the carriage with Pierre (who had been sent for) and Anna Mikhailovna (who found it essential to accompany him) drove into Count Bezukhof's courtyard. When the carriage wheels rolled noiselessly in on the straw scattered under the windows, Anna Mikhailovna turned to her companion with consoling words, but was surprised to find him asleep in the corner of the carriage. She awakened him, and he followed her from the carriage, and then for the first time he thought of the meeting with his dying father that was before him.

"Perhaps the count did not call for me," he said when they reached the upper floor. "I had better go to my room."

Anna Mikhailovna waited till Pierre overtook her.

"Ah, my dear," said she, laying her hand on his arm, just as she had done that morning to her son, "believe that I suffer as much as you, but be a man!"

"Really, had I better go?" asked Pierre, looking affectionately at Anna Mikhailovna through his spectacles.

"Ah, my dear," said she, "forget the wrongs that may have been done you; remember he is your father—perhaps even now dying." She sighed. "I have loved you from the very first like my own son. Trust in me, Pierre. I will not forget your interests."

Pierre did not in the least comprehend, but again he felt quite clearly that all this had to be as it was, and he submissively followed Anna Mikhailovna, who had already opened the door. The door led into the vestibule of the rear apartments. In one corner sat an old manservant of the princesses', knitting a stocking. Pierre had never before been in this part of the house; he was not even aware of the existence of such rooms.

Anna Mikhailovna spoke to a maid whom she saw hurrying along with a carafe on a tray, and calling her by various familiar terms of endearment, asked how the princesses were, and at the same time beckoned Pierre to follow her along the stone corridor.

The first door on the left led into the princesses' private rooms. The chambermaid with the carafe, in her haste (everything was done in haste at this time in the house), failed to close the door, and Pierre and Anna Mikhailovna, as they passed by, involuntarily glanced into the room, where sat the oldest of the nieces in close conference with Prince Vasili. Seeing them passing, Prince Vasili made a hasty movement and drew himself up; the princess sprang to her feet, and in her vexation slammed the door with all her might.

This action was so unlike the princess' habitual serenity, the fear on the prince's face was so contrary to his ordinary expression of pompous dignity, that Pierre paused and looked inquiringly at his guide through his spectacles. Anna Mikhailovna showed no surprise; she merely smiled slightly and sighed, as if to signify that all this was to be expected.

"Be a man, my dear! I will watch over your interests," said she, in answer to his glance, and tripped along the corridor even more hurriedly than before.

Pierre did not comprehend what the trouble was and still less her words "watch over your interests," but he came to the conclusion that all this must be so.

They entered the reception room, with its two Italian windows, its door leading into the "winter garden," a room with a colossal bust and a full-length portrait of the Empress Catherine. The room was filled with the same people in almost the same attitudes, sitting and whispering together. They all ceased talking and stared at Anna Mikhailovna as she entered with her pale, tear-stained face, followed by the stout, burly Pierre, hanging his head.

Not two minutes passed before Prince Vasili, in his belted coat, with three stars on his breast, his head tilted back, came into the room. He seemed thinner than when Pierre had last seen him; his eyes opened wider than usual when he glanced about the room and caught sight of Pierre. He went straight up to him, took his hand (a thing he had never done before), and bent it down as if trying by experiment whether it had any power of resistance.

"Courage, courage, my dear fellow! he has asked to see you. That is good . . ." and he started to move away. But Pierre felt impelled to ask, "How is he?" He stammered, not knowing exactly what to call the dying count; he was ashamed to call him father.

"He had another stroke half an hour ago. Courage, my friend."

Pierre was in such a dazed condition of mind that at the word "stroke" he imagined a blow of some kind. He looked at Prince Vasili in perplexity, and it was only after some time that he was able to gather that "stroke" meant an attack of apoplexy.

Prince Vasili, as he went by, said a few words to Lorrain, the doctor, who was present, and went into the bedroom on his tiptoes. He was not used to walking on his tiptoes and his whole body jerked awkwardly as he walked. He was immediately followed by the oldest princess; then came the confessor and priests; some of the domestics also passed through the door. There was some commotion in the next room, and finally Anna Mikhailovna, with the same pale countenance, firmly bent on the fulfilment of her duties, came running out, and, touching Pierre on the arm, said: "The goodness of God is inexhaustible; the ceremony of divine unction is about to begin. Come!"

Pierre entered the room, treading on the soft carpet, and noticed that the adjutant and a strange lady and one of the servants followed him, as if now it were no longer necessary to ask permission to enter.

Pierre was familiar with this vast room, divided by columns and an arch, all hung with Persian tapestries. The part of the chamber behind the columns, where on one side stood a high mahogany bedstead with silken curtains, and on the other a monstrous shrine with icons, was all brightly and beautifully lighted, just as churches are usually lighted for evening service.

Under the glittering decorations of this shrine stood a long couch, and on the couch, supported by snowy-white cushions, with fresh pillow slips, lay the majestic form of Pierre's father, Count Bezukhof, his hair brushed up on his lofty forehead like a lion's mane, as Pierre remembered it so well, and the same stern deep wrinkles on his handsome, aristocratic face, reddish yellow in color. He was wrapped to the waist in a bright green quilt, and lay directly under the holy pictures; both of his great stout arms were uncovered and reposed on the quilt. In his right hand, which lay palm down, he held a wax taper between the thumb and forefinger, and an old servant, bending over the chair, kept it upright. Around the chair stood the clergy in their magnificent glittering robes, with their long hair streaming down over their shoulders, with lighted tapers in their hands, performing their functions with slow solemnity. A little back of them stood the two younger princesses with handkerchiefs in their hands, pressed to their eyes, and just in front of them was the oldest sister, Catherine, with a spiteful resolute expression, not for a moment letting her eyes wander from the icon, as if she was saying to all that she would not be responsible for her actions if she looked around. Anna Mikhailovna, with an expression of meek grief and pardon to all sinners on her face, stood near the door with the strange lady. Prince Vasili, on the other side of the door, nearer the count, stood behind a carved chair, upholstered in velvet, which he had turned around and on which he rested his left hand with a taper, while crossing himself with his right hand, raising his eyes each time his fingers touched his forehead. His face expressed calm devoutness and submission to the will of God. "If you cannot comprehend these sentiments, so much the worse for you," his countenance seemed to say.

Behind him stood the adjutant, the doctors and the menservants; just as in church, the men and women took opposite sides. No one spoke; all kept crossing themselves; the only sound was the reading of the service, the low subdued chanting of the priests' deep bass voices, and during the intervals of silence the restless movement of feet and deep sighs.

With the noiseless steps of a man possessed of perfect health, the French doctor went over to the sick man, lifted in his white, slender fingers the hand that lay on the green quilt, and bending over, began to count the pulse and grew grave. Something was given to the invalid to drink, there was a slight stir about him; then once more they all took their places and the service proceeded.

At the time of this interruption Pierre noticed that Prince Vasili left his position behind the carved chair and, after the oldest of the princesses joined him, retired with her into the depths of the alcove, to the high bedstead under the silken hangings. From there both the prince and the princess disappeared through the rear door, but before the end of the service both returned to their places, one after the other.

The sounds of the church chant ceased; the voice of the priest was heard respectfully congratulating the sick man on having received the mystery. The count lay as before, motionless and apparently lifeless. Around him there was a stir; footsteps and whisperings were heard; Anna Mikhailovna's voice could be distinguished above the rest. Pierre listened, and heard her say:

"He must be carried instantly to his bed; it will never do in the world for him to . . ."

The doctors, princesses, and servants crowded around the invalid so that Pierre could no longer see that reddish-yellow face with the gray mane of hair, which ever since the service began had constantly filled his vision to the exclusion of everything else. He surmised by the guarded movements of those who crowded around the armchair that they were lifting and carrying the dying man.

"Hold on to my arm! You'll drop him, this way," said one of the servants in a frightened whisper. . . . "Get him lower down!" . . . "Once more," said different voices, and the labored breathing and shuffling of feet growing more hurried seemed to indicate that the load the men were carrying was beyond their strength.

As the bearers, among their number Anna Mikhailovna, came opposite the young man, he caught a momentary glimpse over their heads and backs of his father's strong, full chest uncovered, his stout shoulders lifted above the people holding him under his arms, and his leonine head with its curly mane. The face, with its extraordinary high forehead and cheekbones, its handsome, sensitive mouth and majestic, cold eyes, was undisfigured by the nearness of death. It was just as when Pierre had seen it three months before, when the count had sent him to Petersburg. But the head rolled helplessly to the uneven steps of the bearers, and the cold, indifferent eyes gave no sign of recognition.

There followed a few moments of bustle around the high bedstead; those who had been carrying the sick man withdrew. Anna Mikhailovna touched Pierre on the arm and said, "Come." Pierre went with her to the bed, where the sick man had been placed in a rigid position, evidently in some manner suitable to the sacrament just accomplished. He lay with his head propped high on pillows. His hands lay side by side, palm downward, on the green silk quilt. As Pierre went to him, the count was looking straight at him, but his look had a meaning and significance it was impossible to comprehend. Either that look meant nothing and merely fastened upon him because his eyes must needs look at something, or they had too much to say.

Pierre paused, not knowing what was expected of him, and glanced inquiringly at his guide. Anna Mikhailovna made a hasty motion with her eyes toward the sick man's hand, and with her lips signified that he should kiss it. Pierre bent over carefully so as not to disturb the quilt, and in accordance with her advice touched his lips to the broad, brawny hand. Neither the hand nor a muscle of the count's face moved. Pierre again looked questioningly at Anna Mikhailovna to ask what he should do next. She signed to him with her eyes to sit down in an armchair which stood near the bed. Pierre submissively sat down, his eyes mutely asking if he were doing the right thing. Anna Mikhailovna approvingly nodded her head. Pierre again assumed the symmetrically simple attitude of the Egyptian statue, and evidently really suffered because his awkward, huge frame took up so much space, though he strove with all his might to make it seem as small as possible. He looked at the count. The count was staring at the spot where Pierre had just been standing.

This lasted two minutes, which seemed an hour to Pierre. Suddenly a tremor appeared in the deep, powerful muscles and lines of the count's face. It grew more pronounced; the handsome mouth was drawn to one side (this caused Pierre for the first time to realize how near to death his father was) and from the drawn mouth proceeded an indistinguishable hoarse sound. Anna Mikhailovna looked anxiously into the sick man's eyes and tried to make out what he wanted, pointing first at Pierre, then at a glass of water; then she asked in a whisper if she should call Prince Vasili, then pointed at the quilt. The sick man's face and eyes expressed impatience. He mustered force enough to look at the manservant who never left his master's bedside.

"He wants to be turned over on the other side," whispered the servant, and proceeded to lift and turn the count's heavy body face to the wall.

Pierre got up to help the servant.

Just as they were turning the count over, one of his arms fell back helplessly, and he made a futile effort to raise it. Did the count notice the look of terror in Pierre's face at the sight of that lifeless arm? or did some other thought flash across his dying brain at that moment? At all events, he looked at his disobedient hand, then at Pierre's terror-stricken face, and back to his hand again, and over his lips played a martyr's weak smile, out of character with his powerful features and seeming to express a feeling of scorn for his own lack of strength. At the sight of this smile, Pierre unexpectedly felt an oppression around the heart, a strange pinching in his nose, and the tears dimmed his eyes. The sick man lay on his side toward the wall. He drew a long sigh.

"He is going to sleep," said Anna Mikhailovna to one of the nieces, who had returned to watch. "Let us leave him."

Pierre left the room.

XVII

THERE WAS no one in the reception room except Prince Vasili and the oldest princess, and these two were sitting under the empress' portrait, talking eagerly about something. As soon as they caught sight of Pierre and his guide, they stopped.

"Catherine has had tea made in the little drawing-room," said Prince Vasili, addressing Anna Mikhailovna. "Come, my poor Anna Mikhailovna, you had better have something to eat, or you will collapse."

He said nothing to Pierre, but gave his arm a sympathetic pressure just below the shoulder. Pierre and Anna Mikhailovna went into what Prince Vasili called the little drawing-room.

Around the table were gathered for refreshments all those who were spending this night in Count Bezukhof's mansion. Pierre well remembered this little circular drawing-room, with its mirrors and small tables. In days gone by, when the count gave balls, Pierre, who did not know how to dance, liked to sit in this little room of mirrors and watch the ladies as they passed through in their ball gowns, with diamonds and pearls on their bare necks, glance at themselves in the brightly illuminated mirrors, which reflected back their elegance. Now the room was dimly lighted by a pair of candles.

Pierre did not eat anything, though he was very hungry. He glanced inquiringly at his guide and saw that she was tiptoeing back to the reception room, where they had left Prince Vasili and the oldest niece. Pierre took it for granted that this, also, was as it should be, and after waiting a little while he followed her. Anna Mikhailovna was standing in front of the young lady, and both were talking at once in angry undertones.

"Permit me, princess, to decide what is necessary and what is not necessary," Princess Catherine was saying, evidently still in the same angry frame of mind as when she slammed the door of her room.

"But, my dear young princess," said Anna Mikhailovna in a sweet but conclusive manner, barring the way to the count's chamber, and not allowing the young lady to pass, "will this not be too great an effort for poor uncle at this time, when he so needs rest? At this time any conversation about worldly matters, when his soul has already been prepared . . ."

Prince Vasili still sat in the armchair in his familiar posture, with one leg thrown over the other. His cheeks twitched violently, and seemed to grow flabbier than usual, but he preserved the attitude of a man to whom the altercation of the two women was of no consequence.

"Come, my good Anna Mikhailovna, let Catherine have her way. You know how fond the count is of her."

"I don't even know what is in this paper," said the young princess, turning to Prince Vasili, and pointing to the hand-painted portfolio she had in her hand. "I only know that his last will is in his bureau, but this is a paper he has forgotten."

She tried to pass by Anna Mikhailovna, but Anna Mikhailovna, springing forward, again barred her way.

"I know, my dear good princess," said Anna Mikhailovna, grabbing the portfolio, and so firmly that it was evident she would not let go in a hurry. "My dear princess, I beg of you, I beseech you, have pity upon him."

The young princess said not a word. The only sound was that of the scuffle for possession of the portfolio.

It was obvious that if she opened her mouth to speak, what she would say would not be flattering to Anna Mikhailovna. The latter clung to the portfolio relentlessly, but her voice preserved all its softness, sweetness, and gentleness.

"Pierre, my dear, come here. I think he will not be superfluous in this family council, will he, prince?"

"Why don't you speak, cousin?" suddenly cried the young princess, so loud that those in the little drawing-room heard it, and were startled. "Why don't you speak, when this impertinent creature permits herself to meddle in matters that don't concern her, and make scenes on the very threshold of the death chamber! Vile schemer!" she hissed in a loud whisper, and snatched at the portfolio with all her force; but Anna Mikhailovna took two or three steps forward so as not to let go of it, and succeeded in keeping it in her hand.

"Oh!" cried Prince Vasili, with a look of surprise and reproach. He stood up. "This is absurd! Come, now, let go, I tell you!"

Princess Catherine obeyed.

"You also!"

Anna Mikhailovna paid no attention to him.

"Drop it, I tell you. I will assume the whole responsibility. I will go and ask him. I . . . That ought to satisfy you," said Prince Vasili.

"But, prince," said Anna Mikhailovna, "after receiving the sacrament allow him a moment of repose. Pierre, give us your opinion," said she, turning to the young man, who, coming close to them, looked in amazement at the young princess' angry face, from which all dignity had departed, and at Prince Vasili's twitching cheeks.

"Remember that you will answer for all the consequences," said Prince Vasili, angrily; "you don't know what you are doing."

"You vile woman," screamed the young princess, unexpectedly darting at

Anna Mikhailovna and snatching away the portfolio. Prince Vasili hung his head and flung out his hands.

At this juncture the door, that dread door at which Pierre had been looking so long, and which was usually opened so gently, was hastily and noisily flung back, so that it hit the wall, and the second sister rushed out, wringing her hands.

"What are you doing?" she cried, in despair. "He is dying, and you leave me alone."

Princess Catherine dropped the portfolio. Anna Mikhailovna hastily bent down, and, picking up the precious object, hastened into the death chamber. Princess Catherine and Prince Vasili, regaining their composure, joined her. In a few moments Princess Catherine came out again, the first of all, with a pale, stern face, biting her lower lip. At the sight of Pierre her face expressed uncontrollable hatred.

"Now, now you can rejoice," said she. "You have been waiting for this," and, sobbing, she hid her face in her handkerchief and ran from the room.

The princess was followed by Prince Vasili. Reeling a little, he went to the sofa on which Pierre was sitting and flung himself on it, covering his face with his hands. Pierre noticed that he was pale, and that his lower jaw trembled and shook as if from an attack of ague.

"Ah, my friend," said he, taking Pierre by the elbow, and there was in his voice a sincerity and gentleness that Pierre had never before noticed in it. "How we sin and how we cheat, and all for what? I am sixty years old, my dear. . . . Look at me. . . . Death is the end of all, all! Death is horrible!"

He burst into tears.

Anna Mikhailovna came out last of all. She went straight up to Pierre, with slow, quiet steps.

"Pierre!" said she.

Pierre looked at her inquiringly. She kissed the young man on the forehead, which she wet with her tears. Then after a silence she added:

"He is dead."

Pierre peered at her through his glasses.

"Come, I will take you away. Try to weep. Nothing is so consoling as tears."

She led him into the dark drawing-room, and Pierre was relieved that no one was there to see his face. Anna Mikhailovna left him there, and when she returned he was sound asleep with his head resting on his arm.

The next morning Anna Mikhailovna said to Pierre:

"Yes, my dear, it is a great loss for all of us. I am not speaking of you. But God will give you support; you are young, and at the head of an immense fortune, I hope. The will has not been opened yet. I know you well enough to believe that this will not turn your head, but new duties will devolve upon you, and you must be a man."

Pierre made no reply.

"Perhaps later I will tell you, my dear, that if I had not been here . . . God knows what might have happened. You know uncle, only the day before, promised me that he would not forget Boris. But he did not have the time; I hope, my dear friend, that you will fulfil your father's desire."

Pierre completely failed to see what she was driving at, and, without saying anything and with mortification, looked at Princess Anna Mikhailovna. Having thus spoken with Pierre, she drove back to the Rostofs' and lay down to rest. After her nap, that same morning, she began to tell the Rostofs and all her acquaintances the details of the death of Count Bezukhof. She declared that the count had died as she herself would wish to die, that his end had been not only pathetic but even edifying; the last meeting of father and son had been so touching that she could not recall it without tears, and she could not tell which had borne himself with more composure during these dreadful moments, the father who had had a thought for everything and everyone during those last hours, and had spoken such affectionate and touching words to his son; or Pierre, whom it was pitiful to see, he was so overcome, and yet in spite of it struggled so manfully to hide his grief so as not to pain his dying father.

"Such scenes are painful, but they do one good; it is elevating to the soul to see such men as the old count and his worthy son."

She also spoke of the behavior of Princess Catherine and Prince Vasili, but in terms of censure, and under the promise of the strictest secrecy.

XVIII

THE ARRIVAL of young Prince Andrei and his wife at Lisiya Gori, Prince Nikolai Bolkonsky's estate, was daily expected. But this made no break at all in the strenuous routine of life in the old prince's mansion. Prince Nikolai, a former general-in-chief, nicknamed in society "the King of Prussia," had been banished to his estates during the reign of the Emperor Paul, and had lived like a hermit there ever since with his daughter, Princess Maria, and her hired companion, Mlle. Bourienne. Even after the new reign had begun, although he was free to go wherever he pleased, he continued to live exclusively in the country, saying that if anyone wanted him it was only thirty miles from Moscow to Lisiya Gori, and he himself needed nothing and nobody.

He declared that there were only two sources of human vice, idleness and superstition; and only two virtues, activity and intelligence. He himself undertook his daughter's education, and in order to inculcate both these virtues he gave her lessons up to the age of twenty in algebra and geometry, and apportioned her life into an uninterrupted schedule of occupations. He was constantly engaged in writing his memoirs, or in solving problems in higher mathematics, or in turning snuffboxes on a lathe, or in working in his garden and superintending the erection of buildings, which were always being erected on his estate. As the chief condition of activity is order, order in his scheme of life was enacted to the utmost. His appearance at meals invariably took place under the same circumstances each day, and not only at the same hour but at the same moment. The prince was harsh and so exacting with the people around him, from his daughter to the humblest menial, that while he was not cruel, he inspired an awe and deference such as it would have been difficult for even the cruelest man to exact. Although he was living in seclusion, and now had no influence in matters of state, every official of the province considered it a duty to pay his respects to the prince, and, precisely as the architect or the gardener or Princess Maria, awaited the designated hour for his appearance in the lofty hall. And each of those waiting in this hall experienced the same feeling of awe and fear when the massive door of his study swung open and the form of the little old man appeared, in his powdered wig, with his small, dry hands and overhanging gray eyebrows which sometimes, when he frowned, concealed the gleam of his keen and youthfully glittering eyes.

On the morning of the day when the young couple were expected, Princess Maria, at the regular hour, came down into the hall to wish her father good morning, and with fear and trembling crossed herself and repeated an inward prayer. Each morning she came the same way, and each morning she prayed that their daily meeting might be propitious.

An aged servant in a powdered wig, who was sitting in the hall, got up quietly and addressed her in a respectful whisper: "I beg of you."

Beyond the door could be heard the monotonous hum of the lathe. The princess timidly opened the door, which moved easily and noiselessly on its hinges, and stood at the entrance. The prince was working at his lathe. He looked around and then went on with his work.

The great room was full of objects, apparently in constant use: a huge table whereon lay books and plans; high bookcases with keys in the mirror-lined doors; a large reading desk on which lay an open copybook; a cabinet-maker's lathe, with various kinds of tools and shavings and chips scattered around—all this indicated a constant, varied and regular activity. By the motion of his small foot, shod Tartar fashion in a silver-embroidered boot; by the firm pressure of his sinewy, thin hand, it could be seen that the prince had still the tenacious and undiminished strength of a green old age. Having made a few more turns, he took his foot from the treadle of the lathe, wiped his chisel and put it in a leather pocket attached to the lathe, and going to the table called his daughter to him. He never wasted caresses on his children, and therefore, merely offering his bristly cheek, which had not as yet been shaved for the day, he said, with a severe and at the same time keenly affectionate look:

"Are you well? . . . Now then, sit down."

He took a copybook of geometrical work written out in his own hand, and pushed his chair along with his foot.

"For tomorrow," said he, briskly, turning the page, and marking the paragraphs with his horny nail.

The princess leaned over the table toward the notebook.

"Wait, here's a letter for you," said the old man, abruptly taking an envelope addressed in a feminine hand from the pocket fastened to the table, and tossing it to her.

The princess' face colored in blotches at the sight of the letter. She hastily picked it up and examined it intently.

"From your Héloïse?" asked the prince, with a chilling smile that showed his sound, yellow teeth.

"Yes, from Julie," said the princess, timidly, glancing up.

"I shall allow two more letters to pass, but I shall read the third," said the prince severely. "I fear you write much nonsense. I shall read the third."

"You may read this, father," replied the princess, with a still deeper flush, holding the letter toward him.

"The third, I said, the third," rejoined the prince laconically, pushing away the letter; then, leaning his elbow on the table, he laid the notebook with the geometrical designs before her.

"Well, young lady, these triangles are equal; if you will observe, the angle ABC . . ."

The princess had not the slightest comprehension of what he said, and was so overcome with fear that it really prevented her from comprehending any of her father's instructions, no matter how clearly they were expressed. The teacher may have been at fault, or the pupil may have been, but each day the same thing recurred. The princess made a mistake in her answer.

"Now, how can you be so stupid!" stormed the prince, throwing aside the notebook and hastily turning away; then he rose to his feet, walked up and down, laid his hand on her hair, and again sitting down, drew close to her and proceeded with his instructions.

"No use, princess, no use," said he, as the young lady took the lesson book, and closing it started to leave the room; "mathematics is a great thing, my girl, and I don't wish you to be like our stupid, silly women. By dint of perseverance one learns to like it." He patted her on the cheek. "The dullness will vanish from your brain."

He patted her on the shoulder and, as she went out, closed the door himself.

The young Princess Maria returned to her chamber with the pensive, scared expression that rarely left her and rendered her plain, sickly face still more unattractive. She sat down at her writing table, covered with miniature portraits and cluttered with notebooks and volumes. The princess was just as disorderly as her father was systematic: she threw down her book of problems and hastily broke the seal of the letter, which was from her most intimate friend from childhood; this was no other than the Julie Karagina who was at the Rostofs' on the day of the reception.

Julie wrote as follows:

My dear delightful friend: What a terrible and frightful thing is absence! It is in vain I tell myself that in spite of the distance that lies between us, our hearts are bound to each other by indissoluble ties; mine rebels against my fate, and, notwithstanding all the pleasures and attractions that surround me, I cannot overcome a certain lurking sadness I have felt in the depths of my heart ever since our separation. Why can I not now, as I did three months ago, draw fresh moral strength from your eyes, so sweet, so calm, so penetrating, the eyes I loved so much and which I imagine I see before me as I write.

Having read to this point, Princess Maria sighed and glanced at the pier glass that stood opposite her, reflecting her slight, homely form and thin face. Her eyes, which were generally melancholy, just now looked with a peculiarly hopeless expression at her image in the glass.

"She is flattering me," said the princess to herself, turning away and continuing her reading of the letter. Julie, however, had not flattered her friend; the princess' eyes were really large, deep, and luminous; sometimes a bunch of rays of soft light seemed to gleam from them; and then they were so beautiful that they transfigured her whole face, notwithstanding the plainness of her features, and gave her a charm that was more attractive than mere beauty.

But the young princess had never seen the beautiful expression of her own eyes, the expression they had at times when she was not thinking of herself. Like most people's, her face assumed an affectedly unnatural and ill-favored expression as soon as she looked into the glass.

She went on with the letter:

All Moscow is talking of nothing but the war. Not to speak of my brothers, this war has deprived me of one who is nearest and dearest to my heart; I mean the young Nikolai Rostof, who was so enthusiastic that he was unable to endure inactivity, and has left the university to join the army. Ah, well, my dear Marie, I will confess to you that, notwithstanding his extreme youth, his departure for the army is a great grief to me. Someday I will tell you of our parting and what passed between us. I know very well that Count Nikolai is too young ever to be anything more than a friend to me, but this sweet friendship, this relationship, so poetic and so pure, has become one of the necessities of my heart. But enough of this!

The chief news of the day, which all Moscow is talking about, is the death of old Count Bezukhof and his will. Just imagine: The three princesses get very little, Prince Vasili nothing, and it is Monsieur Pierre who has inherited everything. He has, moreover, been declared legitimate, and is therefore Count Bezukhof, and the possessor of the finest fortune in Russia. It is claimed that Prince Vasili played a very poor part in this whole business, and that he has gone back to Petersburg very much crestfallen.

I confess I have very little understanding of this matter of the bequests and the will; all I know is that since this young man whom we knew as Monsieur Pierre, pure and simple, has become Count Bezukhof and master of one of the greatest fortunes of Russia, I am greatly amused to notice the changed tone and behavior of mamas burdened with marriageable daughters, and even the young ladies themselves, toward this individual, who has always seemed to me to be a poor specimen. As it has been the amusement of many people for the past few years to marry me off, and generally to men I do not even know, *la Chronique matrimoniale* of Moscow now makes me out Countess Bezukhof. You know perfectly well that I have no desire to acquire that position!

Speaking of marriage, do you know that quite recently the "universal auntie," Anna Mikhailovna, has confided to me, under the seal of the strictest secrecy, a marriage project for you; this is neither more nor less than Prince Vasili's son, Anatol, whom it is proposed to discipline by marrying him to a young lady of wealth and distinction, and you are the one on whom the choice of the relatives has fallen. I do not know how you will look upon the matter, but I felt that it was my duty to inform you. They say he is very handsome and a great scapegrace; that is all I have been able to find out about him.

XIX

The gray-haired manservant sat in the study, dozing and listening to the prince's snoring. At this time, a coach and a gig drove up to the entrance door, and from the coach descended Prince Andrei, who handed his little wife down and allowed her to pass ahead of him. The gray-haired Tikhon, in a wig, thrust his head out of the hall door and informed them in a whisper that the prince was asleep and then softly closed the door. Tikhon was well aware that not even the arrival of the son, or any other event, however uncommon, should be allowed to interrupt the order of the day. Prince Andrei knew this as well as Tikhon; he looked at his watch, as if to convince himself that there had been no change in his father's habits since he had seen him, and having satisfied himself on that score, turned to his wife.

"He will be awake in twenty minutes. Let us go to Princess Maria," said he.

The little princess had grown stouter, but her eyes, and her short, downy lip, and her sweet smile were just the same as ever as she exclaimed:

"Why, it is a palace!"

And she looked around with an expression such as people have in congratulating a host on a ball.

"Come along quick, quick!" . . . She smiled at Tikhon and her husband and the footman who was leading the way.

They went to the door of the sitting room, where some bars of a sonata were being repeated again and again. Prince Andrei paused and frowned, as if he were expecting something disagreeable.

The princess went in. The music broke off abruptly; someone exclaimed, and this was followed by the sound of hasty footsteps and kisses. When Prince Andrei went in, the two sisters-in-law, who had met only once for a short time at Prince Andrei's wedding, were still locked in a fond embrace, just as at the first moment of their meeting. Mlle. Bourienne was standing near them with her hand on her heart and a beatific smile on her lips, evidently as ready to cry as to laugh. Prince Andrei shrugged his shoulders and frowned, just as lovers of music frown when they hear a discord. Both the women stood apart; then once again, as if fearing that a moment would be lost, they seized each other's hands and began to kiss them; and not satisfied with kissing each other's hands, they began to kiss each other in the face, and, to Prince Andrei's unqualified surprise, they both burst into tears and again began to kiss each other. Mlle. Bourienne was also greatly moved; it was awkward enough for Prince Andrei, but to the women it seemed perfectly natural to weep.

"Ah, my dear!" . . . "Ah, Maria!" they kept exclaiming, amid laughter and tears. "I dreamed last night." . . . "And so you were not expecting us?" . . . "Ah, Maria, you have grown thin." . . . "And you have grown so stout!"

"I knew the princess the moment I saw her," put in Mlle. Bourienne.

"And here wasn't I thinking of such a thing!" cried Princess Maria . . . "Ah, Andrei, I did not see you!"

Prince Andrei kissed his sister's hand and told her that she was as great a crybaby as ever. Princess Maria turned to her brother, and through her tears her eyes, now large and beautiful and luminous, rested on him with a fond, gentle and sweet expression.

"And are you really going to the war, Andrei?" she asked, with a sigh. Lisa also sighed.

"Yes, and I must be off by tomorrow," replied her brother.

"He leaves me, and God knows why, when he might have been promoted."

Lisa's lip went down. She brought her face near to the young princess', and again unexpectedly burst into tears.

"She needs to rest," said Prince Andrei, scowling; "don't you, Lisa? Take her to her room and I will go to my father. How is he? Just the same as ever?"

"Just the same; but perhaps your eyes will see some change in him," replied the princess, cheerfully.

"The same regular hours, the same walks in the garden, the lathe?" asked Prince Andrei, with a barely perceptible smile which proved that notwithstanding all his love and reverence for his father, he was not blind to his weaknesses.

"Yes, just the same hours, and the lathe, and the mathematics, and my geometry lessons," replied the princess, merrily, as if her geometry lessons were among the great delights of her life.

When the twenty minutes which remained for the prince's nap were over, Tikhon came to summon the young man to see his father. The old man allowed a variation in his mode of life in honor of his son; he commanded to have Prince Andrei come to him in his own room while he was dressing (before dinner). The prince dressed in the old-time costume of a fitted long coat and powdered wig. When Prince Andrei—not with the peevish face and manners he assumed in society, but with a lively expression, such as he had when he was talking with Pierre—went into his father's room, the old man was in his dressing room, sitting in a wide morocco-upholstered armchair in a wrapper, while Tikhon was putting the last touches to his head.

"Ah, my warrior! So you are going to conquer Bonaparte?" cried the old prince, and he shook his powdered head, so far as he was allowed by the pigtail which Tikhon was busy plaiting. "You do well to go against him; otherwise he would soon be calling us his subjects! . . . Are you well?" and he offered his son his cheek.

The old man had awakened from his noon nap in an excellent frame of mind (he was accustomed to say that a nap after dinner was silver, but one before dinner was golden). He squinted cheerily at his son from under his thick, beetling brows. Prince Andrei went and kissed his father on the spot designated. He made no reply to his father's favorite topic of conversation or to his sarcasms on the military men of the present time and especially on Napoleon.

"Yes, I have come to you, father, and with my wife, who expects to be confined soon," said Prince Andrei, watching with eager and reverent eyes all the play of his father's features. "How is your health?"

"Only fools and rakes ever need be unwell, my boy, and you know me; busy from morning till night, and abstemious, and of course, I'm well."

"Thank God," said the son, smiling.

"God has nothing to do with it. Well," continued the old man, returning to his favorite hobby, "tell us how the Germans and Bonaparte have taught us to fight, according to this new science of yours that you call 'strategy'?"

Prince Andrei smiled.

"Let me have time to collect my wits, sir," said he, and his expression showed that his father's foibles did not prevent him from reverencing and loving him. "Why, you see I have not even been to my room yet."

"Nonsense, nonsense," cried the old man, pulling at his little pigtail to assure himself that it was firmly plaited, and grasping his son by the arm. "The quarters for your wife are all ready. Princess Maria will take her there and show them to her, and they will chatter their three basketfuls in their woman's way. I'm glad to have her here. Sit down and talk. I understand Michelson's army and Tolstoy's too. But what's the southern army going to do? What's Sweden going to do?"

Prince Andrei, perceiving the urgency of his father's inquiries, began at first unwillingly, but gradually warming up more and more, to explain the plan of operations determined upon for the campaign. As he spoke, he involuntarily, from very force of habit, kept changing from Russian into French. He explained how an army of ninety thousand was to threaten Prussia and force her to abandon her neutrality and take part in the war; how a portion of this army was to go to Stralsund and unite with the Swedish forces; how two hundred and twenty thousand Austrians, with a hundred thousand Russians, were to engage in active operations in Italy and on the Rhine; and how fifty thousand Russians and fifty thousand English were to disembark at Naples, and how this army, with a total of five hundred thousand men, was to make an attack simultaneously from different sides on the French.

The old prince did not manifest the least interest in the description, any more than if he had not heard it, and continued to dress himself as he walked up and down; though three times he unexpectedly interupted his son. Once he stopped him by crying, "The white one! the white one!" That meant Tikhon had not given him the waistcoat he wanted. The second time he stopped and asked, "And is the baby expected soon?" and reproachfully shaking his head, said, "That's too bad—go on, go on!"

The third time, when Prince Andrei had finished his description, the old man sang in a high falsetto, with the cracked voice of age:

> "*Malbrouck s'en va-t-en guerre.*
> *Dieu sait quand reviendra.*"

The son merely smiled.

"I don't say I approve of this plan," said he; "I am only telling you what it is. Napoleon, of course, has his plan, which is probably as good as ours."

"Well, you haven't told me anything that is in the least new," and the old man thoughtfully continued to hum the refrain: *Dieu sait quand il reviendra.*—"Go into the dining room."

At the appointed hour the prince, powdered and shaved, went to the dining room where his daughter-in-law, Princess Maria, Mlle. Bourienne and his architect were waiting for him. The latter was allowed at the table though a strange caprice of the prince, though from his position this insignificant man would never have been shown such an honor. The prince, who had a firm belief in the gradations of rank, and rarely admitted to his table even the important functionaries of the province, had suddenly selected Mikhail Ivanovitch (who blew his nose in the corner on a checked handkerchief) as a living example of the theory that all men are equal, and more than once assured his daughter that the architect was as good as they were. At the table the prince was very apt to address his conversation mainly to the silent Mikhail Ivanovitch.

In the dining room, tremendously lofty like other rooms in the mansion, the prince's butlers and servingmen, each standing behind a chair, awaited his entrance. The house steward, with a napkin over his arm, glanced to see that the table was properly set, beckoned to the servingmen, and constantly let his troubled eyes wander from the wall clock to the door where the prince was expected to enter. Prince Andrei was looking at a huge gilded frame, which he had never before seen, containing a representation of the genealogical tree of the Bolkonskys, which hung opposite a similar frame with a badly executed painting, evidently perpetrated by some domestic artist and meant to be a portrait of a reigning prince in a crown, showing that he was descended from Rurik and was the originator of the house of Bolkonsky. Prince Andrei was studying this genealogical tree, and shaking his head and laughing, as if the portrait struck him as something ludicrous.

"How like him this all is!" he was saying to Princess Maria, as she came up to him.

Princess Maria looked at her brother in amazement. She could not understand what he could find to amuse him. All that her father did inspired in her a reverence which removed it beyond criticism.

"Every man has his Achilles' heel," continued Prince Andrei. "With his tremendous intellect, the idea of indulging in this absurdity!"

The prince came in briskly, even gaily, as was his custom. From under his thick, overhanging brows, his keen, flashing, stern eyes surveyed all who were present, and then rested on his son's young wife. The young princess instantly experienced that feeling of fear and reverence which this old man inspired in all those around him—a feeling akin to that experienced by courtiers at the appearance of the Tsar.

He smoothed the princess' head, and then, with a clumsy motion, patted her on the back of the neck.

"I am glad to see you, glad to see you," said he; and after looking into her face steadily once more, he turned away and sat down in his place. "Sit down, sit down! Mikhail Ivanovitch, sit down."

He assigned his daughter-in-law the place next him; the servingman pushed the chair up for her.

"Ho! ho!" said the old man, looking at her critically, "your time is coming! Too bad!"

He smiled dryly, coldly, disagreeably, with his lips alone, as usual, and not with his eyes. "You must walk, walk, as much as possible; as much as possible," said he.

The little princess did not hear, or did not wish to hear, his words. She said nothing, and seemed depressed. The prince asked after her father, and she replied and smiled. He asked about common acquaintances; the princess

71

grew more animated, and began to deliver messages and tell the prince the gossip of the town.

"Countess Apraksina, poor woman, has lost her husband, and nearly cried her eyes out," said she, growing still more lively.

The livelier she became, the more sternly the prince looked at her, and suddenly, as if he had studied her enough and had formed a sufficiently clear idea of her mental caliber, he turned abruptly away and began to talk with Mikhail Ivanovitch.

"Well, now, Mikhail Ivanovitch, it is going to go hard with our Bonaparte. As Prince Andrei has been telling me"—he always spoke of his son in the third person—"great forces are collecting against him. But then, you and I have always considered him to be a windbag."

Mikhail Ivanovitch really did not know when he and the prince had ever said any such things about Bonaparte, but perceiving that this was necessary as a preliminary for the prince's favorite subject of conversation, looked in surprise at the young prince and wondered what would be the outcome of it.

"He is great at tactics," said the old prince to his son, referring to the architect. And he began to expatiate on all the blunders that Napoleon, in his opinion, had made in all his wars, and even in his act of administration. His son listened, refraining from engaging in any discussion, and only smiling as he involuntarily wondered how it was possible for this old man, who had lived for so many years like a hermit in the country, to know so thoroughly and accurately all the military and political occurrences that had taken place in Europe during the last years, and be able to form such an opinion of them.

The little princess, during the whole time of the discussion and the rest of the meal, sat in silence, looking in alarm now at her husband's father, now at Princess Maria. After they left the table she took her sister-in-law's arm and drew her into the next room.

"How brilliant your father is," said she. "That's probably the reason I am so afraid of him."

"Ah, he is so good!" exclaimed the princess.

XX

THE NEXT evening Prince Andrei was ready to depart. The old prince, not making any change in his routine, had gone to his room immediately after dinner. The young wife was with Princess Maria. Prince Andrei, having donned a traveling coat without epaulets, was busy packing in his room with his valet. He had personally attended to the carriage and the arrangement of his luggage, and ordered the horses to be put in. Only those things remained in his room that he always took with him: his dressing case, a huge silver bottleholder, two Turkish pistols, and a saber which his father had captured at Ochakof and presented to him.

If men are ever inclined to think about their actions, the moment when they are leaving home and embarking upon some new course of life is certain to induce a serious frame of mind. Generally, at such moments, the past comes up for review, and plans are made for the future. Prince Andrei's face was very thoughtful and tender. With his hands behind his back, he was walking briskly, from corner to corner, up and down the room. Was it terrible for him to be going to the war, or was he a little saddened at the thought of leaving his wife? Perhaps there was a trifle of each feeling. However, on hearing steps in the entry and not wishing to be seen in such a state, he hurriedly unclasped his hands and paused by the table as if engaged in fastening the cover of his dressing case, and his face became, as usual, serene and impenetrable.

The heavy steps he heard were those of Princess Maria.

"I was told that you had ordered the horses put in," said she, panting—she had evidently been running—"and I did so want to have a little talk with you all alone. God knows how long it will be before we see each other again. You are not angry with me for coming? You have changed very much, Andrei darling," she added, as if in explanation of such a question.

She smiled as she called him darling. Evidently it was strange for her to think that this stern, handsome man was the same little Andrei, the slender, frolicsome lad who had been the playmate of her childhood. A smile was his only reply to her question.

"Where is Lisa?" he asked.

"She was so tired that she fell asleep on the couch in my room! Oh, Andrei, what a treasure of a wife you have," she said, as she sat down on the sofa, facing her brother. "She is a perfect child, such a sweet, light-hearted child. I have learned to love her dearly!"

Prince Andrei made no reply, but the princess noticed the ironical and scornful expression her words evoked.

"But you must be tolerant of her little weaknesses; who is without them, Andrei? You must not forget that she was educated and brought up in metropolitan society. And now her life is not all roses. Just think how hard it is on the poor little woman, after the gay life to which she is accustomed, to be parted from her husband and to be left alone in the country, and in her condition! It is very hard!"

Prince Andrei smiled and looked at his sister, as we smile when we look at people whose motives are perfectly transparent to us.

"You live in the country and don't find this life so horrible, do you?"

"I?—but that's quite different. Why should you speak about me? I have no desire for any other life, because I have never known any other life. But think, Andrei, you know what poor company I am for a woman who has been accustomed to sophisticated society. There's only Mlle. Bourienne."

"Your Bourienne does not please me very much," said Prince Andrei.

"Oh, how can you say so? She is very kind and good, and what is more, is greatly to be pitied. She has no relatives, no friends, no one at all. To tell you the truth, I do not really need her at all; if anything, she is in my way. I love to be alone. Father is very fond of her. She and Mikhail Ivanovitch are two people to whom he is always polite and kind, because both of them are under obligation to him. As Sterne says, 'We do not love men so much for the good they do us as for the good we do them.' Father took her in as an orphan from the street, and she is very good, and father loves the way she reads. She always reads aloud to him in the evening. She reads beautifully."

"Now, really, Maria, I am afraid father's temper must be very trying to you sometimes, isn't it so?" asked Prince Andrei suddenly. Princess Maria was at first dumfounded, then terrified, at this question.

"To me . . . me . . . trying?" she stammered.

"He has always been harsh, but now he has become desperately trying, I should think," said Prince Andrei, speaking lightly of his father, apparently for the sake of perplexing or testing his sister.

"You're good to everyone, Andrei, but you have such pride of intellect," said the princess, following the trend of her own thoughts rather than the course of the conversation. "And that is a great sin. Have we any right to judge our father? And even if we had, what other feeling besides veneration could such a man inspire? And I am so happy and content to live with him. I only wish that all were as happy as I am."

Her brother shook his head incredulously.

"There is only one thing that is hard for me—I will tell you the truth about it, Andrei—it is father's approach to religious things. I cannot understand how a man with such immense intellect can fail to see what is as clear as day, and can go so far astray. This is the one thing that makes me unhappy. But even in this I have noticed lately a shade of improvement. Lately his sarcasms have not been quite so pronounced, and there is a monk he allowed to come in and have a long talk with him."

"Well, my dear, I am afraid that you and the monk wasted your powder," said Prince Andrei in a jesting but affectionate way.

"Ah! my dear! All I can do is pray to God and hope He will hear me. Andrei," she said timidly after a moment's silence, "I have one great favor to ask of you."

"What is that, my dear?"

"Promise me that you will not refuse me. It won't be any trouble to you at all and nothing unworthy of you in doing it; but it will be a great comfort to me. Promise me, Andrei darling," said she, thrusting her hand into her reticule and holding something in it but not yet showing it, as if what she held constituted the object of her request and she were unwilling to take this something from the reticule until she was assured of his promise. She looked at her brother with a timid, beseeching glance.

"Even if it required great trouble, I would," replied Prince Andrei, evidently foreseeing what the request was.

"Think whatever you please—I know that you are exactly like father—think whatever you please, but do this for my sake. Please do! My father's father, our grandfather, wore it in all his battles." Not even now did she take from the reticule what she held in her hand. "So, will you promise me?"

"But what is it?"

"Andrei, I give you this little medal with my blessing, and you must promise me that you will never take it off. Will you promise?"

"If it does not weigh a hundred pounds and won't break my neck, I will do it if it will give you any pleasure."

But at that instant, noticing the pained expression that passed over his sister's face at this jest, he regretted it. "With pleasure, really with pleasure, my dear," he added.

"Thank you, my dear."

She kissed him on the brow and again sat down on the couch. Both were silent.

"As I was saying to you, Andrei, be kind and magnanimous as you always used to be. Don't judge Lisa harshly," she began after a while. "She is so sweet, so good! and her position is very hard just now."

"Why, Maria, I have not told you that I have found any fault with my wife, or been vexed with her. Why do you say such things to me?"

Princess Maria flushed in patches and was silent as if she felt guilty.

"I have not said anything to you, but someone has been talking to you. And I am sorry for that."

The red patches flamed still more noticeably on Princess Maria's forehead, neck, and cheeks. She tried to say something, but speech failed her. Her brother had guessed right; his little wife after dinner had wept, and confessed her forebodings about the birth of her baby and how she dreaded it, and poured out her complaints against her fate and her father-in-law and her husband. And after she had cried, she fell asleep.

Prince Andrei was sorry for his sister.

"I wish you to know this, Maria, that I find no fault with my wife, I never have found fault with her and never will, and there is nothing for which I can reproach myself. But if you wish to know the truth . . . do you wish to know whether I am happy? No! Is she happy? No! Why is it? I don't know.". . .

And as he said this he got up, went over to his sister and, bending down, kissed her on the forehead. His handsome eyes showed an unwonted gleam of sentiment and kindliness, though he looked not at his sister, but over her head at the dark aperture of the door.

"Let's go to her, it is time to say good-by. Or, rather, you go ahead and wake her, and I will follow you."

On the way to his sister's room, in the gallery, which connected one part

75

of the house with the other, Prince Andrei met the sweetly smiling Mlle. Bourienne. It was the third time that she had crossed his path that day in the corridor, and with the same enthusiastic and naive smile.

"Ah, I thought you were in your own room," said she, blushing a little and dropping her eyes.

Prince Andrei looked at her sternly. His face suddenly grew wrathful. He gave her no answer, but looked at her forehead and hair, not into her eyes, with such a scornful expression that the little Frenchwoman flushed scarlet and turned away without another word.

When he reached his sister's room his wife was already awake, and her blithe voice was heard through the open door. She was chattering as fast as her tongue would let her, as if she were anxious to make up for lost time, after long repression:

"No, Maria, but just imagine the old Countess Zubova, with her false curls and a mouth full of false teeth, as if she could cheat old age! ha! ha! ha!"

Prince Andrei had heard his wife get off exactly the same phrase about the Countess Zubova at least five times. He went quietly into the room. The princess, plump and rosy, was sitting in an easy-chair with her work in her hands, and was talking an incessant stream, repeating her Petersburg reminiscences and even the familiar Petersburg phrases. Prince Andrei went up to her, smoothed her hair, and asked if she felt rested from her journey. She answered him and went on with her story.

A coach with a six-in-hand was waiting at the front entrance. It was a dark autumn night. The coachman could not see the pole of the carriage. Men with lanterns were standing on the doorsteps. The great mansion was alive with lights, shining through the lofty windows. The domestics were gathered in the entry to say good-by to the young prince; all the household was collected in the hall: Mikhail Ivanovitch, Mlle. Bourienne, Princess Maria, and her sister-in-law. Prince Andrei had been summoned to his father's study, where the old prince wished to bid him good-by privately. All were waiting for their coming.

When Prince Andrei went into the study, the old prince, with spectacles on his nose and wearing his white dressing gown, in which he never received anyone except his son, was sitting at the table and writing. He looked around.

"Are you off?" And he went on with his writing.

"I have come to bid you good-by."

"Kiss me here." He indicated his cheek. "Thank you, thank you."

"Why do you thank me?"

"Because you don't dillydally, because you don't hang on to your wife's petticoats. Service before all! Thank you! thank you!"

And he went on with his writing so vigorously that the ink flew from his sputtering pen. "If you have anything to say, speak. I can pay attention to two things at once," he added.

"About my wife—I am so sorry to be obliged to leave her on your hands."

"What nonsense is that? Tell me what you want."

"When it is time for my wife to be confined, send to Moscow for a good obstetrician. Have him here early."

The old prince paused, and pretending not to understand, fixed his stern eyes on his son.

"I know that no one can help if nature does not do her work," said Prince Andrei, evidently confused; "I am aware that out of millions of cases only one goes amiss; but this is her whim and mine. They have been talking to her, she had a dream, and she is afraid."

"Hm! hm!" growled the old prince, taking up his pen again. "I will do so." He wrote a few more lines, suddenly turned upon his son, and said with a sneer, "Bad business, hey?"

"What is bad, father?"

"Wife!" said the old prince, with laconic significance.

"I don't understand you," said Prince Andrei.

"Well, there's nothing to be done about it, my friend," said the prince. "They are all alike, there's no way of getting unmarried. Don't be disturbed, I won't tell anyone, but you know 'tis so."

He seized his son's hand in his small, bony fingers and shook it, looking him straight in the face with his keen eyes, which seemed to look through a man, and then once more laughed his chilly laugh.

The son sighed, thereby signifying that his father read him correctly. The old man continued to fold and seal his letters with his usual rapidity, and when he had finished, he caught up and put away the wax, the seal, and the paper.

"Well, then, good-by." He offered his son his hand to kiss, and then embraced him. "Remember one thing, Prince Andrei; if you are killed, it will be hard for me to bear; I am an old man . . ." He unexpectedly paused, and then as suddenly proceeded in a tempestuous voice: "But if I should hear that you had behaved in a manner unworthy of a son of Nikolai Bolkonsky, I should be . . . ashamed," he hissed.

"You should not have said that to me, father," replied the son, with a smile.

The old man was silent.

"I have still another request to make of you," Prince Andrei went on to say. "If I should be killed, and if a son should be born to me, don't let him go from you, as I was saying last evening. Let him grow up under your roof, please."

"Not let your wife have him?" asked the old man, and tried to laugh.

Both stood in silence for some moments, facing each other. The old man's keen eyes gazed straight into his son's. There was a slight tremor in the lower part of the old prince's face.

"We have said good-by, now go!" said he, suddenly. "Go!" he cried in a stern, loud voice, opening his study door.

"What is it? What's the matter?" asked Prince Andrei's wife and sister, as the young man came out, and they caught a momentary glimpse of the old prince in his white dressing gown without his wig, and in his spectacles, as he appeared at the door, screaming at his son.

Prince Andrei sighed and made no answer.

"Well?" said he, turning to his wife, and this "well" sounded chillingly sarcastic, as if he had said, "Now begin your little comedy."

"Andrei, already?" said the little wife, turning pale and fixing her terror-stricken eyes on her husband. He took her in his arms, she gave a cry, and fell fainting on his shoulder.

He carefully disengaged himself from her form, looked into her face, and tenderly laid her in an armchair.

"Adieu, Maria," said he gently to his sister, kissed her hand, and hastened out of the room.

The fainting princess lay in the chair; Mlle. Bourienne chafed her temples. Princess Maria, holding her up, was still looking with her lovely eyes dim with tears, at the door through which Prince Andrei had disappeared, and her blessing followed him. In the study the old prince was heard repeatedly blowing his nose with sharp, angry reports, like pistol shots. Prince Andrei had hardly left the room when the study door was hurriedly flung open, and the prince's stern figure appeared in the white dressing gown.

"Has he gone?" he asked. "Well, it is just as well," said he. Then, looking angrily at the unconscious little princess, he shook his head reproachfully and slammed the door after him.

1805

The young Tsar Alexander I, ruler of Russia since the assassination of his father, the mad Tsar Paul, in 1801, has taken the lead in the movement to stop Napoleon. His allies will be weak Emperor Francis of the dying Holy Roman Empire; King Gustavus of Sweden, whose insanity (for which he is to be deposed a few years later) is expressed principally in fear of revolution and hatred of the French; and, of course, Britain, whose war with Napoleon continues. Just as the land campaign is beginning, in October, 1805, Lord Nelson's victory over the French fleet at Trafalgar frees Britain from the threat of invasion. Napoleon invades Austria, and a Russian force under General Kutuzof (now sixty, and an old man for those times) moves southward to the assistance of its ally.

Part Second

In October, 1805, the Russian army was quartered in certain villages and towns in the archduchy of Austria, making a heavy burden for the inhabitants; and still new regiments were on the way from Russia, concentrating around the fortress of Braunau, where Kutuzof, the commander-in-chief, had his headquarters.

One of the many regiments of infantry that had just arrived stopped about half a mile from the city, waiting to be reviewed by the commander-in-chief. Notwithstanding the un-Russian landscape—orchards, stone walls, tiled roofs, and mountains on the horizon—and the un-Russian aspect of the people, who gathered to look with curiosity at the soldiers, this regiment presented exactly the same appearance as every other Russian regiment getting ready for inspection anywhere in the center of Russia.

Along the broad highway, unpaved, shaded with trees, came a high Viennese carriage, painted blue, swinging easily on its springs as its six horses trotted briskly along. Behind it galloped the suite and an escort of Croatians. Next to Kutuzof sat the Austrian general, in a white uniform contrasting strangely with the dark Russian ones. The carriage drew up near

79

the regiment. Kutuzof and the Austrian general were engaged in conversation in low tones, and Kutuzof smiled slightly as he slowly and heavily stepped down from the carriage, exactly as if the two thousand men who were breathlessly gazing at him, and the regimental commander, did not exist.

The word of command rang out; the regiment stirred into life and presented arms. In the dead silence the commander-in-chief's weak voice was heard.

The regiment shouted, "Long life to your hi-i-ighness!" and again all was still.

Kutuzof proceeded down the ranks, occasionally stopping to say a few friendly words to officers or even privates whom he had known during the war with Turkey. Glancing at their shoes, he more than once shook his head mournfully and directed the Austrian general's attention to them with an expression which meant to imply that he would not blame anyone for it, but that he could not avoid seeing how wretched it was. The regimental commander, each time he did so, pushed forward, fearing to lose a single word that his chief might speak regarding his regiment. Behind Kutuzof, just near enough to be able to catch every word, however lightly spoken, that might fall from his lips, followed the twenty men of his suite, talking among themselves and occasionally laughing. Nearest to the commander-in-chief walked a handsome aide. This was Prince Bolkonsky. Next to him went his messmate, Nesvitsky, a tall and remarkably stalwart staff officer with a kindly, smiling, handsome face and liquid eyes.

The third company was the last, and Kutuzof paused, evidently trying to recollect something. Prince Andrei stepped out from the suite and said in French in an undertone:

"You ordered me to remind you of Dolokhof, who was cashiered to this regiment. . ."

"Where is this Dolokhof?"

Dolokhof did not wait to be summoned. Kutuzof saw a well-built soldier with light curly hair and bright blue eyes come forth from the ranks and present arms.

"A grievance?" asked Kutuzof, slightly frowning.

"That is Dolokhof," said Prince Andrei.

"Ah!" exclaimed Kutuzof. "I hope you will profit by this lesson. Do your duty. The emperor is merciful. And I will not forget you, if you deserve well."

The clear blue eyes looked boldly into the chief's face, their expression seeming to rend the veil of rank that so widely separated the commander-in-chief from the private soldier.

"I should like to ask one favor, your high excellency," said Dolokhof deliberately, in his firm, ringing voice; "I beg that you give me a chance to wipe out my fault and show my devotion to his majesty the emperor, and to Russia."

Kutuzof turned away, and frowned, as if he wished to express that all Dolokhof had said to him and all he could possibly say he had known long, long ago and that it was all a bore to him and so much wasted breath. He turned away and went back to the carriage.

The regiment broke up into companies and marched to the quarters assigned them not far from Braunau, where they hoped to get shoes and clothes and rest after their hard marches. A cornet of hussars in Kutuzof's suite fell behind the carriage and drew up alongside of Dolokhof.

Zherkof, this cornet of hussars, had at one time belonged to the same wild set in Petersburg of which Dolokhof was the leader. Here, abroad, Zherkof met Dolokhof in the ranks, but did not find it expedient to recognize him at first. Now, however, since Kutuzof had set the example by talking with the degraded officer, he went to him with all the cordiality of an old friend.

"My dear fellow, how are you?" said he, as he walked his horse abreast of the company.

"How am I?" repeated Dolokhof, coldly. "As you see."

"And how do you get along with your chiefs?" asked Zherkof.

"All right; good fellows. How did you manage to get on the staff?"

"I am attached—on duty."

Neither spoke.

"Say, come to us this evening. You'll have a chance at faro," said Zherkof. "Did you bring much money with you?"

"Come."

"Can't. I've sworn off. I neither drink nor play till I'm promoted."

"Well, that'll come the first engagement."

"We'll see."

Again they relapsed into silence.

"Look in, anyway; if you need anything. The staff will help you."

Dolokhof laughed.

"You'd better not trouble yourself. If I need anything, I won't ask for it; I'll take it."

"Well, I mean . . ."

"Well, and so do I mean."

"Good-by."

"Farewell."

Zherkof put spurs to his horse, which pranced and danced not knowing with which foot to start, and then, with a spring, galloped off, leaving the company far behind, and overtook the carriage.

II

NOTWITHSTANDING the fact that not much time had elapsed since Prince Andrei had left Russia, he had greatly changed. In the expression of his face, in his motions, in his gait, there was almost nothing to be recognized of his former affectation, lassitude, and laziness. He had the appearance of a man who has no time to think about the impression he produces upon others, but is occupied with pleasant and interesting work. His face showed more contentment with himself and his surroundings; his smile and glance were more cheerful and attractive.

Kutuzof, whom he had joined in Poland, received him very warmly and promised not to forget him; treated him with more distinction than his other aides, and had taken him to Vienna and intrusted him with the most important duties. From Vienna Kutuzof sent a letter to his old comrade, Prince Andrei's father:

"Your son," he wrote, "bids fair to become an officer who will be distinguished for his quickness of perception, his firmness, and his faithfulness. I count myself fortunate in having such an assistant."

Coming into the reception room from Kutuzof's room, Prince Andrei approached his colleague, the aide Kozlovsky, who was on duty and was sitting with a book at the window.

"Well, prince?" asked Kozlovsky.

"You are ordered to draw up a memorandum to account for our not advancing."

"But why?"

Prince Andrei shrugged his shoulders.

"Any news of Mack?" asked Kozlovsky.

"No."

"If it were true that he is defeated, the news would have come by this time."

"Probably," rejoined Prince Andrei, and started for the outer door; but at that very instant the door was flung almost into his face, and a tall Austrian general, in an overcoat, with his head swathed in a dark handkerchief, and with the ribbon of Maria Theresa around his neck, hurried into the room, having evidently just arrived from a journey.

Prince Andrei paused.

"Commander-in-chief Kutuzof?" hurriedly asked the newly arrived general, with a strong German accent; and, looking anxiously on all sides, he started without delay for the door of the general's private room.

"The commander-in-chief is engaged," said Kozlovsky, hastening toward the unknown general and barring the way to the study. "Whom shall I announce?"

The unknown general looked scornfully down on the diminutive Kozlovsky, and seemed to be amazed that he was not recognized.

"The commander-in-chief is engaged," repeated Kozlovsky calmly.

The general's face contracted, his lips drew together and trembled.

He drew out a notebook, quickly wrote something in pencil, tore out the leaf, and handed it to the aide; then, with quick steps, walked over to the window, threw himself into a chair, and surveyed those in the room, as if to ask why they stared at him so. The general lifted his head, stretched out his neck as if he were about to say something, and then, affecting to hum to himself, produced a strange sound, instantly swallowed. The office door opened and Kutuzof himself appeared on the threshold. The general with the bandaged head, who had apparently escaped from some peril, bowed and hastened with long swift strides of his thin legs across the room toward Kutuzof.

"You see the unfortunate Mack!" said he, in a broken voice.

Kutuzof's face, as he stood at his office door, remained expressionless for several moments. Then a frown ran like a wave across his brow, and passed off, leaving his face as serene as before. He respectfully bent his head, shut his eyes, silently allowed Mack to pass in front of him into the office, then closed the door behind him.

The rumor, already spread abroad, of the defeat of the Austrians and the surrender of the whole army at Ulm, was thus proved to be correct. Within half an hour aides were flying about in all directions with orders for the Russian army, till now inactive, to prepare with all haste to meet the enemy.

Prince Andrei was one of those uncommon staff officers whose chief interests are the general operations of the war. On seeing Mack and learning the particulars of his defeat, he realized that half of the campaign was lost, realized the difficult situation of the Russian army, and vividly pictured the fate that was awaiting the army and the part he was about to play in it. In spite of himself, he experienced a strong feeling of delight at the thought of the shame that Austria had brought upon herself, and realized that perhaps within a week he would have a chance to witness and take part in an encounter between the Russians and the French, the first since the time of Suvorof. But he feared lest Bonaparte's genius should show itself superior to all the valor of the Russian troops, and at the same time he could not bear the thought of his hero's suffering disgrace.

III

THE PAVLOGRAD regiment of hussars was encamped two miles from Braunau. The squadron in which Nikolai Rostof served as cadet was quartered in the German village of Salzeneck. The squadron commander, Captain Denisof, who was known to the entire cavalry division as "Vaska" Denisof, had been assigned to the best house in the village. Cadet Rostof had shared the captain's quarters ever since he joined the regiment in Poland.

On the very same October day when at headquarters all had been thrown into excitement by the news of Mack's defeat, the camp life of the squadron was going on in its usual tranquil course. Denisof, who had been playing a losing game of cards all night, had not yet returned to his rooms when

Rostof early in the morning rode up on horseback from his foraging tour, going to the cottage he shared with Denisof.

"What is your master doing?" he asked of Lavrushka, Denisof's rascally valet, who was known to the whole regiment.

"He hasn't been in since evening. Probably been losing at cards," replied Lavrushka. "I have learned that if he has good luck he comes in early and in high spirits; but if he does not get in before morning it means he's been losing and he'll come in mad enough. Will you have coffee?"

"Yes, give me some."

In less than ten minutes Lavrushka brought the coffee. "He's coming," said he, "now we'll get it!"

Rostof glanced out of the window and saw Denisof staggering home. He was a little man, with a red face, brilliant black eyes and black mustache, and hair all in disorder. He wore a hussar's cloak unbuttoned, wide, sagging pantaloons, and a hussar's cap crumpled on the back of his head. He came up the steps in a gloomy mood, with hanging head.

"Lavwushka," he cried in a loud, surly voice, "here, you blockhead— take this off!"

"Don't you see I am taking it off?" replied Lavrushka's voice.

"Ah, you are up alweady?" asked Denisof, as he came into the cottage.

"Long ago!" replied Rostof. "I have been after hay and I saw Fräulein Mathilde!"

"So-ho! and there I have been, bwother, losing howibly all night, like a son of a dog!" cried Denisof, flinging his friend a purse containing a few gold pieces. "Wostof, count it, baby! see how much is left, then put it under my pillow," said he, and went out to see the quartermaster.

Rostof took the money, and mechanically making little heaps of the new and old coins, according to their denominations, began to count them.

"Ah! Telyanin! Howdy! Got done up last night!" Denisof was heard saying in the next room.

"Where? At Buikof's—at the Rat's—I heard about it," said a second, thin voice, and immediately after, Lieutenant Telyanin, a young officer of the same squadron, came into the room.

Rostof thrust the purse under the pillow and pressed the little moist hand that was held out to him. Telyanin had been removed from the Guards shortly before the campaign, for some reason or other. He now conducted himself very decently in the regiment, but he was not liked, and Rostof especially could not conquer, or even conceal, his unreasonable antipathy to this officer.

"Well, young man, how does my Grachik suit you?" (Grachik, or Young Rook, was a saddle horse, which Telyanin had sold Rostof.) The lieutenant never looked the man with whom he was talking straight in the eye; his eyes were constantly wandering from one object to another. "I saw you riding him this morning."

"First-rate, he's a good horse," said Rostof, in spite of the fact that the animal, for which he had given seven hundred rubles, was worth only half the price he had paid. "He's begun to go lame in the left foreleg."

"Hoof cracked! That's nothing. I will teach you or show you what kind of a rivet to put on."

"I'll have him brought right around," said Rostof, anxious to get rid of Telyanin, and went out to give his orders. Having given his orders, he returned to Telyanin.

They went out down the front steps to the stable. The lieutenant showed Rostof how to have a rivet made, and then went home.

When Rostof returned, he found Denisof sitting at the table with a bottle of vodka and a sausage before him, and writing with a sputtering pen. He looked gloomily into Rostof's face.

"I'm writing to her," said he. "Do you see, my fwiend, we are asleep when we are not in love. We are childwen of the dust; but when you are in love, then you are like God, you are as pure as on the first day of kweation. Who is there now? Send him to the devil. I have no time!" he cried to Lavrushka, who came up to him, not in the least abashed.

"What can I do? It's your own order. It's the quartermaster come back for the money."

Denisof scowled, opened his mouth to shout something, but made no sound.

"Nasty job," he muttered to himself. "How much money was there left in that purse?" he asked of Rostof.

"Seven new pieces and three old ones."

"Oh, dwat it!—Well, what are you standing there for like a booby; bring in the quartermaster," cried Denisof to Lavrushka.

"Please, Denisof, take some of my money; you see I have plenty," said Rostof, reddening.

"I don't like to bowow of my fwiends. I don't like it," declared Denisof.

"But if you don't let me lend you money, comrade fashion, I'll be offended!" insisted Rostof. "Truly, I have plenty."

"No, indeed, I shan't," and Denisof went to the bed to get the purse from under the pillow.

"Where did you put it, Wostof?"

"Under the bottom pillow."

"It isn't here." Denisof flung both pillows on the floor. There was no purse there. "That's stwange."

"Hold on, didn't you throw it out?" asked Rostof, picking up the pillows and shaking them, and then hauling off the bedclothes and shaking them. But there was no purse.

"I couldn't have forgotten it, could I? No, I remember very well thinking how you kept it like a treasure trove, under your pillow.—Where is it?" he demanded, turning to Lavrushka.

"I haven't been into the room. It must be where you put it."

"But it isn't."

"That is always the way with you. You throw it down, and then forget all about it. Look in your pockets."

"No, if I had not thought about the treasure trove . . ." said Rostof; "and I remember putting it there."

Lavrushka tore the whole bed apart, looked under it, under the table, searched everywhere in the room, and then stood in the middle of the room. Denisof silently followed all his motions, and when Lavrushka in amazement spread open his hands, he glanced at Rostof.

"Wostof, stop your schoolboy twicks. . . ."

Rostof, conscious of Denisof's gaze fixed upon him, raised his eyes and instantly dropped them again. All the blood till then contained somewhere below his throat rushed in an overmastering flood into his face and eyes. He could not get a breath.

"There has been no one in the room except the lieutenant and yourselves. It's nowhere to be found," said Lavrushka.

"Now, you devil's puppet, fly awound, hunt for it," suddenly cried Denisof, growing livid, and starting toward the valet with a threatening gesture. "Find me that purse or I'll soak you! I'll soak you all!"

Rostof, avoiding Denisof's glance, began to button up his jacket, adjusted his saber, and put on his cap.

"I tell you, give me that purse," cried Denisof, shaking his man by the shoulders and pushing him against the wall.

"Denisof, let him go, I know who took it," said Rostof, going toward the door and not lifting his eyes.

Denisof paused, considering a moment, and evidently perceiving whom Rostof meant, he seized him by the arm. "Wubbish!" he cried, the veins on his face and neck standing out like cords. "I tell you, you are beside yourself and I won't have it. The purse is here. I'll take the hide off this waskal and I'll get it."

"I know who took it," repeated Rostof, in a trembling voice, and went to the door.

"But I tell you, don't you dare to do it!" cried Denisof, throwing himself on the cadet to hold him back. But Rostof freed his arm, and, with as much anger as if Denisof were his worst enemy, gave him a direct and heavy blow right between the eyes.

"Do you realize what you are saying?" he cried in a trembling voice. "He is the only person besides myself who has been in the room. Of course if it was not he, then . . ."

He could not finish, and rushed from the room.

"The devil take you and all the west," were the last words that Rostof caught.

He went straight to Telyanin's rooms.

"My master's not at home; he went to headquarters," said Telyanin's man. "Why, has anything happened?" he added, startled by the cadet's distorted face.

"No, nothing!"

"You just missed him," said the man.

Headquarters were two miles from Salzeneck. Rostof, upon returning home, took a horse and galloped off to headquarters.

In the village occupied by the staff was a tavern where the officers resorted. Rostof went to this tavern; at the doorstep he saw Telyanin's horse. The lieutenant himself was sitting in the second room of the tavern with a plate of sausages and a bottle of wine.

"Ah! so you have come too, young man," said he, smiling and lifting his brows.

"Yes," said Rostof, though it required the greatest effort to speak this monosyllable; and he sat down at the next table.

When Telyanin had finished his breakfast, he pulled out of his pocket a double purse, and, with his delicate white fingers which turned up at the ends, slipped up the ring, took out a gold piece, and, lifting his brows, gave it to the waiter.

"Please make haste," said he.

The gold piece was new. Rostof got up and went to Telyanin.

"Allow me to look at your purse," said he, in a quiet, almost inaudible voice.

With wandering eyes and still lifted brows, Telyanin handed him the purse.

"Yes, it's a handsome little purse, isn't it? Yes . . ." said he, and suddenly turned pale. "Look at it, youngster," he added.

Rostof took the purse into his hand and looked at it and at the money that was in it and at Telyanin. The lieutenant glanced around in his usual way, and apparently became suddenly very merry.

"If we ever get to Vienna I shall leave all this there, but there's nothing to get with it in these filthy little towns," said he. "Well, give it back to me, youngster, I must be going."

Rostof said nothing.

"And you? Aren't you going to have some breakfast? Pretty good fare," continued Telyanin. "Give it to me."

He stretched out his hand and took hold of the purse. Rostof let it go. Telyanin took the purse and began to let it slip into the pocket of his riding trousers and his brows went up higher than usual, and his mouth slightly parted as much as to say: "Yes, yes, I will put my purse in my pocket, and it is a very simple matter, and it is no one's business at all."

"Well, what is it, youngster?" said he, sighing and glancing into Rostof's eyes from under his raised brow. Something like a swift electric flash darted from Telyanin's eyes into Rostof's and was darted back again and again and again all in a single instant.

"Come here with me," said Rostof, taking Telyanin by the arm. He drew him almost to the window. "This money is Denisof's! You took it," he whispered in his ear.

"What? . . . What? . . . How do you dare? What?" exclaimed Telyanin. But his words sounded like a mournful cry of despair and a prayer for forgiveness. As soon as Rostof heard this note in his voice it seemed as if a great stone of doubt had fallen from his heart. He was rejoiced, and at the same time felt sincere pity for the unhappy man standing before him; but he was obliged to carry the matter to the end. "There are men here; God knows what they will think," stammered Telyanin, seizing his cap and starting for a small unoccupied room. "We must have an explanation."

"I know this and can prove it," said Rostof.

"I . . ."

All the muscles of Telyanin's scared pale face began to tremble, his eyes kept wandering, though they were fixed on the floor and never once raised to Rostof's and something like a sob escaped from him.

"Count! . . . don't ruin a young man. Here's that wretched money, take it." He threw it on the table. "I have a father who's an old man; I have a mother!"

Rostof took the money, avoiding Telyanin's gaze, and not saying a word, started to leave the room. But at the door he paused and turned back. "My God!" he said, with tears in his eyes; "how could you have done it?"

"Count!" said Telyanin, coming toward the cadet.

"Don't touch me," cried Rostof, drawing himself up. "If you need this money, take it." He tossed him the purse and hurried out of the tavern.

On the evening of the same day a very lively discussion took place in Denisof's rooms among some of the officers of the squadron.

"But I tell you, Rostof, that it's your business to apologize to the regimental commander," said the second cavalry captain, a tall man, with grayish hair, enormous mustache, big features and a wrinkled skin.

This Captain Kirsten had twice been reduced to the ranks for affairs of honor, and twice promoted again.

"I will not allow anyone to call me a liar," cried Rostof, who flushed crimson and was in a great state of excitement. "He told me that I lied, and I told him that he lied. And there the matter rests. He may keep me on duty every day; he may put me under arrest; but neither he nor anyone else can force me to apologize. If he, as regimental commander, considers it improper to give me satisfaction, then . . ."

"Yes, yes, calm yourself, old man, listen to me," interrupted Captain Kirsten in his deep bass voice, calmly twirling his mustaches. "You told the regimental commander, in the presence of other officers, that an officer had stolen . . ."

"It wasn't my fault that the conversation took place before other officers. Maybe it was not best to have spoken before them, but I am not a diplomat. That's why I joined the hussars; I thought that here, at least, such fine distinctions were not necessary; and he told me that I lied. . . . So let him give me satisfaction. . . ."

"That's all very good; no one thinks that you are a coward, but that isn't the point. Ask Denisof—put it to anyone—if a cadet can demand satisfaction of his regimental commander."

Denisof, chewing his mustache, was listening to the discussion with a gloomy expression of countenance, evidently not wishing to take any part in it. In reply to the captain's question, he shook his head.

"In the presence of other officers, you spoke to the regimental commander about this rascality," continued the second captain. "Bogdanitch" (so the regimental commander was called), "Bogdanitch shut you up."

"He did not shut me up; he told me that I was telling a falsehood."

"Well, have it so, but you said foolish things to him and you ought to apologize."

"Not for the world!" cried Rostof.

"I did not think that of you," said the captain, seriously and sternly. "What can the regimental commander do? Must he bring the officer before a court-martial and disgrace the whole regiment? Insult the whole regiment on account of a single rogue?" The captain's voice began to tremble. "Yes, my boy, you, who will perhaps not be in the regiment a year from now, today here, tomorrow transferred somewhere as aide, you don't care a fig if it is said: thieves among the Pavlograd officers. But it isn't all the same to us. What do you say, Denisof? It isn't a matter of indifference, is it?"

"Wight! Devil take it!" screamed Denisof, jumping up. "Now then, Wostof, now then!"

Rostof, flushing and turning pale, looked first at one and then at the other officer.

"No, gentlemen, no . . . you do not think . . . I see that you are completely mistaken in your opinion of me. . . . I . . . for my own sake . . . for the honor of the regiment—what am I saying? And I will prove it, that for my own sake also honor is dear. . . . Well, it's all the same, you're right, I was to blame!" Tears stood in his eyes. "I was to blame, to blame all around. . . . Now what more do you want?"

"That's the way to do it," cried the captain, turning round and slapping him on the shoulder with his big hand.

"I tell you!" cried Denisof, "he's a glowious young fellow!"

"That's the best way, count," repeated the captain, as if giving him his title was a reward for his concession. "Go and apologize, your excellency, that's it."

"Gentlemen, I will do anything. No one shall ever hear another word from me," declared Rostof in a low, supplicating voice, "but I cannot apologize; by God, I cannot! How can you expect it? How can I apologize like a little boy, begging forgiveness?"

Denisof laughed.

"So much the worse for you. Bogdanitch is spiteful. You will pay for your stubbornness," said Kirsten.

"By God! It's not stubbornness! I cannot describe to you what my feelings are, I assure you, I cannot."

"Well, do just as you please," said the captain. "By the way, what has become of that worthless scamp?" asked he, of Denisof.

"He weported himself ill. He's to be stwuck off the list in tomorrow's orders," replied Denisof.

"Well, it is a kind of illness, there's no other way of explaining it," said the captain.

"Whether illness or not, he'd better not come into my sight, I'd kill him," cried Denisof, in a most bloodthirsty manner.

At this instant Zherkof came into the room.

"Why are you here?" exclaimed the officer, addressing the newcomer.

"Active service, gentlemen. Mack and his army have surrendered; it's all up with them."

"Nonsense!"

"I saw him myself."

"What! you saw Mack alive—with his hands and his feet?"

"Active service! active service! give him a bottle, for bringing such news!"

The regimental adjutant came in and confirmed the news brought by Zherkof. The regiment was ordered to break camp the next day.

"Active service, gentlemen."

"Well, glory to God for that. We've lain here long enough!"

I V

KUTUZOF was retreating toward Vienna, destroying the bridges behind him over the river Inn (at Braunau), and over the river Traun (at Linz). On the fourth of November the Russian army was crossing the river Enns. At noon the baggage wagons, the artillery and the columns of the army stretched through the city of Enns, at both ends of the bridge.

It was a mild autumn day, but showery. The wide view commanded by the height, where stood the Russian batteries protecting the bridge, was now suddenly veiled by a muslinlike curtain of slanting rain, then again was suddenly still further broadened so that distant objects stood out distinctly, gleaming in the sunlight as if they were varnished. At their feet lay the little city, with its white houses and red roofs, its cathedral, and the bridge, at both ends of which the Russian troops could be seen, pouring along in dense masses.

On the brow of the hill, among the fieldpieces, stood the general in command of the rear guard, with an officer of his suite, making observations of the landscape with a glass. A little behind them, astride a gun carriage, sat Nesvitsky, who had been sent to the rear guard by the commander-in-chief.

The officer of the suite was pointing out something to the general, who scrutinized it with his field glass.

"Yes, that is so, that is so," said the general, gravely, taking the glass from his eyes and shrugging his shoulders. "You are right, they are going to fire at them as they cross the river. Why do they dawdle so?"

In that direction, even with the naked eye, could be seen the enemy and his battery, from which arose a milk-white puff of smoke. After a while followed the distant report, and it could be seen how the Russian troops were hastening to get across the river.

Nesvitsky, having got his breath, dismounted from the cannon and, with a smile, went up to the general.

"Shall I not go down to them, your excellency?" asked Nesvitsky.

"Yes, do go down, please," replied the general, reiterating orders he had already given. "And tell the hussars to cross last and burn the bridge as I commanded, and see to it that they collect combustible materials on it."

"Very good," said Nesvitsky.

He called the Cossack to bring up his horse and lightly swung his heavy body into the saddle.

The last of the infantry hurriedly marched across the bridge, though they were crowded in the tunnel-like passage at the end. Only the hussars of Denisof's command were left at the end of the bridge toward the enemy. The enemy, though plainly visible from the heights opposite, could not yet be seen from the level of the bridge, since from the valley, through which flows the river Enns, the horizon is bounded by a hill about half a mile distant. Directly in front was a plot of wasteland, over which here and there moved bands of Cossack patrols.

Suddenly, on the height opposite the road, appeared troops in blue uniforms and accompanied by artillery. It was the French!

A patrol of Cossacks came galloping down the road. All the officers and men of Denisof's squadron, though they tried hard to talk of different things and to look in other directions, nevertheless were unable to keep out of their thoughts what was there before them on the hill, and their eyes constantly turned to those patches which were moving against the horizon, and which they knew were the troops of the enemy. The space between them was only a little more than two thousand feet. The enemy had ceased to fire, and all the more distinctly was felt that solemn, ominous gap, unapproachable and inexorable, that divides two hostile armies.

"One step beyond that line, which is like the bourn that divides the living from the dead, and there is the Unknown of suffering and of death. And what is there? Who is there? there, beyond that field, beyond that tree, and that roof, glittering in the sun? No one knows, and no one wishes to know, and it is terrible to pass across that line, and I know that sooner or later I shall have to cross it, and shall then know what is there on that side of the line, just as inevitably as I shall know what is on the other side of death. And yet I am strong, full of life, joy, and exuberant spirits, and surrounded by other men just as full of health and exuberant spirits."

Thus every man feels, even if he does not formulate it in his thoughts, when he comes in sight of the enemy, and this feeling lends a peculiar vividness and distinctness of impression to everything that occurs at such moments.

On the enemy's hill arose a puff of smoke, and a cannon ball, whistling, flew over the heads of the squadron of hussars. The officers, who had been standing together, scattered to their posts; the hussars began to get their horses into regular line. No one spoke in the ranks. All looked intently at the enemy and at the commander, and awaited the word of command. A second, a third shot flew over them. Evidently the enemy were firing at the hussars, but the cannon balls, whistling as they flew swiftly by, went far over their heads and fell somewhere in the rear. The hussars did not look up; but each time they heard the whiz of the ball, the whole squadron, with their monotonously diverse faces, holding their breaths until the cannon shot had passed over, raised themselves in their stirrups as if by orders, and then settled back again. The soldiers, not turning their heads, looked at one another out of the corners of their eyes, each curious to know his neighbor's reaction. On every face, from Denisof's to the trumpeter's, there was around the lips and chin a common expression of internal struggle, excitement, and agitation.

At this moment an officer of high rank appeared on the bridge. Denisof spurred off to meet him.

"Your excellency, let us attack 'em! I will dwive 'em back!"

"Attack them?" cried the officer, showing his annoyance in his voice and frowning as if at a persistent fly. "And why are you delaying here? Don't you see the flankers are withdrawing? Order your squadron back."

The squadron crossed the bridge and retired beyond reach of the shots, not having lost a single man. Behind them came a second squadron which had formed the rear guard, and, last of all, the Cossacks crossed to the farther side.

The two squadrons of the Pavlograd regiment, crossing the bridge one after the other, galloped up the road. The regimental commander overtook Denisof's squadron and walked his horse along not far from Rostof, but without paying him the slightest attention, though it was the first time they had met since their quarrel about Telyanin.

Rostof, who realized, now that he was in line, that he was in the power of the man toward whom he felt guilty, did not take his eyes from the colonel's athletic back, the light hair at the back of his head, and his red neck. Sometimes it seemed to Rostof that Bogdanitch was merely pretending not to notice him, and that his whole aim now was to try the cadet's courage; and he straightened himself up and looked around him gaily. Then again it seemed to him that Bogdanitch rode close to him to display his own courage. Now it occurred to him that his opponent was going to send the squadron into some forlorn hope, in order to punish him. And then again, it occurred to him that after the affray Bogdanitch would come to him and magnanimously extend the hand of reconciliation, in honor of the wound he would receive.

The high-shouldered Zherkof, well known to the Pavlograd boys, having not long since been in their regiment, came riding up to the regimental commander with a message from the commander of the rear guard.

"Colonel," said he, with his most melancholy assumption of gravity, turning to Rostof's opponent and glancing at his comrades, "you are ordered to halt and burn the bridge."

"Who orders it?" asked the colonel, testily.

"Well, I don't know, colonel, who orders it," replied the aide gravely, "but the prince said to me: 'Go and tell the colonel that the hussars are to return as quickly as possible and burn the bridge.'"

Immediately after Zherkof, an officer of the suite rode up to the colonel of the hussars with the same order. And immediately after the officer of the suite came the stout Nesvitsky, galloping up with all his might on his Cossack horse, which could hardly carry him.

"How is it, colonel?" he cried, while still at a distance. "I told you to burn the bridge, but now someone has mistaken the order; everyone here has lost his wits, and there's nothing done right."

The colonel took his time in halting the regiment, and turned to Nesvitsky.

"You told me to burn up the combustibles," said he, "but as to burning the bridge, you did not say a word."

"What's that, my good man?" exclaimed Nesvitsky, reining in his horse, taking off his cap, and with his fat hand brushing back his hair, dripping with perspiration. "How's that? Didn't I say that the bridge was to be burned, when you burned all the combustibles?"

"I won't be called 'my good man' by you, Mister Staff Officer, and you did not tell me to burn the bridge. I know my duties, and I faithfully carry out what I am commanded to do. You said the bridge was to be burned, but who was to do it, by the Holy Ghost, I could not tell."

"Well, that's always the way," cried Nesvitsky, with a wave of the hand. "What are you doing here?" he asked, turning to Zherkof.

"Exactly the same thing as you are! But how wet you are! Let me wring you out!"

"You said, Mister Staff Officer . . ." proceeded the colonel, in an offended tone.

"Colonel," interrupted the officer from the suite, "you must make haste, or else the enemy will be pouring grapeshot into us."

The colonel silently looked at the officer from the suite, at stout Prince Nesvitsky, and at Zherkof, and frowned.

"I will burn the bridge," said he, in a solemn voice, as if to express by it that in spite of all the disagreeable things that happened to him, he was always prepared to do his duty.

Spurring his horse with his long, muscular legs, as if the animal were to blame for everything, the colonel started forward and ordered the second squadron, in which Rostof served, to return under the command of Denisof, and burn the bridge.

"Well, that's the way it is," said Rostof to himself. "He wants to try me." His heart beat and the blood rushed to his face. "Let him see if I am a coward," he thought.

Once more over all the happy faces of the men in the squadron appeared that same serious expression they had worn when they were under fire. Rostof, not taking his eyes from his opponent, the regimental commander, tried to discover in his face a confirmation of his suspicions; but the colonel did not once look at Rostof, but as usual gazed sternly and solemnly along the line. The word of command was heard.

"Lively! Lively!" cried voices around him. With their sabers catching in the reins, with rattling spurs, the hussars dismounted in all haste, not knowing what they were to do. They crossed themselves. Rostof now looked no more at the colonel; he had no time. He was afraid, afraid with a real sinking of the heart, lest he should be left behind by the hussars. His hand trembled as he turned his horse over to the groom, and he felt how the blood was rushing back to his heart. Denisof, on his way back, shouted something to him as he passed. Rostof saw nothing except the hussars running by his side with impeding spurs and rattling sabers.

"The stretchers!" cried some voice behind him, but Rostof did not stop to think what that demand for stretchers meant; he ran on, striving only to be in advance of the others; but at the bridge, not looking where he stepped, slipped in the slimy, sheeted mud, stumbled, and fell on his hands and knees. The others dashed ahead of him.

"At both sides, captain," shouted the regimental commander, who having ridden ahead had reined in his horse not far from the bridge and sat looking on with a triumphant and radiant expression.

Rostof, wiping his soiled hands on his riding trousers, glanced at his opponent and determined to go on, thinking that the farther forward he went the better it would be. But Bogdanitch, without looking at him or even noticing that it was Rostof, cried to him:

"Who is that in the middle of the bridge? Take the right side! Cadet, come back!" he shouted testily, and then turned to Denisof, who, making a show of his foolhardiness, was riding upon the bridge.

"Why run such risks, captain? You'd better dismount," cried the colonel.

"Hey! he always finds someone at fault," replied Vaska Denisof, turning in his saddle.

Meanwhile, Nesvitsky, Zherkof, and the staff officer stood in a little group out of range and watched now the little band of hussars, in yellow shakoes, dark-green roundabouts embroidered with gold lace, and blue trousers, who were swarming over the bridge; and now, in the other direction, the blue uniforms marching down from the distant hill, and the groups with horses, which could easily be recognized as fieldpieces.

"Will they get the bridge burnt or not?" . . . "Who is ahead?" . . .

94

"Will they have time to set the bridge on fire, or will the French fire on them and drive them back?"

Such questions every man involuntarily asked himself, as he looked that bright afternoon at the bridge and at the hussars, and then again, on the other side, at the bluecoats approaching with bayonets and fieldpieces.

"Oh! the hussars will catch it!" exclaimed Nesvitsky. "They're within range of grapeshot now."

"It was useless to send so many men," said the staff officer.

"That's a fact," returned Nesvitsky. "If he'd only sent two smart young fellows, it would have been just as well."

"Ah, your excellency," remarked Zherkof, not taking his eyes from the hussars, but still speaking in his own peculiar fashion, which left it in doubt whether he were serious or in earnest, "ah! your excellency, how can you think so! The idea of sending two men! How then would we get the order of Vladimir and the ribbon? Even if they do get a thrashing, there'll be a chance for the colonel to cite the squadron and get a ribbon for himself. Our Bogdanitch knows a thing or two."

"Now there," said the staff officer, "that's grape!" He pointed at the French fieldpieces, which they were unlimbering and bringing into range.

In the direction of the French, from the groups which had been recognized as the artillery, they saw a puff of smoke arise, then a second, a third almost simultaneously; and by the time the report of the first had reached their ears, a fourth puff arose. Two reports one after the other, and then a third.

"Oh! oh!" groaned Nesvitsky, as if from excruciating agony; and seizing the staff officer's arm: "Look, one fell, fell, one fell!"

"Two, I should think."

"If I were Tsar, there would be no more war," said Nesvitsky, turning away.

Grape pattered and rattled on the bridge. But this time Nesvitsky could not see what took place there. A thick smoke poured up from it. The hussars had succeeded in setting fire to it, and the French fieldpieces were fired at it. The last discharge struck in the middle of the group and hit three hussars.

Rostof, preoccupied by his relations with Bogdanitch, remained on the bridge, not knowing what he had to do. There was no one to cut down—he had always imagined a battle to consist of cutting down—and he could not help fire the bridge either, because he had not provided himself with wisps of straw as the others had. He was standing there and looking on, when suddenly there was a rattling on the bridge as if someone had been scattering hazelnuts, and one of the hussars who happened to be nearest him fell against the parapet with a groan. Rostof and several others ran to him. Again there was a cry for stretchers. Four men grasped the wounded hussar and started to bear him away.

"O-o-o-o! Let me alone for Christ's sake," shrieked the wounded man, but nevertheless they took him up and bore him off.

At that instant the sun went into a cloud; Rostof saw several stretchers being carried before him. The terror of death and of the stretchers, love for the sun and for life, all mingled in one painfully disturbing impression.

"O Lord God! Thou who art there in yonder heaven, save, pardon and defend me!" whispered Rostof in his heart.

The hussars hastened back to their grooms; their voices grew louder and more confident; the stretchers were now out of their sight.

"Well, bwother! so you've smelled powder!" rang Vaska Denisof's voice in his ear.

"It's all over, but I'm a coward, yes, I'm a coward," thought Rostof, and with a heavy sigh he took the bridle from the hands of his groom and mounted his Grachik, which was waiting for him.

"What was it, grapeshot?" asked he of Denisof.

"That's just what it was!" shouted Denisof. "We worked like hewoes. And it was waskally work. A charge is ware sport, you hew down the dogs; but here, the devil only knows what it is, they shoot at you as if you were a target."

And Denisof rode off and joined the colonel, Nesvitsky, Zherkof, and the staff officer, who were talking together a short distance from Rostof.

"One thing's evident, no one noticed it," thought Rostof. And in truth no one had noticed it, because each and every one shared in the sensation the cadet experienced at being under fire for the first time.

"We shall have a splendid report sent," Zherkof was saying. "Do you know, they may give me a lieutenancy."

"Inform the prince that I burned the bridge," said the colonel, with a gay and triumphant expression.

"But suppose someone asks about our loss?"

"A mere trifle," said the colonel, in his deepest tones; "two hussars wounded and one dead," said he, with apparent joy, and scarcely refraining from a contented smile as he brought out with ringing emphasis the happy word, dead.

V

THE RUSSIAN ARMY of thirty-five thousand men, under command of Kutuzof, pursued by the French a hundred thousand strong under Bonaparte himself, meeting with unfriendly natives, no longer having confidence in their allies, suffering from a lack of provisions, and obliged to act in a manner opposed to all preconceived conditions of war, was in hasty retreat down the Danube. It was impossible any longer to think of defending Vienna. In place of the offensive warfare so craftily plotted, the only thing that was left Kutuzof now, unless he were to sacrifice his army as Mack had sacrificed his at Ulm, was to effect a juncture with the troops on their way from Russia, and even this was almost an impossibility.

On the eighth of November, Kutuzof with his army crossed to the left bank of the Danube; and, for the first time, halted, having now put the river between himself and the main body of the French. On the tenth he attacked and defeated the division under Mortier, which was stationed on the left bank of the Danube. In this engagement, for the first time, some trophies were captured: a stand of colors, cannon, and two of the enemy's generals. For the first time, after a fortnight's retreat, the Russian army halted; and at the end of the battle not only held the field of battle, but had driven off the French. Although the army was exhausted and in rags, and reduced a third by the killed, wounded, sick, and stragglers, the halt at Krems and the victory over Mortier signally raised the spirits of the men.

During the battle Prince Andrei had been near by when the Austrian general, Schmidt, was killed. His own horse had been wounded under him and he himself had been slightly grazed by a bullet on the hand. As a sign of special favor from the commander-in-chief he was sent to carry the news of this victory to the Austrian court, which had left Vienna, now threatened by the French, and was established at Brünn. In spite of his apparently delicate constitution, he could endure physical fatigue far better than much stronger men.

Such an errand insured the courier not only a decoration, but pointed infallibly to promotion.

Prince Andrei, notwithstanding his rapid journey and sleepless night, felt as he drove up to the palace in Brünn even more excited than he had the evening before. His eyes gleamed with a feverish light and his thoughts rushed through his mind with extraordinary rapidity and clearness. Vividly all the details of the battle came into his mind, not with any confusion, but in due sequence, word for word as he imagined he would render his account to the Emperor Franz. Vividly he imagined the circumstantial questions that might be asked him and the answers he would make to them. He supposed he would immediately be summoned before the emperor. But at the principal entrance of the palace he was met by an official who, discovering that he was only a courier, sent him around to another entrance.

"Take the corridor at the right, your excellency; there you will find the adjutant who is on duty," said the official. "He will take you to the minister of war."

The adjutant, coming to meet Prince Andrei, asked him to wait while he went to the minister. In five minutes he returned, and, bowing with unusual deference and allowing Prince Andrei to pass in front of him, directed him through a corridor into a private office occupied by the minister of war. The adjutant, by his extravagant politeness, seemed to be trying to defend himself from any attempt at familiarity on the part of the Russian courier.

The minister was sitting between two candles at a great table, and did not even glance at his visitor for the first two minutes. His bald head with its fringe of gray hair was bent over some papers, which he was reading and marking with a lead pencil. He finished reading them, not even lifting his head when the door opened to admit his visitor, though he must have heard the steps.

"Take this and deliver it at once," he said to his secretary, handing him some papers, not even yet recognizing the existence of the courier.

Prince Andrei came to the conclusion that out of all the affairs that preoccupied the minister of war, either the feats of Kutuzof's army interested him the least, or else he felt obliged to give this impression to the Russian courier. "Well, it's all the same to me," said he to himself.

The minister of war sorted the rest of the papers, placing them in regular order, and then at last lifted his head. He had an intelligent and determined face, but at the instant he turned to Prince Andrei this intelligent and firm expression seemed to change as if by purpose and consciously, and in its place came a dull, hypocritical smile, in which there was no pretense even of hiding its hypocrisy—the habitual smile of a man accustomed to receive many petitioners one after the other.

"From General Field Marshal Kutuzof?" he asked. "I hope it is good news. So he's had an encounter with Mortier? A victory? It was time!"

He took the dispatch directed to him and began to read it with a melancholy expression.

"*Ach, mein Gott! mein Gott!* Schmidt!" said he, in German. "What a misfortune! what a misfortune!" Having run through the paper, he laid it on the table and glanced at Prince Andrei, evidently weighing something in his mind. "Ach! what a misfortune! The affair, you say, was decisive? But Mortier was not taken." He pondered. "I'm very glad that you have brought this good news, although the death of Schmidt is a costly price to pay for the victory. His majesty will probably desire to see you, but not this evening. I thank you; go and rest. Tomorrow be at the levee after the parade. However, I will give you due notice."

The dull smile, which had disappeared during this conversation, again appeared on the war minister's face.

V I

PRINCE ANDREI put up at Brünn at the residence of his friend, the diplomat Bilibin.

After his hurried journey, and indeed after this whole campaign, during which he had been deprived of all the comforts and elegances of life, he experienced a pleasant feeling of repose amid these luxurious conditions of existence to which he had been accustomed since childhood. Moreover, it was pleasant, after his reception by the Austrians, to talk, not indeed in Russian, for they spoke in French, but with a Russian who, as he supposed, shared the general Russian aversion, now felt with especial keenness, for the Austrians.

Bilibin was a man of thirty-five, unmarried, and belonged to the same set as Prince Andrei. They had been acquaintances long before in Petersburg, and had become more intimate during Prince Andrei's last visit to Vienna with Kutuzof. Just as Prince Andrei was a young man who promised to make a brilliant career in the military profession, so Bilibin, with even greater probability, was on the road to success in diplomacy. He was still a young man, but he was not a young diplomat, since he had begun his career at the age of sixteen, had been in Paris and in Copenhagen, and now held a very responsible post in Vienna.

"Now, then, tell us your exploits," said he.

Bolkonsky, in the most modest manner, without once referring to himself, told him of the combat and of the minister's behavior.

"I assure you, I cannot understand," he said. "Perhaps there are diplomatic subtleties here that are above my feeble mind, but I cannot understand: Mack has destroyed a whole army, the Archduke Ferdinand and the Archduke Karl are giving no signs of life and are making one blunder after another; finally, Kutuzof is the only one who really gains a victory, breaks the luck of the French, and the minister of war isn't interested enough to inquire about the details!"

"This is the very reason, my dear. What do *we*, I mean the Austrian Court, care for *your* victories! Only bring them your fine news about a victory won by the Archduke Karl or Ferdinand—one archduke is as good as another, as you well know—and even though it were only over a squad of Bonaparte's firemen, that would be another thing; we would proclaim it with the thunder of cannon. But this, as a matter of course, can only vex us. Moreover, even if you had won the most brilliant victory, even if the Archduke Karl had, what change would that make in the course of events? It's too late now, for Vienna has been occupied by the French army."

"What, occupied! Vienna occupied!"

"Not only occupied, but Bonaparte is at Schönbrunn, and the count, our dear friend Count Vrbna, has gone there to him for orders."

Bolkonsky, after his fatigue and the impressions of his journey and his reception, and especially since his dinner, felt that he did not grasp the full meaning of the words he heard.

"But what an extraordinary genius," suddenly cried Prince Andrei, doubling his small fist and pounding the table with it. "And what luck that man has!"

"Who? Buonaparte?" queried Bilibin, knitting his brow and thereby signifying that he was going to get off a witticism. "Buonaparte," he repeated, laying a special emphasis on the *u*. "I certainly think that now when he is laying down the laws for Austria from Schönbrunn, he must be spared that *u*. . . . I am firmly resolved to make the innovation, and I shall call him Bonaparte."

"No, but joking aside," said Prince Andrei, "is it possible that you think the campaign is finished?"

"This is what I think: Austria has been made a fool of and she is not used to that. And she will take her revenge. And she has been made a fool of because in the first place her provinces have been pillaged (it is said the Russians are terrible pillagers), her army is beaten, her capital is taken, and all this on account of the handsome eyes on the Sardinian throne. And in the second place, between us, my dear, I suspect that we are being duped, I suspect dealings with France and a project of peace, a secret peace, separately concluded."

"That cannot be," said Prince Andrei. "That would be too base."

"Whoever lives will learn; you will see," said Bilibin, scowling, this time in a way that signified the ending of the conversation.

When Prince Andrei went to the room that had been prepared for him, and stretched himself between clean sheets on a soft down mattress and on warm perfumed pillows, he felt that the battle of which he had brought the report was far, far away.

He closed his eyes, but instantly his ears were deafened by the cannonading, the musketry, the rumble of the carriage wheels; and now once more the musketeers came marching in scattered lines down the hillside, and the Frenchmen were firing, and he felt how his heart thrilled, and he galloped on ahead, and the bullets whistled merrily around him, and he experienced such a feeling of intensified delight in life as he had not felt since childhood. He awoke with a start. . . .

"Yes, it was all like that!" said he, smiling to himself a happy, childlike smile, and he fell asleep with the sound sleep of youth.

At the levee Prince Andrei, who stood in the place designated him among the Austrian officers, received merely a long unblinking stare from the Emperor Franz, and a slight inclination of his long head. But after the levee, the emperor received him standing in the middle of his room. Before beginning the conversation, Prince Andrei was struck by the evident confusion of the emperor, who reddened and did not know what to say.

"Tell me when the action began," he asked hurriedly.

Prince Andrei told him.

This question was followed by others, no less simple:

"Is Kutuzof well? How long ago did he leave Krems?" and so on.

The emperor spoke as if the whole aim were to ask a certain number of questions. The answers to these questions, as he made only too evident, did not interest him.

"At what hour did the engagement begin?" asked the emperor.

"I cannot tell, your majesty, at what hour the fighting began on the front; but at Durenstein, where I happened to be, the army made the first attack at six o'clock in the evening," said Bolkonsky eagerly, for he supposed that now he had a chance to enter into the carefully prepared and accurate description of all that he had seen and knew. But the emperor smiled and interrupted him.

Prince Andrei left the audience chamber and was immediately surrounded by courtiers coming from all sides. Flattering glances rested on him and flattering words were heard around him. The adjutant reproached him for not having put up at the palace and offered him the use of his rooms. The minister of war came and congratulated him on having received the order of Maria Theresa of the third degree, which the emperor had conferred upon him. The empress' chamberlain invited him to wait upon her majesty. The grand duchess also desired to see him. In spite of Bilibin's prognostications, the news he brought was joyfully hailed. A thanksgiving Te Deum was ordained, Kutuzof was decorated with the grand cross of Maria Theresa, and all the army was rewarded. Bolkonsky was overwhelmed with invitations, and was obliged to spend the whole morning in making calls upon the principal dignitaries of Austria.

Having finished his calls, about five o'clock in the afternoon Prince Andrei, thinking over what he should write his father about the engagement and his visit to Brünn, returned to Bilibin's lodgings. At the door of the house occupied by Bilibin stood a gig half full of luggage, and Franz, Bilibin's valet, was just coming out, laboriously dragging another trunk.

"What does this mean?" asked Bolkonsky.

"Alas, your excellency!" said Franz, with difficulty tumbling the trunk into the gig, "we're going farther off. The rascal is after us again."

"What do you mean? Tell me!" asked Prince Andrei.

Bilibin came out to meet Bolkonsky. His usually tranquil face showed traces of excitement.

"What is the trouble? The trouble is that the French have crossed the bridge at Vienna, and the bridge was not blown up, so that Murat is now hastening down the road to Brünn, and they will be here today or tomorrow."

"Be here? But why was the bridge not blown up, when it was mined?"

"Well, that's what I ask you. No one, not even Bonaparte, knows that."

Bolkonsky shrugged his shoulders.

"But if the bridge is crossed, the army is destroyed; of course, it will be cut off," said he.

"That's the joke of the thing," rejoined Bilibin. "Listen! The French enter Vienna, just as I told you. All very good. On the next day—that is yesterday—Marshals Murat, Lannes and Belliard mount their horses and ride down to the bridge (notice, all three of them are Gascons). 'Gentlemen,' says one of them, 'you know that the Thabor bridge is mined and countermined, and that in front of it is a terrible bridgehead and fifteen thousand men, who are commanded to blow up the bridge and not allow us to pass. But our master, the Emperor Napoleon, would be pleased if we took that bridge. Let us three go therefore and take that bridge.' 'Yes, let's go,' say the others, and they go to it and take it and cross it, and now they are on this side of the

Danube with their whole army, and are in full march against us and against your communications."

"Stop joking," said Prince Andrei in a melancholy and serious tone. This news was sad and at the same time pleasant to him. As soon as he knew that the Russian army was in such a hopeless situation, it occurred to him that he himself was the one called upon to rescue it from this situation—that this was his Toulon, destined to lift him from the throng of insignificant officers and open to him the straight path of glory! Even while he was listening to Bilibin, he was picturing himself going back to the army and there, in a council of war, proposing a plan which alone might save them; and that to him alone it was granted to accomplish this plan.

"No more jesting," said he.

"I am not jesting," insisted Bilibin. "Nothing is more veracious or more melancholy. These gentlemen ride on the bridge without escort, displaying their white handkerchiefs; they assert that there is an armistice, and that they, the marshals, have come over to talk with Prince Auersperg. The officer on guard lets them into the bridgehead. They give him a thousand choice specimens of gasconade; they say the war is ended; that the Emperor Franz has decided on a conference with Bonaparte; that they want to see Prince Auersperg, and a thousand other trumpery lies. The officer sends for Auersperg; these gentlemen embrace the officers, jest, sit astride the cannon, and meantime a French battalion quietly crosses the bridge and flings the bags with the combustibles into the water, and enters the bridgehead. At last the lieutenant general, our dear little Prince Auersperg von Mautern himself, appears on the scene. 'Our dear enemy! Flower of the Austrian army, hero of the Turkish wars! Our enmity is at an end, we can shake hands. The Emperor Napoleon is dying with anxiety to make the acquaintance of Prince Auersperg!'

"In one word, these gentlemen, who are not Gascons for nothing, so bewitch Auersperg with fine words, he is so ravished by this rapidly instituted intimacy with the French marshals, so dazzled by the sight of Murat's mantle and ostrich feathers, that he doesn't see the point, and quite forgets what he himself ought to be pointing at the enemy."

Notwithstanding the vehemence of his remarks, Bilibin did not fail to pause after this pun, so as to allow Bolkonsky time to appreciate it.

"The French battalions run into the bridgehead, spike the cannon—the bridge is theirs! But this is best of all," he went on to say, allowing the fascination of his narrative to keep him calm, "this—that the sergeant who had charge of the cannon, the discharge of which was to explode the mines and blow up the bridge—this sergeant, I say, seeing the French soldiers running over the bridge, was just going to fire the gun, but Lannes pulled away his hand. The sergeant, who evidently had more sense than his general, hastens to Auersperg and says, 'Prince, you are imposed upon, here are the French!'

"Murat sees that their game is played if the sergeant is allowed to speak further. With pretended surprise (true Gascon that he is) he turns to Auersperg: 'I don't see in this anything of your world-renowned Austrian discipline,' says he. 'Do you allow a man of inferior rank to speak to you so?' It was a stroke of genius. Prince Auersperg prides himself on punctilio and has the sergeant put under arrest. But you must confess that all this story of the Thabor bridge is perfectly delightful. It was neither stupidity nor cowardice."

"Perhaps it is treason, though," said Prince Andrei, his imagination vividly bringing up before him the gray cloaks, the wounds, the gunpowder smoke, the sounds of battle, and the glory that was awaiting him.

"Not at all. This puts the court in a most stupid position," continued Bilibin. "It is neither treason nor cowardice nor stupidity, it's just the same as at Ulm." He paused, as if trying to find a suitable expression. "It is—it is Macklike. We are Macked!" he said, at last satisfied that he had coined *un mot*, and a brilliant *mot*, such a one as would be repeated. The wrinkles that had been deeply gathering on his forehead quickly smoothed themselves out, in token of his contentment, and with a slight smile on his lips he began to contemplate his fingernails.

"Where are you going?" he asked, suddenly turning to Prince Andrei, who had got up and was starting for his room.

"I'm off."

"Where?"

"To the army!"

"But you intended to stop two days longer, didn't you?"

"Yes, but now I'm going immediately."

And Prince Andrei, having given his orders for the carriage, went to his room.

"Do you know, my dear fellow?" said Bilibin, coming into his room, "do you know, I have been thinking about you. One of two things will happen to you"—here he managed to gather a fold of wrinkles over his left temple—"either peace will be concluded before you reach the army, or else defeat and disgrace await you with all of Kutuzof's force."

And Bilibin smoothed the skin again, feeling that the dilemma was unavoidable.

"Of that I cannot judge," said Prince Andrei coldly; but he thought in his own mind, "I am going to save the army."

"My dear, you are a hero!" said Bilibin.

VII

KUTUZOF HAD learned on the thirteenth of November, through one of his scouts, that the army under his command was in an almost inextricable position.

The French, according to the report of the scout, had crossed the bridge at

Vienna and were advancing upon Znaim, which lay in the line of Kutuzof's projected retreat, about sixty miles ahead of him. If they could reach Znaim before the French, there was a fair hope of saving the army; but if the French were given a chance to get to Znaim first, it surely meant the disgrace of a surrender like that at Ulm, or else the general destruction of the army.

On the night after receiving this information, Kutuzof sent four thousand men of Bagration's vanguard over the mountains to occupy the road from Vienna to Znaim. Bagration was ordered to make this short cut without pausing to rest; he was to face Vienna and turn his back on Znaim, and if he succeeded in getting there before the French did, he was to do his best to hold them in check. Kutuzof himself, with all the baggage, would hasten on toward Znaim.

Bagration, crossing the mountains, marching without a road, thirty miles on a stormy night, losing a third of his forces in stragglers, came out with his famished, shoeless men at Hollabrunn, on the road from Vienna to Znaim, a few hours before the French reached it from Vienna. It was necessary for Kutuzof to travel a whole day and night with his baggage wagons before reaching Znaim. Therefore, in order to save the army, Bagration, with only four thousand soldiers, hungry and exhausted, was obliged to engage the entire force of the enemy during the course of the twenty-four hours; this was manifestly impossible. But a strange chance made the impossible possible.

Having been successful in the piece of finesse which had given the French the bridge at Vienna without a blow, Murat thought that it would be fine to try a similar deception on Kutuzof. Meeting Bagration's feeble contingent on the road to Znaim, he supposed that it was Kutuzof's whole army. To leave no doubt of his crushing this army, he determined to await the arrival of all the forces that had started out from Vienna, and with this end in view, he proposed an armistice for three days, with the condition that neither army should change its position, or move from its place. Murat asserted that negotiations for peace were already in progress and that, therefore, in order to avoid the useless shedding of blood, he had proposed the armistice. The Austrian general, Count Nostiz, who was posted in the van, placed credence in the words of Murat's emissary, and retired, exposing Bagration.

The armistice was, for Kutuzof, the only means of gaining time. On the receipt of this news, he promptly sent his adjutant general, Winzengerode, who happened to be present, over to the hostile camp. Winzengerode was not only to accept the armistice, but also even to propose terms of capitulation, while, in the meantime, Kutuzof sent his aides back to expedite the movements of the baggage train and of the whole army, and to maintain a firm front against an enemy eight times as strong.

Kutuzof saw that by discussing terms of capitulation, which did not bind him to anything, he would gain time for sending around at least a portion of the heavy baggage, but he also saw that Murat's blunder would be quickly detected. Both of these anticipations were realized.

As soon as Bonaparte, who was at Schönbrunn, sixteen miles from Hollabrunn, read Murat's report and his scheme for an armistice and capitulation, he saw through the hoax, and wrote the following letter to him:

Schönbrunn, Nov. 16, 1805, 8 o'clock A.M.

To Prince Murat: I cannot find words to express my displeasure. You merely command my van, and have no right to conclude an armistice without orders from me. You are making me lose the advantage of a campaign. End the armistice instantly, and march on the enemy. Explain to him that the general who signed this capitulation had no right to do so, that only the Emperor of Russia has this right.

However, if the Russian emperor should ratify the proposed agreement, I also would ratify it. But it is only a trick. March! Destroy the Russian army! You are in a position to capture their baggage and artillery.

The Russian emperor's adjutant general is a ——. Officers are of no account when they are not endowed with any powers; this one had none. The Austrians let themselves be duped about the crossing of the Vienna bridge; you have allowed yourself to be duped by the Russians.

NAPOLEON.

Bonaparte's aide galloped off at headlong speed, to carry this angry letter to Murat. Bonaparte himself, not feeling confidence in his generals, moved toward the field of battle with all his guards, fearing lest he should be cheated of his prey; and the four thousand men under Bagration, cheerfully building bivouac fires, dried and warmed themselves and for the first time in three days cooked their gruel, and not one of the detachment knew or dreamed what was threatening them.

VIII

IT WAS four o'clock in the afternoon when Prince Andrei reached Grund and reported to Bagration. Bonaparte's aide had not yet reached Murat's division, and the battle had not begun. Bagration, knowing that Bolkonsky was the commander-in-chief's favorite and trusted adjutant, received him with the utmost official respect and unusual condescension and assured him that either that day or the next an engagement would probably take place, granting him free choice to be present with him during the battle, or to remain in the rear and superintend the retreat, "which," he said, "would be a very important position."

"However, it is most likely that nothing will happen today," said Prince Bagration, as if to relieve Prince Andrei's anxieties.

At the same time he thought: "If this is only one of the ordinary jack-a-dandies of the staff, sent out to win a decoration, he will get it just as well by staying in the rear; but if he desires to be with me, let him. . . . He will be useful if he is a brave officer."

Prince Andrei gave no definite answer, but asked permission to reconnoiter the position and learn the disposition of the forces, so that in case of necessity he might know where he was. The officer on duty, a handsome man, faultlessly attired and with a diamond ring on his index finger, who spoke French badly but fluently, offered to be Prince Andrei's guide.

Wet and melancholy-looking officers could be seen everywhere, apparently searching for something, and soldiers dragging doors, benches, and fences from the village.

"Here, prince, we cannot get rid of such men as these," said the staff officer, pointing to the soldiers. "The officers let them leave their places. And here again!" the officer pointed to a sutler's tent pitched near them; "they gather around and load. This morning I drove them all out, and look! it's all full again."

They dismounted and went into the sutler's tent, where a few men and a number of officers with flushed and weary faces were sitting around a table, eating and drinking.

"Now what does this mean, gentlemen?" said the staff officer in a tone of vexation, like a man who has been repeating the same thing again and again. "You know it is forbidden to absent yourselves from your posts in this way. The prince has forbidden any such thing. . . . And here you are, Mr. Captain!" said he, turning to a little, lean, dirty artillery officer, who without boots (he had given them to the sutler to dry), in his stocking feet, stood up as the others entered and greeted them with a slightly natural smile. "Well, aren't you ashamed of yourself, Captain Tushin?" demanded the staff officer. "One would think that as an officer you would set a good example, and here you are with your boots off! If an alarm were sounded, you would make a fine show without boots!" The staff officer smiled satirically. "Please go to your places, gentlemen, all, all of you," he added in a tone of command.

Prince Andrei could not help smiling as he looked at Captain Tushin, who, silent and smiling, stood first on one bare foot and then on the other and looked inquiringly with his large, intelligent and good-natured eyes from Prince Andrei to the officer of the day.

"The soldiers say: 'It's easier to go barefooted,'" said Captain Tushin, timid and still smiling, evidently anxious to escape from his awkward predicament by assuming a jesting tone; but he did not say anything further, as if he felt that his joke was not appreciated and was not a success. He grew confused.

"Please go to your places," repeated the staff officer, trying to preserve his gravity.

Prince Andrei once more glanced at the diminutive form of the artillery officer. There was something about it peculiar, utterly unmilitary, and rather comical, but still extraordinarily attractive.

The officer of the day and Prince Andrei remounted their horses and rode on.

After riding along the entire line, from the right flank to the left, Prince Andrei made his way to a battery from which the whole field was visible. Here he dismounted and leaned against the last one of our unlimbered field-pieces. An artilleryman, who was pacing up and down in front of the guns as sentry, started to give Prince Andrei the military salute, but at a sign desisted and once more began his monotonous, tedious march. At a little distance from the outermost gun was a new, wattled hut, in which could be heard the lively voices of officers talking together. Suddenly Prince Andrei was so struck by the note of sincerity in the voices of the officers that he involuntarily began to listen.

"No, my dear fellow," said a pleasant voice, which somehow seemed very familiar to Prince Andrei. "I say that if it were possible to know what will be after death, then none of us would have any fear of death. That's so, my boy."

"But all men are afraid of it."

"Yes, you know so much," said a lusty voice, breaking in upon the others. "You artillerymen know so much because you can take with you, everywhere you go, your tipples of vodka and your rations."

And the possessor of the lusty voice, evidently an infantry officer, laughed.

"Yes, all men are afraid of death," continued the first, familiar voice. "We are afraid of the unknown; that's the point. It's no use saying the soul goes up to heaven; why, we know very well that up yonder there's no heaven, but only the atmosphere."

Again the lusty voice interrupted the artilleryman:

"Come, now, Tushin, let us have some of your liquor."

"So that is the very same captain who was at the sutler's tent in his stocking feet," said Prince Andrei to himself, glad to recognize the pleasant voice of the philosopher.

"The liquor you can have," said Tushin, "but all the same, as to comprehending the life to come . . ."

He did not finish his sentence. At that instant a whiz was heard in the air; nearer and nearer, swifter and louder, louder and swifter, a cannon ball, as if unable to say all it wanted to say, plunged into the earth not far from the hut, tearing up the ground with superhuman violence. The ground seemed to groan with the terrible shock.

In a moment the little Tushin came running out of the hut ahead of the others, with his after-dinner pipe at the side of his mouth; his kind, intelligent face was rather pale. He was followed by the possessor of the lusty voice, a young infantry officer who hurried off to his company, buttoning his coat as he ran.

Prince Andrei mounted his horse, but remained in the battery, trying to distinguish by the smoke the cannon that had sent the projectile. His eyes wandered over the whole landscape. All he could make out was that the hitherto motionless masses of the French were beginning to stir, and that there really was a battery at the left. At the foot of the hill a small but clearly distinguishable column of the enemy was moving, evidently for the purpose of strengthening the lines. The smoke of the first gun had not yet blown away when another puff arose, followed by the report. The action had begun.

Prince Andrei turned his horse and galloped back to Grund to find Prince Bagration.

Lemarrois, with Bonaparte's angry letter, had just dashed up to Murat, and Murat, ashamed of himself and anxious to retrieve his blunder, began immediately to move his army against the center, and at the same time around both flanks, hoping before night and the arrival of the emperor to demolish the insignificant division that opposed him.

"It has begun! Here it is!" said Prince Andrei to himself, feeling his heart beat violently. "But where—how shall I find my Toulon?"

Riding among companies that had been eating their gruel and drinking vodka only a quarter of an hour before, everywhere he found the soldiers hastily moving about, getting into line and examining their guns; on all faces there was the same expression of expectancy that he had in his heart. The face of every soldier and officer seemed to say: "It has begun! Here it is! How terrible! How glorious!"

Before he reached the unfinished earthworks he saw in the twilight of the gloomy autumn day some horsemen riding toward him. The foremost, in a felt cape and a fur cap with insignia, rode a white horse. This was Prince Bagration. He kept his eyes straight ahead, while Prince Andrei was reporting to him what he had seen. The thought, *it has begun; here it is!* could also be read on Bagration's strong, brown face with the half-closed, dull eyes that seemed to show continuous lack of sleep.

IX

A CHARGE OF THE Sixth Jaegers insured the retreat of the right wing. In the center, the action of Tushin's battery, which had succeeded in setting the village of Schöngraben on fire, retarded the advance of the French. They stopped to put out the conflagration, which the wind was spreading, and thus gave time for the Russians to retreat. The retirement of the center through the ravine was accomplished hastily and noisily, but there was no sign of demoralization. But the left wing, consisting of the infantry of the Azof and Podolian regiments and the Pavlograd hussars, which was attacked simultaneously and outflanked by overwhelming numbers of the French under the command of Lannes, was defeated.

Bagration had sent Zherkof to the general in command of the left wing, with orders to retreat slowly. Zherkof, raising his hand to his cap, stuck his spurs into his horse and swiftly dashed off. But he had no more than ridden out of Bagration's sight than his courage began to fail him. Irresistible fear overwhelmed him, and he could not make up his mind to go where it seemed to him so perilous.

He rode over to the army of the left wing, but he did not dare press forward to the front, where there was firing, and he began to search for the general and the officers where there was no possibility of finding them; and so the order was not delivered.

The command of the left wing devolved by order of seniority to the regimental commander of that same brigade which had been reviewed at Braunau by Kutuzof, and in which Dolokhof served as a private. The command of the extreme left wing was intrusted to the colonel of the Pavlograd regiment, in which Rostof served. This led to a serious misunderstanding. The men, from private to general, were not expecting an engagement and were calmly occupied with the ordinary pursuits of peace—the cavalrymen fed their horses, the infantry collected firewood.

"He's my senior, however, in rank," the German colonel of hussars was saying, flushing and addressing the aide who had just ridden up to him, "so let him do as he pleases. I cannot sacrifice my hussars. Bugler, sound the retreat!"

But the battle came upon them in furious haste. Cannonade and musketry, all in confusion, thundered and rattled at their right and center, and the figures of Lannes' sharpshooters could already be seen crossing the mill-dam and forming on this side, two gunshots away. The infantry general, with his tottering gait, went to his horse and, mounting and drawing himself up very straight and tall, rode off to the Pavlograd commander. The two men met with polite bows and with concealed hatred in their hearts.

"Once for all, colonel," said the general, "I cannot leave half of my men in the woods. I beg of you, I really beg of you," he repeated the word, "to draw up in position and meet the charge."

"I beg of you not to meddle in what does not concern you," replied the colonel, angrily. "If you were a cavalryman . . ."

"I am not a cavalryman, colonel, but I am a Russian general, and if you don't know this . . ."

"I know it very well, your excellency," cried the colonel, suddenly starting up his horse and turning purple with rage. "Wouldn't you like to come to the line, and then you can see that this position is as bad as it could be? I do not care to destroy my regiment for your gratification."

"You forget yourself, colonel. I am not seeking my own gratification, and I will not permit you to say such a thing."

The general, accepting the colonel's invitation as a challenge of courage, thrust out his chest, and, frowning, rode forward with him in the direction of the outposts, as if all their dispute were to be settled there at the front, under the fire of the enemy. They reached the outposts; a few bullets flew over them, and they paused and were silent. There was no reason for inspecting the outposts, since, from the place where they had been before, it was perfectly evident that there was no chance for cavalry to maneuver among the bushes and gullies, and that the French were outflanking the left wing.

The general and colonel looked at each other with fierce and unwavering eyes, like two gamecocks all ready for battle, and each waited vainly for the other to show sign of cowardice. Both stood the test. As there was nothing for them to say, and as neither wished to give the other a chance to assert that he had been the first to retire from exposure to the enemy's fire, they would have stood there a long time, each manifesting his bravado, if at this time they had not heard in the forest almost directly behind them the crackling of musketry and distant confused shouting. The French had fallen on the soldiery scattered through the forest gathering firewood. It was now impossible for the hussars to retreat at the same time with the infantry. They were already cut off by the French line at the left. Now, although the locality was most unpropitious, it was absolutely necessary to fight their way through to reach the road beyond.

The squadron in which Rostof served had barely time to mount their horses before they found themselves face to face with the enemy. Again, as at the bridge over the Enns, between the squadron and the line of the enemy there was no one, and between them lay that terrible gap of the unknown and the dreadful, like the bourn that divides the living from the dead. The colonel came galloping along the front, angrily replied to the questions of his officers, and, like a man who in despair insists on his own way, thundered out some command.

"If they would only hurry, hurry," thought Rostof, feeling that at last the time was at hand for participating in the intoxication of a charge, of which he had heard so much from his comrades, the hussars.

"God be with us! Fohwahd, children," rang out Denisof's voice; "twot!"

In the front rank the haunches of the horses began to rise and fall. Grachik began to pull on the reins, and dashed ahead. At the right, Rostof could see the forward ranks of his hussars, but farther in front there was a dark streak, which he could not make out distinctly, but supposed to be the enemy. Reports were heard, but in the distance.

"Charge!" rang the command, and Rostof felt how his Grachik broke into a gallop and seemed to strain every sinew. He realized that his division was dashing forward and the charge became more and more exciting to him. He noticed a solitary tree just abreast of him. At first this tree had been in front of him, in the very center of that line which seemed so terrible. But now he had passed beyond it and there was not only nothing terrible about it, but everything seemed ever more and more jolly and lively.

"Oh! how I will slash at them!" thought Rostof, as he grasped the handle of his saber.

"Hurrah-ah-ah-ah!" rang the cheers in the distance.

"Now let us be at them if ever," thought Rostof, striking the spurs into Grachik; and overtaking the others, he urged him to the top of his speed. The enemy were already in sight before him. Suddenly something like an enormous lash cracked all along the squadron. Rostof raised his saber in readiness to strike, but just at that instant Nikitenko, a hussar galloping in front of him, swerved aside from him, and Rostof felt, as in a dream, that he was being carried with unnatural swiftness forward, and yet was not moving from the spot. A hussar whom he recognized as Bandarchuk was galloping behind him and looked at him gravely. Bandarchuk's horse shied and he dashed by him.

"What does it mean? Am I not moving? Have I fallen? Am I dead?" These questions Rostof asked and answered in a breath. He was alone in the middle of the field. In place of the galloping horses and backs of the hussars, he saw all around him the solid earth and stubble. Warm blood was under him. "No, I am wounded, and my horse is killed."

Grachik raised himself on his forelegs, but fell back, pinning down his rider's foot. From the horse's head a stream of blood was flowing. The horse struggled but could not rise. Rostof tried to get to his feet, but likewise fell back. His sabretache had caught on the saddle. Where our men were, where the French were, he could not tell. There was no one around him. Freeing his leg, he got up.

"Where, in which direction, is now that line that so clearly separated the two armies?" he asked himself, and could find no answer. "Has something bad happened to me? Is this the way things happen? and what must be done in such circumstances?" he asked himself again, as he got to his feet; and at this time he began to feel as if something extra were hanging to his benumbed left arm. His wrist seemed to belong to another person. He looked at his hand, but could find no trace of blood on it. "There now, here are our fellows," he exclaimed mentally, with joy, perceiving a few running toward him. "They will help me."

In front of these men ran one in a foreign-looking shako and a blue cap. He was dark and sunburnt, and had a hooked nose. Two or three others were running at his heels. One of them said something in a language that was strange and un-Russian. Surrounded by a similar set of men in the same sort of shakoes stood a Russian hussar. His hands were held; just behind him they were holding his horse.

"Is our man really taken prisoner? Yes! And will they take me too? Who are these men?" Rostof kept asking himself, not crediting his own eyes. "Can they be the French?" He gazed at the oncoming strangers, and, in spite of the fact that only a second before he had been dashing forward solely for the purpose of overtaking and hacking down these same Frenchmen, their proximity now seemed to him so terrible that he could not trust his own eyes! "Who are they? Why are they running? Are they running at me? And why? Is it to kill me? Me, whom everyone loves so?" He recollected how he was beloved by his mother, his family, his friends, and the idea that his enemies might kill him seemed incredible. "But perhaps . . . they may . . ." For more than ten seconds he stood, not moving from the spot and not realizing his situation.

The foremost Frenchman, with the hooked nose, had now come up so close to him that he could see the expression of his face. And the heated foreign-looking features of this man, who was coming so swiftly down upon him with fixed bayonet and bated breath, filled Rostof with horror. He grasped his pistol, but instead of discharging it, flung it at the Frenchman and fled into the thicket as fast as he could. He ran, not with any of that feeling of doubt and struggle which had possessed him on the bridge at Enns, but rather with the impulse of a hare trying to escape from the dogs.

X

TUSHIN'S BATTERY had been entirely forgotten, and only at the very end of the engagement Prince Bagration, still hearing cannonading at the center, sent thither the first staff officer of the day, and then Prince Andrei, to order the battery to retire as speedily as possible. The covering forces which had been stationed near Tushin's cannon had been withdrawn during the heat of the engagement by someone's orders; but the battery still continued to blaze away, and had not been taken by the French simply because the enemy could not comprehend the audacity of four guns continuing to fire after the supporting columns had been withdrawn. On the contrary, they supposed from the energetic activity of this battery that the principal forces of the Russians were here concentrated in the center. Twice they attempted to storm this point, and both times they were driven back by discharges of grape from these four cannon, standing alone on the hill. As if for a punishment for this misfortune, the enemy established a battery of ten guns a little to the right of Schönbrunn and began to reply to Tushin's fire.

In their childish delight at their successful onslaught upon the French, our gunners did not notice this battery until two cannon balls, followed by four at once, fell among the guns; one of them knocked over two horses, and the other carried away the leg of a powder master. The animation of the men, once aroused, was not dampened, however, but only changed in character. The horses were replaced by two others from the reserve; the wounded were removed, and the four cannon were turned against the ten-gun battery. An officer, Tushin's comrade, had been killed at the beginning of the action, and during the course of the hour, out of forty men serving the guns, seventeen were disabled; but still the gunners were jolly and full of energy. Twice they noticed that below and not far away from them the French were beginning to appear, and they had loaded with grape.

The little captain, with his weak, awkward gestures, kept calling upon his servant for "just one more little pipe," and then, knocking the ashes out, he would leap forward and look from under his little hand at the enemy.

"Let 'em have it, boys!" he would exclaim, and, himself seizing the cannon by the wheel, he would bring it back into position, or he would clean out the bore.

"Now then, our Matveyevna!" said he to himself. It was the great, old-fashioned howitzer that Tushin personified under the name of Matveyevna, daughter of Matthew. He imagined himself a mighty giant of monstrous size, seizing the cannon balls with both hands and hurling them at the French.

"Well, Matveyevna, old girl, don't betray us," he was just saying, and starting away from the cannon, when back of him was heard a voice he did not know: "Captain Tushin! Captain!"

Tushin looked around in alarm. It was the same staff officer who had sent him out of Grund. In a quavering voice, the officer cried:

"Are you crazy? Twice you have been ordered to retire and you . . ."

"Now, why do they bother me?" exclaimed Tushin to himself, looking with dread at the officer. "I . . . I'm all right," he returned, raising two fingers to his visor. "I . . ."

But the colonel did not say all he meant to say. A cannon ball, flying close to him, make him cower down close to his horse. He paused and was just going to repeat his order, when still another cannon ball interrupted him. He wheeled his horse around and galloped away.

"Retire! all of you retire!" he cried from the distance.

The soldiers laughed. In a minute an aide came with the same order. This was Prince Andrei. The first thing he saw, as he reached the little space occupied by Tushin's cannon, was an unharnessed horse, with a broken leg, neighing near the horses that were still hitched up. From his leg the blood was spurting as from a fountain. Among the limbers lay a number of the killed. One cannon ball after another flew over him as he galloped up, and he was conscious of a nervous tremor running down his back. But the mere thought that he was afraid again roused his courage. "I cannot be afraid," he said to himself, and he deliberately dismounted among the fieldpieces. He delivered his message and still lingered in the battery. He resolved that the guns should be removed from their position and brought in under his direction. He and Tushin, stepping among the dead bodies, made the arrangements for limbering the cannon, even while the French were pouring a murderous fire upon them.

"An officer just dashed up here, but he made himself scarce in no time," remarked a gunner to Prince Andrei. "He wasn't like your honor."

Prince Andrei exchanged no words with Tushin. They were both so oc-cupied that it seemed as if they did not see each other. When at last they succeeded in getting two of the four fieldpieces limbered, they started to descend the hill, leaving one fieldpiece dismounted, together with the howitzer. Prince Andrei turned to Tushin. "Well, good-by," said he, offering him his hand.

"Good-by, my dear," returned Tushin. "Farewell, my dear fellow!" exclaimed Tushin, the tears springing to his eyes, though he did not know why.

XI

THE BREEZE had died down; dark clouds hung low over the battlefield, mingling on the horizon with the smoke of gunpowder. It had grown dark, and therefore with all the more clearness the blaze of two burning villages stood out against the sky. The cannonade had slackened, but still the rattle of musketry at the rear and at the right was heard with ever-increasing frequency and distinctness.

As soon as Tushin and his fieldpieces, jolting and constantly meeting wounded men, got out of range and descended into the ravine, he was met by the commander and his aides, among whom were both the staff officer and Zherkof, who had been twice sent but had not once succeeded in reaching Tushin's battery. All of them gave him confused orders and counterorders as to how and where to go, and overwhelmed him with reproaches and criticisms.

Tushin made no arrangements, but rode toward the rear on his artillery jade, not saying a word for fear he would burst into tears, which, without his knowing why, were ready to gush from his eyes. Although the order was to abandon the wounded, many dragged themselves after the troops and begged for a ride on the gun carriages. That very same gallant infantry officer, who before the beginning of the engagement had darted so energetically from Tushin's hut, was stretched out on the carriage of the Matveyevna, with a bullet in his belly. At the foot of the hill, a pale cadet of hussars, holding one arm in his hand, came to Tushin and asked for a seat!

"Captain, for God's sake, my arm is crushed," said he timidly. "For God's sake, I can't walk any longer. For God's sake!"

It was evident that this cadet had more than once repeated his request and been everywhere refused. He asked in an irresolute and piteous voice. "Give me a place for God's sake!"

"Climb on, climb on!" said Tushin. "Spread out a cloak, uncle," he added, turning to his favorite gunner. "But where is the wounded officer?"

"We took him off; he died," replied someone.

"Climb on! Sit there, sit down, my dear fellow, sit there! Spread out the cloak, Antonof!"

The cadet was Rostof. He held his left arm in his right hand; his face was pale, and his teeth chattered with fever. He was assisted to climb on the Matveyevna, to the very same spot from which they had removed the dead officer. There was blood on the cloak which Antonof spread out, and it stained Rostof's riding trousers and hands.

"What! are you wounded, my boy?" asked Tushin, approaching the gun on which Rostof was riding.

"No, only a bruise."

"But where did that blood come from, on the gun cheek?" asked the other.

"That is the officer's, your honor," replied a gunner, wiping away the blood with the sleeve of his cloak, as if he were apologizing for the stain on the gun.

By this time it was quite dark, so that it was impossible at ten paces to distinguish the uniforms of the soldiers; the musketry fire was beginning to slacken. Suddenly shouts and the rattle of shots were heard again near by at the right. The darkness was lighted up by the flashes of the guns. This was the last attack of the French, and the soldiers replied to it as they intrenched themselves in the houses of the village. Once more all hands rushed out from the village, but Tushin's fieldpieces could not be moved, and the gunners and Tushin and the cadet, silently exchanging glances, awaited their fate. Then the firing began to die away once more, and out of a side street came a party of soldiers, engaged in lively conversation.

"Safe and sound, Petrof?" asked one.

"We gave it to them hot and heavy, brother. They won't meddle with us again," returned the other.

"Can't see a thing. How was it? Warmed 'em up a little, hey? Can't see a thing, it's so dark, fellows! Anything to drink?"

Fires were lighted and voices began to grow animated. Captain Tushin, having made his arrangements for his company, sent one of his men to find the temporary hospital, or at least a surgeon for the cadet, and sat down in front of the fire his soldiers had built by the roadside. Rostof also dragged himself up to the fire. The fever caused by his pain, the cold and the dampness shook his whole frame. An irresistible inclination to drowsiness overcame him, but still he could not sleep, owing to the tormenting pain he felt in his arm; it ached, and he found no position that relieved it. Sometimes he closed his eyes; then again, he gazed into the fire, which seemed to him angrily red.

In a cottage that had been made ready for him, not far from the artillery soldiers' fire, Prince Bagration was still sitting at the dinner table.

He thanked the officers of the various divisions and made inquiries about the details of the engagement and the losses. The regimental commander who had commanded the review at Braunau explained to the prince that, as soon as the action began, he had withdrawn from the woods, collected the men engaged in gathering firewood, and sending them back, had charged with two battalions and simply carried the French at the point of the bayonet.

"When I saw that the first battalion was giving way, your excellency, I stood on the road and said to myself, 'I will let them get by first, and then order a running fire,' and that was what I did."

The regimental commander had been so anxious to do this, and so sorry that he had not been successful in doing it, that it now seemed to him that he actually had done so. Indeed, may it not have been so? How was it possible to decide, in the general confusion, what had happened and what had not happened?

"By the way, I ought to observe, your excellency," he went on to say, remembering Dolokhof's conversation with Kutuzof, "that the cashiered private, Dolokhof, took a French officer prisoner under my very eyes, and distinguished himself notably."

"It was there I saw the charge of the Pavlograd hussars, your excellency," remarked Zherkof, looking around uneasily, for he had not that day seen a single hussar, and had only heard about them from an infantry officer! "They broke two formations, your excellency."

Prince Bagration turned to the elderly colonel.

"I thank you all, gentlemen; all parties worked like heroes, infantry, cavalry, and artillery. But how was it two fieldpieces were abandoned in the center?" he demanded, looking round for someone. "I believe I asked you about them?" he said, turning to the staff officer of the day.

"One was dismounted," replied the staff officer; "but the other . . . as to that I myself cannot understand; I was there all the time and gave orders for it to be retired, and immediately I was called away. It was hot there, to be sure," he added modestly.

Someone remarked that Captain Tushin was right here in the village, and that he had already been sent for.

"Ah, but you were there, were you not?" asked Prince Bagration of Prince Andrei.

"Certainly, we almost met there," said the staff officer, giving Prince Andrei an affable smile.

"I did not have the pleasure of seeing you," declared Prince Andrei, coolly and curtly.

All were silent.

Tushin now appeared on the threshold, modestly making his way behind the backs of the generals. Passing around the generals in the narrow room, and confused, as always, in the presence of his superiors, Tushin did not see the flagstaff and stumbled over it. Several laughed.

"How is it the guns were abandoned?" asked Bagration, frowning, but not so much at the captain as at those who were rude enough to laugh, among whom Zherkof's voice was distinguished above the rest. Tushin now, for the first time, at the sight of the stern commander, realized with horror his crime and disgrace at having lost two guns, while he himself was left alive.

He had been so agitated that, till this moment, he had not had time to think of this incident. The laughter of the officers still more threw him off his balance. He stood in front of Bagration with his lower jaw trembling, and could hardly stammer:

"I . . . I . . . don't know . . . your excellency . . . I had no men, your excellency . . ."

"You might have had them from the forces that covered you."

Tushin did not reply that there were no forces covering him, though this would have been the unvarnished truth. He was afraid he might compromise some of his superior officers, and so in silence, with staring eyes, he gazed into Bagration's face as a schoolboy looks in confusion into his master's.

"Your excellency," said Prince Andrei, breaking the silence in his clear voice, "you were pleased to send me to Captain Tushin's battery. I went there and found two-thirds of his men and horses disabled, two of his guns dismounted, and no forces to cover him!"

Prince Bagration and Tushin kept their eyes fixed on Bolkonsky, who was speaking under the influence of restrained excitement.

"And if your excellency will permit me to express my opinion," he went on to say, "we are indebted most of all for the success of this day to the action of this battery and the heroic steadfastness of Captain Tushin and his company," said Prince Andrei; and, without waiting for any reply, he got up and left the table.

Prince Bagration looked at Tushin, and evidently not wishing to show any disbelief in Prince Bolkonsky's outspoken judgment, and at the same time not feeling himself prepared to agree entirely with it, he inclined his head and told Tushin he might go. Prince Andrei followed him.

"Thank you, my boy, you have saved me," said Tushin to him.

Prince Andrei looked at Tushin, and, without saying anything, turned away from him. His heart was heavy and full of melancholy. It was all so strange, so unlike what he had anticipated.

"Who are they? why do they come here? what do they want? and when will all this end?" Rostof asked himself, as he gazed at the shadows which unceasingly passed before him. The pain in his arm grew worse and worse. Unconquerable drowsiness oppressed him. Red circles danced before his eyes, and the impression of these voices and these faces, and the sense of his loneliness, mingled with the sense of his agony. These soldiers, wounded and not wounded, they all did the same thing—they pressed upon him, crushed him, tore his muscles—and burned the flesh in his crushed arm and shoulder. To rid himself of them he closed his eyes.

"I'm of no use to anyone!" thought Rostof. "No one helps me or takes pity on me! If I were only at home, strong, happy, beloved!" He gazed at the snowflakes fluttering down into the fire, and he recalled what winter would be at home in Russia, his warm bright home, with his soft furs, swift sledges, his strong healthy body and the love and care of his family. "And why did I come here?" he asked himself.

On the following day the French did not renew their attack, and the remains of Bagration's division effected a conjunction with Kutuzof's army.

1805

The campaign of 1805 ends disastrously for the coalition against Napoleon. He has destroyed an entire Austrian army at Ulm in October; he has occupied Vienna in November. On December 2 a concentration of Russian and Austrian forces attack the French at Austerlitz, in Moravia, which turns out to be one of Napoleon's most famous victories.

Part Third

PRINCE VASILI was not in the habit of thinking out his plans ahead of time. He never said to himself, for instance: "This man is now in my power, I ought to gain his confidence and friendship and thereby secure myself the advantage of his patronage," or: "Now Pierre is rich, I ought to induce him to marry my daughter, and thus get the forty thousand rubles that I need." But if, by chance, he met a man in power, instinct immediately whispered to him that this man might be profitable to him, and Prince Vasili struck up a friendship with him and at the first opportunity, led by instinct, flattered him, treated him with easy familiarity, and finally brought about the crucial conversation.

Pierre was under his tutelage at Moscow, and Prince Vasili procured for him an appointment as gentleman-in-waiting to the Tsar and insisted that the young man accompany him to Petersburg and take up residence in his own mansion.

Without any exertion, and at the same time taking it absolutely for granted that he was on the right track, Prince Vasili did everything in his power to marry Pierre to his daughter.

Pierre, who had unexpectedly succeeded to Count Bezukhof's wealth and title, found himself, after a life of loneliness and inaction, surrounded and occupied to such a degree that only when he was in bed could he have a moment entirely to himself. He was obliged to sign letters, to show himself at the courthouse in regard to matters of which he had no clear comprehension, to ask questions about this and that of his chief overseer, to ride out to his estate in the suburbs of Moscow, and to receive many people who hitherto had ignored his very existence. He constantly heard such phrases as: "With your extraordinary kindness"; or, "Because of your tender heart"; or "You are so upright, count"; or, "If I were as clever as you are"; and so on, until he actually began to believe in his extraordinary goodness and his extraordinary intelligence, all the more because in the depths of his heart it had always seemed to him that he was really very good and very clever.

Even people who before had been abrupt with him and treated him with undisguised dislike now became sweet and affectionate toward him.

For example, the sharp-tempered elder sister, the princess with the long waist and the phenomenally smooth hair, like a doll's, came into Pierre's room after his father's funeral. Dropping her eyes and flushing deeply, she assured him how sincerely she regretted the misunderstandings that had arisen between them, and asked him as a special favor, though she felt that she had no right to do so, that she might be allowed, after the blow that had befallen her, to remain for a few weeks longer in the house which she loved so well and where she had suffered so much. She could not restrain her tears, and wept freely at these words. Touched by the change that the statuesque princess had undergone, Pierre took her by the hand and begged her forgiveness, though he could not have told for what. That day the princess began to knit Pierre a striped scarf, and her attitude toward him changed completely.

"Do this for her, my dear fellow, for she put up with so many of the late count's whims," said Prince Vasili, giving him a paper to sign for the Princess' benefit.

Prince Vasili had made up his mind that he must cast this die and get this check of thirty thousand rubles for the poor princess, so that it might not enter her head to talk about the part he had taken in the matter of the mosaic portfolio. Pierre signed the check, and from that time forth the princess became still more affectionate to him. The younger sisters also were very flattering; especially the youngest one—the beauty with the mole—who often embarrassed Pierre with her smiles and her embarrassment at the sight of him.

In Petersburg, as in Moscow, Pierre found himself surrounded by an atmosphere of affection and love. Anna Pavlovna Scherer, like everybody else, made Pierre feel the change in society's feelings toward him. Hitherto, in Anna Pavlovna's presence Pierre had constantly felt that whatever he said was unbecoming, wanting in tact, unsuitable. Now, however, everything he said was greeted with the epithet "charming."

At the beginning of the winter of 1805–1806, Pierre received from Anna Pavlovna the usual pink note of invitation, and with this postscript: "The beautiful Helene, whom one never tires of observing, will be with us."

On reading this sentence, Pierre for the first time realized that a peculiar bond had sprung up between him and Helene, recognized by other people, and this thought alarmed him. It seemed to place him under some sort of obligation that he could not fulfil, and at the same time it pleased him as an amusing situation.

Anna Pavlovna's reception was exactly like the former one, except that the dessert with which she regaled her guests was not Montemart as before, but a diplomat who had just arrived from Berlin.

Anna Pavlovna, with her usual art, arranged the groups of her drawing-room. The largest, in which Prince Vasili and the generals were conspicuous, was enjoying the diplomat's conversation. Still another was gathered about the tea table. Pierre was anxious to join the former, but Anna Pavlovna laid her finger on his sleeve.

"Wait, I have designs on you for this evening." She glanced at Helene, and gave her a smile. "My dear Helene, you must be good to my poor aunt, who has conceived a perfect adoration for you. Go and spend ten minutes with her. And lest it should be very tiresome to you, here is our dear count, who certainly will not fail to follow you."

The beauty went over to the aunt, but Anna Pavlovna detained the young man, pretending that she had still some indispensable arrangement to complete.

"Charming! isn't she," said she to Pierre, referring to the stately beauty who was sailing away. "And so much tact for a young girl, such wonderful capability and dignity. Fortunate will be the man who secures her! With her a man even of the humblest position in society could not fail to attain the most brilliant position. Isn't that so? I only wanted to know your opinion."

And Anna Pavlovna released Pierre.

The aunt happened at that moment to be speaking about a collection of snuffboxes which had belonged to Pierre's late father, Count Bezukhof, and she showed him her own snuffbox. Princess Elena asked to see the portrait of her husband painted in miniature on the cover.

"That is apparently the work of Vinnes," remarked Pierre, mentioning the name of a distinguished miniature painter. He leaned over the table to take up the snuffbox, but all the time he was listening to the conversation at the other table. He got up, intending to walk around; but the aunt handed him the snuffbox, passing it directly behind Helene. Helene moved aside to give room, and, as she looked up, she smiled. In accordance with the custom of the day, she wore a dress cut very low both in front and behind. Her bust, which always reminded Pierre of marble, was so near to him that even with his nearsighted eyes he could not help seeing the exquisite beauty of her neck and shoulders, and if he had stooped but a little, his lips would have touched her neck. He was conscious of the warmth of her body, the faint breath of some perfume, and the slight creak of her corset as she moved. He saw not the statuesque beauty which merged so well with the color of her dress, he saw and felt the whole charm of her form, concealed, as it were, only by her clothing. And having once seen this, his eyes refused to see her in any other way, just as it is impossible for us to recall an illusion that has once been explained.

And so you have not noticed before how charming I am? Helene seemed to say. *Have you not noticed that I am a woman? Yes, I am a woman, whom any man might win—even you.* And at that instant, Pierre was conscious that Helene not only might be, but that she must be, his wife, that it could not be otherwise.

He knew this at that moment just as surely as he would have known it had he been standing with her under the bridal crown.

How would this be? and when would it be?

He could not tell; he was not sure that it would be the best thing for him; he even had a dim consciousness that somehow it would not be for the best; but still he knew that it would be. Pierre dropped his eyes, then raised them, and tried once more to see that beauty so far off and foreign to him, as he had seen it every day before; but he found it impossible. She was terribly near to him; already she had begun to wield her power over him. And between him and her there was no longer any barrier except the barrier of his own will.

After he returned home, Pierre was long unable to sleep, for thinking of what had happened to him. What had happened to him? Nothing! All he knew was that a woman he had known as a child, of whom he had often heedlessly said "Yes, she's pretty" when told that Helene was a beauty, might be his.

"But she is stupid; I myself have declared that she is stupid," he said to himself. "There is something revolting in the feeling that she stirs in me, something repulsive. I have been told that her own brother Anatol was in love with her, and that she loved him in return; that there was quite a scandal about it, and that was the reason Anatol was sent away. Ippolit is her brother. Her father— Prince Vasili . . . it's all ugly," he went on thinking, and even while he came to this decision—such considerations are endless —he found himself to his surprise indulging in a smile, and acknowledged that another series of considerations was arising in his mind; that while he was thinking of her faults he was at the same time dreaming how she would be his wife, how she might be in love with him, how she might be quite different, and how all that he had heard and thought about her might be untrue. And again he saw her, not as Prince Vasili's daughter, but as a woman, her form concealed merely by her gray gown. "But why has this idea never entered my mind before?" And again he assured himself that it was impossible; and a sense of horror came over him, lest he had bound himself by dreaming of such a project, a project which was evidently wrong, and which he ought not to have undertaken. But at the very time that he came to this decision, in the other half of his mind arose a vision of her form in all its womanly beauty.

II

In November, 1805, Prince Vasili was obliged to go to four provinces on a tour of inspection. He had secured this commission for himself so as to visit one of his ruined estates, and it was his intention, having picked up his son Anatol, who was with his regiment at one of the places on his route, to go with him on a visit to Prince Nikolai Bolkonsky, so as to marry his son to the daughter of this wealthy old man. But before starting on this journey and undertaking these new duties, Prince Vasili felt called upon to bring Pierre's little affair to a crisis. The truth was Pierre, during these latter days of his visit at Prince Vasili's, had been spending whole days at home, that is to say, at Prince Vasili's where he was staying, and was absurd, agitated, and moping in Helene's presence—the proper condition of a man in love—but still he had not made his declaration.

A fortnight after Anna Pavlovna's reception and the sleepless, agitated night that followed it, when he had made up his mind that to marry Helene would lead to unhappiness and that he should flee from her and go away, Pierre, in spite of this decision, was still at Prince Vasili's, and felt with a sort of horror that each day he was becoming, in the eyes of the world, more and more attached to her; that he could not return to his former way of looking upon her; could not tear himself from her; that it was abominable, but still he must link his fate with hers. Each day he said to himself the same thing: "I must understand her and explain her to myself—what is she? Was I mistaken in her before, or am I mistaken now? No, she is not stupid. No, she is a beautiful girl," he said to himself from time to time. Never did she make a single error; never, by any chance, did she say anything stupid. She spoke little, but what she said was always simple and clear. So she could not be stupid. Never was she agitated or confused. She could not be a vile woman!

Often it chanced that he began to speak with her, or to utter his thoughts in her hearing, but every time she replied with some brief but appropriately worded remark showing that she was not interested, or else with a silent smile and look, which more palpably than anything else proved to Pierre her superiority. She was in the right, for she made it evident that all arguments and reasonings were rubbish in comparison with this smile.

She always treated him with a radiant, confiding and confidential smile, which was meant for himself alone, as though there were in it something more significant than there was in the smile she wore for the world in general. Pierre knew that all were waiting for him at last to speak the one word needful, to step over the certain line, and he knew that sooner or later he would cross it; a strange and invincible horror seized him at the mere thought of this momentous step. A thousand times in the course of this fortnight, during which he felt himself all the time drawn deeper and deeper into the abyss, he said to himself: "What does it mean? What I need is decision! Why do I lack it?"

On the evening of Helene's saint's-day, a small party of friends and relatives—"Our nearest and dearest," as the princess expressed it—took supper at Prince Vasili's. All these friends and relatives were given to understand that on this day the young lady's fate was to be decided. The guests were seated in the dining room. Princess Kuragin, a portly, imposing woman who had once been famous for her beauty, sat at the head of the table. On each side of her were placed the more important guests—an old general, his wife, and Anna Pavlovna Scherer; at the other end of the table were the younger and less honored guests; and there, also, sat the various members of the household—Pierre and Helene side by side.

Prince Vasili did not sit down with the rest; he walked around the table in a jovial mood, stopping to chat now with one, now with another of his guests, speaking some light and pleasant word to all except Pierre and Helene, whose presence he seemed entirely to ignore. Prince Vasili was the very life of the company.

The wax candles burned brightly, the silver and crystal gleamed, the jewels of the ladies and the gold and silver epaulets of the officers sparkled. The clatter of knives and plates and glasses, and the hum of lively conversation, were heard around the table. But Pierre and Helene sat silent, side by side, at the lower end of the table; on the face of each hovered a radiant smile, a smile of bashfulness at their own thoughts. The others might chatter and laugh and jest, but the energies of the whole company were, in reality, devoted to this young couple. Amid the mean, petty and artificial interests uniting this company, there arose the natural feeling of attraction felt for each other by a handsome and healthy young man and woman.

Pierre was conscious that he was the center of everything, and this condition both pleased him and made him uncomfortable. He found himself in the position of a man plunged in some sort of absorbing occupation. He saw nothing, heard nothing, understood nothing clearly. Only occasionally, through his consciousness, flashed fragmentary thoughts and expressions of the reality.

"And so it is all over," he said to himself. "How in the world did it ever happen? It was so sudden! Now I know that not for her sake alone, nor for my own sake alone, but for the sake of all, this must be accomplished without fail. They all expect this so confidently, they are so certain that it will take place, that I cannot, I cannot disappoint them. But how will it take place? I do not know; but it will be, it infallibly must be!" thought Pierre, as he glanced at those shoulders so near him.

Suddenly he heard a voice, a well-known voice, speaking and saying something for the second time. But Pierre was so absorbed that he did not comprehend what was said to him.

"I asked you when you heard last from Bolkonsky," said Prince Vasili for the third time. "How absent-minded you are, my dear fellow!"

Prince Vasili smiled. And Pierre saw that all, all were smiling at him and at Helene. "Well, suppose you all do know!" said Pierre to himself. "What then? It is true," and he smiled his sweet, childlike smile, and Helene also smiled.

"When did you get the letter? Was it from Olmütz?" repeated Prince Vasili, who pretended that he wished to know in order to decide a dispute.

"How can one talk and think about such trifles?" was Pierre's mental exclamation. "Yes, from Olmütz," he replied, with a sigh.

After supper Pierre gave his arm to Helene and led her to the drawing-room in the wake of the others. The guests began to disperse, and some went away without bidding Helene farewell. Others, as if unwilling to tear her away from serious concerns, went up to her for a minute and then hurried away, without allowing her to accompany them to the door. A diplomat preserved a mournful silence as he left the drawing-room. The utter futility of his diplomatic career presented itself in comparison with Pierre's good fortune. The old general growled out a surly reply to his wife when she asked him about the gout in his foot. "Oh! the old fool!" he said to himself, "here's Princess Elena; and she'll be just as much of a beauty at fifty!"

"It seems as if I may congratulate you," said Anna Pavlovna in a whisper to the old princess, and gave her a resounding kiss. "If I hadn't a sick headache, I would stay a little longer."

The princess made no answer; she was tormented by jealousy at her daughter's good fortune.

While the guests were taking their departure, Pierre was left for some time alone with Helene in the little sitting room where they often sat. During the past fortnight he had been often alone with Helene, but he had never said a word to her about love. Now he felt it was indispensable, but still he could not make up his mind to undertake this last step. He felt abashed; it seemed that here in Helene's presence he occupied a place that belonged to someone else. *Not for thee is this good fortune*, some internal voice seemed to whisper. *This happiness is for those who have not what thou hast.*

But it was essential to say something, and he tried to talk. He asked her if she had enjoyed the evening. She replied, with her usual directness, that this saint's-day had been one of the pleasant events of her life.

One or two of the nearest relatives still remained. They were gathered in the great drawing-room. Prince Vasili with leisurely steps came to Pierre. Pierre got up and remarked that it was already late. Prince Vasili looked at him with a gravely questioning face, as much as to imply that what he said was too strange to be heard. But instantly this expression of sternness vanished, and Prince Vasili laid his hand on Pierre's sleeve, made him sit down again, and gave him a flattering smile.

"Well, Helene?" he asked, turning to his daughter, in that easygoing tone of familiarity peculiar to parents who have lived on terms of especial affection with their children ever since their childhood, but which in Prince

Vasili's case had been acquired only through having observed other parents.

"It is absolutely indispensable for me to take this step, but I cannot, I cannot!" said Pierre to himself, and once more he began to talk about irrelevant things.

When Prince Vasili returned to the drawing-room, the princess was engaged in talking in low tones with an elderly lady about Pierre. "Of course, it is a very brilliant match, but happiness, my dear," said she, in the usual mixture of French and Russian.

"Marriages are made in heaven," returned the old lady. Prince Vasili, pretending not to hear what she said, went to the farthest table and sat down on the sofa. He closed his eyes and appeared to be dozing. His head sank forward and then he woke with a start. "Alina," said he to his wife, "go and see what they are doing."

The princess went to the door, passed by it with a significant but indifferent look, and glanced in. Pierre and Helene were still sitting and talking.

"Just the same," she said, in reply to her husband. Prince Vasili scowled and screwed his mouth to one side, and his cheeks began to twitch with that unpleasant, coarse expression so characteristic of him; then with a sudden impulse he sprang to his feet, threw his head back, and with decided steps strode past the ladies into the little sitting room. Swiftly, and with a great assumption of delight, he went straight up to Pierre. His face was so unusually triumphant that Pierre, seeing him, rose to his feet in dismay.

"Thank God! Glory to God!" he cried, "my wife has told me all." He threw one arm round Pierre, the other round his daughter. "My dear boy! Helene! I am very, very glad"—his voice trembled. "I loved your father . . . and she will make you a good wife . . . God bless you." He embraced his daughter, then Pierre again, and kissed him with his malodorous mouth. Tears actually moistened his cheeks. "Princess, come here!" he cried.

The princess came and wept. The elderly lady also wiped her eyes with her handkerchief. They kissed Pierre, and he kissed the lovely Helene's hand several times. After a little they were left alone again.

"All this had to be so, and could not be otherwise," thought Pierre, "and there is no need to ask if it be good or evil. Good, at least, in that it is decided, and I am no longer tortured by suspense."

Pierre silently held the hand of his betrothed, and looked at her fair bosom as it rose and fell.

"Helene!" said he aloud, and then paused. He was aware that something special must be said under such circumstances, but he could not for the life of him remember what was the proper thing to say. He looked into her face, she came nearer to him. Her face grew a deep crimson.

"Oh, take them off. How they . . ." she pointed to his glasses.

Pierre took them off, and his eyes had a scared and entreating look in addition to that strange expression which people's eyes assume when they remove their glasses suddenly. He was about to bend over her hand and kiss it, but she with a quick and abrupt motion of her head intercepted the motion and pressed her lips to his. Her face disturbed Pierre by its changed and unpleasantly passionate expression.

"Now it is too late, it is all decided; yes, and I love her," thought Pierre.

"I love you," he said, at last remembering what was necessary in these circumstances; but these words sounded so meager that he was ashamed of himself.

At the end of a fortnight he was married, the fortunate possessor, as they say, of a beautiful wife and of millions, and settled in the enormous Petersburg mansion of the Counts Bezukhof, newly refurbished for them.

III

THE OLD Prince Nikolai Bolkonsky, in December, 1805, received a letter from Prince Vasili, announcing his arrival with his son on a visit.

"Well, there's no need to bring Marie out, if suitors come to us of their own accord," said the little princess, indiscreetly, when this was mentioned to her. Prince Nikolai frowned and made no reply. Two weeks after the receipt of the letter, Prince Vasili's servants made their appearance in advance of him, and on the next day he and his son arrived.

The old Prince Bolkonsky had a low opinion of Prince Vasili's character, and this had been intensified of late by his great advances in rank and honors under the Emperors Paul and Alexander. On the day that Prince Vasili was expected, Prince Nikolai was especially surly and out of sorts. Whether he was out of sorts because Prince Vasili was coming, or was dissatisfied with Prince Vasili's visit because he was out of sorts, did not alter the fact that he was out of sorts.

"Can sleighs come up?" he asked of his overseer, Alpatitch, a man who was his image in face and actions.

"The snow is deep, your excellency; I have already given orders to have the snow shoveled away from the highway. It was hard to approach, your excellency," he added, "when I heard, your excellency, that your excellency was expecting a minister."

The prince turned around toward his overseer and fastened his gloomy eyes upon him.

"What? A minister. What minister? Who commanded you?" he exclaimed, in his shrill, harsh voice. "The road is cleared, not for the princess, my daughter, but for a minister, is it? We have no ministers at my house."

"Your excellency, I supposed . . ."

"You supposed!" screamed the prince, uttering the words more and more hastily and incoherently. "You supposed . . . cutthroats, blackguards! I will teach you to suppose," and, raising his cane, flourished it over Alpatitch and would have struck him had not the overseer instinctively dodged the blow. "You supposed . . . blackguard!" screamed the prince, but, notwithstanding the fact that Alpatitch, alarmed at his audacity in avoiding the blow, hastened up to the prince and humbly bent before him his bald pate, or possibly for this very reason, the prince continued to scream, "Blackguards! have the snow shoveled back again," but did not raise the cane a second time.

Princess Maria and Mlle. Bourienne, knowing that he was in a bad humor, stood waiting for him to come to dinner. "And the other one not here? Can they have been tattling to her?" wondered the prince when he saw that the little princess was not in the dining room.

"Where is the princess?" he asked. "Is she hiding herself?"

"She is not feeling very well," said Mlle. Bourienne with a radiant smile, "she won't come down. That is natural in her condition."

"Hm! hm! kh! kh!" grumbled the prince, and took his seat at the table. His plate seemed to him not quite clean; he pointed to a spot and flung it away. Tikhon caught it and handed it to the butler.

The little princess was not ill, but she was so desperately afraid of the old prince that when she learned that he was in a bad humor, she resolved not to leave her room.

"I am afraid for my baby," said she to Mlle. Bourienne; "God knows what might happen if I were frightened."

The little princess lived at Lisiya Gori the greater part of the time with a sense of fear and antipathy for her father-in-law, whom she did not understand because her terror so overmastered her that she could not. The prince reciprocated this antipathy for his daughter-in-law, but it was not so strong as his contempt for her. The princess, since her residence at Lisiya Gori, had taken a special fancy to Mlle. Bourienne, spent whole days with her, often begged her to sleep with her, and talked about the old prince with her and criticized him.

"So visitors are coming to see us, prince," said Mlle. Bourienne, as she unfolded her white napkin with her rosy fingers. "His excellency, Prince Kuragin, I understand?" she said, with a questioning inflection.

"Hm—this 'excellency,' as you call him, is a puppy. I secured him his appointment," said the prince, disdainfully, "but why his son is coming is more than I know. Possibly Princess Elizabeth and Princess Maria know, but I don't know what he's bringing his son here for; I don't want him." And he looked at his blushing daughter. "So she isn't very well today? From fear of the 'minister,' I suppose, as that blockhead of an Alpatitch called him today?"

"No, father."

Mlle. Bourienne was not at all put out of countenance but rattled on about the greenhouses, and the prince melted and became more genial.

After dinner he went to see his daughter-in-law. The little princess was sitting by a little table and chatting with Masha, her maid. She turned pale at the sight of her father-in-law. The little princess had very much altered.

One would now much sooner call her ugly than pretty. Her cheeks were sunken, her lip was raised, her eyes had a strained look.

"Yes, a little headache," she replied to the prince's question as to how she felt.

"Do you need anything?"

"No, thank you, father."

"Well, then, very good, very good."

He left the room and went to the office. Alpatitch, with drooping head, was waiting for him there.

"Is the snow shoveled back?"

"It is, your excellency; forgive me, for God's sake, this one piece of stupidity."

The prince interrupted him and smiled his unnatural smile. "Well then, very good, very good." He stretched out his hand for Alpatitch to kiss, and then he went to his study.

Prince Vasili arrived in the evening. He was met on the highway by the coachmen and stable hands, who with loud shouts dragged his covered sledge and sleigh up to the entrance, over snow which had been purposely heaped on the driveway. Separate chambers had been prepared for Prince Vasili and Anatol.

Anatol, in his shirt sleeves and with his arms akimbo, was sitting before a table, at one corner of which he stared absent-mindedly with his large, handsome eyes, while a smile played over his lips. He looked on his life as one unbroken round of gaiety which fate decreed should be prepared for his amusement. And even now he looked in the same way on this visit to a churlish old man and a rich and monstrously ugly heiress. According to his theory, all this might lead to something very good and amusing. And why should he not marry her, if she were so very rich? *That never hurts*, thought Anatol.

He shaved, perfumed himself carefully and coquettishly, and, with an expression of indifference which was innate in him, and holding his head high like a young conqueror, he went to his father's chamber. Two valets were engaged in getting Prince Vasili dressed; he himself looked around him with much animation, and gave a nod to his son as he came in, as much as to say, "Good, that's the way I want you to look!"

"No, but tell me, sir, without joking, is she monstrously ugly?" he asked, as if continuing a subject which had been more than once broached during the course of their journey.

"That'll do! . . . Nonsense! The main thing is to try to be respectful and prudent toward the old prince."

"If he's going to say unpleasant things to me, I shall leave right away," said Anatol. "I can't abide these old men. Hah?"

"Remember, your whole future depends on this."

Meantime, in the maidservants' room, not only was it known that the minister and his son had arrived, but every detail of their personal appearance had been discussed in detail. But Princess Maria sat alone in her room and vainly struggled to conquer her inward agitation.

"Why did they write me? Why did Lisa have to talk to me about this? But, of course, this cannot be!" she said to herself, looking into her mirror. "How can I go down to the drawing-room? Even if he pleased me, I could not now be sure of myself in his presence."

The mere thought of her father's eyes filled her with horror.

"They've come, Maria; did you know it?" said the little princess, waddling along, and dropping heavily into an armchair.

She was no longer in the dressing gown she had worn in the morning, but had put on one of her best dresses. Her hair was carefully brushed and her face was full of animation, which, however, did not make one forget her sunken and livid features. In the finery in which she was accustomed to appear in Petersburg society, it was still more noticeable that her beauty had sadly faded. Mlle. Bourienne had also taken pains to make some improvement in her dress, and this made her pretty, fresh face still more attractive.

"What? and you intend to appear as you are, dear princess?" she exclaimed. "They will be here in a moment to bring word that the gentlemen are in the drawing-room; we must go down; so won't you make just a little change in your toilet?"

The little princess got up, rang for the maid, and hastily and merrily began to devise some adornment for her sister-in-law, and get it arranged.

"No, it's a fact, *ma bonne amie*, that dress isn't becoming," said Lisa, looking critically at her sister-in-law from some little distance. "Try that dark red masaka you have. Really! you know your whole fate, perhaps, depends on this matter. This one is too light; it won't do! no, oh, no! it won't do!"

It was not that the dress was unbecoming, but the princess' face and whole figure were at fault; and yet neither Mlle. Bourienne nor the little princess realized this. It seemed to them that if they put a blue ribbon in her hair, and combed it up, and then added a blue scarf to her cinnamon-colored dress, and made some other such additions, all would be well. They forgot that her scared face and her figure could not be altered, and, therefore, no matter how much they might vary the frame and adornment, the face itself would remain pitiful and unattractive. At last, after two or three experiments, to which Princess Maria patiently submitted, when her hair had been combed high from her forehead (a mode of dressing the hair which absolutely changed her face, and that for the worse), and she was dressed in the masaka dress with the blue scarf, the little princess walked around her twice in succession, adjusted with her dainty fingers some of the folds in the skirt, fluffed out the scarf, looked at her with her head bent now on this side, now on that.

"No, that is impossible," said she decidedly, clasping her hands. "No, Marie, decidedly, this does not do at all. I like you better in your little everyday gray dress. Now, please do this for me. Katya," she said to the maid, "bring the princess her gray dress, and . . . see, Mlle. Bourienne, how I am going to arrange it," she added, with a thrill of anticipation in her artistic pleasure. But when Katya brought the desired garment, Princess Maria sat motionless before the mirror, looking at her face, and the mirror gave back the reflection of eyes full of tears, and a mouth trembling with the premonition of a storm of sobbing.

"Now, dear princess," said Mlle. Bourienne, "just one more little experiment!" The little princess, taking the dress from the maid, went to Princess Maria.

"Well, now we will try something that is simple and becoming," said she. The three voices, hers, Mlle. Bourienne's, and Katya's, who was laughing, mingled into one merry chatter, like the chirping of birds.

"No, let me be," said the princess, and her voice sounded so serious and sorrowful that the chirping of the birds ceased instantly. They looked at her large, beautiful eyes, full of tears and of melancholy, and they knew from their wide and beseeching expression that it was useless, and even cruel, to insist.

"At least, change the style of your hair," said the little princess. "I told you so!" said she, reproachfully, to Mlle. Bourienne. "Maria has one of those faces that can't stand this way of dressing the hair. Not at all, not at all. Change it, please do."

"Let me be, let me be; it's all the same to me," replied the young princess in a weary voice, scarcely restraining her tears.

Mlle. Bourienne and the little princess were obliged to acknowledge to themselves that Princess Maria as they had dressed her was very homely, more so than usual; but now it was too late. She looked at them with the expression they had learned to know so well, an expression of deep thought and sadness. It did not inspire them with any sense of awe of her (for that feeling she never could inspire), but they knew that when her face had this expression, she was silent and immovable in her resolutions.

"You will make the change, won't you?" asked Lisa, but when Princess Maria made no reply, Lisa left the room.

Princess Maria was left alone. She did not comply with Lisa's request, and not only did she not change the style of her hair, but did not even look at herself in the glass. With downcast eyes she let her hands fall, and sat and pondered. She saw in her imagination what her husband should be: a man, a strong, commanding, and strangely attractive being, who would suddenly carry her off into his own world, so different from hers, so full of happiness. She imagined herself pressing to her bosom her own child, just such a baby as she had seen the evening before with the daughter of her old nurse. Her husband stood looking affectionately at her and at their baby—"But no, this is impossible, I am too homely," she said to herself.

"Please come to tea. The prince will be down in a moment," said the voice of the chambermaid outside the door. She started up from her daydream, and was horror-struck at her own thoughts. And before she went downstairs she went into the chapel, and pausing before the face of the great image of the Saviour, lighted by the flames of the candles, she stood there for several moments with folded hands. Her heart was filled with painful forebodings. Could it be that for her there was the possibility of the joy of love, of earthly love for a husband? In her imaginings concerning marriage, Princess Maria dreamed of family happiness and children, but her principal dream, predominating over all others, though unknown to herself, was that of earthly love. The feeling was all the stronger the more she tried to hide it from others, and even from herself.

"My God," she cried, "how can I crush out in my heart these thoughts inspired by the devil? How can I escape once and for all from evil imaginings, and calmly fulfil Thy will?" And she had hardly offered this prayer ere God gave an answer in her own heart. "Desire nothing for thyself, seek not, disturb not thyself, be not envious. The future and thy fate must needs be hidden from thee; but live so as to be ready for anything. If it please God to try thee in the responsibilities of marriage, be ready to fulfil His will."

With this consoling thought—but still with a secret hope that her forbidden, earthly dream might be realized—Princess Maria, with a sigh, crossed herself, and went downstairs, thinking not of her dress, or of her hair, or of how she would make entrance, or of what she should say. What did all that signify in comparison with the preordination of God, without Whose will not a hair can fall from a man's head?

I V

When Princess Maria came down, Prince Vasili and his son were already in the drawing-room, talking with the little princess and Mlle. Bourienne. When she came in with her heavy gait, treading on her heels, the gentlemen and Mlle. Bourienne stood up, and the little princess exclaimed, "Here is Maria!" Princess Maria saw them all, and saw them distinctly. Prince Vasili was the first to greet her, and she kissed the bald forehead bending over her hand, and answered his question by assuring him that, on the contrary, she remembered him very well. Then Anatol came to her. She could not as yet see him at all. She was conscious only of a soft hand holding hers, while she lightly touched with her lips a white brow under a thatch of beautiful brown hair perfumed with pomade. When she looked at him his beauty dazzled her.

Anatol, hooking the thumb of his right hand behind one button of his uniform, stood with his chest thrust out and his back bent in, resting his weight on one leg and slightly inclining his head, and looked at the princess cheerily, but without speaking. He was evidently not thinking of her at all. Anatol was not quick-witted or a ready talker, but, on the other hand, he had that gift of composure which is so valuable in society, and a self-confidence which nothing could disturb.

Moreover, Anatol had in his behavior toward women that manner which strongly piques curiosity, and excites fear and even love in them—a sort of scornful consciousness of his own superiority. His look seemed to say to them: *I know you, I know what is disturbing you. Ah, how happy you would be if* . . . Possibly he did not think any such thing when he met women (and there is considerable ground for such a supposition, because he thought very little), but this was what was expressed by his look and manner. The princess felt it, and apparently wishing to show him that she did not venture to do such a thing as engage his attention, she turned to his father.

The conversation became general, and rather lively, thanks to the merry voice of the little princess, who kept lifting up her downy lip and showing her white teeth. She met Prince Vasili with that peculiarly vivacious manner which is often employed by people of merrily loquacious moods, and consists, in the interchange between you and your acquaintance, of the regular stock witticisms of the day, and of pleasant and amusing reminiscences which it is taken for granted are not understood by all people, comical reminiscences of things that they have never experienced together; and so it was with the little princess and Prince Vasili. Prince Vasili willingly adapted himself to this spirit; the little princess managed to include Anatol as well, though she scarcely knew him, and soon found herself sharing with him recollections of ridiculous occurrences, events that in some cases had never happened at all. Mlle. Bourienne also took part in these general recollections, and even Princess Maria had a sort of satisfaction in feeling herself drawn into this light gossip.

Seeing how pretty *la Bourienne* was, Anatol decided that, after all, it would not be so very stupid here at Lisiya Gori. "Not at all bad looking," he said to himself, as he looked at her; "very far from it. I hope that when she marries me she will take this companion with her, she's a pretty little girl!"

The old prince took his time about dressing, and he frowned as he thought what he should do. The coming of these guests annoyed him. For Prince Nikolai, life without his daughter, little as he outwardly seemed to appreciate her, was almost unthinkable. "And why should she get married?" he asked himself. "Probably to be unhappy. Here is Lisa—certainly it would be hard to find a better husband than Andrei—and yet is she contented with her lot? And who would take Maria from mere love? She is homely, awkward! And can't girls live unmarried? They'd be much happier."

Thus thought Prince Nikolai, as he performed his toilet in his room, and still at the same time the ever-procrastinated question now demanded an immediate solution. Prince Vasili had brought his son, evidently with the intention of making a proposal; therefore this very day or the next he would have to give a direct answer. Anatol's name, his position in the world, were excellent.

"Well, I've no objection," said the prince to himself. "But let him prove himself worthy of her. Well, we shall see. Yes, we shall see!" he exclaimed aloud. "Yes, we shall see how it is," and with his usual firm step he went into the drawing-room, took in all present with a sweeping glance, noticed even the change that the little princess had made in her dress, and Mlle. Bourienne's ribbon, and Princess Maria's ugly headdress, and her isolation in the general conversation, and Bourienne's and Anatol's exchange of smiles.

"She is dressed up like a fool," he said to himself, giving his daughter a wrathful glance. "She has no sense of shame, and he—he does not care anything about making her acquaintance."

He went straight to Prince Vasili: "Well, how are you, how are you? Glad to see you!"

"Friendship laughs at distance," exclaimed Prince Vasili, quoting the familiar proverb with ready wit, and with his usual self-confident familiarity. "Here is my second son; grant him your friendship, I beg of you." Prince Nikolai surveyed Anatol.

"Fine young fellow! Fine young fellow," said he. "Now come, give me a kiss," and he offered him his cheek. Anatol kissed the old man and looked at him curiously, but with perfect composure, expecting soon to hear one of those droll remarks of which his father had told him. Prince Nikolai sat down in his usual place in one corner of the divan, drew up an armchair for Prince Vasili, waved him to it, and began to ask him about the news in the political world. He listened with apparent attention to what Prince Vasili had to say, but he kept glancing at Princess Maria.

"So that's what they write from Potsdam, is it?" said he, repeating Prince Vasili's last words; and then suddenly getting up, he went over to his daughter. "So this is how you dress for company, hey?" exclaimed he. "Excellent, admirable! You appear before folks with your hair done up in this newfangled way, and I tell you, in the presence of these same folks, never again, without my leave, to rig yourself up in such a fashion!"

"It was my fault, father," said the little princess, blushing, and coming to her sister-in-law's rescue.

"You may do as you please," said Prince Nikolai, making a low bow before his son's wife. "But she has no right to disfigure herself; she's ugly enough without that." And he once more resumed his place, paying no further heed to his daughter, who was ready to weep.

"On the contrary, that way of dressing her hair is very becoming to the princess," said Prince Vasili.

"Well, my boy—my young prince—what is his name?" said Prince Nikolai, turning to Anatol, "come here. Let us have a little talk, and get acquainted."

"Now the sport begins," thought Anatol, and with a smile he took a seat by the old prince.

"Well, now, my boy, you have been educated abroad, somewhat differently from your father and me, who had the parish clerk teach us our *ABC's*.

Tell me, my dear boy, you serve in the Horse Guards, don't you?" asked the old prince, scrutinizing Anatol closely and keenly.

"No, I have been transferred to the line," replied Anatol, scarcely able to keep from laughing.

"Ah, excellent thing! It's wartime. Such fine young men as you ought to be in the service. At the front, I suppose?"

"No, prince; our regiment has gone, but I was detached. What was I detached for, papa?" asked Anatol, turning to his father with a laugh.

"Famous way of serving, I must confess. 'What am I detached for?' ha! ha! ha!" roared Prince Nikolai, and Anatol joined in still more vociferously. Suddenly Prince Nikolai began to scowl. "Well, off with you," said he to Anatol.

Anatol, with a smile, went and rejoined the ladies.

As usually happens in the case of women who have been long deprived of the society of men, all three of the women at Prince Nikolai's, now that they had Anatol in their midst, felt that hitherto life had not been life for them. The powers of feeling, thinking, loving, were instantly multiplied tenfold in each one of them, so that their existence, which had been till now, as it were, spent in darkness, was suddenly filled by a new light, full of rich significance.

Princess Maria no longer gave a thought to her looks or her coiffure. Her whole attention was absorbed by the handsome open face of the man who perhaps would be her husband. He seemed to her good, brave, resolute, manly, and noble. She was quite convinced of this. A thousand dreams of the family life she would enjoy in the future persistently rose in her mind. She tried to banish them, and keep them out of her imagination.

"But was I too cool toward him?" queried Princess Maria. "I try to be reserved, because I feel in the depths of my soul that he is already too near to me; but, of course, he cannot know all that I think about him, and he may imagine that I do not like him."

And Princess Maria strove, and yet was unable to be amiable to her new guest.

"Poor girl! she is devilishly ugly!" Such was Anatol's uncomplimentary thought of her.

Mlle. Bourienne, whom Anatol's arrival had thrown into a high state of excitement, allowed herself to have quite different thoughts. Of course, being a pretty young girl, without any stated position in society, without relatives and friends, and far from her native land, she had no intention of devoting her whole life to the service of Prince Nikolai, reading books to him, and playing the part of companion to Princess Maria. Mlle. Bourienne had been long waiting for the Russian prince who would immediately have wit enough to appreciate her superiority to these homely, unbecomingly dressed and awkward Russian princesses, would fall in love with her, and elope with her; now, at last, the Russian prince had come. Mlle. Bourienne knew a story her aunt had once told her, which, in imagination, she liked to repeat to the end, with herself in the heroine's place. The story was about a young girl who had been seduced, and whose poor mother, finding where she was, came and heaped her with reproaches because she had gone to live with a man to whom she was not married. Mlle. Bourienne was often melted to tears by imagining herself telling *him,* her seducer, this story. And now this *he,* this genuine Russian prince, had made his appearance. He would elope with her, then her poor mother would appear, and he would marry her.

The little princess (forgetting her condition instinctively), and like an old war horse at the sound of the trumpet, made ready to flirt at headlong speed, without meaning anything by it, but with her usual naive and light-hearted spirit of fun.

Although Anatol in the society of women generally affected the attitude of a man who considers it a bore to have them running after him, still he felt a thrill of gratified vanity when he realized his power over these three women. Moreover, he began to feel for the pretty and enticing Bourienne a real animal passion, such as sometimes overcame him with extraordinary rapidity and impelled him to commit the coarsest and most audacious actions.

After tea they all went into the sitting room, and Princess Maria was invited to play on the clavichord. Anatol leaned on his elbows in front of her, near Mlle. Bourienne, and, with eyes full of mirth and gaiety, looked at Maria, who felt his gaze with a painful and at the same time joyous emotion. Her favorite sonata bore her away into a most genuinely poetic world, and the consciousness of that glance endowed this world with even more poetry. In reality, however, Anatol, though he looked in her direction, was not thinking of her, but was occupied with the motion of Mlle. Bourienne's foot, which he was at this moment pressing with his under the piano. Mlle. Bourienne was also looking at the princess, but her beautiful eyes had an expression of timid happiness and hope, which Princess Maria had never seen in them before.

"How fond she is of me," thought Princess Maria. "How happy I am now, and how happy I might be with such a friend and such a husband! Husband! Can it be possible?" she asked herself, not daring to look at him, but, nevertheless, feeling his gaze fixed on her face.

After supper, when they were about to separate for the night and Anatol kissed the young princess' hand, she herself did not know how she dared do such a thing but she looked straight into his handsome face as it approached her shortsighted eyes.

Turning from the princess, he went and kissed Mlle. Bourienne's hand. This was contrary to etiquette, but he did everything with such confidence and simplicity! Mlle. Bourienne flushed and glanced in dismay at the princess.

"How considerate of him," thought the princess. "Can it be that Amélie" —so she called Mlle. Bourienne—"thinks that I should be jealous of her, and do not appreciate her affection and devotion to me?" She went straight to Mlle. Bourienne and gave her an affectionate kiss. Anatol was about to kiss the little princess' hand also.

"No! no! no! when your father writes me that you are behaving beautifully, then I will let you kiss my hand. Not before."

And, shaking her finger at him, she left the room with a smile.

V

ALL HAD GONE to their rooms, but, with the exception of Anatol, who went to sleep as soon as he got into bed, it was long before anyone could close an eye that night.

"Is he really to be my husband, this handsome stranger, who seems so good; ah, yes, above all, so good!" thought Princess Maria; and a feeling of fear, such as she had scarcely ever experienced before, came upon her. She was afraid to look around; it seemed to her as if someone were standing there behind the screen in the dark corner. And this someone was he —the devil—and he was this man with the white forehead, the black eyebrows, and the rosy lips.

She called her maid and begged her to sleep in her room.

Mlle. Bourienne that same evening walked for a long time up and down the winter garden, vainly expecting someone, now smiling at her own thought, now stirred to tears by imagining the words which "her poor mother" would say in reproaching her after her fall.

The little princess scolded her maid because her bed was not comfortable. It was impossible for her to lie on her side, or on her face. Any position was awkward and uncomfortable. She felt more than ever tried today, especially because Anatol's presence brought back so vividly the days before she was married, when she was light-hearted and merry. She reclined in her easy-chair, in her dressing jacket and nightcap. Katya, half asleep and with her hair hanging down in a braid, was turning the heavy mattress for the third time and shaking it up, muttering to herself.

"I told you that it was all humps and hollows," insisted the little princess. "I should like to go to sleep myself; I'm sure it isn't my fault," and her voice trembled as if she were a child getting ready to cry.

The old prince, also, could not sleep. Tikhon, as he napped, heard him stamping wrathfully up and down and snorting. It seemed to the old prince that he had been insulted through his daughter. The insult was painful because it was directed not to himself, but to another, to his daughter, whom he loved better than himself. He kept telling himself that he would calmly think the whole matter over, and decide how in justice to himself he must act; but instead of so doing, he grew more and more vexed with himself.

"Let the first young man come along, and she forgets father and all! and she runs upstairs, combs up her hair and prinks, and is no longer like herself. Glad to throw her father over. And she knew that I noticed it. Fr!—fr!—fr! and then, haven't I eyes to see that that simpleton has no eyes for anyone except the little Bourienne (I must get rid of her!). And how is it she hasn't enough pride to see it herself? If not for her own sake, she might at least show some for mine. I must show her that this booby doesn't think of her at all, but stares only at Bourienne. She has no pride, but I'll prove this for her."

The old prince knew that if he told his daughter that she was laboring under a delusion, that Anatol was bent on flirting with Bourienne, he would in this way appeal to his daughter's pride, and his game would be played; for he was anxious not to part with his daughter. This consideration served to quiet him. He summoned Tikhon and began to undress.

"Have they gone to bed?" asked the prince.

Tikhon, after the manner of all well-trained valets, knew by intuition what his master was thinking about. He judged that the question referred to Prince Vasili and his son.

"They have deigned to go to bed, and their lights are out, your excellency."

"No reason why they shouldn't," briskly exclaimed the prince, and, thrusting his feet into his slippers and his arms into his dressing gown, he went to the couch where he usually slept.

Although but few words had been exchanged by Anatol and Mlle. Bourienne, they thoroughly understood each other as to the first chapter of the romance, up to the appearance of the poor mother; they understood that they had much to say to each other in secret, and therefore early in the morning they both sought an opportunity for a private interview. While the young princess was going at the usual hour to meet her father, Mlle. Bourienne and Anatol met in the winter garden.

Princess Maria on this particular day went with unusual trepidation to the door of her father's study. It seemed to her that everyone knew that this day her fate was to be decided, and also knew what she herself felt about it. She read this expression on Tikhon's face, and on the face of Prince Vasili's valet, who met her in the corridor on his way with hot water for the prince, and made her a low bow.

The old prince this morning was affectionate and kind in his behavior to his daughter. Princess Maria well knew this expression of kindness. It was the expression his face generally wore when his nervous hands doubled up with vexation because she did not understand her arithmetical examples, and he would spring to his feet, walk away from her, and then repeat the same words in a low, gentle voice.

He immediately addressed himself to the business in hand, and began to explain it to her.

"I have received an offer for your hand in marriage," said he, with a strained smile. "I suppose you did not imagine," he went on to say, "that he came here and brought his pupil"—for some inexplicable reason, Prince Nikolai called Anatol a "pupil"—"for the sake of 'my handsome eyes.' Last evening he proposed for your hand. And, as you know my principles, I refer it to you."

"How am I to understand you, father?" she exclaimed, turning pale and then blushing.

"How understand me!" cried her father, wrathfully, "Prince Vasili is satisfied with you for a daughter-in-law, and has proposed for your hand on behalf of his pupil. That's what it means. 'How understand it!' That I ask you."

"I do not know as well as you, father," whispered the princess.

"I? I? What have I to do with it? Consider me out of the question. I'm not the one who is going to be married. What's your opinion? That is what must be known."

The princess saw that her father did not regard the matter very favorably, but at the same time the thought occurred to her that now or never her whole future hung in the balance. She dropped her eyes so as not to see his face, because she knew that she could not think if she were under its dominion, but could only be subject to him, and she said: "I desire only one thing, to fulfil your will; but if it be necessary for me to express my desire . . ."

She had no time to finish her sentence. The prince interrupted her.

"That's admirable," he cried. "He will take you for your fortune, and, by the way, hook on Mlle. Bourienne! She will be his wife, and you . . ." the prince paused. He noticed the effect produced on his daughter by his words. She hung her head and was ready to burst into tears.

"Well, well, I was only jesting," said he. "Remember this one thing, princess; I stick to my principles that a girl has a perfect right to choose for herself. I give you your freedom. Remember this, though, the happiness of your whole life depends upon your decision. Leave me out of the consideration."

"But I do not know . . . father."

"There's nothing to be said. He will marry as he is told, whether it be you or somebody else, but you are free to choose. Go to your room; think it over, and at the end of an hour come to me and tell me in his presence what your decision is, yes or no. I know that you'll have to pray over it. Well, pray if you like. Only you'd better use your reason. Get you gone . . . Yes or no, yes or no, yes or no!" cried he, as the princess, still as if in a trance, left the room with tottering steps.

Her fate was already decided, and happily decided. But what her father said about Mlle. Bourienne—that insinuation was horrible. False, perhaps, but still it was horrible, and she could not keep it out of her thoughts. She started directly to her room through the winter garden, seeing nothing and hearing nothing, when suddenly Mlle. Bourienne's well-known chatter struck her ear and woke her from her dreaming. She raised her eyes and, two paces away, saw Anatol with the Frenchwoman in his arms, and whispering something in her ear. With a terrible expression on his handsome face he looked at Princess Maria, and at first did not release Mlle. Bourienne, who had not seen the princess at all.

"Who is here? What is the trouble? Just wait a little," Anatol's face seemed to say. Princess Maria silently gazed at them. She could not comprehend it. Then Mlle. Bourienne uttered a cry and fled. Anatol, with an amused smile, bowed to the princess, as if asking her to look on the ridiculous side of this strange behavior, and, shrugging his shoulders, disappeared through the door that led to his own quarters.

At the end of an hour Tikhon came to summon Princess Maria. He conducted her to her father's room, and told her that Prince Vasili was also there. When Tikhon came for her, the princess was sitting on a sofa in her room, with her arm around Mlle. Bourienne. The latter was weeping, and the princess was softly stroking her hair. The princess' beautiful eyes, with all their usual calmness and brilliancy, gazed with affectionate love and sympathy into Mlle. Bourienne's pretty face.

"No, princess, my place is forever gone from your heart," said Mlle. Bourienne.

"Why, I love you more than ever," replied Princess Maria, "and I will try to do all that is in my power for your happiness."

"But you despise me! You, who are so pure, will never understand this frenzy of passion. Ah! my poor mother!"

"I understand it all," replied the princess, with a melancholy smile. "Compose yourself, my friend, I am going to see my father," said she, and left the room.

Prince Vasili, with one leg thrown across his knee, holding his snuffbox in his hand, excited, and seeming to feel a sort of pity for himself while amused at his own emotion, was sitting with an anxious smile on his face as Princess Maria entered the room. He hastily applied a pinch of snuff to his nose.

"Ah! my lovely, my lovely!" he exclaimed, rising and seizing her by both hands. He sighed, and added, "My son's fate is in your hands. Decide, my lovely, my dear, my sweet Maria! I have always loved you as if you were my own daughter." He turned away. Genuine tears stood in his eyes.

"Fr! . . . fr!" . . . snorted Prince Nikolai. "The prince in the name of his pupil . . . I mean his son . . . makes you an offer. Will you or will you not be the wife of Prince Anatol Kuragin? Speak: yes or no," cried he. "And then I reserve to myself the right of giving my opinion also. Yes, my opinion, and my opinion only," added Prince Nikolai, in reply to Prince Vasili's beseeching expression. "Yes or no?"

"My desire, father, is never to leave you, never to part from you as long as we live. I do not wish to marry," said she with firm deliberation, fixing her lovely eyes on Prince Vasili and on her father.

"Folly! nonsense! nonsense! nonsense!" cried Prince Nikolai, frowning;

he drew his daughter to him, yet he did not kiss her, but merely brought his forehead close to hers, and squeezed her hand, which he held in his, so that she cried out with pain.

Prince Vasili arose.

"My dear, I will tell you that this is a moment that I shall never forget, never! but, my dear, can't you give us a little hope of ever touching your kind and generous heart? Say that perhaps . . . the future is so long. Only say 'perhaps.'"

"Prince, what I have told you is all that my heart can say. I thank you for the honor, but I can never be your son's wife."

"Well, that ends it, my dear fellow. Very glad to have seen you. Very glad to have seen you. Go to your room, princess, go to your room," said the old prince. "Very, very glad to have seen you," he reiterated, embracing Prince Vasili.

"My vocation is different," said Princess Maria to herself; "my vocation is to be happy in the happiness of others; a different sort of happiness, the happiness of love and self-sacrifice. And as far as within me lies, I will bring about the happiness of poor Amélie. She loves him so passionately. She repents her conduct so bitterly. I will do everything to bring about a marriage between them. If he is not rich, I will give her the means, I will petition my father, I will ask Andrei. And I shall be so happy when she becomes his wife. She is so unfortunate, lonely and helpless in a strange land. And good heavens! how passionately she must love him, if she can so far forget herself. Maybe I myself would have done the same thing!" . . . thought Princess Maria.

VI

ON THE TWENTY-FOURTH of November Kutuzof's fighting army, bivouacked near Olmütz, made ready to be reviewed on the following day by the Emperor of Russia and the Emperor of Austria.

Nikolai Rostof on that day had received a note from Boris informing him that the Izmailovsky regiment was going to encamp about ten miles away, and that he wanted to see him to give him some letters and some money. Rostof had just celebrated his promotion from cadet to cornet, had bought Denisof's horse Bedouin, and was in debt to his comrades and the sutlers on every side. On receipt of the note from Boris, Rostof rode into Olmütz with some comrades, dined there, drank a bottle of wine, and rode off alone to the guards' camp to find the friend and companion of his youth.

Rostof had not as yet had a chance to obtain his new uniform. He wore a cadet's jacket well soiled, with a private's cross, his ordinary much-worn, leather-seated riding trousers, and an officer's saber with the swordknot. The horse he rode was a Don pony he had bought from a Cossack, during the campaign; his crumpled cap was rakishly set sidewise on the back of his head. When he reached the camp of the Izmailovsky regiment, he thought how much he would surprise Boris and all his comrades of the Guard by appearing before them as a veteran who had been under fire.

Boris, during the whole campaign, had marched and halted with Berg, who had risen to the rank of captain. Berg, having been given a company, had succeeded by his promptness and punctuality in winning the good will of his superiors, and his financial affairs were now in very good shape. Boris had made many acquaintances with men who might be of service to him, and, by means of a letter of introduction given him by Pierre, had become acquainted with Prince Andrei Bolkonsky, through whom he hoped to obtain a place on the staff of the commander-in-chief.

Berg and Boris, neatly and elegantly dressed, were resting after their day's journey and were playing checkers at a small round table, when the door opened.

"Ah, there he is at last," cried Rostof. "And Berg here too! Ah, you 'leetle cheeldren go bed, go sleep!'" he cried, quoting the words of their old nurse, in which he and Boris always found great amusement.

"Goodness! How you have changed!"

Boris arose to meet Rostof, but as he did so he took pains to pick up and replace the checkers that had fallen, and he was about to embrace his friend, but Nikolai slipped out of his grasp. With that feeling peculiar to youth, which suggests the avoidance of beaten paths and the expression of feelings like everyone else, and especially that often hypocritical fashion of our elders, Nikolai wanted to do something unusual and original on the occasion of meeting his friends; he wanted to give Boris a punch or a shove, anything except kiss him, as was universally done.

Boris, on the contrary, threw his arms around Rostof in a composed and friendly fashion, and kissed him three times. They had not met for almost six months, and in such an interval, when young men have been taking their first steps on the pathway of life, each finds in the other immense changes, due to surroundings so entirely different from those in which they took the first steps of life. Both had changed greatly since they had last met, and each was equally anxious to show the changes to the other.

"Oh! you cursed dandies! Spruce and shiny, just in from a promenade! Not much like us poor sinners of the line!" exclaimed Rostof, with baritone notes in his voice and with brusque army manners quite new to Boris, and he exhibited his own dirty and bespattered trousers.

"What makes you shout so?" said Boris. "I wasn't expecting you today," he added. "It was only this afternoon that I sent my note to you through an acquaintance of mine, Kutuzof's aide, Bolkonsky. I didn't think of its reaching you so soon. Well, how are you? So you've been under fire already, have you?" asked Boris.

Rostof said nothing in reply, but shook the cross of St. George on the lace of his coat, and, pointing to the arm he carried in a sling, looked at Berg with a smile. "As you see," said he.

"Well, well, so you have!" returned Boris with a smile, "and we also have had a glorious campaign. You know his imperial highness was most of the time near our regiment, so that we had all sorts of privileges and advantages. What receptions we had in Poland, what dinners and balls! I can't begin to tell you! and the heir apparent was very courteous to all of us officers."

Then the two friends related their experiences; the one telling of the good times with the hussars, and his campaign life; the other of the pleasures and advantages of serving under the direct command of men high in authority and so on.

"Oh, you guardsmen!" cried Rostof. "But come now, send out for some wine."

Boris scowled. "Certainly, if you really wish it," and going to his couch he took a purse from under the clean pillow and ordered his man to bring wine. "Oh, yes; and I will deliver to you some letters and your money," he added.

Rostof took his packet and, flinging the money on the sofa, leaned both elbows on the table and began to read. He read a few lines and then gave Berg a wrathful glance. Berg's eyes, fastened upon him, annoyed him, and he shielded his face with the letter.

"Well, they've sent you a good lot of money," exclaimed Berg, glancing at the heavy purse, half buried in the sofa. "And here we have to live on our salaries, count! Now I will tell you about myself."

"Look here, Berg, my dear fellow," said Rostof, "whenever I find you with a letter just received from home, and with a man you want to talk to about all sorts of things, I will instantly leave you so as not to disturb you. Hear what I say, go away anywhere, anywhere; to the devil," he cried, and then seizing him by the shoulder and giving him an affectionate look full in the face, evidently for the purpose of modifying the rudeness of his words, he added, "Now see here, don't be angry with me, my dear, I speak frankly because you are an old acquaintance."

"Oh, for heaven's sake, count! I understand perfectly," said Berg, getting up and swallowing down his throaty voice.

"Go and see our hosts; they have invited you," suggested Boris.

Berg put on his immaculate, neat and speckless coat, went to the mirror, brushed the hair up from his temples after the style of the emperor, and, being persuaded by Rostof's looks that his coat was noticeable, left the room with a smile of satisfaction.

Among the home letters there was inclosed a note of recommendation to Prince Bagration, which the old countess at Anna Mikhailovna's suggestion had obtained from some acquaintance and sent to her son, urging him to present it and get all the advantages that he could from it.

"What nonsense! Much I need this!" said Rostof, flinging the letter on the table.

"Why did you throw it down?" said Boris.

"Oh! it was a letter of recommendation; what the deuce do I want with such a letter!"

"Why do you say that?" asked Boris, picking up the letter and reading the inscription. "This letter might be very useful to you."

"I don't need anything, and I don't care to become anyone's aide!"

"Why not, pray?" asked Boris.

"It's a lackey's place!"

"You still have the same queer notions, I see," rejoined Boris, shaking his head.

"And you're the same old diplomat. However, that's beside the point. How are you?" asked Rostof.

"Just exactly as you see! So far, all has gone well with me. But I confess I would very much like to be an aide, and not stick to the line."

"Why?"

"Because, having once entered upon the profession of arms, it is best to make one's career as brilliant as possible."

"Yes, that's true," said Rostof, evidently thinking of something else. He gave his friend a steady, inquiring look, evidently trying in vain to find in his eyes the answer to some puzzling question.

Old Gavrilo brought the wine.

"Hadn't we better send now for Lieutenant Berg?" asked Boris. "He will drink with you, for I can't."

"Yes, do send for him! But who *is* this Dutchman?" asked Rostof, with a scornful smile.

"He's a very, very nice, honorable, and pleasant man," explained Boris.

Rostof once more looked steadily into Boris' eyes and sighed. Berg came back, and over the bottle of wine the conversation between the three officers grew more lively. Rostof described his action at Schöngraben exactly in the way those who take part in battles always describe them—that is, in the way they would like to have had them happen—so that his story agreed with all the other accounts of the participants, but was very far from being as it was. Rostof was a truthful young man; not for anything in the world would he have deliberately told a falsehood. He began with the intention of telling it exactly as it happened, but imperceptibly, involuntarily, and unavoidably, as far as he was concerned, he fell into falsehood.

In the midst of his tale, just as he was saying the words, "You can't imagine what a strange sensation of frenzy you experience during a charge," Prince Andrei Bolkonsky, whom Boris had been expecting, came into the room.

Prince Andrei, who liked to bear a patronizing relationship toward young men, was flattered by having Boris consigned to his protection, and was very well disposed toward him. Boris had succeeded in making a pleasant impression upon him, and he had made up his mind to have the young man's desire gratified. When he came in and found there a hussar of the line, relating his military experiences, the sort of individual whom Prince Andrei could not endure, he gave Boris an affectionate smile, scowled at Rostof, half closing his eyes, and, with a stiff little bow, took his seat wearily and indifferently on the sofa. He was disgusted at finding himself in uncongenial society. Rostof, feeling this instinctively, instantly grew angry. But it was all the same to him; it was a stranger. He looked at Boris, and saw that he seemed to be ashamed of being in company with a hussar of the line.

Notwithstanding Prince Andrei's disagreeable, mocking tone, notwithstanding the general scorn that Rostof, from his point of view as a hussar of the line, had for staff aides, to which number evidently belonged the gentleman who had just entered, Rostof felt overwhelmed with confusion, reddened, and grew silent. Boris asked what was the news at headquarters and whether it was indiscreet for him to inquire about future movements.

"Probably we shall advance," replied Bolkonsky, evidently not wishing to commit himself further in the presence of strangers. Berg took advantage of his opportunity to ask, with his usual politeness, whether it was true, as he had heard, that double rations of forage were to be supplied to captains of the line. At this Prince Andrei smiled, and replied that he could not discuss such important questions of state, and Berg laughed heartily with delight.

"In regard to that business of yours," said Prince Andrei, turning to Boris again, "we will talk about it by and by," and he glanced at Rostof. "You come to me after review; we will do all that is in our power." And glancing around the room, he addressed himself to Rostof, pretending not to notice his state of childish confusion, which was rapidly assuming the form of ill temper.

"I suppose you were telling about the affair at Schöngraben? Were you there?" he asked.

"I was there," replied Rostof curtly, as if he desired by his tone to insult the aide. Bolkonsky noticed the hussar's state of mind, and it seemed to him amusing. A slightly scornful smile played over his lips.

"Yes, there are many stories circulating now about that affair!"

"Stories, indeed!" exclaimed Rostof, in a loud voice, turning his angry eyes on Boris and Bolkonsky. "Yes, many stories; but the stories we tell are the accounts of those who were under the hottest fire of the enemy. Our accounts have some weight, and are very different from the stories of those staff officers, milk suckers, who win rewards by doing nothing."

"Do you mean to insinuate that I am one of them?" asked Prince Andrei, with a calm and very pleasant smile.

A strange feeling of anger and at the same time of respect for the dignity of this stranger were at this moment united in Rostof's mind.

"I was not speaking of you," said he. "I do not know you, and I confess I have no desire to know you. I merely made a general remark concerning staff officers."

"And I will say this much to you," said Prince Andrei, interrupting him, a tone of calm superiority ringing in his voice. "You wish to insult me, and

I am ready to have a settlement with you, a matter easy to bring about, if you have not sufficient self-respect; but you must agree with me that the time and place are exceedingly unpropitious for any such settlement. We are all soon to take part in a great and far more serious duel, and moreover, Drubetskoy here, who says that he is an old friend of yours, cannot be held accountable for the fact that my face was unfortunate enough to displease you. However," he continued, as he got up, "you know my name, and you know where to find me; but don't forget," he added, "that I consider that neither you nor I have any ground for feeling insulted, and my advice, as a man older than you, is not to let this matter go any farther. Well, Drubetskoy, on Friday, after the review, I shall expect you; good-by!" said Prince Andrei, and went out with a bow to both of them.

It was only after Prince Andrei had left the room that Rostof remembered what reply he should have made. And he was still more out of temper because he had not had the wit to say it. He immediately ordered his horse brought round, and, bidding Boris farewell rather dryly, rode off to his own camp. Should he go next day to headquarters and challenge this captious aide, or should he follow his advice and leave things as they were? That was the question that tormented him all the way. At one moment he angrily imagined how frightened this little, feeble, bumptious man would look when covered by his pistol; the next, he confessed with amazement, that of all the men whom he knew, there was none he would be more glad to have as his friend than this same aide he detested!

VII

ON THE DAY following the review, Boris, dressed in his best uniform, and accompanied by the wishes of his comrade Berg for his success, rode off to Olmütz to find Bolkonsky, anxious to take advantage of his good will and secure a most brilliant position, especially the position of aide to some important personage, as this seemed to him the most attractive branch of the service. "It's fine for Rostof, whose father sends him ten thousand at a time, to argue that he would not accept favors of anyone, or be anyone's lackey; but I, who have nothing except my brains, must pursue my career and not miss opportunities, but take advantage of them."

At the moment that Boris came in, Prince Andrei, with a contemptuous frown on his face and that peculiar look of well-bred weariness which says louder than words that "if it were not my duty, I would not think of wasting any more time talking with you," was listening to an old Russian general with orders on his breast, who was standing upright, almost on his tiptoes, and, with the servile expression characteristic of the military on his purple face, was laying his case before Prince Andrei.

"Very good, be kind enough to have patience," he was saying to the general in Russian, but with the French accent he affected when he wished to speak rather scornfully; then, catching sight of Boris, and making no further reply to the general, who hastened after him with his petition, begging him to let him say just one thing more, Prince Andrei with a radiant smile and wave of his hand went to meet Boris.

Boris at this instant clearly understood what he had suspected before, that in the army, above and beyond the subordination and discipline taught by the code, and which they in the regiments knew by heart, and which he knew as well as anyone else, there was another still more essential form of subordination, one that compelled his anxious general with the purple face to wait respectfully while Captain Prince Andrei, for his own satisfaction, found it more interesting to talk with Ensign Drubetskoy. More than ever Boris decided henceforth not to act in accordance with the written law, but with this unwritten code. He now felt that merely through the fact of having been sent to Prince Andrei with a letter of recommendation he was allowed to take precedence over this old general, who in other circumstances, at the front for instance, might utterly humiliate him—a mere ensign of the Guards.

Prince Andrei came to meet him and took him by the hand.

"Well, now, my dear, so you would like to become an aide, would you? I was just thinking about you."

"Yes," replied Boris, in spite of himself reddening at the very thought. "I was thinking of calling on the commander-in-chief; he has had a letter in regard to me from Prince Kuragin; I wanted to ask that favor," he added, as if by way of apology, "because I was afraid the Guards would not take part in any action."

"Very good, very good! We will talk it over," said Prince Andrei. "Only let me finish up this gentleman's business and I will be at your service."

While Prince Andrei went to report on the business of the purple-faced general, this general, evidently not sharing Boris' attitude toward the advantages of the unwritten code, glared so fiercely at the audacious young ensign who had interrupted his conversation that Boris grew uncomfortable. He turned away and waited impatiently for Prince Andrei's return from the commander-in-chief's private room.

"Well, my dear fellow, as I said, I was just thinking of you," said Prince Andrei, as they went into the big room where the clavichord was. "There is no use in your going to call on the commander-in-chief," he went on to say; "he will make you pleasant enough speeches, he will have you invited to dinner"—("That would not be so bad according to this other code," thought Boris, in his own mind)—"but nothing more would come of it; if it did, there would soon be a whole battalion of us aides and orderlies. But I'll tell you what we'll do; I have a good friend who is general adjutant and a splendid man, Prince Dolgorukof—and perhaps you may not know this, but it is a fact, that just now Kutuzof and his staff and all of us are of mighty little consequence; everything at the present time is centered on the emperor—so let us go to Dolgorukof; I have an errand to him anyway, and I have already spoken to him of you, so we will see whether he can't find the means of giving you a place on his own staff, or somewhere even nearer to the sun."

Prince Andrei always showed great energy when he had the chance to lend a young man a hand and help him to worldly success. Under cover of the assistance granted another, and which he would have been too proud to accept for himself, he came within the charmed circle which was the source of success and in reality a powerful attraction for him. He very readily took Boris under his wing and went with him to Prince Dolgorukof.

It was already quite late in the afternoon when they reached the palace of Olmütz, occupied by the emperors and their immediate followers. On this very day there had been a council of war in which the two emperors had taken part. In the council it had been decided, contrary to the advice of the old generals, Kutuzof and Schwartzenberg, to act immediately on the offensive and offer Bonaparte general battle. The council had only just adjourned when Prince Andrei, accompanied by Boris, entered the palace in search of Prince Dolgorukof. Already the magic impression of this war council, which had resulted in victory for the younger party, could be seen in the faces of all whom they met at headquarters. The voices of the temporizers, who advised further postponement of the attack, had been so unanimously drowned out and their arguments confuted by such indubitable proofs of the advantage of immediate attack, that the subject of their deliberations—that is, the impending engagement and the victory which would doubtless result from it—seemed to be a thing of the past rather than of the future.

All the advantages were on our side. The enormous forces of the allies, doubtless far outnumbering Napoleon's forces, were concentrated at one point; the armies were inspired by the presence of the emperors and eager for action; the "strategic point" where the battle was to be fought was known in its minutest details to the Austrian General Weirother, who would take command of the army; it happened also, by a fortunate coincidence, that the Austrian army had maneuvered the previous year on these very plains where now it was proposed that they should meet the French in battle; all the features of the ground were well known and accurately delineated on the maps, and Bonaparte, evidently weakened, was making no preparations to meet them.

Dolgorukof, one of the most fiery advocates of immediate attack, had just returned from the council, weary and jaded, but full of excitement and proud of the victory won. Prince Andrei introduced the young officer he had taken under his protection, but Prince Dolgorukof, though he politely and even warmly pressed his hand, said nothing; and evidently being unable to refrain from expressing the thoughts that occupied him to the exclusion of everything else, turned to Prince Andrei and said in French:

"Well, my dear fellow, what a struggle we've been having! May God only grant that the one which will result from it will be no less victorious! One thing, my dear fellow," said he, speaking eagerly and brusquely, "I must confess my injustice to these Austrians, and especially to Weirother! What exactitude and care for minutiæ! What accurate knowledge of the localities! What foresight for contingencies! What attention to the minutest details! No, my friend, nothing more advantageous than our position could possibly be imagined. Austrian accuracy and Russian valor combined! What more could you desire?"

"So an engagement has been actually determined on?" asked Bolkonsky.

"And do you know, my boy, it seems to me that really Bonaparte 'has lost his Latin.' Did you know a letter was received from him today addressed to the emperor?"

Dolgorukof smiled significantly.

"What's that? What did he write?" asked Bolkonsky.

"What could he write? Tra-la-la-la and so forth . . . merely for the sake of gaining time; that's all. I tell you, he's right in our hands; that's certain! But the most amusing thing of all," said he, with a good-natured smile, "was this, that no one could think how it was best to address the reply to him! Not as 'consul' and still less as emperor, of course; I supposed it would be to General Bonaparte."

"But there is considerable difference between not recognizing him as emperor and addressing him as General Bonaparte," said Bolkonsky.

"That's the very point," said Dolgorukof, interrupting him with a laugh, and speaking rapidly. "You know Bilibin—he's a very clever man—he proposed to address him as 'Usurper and Enemy of the Human Race'."

Dolgorukof broke into a hearty peal of laugher.

"Was that all?" remarked Bolkonsky.

"But in the end it was Bilibin who invented a serious title for the address. He's a shrewd and clever man!"

"What was it?"

" 'Head of the French Government'—*au chef du gouvernement français*," replied Prince Dolgorukof, gravely, and with satisfaction. "Now, wasn't that good?"

"Very good, but it won't please him much," replied Bolkonsky.

"Oh, not at all! My brother knows him; he's dined with him more than once—with the present emperor at Paris—and told me that he never saw a more refined and shrewd diplomat! French finesse combined with Italian astuteness, you know! You've heard the anecdotes about him and Count Markof, haven't you? Count Markof was the only man who could meet him on his own ground. You know the story of the handkerchief? It's charming!"

And the loquacious Dolgorukof, turning now to Boris, now to Prince Andrei, told how Bonaparte, wishing to test Markof, our ambassador, purposely dropped his handkerchief in front of him and stood looking at him, apparently expecting Markof to hand it to him, and how Markof instantly dropped his handkerchief beside Bonaparte's and stooping down, picked it up, leaving Bonaparte's where it lay.

"Charming!" exclaimed Bolkonsky. "But prince, I have come as a petitioner in behalf of this young man here. Do you know whether . . ." but before Prince Andrei had time to finish, an adjutant came into the room with a summons for Prince Dolgorukof to go to the emperor.

"What a nuisance!" exclaimed Dolgorukof, hurriedly rising and shaking hands with Prince Andrei and Boris. "You know I should be very glad to do all in my power either for you or for this charming young man." Once more he pressed Boris' hand with an expression of good-natured frankness and mercurial heedlessness. "But we'll see about it. . . . See you another time!"

On the next day the armies were set in motion, and Boris had no opportunity, until the Battle of Austerlitz itself, to meet either Prince Bolkonsky or Dolgorukof, and remained for the time being in the Izmailovsky regiment.

VIII

At dawn on the twenty-eighth, Denisof's squadron, in which Nikolai Rostof served, and which belonged to Prince Bagration's division, marched out from its bivouac to battle, as it was said, and after proceeding about a mile, behind the other columns, was halted on the highway.

Rostof saw the Cossacks riding forward past them; then the first and second squadron of hussars and battalions of infantry and artillery; and then the generals, Bagration and Dolgorukof, and their adjutants also rode by. All the fear which, just as at the previous battles, he had experienced before the action, all the internal conflict by means of which he had overcome this fear, all his dreams of how he would distinguish himself, hussar fashion, were wasted this time. Their squadron was stationed in the reserve, and Nikolai Rostof spent that day bored and anxious.

About nine o'clock in the morning he heard at the front the sounds of musketry firing, huzzas and shouting; he saw some wounded men carried to the rear (there were not many of them), and at last he beheld a whole division of French cavalrymen conducted by in charge of a hundred Cossacks. Evidently the action was at an end, and though it appeared to have been of small magnitude, it was attended with success. The soldiers and their officers, as they returned, narrated the story of their brilliant victory, resulting in the occupation of the city of Wischau and the capture of a whole squadron of the French.

The officers gathered in a circle around Denisof's canteen, eating their lunch and chatting.

"Here they come, bringing another!" exclaimed one of the officers, pointing to a French dragoon who had been made a prisoner and was walking along under guard of two Cossacks. One of them was leading by the bridle a large, handsome French horse which had been taken from the prisoner.

"Sell us the horse?" cried Denisof to the Cossack.

"Certainly, your honor."

The Cossacks sold the horse for two gold pieces, and Rostof, who just now had plenty of money, and was the richest of the officers, bought it.

"The emperor! the emperor!" was suddenly heard among the hussars. All was hurry and confusion as the officers scattered, and Rostof saw a number of horsemen with white plumes in their hats riding toward them. In a moment all were in their places and waiting.

Rostof did not remember and had no consciousness of how he got to his place and mounted his horse. Instantly his disappointment at not being present at the skirmish, his mutinous frame of mind during the hours of inaction, passed away; every thought about himself instantly vanished; he was completely absorbed in the sense of happiness arising from the proximity of his sovereign! He felt himself compensated by this mere fact for all the loss of the day. He was as happy as a lover in expectation of the wished-for meeting! Not daring to look down the line or glancing around, he felt the sovereign's approach by a sense of rapture. And he felt this, not alone by the mere trampling of the horses' hoofs as the cavalcade rode along, but because in proportion as they drew near everything around him grew brighter, more radiant with joy, more impressive and festive. Nearer and nearer came what was the sun for Rostof, scattering rays of blissful and majestic light, and now at last he realized that he was enveloped by these rays; he heard *his* voice, that affable, serene, majestic, and at the same time utterly unaffected voice. A dead silence ensued, just as Rostof felt ought to be the case, and this silence was broken by the sound of his sovereign's voice:

"The Pavlograd hussars?" he asked in French.

"The reserves, your majesty," replied some other voice, a merely human voice after the superhuman one that had asked if they were the Pavlograd hussars.

The emperor came near to where Rostof was and reined in his horse. Alexander's face fairly beamed with delight and youthful spirits—such innocently youthful spirits that it reminded one of the sportiveness of a fourteen-year-old lad; and yet, nevertheless, it was the face of a majestic emperor! Chancing to glance down the squadron, the sovereign's eyes met Rostof's and for upward of two seconds gazed into them. Maybe the sovereign read what was passing in Rostof's soul; it certainly seemed to Rostof that he must know it; at all events, he fixed his blue eyes for the space of two seconds on Rostof's face. A sweet and gentle light seemed to emanate from them. Then suddenly his eyebrows contracted, and with a brusque movement of his left foot he spurred his horse and galloped forward.

The young emperor could not restrain his desire to be present at the battle, and in spite of all the objections of his courtiers he managed about twelve o'clock to leave the third column, under whose escort he had been moving, and spurred off to the front. But before he reached the hussars he was met by some of his aides with the report of the happy issue of the skirmish. The engagement, which was merely the capture of a squadron of the French, was represented as a brilliant victory, and consequently the sovereign and the whole army, especially before the smoke had cleared away from the field of battle, were firmly convinced that the French were conquered and were in full retreat.

A few minutes after the passing of the sovereign, the division of the Pavlograd hussars was ordered to advance. In the little German town of Wischau, Rostof saw the emperor yet a second time. In the town square, where just before the sovereign's arrival there had been a lively interchange of shots, still lay a number of men, killed and wounded, whom there had not as yet been time to remove. The sovereign, surrounded by his suite of military and civil attendants, and riding a chestnut mare groomed in English style, leaning over and gracefully holding a gold lorgnette to his eyes, was looking at a soldier stretched out on the ground, without his shako and with his head all covered with blood. The soldier was so filthy, rough, and disgusting that Rostof was quite affronted that he should be so near his majesty. Rostof saw how the sovereign's stooping shoulders contracted, as if a chill ran down his back, and how his left heel convulsively pressed the spur into the horse's side, and how the admirably trained animal looked around goodnaturedly and did not stir from his place. An adjutant dismounted, and taking the soldier under the arm assisted to lift him to a stretcher that had just been brought. The soldier groaned.

"Gently, gently! Can't you lift him more gently?" exclaimed the sovereign, apparently suffering more keenly than the dying soldier, and he rode away.

Rostof saw the tears that filled his monarch's eyes, and heard him say in French to Czartorisky as he rode away:

"What is so terrible as war! What a terrible thing!"

The vanguard had been stationed in front of Wischau, in sight of the enemy's pickets, who had abandoned the place to the Russians after desultory firing that had lasted all day. The vanguard had been personally congratulated and thanked by the emperor, rewards had been promised, and a double portion of vodka had been dealt out to the men. The bivouac fires crackled even more merrily than the night before, and the soldiers' songs rang out with still greater gusto.

Denisof that night gave a supper in honor of his promotion to major, and Rostof, who had already taken his share of wine, at the end of the merrymaking proposed a toast to the sovereign's health:

"Not the sovereign emperor, as he is called in official circles," said he, "but the health of the sovereign as a kind-hearted, lovable, and great man. Let us drink to his health, and to our probable victory over the French. If we fought well before," he went on to say, "and gave no quarter to the French at Schöngraben, will not this be the case now when he himself leads us? We will all die, gladly die for him! Isn't that so, gentlemen? Perhaps I do not express myself very well, for I have been drinking a good deal, but that's what I feel, and so do you all! To the health of Alexander the First! Hurrah!"

"Hurrah! Hurrah!" rang the hearty voices of the officers. And the old Captain Kirsten shouted just as heartily and no less sincerely than the twenty-year-old Rostof.

Late that night, when all had separated, Denisof laid his stubby hand on his favorite Rostof's shoulder:

"In the field, no woom for love affairs, when one's so much in love with the Tsar!" said he.

"Denisof! don't jest on this subject!" cried Rostof. "This is such an exalted, such a noble feeling, that . . ."

"I agwee with you, I agwee with you, my fwend, I understand, I appwove . . ."

"No, you can't understand it!"

And Rostof got up and began to wander among the watch fires, and dreamed of what bliss it would be to die—as to losing his life, he did not dare to think of that!—but simply to die in the presence of his sovereign. He was really in love, not only with the Tsar, but also with the glory of the Russian army and the hope of impending victory. And he was not the only one who experienced this feeling on the memorable days that preceded the Battle of Austerlitz: nine-tenths of the men composing the Russian army were at that time in love, though perhaps less ecstatically, with their Tsar and the glory of the Russian army.

IX

AT DAYBREAK on the twenty-ninth, a French officer with a flag of truce passed the sentinels and was brought into Wischau, demanding a personal interview with the Russian emperor. This officer was Savary. It was soon reported that the purpose of his mission was a proposal for a meeting of the emperor with Napoleon. This personal meeting was refused, much to the gratification and delight of the whole army, and in the sovereign's place Prince Dolgorukof, the conqueror of Wischau, was delegated to confer with Napoleon if, contrary to anticipation, these conferences had for their object a genuine desire for peace.

In the evening Dolgorukof returned, went directly to the sovereign, and was closeted a long time with him alone.

Up to the afternoon of the first, the movement, the excited conversations, the galloping about and carrying of messages, was confined to the headquarters of the two emperors; in the afternoon of the same day the excitement was communicated to Kutuzof's headquarters and to the staffs of the division commanders. About six o'clock in the evening Kutuzof came to the headquarters of the emperors, and, after a short audience with his sovereign, went to see Count Tolstoy, the Grand Marshal, the master of supplies. Bolkonsky took advantage of this time to run into Dolgorukof's to find out about the impending engagement.

"Well, how are you, fellow?" exclaimed Dolgorukof, who was drinking tea with Bilibin. "The celebration comes tomorrow! What's the matter with your old man? Is he out of sorts?"

"I wouldn't say he was out of sorts, but I think he would like to have been listened to."

"Well, he was listened to at the council of war, and he will be when he is willing to talk business; but to be temporizing and waiting for something, now that Bonaparte fears a general engagement more than anything else, is impossible."

"And so you've seen him, have you?" asked Prince Andrei. "Well, what sort of a man is this Bonaparte? What impression did he produce upon you?"

"Yes, I have seen him, and I am convinced that he is more afraid of a general engagement than of anything else in the world," replied Dolgorukof, evidently putting great importance on this general conclusion drawn from his interview with Napoleon. "If he were not afraid of a general battle, why should he have demanded this interview, and entered into negotiations and above all retreated, when retreating is contrary to his entire method of carrying on war? Believe me, he is afraid—afraid of a general engagement; his hour is at hand! Mark my words!"

"But tell me about him, what kind of man is he?" insisted Prince Andrei.

"He is a man in a gray overcoat, very anxious for me to address him as 'your majesty,' and very much affronted because I gave him no title at all. That's the kind of man he is, and that's all I can say!" replied Dolgorukof, looking at Bilibin with a smile. "In spite of my perfect confidence in old Kutuzof," he went on to say, "we would all be in a fine state if we kept on waiting for something to happen, thereby giving him the chance to outflank us or play some trick upon us, now when he's evidently right in our hands. No, it's not a good thing to forget Suvorof and his rule: 'It's a better policy to attack than to be attacked.' Believe me, in war the energy of young men often points the way more wisely than all the experience of old tacticians."

"But in what position are we going to attack him? I was at the advanced posts today, and it is impossible to make out where his main force is stationed," said Prince Andrei. He was anxious to explain to Dolgorukof a plan of attack he himself had devised.

"Oh, it is of absolutely no consequence," replied Dolgorukof, hastily getting up and spreading a map on the table. "All contingencies are foreseen. If he is posted at Brünn . . ."

On the way back to their quarters, Prince Andrei could not refrain from asking Kutuzof, who sat in moody silence beside him, what he thought of the approaching engagement.

Kutuzof looked sternly at his aide, and after a moment of silence replied: "I think the battle will be lost, and so I told Count Tolstoy, and begged him to repeat it to the sovereign, and what do you think was the answer he gave me? 'Ah, my dear general, rice and cutlets interest me; you attend to the affairs of war!' Yes, that's the way they answer me!"

Rostof that same night was with his platoon in the line of scouts stationed in front of Bagration's division. His hussars were posted two and two along the line; he himself kept riding his horse the whole length of the line, struggling to overcome his irresistible inclination to drowsiness. Suddenly a distant shout startled him. He awoke and opened his eyes.

At that instant he heard in front of him, in the direction of the enemy, the prolonged shouts of thousands of voices. His horse and those of the hussars stationed near him pricked up their ears at these sounds. On the spot from which the cries proceeded, one point of fire after another flashed and died, and along the whole line of the French army, stretching up the hills, gleamed those fires, while the shouts grew louder and louder. Rostof made out that it was French, but could not distinguish the words. There was too great a roar of voices. All that it sounded like was a confused *a.a.a.a.!* and *rrrrrr!*

"What's that? What do you think it is?" asked Rostof, turning to his neighbor, the hussar. "It's from the enemy, isn't it?"

The hussar made no reply.

"What! didn't you hear anything?" asked Rostof, after waiting for some time for the hussar to speak.

"How can anybody tell, your honor," replied the hussar in a non-committal way.

"Judging from the direction, it must be the enemy?" inquired Rostof.

"Maybe it is, and maybe it isn't," exclaimed the hussar. "You see, it's night. There now, steady," he cried to his horse, which was growing restive. Rostof's horse also became excited and pawed the frozen ground, as he listened to the shouting and glanced at the flashing fires.

The shouts of the voices constantly increased in volume and mingled in a general roar that could have been produced only by an army of many thousand men. The fires spread out more and more, until at last they seemed to extend throughout the French camp. Rostof had now lost all inclination to sleep. The joyful, enthusiastic huzzas in the enemy's army had a most stimulating effect upon him. *Long live the emperor! the emperor!* were the words he could now clearly distinguish.

The shouts and cries arose from the fact that while Napoleon's general order was being read throughout the army, the emperor himself came on horseback to inspect the bivouacs. The soldiers, seeing the emperor, lighted trusses of straw and followed him with the cries of *Long live the emperor!* Napoleon's order was as follows:

Soldiers! The Russian army has come against us to avenge the Austrian army of Ulm. These are the same battalions which we defeated at Hollabrünn, and which, since that time, we have been constantly following up.

The position we occupy is paramount, and as soon as they attempt to outflank my right they will expose their own flank.

Soldiers! I myself will direct your battalions. I will keep out of range of the firing, if you, with your usual gallantry, carry confusion and consternation into the ranks of the enemy; but if the combat becomes for one instant doubtful, you will see your emperor exposing himself at the front to the blows of the enemy, since there can be no hesitation in the victory, especially today when the honor of the French infantry, in whose hands lies the honor of the nation, is at stake. Do not break the ranks under pretext of carrying away the wounded. Let each man be animated by the thought that we must conquer these mercenaries of England, filled with such hatred against our nation. This victory will bring the campaign to an end, and we can retire to winter quarters where we will be joined by the fresh troops that are mobilizing in France. And then the peace I shall conclude will be memorable for my people, for you, and for me.

NAPOLEON.

X

AT FIVE O'CLOCK in the morning it was still completely dark. The troops of the center, of the reserves, and of the right wing, under Bagration, were as yet immobilized; but on the left wing the columns of infantry, cavalry, and artillery, ordered to be the first to descend from the heights and attack the enemy's right flank and drive him back into the mountains of Bohemia, according to the "disposition," were already stirring and beginning to rise from where they lay. The smoke from the fires, into which they were throwing everything superfluous, made their eyes smart. It was cold and dark. The officers were hastily drinking their tea and breakfasting; the soldiers were munching their biscuits, kicking the round cannon balls, and crowding about in front of the fires, throwing in the remains of their huts, chairs, tables, wheels, buckets, and everything that could not be taken with them. The Austrian guides were wandering about among the Russian troops and serving as starters of the forward movement. As soon as an Austrian officer made his appearance near the quarters of a regimental commander, the columns were set in motion; but they knew not whither they were going, and owing to the throngs that surrounded them, and the smoke and the thickening fog, they could not see either the place they were leaving or that to which they were being sent.

The soldier in a military movement is as much surrounded, limited, and fettered by his regiment as a sailor is by his ship. However far he goes, into whatever strange, unknown and terrible distances he is sent, around him are always and everywhere the same comrades, the same ranks, the same sergeant Ivan Mitrich, the same company dog, Zhutchka, the same officers; just as for the sailor there are the same decks, the same masts, the same cables. The sailor rarely cares to know the distances over which his ship has sailed; but on the day of a military movement God knows how or whence or in what world of mystery the soldiers hear a stern note, which is the same for all, and which signifies the nearness of something decisive and solemn and induces them to speculate on what they do not usually think about. The soldiers on the day of a military movement are excited, and strive to think beyond the petty interests of their own regiment; they are all ears and eyes, and greedily ask questions about what is going to take place before them.

The fog was so dense that, though it had grown lighter, it was impossible to see ten paces ahead. Bushes seemed like huge trees, level places gave the impression of being precipices and slopes. Anywhere, at any moment, they might meet the enemy, who would be utterly invisible within ten paces. But the columns marched for a long time in the same fog, up hill and down dale, skirting gardens and orchards, past places where none of them had ever been before, and still they found no enemy. On the other hand, in front of them, behind them, on all sides of them, the soldiers were made conscious that our Russian columns were all marching in the same direction. Each soldier felt a thrill in his heart at the knowledge that many, many others of our men were going where he was going: that is, he knew not whither.

"See there! The Kursk men have started," said various voices in the ranks.

"Terrible lot of our troops collected here, messmates! Last evenin' I looked around when the fires were lit; couldn't see the end of 'em! Like Moscow, one might say!"

But after they had been marching for about an hour, all the time in thick fog, they were ordered to halt, and an unpleasant consciousness of disorder and confusion in the operations spread through the ranks. It would be very difficult to explain how such a consciousness got abroad; but there was no doubt that it was transmitted and spread with extraordinary rapidity; the uncertainty became certainty, gaining with irresistible force, as water rushes down a ravine.

The cause of the confusion was this: After the Austrian cavalry on the left wing had started forward, those who had charge of it came to the conclusion that the Russian center was too widely separated from the right, and all the cavalry was commanded to cross over to the right side. Several thousand cavalrymen rode across in front of the columns of infantry, and the infantry had to wait till they passed.

Meantime the army was growing impatient and losing spirit. At last, after an hour's delay, the troops began to move forward once more, and found themselves descending into the valley. The fog, which had been scattering on the heights, was as thick as ever on the lower lands where they were now marching. In front of them in the fog, one shot, then a second, was fired, incoherently and at different points, *trat-ta-tat*; and then the firing became more regular and rapid, and the engagement fairly began over the brook called Holdbach.

It was now nine o'clock. The fog like a fathomless sea spread over the valley, but in front of the village of Schlapanitz, on the height where Napoleon stood surrounded by his marshals, it was quite clear. Over them was the blue bright heaven, and the mighty sun, like a gigantic inflated magenta balloon, was just rising above the milk-white sea of fog. The French troops and Napoleon himself with his staff were not on the farther side of the brook and the hollows of Sokolnitz and Schlapanitz behind which we had expected to take up our position and begin the engagement, but they had all come over to the hither side and were so near our troops that Napoleon with his naked eye could distinguish in our army a horseman from an infantry soldier.

Napoleon, mounted on his little gray Arab horse and wearing the same blue cloak in which he had made the whole Italian campaign, was standing a little in advance of his marshals. He was silently gazing at the summits of the hills that emerged like islands from the fog and was watching the Russian troops as they moved along in the distance, and listening to the sounds of firing in the valley. Not a muscle of his face—it was still thin—moved; his glittering eyes were steadfastly fixed on one spot.

His anticipations seemed to be justified. By the reports that had been brought him the evening before, by the sounds of wheels and footsteps that had been heard during the night along the vanguard, by the disorderly movements of the Russian columns, by all the indications, he clearly saw that the allied armies supposed him to be posted a long distance from them, that the moving columns constituted the center of the Russian army, and that this center was weak enough to justify him in giving it attack. But not even yet did he begin the battle.

That was a solemn day for him, the anniversary of his coronation. Just before morning he had taken a nap for a few hours, and then waking, healthy, jovial, fresh, and in that happy frame of mind in which everything seems possible, success certain, he mounted his horse and rode out into the field. He stood motionless, gazing at the hills becoming visible through the fog, and into his cold face there came that peculiar shade of self-confident, well-deserved happiness, such as is sometimes seen on the face of a young lad who is happy and in love. His marshals were grouped behind him and did not venture to distract his attention. He gazed now at the heights above Pratz, now at the sun swimming out from the fog.

When the sun had risen, and its dazzling radiance spilled over the fields and the fog, as if this were the signal for which he was waiting, he drew off the glove from his handsome white hand, beckoned to his marshals, and gave the order to begin the battle. The marshals, accompanied by their aides, galloped off in different directions, and within a few minutes the chief forces of the French army were in rapid motion toward those same heights of Pratz that the Russian troops were abandoning more and more as they filed to the left and into the vale.

XI

AT EIGHT O'CLOCK that morning, Kutuzof had ridden up toward Pratz, at the head of the division—Miloradovitch's—that was to take the place of the columns of Prschebiszewsky and De Langeron, which were now on their way down into the valley. He greeted the men of the foremost regiment and gave the word of command, thereby signifying that he intended to lead that column in person. When he reached the village of Pratz, he halted. Prince Andrei, forming one of his large staff, stood just behind him. Prince Andrei felt stirred and excited, and at the same time self-confident and calm, as is apt to be the case with a man at the arrival of the moment he has been anxiously awaiting. He was firmly convinced that this day was to be his Toulon, or his bridge of Arcola. How it would come about he had not the faintest idea, but he was firmly convinced that it would be.

Toward the left, in the valley below, where the fog lay, could be heard the musket fire of the unseen opponents. There, so it seemed to Prince Andrei, the fighting would be hottest, there the obstacles would be met with; "and there I shall be sent," he said to himself, "with a brigade or division; and with the standard in my hand, I shall rush on and conquer everything before me."

The commander-in-chief stationed himself at the entrance of the village and allowed the troops to file past him. Kutuzof that morning appeared fatigued and irritated. The infantry filing by him came to a halt without any orders, apparently because they had come in contact with some obstacle ahead of them.

"Go and tell them to form into battalions and get outside the village," said Kutuzof to a general who came riding along. "How is it you do not understand, your excellency, my dear sir, that it's impossible to open ranks so, along a village street, when we are moving against the enemy?"

"I propose to form behind the village, your eminence," replied the general. Kutuzof gave him a saturnine smile.

"You'd be in a fine condition, deploying your front in the presence of the enemy; very fine idea!"

"The enemy are still a long way off, your eminence. According to the plan . . ."

"The plan!" cried Kutuzof bitterly, "and who told you that? Be good enough to do as I tell you."

"I obey."

"My boy," whispered Nesvitsky to Prince Andrei, "the old man is as surly as a dog."

An Austrian officer, in a white uniform, with a green plume in his hat, galloped up to Kutuzof and asked him, in the name of the emperor, if the fourth column was taking part in the action.

Kutuzof, without answering him, turned around, and his glance fell accidentally on Prince Andrei, who was stationed near him. When he noticed Bolkonsky, the vicious and acrimonious expression of his face softened, as if to signify that he was not to blame for what was taking place. And still without answering the Austrian aide, he turned to Bolkonsky and said in French: "Go and see, my dear fellow, if the third division has passed the village yet; command them to halt and await my orders."

As soon as Prince Andrei started, he called him back:

"And ask if the skirmishers are posted and what they are doing. What they are doing," he repeated to himself, still paying no attention to the Austrian.

Prince Andrei galloped off to execute this order.

Outstripping the battalions, which were all the time pressing forward, he halted the third division and convinced himself that no skirmishers had been thrown out in front of our columns. The general in command of the foremost regiment was greatly amazed at the order from the commander-in-chief to throw out sharpshooters. The regimental commander was firmly assured in his own mind that other troops were in front of him and that the enemy could not be less than six miles distant. In reality, nothing could be discerned in front of them except waste ground which sloped down and was shrouded in fog. After giving him the commander-in-chief's orders to repair his negligence, Prince Andrei galloped back. Kutuzof was still in the same place, his fat body sitting in a dumpy position in his saddle, and was yawning heavily, with his eyes closed. The troops had not yet moved, but stood with grounded arms.

"Good, very good," said he to Prince Andrei, and turned to the general, who, holding his watch in his hand, said that it must be time to move, since all the columns had already gone down from the left wing.

"Time enough, your excellency," said Kutuzof. "We shall have time enough," he repeated.

At this time, behind Kutuzof were heard the sounds of the regiments in the distance cheering, and these voices quickly ran along the whole line of the Russian columns under march. It was evident that whoever they were greeting was approaching rapidly. When the soldiers of the regiment behind Kutuzof began to cheer, he rode a little to one side and glanced around with a frown. Along the road from Pratz came what appeared to be a squadron of gaily dressed horsemen. Two of them rode side by side at a round gallop, ahead of the others. One was in a black uniform with a white plume, on a chestnut horse groomed in the English style; the other in a white uniform on a coal-black steed. These were the two emperors with their suite.

Kutuzof, with an affectation of "the thorough soldier" found at his post, shouted "Halt! eyes front!" to the soldiers halting near him, and, saluting, rode toward the emperor. His whole figure and manner had suddenly undergone a change. He had assumed the mien of a subordinate, of a man ready to surrender his own will. With an affectation of deference which evidently was not pleasing to the Emperor Alexander, he came to meet him and saluted him.

This impression crossed the young and happy face of the emperor, and disappeared like the mist wreaths in the clear sky. His face was a trifle flushed after his gallop of two miles and as he reined in his horse he drew a long breath and glanced around into the faces of his suite, all young men like himself, and like himself all full of life. Czartorisky and Novosiltsof and Prince Volkonsky and Stroganof and many others, all richly dressed, jovial young men on handsome, well-groomed, fresh-looking and slightly sweating horses, chatting and laughing together, formed a group behind the sovereign.

The Emperor Franz, a florid young man with a long face, sat bolt upright in his saddle on his handsome black stallion and slowly glanced around him with an anxious expression. He beckoned to one of his white-uniformed aides and asked him some question. "Probably he asked at what hour they started," thought Prince Andrei, gazing at his old acquaintance with a smile he could not repress when he thought of his audience. The emperor's suite was composed of young orderlies, Austrian and Russian, selected from the regiments of the Guards and of the line. Grooms had brought with them handsome reserve horses in embroidered caparisons for the emperors.

Just as when a fresh breeze from the fields breathes through an open window into a stuffy chamber, so these brilliant young men brought with them to Kutuzof's dispirited staff the sense of youth and energy and confidence in victory.

"Why don't you begin, Mikhail Ilarionovitch?" impatiently demanded the Emperor Alexander, turning to Kutuzof, at the same time looking courteously toward the Emperor Franz.

"I was waiting, your majesty," replied Kutuzof, deferentially bowing low.

The emperor leaned toward him, frowning slightly and giving him to understand that he did not hear.

"I was waiting, your majesty," repeated Kutuzof, and Prince Andrei noticed that Kutuzof's upper lip curled unnaturally when he repeated the words "I was waiting."—"The columns have not all assembled, your majesty."

The sovereign heard, but the answer evidently displeased him; he shrugged his drooping shoulders, glanced at Novosiltsof, who was standing near him, and his glance seemed to imply a certain compasssion for Kutuzof.

"We are not on the Empress' Field, Mikhail Ilarionovitch, where the review is not begun until all the regiments are present," said the emperor, again glancing into the Emperor Franz' eyes, as if to ask him to take part so that he might listen to what he might say; but the Emperor Franz, who was still gazing about, did not heed him.

"That's the very reason I do not begin, sire," said Kutuzof in a ringing voice, seeming to anticipate the possibility that the emperor might not see fit to hear him, and again a peculiar look passed over his face. "That's the very reason that I do not begin, sire, because we are not on parade and not on the Empress' Field," he repeated, clearly and distinctly.

The faces of all those composing the emperor's suite expressed annoyance and reproach, as they hastily exchanged glances on hearing these words. "No matter if he is old, he ought not, he never ought to speak in that way," the faces seemed to say.

"However, if you give the order, your majesty," said Kutuzof, raising his head and again assuming that former tone of a general ready to listen to orders and to obey. He turned his horse, and beckoning to Division Commander Miloradovitch he gave him the order to attack.

The troops were again set in motion, and two battalions of the Novgorod regiment and one battalion of the Apsheron regiment filed forward past the emperor.

XII

KUTUZOF, accompanied by his aides, rode slowly after the carabiniers. The fog began to disperse and already a mile and a half away could be seen, though as yet indistinctly, the ranks of the enemy on the heights opposite. Down in the valley at the left the firing was growing more violent. Kutuzof halted, discussing some point with the Austrian general. Prince Andrei, sitting on his horse a little distance behind, gazed at them and then, wishing to obtain the use of a field glass, turned to one of the aides who had one.

"Look! look!" exclaimed this aide, turning his glass not at the distant host, but to the hill nearly in front of them. "Look, there are the French!"

The two generals and the adjutants reached after the glass, one taking it from the other. All the faces suddenly changed, and an expression of dismay came into them. They expected to find the French a mile and a half away, and there they were unexpectedly appearing right at hand.

"Is that the enemy?" . . . "It can't be!" . . . "Yes, look, they . . ." "Certainly it is." . . . "What does it mean?" exclaimed various voices.

Prince Andrei with his naked eye could see a dense mass of the French moving up at the right to meet the Apsheron boys, not more than five hundred paces from the very spot where Kutuzof was standing.

"Here it is! The decisive moment is at hand! my chance has come!" said Prince Andrei, and starting up his horse he approached Kutuzof. "The Apsheron men ought to be halted, your eminence," he cried. But at that very instant all became veiled in smoke; the rattle of musketry sounded near them, and a naively terrified voice only two steps from Prince Andrei cried: "Well, brothers, it's all up with us!" and this voice seemed to be a command. At this voice all started to run.

Confused but still constantly increasing throngs ran back by the very same place where five minutes before the troops had filed so proudly past the emperors. Not only was it hard to arrest these fugitives, but it was even impossible not to be borne back by the mob. Bolkonsky could only struggle not to let them pass him, and he gazed around, finding it quite out of the question to understand what was taking place at the front. Nesvitsky, with angry face, flushed and quite unlike himself, cried to Kutuzof that if he did not instantly come away, he would be probably taken prisoner. Kutuzof still stayed in the same place, and without answering took out his handkerchief. A stream of blood was trickling from his face. Prince Andrei forced his way through to where he was.

"You are wounded?" he asked, scarcely controlling the trembling of his lower jaw.

"The wound is not here, but yonder," said Kutuzof, pressing his handkerchief to his wounded cheek, and pointing to the fugitives. "Halt them!" he cried, and at the same time, evidently convinced that it was an impossibility to bring them to a halt, he gave spurs to his horse and rode off to the right. New masses of fugitives came pouring along like a torrent, engulfed him, and bore him along with them.

The troops were pouring back in such a dense throng that, once entangled in the midst of it, it was very difficult to extricate oneself. Some shouted: "He's coming, why don't you let him pass?" Others turned around and fired their muskets into the air; others struck the horse on which Kutuzof rode, but by the exercise of supreme force Kutuzof—accompanied by his staff, diminished by more than half—struggled through to the left and rode off in the direction of cannonading heard not far away. Prince Andrei, also forcing his way through the throng of fugitives and endeavoring not to become separated from Kutuzof, could make out through the reek of gunpowder smoke a Russian battery on the side of the hill, still blazing away vigorously, while the French were just marching against it. A little higher up stood the Russian infantry, neither moving forward to the aid of the battery nor back in the same direction as the fugitives. A general spurred down from this brigade of infantry and approached Kutuzof. Out of Kutuzof's staff only four men were left, and all were pale and silently exchanged glances.

"Stop those cowards!" cried Kutuzof, all out of breath, as the regimental commander came up to him, and pointing to the fugitives; but at that very second, as if for a punishment for those words, like a bevy of birds a number of bullets flew buzzing over the heads of the regiment and of Kutuzof's staff. The French were charging the battery, and when they caught sight of Kutuzof they aimed at him.

At this volley, the regimental commander suddenly clapped his hand to his leg; a few soldiers fell and an ensign standing with the flag dropped it from his hand; the flag reeled and fell, catching on the bayonets of the soldiers near him. The men began to load and fire without orders.

"O-o-o-oh!" groaned Kutuzof, with an expression of despair, and glanced around. "Bolkonsky," he whispered, his weak old man's voice trembling with emotion, "Bolkonsky!" he whispered, pointing to the demoralized battalion and at the enemy, "what does this mean?"

But before he had uttered these words, Prince Andrei, conscious of the tears of shame and anger choking him, had already leaped from his horse and rushed toward the standard.

"Boys, follow me!" he cried in his youthfully penetrating voice. "Here it is," thought Prince Andrei as he seized the flagstaff; and he listened with rapture to the whiz of the bullets that were evidently directed straight at him. A number of the soldiers fell.

"Hurrah!" cried Prince Andrei, instantly seizing the flag and rushing forward with unfailing confidence that the whole battalion would follow him.

In fact he ran on only a few steps alone. Then one soldier was stirred, and then another, and the whole battalion with huzzas dashed forward and overtook him.

A noncommissioned officer of the battalion, darting up to him, seized the standard, which from its weight shook in Prince Andrei's hand, but he was instantly shot down. Prince Andrei again grasped the flag and, dragging it along by the staff, hurried on with the battalion. In front of him he saw our artillerymen, some fighting, others abandoning the guns and running toward him; he also saw the French infantry, who had seized the artillery horses, and were reversing the fieldpieces. Prince Andrei and the battalion were now only twenty paces distant from the battery. He heard the incessant ping of the bullets over his head, and the soldiers constantly groaning and falling at his left and at his right. But he did not look at them; his eyes were fastened only on what was going on in front of him, where the battery was. He now saw distinctly the figure of a red-headed artilleryman, with his shako half knocked off, and dragging with him a long-handled cannon brush, while a French soldier was trying to pull it away from him. Prince Andrei distinguished clearly the distorted and angry faces of these two men, who evidently were not aware of what they were doing.

"What are they up to?" thought Prince Andrei, as he looked at them. "Why doesn't the red-headed artillerist run, if he has no weapons, and why doesn't the Frenchman finish him? He wouldn't have time to get any distance, though, before the Frenchman would recover his musket and put an end to him."

In point of fact, another Frenchman, clubbing his musket, ran up to the combatants, and the fate of the red-headed artillerist, who had no idea of what was coming upon him and had just triumphantly made himself master of the brush, must have been sealed. But Prince Andrei did not witness the end of the struggle. It seemed to him that one of the approaching soldiers struck him in the head with the full weight of a heavy cudgel. It was rather painful, but his chief sensation was that of displeasure because the pain distracted his attention and prevented him from seeing what he had been looking at.

"What does this mean? Am I falling? Surely my legs are giving way," he said to himself, and he fell on his back. He opened his eyes, hoping to see how the struggle between the artilleryman and the Frenchman ended, and anxious to know whether or not the red-headed artillerist was killed, and the cannon saved or captured. But he could see nothing of it. Over him he could see only the sky, the lofty sky; not clear, but still immeasurably lofty, and with light gray clouds slowly wandering over it.

"How still, calm, and solemn! How entirely different from when I was running," said Prince Andrei to himself. "It was not so when we were all running and shouting and fighting; how entirely different it was when the Frenchman and the artilleryman, with vindictive and frightened faces, were struggling; the clouds then were not floating over those infinite depths of sky as they are now. How is it that I never before saw this lofty sky? and how glad I am that I have learned to know it at last! Yes! all is empty, all is deception, except these infinite heavens. Nothing, nothing at all besides! And even that is nothing but silence and peace! And glory to God! . . ."

XIII

By FIVE O'CLOCK in the evening the battle was lost at every point. More than a hundred cannon had already fallen into the hands of the French. Prschebiszewsky and his corps had laid down their arms. The other columns, having lost more than half their effectives, were retreating in disorderly, demoralized throngs.

The remains of Langeron's and Dokhturof's forces, all in confusion, were crowded together around the ponds, on the dikes and banks of the village of Augest.

By six o'clock the only cannonading that was heard was directed at the dike of Augest by some of the French, who had established a large battery on the slopes of the hill and were trying to cut down our men as they retreated. At the rear, Dokhturof and some others, having collected their battalions, made a stand against the French, who were pursuing our troops.

It was already quite dark. On the narrow dike of Augest, where for so many years the little old miller had peacefully sat with his hook and line while his grandson with rolled-up shirt sleeves played in the water can with the flapping silver fish; on that dike, over which the Moravians in shaggy caps and blue blouses had driven their two-horse teams loaded down with spring wheat, and had returned dusted with flour and with whitened teams; along this same dike, this narrow dike, among vans and fieldpieces, under the feet of horses and between the wheels, crowded a throng of men, their faces distorted with fear of death, pushing one another, expiring, trampling on the dying and dead, and crushing one another, only to be themselves killed a few steps farther on.

Every ten seconds a cannon ball flew by, sucking in the air, or a shell came bursting amid this dense throng, dealing death and spattering with blood those who stood near by. Dolokhof, wounded in the arm, on foot, with ten men of his company—he was now an officer again—and his regimental commander, on horseback, constituted the sole survivors of the whole regiment. Carried along in the throng, they were crowded together at the very entrance of the dike, and, pressed on all sides, were obliged to halt because a horse attached to a field piece had fallen and men were trying to drag it along.

One cannon ball struck someone behind them, another struck just in front and spattered Dolokhof with blood. The crowd, in desperation, pressed on, squeezing together, and then after advancing a few steps, halted again.

"If we could only make those hundred paces, safety is sure; if we stay here two minutes longer, our destruction is certain!" said each one to himself.

Dolokhof, standing in the midst of the throng, forced his way through to the edge of the dike, knocking down two soldiers, and sprang out on the slippery ice that covered the pond.

"Turn out this way!" he cried, sliding along on the ice, which cracked under his weight. "Turn out," he cried to the gunner, "it will hold! it will hold!"

The ice held him, but it yielded and cracked, and it was evident that it would immediately give way, if not under his weight alone, certainly under that of the fieldpiece or the throng of men. They looked at him, and crowded along the shore, not venturing to step upon the ice. The commander of the regiment, sitting on horseback at the entrance, was just raising his hand and opening his mouth to speak to Dolokhof, when suddenly a cannon ball flew so close over the men that they all ducked their heads. There was a thud as if something soft were struck, and the general fell from his horse in a pool of blood. No one looked at the general or thought of picking him up.

"Get on to the ice!" . . . "Cross the ice!" . . . "Come on!" . . . "Move on! Don't you hear? Come!" was heard suddenly from innumerable voices after the cannon ball had struck the general, though the men knew not what or why they were yelling.

One of the last fieldpieces to enter on the dike ventured on the ice. A throng of soldiers started down to the frozen pond. One of the rearmost soldiers broke through, one leg slumping down into the water. He tried to save himself and sank up to his belt. The men who stood nearest held back; the driver of the fieldpiece drew in his horses, but still behind them men were shouting:

"Take to the ice!" . . . "What are you stopping for?" . . . "Take to the ice!" . . . "Take to the ice!" and cries of horror were heard among the throng. The soldiers surrounding the gun gesticulated over their horses and beat them to make them turn and go on. The horses struck out from the shore. The ice, which might have held the foot soldiers, gave way in one immense sheet, and forty men who were on it threw themselves, some forward and some back, trampling on one another.

All the time the cannon balls kept regularly whistling by and falling on the ice, into the water, and, most frequently, into the mass of men that covered the dike, the pond, and the banks.

XIV

ON THE HILL above Pratz, in the same spot where he had fallen with the flagstaff in his hand, lay Prince Andrei Bolkonsky, his lifeblood oozing away, and unconsciously groaning with light, pitiful moans, like an ailing child.

By evening he ceased to groan, and lay absolutely still. He did not know how long his unconsciousness continued. Suddenly he became conscious that he was alive, and suffering from a burning and tormenting pain in his head.

"Where is that lofty heaven that I had never seen before and saw today?" That was his first thought. "And I never knew such pain as this, either," he said to himself. "Yes, I have never known anything, anything like this, till now. But where am I?"

He tried to listen, and heard the trampling hoofs of several horses approaching, and the sounds of voices speaking French. He opened his eyes. Over him still spread the same lofty sky, with clouds sailing through it in still loftier heights, and beyond them he could see the depths of endless blue. He did not turn his head or look at those who, to judge from the hoofbeats of the horses and the sounds of the voices, rode up to him and paused.

These horsemen were Napoleon, accompanied by two aides. Bonaparte, who had been riding over the field of battle, had given orders to strengthen the battery cannonading the dike of Augest, and was now looking over the killed and wounded left on the battlefield.

"Handsome men!" said Napoleon, gazing at a Russian grenadier who lay on his belly with his face half buried in the soil, his neck turning black and one arm flung out and stiffened in death.

"The ammunition for the field guns is exhausted, sire!"

"Have that of the reserves brought," said Napoleon, and then a step or two nearer he paused over Prince Andrei, who lay on his back with the flagstaff clutched in his hands (the flag had been carried off by the French as a trophy).

"There's an honorable death," said Napoleon, gazing at Bolkonsky. Prince Andrei realized that this was said of him, and that it was spoken by Napoleon. He heard them address the speaker as "sire." But he heard these words as if they had been the buzzing of a fly. He was not only not interested in them, but they made no impression upon him, and he immediately forgot them. His head throbbed and burned; he felt that his lifeblood was ebbing, and he still saw far above him the distant, eternal heavens. He knew that this was Napoleon, his hero; but at this moment, Napoleon seemed to him merely a small, insignificant man in comparison with that lofty, infinite heaven, with the clouds flying through it. It was a matter of utter indifference to him who stood looking down on him, or what was said about him at that moment. He was merely conscious of a feeling of joy that people had come to him, and of a desire for these people to give him assistance and bring him back to life, which now seemed to him so beautiful because he understood it so differently. He collected all his strength to move and make some sound. He managed to move his leg slightly, and uttered a weak, feeble, sickly moan which stirred pity even in himself.

"Ah! he is alive!" said Napoleon. "Take up this young man and take him to the temporary hospital."

Having given this order, Napoleon rode on to meet Marshal Lannes, who, removing his hat and smiling, rode up and congratulated him on the victory.

Prince Andrei recollected nothing further; he lost consciousness from the terrible pain of being placed on the stretcher, and from the jolting as he was carried along, and from the probing of the wound. He recovered it again only at the very end of the day, as he was carried to the hospital together with other Russians wounded and taken prisoner. At this time, he felt a little fresher and was able to glance around and even to speak.

The first words he heard after he came to were spoken by a French officer in charge of the convoy, who said:

"We must stop here; the emperor is coming by immediately; it will give him pleasure to see these prisoners."

"There are so many prisoners today—almost the whole Russian army—I should think it would have become a bore to him," said another officer.

"Well, at all events, this man here, they say, was the commander of all Emperor Alexander's Guards," said the first speaker, indicating a wounded Russian officer in a white Cavalier-guards uniform. Bolkonsky recognized Prince Repnin, whom he had met in Petersburg society. Next to him was a youth of nineteen, an officer of the Cavalier-guard, also wounded. Bonaparte, coming up at a gallop, reined in his horse.

"Who is the chief officer here?" he asked, looking at the wounded.

They pointed to Colonel Prince Repnin.

"Were you the commander of Emperor Alexander's horse-guard regiment?" asked Napoleon.

"I commanded a squadron," replied Repnin.

"Your regiment did its duty with honor," remarked Napoleon.

"Praise from a great commander is the highest award a soldier can have," said Repnin.

"It is with pleasure that I give it to you," replied Napoleon. "Who is this young man next to you?"

Prince Repnin named Lieutenant Sukhtelen.

Napoleon glanced at him and said with a smile: "He is very young to oppose us."

"Youth does not prevent one from being brave," replied Sukhtelen in a broken voice.

"A beautiful answer," said Napoleon. "Young man, you will get on in the world."

Prince Andrei, who had been placed also in the front rank under the eyes of the emperor, so as to swell the number of those who had been taken prisoner, naturally attracted his attention. Napoleon evidently remembered having seen him on the field, and turning to him he used exactly the same expression, "young man," as when Bolkonsky had the first time come under his notice.

"Well, and you, young man?" said he, addressing him. "How do you feel, *mon brave?*"

Although five minutes before this Prince Andrei had been able to say a few words to the soldiers who were bearing him, now he fixed his eyes directly on Napoleon, but had nothing to say. . . . To him at this moment all the interests occupying Napoleon seemed so petty; his former hero himself, with his small vanity and delight in the victory, seemed so sordid in comparison with that high, true, and just heaven which he had seen and learned to understand; and that was why he could not answer. Yes, and everything seemed to him so profitless and insignificant in comparison with that stern and majestic train of thought induced by his lapsing strength as his lifeblood ebbed away, by his suffering and the near expectation of death. As Prince Andrei looked into Napoleon's eyes, he thought of the insignificance of majesty, of the insignificance of life, the meaning of which no one could understand, and of the still greater insignificance of death, the meaning of which no one could comprehend or explain.

The emperor, without waiting for an answer, turned away, and as he started to ride on said to one of the officers:

"Have these gentlemen looked after and conveyed to my bivouac; have Doctor Larrey himself look after their wounds. *Au revoir*, Prince Repnin," and he touched the spurs to his horse and galloped away.

His face was bright with self-satisfaction and happiness.

The soldiers carrying Prince Andrei had taken from him the golden religious medal that Princess Maria had hung around her brother's neck; but when they saw the flattering way in which the emperor treated the prisoners, they hastened to return the medal. Prince Andrei did not see how or by whom the medallion was replaced, but he suddenly discovered on his chest, outside of his uniform, the little image attached to its slender golden chain.

"It would be good," thought Prince Andrei, letting his eyes rest on the medallion which his sister had hung around his neck with so much feeling and reverence, "it would be good if everything were as clear and simple as it seems to Princess Maria. How good it would be to know where to find help in this life, and what to expect after it, beyond the grave! How happy and serene I would be if I could say now, 'Lord, have mercy on me!' But to whom can I say that! Is it the great Power, impalpable, incomprehensible, which I cannot turn to, or even express in words; is it the great All or Nothingness," said he to himself, "or is it God who is sewed in this amulet that Princess Maria gave me? Nothing, nothing is certain, except the insignificance of all within my comprehension and the majesty of that which is incomprehensible but all-important."

The stretcher started off. At every jolt he again felt the insufferable pain, his fever grew more violent, and he began to be delirious. The dreams about his father, his wife, his sister, and his unborn son, and the feeling of tenderness he had experienced on the night before the battle, the figure of the little insignificant Napoleon, and above all the lofty sky, formed the principal content of his feverish imaginations. He seemed to be living a quiet life amid calm, domestic happiness at Lisiya Gori. He was beginning to take delight in this blissful existence, when suddenly the little Napoleon appeared with his unsympathetic, shallow-minded face, expressing happiness at the unhappiness of others; and once more doubts began to arise and torment him, and only the skies seemed to promise healing balm. Toward morning all his imaginings were utterly confused and blurred in the chaos and fogs of unconsciousness and forgetfulness, which in the opinion of Doctor Larrey, Napoleon's physician, were much more likely to end with death than with recovery. "He is of a nervous and bilious temperament—he won't recover."

Prince Andrei, together with other prisoners hopelessly wounded, was turned over to the care of the natives of the region.

1806

Austria, her capital fallen, her armies routed at Austerlitz, has been forced into a separate peace at the end of 1805. The other combatant armies are in winter quarters; Britain is active only on the sea, and the war in 1806 assumes the nature of an armed truce. But politically the prosecution of the war continues; Britain maintains a blockade directed against enemy and neutrals alike; Napoleon forbids trade between England and continental countries friendly to France. One of these, Prussia, at the end of 1806 breaks away, joins the coalition against Napoleon, and declares war. Napoleon contemptuously vanquishes Prussia in a month, occupies Berlin, and moves on against Russia.

Part Fourth

AT THE beginning of the year 1806, Nikolai Rostof went home on furlough. Denisof was also going to his home in Voronezh, and Rostof persuaded him to accompany him to Moscow and make him a visit. At the next-to-last post station, Denisof fell in with a comrade and drank three bottles of wine with him; and on the way to Moscow, in spite of the cradle holes on the road, he did not once wake up, but lay stretched out in the bottom of the hired sleigh next to Rostof, who, in proportion as they approached the city, grew more and more impatient.

"Faster! faster! oh, those intolerable streets, shops, fresh rolls, lanterns, cabdrivers!" thought Rostof, when having left their names at the city gates as visitors on furlough they had actually entered the city.

At last the sleigh drew up at an entrance at the right. Over his head, Rostof saw the well-known cornice with the peeling stucco, the front doorsteps, the curbstone. He leaped out before the sleigh had stopped, and rushed into the entry. There was still the same old door handle, the untidiness of which always annoyed the countess, as loose and as much askew as ever. In the anteroom burned a single tallow candle.

The old Mikhaila was asleep on the chest. Prokofi, the hall boy, who was so strong he could lift a coach, was sitting making felt overshoes out of odd bits of cloth. As the door opened he looked up, and his sleepy, indifferent expression suddenly changed to one of awe and even fright.

"Heavens and earth! The young count!" he cried, as soon as he recognized his young master. "How does this happen, my dear boy?"

And Prokofi, trembling with emotion, rushed through the door into the drawing-room, evidently with the intention of announcing the good news; but then, on second thought, he came back and fell on the young master's neck.

"All well?" asked Rostof, drawing away his arm.

"Yes! glory to God, glory to God!"

Rostof, entirely forgetting about Denisof, and not wishing anyone to announce his arrival, pulled off his fur coat and ran on tiptoe into the great dark drawing-room. Hardly had he entered the room before something flew out from one of the adjoining rooms like a tornado, hugged him and began to kiss him. Then a second and still a third creature came rushing out of a second and third side door; more embraces, more kisses, more exclamations, more tears of joy. He could not tell which was papa, or which was Natasha, or which was Petya. All were shouting, talking, and kissing him at one and the same time. Suddenly, he discovered that his mother was not among them.

"And here I knew nothing about it . . . Kolya darling! . . . my darling!"

"Here he is . . . ours again . . . my darling Kolya! . . . How you have changed! . . . There are no lights! Bring tea!"

"Now kiss me!"

"Sweetheart! . . . and me too!"

Sonya, Natasha, Petya, Anna Mikhailovna, Vera, the old count, all were embracing him; and the servants and the maids, crowding into the room, were exclaiming and oh-ing and ah-ing.

Petya, clinging to his legs, kept crying, "Me too!"

Natasha, after having thrown her arms around him and kissed him repeatedly all over his face, ran behind him, and seizing him by the tail of his coat, was jumping up and down like a kid in the same spot, and squealing at the top of her voice.

On all sides of him were eyes gleaming with tears of joy and love; on all sides were lips ready to be kissed.

Sonya, red as turkey twill, also held him by the hand, and, all radiant with affection, gazed into the eyes she had been so longing to see. Sonya was now just past sixteen, and was very pretty, especially at this moment of joyous, triumphant excitement. She looked at him without dropping her eyes, smiling, and almost holding her breath. He glanced at her gratefully, though he was waiting and looking for someone else. The old countess had not yet made her appearance.

And now steps were heard at the doorway—steps so quick that they could not be his mother's.

But it was his mother, in a gown he had never seen before, one that had been finished since he was gone. All made way for him, and he ran to her. When they met, she fell on his breast, sobbing. She could not lift her face, and only pressed it against the cold silver braid of his Hungarian coat. Denisof, coming into the room unobserved by anyone, stood there also, and as he looked at them, he wiped his eyes.

"Vasili Denisof, the fwiend of your son," said he, introducing himself to the count, who looked at him with a questioning expression.

"I beg your pardon. I know, I know," said the count, embracing Denisof and kissing him. "Nikolai wrote . . . Natasha, Vera, here is Denisof."

The same happy, enthusiastic faces were turned upon Denisof's shaggy figure, and crowded around him.

"My dear Denisof," screamed Natasha; and forgetting herself in her excitement and running to him, she threw her arms around him and kissed him. All were abashed at Natasha's behavior. Denisof blushed, but smiled, and taking Natasha's hand, kissed it.

The next morning the travelers slept till ten o'clock.

In the adjoining room there was a confusion of sabers, valises, sabretaches, opened trunks, muddy boots. Two pairs of boots, cleaned and with polished spurs, had just been brought up and set along the wall. Servants were carrying basins, hot water for shaving, and well-brushed clothes. There was an odor of tobacco and of men.

"Hey! Gwishka! bwing my pipe!" cried Vaska Denisof, in his hoarse voice. "Wostof, wouse you'self!"

Rostof, rubbing his sleepy eyes, lifted his disheveled head from his warm pillow.

"What is it? Late?"

"Late! It's after ten o'clock," cried Natasha's voice in answer to his question, and in the next room was heard the rustling of starched dresses and whispering and giggling of the girls.

"Kolya, come out in your dressing gown!" said Natasha's voice.

Rostof hastily put on his shoes and stockings, threw his dressing gown over his shoulders, and went out. Natasha had put on one of his spurred boots and was just slipping her foot into the other. Sonya, as he came in, was whirling around and trying to make a balloon of her skirts and then squat down. Both were dressed alike in new blue dresses, and were fresh, rosy, full of spirits. Sonya ran away, but Natasha, putting her arm in her brother's, drew him into the sitting room and the two began to talk. Natasha laughed at every word he said and every word she said, not because there was anything to laugh at but because she was happy, and because she had not the ability to restrain the joy that expressed itself in laughter.

"No, listen, you are now a grown-up man, aren't you? I am awfully glad you are my brother!" She touched his mustache. "I want to know what you men are like! Are you like us? No?"

"What made Sonya run away?" asked Rostof.

"Oh, that is a whole long story! I will tell you why some other time. Well, then, I will tell you now. You know that Sonya is my dearest friend, such a friend that I have burnt my arm for her sake. Just look here!" She turned up her muslin sleeve and showed him a red spot on her long, thin, delicate arm below the shoulder and considerably above the elbow, in a place where it would be hidden even by a ball dress.

"I burnt that spot to prove how much I loved her! I simply heated a ruler in the fire and held it there!"

As he sat in what had formerly been his classroom, on the sofa with the cushion on the arms, and gazed into Natasha's desperately lively eyes, Rostof again fell back into that old world of his childhood, of his home, which no one besides himself could understand, but which appeared to him replete with some of the sweetest joys of life. And the burning of the arm with the ruler, for the sake of exhibiting love, seemed to him not so senseless; he understood it, and was not surprised.

"So that was what you did? was that all?" he asked.

"We are such friends, such friends! That business of the ruler was a mere trifle; but we are to be friends forever. When she loves anyone it is forever; but I can't understand that; I forget right away."

"Well, what then?"

"Well, she loves you just as she does me." Natasha suddenly blushed. "Well, you remember what happened just before you went away. And so she says that you have forgotten all about it—she says: 'I shall love him always, but he must be left to his own free choice.' That is a fact, and isn't it splendid and noble of her? Now, isn't it? very noble! Isn't it?" asked Natasha, so seriously and so full of emotion that obviously what she said now she had spoken of before, with tears.

Rostof was lost in thought.

"I will not retract the words that I have given," said he. "And, besides, Sonya is so charming that anyone would be a fool to refuse such happiness."

"No, no!" cried Natasha, "she and I have already discussed that. We knew you would say so. But it is impossible, because, you understand, if you say so, you will consider yourself bound by your word; it would seem as if she had said this on purpose. It would seem as if you had married her under compulsion, and that wouldn't do at all."

Rostof saw that all this had been well decided by them. Sonya had struck him the evening before by her beauty. Today, when he had just caught a glimpse of her, she seemed to him still prettier. She was a charming girl of "sweet sixteen," evidently passionately in love with him; that he did not doubt for a single instant. "Why shouldn't I love her, and even marry her?" thought Rostof. "But just now there are so many pleasures and occupations still before me! . . . Yes, they have made a wise decision," said he to himself, "I must remain free."

"Well, all right," said he, after their talk. "But how glad I am to see you!"

he added. "Well, and tell me, have you changed toward Boris?" asked he.

"Oh, that's all nonsense," cried Natasha, laughing. "I don't trouble myself about him or anyone else, and I don't want to hear about it."

"Hear the girl! Then who is it that you . . . ?"

"I?" asked Natasha in her turn, and a smile of happiness spread over her face, "have you ever seen Duport?"

"No."

"Never seen Duport, the famous dancer! Then you can't understand. Well, that's what I am going to be!" Natasha picked up her skirt as dancers do, and, curving her arms, ran off a few steps, turned around, cut a caper, whirled one leg around the other, and standing on the very tips of her toes glided forward several feet. "See how I can pose! That's the way," said she. But she did not, could not, keep herself on tiptoe. "That's what I'm going to be. I am never going to marry anyone, but I am going to be a ballet dancer! But don't you tell anyone!"

Rostof laughed so loud and merrily that Denisof in his room really envied him.

When Rostof met Sonya in the drawing-room, he reddened. He did not know how to behave toward her. The evening before they had kissed each other, in the first joyful moment of meeting again; but today they both felt that it was impossible to do so; he imagined that everyone, his mother and his sisters, was looking inquisitively at him, and wondering how he would conduct himself toward her. But their eyes met and expressed the kisses that were not exchanged. Her glance seemed to ask forgiveness for having, through the mediation of Natasha, dared to remind him of his promise, and thanked him for his love. He, with his glance, in turn, thanked her for offering him his freedom and assured her that he would never cease to love her, since it was impossible not to love her.

I I

THIS YEAR the old count had plenty of money, having mortgaged all his possessions, and consequently Nikolai, who kept his own fast trotter, and wore the most stylish riding trousers of the latest cut, such as had never before been seen in Moscow, and likewise the most fashionable boots, with very pointed toes and little silver spurs, could spend his time very agreeably. It seemed to him that he had grown to be very much a man. His despair at not having been able to pass his examination in the catechism, his borrowing of money from Gavrilo to pay for a hired carriage, his clandestine kisses with Sonya, all came back to him as remembrances of a childhood from which he was now immeasurably separated. Now he was a lieutenant of hussars, in a silver-laced jacket, with the cross of St. George, and he could pit his own racer against well-known, experienced and respected amateurs. There was a lady of his acquaintance on the boulevard, with whom he liked to spend his evenings. He took the lead of the mazurka at the Arkharofs', discussed war with Field Marshal Kamiensky, was a habitué of the English Club, and was on intimate terms with a colonel of forty years to whom Denisof had introduced him.

Instead of growing nearer to Sonya, he rather drifted away from her. She was very pretty and sweet, and was evidently deeply in love with him; but he had reached that period of young manhood when there seem to be so many things to do that no time is left for this, and the young man is afraid of binding himself irrevocably and learns to prize his freedom, since it is necessary to him for other things. When he thought of Sonya during these days of his visit at home, he would say to himself: "Eh! there are many, many more as good as she is whom I have not had a chance to see as yet. I shall have time enough whenever I want to engage myself and fall in love, but now I will have none of it."

Moreover, it seemed to him that it was somehow derogatory to his manhood to spend his time in the society of the ladies. If he went to balls and into the society of women, he pretended that he did so against his will. Races, the English Club, junketing with Denisof, and visits *there*, were quite a different affair; such things were becoming to a gay young hussar!

About the middle of March, the old Count Ilya Rostof was occupied with the preparations for a dinner to be given at the English Club in honor of Prince Bagration.

The count in his dressing gown was walking up and down his drawing-room, giving orders to the club steward and the famous Feoktist, the old cook of the English Club, in regard to asparagus, fresh cucumbers, strawberries, veal and fish for the dinner to the prince. The cook and steward of the club listened to the count's orders with happy faces, because they knew of no easier person for whom to manage a dinner costing several thousand rubles, which need not be accounted for in detail.

"Now see here, put esparcette in the turtle soup, esparcette, you know."

"Must there be three kinds of cold dishes?" asked the cook.

The count pondered: "Certainly not less than three—mayonnaise salad, one . . ." he began to count them on his fingers.

"Do you wish me to order some large sturgeon?" interrupted the steward.

"What shall we do if there are no good ones? Yes, certainly—I came near forgetting. See here, we must have another entrée on the table. Oh, dear me!" he put his hands to his head. "Now who is going to get me flowers? . . . Mitenka! ah! Mitenka—hurry off, Mitenka!" he cried to the overseer, who came in at his call, "hurry off to our country house and tell Maksimka, the gardener, to get up the decorations. Tell him to have all the greenhouses stripped and the flowers sent up, well wrapped in cotton. Let him have two hundred flowerpots here by Friday."

Having given a profusion of various other orders, he was just going to the "little countess'" room to rest, but remembering some important item he had turned around, called back the steward and the cook, and began to give still further orders.

Just then in the doorway was heard the light step of a man, and the jingling of spurs, and the young count, handsome, ruddy-faced, with dark mustache, came into the room; it was evident that the lazy, easygoing life in Moscow agreed with him.

"Ah! my dear boy, how my head whirls!" said the old man, smiling at his son with a sort of humble expression. "Come now, if you'd only help me! We really must have some more singers. I shall have my own orchestra, but what would you think of getting the gypsies? Your military men like them."

"It's a fact, dear papa! I think that Prince Bagration, when he was getting ready for the Battle of Schöngraben, did not make such hard work of it as you are doing now," said the young man with a smile.

The old count pretended to be angry:

"Yes, you talk, just try it yourself!"

And the count turned to the cook, who with an intelligent and respectful face was looking on with friendly and flattering eyes at the father and son.

"That's the way with the young men, hey, Feoktist?" said he. "Always making sport of us old fellows!"

"That's so, your excellency, all they want is to have good things to eat and drink, but how it's got and served is no concern of theirs."

"That's it, that's it," cried the count, and gaily seizing his son's two hands, cried: "Now this is what I want, since I have you. Take the sleigh and pair and hurry off to Bezukhof's and tell him your father sent to ask for some fresh strawberries and pineapples. No one else has any. If he himself is not there, mind you, drive to the Razgulyai—Ipatka, the coachman, will know the way—and there find Ilyushka the gypsy, the one who danced and sang in a white coat at Count Orlof's, you remember, and bring him with you to me here."

"Shall I bring some of the gypsy girls with him too?" asked Nikolai, laughing. "There! there!"

At this moment, with noiseless steps, and with her indefatigable and anxious, and at the same time, sweet and Christian expression, which never deserted her, Anna Mikhailovna came into the room. In spite of the fact that Anna Mikhailovna every day discovered the count in his dressing gown, each time he was much abashed and offered her apologies for his costume.

"No matter, count, my dear," said she, blandly closing her eyes. "I myself am going to the Bezukhofs'. Pierre has come, and now we can get anything from his greenhouses. I have been wanting to see him. He sent me a letter from Boris. Glory to God!—Boris is now on the staff."

The count was delighted to have one part of his commission undertaken by Anna Mikhailovna, and bade her make use of the brougham.

"You tell Bezukhof to come. I will write him a note. How are he and his wife getting along?" asked the count.

Anna Mikhailovna rolled up her eyes, and her face expressed deep affliction.

"Ah, my dear! he's very unhappy," said she; "if it is true, what we have
heard, it is terrible! And could we have dreamed of such a thing, when we
rejoiced so in his happiness! And such a lofty, heavenly soul this young
Bezukhof is! Yes, I pity him from the bottom of my heart! and I mean to do
all in my power to give him consolation."

"Tell us, what is it?" asked both the Rostofs, elder and younger.

Anna Mikhailovna drew a deep sigh.

"Dolokhof, Marya Ivanovna's son," said she, in a mysterious whisper, "has,
so they say, absolutely compromised her. Pierre introduced him to her, took
him to his own house in Petersburg, and now . . . she came here and that
madcap fellow followed her," said Anna Mikhailovna, trying to express her
sympathy for Pierre, but involuntarily, by the inflections of her voice and by
the half-smile on her face, showing more sympathy for the "madcap fellow,"
as she called Dolokhof. "They say Pierre is broken-hearted about the situation."

"Well, then, be sure to tell him to come to the club. It will help to distract him. It will be a stunning banquet!"

III

On the next day, the fifteenth of March, at two o'clock in the afternoon,
two hundred and fifty members of the English Club and fifty guests were
assembled to meet their distinguished guest, Prince Bagration, the hero of
the Austrian campaign.

Just before the dinner began, Count Rostof presented his son to the
prince. Bagration, recognizing him, mumbled a few words, awkward and
incoherent, like everything else that he said that day. Count Rostof looked
around gleefully and proudly while Bagration was talking to his son.

Pierre sat opposite Dolokhof and Nikolai Rostof. He ate much and
greedily, and, as usual, drank much. But those who knew him intimately
observed that day that a great change had come over him. He said nothing
all during dinner; scowling and frowning, he looked about him, or, with
downcast eyes and a look of absolute abstraction, picked at his nose with
his finger. His face was gloomy and dismal. Apparently he did not see or
hear anything going on around him, and was absorbed in some disagreeable
and unsolvable problem.

This unsolvable problem that tormented him was caused by the hints of
the princess in Moscow in regard to Dolokhof's intimacy with his wife, and
by an anonymous letter received that very morning, wherein it was said, in
that dastardly mocking tone characteristic of anonymous letters, that his
spectacles did him very little good, and that his wife's disgraceful intimacy
with Dolokhof was a secret to him alone. Pierre resolutely refused to heed

the princess' insinuations or the letter, but it was terrible for him to look now at Dolokhof, sitting opposite him. Every time his glance fell accidentally upon Dolokhof's handsome, insolent eyes, he was conscious of something terrible and ugly arising in his soul, and he would quickly turn away. Involuntarily remembering all his wife's past, and her behavior toward Dolokhof, Pierre saw clearly that what was expressed so brutally in the letter might very well be true; might, at least, seem true, if it did not concern his wife! Pierre could not help recalling how Dolokhof, on being restored to his rank after the campaign, had returned to Petersburg and come to him. Taking advantage of the friendship arising from their former sprees together, Dolokhof had come straight to his house, and Pierre had taken him in and lent him money. Pierre remembered how Helene, with her set smile, had expressed her discontent at having Dolokhof living under their roof; and how Dolokhof had cynically praised his wife's beauty to him, and how, from that time forth until his coming to Moscow, he had not budged from their house.

"Yes, he is very handsome," thought Pierre, "I know him. In his estimation it would be admirable sport to besmirch my name and ridicule me, just for the very reason that I was doing so much for him, and taking care of him and helping him. I know, I understand, what spice it would add in his estimation to his villainy, if this were true! Yes, if it were true; but I don't believe it! I have no right to believe it, and I cannot!"

He remembered the expression Dolokhof's face had borne at times when he was engaged in his acts of deviltry, as for instance when they had tied the policeman to the bear and flung them into the river, or when, without any provocation, he had challenged men to fight duels, or shot the post-driver's horse dead with his pistol. This expression he had often noticed lately on Dolokhof's face.

"Yes, he's a bully," said Pierre to himself; "he would think nothing of killing a man; it is essential for him to think everyone is afraid of him; this must be pleasant to him. He must think I am afraid of him. And in fact I am afraid of him," thought Pierre, and again at these suggestions the horrible and ugly *something* arose in his mind.

Dolokhof, Denisof, and Rostof were still sitting opposite Pierre, and seemed to be very lively. Rostof was gayly chatting with his two friends, one of whom was a clever hussar, the other a well-known bully and madcap, and occasionally he glanced rather mockingly at Pierre, who had impressed him by the concentrated, abstracted and stolid expression of his countenance. Rostof looked at Pierre with a malevolent expression, in the first place because Pierre, in the eyes of a hussar like him, was merely a millionaire civilian, the husband of a pretty woman, and moreover was a *baba*—an old woman! in the second place, because Pierre, in his abstracted state of mind, did not recognize Rostof or return his bow. When they stood up to drink the toast to the emperor, Pierre was so lost in his thoughts that he forgot to get up with the others, and did not lift his wineglass.

"What's the matter with you?" shouted Rostof, his eyes flashing with righteous indignation as he looked at him. "Why don't you pay attention? the health of our sovereign, the emperor!"

Pierre, with a sigh, humbly got to his feet, drained his glass, and then, after they had all sat down, he turned to Rostof with his good-natured smile: "Ah! I did not recognize you," said he.

But Rostof was engaged in shouting "Hurrah!" so that this was lost on him. "Aren't you going to renew the acquaintance?" asked Dolokhof of Rostof.

"Curse the fool!"

"One must cawess a pwetty woman's husband," said Denisof. Pierre did not catch what was said, but he knew that they were talking about him. He reddened, and turned away.

"Well, now to the health of the pretty women!" said Dolokhof, and with a serious expression, though a smile lurked in the corners of his mouth, he lifted his glass to Pierre. "To the health of the pretty women, dear Pierre, and—their lovers!" he added.

Pierre, dropping his eyes, sipped his wine, without looking at Dolokhof or making any reply.

A lackey who was distributing copies of Kutuzof's cantata handed one to Pierre as one of the more distinguished guests. Pierre was going to take it, but Dolokhof leaned over, snatched the sheet from his hand, and began to read it. Pierre stared at Dolokhof; his pupils contracted; that terrible and ugly something that had been tormenting him all during dinner now arose in him and overmastered him. He leaned his heavy frame across the table.

"Don't you dare take it!" he cried.

Nesvitsky and his right-hand neighbor, hearing Pierre speak in such a tone of voice and seeing whom he was dealing with, were filled with alarm and hastily tried to calm him.

"That's enough!" . . . "Be careful!" . . . "Think what you're doing!" whispered anxious voices.

Dolokhof stared at Pierre with his bright, merry, insolent eyes, and with that smile of his that seemed to say, "This is what I like."

"I will not give it back," he said, measuring his words.

Pale, with twitching lips, Pierre snatched back the sheet of paper. "You . . . you . . . blackguard! . . . I will call you to account for this!" he cried, and pushing away his chair, rose from the table. At the very instant that he did this and pronounced these words, Pierre felt that the problem of his wife's guilt, which had been torturing him for the past twenty-four hours, was finally and definitely settled beyond a peradventure. He hated her, and the breach between them was widened irrevocably.

In spite of Denisof's urgency that Rostof should not get mixed up in this affair, Rostof consented to act as Dolokhof's second, and after dinner he arranged with Nesvitsky, Bezukhof's second, the conditions of the duel.

Pierre went home, and Rostof, together with Denisof and Dolokhof, stayed at the club till late, listening to the gypsies and the singers.

"Well, then, till tomorrow, at Sokolniki," said Dolokhof, taking his leave of Rostof on the club steps.

"And you are confident?" asked Rostof.

Dolokhof paused.

"Now, see here, I will give you in two words the whole secret of dueling. If you are going to fight a duel, and write your will and affectionate letters to your father and mother, if you get it into your head that you are going to be killed, then you are an idiot, and deserve to fall; but if you go with firm intention to kill him as quickly and certainly as you can, then you are all right, as our Kostroma bear driver told me. 'How can you help being afraid of the bear?' says he; 'yes, but when you once see him, your only fear is that he will get away.' Well, that's the way it is with me! Till tomorrow, my friend!"

Next morning at eight o'clock, Pierre and Nesvitsky drove to the woods of Sokolniki and found there Dolokhof, Denisof and Rostof waiting for them. Pierre had the aspect of a man entirely absorbed in his reflections and absolutely unaware of the affair before him. His countenance was haggard and yellow. He had evidently not slept the night before. He glanced around him vaguely and frowned as if he were blinded by the bright sun. Two considerations exclusively occupied him: his wife's guilt, of which, after his sleepless night, he had no longer the slightest doubt; and the innocence of Dolokhof, who had no reason to guard the honor of a stranger.

"Maybe I would have done the same thing if I had been in his place," said Pierre to himself; "I am perfectly certain that I would; why then this duel, this homicide? Either I shall kill him, or he will put a bullet through my head, in my elbow, or my knee. Can't I get out of it somehow, run away, hide myself somewhere?"

This thought came into his mind. But at the very instant that these suggestions were offering themselves to him, he, with his usual calm and absent-minded expression, which aroused the respect of those who saw him, was asking if all were ready and they would begin soon.

When all had been arranged, and the swords stuck upright in the snow to mark the limits for them to advance, and the pistols loaded, Nesvitsky went up to Pierre.

"I should not be doing my duty, count," said he, in a faltering voice, "or be worthy of the confidence and honor you confide in me at this moment, this most serious moment, if I did not tell you the whole truth. I consider that this affair has not sufficient reason, and does not warrant the shedding of blood. You were in the wrong, absolutely, you were in a passion . . ."

"Oh, yes, it was horribly foolish," said Pierre.

"Then allow me to offer your regrets, and I am sure that your opponent will be satisfied to accept your apologies," said Nesvitsky, who, like the other participants, and like all men in similar affairs, did not believe even now that it would actually come to a duel. "You know, count, that it is far more noble to acknowledge one's fault than to carry an affair to its irrevocable consequences. The insult was not wholly on one side. Let me confer."

"No! there's nothing to be said about it," said Pierre. "It's all the same to me. . . . Is everything ready?" he asked. "Only tell me where I am to stand and where to fire," he added, with an unnaturally sweet smile. He took the pistol and began to ask about the working of the trigger, for he had never before held a pistol in his hands, though he was unwilling to confess it. "Oh, yes, that's the way . . . I know . . . I had only forgotten," said he.

"No apologies, decidedly not," said Dolokhof to Denisof, who also on the other side proposed to effect a reconciliation, and he also went to the designated place.

The place selected for the duel was a small clearing in the fir woods, covered with what remained of the snow after the recent thaw, and about eighty paces from the road where the sledges had been left. The opponents stood about forty paces apart on the border of the clearing. The seconds, while measuring off the distance, had trampled down the deep, wet snow between the place where they stood and Nesvitsky's and Denisof's sabers, stuck upright ten paces apart to make the bounds. It was thawing, and the mist spread around; nothing could be seen forty paces away. For three minutes all had been ready, and still they hesitated about beginning; no one spoke.

"Well, begin," said Dolokhof.

"All right," said Pierre, still smiling as before.

It was a solemn moment. It was evident that the affair, which at first had been so trivial, could no longer be averted, but was now bound to take its course to the very end, irrespective of the will of the men. Denisof first went forward to the barrier and announced:

"As the adve'sewies have wefused to agwee, we may pwoceed. Take youah pistols, and at the word thwee, advance and fiah."

"Uh—one!—two!—thwee!" cried Denisof sternly, and stepped to one side. The two men advanced along the trodden path, coming closer and closer, their faces growing more and more distinct to each other in the fog. The antagonists had the right to fire at any moment before reaching the barrier. Dolokhof advanced slowly, not raising his pistol, but fastening his bright, glittering blue eyes on his opponent's face. His lips as usual wore what seemed like a smile.

"So it seems I can fire when I please," said Pierre to himself, and at the word "three" he advanced with quick strides, leaving the beaten path and pushing through the untrodden snow. He held the pistol in his right hand, out at arm's length, apparently afraid of killing himself with it. His left hand he strenuously kept behind his back because he felt such a strong desire to support his right arm with it, which he knew was out of the question.

After he had gone six steps and had left the trodden path, he looked down at his feet, then gave a quick glance at Dolokhof, and, pulling the trigger as he had been told to do, fired. Not anticipating such a loud report, Pierre jumped, and then, smiling at his own sensations, stood stock still. The smoke, made heavier by the misty atmosphere, prevented him from seeing anything at first; but there was no second report, as he had expected. All he could hear was Dolokhof's hasty steps, and then his form loomed up through the smoke. He was holding one hand to his left side; with the other he clutched the pistol, which he did not raise. His face was pale. Rostof had rushed up to him, and was saying something.

"N . . . no," hissed Dolokhof through his teeth. "No, I'm not done yet," and, making a few tottering, staggering steps toward the saber, he fell on the snow, near it. His left arm was covered with blood. He wiped it on his coat and supported himself with it. His face was pale and contracted, and a spasm passed over it.

"I beg of you . . ." began Dolokhof, but he could not speak coherently. "Please . . ." said he, with difficulty.

Pierre, hardly restraining his sobs, started to run to Dolokhof and was just crossing the line when Dolokhof cried, "Stop at the barrier;" and Pierre, realizing what he meant, paused near the saber. They were only ten paces apart. Dolokhof bent his head over to the snow, greedily ate a mouthful, lifted his head again, straightened himself up, tried to get to his feet, and sat down, in his effort to recover his equilibrium. He swallowed the icy snow and sucked it; his lips twitched; but he still smiled, and his eyes gleamed with concentrated hatred as he tried to collect his failing strength. He raised the pistol and tried to aim.

"Stand sidewise; protect yourself from the pistol," cried Nesvitsky.

"Pwotect you'self," instinctively cried Denisof, though he was the other's second.

Pierre, with his sweet smile of compassion and regret, helplessly dropping his arms and spreading his legs, stood with his broad chest exposed directly to Dolokhof, and looking at him mournfully. Denisof, Rostof, and Nesvitsky shut their eyes.

They heard the report, and simultaneously Dolokhof's wrathful cry.

"Missed!" cried Dolokhof, and lay back feebly on the snow, face down. Pierre clutched his temples, and turning back, went into the woods, trampling down the virgin snow and muttering incoherent words.

"Folly! Folly! Death! Lies!" he kept repeating, with scowling brows. Nesvitsky called him back and took him home.

Rostof and Denisof lifted the wounded Dolokhof. They put him in the sleigh, where he lay with closed eyes and without speaking or making any reply to their questions; but when they reached Moscow, he suddenly roused himself, and, with difficulty raising his head, seized the hand of Rostof, who was sitting next him. Rostof was struck by the absolutely changed and unexpectedly softened expression of Dolokhof's face.

"Well? How do you feel now?" asked Rostof.

"Wretched; but that is no matter. My dear," said Dolokhof, in a broken voice, "where are we? We are in Moscow, I know it. It's no matter about me, but I have killed her, killed her; she won't get over this. She won't survive."

"Who?" asked Rostof.

"My mother. My mother, my good angel, my adored angel, my mother," and Dolokhof burst into tears, pressing Rostof's hand. When he had grown a little calmer, he explained to Rostof that he lived with his mother, and that if his mother should see him dying, she would not survive it. He begged Rostof to go and break the news to her.

Rostof rode on ahead to attend to this, and to his great surprise discovered that Dolokhof, this insolent fellow, this bully Dolokhof, lived with his old mother and a hunchbacked sister, and was a most affectionate son and brother.

IV

PIERRE HAD rarely of late seen his wife alone. Both in Petersburg and in Moscow their house was constantly full of company. On the night following the duel he did not go to his bedroom, but, as was often the case, stayed in the vast room where his father, Count Bezukhof, had died.

He stretched himself out on the sofa with the idea of forgetting all that had taken place; but this he couldn't do. Such a tornado of thoughts, feelings, recollections, suddenly arose in his mind that he not only could not sleep, but could not keep still; and he was compelled to spring up from the sofa and walk the room with rapid strides. Now she seemed to come up before him as she was during the first few weeks after their marriage, with her bare shoulders and her languid, passionate eyes; and then immediately he would see Dolokhof by her side—Dolokhof, with his handsome, impudent, mocking face, as he had seen it at the banquet, and then the same face, pale, convulsed, and agonized, as it had been when he reeled and fell on the snow.

"What was it?" he asked himself. "I have killed her paramour! yes, I have killed my wife's paramour. Yes, that was it. Why? How did it come to this?"

"Because you married her," replied an inward voice.

"But wherein was I to blame?" he asked again.

"Because you married her without loving her; because you deceived yourself and her."

And then he vividly recalled the moment after the dinner at Prince Vasili's, when he had murmured those words, "I love you," that had come with so much difficulty.

"It was all from that. Even then I felt," said he to himself, "even then I felt that this was wrong, that I had no right to do it, and so it has proved."

He recalled their honeymoon, and reddened at the recollection. Extraordinarily vivid, humiliating, and shameful was the recollection of how one time, shortly after their marriage, he had gone in his silk dressing gown, at noon, from his bedroom to his library, and found there his head overseer, who, with an obsequious bow, glanced at Pierre's face and at his dressing gown, while a shadow of a smile passed over his face, as if he thereby expressed his humble sympathy in the happiness of his master.

"And yet how many times I have been proud of her, proud of her majestic beauty, of her social tact," he went on thinking, "proud of my house, where she received all Petersburg, proud of her inaccessibility and radiance. Yes, how proud I was of it all! then I thought that I did not understand her. How often, when pondering over her character, I said to myself that I was to blame, that I did not understand her, did not understand her habitual repose, self-satisfaction, and lack of all interests and ambition, and now I have found the answer in that terrible expression: she is a lewd woman. Now I have said to myself that terrible word, all has become clear!

"Anatol came to her to borrow some money, and kissed her on her naked shoulder. She did not let him have the money, but she was willing for him to kiss her. Her father, in jest, tried to make her jealous, and she, with her calm smile, replied that she was not so stupid as to be jealous: 'Let him do as he pleases,' said she about me. I asked her once if she saw no signs of approaching maternity. She laughed scornfully and replied that she was not such a fool as to want children, and that I should never get any children by her."

Then he recalled the coarseness and frankness of her thoughts, the vulgarity of the expressions that came natural to her, in spite of her education in the highest aristocratic circles. "I am no such fool," "Go try it on yourself," "Go take a walk," and similar slang she was fond of using.

Pierre, witnessing her success in the eyes of old and young, men and women, had often found it hard to understand why he did not love her.

"Yes, and I have never really loved her," said Pierre to himself. "I knew that she was a lewd woman," he kept repeating to himself, "but I did not dare to acknowledge it to myself. And now there is Dolokhof sitting in the snow and trying to smile, and dying maybe, and responding to my repentance with pretended bravado!"

Pierre was a man who, notwithstanding his affectionate nature, which some would call weakness of character, would never seek a confidant for his troubles. He worked out his sufferings by himself.

"She is to blame, the only one to blame for all," said he to himself. "But what was back of that? That I married her, that I said to her 'I love you,' which was a lie, and even worse than a lie," said he to himself. "I am to blame and must suffer . . . what? The besmirching of my name? the unhappiness of my life? eh! that's all nonsense," he continued, "the disgrace to my name and honor, all that is conditional, absolutely independent of me."

At night he summoned his valet and ordered him to pack up in readiness to go to Petersburg. He could not imagine himself having anything more to say to her. He had decided to take an early departure the next day, leaving her a letter in which he should explain his intention of living apart from her forevermore.

The next morning, when the valet, bringing him his coffee, came into the room, Pierre was lying on an ottoman asleep, with an open book in his hand.

He aroused himself and looked around for some time with a startled expression, wholly unable to understand where he was.

"The countess commanded me to ask if your excellency were at home," said the valet.

But before Pierre had time to decide what answer to give, the countess herself, in a morning gown of white satin embroidered in silver, and her hair dressed in the simplest style—two enormously long braids wound twice, *en diadème*, around her graceful head—came into the room calmly and majestically; only on her marble forehead, which was a little too prominent, there was a deep frown of fury. With complete self-restraint, she did not say a word in the valet's presence. She had heard of the duel and had come to speak about it. She waited until the valet had set down the coffee and left the room. Pierre looked at her timidly over his spectacles, and, like a hare surrounded by dogs, which lays back its ears and crouches motionless before its enemies, so he also pretended to take up his reading again; but he was conscious that this was a senseless and impossible thing to do, and again he looked at her. She did not sit down, but with a scornful smile stared at him, waiting until the valet should be out of the room.

"Well, now, what's this latest? What have you been doing? I demand an answer!" said she, sternly.

"I . . . what have I . . . ?" stammered Pierre.

"Playing the hero, hey? Come now, answer me; what about this duel? What did you mean to imply by it? What? I demand an answer!"

Pierre turned heavily on the sofa, opened his mouth, but could not make a sound.

"If you won't answer, then I will tell you," continued Helene. "You believe everything that is told you: you were told," Helene laughed, "that Dolokhof was my lover," said she in French, with her uncompromising, explicit manner of speech, pronouncing the word *amant* like any other word. "And you believed it! And what have you proved by it? What have you proved by this duel? That you are a fool! And that's what everyone calls you! What will be the result of it? This!—that you have made me the laughingstock of all Moscow; this! that everyone will say that you, while in a drunken fit, and not knowing what you were about, challenged a man of whom you were jealous without any reason"—Helene kept raising her voice and growing more and more excited—"a man superior to you in every sense of the word . . ."

"Hm . . . hm," bellowed Pierre, scowling, but not looking at her or stirring.

"And why did you believe he was my lover? Why was it? Because I liked his society? If you had been brighter and more agreeable, I would have preferred yours."

"Do not speak to me, I beg you," whispered Pierre, hoarsely.

"Why shouldn't I speak to you? I have a right to speak, and I tell you up and down that it's rare to find a woman with a husband like you who doesn't console herself with lovers, and that is a thing I haven't done," said she.

Pierre started to say something, looked at her with strange eyes whose expression she could not understand, and again threw himself back. At that moment he was suffering physical pain; his chest was oppressed, and he could not breathe. He knew that he had to do something to put an end to his torment, but what he wanted to do was too horrible.

"We had better part," he exclaimed in a broken voice.

"By all means, part, provided only you give me enough," said Helene. "Part! That's nothing to scare one!"

Pierre sprang from the sofa and staggered toward her.

"I will kill you!" he cried, and seizing from the table a marble slab, with a force he had never before possessed, rushed toward her brandishing it in the air.

Helene's face was filled with horror; she screamed and sprang away from him. His father's nature suddenly became manifest in him. Pierre experienced the rapture and fascination of frenzy. He flung down the marble, breaking it in fragments, and with raised arms flew at her crying, "Away!" with such a terrible voice that it rang through the whole house and filled everyone with horror. God knows what Pierre would have done at that moment if Helene had not escaped from the room.

At the end of a week, Pierre had given to his wife power of attorney for the control of all his Great Russian possessions, which amounted to a large half of his property, and returned alone to Petersburg.

V

Two months had elapsed since news of the Battle of Austerlitz and the death of Prince Andrei had been received at Lisiya Gori, and in spite of all the letters sent through the diplomatic service, and all inquiries, his body had not been recovered and his name was not on the list of prisoners. A week after the receipt of the newspapers which informed the old prince of the Battle of Austerlitz, a letter came from Kutuzof, who announced the fate that had befallen his son.

"Your son," wrote Kutuzof, "fell before my eyes at the head of his regiment with the standard in his hands, like a hero worthy of his father and his fatherland. To the universal regret of all the army, including myself, it is as yet uncertain whether he is alive or dead. I comfort myself with the hope that your son is still alive, for, in the contrary case, he would certainly have been mentioned among the officers found on the field of battle, the list of whom was brought me under flag of truce."

Receiving this news late in the afternoon when he was alone in his study, the old prince as usual went the next day to take his morning promenade, but he had nothing to say to the overseer, the gardener, or the architect, and though his countenance was lowering, there was no outbreak of wrath.

When, at the accustomed time, Princess Maria went to him, he was standing at his bench and driving his lathe, but he did not glance up at her as usual when she entered the room.

"Ah! Princess Maria," suddenly said he, in an unnatural tone, and threw down his chisel. The wheel continued to revolve from the impetus. Princess Maria long remembered this dying whir of the wheel, which was associated for her with what followed. Princess Maria approached him and looked into his face, and suddenly something seemed to tug at her heartstrings. Her eyes ceased to see clearly. By her father's face, which was not sorrowful or downcast, but wrathful and working unnaturally, she saw that now, now some terrible misfortune was threatening to overwhelm her, a misfortune worse than any in life, more irreparable and incomprehensible, such a misfortune as she had never yet experienced—the death of one she loved.

"Father! Andrei!" said the princess, and she who was ordinarily so clumsy and awkward became endowed with such inexpressible charm of grief and self-forgetfulness that her father could not endure her glance, and, with a sob, turned away.

"I have had news. He's not among the prisoners, he's not on the list of the dead. Kutuzof has written me," he cried in a shrill voice, as if he desired by this cry to drive the princess away. "He is killed!"

The princess did not fall; she did not even feel faint. She was pale to begin with, but when she heard these words her face altered and a light seemed to gleam in her beautiful lustrous eyes. Something like joy, a super-human joy independent of the sorrows and joys of this world, took the place of the violent grief that filled her heart. She forgot all her fear of her father and went up to him, took him by the hand, drew him to her, and threw her arm around his thin, sinewy neck.

"Father!" said she, "do not turn away from me; let us weep together!"

"Villains! Scoundrels!" cried the old man, averting his face from her. "To destroy the army, to destroy men! What for? Go, go and tell Lisa."

The princess fell back feebly in the armchair near her father, and burst into tears. She could now see her brother as he looked at the moment when he bade her and Lisa farewell, with his affectionate and at the same time rather haughty face. She could see him as he tenderly and yet scornfully hung the medallion round his neck. Had he come to believe? Had he repented of his unbelief? Was he yonder now, yonder in the mansions of eternal calm and bliss? These were the questions that filled her thoughts.

"Father, tell me how it happened?" said she, through her tears.

"Go, go; he was killed in that defeat where the best men of Russia and Russian glory were led out to sacrifice. Go, Princess Maria. Go and tell Lisa. I will follow."

When Princess Maria left her father, she found the little princess sitting at her work with that expression of inward calm and happiness peculiar to women in her condition. She looked up as her sister-in-law came in. It was evident that her eyes did not see Princess Maria, but rather were profoundly searching into the tremendous and blessed mystery that was taking place within her.

"Maria," said she, turning from her embroidery frame and leaning back, "let me have your hand."

She took the princess' hand and laid it just below her heart. Her eyes smiled with anticipation; the short, downy lip was raised in a happy, childlike smile.

Several times in the course of the morning Princess Maria attempted to break the news to her sister-in-law, and each time she had to weep. These tears, the cause for which the little princess could not understand, alarmed her, unobservant as her nature was. Before dinner the old prince came into her room and went right out again without saying a word; she was always afraid of him, but now his face was so disturbed and stern that she gazed at Princess Maria, then fell into a brown study, with her eyes, as it were, turned inward with that expression so characteristic of pregnant women, and suddenly burst into tears.

"Have you heard anything from Andrei?" she asked.

"Nothing," replied Princess Maria, letting her lustrous eyes rest unflinchingly on her sister-in-law.

She had made up her mind not to tell her, and had persuaded her father to conceal the terrible tidings from her until her confinement, which was due before many days. Princess Maria and the old prince, each according to his own nature, bore and hid their grief. The old prince was not willing to indulge in hopes; he had made up his mind that Prince Andrei was killed, and, although he sent an official to Austria to make diligent search for traces of his son, he commanded him to order in Moscow a gravestone to be erected in his garden, and he told everyone that his son was dead. He himself aged rapidly; he still carried out the rigorous routine of his life, but his strength failed him; he took shorter walks, ate less, slept less, and each day grew weaker. Princess Maria still hoped. She prayed for her brother as if he were alive, and all the time was on the lookout for news of his return.

VI

It was one of those March nights when winter seems determined to return and scatters with rage and despair the last snows and gusts of wind. A relay of horses had been sent along the highway to meet the German doctor from Moscow, who was expected momentarily, and horsemen with lanterns were sent out to the junction of the crossroad to guide him safely through the pitfalls and watery hollows.

Princess Maria was sitting in perfect silence, with her lustrous eyes fastened on her old nurse's wrinkled face, every line of which she knew so well; on the little tuft of gray hair that had escaped from under her kerchief and on the loose flesh hanging under her chin.

Nyanya Savishna, with her unfinished stocking in her hand, was telling in a low voice, without heeding her own words, the story that she had told a hundred times about the late princess, and how she had been delivered of Princess Maria in Kishenef, with an old Moldavian peasant woman for a midwife.

"God is merciful; doctors are never needed," she was saying.

Suddenly a gust of wind beat violently against the window frame (it was always a whim of the princess to have the double windows taken off from at least one of the windows in each room as soon as the larks made their appearance) and burst the carelessly pushed bolt, while a draft of cold air laden with snow shook the silken curtains and snuffed the light. The princess shuddered. The old nurse, laying down her stocking, went to the window and, leaning out, tried to shut it again. The cold wind fluttered the ends of her kerchief and the gray locks of her disheveled hair.

"Princess! someone's coming up the drive," cried she, getting hold of the window, but not closing it, "with lanterns! It must be the doctor!"

"Ah! glory to God!" exclaimed Princess Maria. "I must go and meet him; he won't be able to speak Russian."

Princess Maria wrapped her shawl around her and hastened down to meet the newcomer. A voice that struck her as strangely familiar was saying something.

"Thank God—" said the voice, "and my father?"

"He has gone to bed," replied the voice of Demyan, the steward, who had by this time come down.

"It is Andrei!" said the princess to herself. "No, it cannot be! It would be too extraordinary," she thought, and at the very moment this thought occurred to her, on the landing where stood the servant with the candle, appeared Prince Andrei's form, enveloped in a fur coat, the collar all powdered with snow. Yes, it was he; but pale and thin, and with an altered and strangely gentle but anxious expression. He ran up the stairs and clasped his sister in his arms.

"You didn't receive my letter?" he asked, and not waiting for her reply, which, indeed, he would not have heard, for the princess was too moved to speak, he turned back, and joined by the obstetrician, who had come with him (he had overtaken him at the last post station), with hasty steps flew up the stairs again and again embraced his sister.

"What luck!" he cried, "dear Maria!" and flinging off his coat and boots, he went to his wife's room.

The little princess, in a white cap, was lying on the pillows. (For the moment she was a little easier.) Her dark locks fell in disorder over her flushed cheeks, wet with perspiration; her rosy, fascinating mouth, with its downy upper lip, was open, and she wore a smile of joy.

Prince Andrei went into the room and paused in front of her, at the foot of the couch on which she lay. Her brilliant eyes, looking at him with childish trepidation and anxiety, rested on him without change of expression. *I love you all; I haven't done anyone any harm; why must I suffer so? Help me!* her expression seemed to say.

She saw her husband, but seemed to have no comprehension of the significance of his appearance just at this moment.

Prince Andrei went round to the side of the sofa and kissed her on the forehead.

"My darling heart—my love," he said. He had never called her by this endearing term before. "God is merciful . . ."

She looked at him with a questioning, childishly offended expression.

I expected help from you, and none comes, none comes! her eyes seemed to say. She was not surprised at his coming; she did not even realize that he had come. His appearance had nothing to do with her agony and the assuagement of it.

The obstetrician entered the room. Prince Andrei went out, and meeting his sister he again joined her. They began to talk in a whisper, but the conversation was constantly interrupted by silences. They kept waiting and listening.

"Come, my friend," said Princess Maria.

He began to pace up and down the room. The cries had ceased; a few seconds more passed, when suddenly a terrible scream—it could not be his wife's, she could not shriek like that—rang through the next room. Prince Andrei hastened to the door; this cry ceased; a baby's wailing was heard.

"What have they brought a baby in there for?" was Prince Andrei's query at first. "A baby? What baby? . . . Why a baby there? . . . Or can my baby have been born?"

Then he suddenly realized all the joyful significance of this cry; tears choked him, and leaning both his elbows on the window seat, he wept and sobbed as children weep.

The door opened. The doctor, with his shirt sleeves rolled up, without his coat, pale, and with trembling jaw, came from the room. Prince Andrei went to him, but the doctor looked at him with a strange expression of confusion, and without saying a word passed by him. A woman came running out, but, when she saw Prince Andrei, stopped short on the threshold. He went into his wife's room.

She was dead, lying in the same position in which he had seen her five minutes before, and notwithstanding the fixity of her eyes and the pallor of her cheeks, that charming little childish face, with the lip shaded with dark hairs, wore the same expression as before.

I love you all, and I have done no one any harm, and what have you done to me? said her lovely face, pitifully pale in death. In the corner of the room a small red object was screaming and wailing.

Two hours later Prince Andrei, with noiseless steps, went to his father's study. The old prince had already been informed of everything. He was standing near the door, and as soon as it was thrown open, the old man, without speaking, flung his rough, aged hands around his son's neck and held him as in a vise and sobbed like a child.

Three days later the little princess was buried and Prince Andrei went up the steps to the coffin to take his last farewell. And there also in the coffin lay the same face, though with closed eyes.

Ah, what have you done to me? it all seemed to say. Prince Andrei felt that his heartstrings were torn within him, that he had done a wrong that could never be repaired or forgotten. He could not weep. The old prince also came and kissed her waxen hand, placidly folded on her breast, and to him her face seemed to say: *Ah! and why have you done this to me?* And the old man, after looking into her face, abruptly turned away.

Then, five days later, they christened the baby Prince Nikolai Andreyitch. The wet nurse held up the swaddling clothes against her chin while the priest, with a goose quill, annointed with holy oil the infant's wrinkled little pink palms and soles. His grandfather, who acted as sponsor, with tottering steps, and afraid of dropping him, carried the little prince around the tin-lined font, and handed him over to his godmother, Princess Maria. Prince Andrei, in deadly apprehension lest they should drop the child, sat in the next room waiting for the conclusion of the sacrament. He looked joyfully at his baby when the nurse brought it to him, and nodded his head with great satisfaction when the nurse confided to him that the lump of wax with some of the infant's hairs on it, when thrown into the font, did not sink, but floated.

VII

THE PART PLAYED by Rostof in the duel between Dolokhof and Bezukhof was ignored through the old count's efforts, and the young man, instead of being cashiered as he anticipated, was appointed aide to the governor-general of Moscow. As a result, he was unable to go to the country with the rest of the family, but was kept in Moscow all summer, engaged in his new duties. Dolokhof recovered, and he and Rostof became great friends during the time of his convalescence.

In the autumn the Rostof family returned to Moscow. Early in the winter Denisof also came back and stayed with the Rostofs. The first months of this winter of 1806, which Nikolai Rostof spent in Moscow, could not have been happier or gayer for him and for all his family. Nikolai brought home with him many young men. Vera was a pretty young lady of twenty summers. Sonya was just sixteen, and had all the charm of an unfolding flower. Natasha, half child and half woman, at one moment was full of innocent merriment, at the next showing all the wiles of a young lady.

The house of the Rostofs at this time seemed to be full of the peculiar charm characteristic of homes where there are very pretty and very young ladies. Every young man who came there and saw these bright, impressionable, girlish faces, smiling apparently from sheer happiness, and the merry running to and fro; and heard that continual chatter of girlish voices, light, illogical, kindly to everyone, ready for anything and full of hope; and listened to these inconsequential sounds, now of singing, now of instrumental music, must have experienced the very same feeling of anticipation of love and promised happiness that the young people of the Rostof household themselves experienced.

Among the young men, and one of the first whom Rostof introduced at home, was Dolokhof, and everyone, with the exception of Natasha, was pleased with him. She almost quarreled with her brother about Dolokhof. She insisted that he was a bad man, that Pierre was in the right in his duel with Dolokhof, and the other in the wrong; and that he was disagreeable and insincere.

"There's nothing for me to understand," cried Natasha, with stubborn self-will; "he is bad and lacks sensitivity. Now, for instance, I like your Denisof; he may be a spendthrift, and all that, but still I like him, and I certainly understand him. I don't know how to express it to you, but everything Dolokhof does has some ulterior object. And do you know, he's in love with Sonya?"

"What nonsense!"

"I'm certain of it, you can see for yourself."

Natasha's prognostication was justified. Dolokhof, though he did not like the society of ladies, had begun to be a frequent visitor at the Rostofs', and the reason for his visits was quickly discovered, though no one ventured to remark upon it. He came on account of Sonya. And Sonya, though she would never have dared to acknowledge such a thing, knew it very well, and every time that Dolokhof was announced blushed as red as a poppy.

It was obvious that this strong, strange man was coming under the irresistible influence of the gracious, dark-eyed girl, who all the time was in love with someone else.

On the third day of the Christmas holidays Nikolai dined at home—a thing he had rarely done of late. It was a sort of farewell dinner, as he and Denisof were going to start for their regiments after Epiphany. There were about twenty at the table, among them Dolokhof and Denisof.

Never at the Rostofs' had that enchanting tremor of passion and that mood of love been felt so strongly as during these days of the Christmastide. "Seize these moments of happiness; let yourself drift into love; become enamored yourself. This is the only genuine bliss in the world; everything else is dross. And with this alone all of us here are exclusively occupied," said this mood.

Nikolai, as always, tired out two spans of horses and yet had not had time enough to go to all the places where he was needed and summoned; he came home just before dinnertime. As soon as he came in, he noticed and felt this atmosphere charged with the electrical tension of love, but more especially he remarked a strange embarrassment which seemed to exist among several of those gathered in the drawing-room.

"There must be something brewing," he said to himself, and he was still further confirmed in this impression by the fact that Dolokhof took his departure immediately after dinner. He called Natasha to him and asked what the matter was.

"And I was just looking for you," exclaimed Natasha, running to him. "I told you so, but you would not believe me," said she triumphantly. "He has proposed to Sonya."

Little as Sonya had occupied Nikolai's thoughts during these last weeks, still he felt a sort of pang when he learned this. Dolokhof was a suitable, and in some respects a brilliant, match for the dowerless orphan Sonya. From the old countess' standpoint, and that of society, it was simply madness to refuse him. Therefore, Nikolai's first feeling on hearing this piece of news was indignation against the girl.

He had it on his tongue's end to say, "And it is an excellent thing, of course, for her to forget her old promises and accept this first proposal," but before he spoke, Natasha went on:

"And can you imagine it, she refused him?—absolutely refused him! She told him that she loved someone else," she added, after a moment's silence.

"Yes, and could my Sonya have done anything else!" thought Nikolai.

"In spite of all mama's arguments, she refused him, and I know that she won't change her decision if she said that."

"And mama tried to persuade her?" he asked reproachfully.

"Yes," said Natasha. "And now, Kolya darling—and don't be vexed—but I know you will never marry her. I am sure of it, God knows why, but I am perfectly certain that you will never marry her."

"Well, you know nothing about it at all," said Nikolai. "But I must have a little talk with her. How charming she is! our Sonya," he added, with a smile.

"Charming! indeed she is. I will send her to you."

And Natasha, kissing her brother, ran away.

In a moment Sonya came in, alarmed and abashed, as if she had been doing something wrong. Nikolai went to her and kissed her hand. This was the first opportunity they had enjoyed for some time of being alone together and talking about their love.

"Sonya," said he, timidly, and then growing more and more confident. "If you have seen fit to refuse an offer not only so brilliant, but so very advantageous . . . he is a splendid, noble fellow; and he is a friend of mine."

Sonya interrupted him.

"I have already refused him," said she, hastily.

"If you have refused him for my sake, then I am afraid that I . . ."

Sonya again interrupted him. She looked at him with beseeching, frightened eyes.

"Nicholas, don't speak of that, please," said she.

"But I must. Maybe it is unbounded conceit on my part, but it is better to speak. If you have refused him for my sake, then I ought to tell you the whole truth. I love you, I think, more than all . . ."

"That is all I want," said Sonya, with a sigh.

"No! I have fallen in love a thousand times, and I shall fall in love again, and I shall never find anyone so friendly, so true, so lovely as you. But then, I am young. Mama does not approve of this. So, then, simply I can't make any promises. And I beg of you to reconsider Dolokhof's proposal," said he, finding it hard to speak his friend's name.

"Don't mention such a thing. I have no desires at all. I love you as if you were my brother, and shall always love you, and that is quite enough for me."

"You are an angel! I am not worthy of you, but what I am afraid is that I might give you a wrong impression!" Nikolai once more kissed her hand.

VIII

For two days Rostof had not seen Dolokhof at his house, or found him at home; on the third day he received a note from him:

"As I intend never to visit your house again, for reasons which you may appreciate, and as I am about to rejoin my regiment, I am going to give a farewell supper this evening for my friends. Come to the English hotel."

At ten o'clock that evening, after the theater, where he had been with Denisof and his family, Rostof repaired to the place Dolokhof had designated. He was immediately shown into the handsomest room of the hotel, which Dolokhof had engaged for the occasion. A score of men were gathered around the table, at the head of which sat Dolokhof between two candles. There was a pile of gold and bills on the table, and Dolokhof was keeping the bank.

Since Dolokhof's proposal and Sonya's refusal, Nikolai had not seen him, and he felt a slight sense of confusion at the thought of their meeting. Dolokhof's keen, cold eyes met Nikolai's the moment he entered the room, as if he had been waiting for him for some time.

"We have not met for several days," said Dolokhof, "thank you for coming. Here, I will only finish this hand. Ilyushka and his chorus are coming."

"I have called at your house," said Rostof, reddening.

Dolokhof made no answer.

"You may bet," he said.

Rostof recalled a strange conversation he had once had with Dolokhof. "Only fools play on chance," had been Dolokhof's remark at the time.

"But perhaps you are afraid to play with me," said Dolokhof now, as if he read Rostof's thought, and he smiled.

By his smile Rostof could plainly see that he was in the same frame of mind as he had been at the time of the dinner at the club, or, one might say, at any of those times when Dolokhof, bored by the monotony of life, felt the necessity of escaping from it by some strange and outrageous action. Rostof felt ill at ease. He racked his brain, but was unable to find an appropriate repartee for Dolokhof's words. But before he had a chance to reply, Dolokhof, looking straight into Rostof's face, said slowly, with deliberate intervals between the words, so that all might hear:

"Do you remember you and I were talking once about gambling? . . . 'It's a fool who is willing to play on chance. One ought to play a sure hand,' but I am going to try it."

"Try the chance, or the sure thing—I wonder which," thought Rostof.

"Well, you'd better not play," he added, and springing the freshly opened pack of cards, he cried: "Bank, gentlemen!"

Pushing the money forward, Dolokhof prepared to start the bank. Rostof took a seat near him, and at first did not play. Dolokhof glanced at him.

"What? Won't you take a hand?" and strangely enough Nikolai felt it incumbent upon him to select a card and stake an insignificant sum on it, and thus begin to play.

"I have no money with me," he said.

"I will trust you."

Rostof staked five rubles on his card and lost; he staked again, and again he lost. Dolokhof took Rostof's stake ten times running.

"Gentlemen," said he, after he had been keeping the bank some time, "I beg of you to lay your stakes on the cards, otherwise I may become confused in the accounts."

One of the players ventured the hope that he was to be trusted.

"I trust you, certainly, but I am afraid of getting the accounts mixed. I beg of you to lay your money on the cards," replied Dolokhof. "Don't you worry, you and I will settle our accounts afterwards," he added, turning to Rostof.

The game went on; the servant kept filling their glasses with champagne. All Rostof's cards failed to be matched, and his losses amounted to eight hundred rubles. He was just writing down on the back of a card "eight hundred rubles" but, as it happened that at that moment a glass of champagne was handed him, he hesitated, and once more staked the sum that he had been risking all along, that is, twenty rubles.

"Make it that," said Dolokhof, though he was apparently not looking at Rostof. "You'll win it back all the quicker. The others win but you keep losing. Or are you afraid of me?" he insisted.

Rostof acquiesced, staked the eight hundred which he had written down on a seven of hearts with a bent corner, which he had picked up from the floor. He remembered it well enough afterwards. He laid down this seven of hearts, after writing on the broken part, the figures "eight hundred rubles" in large, distinct characters; he drank the glass of foaming champagne handed him by the waiter, smiled at Dolokhof's words, and, with a sinking at the heart, while hoping that a seven would turn up, watched the pack of cards in Dolokhof's hands.

The gain or loss dependent on this seven of hearts would have very serious consequences for Rostof. On the preceding Sunday, Count Rostof had given his son two thousand rubles, and, although he generally disliked to speak of his pecuniary difficulties, had told him that he could not have any more till May, and therefore begged him, for this once, to be rather economical. Nikolai had told him that two thousand rubles would be ample, and gave him his word of honor not to ask for any money till spring.

And now, out of that sum, only twelve hundred rubles were left. Of course that seven of hearts, if he lost on it, would signify not only the loss of sixteen hundred rubles, but also the necessity of breaking his word to his father. With a sinking of the heart, therefore, he watched Dolokhof's hands, and said to himself:

"Now let him hurry up and give me this card, and I will put on my cap and go home to supper with Denisof, Natasha, and Sonya, and truly I will never, as long as I live, take a card into my hands again."

At that instant his home life, his romps with Petya, his talks with Sonya, his duets with Natasha, his game of piquet with his father, and even his peaceful bed in his home on the Povarskaya, came to him with such force and vividness and attraction that it seemed to him like an inestimable bliss which had passed and been destroyed forever. He could not bring himself to believe that stupid chance, by throwing the seven of hearts to the right rather than to the left, might deprive him of all this happiness and plunge him into the abyss of a wretchedness never before experienced, and of which he had no adequate idea. It could not be so, and yet, with a fever of expectation, he watched every motion of Dolokhof's hands. Those coarse reddish hands, with heavy knuckles and hairy wrists showing from under his shirt cuffs, laid down the pack of cards, took up the champagne glass that had been handed him, and put his pipe in his mouth.

"And so you are not afraid to play with me?" repeated Dolokhof, and, as if for the purpose of telling some humorous story, he laid down the cards, leaned back in his chair, and with a smile deliberately began to speak:

"Yes, gentlemen, I have been told that there is a report current in Moscow that I am a sharper, and so I advise you to be on your guard against me."

"Come now, deal," said Rostof.

"Oh! these Moscow old ladies!" exclaimed Dolokhof, and with a smile he took up the cards.

"O-o-oh!" almost screamed Rostof, clasping his head with both hands. The seven he needed already lay on top, the very first card in the pack. He had lost more than he could pay.

"Now, don't ruin yourself!" said Dolokhof, giving Rostof a passing glance, and proceeded to deal the cards.

IX

During the next hour and a half the majority of the gamblers watched idly their own play. The whole game centered on Rostof alone. Instead of the sixteen hundred rubles against him there was already a long column of figures which he had reckoned to be at least ten thousand rubles, and which he now vaguely imagined to be perhaps fifteen thousand. In reality the sums added up to more than twenty thousand.

Dolokhof no longer listened to stories or told them himself; he watched each motion of Rostof's hands, and occasionally cast hasty glances at the paper containing Rostof's indebtedness. He had made up his mind to keep playing until Rostof's losses reached forty-three thousand rubles. He had selected this number because forty-three represented the sum of his and Sonya's ages. Rostof, supporting his head in both hands, sat in front of the table, now all written over, wet with wine, and littered with cards. One painful impression filled his mind: those wide-jointed, red hands with the hairy wrists, those hands which he loved and also hated, held him in their power.

"Six hundred rubles, ace, nine-spot . . . impossible to win it back . . . and how gay it would be at home!—Knave, five—it cannot be.—And why is he treating me so?" said Rostof to himself, mingling his thoughts and recollections.

Sometimes he would stake a large sum and Dolokhof would refuse to accept it and himself name the stake. Nikolai would submit, and then pray God, just as he had prayed on the battlefield; then it would occur to him that perhaps the first card he might draw from the pile of rejected cards on the table would save him; then he would count up the number of buttons on his jacket and select a card with the same number for a stake double what he had already lost; then, again, he would look for aid to the other players, or glance into Dolokhof's face, now so cold, and try to read what was passing in his mind.

"Of course, he knows what this loss means for me. It cannot be that he wants me to lose like this. For he was my friend. For I loved him . . . But of course it isn't his fault; how can he help it if luck favors him? And neither am I to blame," said he to himself. "I have done nothing wrong. Have I killed anyone, or insulted anyone, or wished anyone evil? Why, then, this horrible misfortune? And when did it begin? It was only such a short time ago that I came to this table with the idea of winning a hundred rubles to buy that jewel box for mama's birthday, and then go home. I was so happy, so free from care, so gay! And I did not realize then how happy I was! When did it all end, and when did this new, this horrible state of things begin? What does this change signify? And here I am, just the same as before, sitting in the same place at this table, choosing and moving the same cards, and looking at those heavy-knuckled, dexterous hands. When did this take place and what is it that has taken place? I am well, strong, and just the same as I was, and in the selfsame place! No, it cannot be! Surely this cannot end in such a way!" His face was flushed, he was in a sweat, though it was not warm in the room. And his face was terrible and pitiable, especially because of his futile efforts to seem composed.

The list of his losses was nearing the fatal number of forty-three thousand. Rostof had in readiness a card with the corner turned down as the quarter-stakes for three thousand rubles, which he had just won, when Dolokhof, rapping with the pack, flung it down, and taking the lump of chalk began swiftly to reckon up the sum total of Rostof's losses with his firm, legible figures, breaking the chalk as he did so.

"Supper, it's time for supper, and here are the gypsies!"

It was a fact; at that moment a number of dark-skinned men and women came in, bringing with them a gust of cold air and saying something in their gypsy accent. Nikolai realized that all was over; but he said, in an indifferent tone: "What, can't we play any more? Ah, but I had a splendid little card all ready!"

Just as if the mere amusement of the game was what interested him the most.

"All is over! I have lost!" was what he thought. "Now a bullet through my brain—that's all that's left," and yet he said, in a jocund tone, "Come now, just this one card!"

"Very well," replied Dolokhof, completing the sum total, "very good! Make it twenty-one rubles then," said he, pointing to the figures twenty-one, which was over and above the round sum of forty-three thousand; and, taking up the pack of cards, he began to shuffle them. Rostof obediently turned back the corner and, instead of the six thousand which he was going to wager, carefully wrote twenty-one.

"It's all the same to me!" said he, "all I wanted to know was whether you would give me the ten or not."

Dolokhof gravely began to deal. Oh, how Rostof at that moment hated those red hands, with the short fingers and the hairy wrists emerging from the shirt cuffs, those hands that had him in their grasp!

The ten-spot fell to him.

"Well, you owe me just forty-three thousand, count," said Dolokhof, getting up from the table and stretching himself. "One gets tired sitting still so long," he added.

"Yes, I'm worn out too," said Rostof.

Dolokhof, as if to remind him that it was not seemly to jest, interrupted him:

"When do you propose to pay me this money, count?"

Rostof, coloring with shame, drew Dolokhof into another room. "I cannot pay you at such short notice, you must take my note," said he.

"Listen, Rostof," said Dolokhof, with a frank smile, and looked into Nikolai's eyes, "you know the proverb: 'Lucky in love, unlucky at cards.' Your cousin is in love with you, I know."

Oh! how horrible it is to be in this man's power, thought Rostof. He realized what a blow it would be to his father, to his mother, to learn that he had been gambling and had lost so much. He realized what happiness it would be if he could only have avoided doing it, or could escape confessing it, and he realized that Dolokhof knew how easily he might save him from this shame and pain, and yet here he was playing with him as a cat plays with a mouse.

"Your cousin . . ." Dolokhof started to say; but Nikolai interrupted him.

"My cousin has nothing to do with this, and there is no need to bring her in," he cried in a fury.

"Then when will you pay me?" demanded Dolokhof.

"Tomorrow," replied Rostof, and he left the room.

X

To say "tomorrow," and to preserve the conventional tone of decorum, was not hard; but to go home alone, to see his brother and sisters, his father and mother, to confess his fault and ask for money to which he had no right, after giving his word of honor, was horrible.

When Nikolai reached home the family were still up. The young people on their return from the theater had had supper and were now sitting at the clavichord. As soon as he entered the music room he felt himself surrounded by that romantic atmosphere of love which had reigned all winter in his home, and which now seemed to hang breathlessly around Sonya and Natasha, like the air before a thunderstorm.

Sonya sat at the clavichord playing the introduction to the barcarole which was Denisof's special favorite. Natasha was getting ready to sing. Denisof gazed at her with ecstatic eyes.

Nikolai began to pace up and down the room.

"Now, why should they want to make her sing? What can she sing? There's nothing here to make a fellow feel happy!" said Nikolai to himself.

Sonya struck the first chord of the prelude.

"My God, I am a ruined, dishonorable man! A bullet through my brain, that is the only thing left for me, and not singing!" his thoughts went on. "Go away? But where? Very well, let them sing!"

Nikolai continued to stride up and down the room, glancing at Denisof and the girls, but avoiding their eyes.

"Nikolai dear, what is the matter?" Sonya's eyes, fixed on him, seemed to ask. She had immediately seen that something unusual had happened to him.

Nikolai turned away from her. Natasha also, with her quickness of perception, had instantly noticed her brother's preoccupation. She had observed it, but she felt so gay at that time, her mood was so far removed from grief, melancholy, and reproaches, that (as often happens in the case of young girls) she purposely deceived herself. "No, I'm too happy now to disturb my joy by trying to sympathize with the unhappiness of another," was her feeling, and she said to herself: "No, of course I am mistaken. It must be that he is as happy as I am myself."

Natasha this winter had for the first time begun to take singing seriously; this was really because Denisof had been so enthusiastic about her voice. In it there was a girlish sensitivity, an unconsciousness of its own power, and an untrained velvet tone, so combined with lack of knowledge of the art of singing that it seemed it would be impossible to change anything in that voice without ruining it.

"What does this mean?" queried Nikolai, as he listened to her voice and opened his eyes wide. "What has come over her? How she sings tonight!" he said to himself. And suddenly all the world for him was concentrated on the expectation of the following note, the succeeding phrase, and everything in the world was divided into those three beats: *"Oh mio crudele affetto"* . . . one, two, three; one . . . two . . . three . . . one. It was long since Rostof had experienced such delight from music as he did that night. But as soon as Natasha had finished her barcarole, grim reality again came back to him. Without saying a word to anyone, he left the room and went up to his own chamber. A quarter of an hour later the old count came in from the club cheerful and satisfied. Nikolai, finding that his father had returned, went to his room.

"Well, have you had a pleasant day?" asked the count, smiling gaily and proudly at his son. Nikolai wanted to say "yes," but he found it impossible; it was as much as he could do to keep from bursting into tears. The count began to puff at his pipe, and did not perceive his son's state of mind.

"Well, it can't be avoided," said Nikolai to himself, for the first and last time. And suddenly, in a negligent tone which seemed to him utterly shameful, he said to his father, just as if he were asking for the carriage to drive down town:

"Papa, I came to speak to you about business. I had forgotten all about it. I need some money."

"What's that?" said the father, who had come home in a peculiarly good-natured frame of mind. "I told you that you wouldn't have enough. Do you need much?"

"Ever so much," said Nikolai, reddening, and with a stupid, careless smile for which he could not pardon himself for a long time. "I have been losing a little; that is, considerably; I might say a great deal—forty-three thousand . . ."

"What? To whom? You are joking!" cried the count, flushing as elderly men are apt to flush, with an apoplectic rush of blood coloring his neck and the back of his head.

"I promised to pay it tomorrow," continued Nikolai.

"Well!" said the old count, spreading his hands and falling helplessly back upon the divan.

"What's to be done? It's what might happen to anyone!" said the son, in a free and easy tone of banter, while all the time in his heart he was calling himself a worthless coward who could not atone by his whole life for such an act. He felt an impulse to kiss his father's hands, to fall on his knees and beg his forgiveness, but still he assured his father in that careless and even coarse tone that this was a thing liable to happen to anyone!

Count Rostof dropped his eyes when he heard his son's words, and fidgeted about as if he were trying to find something.

"Yes, yes," he murmured, "it'll be hard work, I'm afraid . . . hard work to raise so much . . . it happens to everyone, yes, yes, it happens to everyone."

And the count, with a swift glance at his son's face, rose to leave the room.

Nikolai was prepared for a refusal, but he had never expected this.

"Papa! pa-pa dear!" he cried, hastening after him with a sob, "forgive me!" and, seizing his father's hand, he pressed it to his lips and burst into tears.

While father and son were having this conversation, a no-less-important confession was taking place between the mother and daughter. Natasha in great excitement had run to where her mother was.

"Mama! . . . mama! . . . He has done it!"

"Done what?"

"He has done it! He has made me an offer; mama! mama!" she cried.

The countess did not believe her ears. Denisof propose! To whom? To this little chit of a Natasha, who only a short time since was playing with her dolls, and even now was only a schoolgirl?

"Natasha! Come now! No nonsense!" said she, still hoping that it was a joke.

"Why do you say 'nonsense'? I'm telling you exactly what happened," said Natasha, indignantly. "I came to ask you what I should do about it, and you call it 'nonsense.'"

The countess shrugged her shoulders. "If it is true that Monsieur Denisof has made you an offer, then tell him that he is a fool, and that's all there is of it!"

"No, he is not a fool," replied Natasha in a serious and offended tone.

"Well, then, what do you wish? It seems to me that these days all of you are falling in love. Well, if you love him, then marry him," exclaimed the countess with an angry laugh. "Good luck to you!"

"No, mama, I'm not in love with him; it can't be that I am!"

"Well, then, go and tell him so!"

"Mama, are you annoyed? Don't be annoyed, sweetheart; now how, I should like to know, was I to blame?"

"No, but what do you wish, my dear? Shall I go and tell him?" asked the countess, smiling.

"Certainly not, I will answer him myself, only tell me what to say. Everything comes so easy to you," she added, with an answering smile. "And if you had only heard how he said it to me! Do you know, I am sure that he did not mean to say it, but it came out accidentally."

"Well, in that case you certainly should refuse him."

"No, not refuse him! I feel so sorry for him! He is such a nice man!"

"Well, then, accept his proposal. Indeed, it is time you were married," exclaimed her mother in a sharp derisive tone.

"No, mama, I pity him so. I don't know how to tell him!"

"Well, then, if you can't find anything to say, I myself will go and speak with him," said the countess, stirred to the soul that anyone dare to look upon her little Natasha as already grown up.

"No, not for anything; I will tell him myself, and you may listen at the door," and Natasha started to run through the drawing-room into the music room, where Denisof was still sitting on the same chair by the clavichord with his face in his hands. He sprang up the moment he heard her light steps.

"Natasha," said he, going toward her with quick steps, "decide my fate. It is in your hands."

"Vasili, I am so sorry for you . . . Really! you are so splendid . . . But it cannot be . . . it is . . . but I shall always, always love you."

Denisof bent over her hand, and she heard strange sounds which she could not understand. She kissed him on his dark, curly, disordered hair. At this instant they heard the hurried rustle of the countess' gown. She came toward them.

"Captain Denisof, I thank you for the honor," said the countess, in a troubled tone of voice, though it seemed to Denisof to be stern. "But my daughter is so young, and I should have thought that you, as a friend of my son's, would have addressed me first. In that case you might not have forced me to an unavoidable refusal."

"Countess," said Denisof with downcast eyes and a guilty look, and vainly trying to stammer something more.

Natasha could not look with any composure upon him, he looked so pitiful. She began to sob aloud.

"Countess, I have done w'ong," at last he managed to articulate, in a broken voice. "But pway believe me, I adoah your daughteh and all your family, and I would gladly sacwifice my life twice oveh—" He looked up at the countess and seeing her stern face, "Well, good-by, countess," he added, kissing her hand and without even looking at Natasha he left the room with quick, resolute steps.

Rostof spent the next day making calls with Denisof, who would not hear of staying any longer in Moscow. All his Moscow friends gave him a send-off at the gypsies', and he had no recollection of how he was packed into his sleigh or how he rode the first three stages.

After Denisof's departure, Rostof spent a fortnight longer at home, waiting for the money, which the old count was unable to raise at such short notice; he did not leave the house, and spent most of his time with the girls. Sonya was more affectionate and devoted to him than ever. It seemed as if she were anxious to show him that his gambling losses were quite an exploit, for which she could only love him the more, but Nikolai now felt that he was unworthy of her. He filled the girls' albums with verses and music, and at last, toward the end of November, after paying over the forty-three thousand rubles and receiving Dolokhof's receipt for it, he started off without taking leave of any of his acquaintances, to rejoin his regiment, which was now in Poland.

1807

An indecisive battle at Eylau has begun the campaign of 1807; the Russians are deemed victorious, yet the French advance. In June the opposing Russian and French forces draw up at Friedland, far into East Prussia. It is another great victory for Napoleon. Now peace is forced on Russia by military exigency; but beyond that, the Tsar Alexander is physically ready for it. He admires Napoleon's strength, and many of Napoleon's reforms appeal to the young (thirty years old), liberally inclined Tsar. Napoleon and Alexander meet as brother-emperors at Tilsit. In the peace that results Napoleon emerges as the undisputed master of the continent. Only the British fight on.

Part Fifth

AFTER his settlement with his wife, Pierre went to Petersburg. At the post-station at Torzhok there were no horses, or the stationmaster was unwilling to furnish them. Pierre was obliged to wait. While undressing, he stretched himself out on the leather divan before a circular table, put his big feet in warm boots on it, and pondered.

"Will you have the trunks brought in? Shall I make up a bed? Do you wish tea?" asked the valet.

Pierre made no answer, for he heard nothing and saw nothing. He had begun to ponder while at the last station, and still he went on, propounding the same questions, much too important for him to pay any attention to what was going on around him. He did not in the least care whether he reached Petersburg sooner or later, or whether he spent a few hours or his whole life at this station.

The stationmaster came in and began obsequiously to ask his excellency to deign to wait only two "little hours," and then he could have for his excellency, come what would, post horses for his service. The stationmaster was evidently lying, and his sole idea was to get as much money as possible from the traveler.

"Is this right, or is it wrong?" Pierre asked himself. "As far as I am concerned, it is good, but it is bad for the next traveler; but the stationmaster can't help himself, because he has nothing to eat; he told me that some officer had given him a thrashing because of a delay. But perhaps the officer thrashed him because it was necessary for him to hasten away. And I shot at Dolokhof because I considered myself insulted, and Louis XVI was beheaded because he was convicted as a criminal; but within a year those who had beheaded him were also put to death for something or other. What is wrong? What is right? What must one love? What must one hate? What is the purpose of life, and what am I? What is life, and what is death? What is the Power that directs all things?" he asked himself. And there was no answer to any one of the questions, except the one, the illogical answer which did not in reality fit any of these questions.

The answer was: "Thou shalt die—all will come to an end! Thou shalt die and know all, or else cease to question." But the mere thought of death was terrible to him.

A Torzhok peddler woman, in her piping voice, offered her wares and called especial attention to her goatskin slippers.

"I have hundreds of rubles that I don't know what to do with, and she in her ragged coat stands there and looks at me timidly," thought Pierre. "And what good would this money do her? Would this money of mine add the value of a single hair to her happiness, to her peace of mind? Can anything on earth make her or me in the least degree less susceptible to evil and death? Death, which ends all, and which may come today or tomorrow; everything is of equal unimportance in comparison with eternity."

"May I venture to ask your excellency to make a little room for this gentleman here?" asked the stationmaster, coming into the room and introducing another traveler, delayed also by the lack of horses. The newcomer was a thickset, big-boned, little old man, yellow and wrinkled, with gray, beetling brows which shaded glittering eyes of an indefinable grayish hue.

Pierre took his feet from the table, got up, and threw himself down on the bed that had been made ready for him, occasionally glancing at the stranger, who, with a morose tired air, without paying any heed to Pierre, allowed his servant to help him take off his wraps.

The old man sat down on the divan. He had on a well-worn, nankeen-lined sheepskin jacket, and felt boots on his thin, bony legs; his head was large and very broad in the temples, and his hair was closely cropped. Sitting thus, and leaning back against the sofa, he glanced at Bezukhof. The grave, intelligent and penetrating expression of his glance struck Pierre. He sat motionless, with his wrinkled old hands folded. On one finger he wore a heavy iron ring with a death's head for a seal.

The stranger's servant was also a little old man, all covered with wrinkles, without mustache or beard, not because they had been shaven, but because they seemed never to have grown. This agile old servant opened the traveling case, prepared the tea table, and brought in the boiling samovar.

"If I am not mistaken, I have the pleasure of addressing Count Bezukhof," said the stranger in a loud and deliberate voice.

Pierre, without speaking, gave his neighbor an inquiring glance over his spectacles.

"I have heard of you," continued the traveler, "and of the misfortune that has befallen you, my dear sir."

He seemed to lay a special stress on the word "misfortune," as much as to say: *Yes, misfortune, whatever you may call it, for I know that what happened to you in Moscow was a misfortune.* "I have a great sympathy for you, my dear sir."

Pierre flushed, and, hastily putting down his legs from the bed, bent toward the old man, smiling with a timid and unnatural smile.

"Not from mere curiosity do I speak to you of this, my dear sir, but for a much more important reason."

He paused, though his eyes were still fixed on Pierre, and he moved along on the divan, signifying by this action that Pierre should sit down by his side. It was not particularly agreeable for Pierre to enter into conversation with this old man, but, involuntarily submitting, he came and sat down by his side.

"You are unhappy, my dear sir," pursued the stranger. "You are young, I am old. I should like, as far as in me lies, to help you."

"Ah! yes!" replied Pierre, with the same unnatural smile. "I am very grateful to you. Have you been traveling far?"

The stranger's face was not genial; on the contrary, it was even cold and stern; nevertheless, his face and his speech had an irresistible attraction for Pierre.

"Now, if for any reason it is disagreeable for you to talk with me," said the old man, "tell me frankly, my dear sir." And he suddenly smiled, an unexpected, a paternally affectionate smile.

"No! no, not at all; on the contrary, I am very happy to make your acquaintance," said Pierre, and, glancing once more at his new acquaintance's hand, he looked more carefully at the ring. He perceived on it the death's head, the symbol of Masonry.

"Allow me to ask," said he, "are you a Mason?"

"Yes, I belong to the Brotherhood of the Freemasons," said the traveler, looking deeper and deeper into Pierre's eyes. "And on my own account and that of the craft, I offer you the hand of fellowship."

"I fear," said Pierre, smiling and hesitating between the confidence inspired in him by the Freemason's personality and the current disapprobation of the doctrines of the order . . . "I fear that I am very far from being able to express myself; I fear that my whole system of thought in regard to the world in general is so opposite to yours that we would not understand each other."

"I know your system of thought," replied the Freemason, "and this system you mention, and which seems to you the product of your brain, is that

common to most men; it is uniformly the fruit of pride, idleness and ignorance. Excuse me, my dear sir; if I had not known this, I would not have
addressed you. Your system of thought is a grievous error."

"In exactly the same way, I can imagine that it is you who are in error,"
said Pierre, with a feeble smile.

"I never venture to assert that I know the truth," said the Mason, im-
pressing Pierre more and more by the precision and assurance of his discourse. "No one can alone attain to the truth; it must be stone upon stone,
all lending their aid, millions of generations, from the first Adam even
down to our day, building the temple which is destined to be the suitable
abiding-place for the Most High God," said the Mason, and he shut his
eyes.

"I must tell you, I do not believe . . . do not believe in God," said Pierre,
with an effort and a sense of regret, but feeling it indispensable to confess
the whole truth.

The Mason looked earnestly at Pierre and smiled, much as a rich man
with millions might smile upon a poor man who told him that five rubles
would make him the happiest of men.

"Yes, you do not know Him, my dear sir," said the Mason. "You cannot
know Him—you cannot know Him; therefore, you are unhappy."

"Yes, yes, I am unhappy," repeated Pierre. "But what am I to do?"

"You do not know Him, my dear sir, and therefore you are very unhappy.
You do not know Him, but He is here; He is in me, He is in my words;
He is in you, and even in those blasphemous words that you have just
uttered," said the Mason, in his stern sonorous voice.

He paused and sighed, evidently trying to master his emotion.

"If He did not exist," said he, gently, "you and I would not be speaking
about Him, my dear sir. Of what, of whom, have we been speaking? Whom
didst thou deny?" he suddenly asked, with a tone of enraptured sternness
and power in his voice. "Who could have invented Him if He did not
exist? How camest thou to have the hypothesis that such an incomprehensible being exists? How came you and all the world to suppose the existence
of an incomprehensible Being—a Being omnipotent, eternal, and infinite
in all His attributes?"

He paused, and remained silent for some time.

Pierre could not and would not break in upon his silence.

"He is, but it is hard to comprehend Him," said the Mason at last, looking
not into Pierre's face, but straight ahead, while his aged-looking hands,
which he could not keep quiet owing to his internal excitement, kept turning over the leaves of his book. "If it were a man whose existence thou
disbelieved, I could bring this man to thee, I would take him by the hand
and show him to thee. But how can I, an insignificant mortal, show all
His omnipotence, all His infinity, all His goodness, to him who is blind,
or to him who shuts his eyes in order not to see, not to comprehend Him,
and not to see and not to comprehend all his own vileness and depravity?"

He paused again. "Who art thou? What art thou? Thou imaginest that thou art heroic because thou canst utter those blasphemous words," said he, with a saturnine and scornful laugh. "And thou art stupider and less intelligent than a little child, who, playing with the artistically constructed parts of a clock, should dare to say that because he did not understand the clock, he did not believe in the artificer who made it. To comprehend Him is hard. For ages, since our first ancestor Adam even down to our own days, we have been striving to comprehend Him, and we are still infinitely far from the attainment of our purpose; but, while we cannot comprehend Him, we see only our feebleness and His majesty."

Pierre, with agitated heart and burning eyes, looked at the Mason, listening to his words, not interrupting him or asking him any questions; but with all his soul he believed in what this strange man told him. Whether he was convinced by the reasonable arguments that the Mason employed, or was persuaded, as children are, by the conviction, by the sincerity expressed by the Mason's intonations, by the trembling voice which sometimes almost failed him, or by the brilliant eyes that had grown old in this conviction, or by that calmness, security, and belief in his own mission which radiated from the Mason's whole being and which especially impressed him when he compared it with his own feeble convictions and hopelessness—he could not tell; at all events, he desired with all his soul to believe, and he did believe, and experienced a joyous sense of calmness, regeneration, and restoration to life.

"It is not by the intellect that He is comprehended, but by life," said the Mason.

"I do not understand," said Pierre, finding with dread his doubts arising in him again. He was afraid lest he might detect some weakness and lack of clarity in his new friend's arguments; he was afraid not to believe in him. "I do not understand," said he, "how the human mind can attain that knowledge of which you speak."

The Mason smiled his sweet, paternal smile.

"The highest wisdom and truth is like the purest elixir of the gods, which we should wish to receive into our very selves," said he. "Can I, an unclean vessel, accept this pure elixir and judge of its purity? Only through the cleansing of my inner nature can I, to a certain extent, receive this baptismal consecration."

"Yes, yes, that is so," said Pierre, joyfully.

"Look with the eyes of your spirit at your inner man, and then ask yourself if you are content with your life. What do you attain when you put yourself under the guidance of the intellect alone? What are you? You are young, you are intelligent and educated, my dear sir. What have you been doing with all those blessings that have been put into your hands? Are you content with yourself and your life?"

"No, I detest my life," exclaimed Pierre, with a scowl.

"If you detest it, then change it, undergo self-purification, and in accordance, as you accomplish it, you will learn wisdom. Examine your life, my dear sir. What sort of life have you been leading? Wild revels and debauchery! Receiving everything from society, and giving nothing in return. You have become the possessor of wealth—how have you used it? What have you done for your neighbor? Have you had a thought for your tens of thousands of serfs? Have you helped them, physically or morally? No! You have taken advantage of their labor to lead a dissipated life. That is what you have been doing! Have you chosen a lifework that might enable you to be of help to your neighbor? No! You have been spending your life in idleness. Then, my dear sir, you got married; you assumed responsibilities for the guidance of a young woman, and how have you carried them out? You have not aided her, my dear sir, to find the path of truth, but you have hurled her into the abyss of falsehood and wretchedness. A man insulted you, and you fought with him, and you say that you do not know God, and that you detest your life. There is no wisdom in that, my dear sir!"

After saying these words, the Mason, as if wearied by this long speech, again leaned against the back of the sofa and closed his eyes. Pierre looked at the stern, impassive, almost lifeless face of the old man, and moved his lips without making any sound. He wanted to say, "Yes, my life is shameful, idle, dissipated," but he did not dare break the silence.

The Freemason coughed, a hoarse, decrepit cough, and summoned his servant.

"How about the horses?" he asked, without looking at Pierre.

"Those that were ordered have been brought," replied the servant. "Do you not wish to rest?"

"No, have them harnessed."

"Can it be that he is going to leave me here alone, and not tell me all, and not promise me help?" wondered Pierre, getting up, and beginning to pace up and down the room with bowed head, though he occasionally glanced at the Mason.

Yes, I had never thought about it before. I lead a contemptible, depraved life, but I do not love it and have no desire to continue it, thought Pierre. *And this man knows the truth, and if he had the desire he might enlighten me.*

Pierre wished, but he had not the courage, to say this to the Mason. The traveler, gathering up his effects with his skilful, aged hands, began to button up his sheepskin coat. Having accomplished these tasks, he turned to Bezukhof, and said to him in a polite, indifferent tone: "Where are you going now, my dear sir?"

"I? . . . I am going to Petersburg," replied Pierre, in a childish, irresolute voice. "I am grateful to you. I agree with what you have said. But pray do not think that I am all bad! I wish with all my soul that I were what you wish me to be—but I have never found any help to become such . . .

however, I am, above all, to blame for my faults. Help me! teach me, and maybe I might . . ."

Pierre could not speak further. There was a strange sound in his nose, and he turned away.

The Mason did not speak for some time, evidently lost in thought.

"Help is given only from God," said he. "But that measure of help which it is within the power of our craft to give you, it will be glad to give, my dear sir. When you reach Petersburg, give this to Count Villarski."

He took out a pocketbook, and on a large sheet of paper, folded twice, he wrote a few words.

"Allow me to give you one piece of advice. When you reach the capital, consecrate your first hours to solitude, to self-examination, and do not again enter into your former paths of life. And now I wish you a happy journey, my dear sir," said he, perceiving that his servant had entered the room, "and all success."

The traveler was Ossip Alekseyevitch Bazdeyef, as Pierre discovered from the stationmaster's record book. Pierre, after his departure, without lying down to sleep or asking for horses, long paced up and down the room of the station house, thinking over his vicious way of living and, with the enthusiasm of regeneration, imagining to himself the blessed, irreproachable and beneficent future which now seemed to him so easy. He was, so it seemed to him, wicked only because he had forgotten how good it was to be righteous. Not a trace of his former doubts remained in his mind. He had a firm faith in the possibility of a brotherhood of men, united in one common aim of keeping each other in the path of righteousness, and such a brotherhood Masonry now seemed to him to be.

I I

ON REACHING Petersburg, Pierre informed no one of his presence, went nowhere, and spent whole days in reading Thomas à Kempis, which someone—he did not know who—had sent him. One thing, and only one thing, Pierre understood in reading that book: the hitherto unknown delight of faith in the possibility of attaining perfection and in the possibility of active brotherly love among men which Bazdeyef had revealed to him. Within a week after his return, the young Polish Count Villarski, whom Pierre had known slightly in Petersburg society, came one evening into his room with the same sort of official and solemn air with which Dolokhof's second had approached him; closing the door behind him, and assuring himself that no one except Pierre was in the room, he thus addressed him:

"I have come to you, count, for the purpose of laying a proposition before you," said he, not sitting down. "An individual of very high degree in our brotherhood has interested himself in having you admitted in due course, and he has proposed that I should be your sponsor. I consider it a sacred duty to fulfil this person's desires. Do you wish to join the brotherhood of Freemasons under my sponsorship?"

Pierre was amazed at the cold and severe tone of this man, whom he had seen almost always at balls, with a gallant smile, in the society of the most brilliant ladies.

"Yes," said Pierre, "I do wish it."

Villarski inclined his head.

"Still one further question, count," he said, "which I will beg of you to answer with all frankness, not as a future Mason, but as a man of honor: Have you renounced your former convictions? Do you believe in a God?"

Pierre hesitated.

"Yes . . . yes, I believe in a God," said he.

"In that case . . ." began Villarski, but Pierre interrupted him.

"Yes, I believe in God," said he once more.

"In that case we may start, then," said Villarski. "My carriage is at your service."

Villarski sat in silence all the way. To Pierre's questions as to what he had to do and how he must answer, Villarski contented himself with replying that brethren more suitable than himself would examine him and that all Pierre had to do was to speak the truth.

They entered the courtyard of a large mansion where the lodge met, and after mounting a dark staircase they came into a small, brightly lighted anteroom, where they removed their cloaks without the aid of servants. Through an entry they passed into another room. Here a man in a strange garb made his appearance at the door. Villarski, going forward to meet him, said something to him in French in an undertone, and went to a small wardrobe in which Pierre observed trappings such as he had never seen before. Taking from the wardrobe a handkerchief, Villarski bound it around Pierre's eyes and tied a knot behind in such a way that his hair was caught in it and hurt him.

After leading him half a score of paces, Villarski paused.

"Whatever happens to you," said he, "you must courageously endure it all if you are firmly resolved to enter our brotherhood."

Pierre nodded assent.

"When you hear a rap on the door you can take off the handkerchief," added Villarski. "I wish you good courage and success."

And pressing Pierre's hand, Villarski went away.

Left alone, Pierre still continued to smile as before. Twice he shrugged his shoulders, raised his hand to the handkerchief as if inclined to remove it, and again let it fall. The five minutes he spent with bandaged eyes seemed to him like an hour. His hands swelled, his legs trembled; he had the sensation of being tired. He had the most complex and varied feelings. What was going to happen to him seemed to him terrible, and he was still more afraid that he should show his fear. He was filled with curiosity to know what was going to take place, what was going to be revealed to him;

but, above all, it was delightful for him to think that the moment had come when he had definitely entered upon the path of regeneration and of an active, beneficent life.

Loud raps were heard at the door. Pierre took off the bandage and looked around him. A door opened and someone entered.

By the feeble light Pierre could just manage to make out a short man. Coming from light into darkness, this man paused a moment, then, with cautious steps, he approached the table and placed on it his small hands covered with leather gloves.

"Why have you come hither?" asked the new man, approaching Pierre, who had made a slight noise. "Wherefore do you, who believe not in the truth of light and have never seen the light, wherefore have you come hither? What do you desire of us? Wisdom? virtue? enlightenment?"

With his heart beating so that he could hardly breathe, Pierre went toward the Rhetor, as the Masons call the brother whose duty it is to prepare the candidate for admission into the confraternity.

"I . . . hope for . . . guidance . . . for help . . . toward regeneration," said Pierre in a trembling voice, and finding a difficulty in speaking which arose from his emotion as well as from his lack of practice in speaking in Russian on abstract themes.

"What knowledge have you of Freemasonry?"

"I suppose that Freemasonry is fraternity and equality of all men who have virtuous aims," said Pierre, with a feeling of shame overwhelming him at the unfitness of his words at such a solemn moment. "I suppose . . ."

"Good," said the Rhetor in haste, evidently perfectly satisfied with this reply. "Have you found in religion means for the attainment of these ends?"

"No, I have considered religion opposed to truth, and I have spurned it," said Pierre, so low that the Rhetor did not hear him and asked him what he said. "I have been an atheist," replied Pierre.

The Rhetor coughed, folded his gloved hands on his chest, and began to discourse:

"It is now my duty to unfold to you the chief aim of our brotherhood," said he. "If this aim coincides with yours, then you will find it an advantage to join our fraternity. The first and principal aim, and at the same time the foundation of our confraternity, on which it stands firm and which no human violence can shape, is the conservation and handing down to posterity of a certain important mystery which has been handed down to us from the remotest antiquity, even from the first man, on which mystery perhaps depends the destiny of the human race. But as this mystery has the peculiarity that no one can know it and get advantage from it except through a long and assiduous course of self-purification, therefore not everyone can hope speedily to discover it. Consequently we have a secondary aim and object, which consists in preparing our fellow members, as far as in us lies, to correct their hearts, to purify and enlighten their reason, by those means which have been handed down to us by tradition from men who labored to probe those mysteries, and thereby be qualified to receive the knowledge.

"By purifying and correcting our members, we endeavor, in the third place, to correct also the whole human race, presenting in our own members an example of honor and virtue, and therefore we endeavor, by all means in our power, to counteract the evil that rules in the world. Think this over, and I will come to you again," said he, and he left the room.

"To counteract the evil that rules the world," repeated Pierre, and he imagined his future activity in this great field.

Within half an hour the Rhetor returned to instruct the candidate in the seven virtues, symbolized by the seven steps of Solomon's Temple, which every Mason must make his especial practice. These virtues were:

1. Modesty, the observation of the secrets of the order.
2. Obedience to the higher degrees of the fraternity.
3. Good temper.
4. Love for mankind.
5. Courage.
6. Generosity.
7. Love of death.

"Apply yourself to the seventh," said the Rhetor. "By frequent thoughts of Death, bring yourself to feel that he is no more a terrible enemy, but a friend who frees the soul, wearied by works of beneficence, from the wretchedness of this life and leads it into the place of rewards and rest."

"Yes, this ought to be so," thought Pierre when the Rhetor, after delivering himself of this message, again retired, leaving him to solitary reflection. "This ought to be so, but I am still so feeble as to love my life, the meaning of which has only just been to some small degree revealed to me."

For the third time the Rhetor returned, this time more promptly than before, and asked Pierre if he was still firm in his convictions and resolved to undergo all that might be required of him.

"I am ready for anything," said Pierre.

"If you are resolved, then it is my duty to proceed to the initiation," said the Rhetor, coming closer to Pierre. "As a sign of your generosity, I shall ask you to give me everything of value that you have."

"But I have nothing with me," said Pierre, supposing that he was to be required to make over all that he possessed.

"Well, what you have on you: your watch, money, rings . . ."

Pierre hastily took out his pocketbook, his watch, and struggled for some time to remove his wedding ring from his stout finger. When this was accomplished, the Mason said:

"As a sign of obedience, I will ask you to strip."

Pierre took off his coat, waistcoat, and left shoe at the Rhetor's direction. The Mason opened the shirt over his left breast, and, bending over, lifted his trousers above the knee of his left leg. Pierre hastily began to take off his right shoe also, and to tuck up his trousers, so as to save this stranger the trouble, but the Mason assured him this was unnecessary, and gave him a slipper for his left foot. With an involuntary, childlike smile of shame, doubt, and derision at his own awkwardness, Pierre stood up, dropping his arms and spreading his legs, and faced the Rhetor, waiting his next commands.

"And finally, as a sign of sincerity, I will ask you to reveal to me your chief predilection," said he.

"My predilection? But I used to have so many of them!" exclaimed Pierre.

"The predilection which more than all others has caused you to waver in the path of virtue," said the Mason.

Pierre paused, trying to think.

"Wine? Gluttony? Slothfulness? Impetuosity? Anger? Women?" He passed his faults in review, mentally considering them, and not knowing which to take in preference.

"Women," said he, in a voice so low that it was scarcely audible. The Mason did not move and did not speak until long after this reply. At last he approached Pierre, took up the handkerchief that was lying on the table, and again blindfolded his eyes.

"For the last time I say to you: 'Examine yourself with all attention! Put a bridle on your feelings, and seek your happiness, not in your passions, but in your heart. The fountainhead of happiness is not without, but within us.'" . . .

Pierre had already begun to feel in himself this refreshing fountain of happiness, which now filled his soul to overflowing with bliss and emotion.

III

ON THE DAY following his reception into the Masonic lodge, Pierre was sitting at home reading a book and trying to penetrate the meaning of the square formed on one side by God, on the second by the spiritual world, on the third by the physical, and on the fourth by a mixture. Occasionally his attention wandered from his book and square, and in his imagination he began to formulate a new plan of life for himself.

The evening before, at the lodge, he had been told that the emperor had heard of his duel, and that it would be to his advantage to leave Petersburg for a time. Pierre proposed to go to his southern estates and look after the welfare of his peasantry. He was joyfully thinking about this new life when Prince Vasili unexpectedly came into the room.

"My dear, what have you been doing in Moscow? Why, my dear fellow, what made you quarrel with Helene? You are in the wrong," said the prince, as he came in. "I have known all about it, and I can tell you honestly that Helene is as innocent toward you as Christ toward the Jews."

Pierre started to reply, but Prince Vasili cut him short.

"And why didn't you come right to me in all frankness, as to a friend? I know how it was, I understand it," said he. "You behaved as a man who prizes his honor; perhaps, too, you acted too hastily, but we won't discuss that now. Just think of this, though: in what a position you have put her and me in the eyes of society, and especially of the court," he added, lowering his voice. "She is living in Moscow, you here. Remember, my dear"—he made him sit down—"this is a mere misunderstanding; you yourself will feel so, I am sure. Now join me in writing a letter; and she will come back—everything will be explained; but if you don't, I will tell you, you may very easily repent of it, my dear."

Prince Vasili gave Pierre a very suggestive look. "I have it from the very best sources that the empress dowager takes a lively interest in all this matter. You know that she is very favorably disposed to Helene."

Several times Pierre collected himself to speak, but on the one hand Prince Vasili did not give him a chance; on the other, Pierre himself was afraid to take that tone of determined refusal with which he had definitely made up his mind to answer his father-in-law. Moreover, the words of the Masonic ritual, "Be courteous and genial," occurred to him. He scowled, flushed, got up and sat down again, struggling to perform the hardest task that had ever come to him in his life—to say something unpleasant to a man's face, to say exactly the opposite of what this man expected. He was so accustomed to giving in to Prince Vasili's tone of easygoing self-confidence, that even now he felt he had not the force of mind necessary to oppose him; but he felt that what he was going to say now would decide the whole destiny of his life: was he to go back to the old path of the past, or to go on to that new one which had been opened before him in so attractive a light by the Masons, and where he firmly believed he would find regeneration.

"Well, my dear," said Prince Vasili in a jocose tone, "tell me 'yes,' now, and I will write her the letter and we will kill the fatted calf."

But Prince Vasili had not time to finish his joke, before Pierre, not looking at Prince Vasili, and with a flash of rage which made him resemble his father, exclaimed in a whisper:

"Prince, I did not invite you to come; please go, go!" He sprang up and flung the door open. "Go!" he repeated, not believing in himself and rejoicing in the expression of confusion and terror on Prince Vasili's face.

"What is the matter with you, are you ill?"

"Go!" he cried once more in a trembling voice. And Prince Vasili was obliged to go without bringing about any settlement.

In a week's time, Pierre, bidding his new friends, the Masons, farewell, and leaving in their hands large sums for charities, departed for his estates. The brotherhood gave him letters to the Masons of Kiev and Odessa and promised to write and guide him in his new activity.

IV

PIERRE's DUEL with Dolokhof was hushed up, and in spite of the emperor's strictness in regard to dueling, neither the two principals nor their seconds were punished. But the story of the duel, confirmed by Pierre's rupture with his wife, was noised abroad in society. Pierre, who when he was an illegitimate son had been looked upon with patronizing condescension, who when he was the best match in the Russian empire had been flattered and glorified, had lost much of his importance in the eyes of the world since his marriage; and young ladies and their mothers had nothing more to expect from him, the more because he could not and would not ingratiate himself into the favor of fashionable society. Now he alone was blamed for this occurrence; it was said that he was a jealous blockhead, liable to exactly the same fits of ferocious temper as his father.

And when, after Pierre's departure, Helene returned to Petersburg she was received by all her acquaintances not only gladly, but even with a shade of respectful deference due to her unhappiness. When her husband was mentioned in conversation, Helene put on a dignified expression, which, without her realizing its significance, she managed with that consummate tact of hers to make peculiarly becoming. This expression signified that she had made up her mind to endure her unhappiness without complaining, and that her husband was a cross sent her from God.

Prince Vasili expressed his feelings more openly. He would shrug his shoulders when the conversation turned to Pierre, and, pointing to his forehead, he would say:

"I have always said he was cracked."

Toward the end of the year 1806, when the melancholy news of Napoleon's defeat of the Prussian army at Jena and Auerstadt and the surrender of the majority of the Prussian fortresses had been received, when our armies had just crossed over into Prussia, and our second campaign with Napoleon was beginning, Anna Pavlovna gave an "at home." The person whom Anna Pavlovna served up this evening as a choice "first-fruit" for the edification of her guests was Boris Drubetskoy, who had just arrived on a special mission from the army in Prussia and was now enjoying the position of aide to a very great personage.

Boris, in an elegant uniform, fresh and ruddy, and grown to man's estate, came with easy assurance into the drawing-room and was led up, according to custom, to salute the aunt, and then brought back to the general circle of guests.

Anna Pavlovna gave him her withered hand to kiss, introduced him to a number of the company with whom he was not acquainted, and of each she would say in a whisper:

"Prince Ippolit Kuragin, a charming young man; Monsieur Krouq, chargé d'affaires from Copenhagen, a deep thinker"; or simply, "Monsieur Sitof, a man of great ability," giving each one a word of flattery.

Since Boris had been in the service he had succeeded, thanks to Anna Mikhailovna's efforts and to his own tastes and habit of self-control, in obtaining a very advantageous position. He had thoroughly mastered that unwritten system of subordination which had pleased him so much at Olmütz, according to which the ensign may stand incomparably higher than a general. The consequence of this discovery was that his whole mode of life, and all his relations to former friends and acquaintances, and all his plans for the future, were entirely and completely changed. He was not rich, but he would spend his last penny to be better dressed than others; he preferred to deprive himself of many pleasures rather than allow himself to ride in a shabby carriage or appear in anything but an immaculate uniform in the streets of Petersburg. He frequented only the society of those who were above him and might be of advantage to him. He liked Petersburg and despised Moscow. His recollection of his home with the Rostofs and his boyish love for Natasha were unpleasant to him, and since his first departure for the army he had not once been to see the Rostofs.

On reaching Anna Pavlovna's drawing-room, an invitation which he considered equivalent to a rise in the service, he immediately understood what part he had to play, and he allowed Anna Pavlovna to make the most of the interest that centered upon him, while he attentively studied each face and took mental stock of what might be the possibilities of getting advantage from each. He sat down in the place assigned to him next the beautiful Helene, and though he began to listen attentively to the conversation, nevertheless he was able to look several times at Helene, who, with a smile, more than once exchanged glances with the handsome young adjutant.

Quite naturally, while speaking of the position of Prussia, Anna Pavlovna begged Boris to tell about his visit to Glogau and the state in which he found the Prussian army. Helene more than anyone else gave her undivided attention to what Boris had to say. Several times she asked him about certain details of his journey, and was apparently greatly interested in the position of the Prussian army. As soon as he had finished, she turned to him with her usual smile, and said:

"You must be sure to come and see me." She spoke in a tone which seemed to imply that circumstances of which he could know nothing made it absolutely imperative.

"Tuesday, between eight o'clock and nine. You will give me great pleasure."

Boris promised to comply with her wishes and was about to engage her in further conversation, when Anna Pavlovna called him away under the pretext that her old aunt wanted to speak with him.

"You used to know her husband, didn't you?" asked Anna Pavlovna, closing her eyes and making a melancholy gesture toward Helene. "Ah!

she is such an unhappy and charming woman. Don't speak to her about him, please be careful about it. It is too painful for her."

When all got up to leave, Helene, who had spoken very little all the evening, addressed Boris again and begged him with the most flattering and significant expression to come to see her the following Tuesday.

"It will be a very great favor to me," said she with a smile, glancing at Anna Pavlovna, and Anna Pavlovna, with the same melancholy expression as the one with which she always spoke of her august protectress, corroborated Helene's request.

It seemed that from certain words spoken by Boris that evening concerning the Prussian army, Helene had suddenly conceived a powerful determination to see him. She practically promised him that when he came on the following Tuesday she would tell him what it was that made her wish see him.

But when, on the Tuesday evening, Boris reached Helene's salon, he received no explanation as to why he had been so urgently invited. There were other guests; the countess talked very little with him, and only when he was leaving, just as he was kissing her hand, she unexpectedly whispered to him, without any smile, which was strange for her—

"Come tomorrow evening to dinner. You really must come!"

Thus with his first visit to Petersburg began Boris' intimacy at the house of the Countess Bezukhof.

V

THE WAR WAS growing fiercer and its theater was approaching the Russian frontiers. Everywhere could be heard curses against Bonaparte, the enemy of all the human race. In all the villages of the empire, veterans and raw recruits were forming companies, and from the theater of war came conflicting rumors, usually false, and consequently interpreted in various ways.

The life of the old Prince Bolkonsky, Prince Andrei, and Princess Maria had changed in many ways since the year 1805.

In 1806 the old prince was appointed one of the eight commanders-in-chief for the militia at that time recruiting all over Russia. The old prince, in spite of the weaknesses of age, which had become especially noticeable at the period when he supposed his son was killed, felt that he had no right to refuse the duty to which he had been called by the sovereign in person, and this new activity stimulated and strengthened him. He was constantly engaged in traveling about the three provinces intrusted to him; he carried his regulations even to pedantry; he was stern and strict even to cruelty with his subordinates, and he himself looked into the smallest details of his work.

Shortly after Prince Andrei's return, the old prince had quarreled with his son and made over to him the large estate of Bogucharovo, situated about twenty-five miles from Lisiya Gori. Partly on account of the sad recollections associated with Lisiya Gori, partly because Prince Andrei always felt himself unable to endure his father's idiosyncrasies, and partly also because he felt the need of solitude, he took possession of Bogucharovo, established himself there, and there spent a large part of his time.

After the battle of Austerlitz, Prince Andrei had resolutely made up his mind never to go back into military service again; and when the war began and all were obliged to enlist in order to escape active service, he accepted a position under his father's command in the recruiting of the militia.

On the tenth of March, 1807, the old prince started on one of his circuits. Prince Andrei, as usual during his father's absences, stayed at Lisiya Gori. The dear little Nikolusha had not been quite well for several days. The coachman who had driven the old prince to the next town returned and brought documents and letters for Prince Andrei.

The old prince, in his large scrawly hand, sometimes employing abbreviations and quaint archaic words, wrote on blue paper as follows:

I have just at this moment received very agreeable news—unless it's a canard. Benigsen is said to have gained a complete victory over Bonaparte at Eylau. They are wild with delight at Petersburg, and endless rewards have been distributed in the army. When mischief-makers do not meddle, then even a German can beat Bonaparte. They say he is retreating in great disorder.

Prince Andrei sighed and tore open another envelope. This was a closely written letter from Bilibin, covering two sheets. He folded it up without reading it, and again perused the letter from his father.

"Yes, what in the name of goodness was that disagreeable thing that he wrote?" asked Prince Andrei. "Oh, yes. Our men have won a victory over Bonaparte, now that I am not there to take part. Yes, yes; he will have a good chance to make sport of me; well, let him if he wants."

And he began to read Bilibin's letter, which was in French.

Bilibin was now acting as a diplomatic official at the headquarters of the army, and though he wrote in French with French jests and phraseology, still he described the whole campaign with genuine Russian frankness, not sparing reproaches or sarcasms. He wrote that the discretion imposed upon him by the necessities of diplomacy annoyed him, and that he was glad to have in Prince Andrei a disinterested correspondent, to whom he was able to pour out all the spleen that had been accumulating in him at the sight of what was going on in the army. This letter was of somewhat ancient date, having been penned even before the Battle of Preussisch-Eylau. Bilibin wrote as follows:

Since our great success at Austerlitz, my dear prince, I have been, as you may know, constantly at headquarters. I have conceived a decided taste for war, and so much the better for me. What I have witnessed these past three months is beyond belief!

I will begin at the very beginning. The "enemy of the human race," as you are well aware, has been attacking the Prussians. The Prussians are our faithful allies, who have only duped us three times within three years. Consequently, we take up their cause. But it proves that the "enemy of the human race" pays no attention to our fine speeches, and, in accordance with his rough and untrained nature, flings himself on the Prussians without allowing them to finish their parade, in short shrift beats them all hollow, and makes himself at home in the palace at Potsdam.

"I have the most earnest desire," writes the King of Prussia to Bonaparte, "that your majesty should be received and treated in my palace as would be most agreeable to you, and I hasten to take all measures to this end that circumstances permit. I only hope that I have been successful."

The Prussian generals make it a point of honor to be gracious toward the French and lay down their arms at the first summons.

The principal officer of the garrison of Glogau, with ten thousand men, asks the King of Prussia what he shall do if he is called upon to surrender. Fact!

In short, while hoping to make a great impression solely by our military attitude, lo and behold! here we are in for a real war and what is worse, for a war on our own frontiers.

Everything is all ready; we lack only one trifling thing, that is, a general-in-chief. As it has been discovered that the success of Austerlitz might have been more significant if only the general-in-chief had been older, all the octogenarians have been brought forward, and between Prosorovsky and Kamiensky, the preference has been given to the latter. The general comes to us in a little covered wagon after the style of Suvorof, and is received with acclamations of joy and triumph.

On the fourth comes the first courier from Petersburg. The mail is brought into the marshal's study, as he likes to do everything personally. I am summoned to help sort the letters and take those addressed to ourselves. The marshal looks on while we work and waits for the packages addressed to him. We search them over, but there is not one. The marshal becomes impatient and sets to work himself and finds letters from the emperor for Count T., for Prince V., and others. Then lo and behold! he goes off into one of his blue rages. He shoots fire and flames against everybody; he seizes the letters, breaks their seals, and reads those which the emperor has written to others.

"So that's the way I am treated! They have no confidence in me! Ah, that's a fine notion, setting others to watch my actions! Away with you." And he writes his famous order of the day to General Benigsen:

"I am wounded, and cannot ride on horseback, and consequently cannot command the army. You have taken your defeated army into Pultusk; there it is exposed, and lacks firewood and provender, and, as you yourself reported last evening to Count Buxhovden, you must devise measures for retiring beyond our frontier; see that this is done today."

"Owing to all my riding on horseback," he writes to the emperor, "I have become galled by the saddle, which, in addition to my former infirmities, entirely prevents me from riding on horseback and commanding such an extensive army, and therefore I have transferred the command to Count Buxhovden, who is next in seniority to myself, giving him the whole charge, and advising him, in case he cannot obtain bread, to move nearer to the interior of Prussia, since only enough bread is left for one day, and some of the regiments have none at all—according to the reports of the division commanders, Ostermann and Sedmoretsky—and the peasants, also, have nothing left. And I myself shall remain in the hospital at Ostrolenko until I am well. In offering, most respectfully, this report, I would add that if this army remains another fortnight in its present bivouac, by spring there will not be a single sound soldier left.

"Permit an old man to retire to the country, since he is now so feeble that he finds it impossible to fulfil the great and glorious duty for which he was chosen. I shall await your all-gracious permission here in the hospital, so as not to play the rôle of a clerk instead of commander at the head of the army. Of men like myself there are thousands in Russia."

The marshal is vexed with the emperor, and punishes all of us for it. Isn't that logical?

Thus ends the first act. In those that follow, the interest and the absurdity increase in proper degree. After the marshal's departure, it is discovered that we are in sight of the enemy and must fight. Buxhovden is commander-in-general-in-chief by order of seniority, but General Benigsen is not of this opinion; all the more because it is he and his corps who are in sight of the enemy, and he is anxious to profit by the occasion to fight a battle on his own account. He does so. This is the battle of Pultusk, which is reported to be a great victory, but which, in my opinion, was no victory at all. We civilians have, as you are well aware, a very wretched habit of making up our own minds in regard to the gain or loss of a battle. The one who retires after the battle is the loser, so we say, and in this respect we lost the battle of Pultusk.

In short, we retreat after the battle, but we send a courier to Petersburg to carry the news of the victory, and the general refuses to surrender the chief command to Buxhovden, hoping to receive from Petersburg the title of general-in-chief as a reward for his victory.

During this interregnum, we begin an excessively interesting and original scheme of maneuvers. Our design consists not, as it should have been, in avoiding or attacking the enemy, but solely of avoiding General Buxhovden, who by right of seniority should be our chief. We pursue this plan with so much energy that even in crossing an unfordable river we burn our bridges to cut off the enemy, who for the nonce is not Bonaparte but Buxhovden. General Buxhovden just misses being attacked and taken by overwhelming forces of the enemy by reason of one of our pretty maneuvers to save ourselves from him. Buxhovden pursues us, we sneak away. As soon as he crosses to our side of the river we cross back again. At last our enemy, Buxhovden, catches up with us and attacks us. The two generals have a quarrel. Buxhovden even goes so far as to send a challenge, and Benigsen has an attack of epilepsy.

But at the critical moment the courier who carried the news of our victory at Pultusk returns with our nomination as general-in-chief, and our enemy No. 1 is done for. We can think of No. 2, Bonaparte. But what do you suppose? Just at this moment there rises before us a third enemy—the orthodox army—loudly clamoring for bread, for meat, for crackers, for hay, and whatnot! The stores are empty; the roads impassable. The orthodox troops start marauding and in a way of which the last campaign would not give you the slightest notion. Half the regiments form themselves into freebooters, scouring the country and putting everything to fire and sword. The natives are ruined, root and branch; the hospitals overflowing with sick, and famine is everywhere. Twice the headquarters have been attacked by troops of marauders, and the general-in-chief has himself been obliged to ask for a battalion to drive them off. In one of these attacks my empty trunk and my dressing gown were carried off. The emperor has consented to grant all the divison chiefs the right to shoot the looters, but I very much fear that such a course would oblige one half of the army to shoot the other half.

V I

SHORTLY AFTER his reception into the Masonic brotherhood, Pierre, with full written instructions given him for his guidance in managing his estates, reached the province of Kiev, where the larger number of his serfs were to be found.

When he reached Kiev, he summoned all his overseers and explained his intentions and desires. He told them that measures would be immediately taken for the unconditional emancipation from servitude of all his serfs; that till this was done the peasants must not be constrained to hard work, that the women and children must not be required to work at all; that assistance was to be freely rendered the peasantry; that corporal punishment was not to be practiced, but reprimands should replace it, and that hospitals, asylums and schools were to be established on each of his estates.

Some of the overseers—and in the number were half-educated stewards —listened with dismay, supposing that the young count's speech meant that he was dissatisfied with their management or had discovered how they had been embezzling his funds. Others, after their first panic, found amusement in Pierre's thick, stumbling speech and the new words which they had never before heard; a third set found simply a certain sense of satisfaction in hearing their master talk; a fourth, and these were the sharpest, and at their head the chief overseer, perceived from this talk how it behooved them to deal with their landowner so as to serve their own ends.

The chief overseer expressed great sympathy with Pierre's proposed plans; but he remarked that, over and above these reforms, it was indispensable to make a general investigation of his affairs, which were in an unfortunate state.

In spite of Count Bezukhof's enormous wealth at the time when Pierre entered upon his inheritance—and it was said that he had an income of five hundred thousand rubles a year—he felt himself much poorer than when he received an allowance of ten thousand a year from his late father. He had a general dim idea that his expenses were somewhat as follows: interest to the bank, about eighty thousand rubles; about thirty thousand for the maintenance of his house in Moscow and his country home near Moscow, and the support of the three princesses; about fifteen thousand in pensions; as much more to various charitable institutions; one hundred and fifty thousand for support of the countess; about seventy thousand in interest on his debts; the building of a church which he had begun two years before, about ten thousand a year; the rest, not far from one hundred thousand, was expended, he himself knew not how, and almost every year he found himself obliged to borrow. Moreover, each year his chief overseer had written to him about fires, about bad harvests, about the necessity of building new factories and works. And thus Pierre was at the very first confronted by the settlement of his affairs, for which he had not the slightest taste or capacity.

Pierre each day spent some time with his chief overseer in this business; but he was conscious that his efforts did not advance his interests a single step. He felt that his efforts were wasted, that they did not have the slightest influence on his affairs and were not calculated to help him with his schemes. On the one hand, his head overseer pictured his affairs in the gloomiest colors, pointing out the absolute necessity of paying his debts and undertaking new enterprises with the labor of his peasantry, a thing to which Pierre refused to listen; on the other hand, Pierre insisted on the project of emancipating his serfs, but to this the overseer opposed the urgent necessity of first paying the mortgages, and consequently the impossibility of accomplishing the business rapidly.

The overseer did not say that this was absolutely impossible; he proposed to bring it about by selling certain forests in the province of Kostroma, some river lands, and an estate in the Crimea. But all these operations proposed by the overseer entailed complicated legal proceedings, replevins, permits, licenses, and so forth, so that Pierre quite lost his wits, and merely said, "Yes, yes, do so, then."

Pierre was not possessed of that practical bent for business which would have enabled him to grasp the whole matter immediately, and consequently he disliked it all and merely pretended to take an interest in it in the overseer's presence. The overseer, on his side, pretended to consider all these efforts advantageous for the proprietor and troublesome for himself.

In the large city of Kiev, the capital of the province, Pierre had some acquaintances; those he did not know made haste to pay their respects to him and gladly welcomed the millionaire, the largest landowner of the whole region. The temptations that assailed Pierre in his principal weakness—the one he had confessed at the time of his entrance into the lodge—were also so powerful that he could not resist them. Again whole days, weeks, months, of his life sped away constantly occupied with parties, dinners, breakfasts, balls, just as it had been in Petersburg, so that he had no time whatever for serious thoughts. Instead of the new life he had hoped to lead, he still went on with the same old routine, only in different surroundings.

Of the three obligations of Freemasonry, Pierre acknowledged that he was not fulfilling the one that enjoined upon every Mason to be a model of moral living; and of the seven precepts of virtue, two he had not taken to heart—virtuous living and love for death. He comforted himself with the thought that he was fulfilling one of the other obligations, the reformation of the human race, and that he possessed the other virtues, love of his neighbor and particularly generosity.

In the spring of the year 1807 Pierre determined to return to Petersburg, making on his way a visit to all of his possessions so as to assure himself of what had been done toward carrying out his orders and personally to learn the condition of the peasantry intrusted to him by God and whom he was striving to benefit.

His head overseer, who considered all of the young count's ideas completely fantastic—disadvantageous for the count, for the overseer, for the peasants themselves—had made some concessions. Though he still maintained that the emancipation of the serfs was an impossibility, he had made arrangements for the extensive erection on all the estates of schools, hospitals, and asylums, against the coming of the owner; everywhere he made arrangements for receptions, not, to be sure, on a sumptuous and magnificent scale which he knew would displease the young count, but rather semireligious and thanksgiving processions, with sacred images and the traditional bread and salt—the Russian symbol of hospitality; such demonstrations, in fact, as he was certain from his knowledge of his employer's character would deeply touch him and delude him.

The southern spring, the comfortable, rapid journey in his Vienna carriage, and the lonely roads had made a most pleasant impression on Pierre. These estates, none of which he had ever seen before, were each more picturesque than the other; the peasantry everywhere appeared prosperous and touchingly grateful to him for the benefits he was heaping upon them. Everywhere they met him with processions and receptions which, though they embarrassed him, filled his heart with a pleasant sensation. In one place the peasants brought him the bread and salt and a holy picture of Peter and Paul, and besought his permission to add at their own expense, in honor of his saint's-day and as a sign of their love and gratitude to him, a new chantry to the church. In another place he was met by women with children at the breast, who thanked him for freeing them from hard work. On a third estate he was met by a priest carrying a cross and surrounded by children to whom, through the count's liberality, he was teaching reading and religion. On all his estates he saw with his own eyes the massive stone foundations of edifices for hospitals, schools and almshouses, built or almost built, and ready to be opened in a short time. Everywhere Pierre saw from the accounts of his overseers that enforced labor had been greatly reduced from what it had been, and he listened to the affecting expressions of gratitude from deputations of serfs in their blue coats.

But Pierre did not know that where he had been met with the bread and salt, and where they were building the chantry of Peter and Paul, it was a commercial village where a yarmarka, or annual bazaar, was held on Saint Peter's day; that the chantry had been begun long before by some well-to-do peasants of the village, the very ones in fact who came to meet him, while nine-tenths of the peasants of this same village lived in the profoundest destitution. He did not know that in consequence of his order to cease employing nursing women at work on his fields, these very same women were forced to do vastly harder work on their own bits of communal land. He did not know that the priest who came to meet him with his cross oppressed the villagers with his penances, and that the pupils who accompanied him were placed with him at the cost of tears and were often ransomed back by their parents for large sums of money. He did not know that the edifices built, according to his plan, of stone were the work of his own laborers and greatly increased the forced service of his serfs, which were really diminished only on paper. He did not know that where the overseers pointed out to him on the books the reduction of the serfs' money payments by one-third, an amount corresponding was added to the forced labor of the peasantry. And so Pierre was in raptures over his tour among his estates, and he returned to that philanthropical frame of mind in which he had left Petersburg and wrote enthusiastic letters to his "preceptor-brother," as he called the Grand Master.

"How easy it is, how little strength it requires, to do so much good," said Pierre to himself. "And how little we trouble ourselves about it!"

He was happy at the gratitude, but felt mortified to be the recipient of it.

This gratitude made him think how very much more he might have easily done for these simple-hearted, kindly people.

The chief overseer, an obstinate and wily man, perfectly comprehending the intelligent but innocent young count and playing with him as with a toy, when he saw the effect produced upon Pierre by the receptions that he had himself so skilfully arranged, approached him all the more resolutely with arguments for the impossibility and, above all, the uselessness of emancipating the serfs, who were perfectly happy and contented as they were.

Pierre, in the depths of his soul, agreed with the overseer that it would be hard to imagine people more happy and contented, and that God only knew what would happen to them if they had their freedom; but still, though against his better judgment, he insisted upon what he felt was only justice. The overseer promised to do all in his power to carry out the count's desires, clearly comprehending that the count would never be in a position to assure himself whether all his plans for redeeming his mortgages had been carried out, or would ever ask or know how his costly edifices would stand empty and the peasants would continue to contribute their labor and money, just as they did on other estates, that is, the utmost that they could give.

VII

Rostof, returning from his furlough, for the first time felt and realized how strong were the ties that bound him to Denisof and all his regiment.

When he went back to his regiment he felt a sensation like the one that had come over him on his return home. When he saw the first hussar of his regiment, with unbuttoned uniform, when he recognized the redheaded Dementyef, when he caught sight of the roan horses picketed, when Lavrushka joyfully shouted to his gentleman, "The count has come," and the tattered Denisof, who had been having a nap, came running out from his earth hut and threw his arms around him, and the officers all came out to greet him, Rostof felt very much as he had when his mother and father and sister welcomed him home; tears of joy filled his throat and choked his voice. The regiment was also his home, and as sweet and dear to him as the home of his childhood.

There was nothing more of that mad confusion of the outside world in which he found himself out of place and often engaged in questionable actions. In the regiment everything was known: Who was lieutenant, who was captain, who was a good fellow, who was a rascal, and above all, who was his messmate. The sutler sold on credit, the pay was given quarterly. There was no necessity for thought or decision, provided only one did nothing that was considered dishonorable. Fulfil your duty, do what is commanded you in clear, explicit and unmistakable language, and all will be well.

Rostof had determined ever since the time of his gambling escapade to pay back his debt to his parents within five years. They sent him ten thousand rubles a year; now he resolved to take only two and to apply the remainder to covering the debt.

Our army, after repeated marches and countermarches, with skirmishes at Pultusk and at Preussisch-Eylau, was concentrated in the vicinity of Bartenstein, where it was awaiting the arrival of the emperor and the beginning of a new campaign.

During the month of April, the Pavlograd regiment was stationed for several weeks without moving, in the vicinity of an utterly dilapidated and deserted German village. It was thawing and cold; the rivers were beginning to break up; the roads were impassable owing to the mud; for many days no provisions had been brought for horses or men. As it seemed an impossibility for transport trains to arrive, the men scattered about among the pillaged and deserted villages in search of potatoes, but even these were scarce. Everything had been devoured and all the inhabitants had fled. Those who were left were worse than poverty-stricken; there was indeed nothing to take from them, and even the usually pitiless soldiers often let them keep the little they had, instead of appropriating it for themselves.

The Pavlograd regiment had lost only two men wounded in engagements, but they had lost almost half their numbers from sickness and starvation. Death was so certain if they went into the hospitals that the soldiers suffering from fevers and swellings caused by bad food preferred to stay in the ranks—dragging themselves by sheer strength of will to the front rather than take their chances in the hospitals. As spring opened they began to find a plant just showing above the ground; it resembled asparagus, and for some reason they called it "Mashka's sweetwort," though it was very bitter. They hunted for it all over the fields and meadows, digging it up with their sabers and devouring it, in spite of the injunction not to eat this poisonous plant. Later a new disease broke out among the soldiers, a swelling of the arms, legs, and face, and the physicians attributed it to the use of this root.

The horses also had been subsisting for a fortnight on thatching straw taken from the roofs, and had become shockingly emaciated, and, even before the winter was over, covered with tufts of uneven hair.

Yet, in spite of this terrible destitution, officers and men lived just the same as usual. Just as always, though with pale and swollen faces and in ragged uniforms, the hussars attended to their duties, went after forage and other things, groomed their horses, cleaned their arms, tore the thatch from roofs to serve as fodder, and gathered around the kettles for their meals, from which they got up still hungry, while they joked over their wretched fare and hunger. And just as usual during the hours when they were off duty, the soldiers built big fires, stripped and stood around them steaming themselves, smoked their pipes, sorted and baked their rotten, sprouting potatoes, and told stories about the campaigns of Potemkin and Suvorof, or legends of Alyosha the Cunning, or of Mikolka Popovitch the Journeyman.

The officers, also as usual, lived in couples or in threes in unroofed and half-ruined houses. The older ones looked after the procuring of straw and potatoes and other means of victualing the men. The younger ones were occupied as usual, some with card-playing (money was plentiful if provisions were not), some with innocent games—svaïka, a kind of ring toss, and quoits or skittles. Little was said about the general situation, partly because nothing positive was known, partly because there was a general impression that the war was going badly.

In the month of April the troops were cheered by the news that the sovereign was coming to the army. Rostof did not have the privilege of taking part in the review made by the emperor at Bartenstein, for it happened that the Pavlograd regiment was stationed at the advanced posts a considerable distance in front of Bartenstein. They were established in bivouacs. Denisof and Rostof lived in an earth hut excavated for them by their soldiers and covered with boughs and turf.

This earth hut was constructed according to a plan much in vogue at that time: a trench three and a half feet wide, a little less than five deep, and about eight long was dug. At one end steps were constructed, and this formed the entry, the "grand staircase"; the trench itself constituted the abode, in which those who were fortunate, as, for instance, the squadron commander, had a board set on posts on the side opposite the entrance; this served as a table. On each side along the trench the earth was hollowed away to half its depth, making a bed and divan. The roof was so constructed that in the middle it was possible to stand erect under it, and one could sit up on the beds by leaning over toward the table. Denisof, who lived luxuriously because the men of his squadron were fond of him, had an extra board in the pediment of the roof, and in this board was a broken but mended piece of glass. When it was very cold, coals from the soldiers' fires were brought on a bent piece of sheet iron and set on the steps in the "reception room," as Denisof called this part of the hovel, and this made it so warm that the officers who used to come in great numbers to visit Denisof and Rostof could sit there in their shirt sleeves.

In April Rostof happened to be on duty. One morning about eight o'clock, returning home after a sleepless night, he ordered some coals to be brought, changed his linen, which had been wet through by the rain, went through his devotions, drank his tea, got thoroughly warm, put his belongings in order in his own corner and on the table, and, with his face flushed by the wind and the fire, threw himself down on his back, in his shirt sleeves with his arms for a pillow. He was indulging in pleasant anticipations of the promotion which was likely to follow his last reconnoitering expedition and was waiting for the return of Denisof, who had gone off somewhere. Rostof was anxious to have a talk with him.

Behind the hut he heard Denisof's high-pitched voice; he had evidently returned in a bad humor. Rostof went to the "window" to look out and see whom he was berating; he recognized the quartermaster, Topcheyenko.

"I have given you special orders not to let them eat that woot, Mashka's what-you-call-it," cried Denisof. "And here I've seen it with my own eyes; Lazarchuk was bwinging some in fwom the field."

"I have given the order, your excellency, but they won't listen to it," replied the quartermaster.

Rostof again lay down on his bed and said to himself with a feeling of content: "Let him kick up a row and make as much fuss as he pleases; I've done my work and now I'll lie down; it's first-class!"

He heard Lavrushka, Denisof's shrewd and rascally valet, join his voice to the conversation going on outside the hut. Lavrushka had something to tell about oxcarts laden with biscuits which he had seen as he was going after provisions.

Denisof's sharp voice was again heard behind the hut, and his command, "Second platoon to saddle!"

"What can be up?" wondered Rostof.

Five minutes later Denisof came into the hut, climbed up with his muddy boots on his bed, lighted his pipe in grim silence, tossed over all his belongings, got out his whip and saber, and started from the hut. In reply to Rostof's question, "Whither away?" he gruffly and carelessly replied that he had something to attend to.

"May God and the soveweign be my judges!" he exclaimed as he went out, and then Rostof heard the hoofs of several horses splashing through the mud. Rostof did not take any pains to inquire where Denisof had gone. Warm and comfortable in his corner, he soon fell asleep, and it was late in the afternoon when he left the hut.

Denisof had not yet returned. The weather had cleared up and was bright and beautiful. Near a neighboring hut two officers and a cadet were playing svaïka, merrily laughing as they drove the redki, or mumbletypegs, into the loose, muddy ground. Rostof joined them. In the midst of the game the officers saw a train approaching them; fifteen hussars on emaciated horses followed the wagons. The teams, convoyed by the hussars, approached the picketing station, and a throng of hussars gathered round them.

"There, now, Denisof has been mourning all the time," said Rostof, "and here are provisions after all!"

"See there!" cried the officers. "Won't the men be happy!"

A short distance behind the hussars rode Denisof, accompanied by two infantry officers with whom he was engaged in a heated discussion. Rostof started down to meet them.

"I was ahead of you, captain," declared one of the officers, a lean little man evidently beside himself with passion.

"See here! I have told you that I would not weturn 'em!" replied Denisof.

"You shall answer for it, captain; this is violence—to rob an escort of their wagons. Our men have not had anything to eat for two days."

"And mine have not had anything to eat for two weeks," replied Denisof.

"This is highway robbery. You'll answer for it, my dear sir," repeated the infantry officer, raising his voice.

"What are you bothewing me for! Hey?" screamed Denisof, suddenly losing his temper. "I am the one who is wesponsible, and not you. What is the object of all your gwumbling here? Forward! . . . March!" he cried to the officers.

"Very good!" screamed the little officer, not quailing and not budging. "If you insist on pillage, then I . . ."

"Take yourself off to the devil! Get out of here!" and Denisof rode his horse straight at the officer.

"Very good, very good," reiterated the officer, with an oath, and turning his horse, he rode off at a gallop, bouncing in his saddle.

"A dog in a manger, a weal dog in a manger," shouted Denisof as he rode away. This was the most insulting remark that a cavalryman could make to a mounted infantryman. Then as he joined Rostof he burst into a loud laugh.

"I wescued 'em from the infantwy, I cawied off their 'twansport' by main force," said he. "What! do they think I would let my men pewish of starvation?"

The wagons which had been brought to the hussars were consigned to the infantry regiment, but Denisof, learning through Lavruskha that the "transport" was proceeding alone, had ridden off with his hussars and intercepted it. The soldiers had as many biscuits as they wished, and even enough to share with other squadrons.

The next day the regimental commander summoned Denisof, and covering his eyes with his spread fingers, he said:

"This is the way I look at it: I know nothing about it and I have nothing to do with it; but I advise you to go instantly to headquarters and report this affair to the commissary department, and, if possible, give a receipt for so many provisions received; unless you do, the requisition will be put down to the infantry: the matter will be investigated, and may end badly."

Denisof went straight from the regimental commander's to headquarters with the sincere intention of adopting his advice. In the evening he returned to his hut in a state such as Rostof had never seen Denisof in before. He could hardly speak or breathe. When Rostof asked him what the matter was, he only broke out in incoherent oaths and threats in a weak and husky voice.

Alarmed at Denisof's condition, Rostof advised him to undress, drink some cold water, and send for a physician.

"They are going to twy me for wobbewy—oh! Give me a dwink of water; let 'em twy me, I will beat the waskals evewy time, and I'll tell the empewor. Give me some ice," he added.

The regimental surgeon came in and said that it was absolutely necessary to take some blood from him. He filled a soup plate with dark blood from

Denisof's hairy arm, and then only was he in a condition to tell all that had taken place.

"I get there," said Denisof, telling his story. " 'Where is your head man here?' They show me. 'Can't you wait?' 'I have pwessing business; came twenty miles, impossible to wait; let me see him!' Vewy good; out comes the wobber-in-chief; he, too, undertakes to lecture me: 'This is highway wobbewy.' 'A man,' says I, 'is not a wobber, who takes pwovisions to feed his soldiers, but one who fills his own pockets.'—'Will you please keep quiet!' 'Vewy good.' 'Sign a weceipt at the commissioner's,' says he, 'and your affair will take its due course.' I go to the commissioner's, I go in. And there at the table, who do you suppose? No! Guess . . . Who has been starving us?" screamed Denisof, gesticulating his wounded arm, and pounding the table with his fist so violently that the board almost split and the glasses on it jumped up. "Telyanin!—'So it's you, is it, who's been starving us? Once before you had your snout slapped for you, and got off cheap at that. Ah! what a . . . what a . . . ' and I began to give it to him. I enjoyed it, I can tell you," cried Denisof, angrily and yet gleefully showing his white teeth under his black mustache. "I would have killed him if they had not sepawated us."

"Here, here, what are you shouting so for? Calm yourself," said Rostof. "You've set your arm bleeding again. Wait, it must be bandaged."

They bandaged Denisof's arm, and got him off to bed. The following day he woke cheerful and calm.

But at noon the adjutant of the regiment, with a grave and regretful face, came into Rostof's and Denisof's earth hut, and with real distress served upon Major Denisof a formal document from the regimental commander, who had been called to account for the proceedings of the day before. The adjutant informed them that the affair was likely to assume a very serious aspect, that a court-martial commission had been convened, and that on account of the severity with which just at that time rapine and lawlessness were treated, he might consider himself fortunate if the affair ended with mere degradation.

Those who felt themselves aggrieved represented the affair in somewhat this way: that after the pillage of the transport Major Denisof, without any provocation and apparently drunk, had made his appearance before the "commissary," called him a thief, threatened to thrash him, and when he was dragged away he had rushed into the office, struck two officials, and sprained the arm of one of them.

Denisof, in reply to a fresh series of questions from Rostof, laughed and said that he thought someone else had been there in that condition; but that all this story was rubbish, fiddle-faddle, that he was not afraid of any court-martials, and that if these villains dared to pick a quarrel with him, he would answer them in a way they would not soon forget.

Denisof spoke with affected indifference about the whole affair; but Rostof knew him too well not to perceive that at heart—though he hid it from the rest—he was afraid of a court-martial, and was really troubled by this affair, which evidently might have sad consequences. Every day inquiries, summonses, and other documents kept coming to him, and on the first of May he was required to turn over his command to his next in seniority, and appear at the headquarters of the division to make his defense in the matter of pillaging the provision train. On the evening preceding the day of the trial, Platof made a reconnaissance of the enemy with two regiments of Cossacks and two squadrons of hussars. Denisof, as usual, went out beyond the lines, in order to make an exhibition of his gallantry. A bullet from a French musket stuck him in the fleshy upper portion of his leg. Most likely Denisof, in ordinary circumstances, would not have left the regiment for such a trifling wound, but now he profited by this occurrence, gave up his command of the division, and went to the hospital.

VIII

In the month of June occurred the Battle of Friedland, in which the Pavlograd regiment took no part, and this was followed immediately by an armistice.

Rostof grievously missed his friend, and as he had not had any news of him since he left the regiment and was doubly uneasy about his trial and the result of his wound, he took advantage of the armistice and went to the hospital to make inquiries about Denisof.

The hospital was established in a small Prussian village which had twice been sacked by the Russian and French armies. For the very reason that it was summer, when everything in nature was beautiful, this village with its ruined rooftrees and fences and its filthy streets, its ragged inhabitants and the invalid and drunken soldiers wandering about, presented an especially gloomy appearance.

The hospital had been established in a stone mansion with many broken panes and window frames, situated in a yard with the remains of a ruined fence.

A number of pale-looking soldiers, bandaged and puffy, were walking up and down or sitting in the sun in the yard.

As soon as Rostof entered the house, he was enveloped by the odor of putrefaction and disease. On the doorstep he met the Russian military surgeon with a cigar in his mouth. The surgeon was followed by a Russian assistant.

"What are you doing here? Because a bullet hasn't touched you, do you want to be carried off by typhus? This is the house of leprosy!"

"What do you mean?" asked Rostof.

"Typhus, my boy! It's death for whoever comes in here. Makeyef," he pointed to his assistant, "Makeyef and I are the only two left to wriggle! Five of our brother doctors have died already. When a new man comes, it's all up with him in a week," said the doctor, with apparent satisfaction.

"The Prussian doctors were invited, but our allies did not like it at all."

Rostof explained his anxiety to find Major Denisof of the hussars.

"I don't know; I don't remember him. You can imagine: I have charge of three hospitals; four hundred sick are too many. It's a very good thing for benevolent Prussian ladies to send us coffee and lint at the rate of two pounds a month; if they didn't, we should be utterly lost." He laughed. "Four hundred, my boy! and they send me all the new cases. There are four hundred, aren't there? Hey?" he asked of the assistant. His assistant looked annoyed. It was evident that he was impatient for the loquacious doctor to make haste and take his departure.

"Major Denisof," repeated Rostof. "He was wounded at Moliten."

Rostof described Denisof's appearance.

"Yes, there was, there certainly was such a person," exclaimed the doctor, seeming to show a gleam of satisfaction. "But that person, I'm sure, must have died; however, I'll make inquiries; I had the lists; you have them, Makeyef, haven't you?"

"The lists are at Makar Alekseyevitch's," replied the assistant. "But you might inquire in the officers' ward; there you would find out for yourself," he added, turning to Rostof.

"You'd better not go," said the surgeon. "You wouldn't like to be kept here!"

Rostof, however, took leave of the surgeon, and begged the assistant to show him the way.

The first person Rostof met in the officers' ward was a slim little man with one arm gone, wearing a cap and dressing gown, who was walking up and down the first room with a pipe in his mouth. Rostof, on catching sight of him, racked his brains to remember where he had seen him.

"What a place for God to bring us together again!" exclaimed the little man. "I'm Tushin, Tushin, don't you remember? I brought you back safe at Schöngraben! Well, they've lopped off a little morsel, see here!" said he, smiling, and pointing to the empty sleeve of his dressing gown. "And you're hunting for Denisof. He's one of our chums!" he said, on learning whom Rostof wanted. "Here, here," and Tushin drew him into the second room, where several men were heard laughing loudly.

"I declare! how can they think of living here, much less of laughing?" wondered Rostof, with the odor of dead bodies still in his nostrils.

Denisof, with his head buried under the bedclothes, was sound asleep on his bed, although it was noon.

"What? Wostof? How are you, how are you?" he cried, in exactly the same voice as when he was with the regiment; but Rostof observed with pain that hidden under this show of ease and vivacity there was a shadow of a new and disagreeable asperity in Denisof's expression, and in his words and tones. It seemed as if he were trying to forget his former life, and the only thing that interested him was his quarrel with the commissary officials.

In reply to Rostof's question as to how the affair was going, he immediately pulled out from under his pillow a document which he had received from the commission, and the rough draft of his own reply to it. He brightened as he began to read his document, and he called Rostof's attention to the keen things which he said against his enemies in his reply.

His neighbor on the next bed, a stout Uhlan, interrupted Denisof.

"Now, it's my opinion," said he, turning to Rostof, "that the only thing to do is simply to petition the sovereign for pardon. They say now there are going to be great rewards, and a mere matter of a pardon . . ."

"I petition the soveweign!" exclaimed Denisof, in a voice in which he tried hard to maintain his old-time energy and vehemence, but which sounded helplessly feeble. "What for? If I had been a highway wobber I might petition for pardon, but here I am court-martialed because I 'cawy these wobbers thwough clean water,' as the saying is. Let 'em twy me, I'm not afwaid of 'em! I have served my Tsar honowably, and my countwy, and I have not been a thief! and they degwade me, and . . . See here! listen to what I wite 'em in stwaightforward language. This is what I wite: 'If I had been an embezzler . . .'"

"It's cleverly written, no question about that," said Tushin. "But this is not the point." He turned also to Rostof. "He must give in, and this is what Denisof will not hear of doing. Now, look, the auditor himself told you that it was bad business."

"Let it be bad business, then!" exclaimed Denisof.

"And the auditor wrote a petition for you," continued Tushin, "and you had better sign it and give it to him. He"—meaning Rostof—"has influence at headquarters. You won't find a better chance."

"Yes, but haven't I told you that I won't stoop to cwinge," interrupted Denisof, and once more he set out to finish his document.

Rostof did not dare to argue with Denisof, although he felt instinctively that the course indicated by Tuskin and the other officers was the one advisable, and he would have counted himself happy to find a chance to render Denisof a service.

Late in the afternoon Rostof got up to go, and asked Denisof if there was anything he could do for him.

"Yes, wait," said Denisof, glancing at the officers, and, pulling some papers out from under his pillow, he went to the window, where stood an inkstand, and began to write.

"You can't split an axhead with a whip," said he as he came away from the window, and gave Rostof a large envelope. This was the petition to the emperor, which the auditor had written for him; in it nothing was said whatever about the faults of the commissary department, but he simply craved pardon.

"Hand it in; it's evident . . ." he did not finish his sentence, and smiled a painfully unnatural smile.

IX

On his return to the regiment, after having made his report to the commander in regard to Denisof's condition, Rostof set out for Tilsit with the petition to the sovereign.

On the twenty-fifth of June the French and Russian emperors had met at Tilsit. Boris Drubetskoy begged the distinguished individual to whose staff he was attached for permission to be present at the conference which was to be held at Tilsit.

"I should like to see the great man with my own eyes," said he, speaking of Napoleon, whom he, like everyone else, had always hitherto called Bonaparte.

"You mean Bonaparte?" asked the general, with a smile.

Boris looked inquiringly at his general, and immediately perceived that the general was trying to quiz him.

"Prince, I am speaking of the Emperor Napoleon," he replied.

The general, with a smile, tapped him on the shoulder. "You'll get on," said he, and took him along.

Boris was one of the few who were there at the Niemen on the day when the emperors met; he saw the rafts with the monograms; he saw Napoleon ride down the bank past the French Guards; he saw the Emperor Alexander's thoughtful face, as he sat in silence in the inn on the bank of the river, waiting for Nepoleon to come; he saw the two emperors get into the boats, and Napoleon, who was the first to reach the raft, go forward with swift steps to meet Alexander, give him his hand, and then disappear with him under the pavilion.

Boris felt that his position was henceforth secured. He was not only known by name, but was always seen and taken for granted. Twice he was sent on errands to the emperor himself, so that the emperor came to know his face, and the inner circle not only ceased to shun him as a "new person," as before, but would have been surprised at his absence.

Boris lodged with another aide, the Polish Count Zhilinski. Zhilinski, though a Pole, had been educated in Paris, was rich, and was passionately fond of the French. Almost every day during the time of the interview at Tilsit, he and Boris used to have the officers of the Guards and members of the imperial French staff to breakfast and dinner with them.

On the evening of the sixth of July, Count Zhilinski was giving a dinner to some of his French acquaintances. The guest of honor was one of Napoleon's aides; there were a number of the officers of the Imperial Guard, and a young lad belonging to an old aristocratic French family, who was Napoleon's page. That same day Rostof, profiting by the darkness to pass unrecognized, proceeded to Tilsit in civilian dress and went to the apartment occupied by Zhilinski and Boris.

Rostof, in common with the whole army from which he came, was as yet far from experiencing that change which had taken place at headquarters and in Boris, in regard to Napoleon and the French—who now looked upon them as friends rather than foes. It struck Rostof strangely, therefore, to see in Boris' rooms French officers in the very same uniforms which he had been in the habit of viewing in an utterly different light, across from the skirmishers' lines. He paused at the threshold and asked in Russian if Drubetskoy lived there.

Boris heard the strange voice in the entry and came out to meet him. At the first moment, on recognizing Rostof, a shade of annoyance crossed his face.

"Ah! is it you? Very glad, very glad to see you," said he, nevertheless, coming toward him with a smile. But Rostof had noticed his first impression.

"It seems I have come at the wrong time," said Rostof. "I should not have come, but I had business," he added coldly.

"No, I was only surprised that you had got away from your regiment. I'll be with you in a moment," he shouted, in reply to someone calling him from within.

"I see that my visit is untimely," repeated Rostof.

The expression of annoyance had entirely disappeared by this time from Boris' face; apparently having considered and made up his mind what course to pursue, he seized his visitor by both hands, with remarkable ease of manner, and drew him into the adjoining room. Boris' eyes, fixed calmly and confidently on Rostof, seemed to be shielded by something—as if there were a screen, the blue spectacles of high society, placed in front of them.

"Oh, please say no more about coming inopportunely," said Boris. He drew him into the room where the table was set for dinner, introduced him to the guests, calling him by name and explaining that he was not a civilian, but an officer of the hussars, and an old friend of his.

Rostof's ill-humor had sprung up immediately on noticing the annoyance expressed in Boris' face, and, as usually happens with people who are out of sorts, he imagined that all were looking at him with unfriendly eyes and that he was in their way. And, in truth, he was in their way, for he took no part in the conversation that was just beginning.

"And why is he sitting there?" the glances that were fixed on him seemed to say. He got up and went to Boris.

"I know I am a burden to you," said he, in a whisper. "Come, let me tell you about my business and I will be going."

"No, not in the least," replied Boris. "But if you are tired, let us go into my room, and you can lie down and rest."

"Well, really . . ."

They went into Boris' little bedroom. Rostof, without sitting down, began in a pettish tone—as if Boris were in some way to blame for the matter—to tell him about Denisof's affair, and asked him if he could and would send in the petition for Denisof through the general on whose staff he was serving, and see to it that Denisof's letter reached the emperor.

When the two were alone together, Rostof, for the first time, found it awkward to look into Boris' eyes. Boris, sitting with his legs crossed and pressing the slender fingers of his right hand into his left, listened to Rostof in the same way as a general listens to a report from his subordinate; sometimes he glanced around, and then again looked into Rostof's face with that peculiar veil of impenetrability over his eyes. Rostof felt awkward every time he did so, and looked down.

"I have heard of things like that, and I know that the sovereign is very strict in such cases. I think it would be best not to bring it to his majesty's attention. In my opinion, it would be better to give the petition directly to the commander of the corps . . . And, as a general thing, I think . . ."

"Then you don't care to do anything. Why not say it right out!"

Rostof almost shouted, not looking at Boris' eyes.

Boris smiled. "On the contrary, I will do all that is in my power. But I thought . . ."

At this moment, Zhilinski's voice was heard, calling Boris back.

"Well, go, go, go!" said Rostof, and excusing himself from the supper and remaining alone in the little chamber, he paced for a long time up and down and listened to the lively French conversation in the adjoining room.

No day could have been more unfavorable for presenting Denisof's petition to the emperor than that on which Rostof went to Tilsit. He himself could not appear in the presence of the general-in-charge, for the reason that he was in civilian dress and had come away without leave of absence; and Boris, even if he had had the best will in the world, could not do this on the day that followed Rostof's arrival at Tilsit. On that day, the ninth of July, the preliminary articles of peace were signed; the emperors exchanged orders, Alexander received that of the Legion of Honor and Napoleon that of Saint Andrew of the first degree; and on that same day a dinner was to be given to the Preobrazhensky battalion by the battalion of the French Guards. The emperors had both agreed to be present at the banquet.

"Boris isn't willing to help me, and I won't have anything more to do with him, that's settled," said Nikolai to himself. "It's all over between us; but I won't leave town until I have done the best I could for Denisof, and at least handed his petition to the sovereign. To the sovereign? . . . He is there!" said Rostof to himself, involuntarily wandering back to the mansion occupied by Alexander.

In front of the door stood saddle horses, and the suite were assembling, evidently for the purpose of escorting his majesty on a ride.

"At any moment I may see him," said Rostof to himself. "If I could only put the letter straight into his hands! But wouldn't they arrest me on account of being out of uniform? Impossible! He would understand on whose side justice lay. He understands everything, he knows everything!

"I will fall at his feet and beseech him. He will raise me, listen to me, and even thank me. 'I am glad of any opportunity of doing good, but to right wrongs is my greatest happiness,'" said Rostof, imagining the words his sovereign would say to him. And, though he had to run the gauntlet of the inquisitive glances fastened upon him, he went up the front steps of the imperial residence.

From the porch a broad staircase led straight upstairs. At the right was a half-open door. Below, at the foot of the staircase, was still another door leading to the ground floor.

"What do you wish?" asked someone.

"To give a letter, a petition, to his majesty," said Rostof in a trembling voice.

"A petition? It should go to the general-in-charge; please come this way," he indicated the door leading to the ground floor. "But he won't receive it."

On hearing this voice, so cold and unconcerned, Rostof was panic-stricken at his audacity; the thought that he might at any moment meet his majesty was so entrancing, and at the same time so terrible to him, that he felt like running away, but the orderly who came to meet him opened the door into the general's office, and Rostof went in.

"Well, my boy, what are you doing here without a uniform?" demanded a deep bass voice.

This was a general of cavalry, formerly commander of the division in which Rostof served. During that campaign he had won the signal favor of the sovereign.

Rostof was startled and began to make his excuses, but when he saw the general's good-natured, jovial face, he drew him to one side and began, in a voice choked by emotion, to lay his whole case before him, and begged the general to take the part of Denisof, who was well known to him. The general listened to Rostof's story and shook his head gravely. "Pity, pity; he's a brave fellow; give me his letter."

Rostof had only just handed him the petition and finished telling Denisof's whole story, when quick steps and a jingling of spurs were heard on the staircase, and the general, leaving him, hurried to the steps. Forgetting his apprehension of being recognized, Rostof, with many other curious spectators from among the natives, went close to the doorway, and again, though two years had passed, he recognized those adored features, the same face, the same glance, the same gait, the same union of majesty and sweetness. And that feeling of enthusiasm and love for his sovereign rose in Rostof's soul with all its former force.

The emperor wore the Preobrazhensky uniform, white chamois leather breeches, Hessian boots, with the star of an order Rostof did not know. It was the Legion of Honor. As he came out on the steps, he held his cap under his arm and was putting on his gloves. He paused, glanced around, and his glance seemed to light up all about him. He said a few words to one of the generals. He also recognized the general who had been formerly commander of Rostof's division, gave him a smile, and beckoned to him.

All the suite moved away from them, and Rostof noticed that this general held a rather long conversation with the sovereign.

The emperor said a few words in reply, and took a step toward his horse. Again the crowd of the suite and the crowd of spectators, with Rostof in their number, followed after the emperor. Standing by his steed, with his arm thrown over the saddle, the sovereign turned to the cavalry general, and spoke in a loud voice, evidently intending that he should be heard by all:

"I cannot, general, and I cannot because the law is more powerful than I," said the emperor, and he put his foot in the stirrup. The general respectfully inclined his head; the emperor got into the saddle and rode at a gallop down the street. Rostof, forgetting himself in his enthusiasm, joined the crowd and ran after him.

1808-1810

Having made peace with Napoleon, the Tsar espouses his cause. When France and Sweden fight in 1808, Russia invades Sweden and for her pains is permitted to annex Finland. When Austria again defies Napoleon in 1809, Russia is on the French side. Meanwhile Napoleon is at war against Spain and Portugal, and there on the Iberian penisula an army under Arthur Wellesley (later to become Duke of Wellington) begins Britain's first large-scale participation in the continental land fighting. But in this campaign Russia is not involved, and by the standards of those troubled times is enjoying peace and tranquillity.

Part Sixth

IN THE YEAR 1808 the emperor went to Erfurt for another interview with the Emperor Napoleon, and in the upper circles of Petersburg much was said about the magnificence of this solemn meeting.

In 1809 the intimacy between these two "arbiters of the world," as Napoleon and Alexander were called, reached such a point that when Napoleon that year declared war against Austria, the Russian troops crossed the frontier to support their former enemy, Bonaparte, against their former ally, the emperor of Austria; and there was also talk in high society of a possible marriage between Napoleon and one of the Emperor Alexander's sisters.

But besides these external political combinations, the attention of Russian society was at this time especially occupied with the internal reforms that were being inaugurated in all parts of the imperial dominion.

In the meantime, life—the ordinary life of men—with its own concerns of health, illness, labor, recreation, with its interest in philosophy, science, poetry, music, love, friendship, hatreds, sufferings, went on as always, independent and outside of political alliance or enmity with Napoleon Bonaparte, and outside of all prospective reforms.

Prince Andrei had been living uninterruptedly for two years in the country. All those enterprises that Pierre had devised on his estates and had brought to no result, constantly changing as he did from one plan to another, had been accomplished by Prince Andrei without any display and without noticeable exertion. He had to a high degree that practical tenacity of purpose which Pierre lacked, and which gave impetus to any enterprise without oscillation or undue effort on his own part.

On one of his estates the three hundred serfs were enrolled as free farmers; this was one of the first instances of the sort in Russia. On others, the forced husbandry service was commuted for quitrent. At Bogucharovo, a midwife was engaged at his expense to help in cases of childbirth, and a priest was employed at a salary to teach the children of the peasants and household servants.

Half of his time Prince Andrei spent at Lisiya Gori with his father and son, who was still in the care of nurses; the other half he spent at his "Bogucharovo monastery," as his father called his estate.

He eagerly followed all the outside events of the world; he read many books, and was often amazed to remark when men came fresh from Petersburg, from the very vortex of life, to visit his father or himself, that these men were far behind him in their knowledge of what was going on in politics at home and abroad, though he had not once left the country. In addition to his enterprises on his estates, and his general occupation in reading the most varied books, Prince Andrei spent his spare time in composing a critical account of our last two unfortunate campaigns, and a project for a change in our military code and regulations.

In the spring of 1809 Prince Andrei went to the neighborhood of Riazan, where his son, whose guardian he was, had estates.

He was compelled by his obligations as trustee of the Riazan property to call upon the district marshal of the nobility. The marshal was Count Ilya Andreyitch Rostof; about the middle of May, Prince Andrei went to see him.

By this time the weather had become very warm. The woods were now in full leaf, it was dusty, and it was so hot that as he drove by water he had a powerful desire to go swimming.

Prince Andrei, in anything but a happy frame of mind and absorbed in thinking of the business he had to transact with the marshal, drove into the tree-shaded avenue leading up to the mansion of the Rostofs at Otradnoye. At his right, he heard behind the trees the gay sounds of women's voices, and saw a bevy of young girls running down as if to cut off his advance. In front of the others, and therefore nearest to him, ran a very slender, indeed a strangely slender, girl, with dark hair and dark eyes, in a yellow chintz dress, with a white handkerchief around her head, the locks escaping from it in ringlets. The girl shouted something as she approached the carriage; then, seeing that it was a stranger, she ran back again with a merry laugh, not looking at him.

Something akin to pain affected Prince Andrei at this incident. The day was so beautiful, the sun so bright, everything all around was so cheerful! But this slender, pretty young girl did not know and had no wish to know anything of him, and was content and happy in her separate, most likely stupid, but still gay and careless existence. What was there for her to be merry about? What were her thoughts? Certainly not about the military code or about Riazan quitrents! What, then, was she thinking about? And why was she happy? Such questions involuntarily arose in Prince Andrei's mind.

Count Rostof was spending the summer of 1809 at Otradnoye just as he always had; that is, entertaining almost all the residents of the province with hunting parties, theatricals, dinners, and music. He welcomed Prince Andrei most hospitably, as he did every new guest, and almost by main force compelled him to stay for the night.

During the course of the wearisome day, monopolized by his elderly host and the most distinguished of the guests, who happened to be present in large numbers on account of the old count's approaching saint's-day, Bolkonsky many times was attracted to Natasha, who was among the merriest and most entertaining of the younger members of the household, and kept asking himself, "What can she be thinking about? Why is she so gay?"

At last finding himself alone that night, in a strange place, he could not at once go to sleep. He read for a time, then put out his candle, then lighted it again. It was hot in the room with the shutters closed from within. He was annoyed at "that stupid old man," as he called Rostof, for having detained him by the excuse that the necessary papers had not yet come from the city; and he was vexed with himself for having remained.

He got up and went to the window to open it. As soon as he threw back the shutters, the moonlight, as if it had been on the watch at the window and long waiting the opportunity, came pouring into the room. He opened the window. The night was cool and calmly beautiful. In front of the window was a row of clipped trees, dark on one side and silver-bright on the other. At the foot of the trees was some sort of succulent, rank vegetation, the leaves and stalks covered with silvery dew. Farther away, beyond the trees, was a roof glittering with dew. Farther to the right, a tall tree with wide-spreading branches showed a brilliant white bole and limbs; and directly above it the moon, almost at her full, shone in the bright, almost starless, spring night. Prince Andrei leaned his elbows on the window sill and fixed his eyes on the sky.

His room was on the second floor; the rooms overhead were also occupied, and by people who were not asleep. He overheard women's voices above him.

"Only just once more," said a voice that Prince Andrei instantly recognized.

"But when are you going to sleep?" replied a second voice.

"I will not, cannot sleep; what can I do? Come! this is the last time." The two female voices broke out into a snatch of song, forming the final phrase of a duet.

"Ah! how charming! Now then, let's go to sleep; that's the end of it!"

"You go to sleep, but I can't," replied the first voice, approaching the window. She evidently thrust her head out of the window, because the rustling of her dress was heard, and even her breathing. Everything was calm and stone-still, like the moon and her light, and the shadows. Prince Andrei feared to stir, lest he should betray his involuntary presence.

"Sonya! Sonya!" again spoke the first voice. "Now, how can you go to sleep! Just see how lovely it is! Oh, how lovely! Come, wake up, Sonya!" said she again, with tears in her voice. "Come, now, such a lovely, lovely night was never seen!"

Sonya made some answer expressive of her disapproval.

"No, but do look! What a moon! Oh, how lovely! Do come here! Sweetheart! Darling, come here! There, now, do you see? If you would only sit down this way, and rest yourself on your knees . . . a little closer . . . we must squeeze together more . . . there, if one tried, one might fly away! Yes, that's the way!"

"Look out! You'll fall!"

A little scuffle was heard, and then Sonya's discontented voice saying: "Look, it's two o'clock!"

"Oh, you only spoil it all for me! Now go away, go away!"

Again all became still, but Prince Andrei knew she was still there; he could hear from time to time a little rustling, from time to time her sighs.

"Oh, dear me! Dear me! It's too bad! To bed, then, if I must!" and the window was closed.

"And my existence is nothing to her!" thought Prince Andrei while he was listening to their talk, somehow or other hoping and fearing that she would say something about him. "It's the same old story! And done on purpose!" he thought. And suddenly there arose in his soul such an unexpected throng of youthful thoughts and hopes, opposed to the whole current of his life, that he felt himself too weak to analyze his condition, and so he went to sleep immediately.

On his return from his journey, Prince Andrei made up his mind to go to Petersburg in the autumn, and he devised various reasons in support of this decision. A whole series of convincing and logical arguments in favor of his return to Petersburg, and even reëntering the army, were all the time coming to his aid. It was now beyond his comprehension that he could ever have doubted the necessity of going back to active life, just the same as a short month before he could not comprehend how the idea could ever occur to him of leaving the country.

It seemed clear to him that all his experiments of life would surely be wasted and pointless unless he were to put them into effect and once more take an active part in life. He now could not understand how, on the strength of such wretched arguments, he had convinced himself that it would be humiliating himself, after all his lessons in life, to believe in the possibility of success and the possibility of happiness and love. Now his reason showed him the exact contrary.

After this journey of his, Prince Andrei began to feel tired of the country; his former occupations no longer interested him; and often, as he sat alone in his study, he would get up, go to the mirror, and look long at his own face. Then he would turn away and gaze at the portrait of his late wife, Lisa, who, with her little curls à la grecque, looked down upon him with an affectionate and radiantly happy expression from the gilded frame. She seemed no longer to say to her husband those terrible words she had once uttered; she simply gazed at him with a merry and quizzical look. And Prince Andrei, clasping his hands behind his back, would walk long up and down the room, sometimes scowling, sometimes smiling, thinking over the preposterous, inexpressible, mysterious, almost criminal ideas connected with Pierre, with glory, with the girl at the window, with the beauty of women, and love, which were changing his whole life.

II

Two YEARS before this, Pierre, on his return to Petersburg from a tour among his estates, found himself involuntarily at the head of the Petersburg Freemasons. He established dining lodges and burial lodges, he enrolled new members, and he labored for the union of various lodges and for the acquisition of original documents. He gave his money freely toward the building of a Masonic temple and, as far as he could, promoted collections for charity, to which the majority of the members subscribed sparsely or irregularly. He supported almost unaided the almshouse established by the order in Petersburg.

His life, in the meantime, went on the same as before, with the same inclinations and dissipations. He liked the pleasures of the table—good eating and wines; and although he looked upon it as immoral and degrading, he could not keep himself from the amusements of the bachelor friends with whom he mingled.

Amid the fog of all his various occupations and enterprises, however, Pierre before a year was over began to be conscious that the Masonic ground on which he stood was giving way faster and faster under his feet, the more he tried to maintain himself on it. At the same time he felt that the more the ground on which he stood yielded under him, the more inextricably he was committed to it. When he first entered Freemasonry he experienced the sensations of a man who unquestioningly sets foot on the smooth surface of a bog. On trusting his weight to it, he begins to sink. In order fully to persuade himself of the solidity of the ground whereon he stands, he sets down another foot and slumps in more deeply than before; and, being caught in it, in spite of himself he wades in to the knee.

At this time he received a letter from his wife, who begged him to grant her an interview, and described her sorrow at what had happened and her desire to devote her whole life to him. At the end of the letter she informed him that she was about to return to Petersburg from abroad.

Shortly after his receipt of the letter, one of the Masonic brethren whom he respected less than the others broke in on his solitude and, leading the conversation to Pierre's domestic grievances, took it upon himself to say to him, by way of brotherly advice, that his severity toward his wife was unjust and that Pierre had deviated from the first rules of the brotherhood by not pardoning the penitent.

At the same time, his mother-in-law, the wife of Prince Vasili, sent for him, begging him to call on her, if only for a few minutes, in regard to a matter of supreme importance. Pierre saw that he was destined to be over-ruled, that they were set on reconciling him to his wife; and indeed this was not wholly disagreeable to him in the state of mind in which he found himself. It was all the same to him. He now felt that nothing in life was of great importance; and under the influence of the depression which engulfed him, he prized neither his own freedom nor his obstinate determination to punish his wife.

"No one is right, no one is to blame, and of course she was not to blame," he said to himself. If Pierre did not immediately agree to a reconciliation with his wife, it was simply because in his condition of melancholy he had not the energy to take the first step in the matter. If his wife had come to him, he would simply not have driven her away. In comparison with what now occupied him, was it not a matter of supreme indifference to him whether or not he lived with his wife? This is what he wrote in his diary:

Petersburg, November 23.

Again I am living with my wife. My mother-in-law, with tears in her eyes, came to me and said that Helene had returned and that she begged me to hear her; that she was innocent; that she was unhappy at my sending her away, and many such things. I was well aware that if I once allowed myself to see her, I would not have the strength to refuse her request. In my perplexity, I did not know whose help and advice to seek. If the benefactor had been here, he would have told me. I shut myself up alone in my room, read over Bazdeyef's letters, re-called my conversations with him, and, taking all things together, I came to the conclusion that I had no right to refuse her request; and that if it was my duty to offer the hand of help to everyone, all the more was it so with a person so closely united to me, and that I was in duty bound to bear my cross. But if I pardoned her for the sake of right-doing, then my reunion with her must have merely a spiritual end and aim. I told my wife that I would beg her to forget all the past, that I would beg her to pardon me for anything in which I had been blameworthy toward her, and that I had nothing to forgive. It was a pleasure for me to tell her that. No need for her to know how trying it was for me to see her again. I have taken up my abode in the upper rooms of the great mansion, and I rejoice in a pleasant sense of regeneration.

In those days, as has always been the case, "high society," which met at court and at the fashionable balls, was divided into a number of inner circles, each having its own distinctive peculiarities. The most popular of these cliques was the "French circle," which advocated the Napoleonic alliance and was led by Count Rumyantsof and Caulaincourt. Helene played a prominent part in this clique as soon as she and her husband began living together again at Petersburg. Her salon was frequented by the gentlemen of the French legation and by a great number of people distinguished for their amiability and wit who belonged to that set.

Helene had been at Erfurt at the time of the notable meeting between the emperors, and had there made the acquaintance of all the Napoleonic celebrities of Europe. She had enjoyed a most brilliant success. Napoleon himself remarked her presence at the theater and said of her, "*C'est un superbe animal.*"

Pierre was not surprised at her success as far as beauty and elegance were concerned, because as time went on she grew even more beautiful than before. But he was amazed that his wife in the course of two short years should have succeeded in acquiring the reputation of being a "charming woman, as clever as she is beautiful." The distinguished Prince de Linge wrote her eight-page letters. Bilibin treasured up his witticisms so as to get them off for the first time at Countess Bezukhof's. To be received in her salon was regarded as equivalent to a diploma of cleverness. Young men read books previous to making their appearance there, so as to have some special subject to talk about; and the secretaries of the legation, and even ambassadors, confided diplomatic secrets to her, so that Helene was a power in a certain way.

Pierre, who knew that she was really stupid, had a strange feeling of perplexity and fear when he appeared, as he sometimes did, at her receptions and dinner parties, where the conversation ran on politics, poetry and philosophy. On such occasions he experienced such a feeling as a conjurer must have who is constantly afraid lest somehow or other his tricks will be discovered. But either because stupidity is the one thing needful in the management of such a salon, or because those who are deceived find a certain amount of satisfaction in the deception itself, the secret was not betrayed, and Countess Elena Vasilyevna Bezukhof's reputation of being "a clever, charming woman" was so firmly established that she could utter the most astonishing trivialities, and all professing to be charmed with every word that fell from her lips, discovered in them a depth of thought which she herself did not begin to suspect.

Pierre was precisely the kind of husband that such a brilliant woman of the world ought to have. He was a queer, absent-minded fellow, a *grand seigneur* of a husband, interfering with no one, and not only not spoiling the lofty tone proper to such a drawing-room, but serving as an admirable background against which to display his wife's elegance and tact. Pierre during these two years—in consequence of perpetually concentrating on transcendental interests and his genuine contempt for all things else—had assumed, in the (to him) uninteresting society which his wife gathered round her, that tone of abstraction and absent-mindedness, combined with affability toward all, which cannot be acquired by art and which somehow commands involuntary respect. He walked into his wife's drawing-room as if it were the theater; he knew everyone, toward all he was equally cordial and equally reserved. Sometimes he joined in the conversation if it interested him, and then he blurted out his opinions with that thick utterance of his, regardless of the inappropriateness of his ideas or the presence of the gentlemen from the embassies. But it was a foregone conclusion in regard to "that queer husband" of the most distinguished woman in Petersburg that no one would take his idiosyncrasies seriously.

Among the young men who daily frequented Helene's mansion after her return from Erfurt, Boris Drubetskoy, who was now on the highroad to success in the service, was the most assiduous in his visits at the Bezukhofs'. Helene called him "my page" and treated him as if he were a boy. The smiles she gave him were just like the ones she showered on all the rest, but occasionally Pierre had an unpleasant feeling at the sight of them together.

Boris treated Pierre with a peculiar dignified and rather grave deference. This shade of deference also disquieted Pierre. He had suffered so keenly, three years before, from the affront his wife had put on him, that now he saved himself from the possibility of a repetition of it, in the first place by renouncing the idea of being his wife's husband, and in the second place by not allowing a suspicion of her to enter his head.

"No, now that she has become a bluestocking, she will never be troubled again with such temptations," he would say to himself. "There is no example of a bluestocking's having love affairs," he would assure himself, as if it were an axiom in which he must infallibly believe, though he could not have told where he had acquired it.

But strangely enough, Boris' presence in his wife's drawing-room—and he was there almost constantly—affected him physically: it seemed to paralyze his limbs, to waken all his self-consciousness and take away his freedom of motion.

"Such a strange antipathy," thought Pierre, "and yet he used to please me very much."

In the eyes of the world Pierre was a great gentleman, the somewhat blinded and ridiculous husband of a distinguished wife, a queer genius who accomplished nothing, did no one any harm, and was on the whole a very fine and good young man. But in the depths of Pierre's soul during all this time there was going on the complicated and arduous labor of internal development, which brought him a perception of many secrets, and made him experience many joys and many doubts.

247

III

THE ROSTOFS' financial affairs had not improved in the course of the two years they had been living wholly in the country.

Although Nikolai had persistently kept to his resolve and continued to serve in an obscure regiment where he had no chance of advancement, and therefore spent comparatively little money, still the scale of life at Otradnoye was so lavish and, above all, Mitenka's management so bad, that the debts rolled up more and more each year. The old count evidently saw but one means of relief—a government position; and he went to Petersburg to get one, and at the same time, as he expressed it, to give the girls one last season's amusement.

Shortly after the Rostofs reached Petersburg Berg proposed to Vera, and his proposal was accepted.

In spite of the fact that in Moscow the Rostofs moved in the highest society without thinking or inquiring what the society was to which they belonged, they found in Petersburg that their position was somewhat absurd and vague. In Petersburg they were regarded as provincials, and many people who had accepted their hospitality at Moscow without question now did not deign to notice them.

The Rostofs entertained as freely in Petersburg as they had done in Moscow, and around their board gathered a very mixed company: neighbors of theirs from Otradnoye, landed proprietors of good standing but not rich, and their daughters, and a lady in waiting of the empress, a Madame Peronski; Pierre Bezukhof, and the son of their district postmaster, who had a government appointment at Petersburg. Among the men who were on a footing of familiarity at the Rostofs' were Boris; Pierre, whom the old count had met on the street one day and brought home with him; and Berg, who spent whole days at the Rostofs', and showed the Countess Vera those attentions every young man is expected to show on the eve of a proposal.

Not without effect had Berg shown everyone the right arm wounded at Austerlitz, demonstratively holding his wholly unnecessary sword in his left hand. He described the occurrence so persistently and made it a matter of such grave importance that all came to believe in the gallantry and merit of his action, and Berg received two decorations after Austerlitz.

In the campaign in Finland he had also succeeded in distinguishing himself. He picked up a fragment of shell which had just killed one of the general-in-chief's aides, and carried this fragment to the chief. And in exactly the same way as after Austerlitz, he persisted in giving everyone such detailed accounts of his behavior, that all came finally to believe with him; and again, after the war in Finland, he received two citations. In 1809 he was already captain of the Guard, and held a most advantageous position in Petersburg.

Though there were some skeptics who smiled significantly when Berg's merits were mentioned in their presence, it was impossible not to admit that Berg was a well-disciplined, brave officer of excellent standing at headquarters, and a highly moral young man with a brilliant career before him who already enjoyed an exceptional position in society.

Four years before, Berg happened to meet with a comrade, also a German, in one of the Moscow theaters, and calling attention to Vera Rostof, said in German, "She is to be my wife." From that moment he laid his plans to marry her. Now that they were in Petersburg together, he compared his own position with the Rostofs' and came to the conclusion that his time had come, and he proposed.

Berg's proposal was received at first with a surprise not flattering to him. It seemed at first thought strange that the son of an obscure Lithuanian nobleman should offer himself to a Countess Rostof! But one of Berg's most characteristic traits was such a naive and good-natured egotism that the Rostofs began involuntarily to feel that it would be an excellent arrangement, if he himself were so firmly convinced that it was an excellent, a very excellent arrangement! Moreover, the Rostofs' affairs were in great disorder, so that there was little attraction for wooers; and worst of all, Vera was twenty-four and, although she had been everywhere and was undoubtedly pretty and sensible, she had never before received an offer. So the consent was granted.

"Now you see," said Berg to a comrade whom he called his "friend," simply because he knew it was fashionable for men to have friends, "you see I have weighed it all carefully, and I should not think of marrying if I had not thought it all over, or if it interfered with anyone. But now, on the contrary, my father and mother are provided for. I have secured for them that leasehold on the Baltic frontier, and I can live in Petersburg on my salary, together with what comes from her estate, for I am careful and economical. We can live very well. I don't marry her for her money; I don't call that sort of thing honorable, but it's no more than fair for the wife to contribute her portion and the husband his. I have my appointment; she, her connections and her little property. That's something in these days, isn't it? But, best of all, she is a lovely girl, of good character, and she loves me."

Berg reddened, and added with a smile, "And I love her because her character is well balanced . . . very admirable. Now there's her sister, of the same family, but a very different person . . . a most disagreeable character and no sense at all, and that kind of thing, you know . . . disagreeable. But my affianced . . . well," continued Berg, "you'll come to us some day to see her." He had it in mind to say "to dine," but he bethought himself and said "to tea," and, curling his tongue, he deftly sent forth a little ring of tobacco smoke, absolutely typical of his dreams of happiness.

After the first feeling of dissatisfaction that Vera's parents felt at Berg's proposal, the festivity and happiness usual in such circumstances were redoubled; but the joy was not genuine, it was artificial. In the emotions of the relatives regarding this alliance there were mingled elements of perplexity and mortification. Their consciences pricked them because they had never been fond of Vera and were now so glad to get her off their hands. The old count, most of all, was perplexed. He probably would not have been able to state the cause of this perplexity, but the real cause of it was his finances. He really did not know how he stood or how much he owed, and what he would be able to give as Vera's dowry. When the daughters were born each had received as a portion about three hundred serfs; but one of the estates had been already sold, and the other was mortgaged and the payments were so far behind that it was bound to be foreclosed, and therefore could not be granted as a dower. Nor was there any money to spare.

Berg had already been the accepted bridegroom for more than a month, and only a week remained before the wedding, and still the count had not been able to face the dreaded question of the dowry, and had not broached the subject to his wife. At one time the count thought of giving Vera his Riazan property; at another of selling a forest; then of raising money on a note.

One morning a few days before the wedding, Berg came early to the count's private room, and with a pleasant smile respectfully asked his future father-in-law what he was going to give as the Countess Vera's marriage portion. The count was so confused at this long-anticipated question that he answered at haphazard whatever first came into his head.

"I like it in you that you are careful, I like it; you shall be satisfied . . ."

And patting Berg on his shoulder, he got up, thinking to end the conversation then and there. But Berg, still smiling pleasantly, explained that unless he could know definitely what would be Vera's dowry, and unless a portion of it, at least, were paid over beforehand, he would be under the necessity of withdrawing from the offer.

"You will certainly agree with me, count, that if I should permit myself to marry without having a definite knowledge of what means I shall have for the maintenance of my wife, I should be acting very badly."

The conversation ended when the count, who wished to be generous, and also avoid future demands, said that he would give him a note for eighty thousand rubles. Berg, sweetly smiling, kissed him on the shoulder and declared that he was very grateful, but that he could never make himself ready for his new life unless he had thirty thousand in ready cash. "Or only twenty thousand would do, count," he added. "And in that case, the note would be for only sixty thousand."

"Well, very good," said the count, hastily. "Only you will allow me, my dear fellow, to give you the twenty thousand, and the note for eighty thousand besides. That's the way we'll do it! Kiss me!"

I V

Natasha was now sixteen, and the year 1809 was the very one to which she had counted up on her fingers four years before, when she and Boris had exchanged kisses. Since that time she had not once seen Boris. Before Sonya, and always with her mother, when Boris was mentioned, she had freely declared that what had gone before was childish nonsense, as if it were a settled matter of which there was no use talking, and long ago forgotten. But in the deepest depths of her heart she was tormented by the question of whether the promise that bound her to Boris was to be considered in jest or in earnest.

From the very time when in 1805 Boris had first left Moscow and joined the army, he had not met the Rostofs. He had been in Moscow several times, and had passed not very far from Otradnoye, but not once had he been to see his old friends.

It had several times occurred to Natasha that he was trying to avoid her, and her surmises had been strengthened by the melancholy tone in which her elders spoke of him.

"In these degenerate days, old friends are easily forgotten," said the countess more than once when Boris was mentioned.

Anna Mikhailovna had also been more rarely of late at the Rostofs'; she seemed to behave with especial dignity, and always spoke enthusiastically and boastfully of her son's accomplishments and the glittering career he was now pursuing.

When the Rostofs came to Petersburg, Boris went to call on them.

He went to their house with some emotion. His romance with Natasha was the most poetical recollection of his youth. But at the same time he went there with a firm determination to let both her and her parents clearly understand that those youthful relations between him and Natasha could not be considered binding to either of them. He had a brilliant position in society, thanks to his intimacy with Countess Bezukhof; a brilliant position in the service, thanks to the patronage of an eminent personage whose confidence he enjoyed; and he had now completed plans for a marriage with one of the wealthiest heiresses in Petersburg, an achievement which, indeed, he might very easily pull off.

When Boris reached the Rostofs', Natasha was in her room. When she was informed of his presence she went to the drawing-room almost on the run, blushing and beaming with a more than gracious smile.

Boris remembered Natasha as a little girl, in a short gown, with dark, flashing eyes under her curly hair, and with a spontaneous, merry laugh. That was just as he had last seen her, four years before; and consequently, when an entirely different Natasha came into the room he was taken aback, and his face expressed solemn amazement. This expression on his face delighted Natasha.

"Well, would you have known your mischievous little playmate?" asked the countess. Boris kissed Natasha's hand, and said that he noticed a great change in her.

"How handsome you have grown!"

"Why shouldn't I?" replied Natasha's mocking eyes.

"Don't you think that papa seems much older?" she asked.

Natasha sat there without joining in the conversation between Boris and the countess, and silently studying her childhood ideal, even to the minutest particulars. Boris was conscious of her steady and affectionate gaze fixed upon him, and occasionally he stole a glance at her.

His uniform, his spurs, his cravat, the cut of his hair, all were most fashionable and correct. Natasha instantly noticed this. He sat somewhat toward the edge of the armchair nearest the countess, with his right hand smoothing the immaculate, neat-fitting glove that he wore on his left, and he spoke with a peculiarly delicate compression of the lips about the amusements of Petersburg high life, and called to mind the old times in Moscow and his Moscow acquaintances with a gentle irony. Natasha felt sure that not without design he mentioned the names of the highest aristocracy, whom he had met at the ambassador's ball, or his invitations to the N. N.'s and the S. S.'s.

Natasha sat silent all the time, looking keenly at him. This glance of hers confused and troubled Boris more and more. He kept turning toward her, and stumbling in the midst of his stories. He did not stay more than ten minutes, and then got up to take his leave. All the time those keen inquisitive eyes, full of mockery, looked at him with a peculiar challenging expression.

After this first visit of his, Boris confessed to himself that Natasha was just as fascinating to him as ever, but that it was his duty to renounce this feeling, because to marry her, an almost dowerless girl, would be the ruin of his career; and the renewal of their former friendship without intention of marrying her would be a base trick. Boris resolved in his own mind to avoid meeting Natasha; but notwithstanding this resolution, he went again in a few days, and kept going more and more frequently, and at last spent whole days at the Rostofs'. He kept trying to persuade himself that he would soon have a chance to come to an explanation with Natasha and tell her that what was past must be forgotten, that, in spite of everything, she could not be his wife, that he had no property and their friends would never consent to their union. But he kept putting it off, and found it more and more awkward to bring about this explanation. Each day he became more and more perplexed.

In the opinion of her mother and Sonya, Natasha was just as much in love with Boris as ever she had been. She sang for him all her favorite pieces; she showed him her album, begging him to write in it; but she never allowed him to talk about the past, giving him to understand how charming the new relationship was, and each day he entered deeper into the fog, never saying what he had resolved to say, not knowing what he was doing, or why he went there, or how it would all end. He even ceased to frequent Helene's, though he daily received reproachful notes from her; he spent most of his spare time at the Rostofs'.

One evening when the old countess, in nightcap and dressing gown, with her false curls removed and with one thin little wisp of white hair escaping from under her white calico cap, was performing the low obeisances of her evening devotions on a rug, sighing and groaning, the door of her room creaked on its hinges and Natasha came running in, with her bare feet in slippers, and also in dressing jacket and curl papers.

The countess glanced around and frowned. She went on repeating her last prayer, "If this couch become my tomb." Her devotional frame of mind was destroyed. Natasha, with rosy cheeks and full of animation, when she saw her mother at her devotions, suddenly paused, made a curtsy, and involuntarily poked out her tongue to express her annoyance at her carelessness. Then, perceiving that her mother still went on with her prayer, she ran to the bed on tiptoe, kicked off her slippers by rubbing one dainty little foot against the other, and sprang onto that couch which the countess was so afraid would be her tomb. This couch was a lofty feather bed with five pillows, each smaller than the next. Natasha jumped into the middle, sinking deep into the feather mattress, rolled over next to the wall and began to creep under the bedclothes, snuggling down, tucking her knees up to her chin, then giving animated little kicks and laughing almost aloud, now and again uncovering her head and looking at her mother.

The countess finished her prayers, and with a stern face came to the bed; but seeing that Natasha's head was hidden under the bedclothes, she smiled her good, amiable smile.

"Well, well, well," said the mother.

"Mama, can we talk now? Say yes!" cried Natasha. "There now, one kiss, on the neck; just one more and that will satisfy me!" and she threw her arms around her mother and kissed her under the chin. In her treatment of her mother, Natasha seemed to be very rough in her manner; but she was so dexterous and graceful that whenever she seized her mother in her arms she always did it in such a way as not to hurt her or disturb her at all.

"Well, what have you to tell me tonight?" asked the countess, settling back on the pillows and waiting for Natasha, rolling over and over, to nestle down close to her, drop her hands, and become serious.

These visits from Natasha, which took place every night before the count came from his club, were a great delight to both mother and daughter.

"What is there to tell tonight? I want to tell you about . . ."

Natasha stopped her mother's mouth with her hand.

"About Boris? . . . I know," said she, gravely. "That's why I came. Don't speak, I know! No, but you may tell me." She took away her hand. "Go on, mama; he's a dear, isn't he?"

"Natasha, you are sixteen years old; at your age I was already married. You say that Boris is a dear. He is a very dear boy, and I love him like a son, but what do you wish? . . . What are you thinking about? You have entirely turned his head, that's evident."

As she said this, the countess looked at her daughter. Natasha lay looking fixedly at one of the carved mahogany sphinxes that ornamented the bed-posts. The countess could see only her daughter's profile. It seemed to her that the sweet face had a peculiarly grave and thoughtful expression.

Natasha was listening and pondering.

"Well, what is it?"

"You have entirely turned his head. What made you do so? What do you want of him? You know that you cannot marry him."

"Why not?" asked Natasha, without altering her position.

"Because he is young, because he is poor, because he is a relative . . . because you are not in love with him."

"How do you know I'm not in love with him?"

"I know. Now, this is not right, darling."

"But if I wish . . ." began Natasha.

"Do stop talking nonsense!" said the countess.

"But if I wish . . ."

"Natasha, I am in earnest."

Natasha did not allow her to finish; she seized the countess' plump hand and kissed it on the back and then on the palm; then turned it over again and began to kiss it on the knuckle of each finger in succession, then on the middle joints, then again on the knuckles, repeating in a whisper, "January, February, March, April, May . . . Tell me, mama, why don't you go on? Speak!" said she, looking at her mother, who with affectionate eyes gazed at her daughter, becoming so engrossed in this contemplation that she apparently forgot what she was going to say.

"It isn't proper, darling! People won't remember anything about your affections as children, but if he is seen to be so intimate with you now, it might injure you in the eyes of other young men who come to the house; and, worst of all, it is torturing him all for nothing. Perhaps he might, by this time, have found some rich girl to marry, but now he is quite beside himself."

"Beside himself?" repeated Natasha.

"I will tell you my own experience. I once had a cousin . . ."

"I know—Kirill Matveyitch, but he's an old man, isn't he?"

"He hasn't always been old! But see here, Natasha, I am going to talk with Boris. He must not come here so often."

"Why mustn't he, if he likes to?"

"Because I know that this cannot come to any good end."

"How do you know? No, mama! You must not speak to him. What nonsense!" exclaimed Natasha, in the tone of one who is about to be deprived of a possession. "Well, I won't marry him; but do let him come, for he enjoys it, and so do I." Natasha looked at her mother with a smile. "Not with any intentions, but this way," she repeated.

"What do you mean, my dear?"

"Why, this way. It is perfectly understood that he is not to marry me . . . but this way!"

"Yes, this way, this way," repeated the countess; and she went into an unexpected fit of good-natured laughter, her whole body shaking.

"Come, mama, stop laughing at me!" cried Natasha. "You make the whole bed shake. You are awfully like me. You laugh just as easily as I do . . . Do stop!"

She seized the countess' two hands, kissed the joint of the little finger of one of them for June, and went on kissing July and August on the other hand.

"Mama, but is he ever and ever so much in love? . . . you think so, do you? . . . Was anyone ever as much in love with you? . . . And he's a dear boy, a very, very dear boy, isn't he? Only, he's not quite to my taste—he's so narrow, just like the dining-room clock. You know what I mean, don't you? Narrow, you know . . . grayish and polished . . ."

"What nonsense you do talk!" exclaimed the countess.

Natasha went on: "Don't you understand what I mean? Nikolai would understand me. There's Bezukhof—he's blue, dark blue and red, and he is four-square."

"And are you coquetting with him too?" asked the countess, laughing again.

"No; he's a Freemason; I found it out. He is splendid, dark blue and red. How can I make you see it? . . ."

"Little countess! Aren't you asleep yet?" cried the count at this moment at the door. Natasha jumped out of bed, seized her slippers in her hand, and escaped barefooted to her own room.

It was long before she could go to sleep. She kept thinking how strange it was that no one could ever understand things as she understood them, or read what was in her mind.

"Sonya?" she thought, gazing at the young girl who, with her hair in a tremendous long braid, lay asleep curled up like a little kitten. "No, not even she! She is amiable! She is in love with Nikolai, and that's all she cares about. And mama can't understand either! . . . It is so strange; how clever I am and how . . . she is pretty," Natasha went on, speaking of herself in the third person, and imagining that some very intelligent, some most intelligent and most handsome man, was saying this about her. "She has everything, everything," this man of her imagination was saying, "She is extraordinarily clever, lovable, and pretty, besides . . . extraordinarily pretty and graceful; she can swim, she can ride horseback splendidly, and what a voice! One might say, a marvelous voice!"

She sang her favorite snatch from a Cherubini opera, threw herself into bed, smiling at the happy thought that she would be asleep in a moment, called to Dunyasha to put out the light; and even before Dunyasha had left the room, she had already passed across into that other, still happier world of dreams, where all things were just as bright and beautiful as in reality, but still more fascinating because so different.

On the next day the countess, calling Boris to her, had a talk with him, and from that time forth he ceased to be a frequent visitor at the Rostofs'.

V

On the thirty-first of December, on the eve of the new year, 1810, a ball was given by a grandee of Catherine's time. The diplomatic corps and the emperor had promised to be present.

The grandee's splendid mansion on the English Quay was illuminated with countless windows all ablaze. At the brilliantly lighted, red-carpeted entrance stood a guard of police, including even the chief of police and half a score of officers. Carriages drove away and new ones kept taking their places, with red-liveried lackeys and lackeys with plumes in their hats. From the carriages descended men in uniforms and men adorned with stars and ribbons; and, as the steps were let down with a bang, ladies in satins and in ermine cloaks hastily and noiselessly went up the carpeted entrance.

Almost every time a new equipage drove up, a flurry of excitement ran through the crowd, and hats were removed.

"The sovereign?" . . . "No, a minister." . . . "Prince so and so." . . . "An ambassador." . . . "But did you see his plume?"

Such were the remarks heard in the crowd. There was one man, better dressed than the rest, who seemed to know who everybody was and called by name the famous grandees of the time.

Already a third of the guests had arrived; but at the Rostofs', who were also invited, hasty preparations were still being made.

In the Rostof family there had been much discussion and excitement over this ball; many were the apprehensions lest they should not get their invitation, lest their dresses should not be ready, lest everything should not be as it ought to be.

Marya Ignatyevna Peronski, an old friend and relative of the countess, was to accompany the Rostofs to the ball. She was a lean and sallow lady in waiting to the empress dowager, and took charge of her country cousins, the Rostofs, in their entry into Petersburg high life. They were to call for her at ten o'clock in the evening, and now it lacked only five minutes of ten, and the ladies were not yet dressed.

This was to be the first great ball Natasha had ever attended. She had got up at eight o'clock that morning and had been all day long in a state of the wildest excitement and bustle. All her energies from earliest morning had been expended in the effort to have all of them—herself, Sonya and the countess—dressed to perfection. Sonya and the countess trusted themselves entirely to her hands. The countess was to wear a dark red velvet gown; the two girls, white crêpe gowns with pink silk overskirts, and roses in their corsages; their hair was to be arranged *à la grecque.*

The most important part had been already done: their feet, hands, arms, necks and ears had been washed, perfumed and powdered with extraordinary care. On their feet they wore open-work silk stockings and white satin slippers with bows. Their toilets were almost finished. Sonya was already dressed and so was the countess; but Natasha, who had been helping the others, was behind. She was still sitting in front of the mirror in a peignoir that covered her slender shoulders. Sonya was standing in the middle of the room fastening on a last bow with a pin that hurt her dainty fingers as she tried to press it, squeaking, through the ribbon.

"Not that way, not that way, Sonya," cried Natasha, turning her head suddenly, and putting her hands up to her hair, which the maid who was dressing it had not yet had time to finish. "Don't put the bow that way, come here!"

Sonya sat down in front of her. Natasha pinned the bow in a different position.

"If you please, Miss, I can't arrange your hair this way," exclaimed the maid, still holding Natasha's braids.

"Oh, good gracious, wait then! There, that's the way, Sonya!"

"Are you almost ready?" the countess was heard asking. "It's ten o'clock already."

"In a minute, in a minute. And are you all ready, mama?"

"Only have my toque to put on."

"Don't you do it without me!" cried Natasha. "You won't get it right!"

"Yes, but it's ten o'clock!"

It had been decided upon that they should reach the ballroom at half-past ten, and Natasha still had to get on her gown, and they had to pick up Madame Peronski.

As soon as her hair was done, Natasha, in her short petticoat which showed her ball slippers, and wearing her mother's dressing jacket, ran to Sonya and examined her critically; then she hurried to her mother. Bending her head down she put the toque on it, and giving her gray hair a hasty kiss, she scurried back to the maids, who were putting the last touches to her skirt.

The delay had been caused by Natasha's skirt, which was too long; two maids were at work on it, hastily biting off the ends of the thread. A third, with her mouth full of pins, was hastening from the countess to Sonya; and a fourth was holding up high in the air the complete crêpe gown.

"Mavrushka, hurry up, you old darling."

"Give me the thimble, Miss."

"Are you almost ready?" asked the count, coming to the door. "Here is some perfume for you. Madame Peronski will be in a fume."

"There! it is done!" cried the maid, lifting up with two fingers the completed crêpe dress and giving it a puff and a shake, by this motion expressing her sense of the airiness and purity of what she held.

Natasha began to put the garment on.

"In a minute, in a minute; don't come in, papa," she cried to her father, who was just opening the door. Her head at that very moment was disappearing under the cloud of crêpe. Sonya closed the door. But in a moment the count was admitted. He wore a blue dress coat, knee breeches, and buckled shoes, and was scented and pomaded.

"Oh! papa, how handsome you look! Charming!" cried Natasha, as she stood in the middle of the chamber and adjusted the folds of her skirt.

"Mercy on us!" cried Sonya, with despair in her voice, scrutinizing Natasha's dress. "Mercy on us! it's too long now!"

Natasha made a few steps so as to look into the pier glass. The skirt was indeed too long.

"Good gracious! Miss, it isn't too long at all," said Mavrushka, crawling along on the floor after her young mistress.

"Well, if it's too long, then let us tack it up; we can do it in a second," said Dunyasha in a decisive tone, taking a needle from the bosom of her dress, and again sitting on the floor to baste up the bottom of the skirt.

At this instant the countess, in her toque and velvet dress, came timidly into the room with noiseless steps.

"Oo! Oo! my beauty!" cried the count. "You are the best of them all!" He tried to give her a hug and a kiss, but she blushed and pushed him away, so as not to rumple her dress.

"Mama, your toque should be more to one side," cried Natasha. "I will pin it on."

"Oh, my beauty! a real queen!" cried the old nurse looking in at the door. "And little Sonya, too; well, they are beauties!"

By a quarter past ten, finally, all were seated in the carriage and on their way. But they still had to call for their friend.

Madame Peronski was ready and waiting for them. Notwithstanding her advanced age and her lack of charms, almost exactly the same thing had taken place in her case as with the Rostofs, though, of course, with no haste and flurry, for this was an old story with her; but her unbeautiful old body had been washed and scented and powdered in just the same way, and she had been just as scrupulous in washing behind her ears; and just as at the Rostofs', her ancient maid had enthusiastically contemplated the adornment of her mistress when, dressed in her yellow dress with the royal insignia of a lady in waiting, she had come down into the drawing-room.

She praised the Rostofs' toilets and the Rostofs extolled her taste and her toilet; and at last, at eleven o'clock, taking great care of their hair and their gowns, they stowed themselves away in the carriages and drove off.

VI

NATASHA HAD NOT had a moment's freedom since that morning; and not once had she taken time to think of what was before her.

In the raw, chill atmosphere, in the narrow, dimly lighted, swaying carriage, for the first time she vividly saw in her imagination what was waiting for her there at the ball, in the lighted halls—the music, the flowers, the dances, the sovereign, all the brilliant youth of the city. Fancy pictured it in such attractive colors that she could hardly believe it was going to be realized; it was all in such vivid contrast with the impression of the chill, the narrowness and darkness of the carriage. She realized all that was awaiting her only at the moment when, having passed along the red-carpeted entrance, she went into the vestibule and took off her cloak, and, together with Sonya, preceded her mother up the grand staircase lined with flowering plants. Then only it came over her with what propriety she must behave at a ball, and she tried to assume the dignified manner she felt to be the proper thing for a young girl on such an occasion.

But, fortunately for her, she was conscious that her eyes were wandering; she could not distinguish anything clearly; her heart was beating a hundred a minute, and her pulses throbbed almost painfully. It was impossible for her to assume any such manner, and it would have been ridiculous in her; and so she walked along, trembling with excitement, and trying with all her might to hide it; and this was the very manner which, more than any other, was becoming to her.

Behind them and in front of them, other guests were mounting the stairs, also talking in low tones, and dressed in ball costumes. The mirrors on the landings reflected visions of ladies in white, blue and pink gowns, with diamonds and pearls on their bare arms and bosoms. Natasha glanced into the mirrors, but in the reflection she could not distinguish herself from the others; all were commingled and confused in one glittering procession. As they reached the door leading into the first ballroom, an unbroken roar of voices, footsteps and greetings deafened Natasha; the lights and brilliant toilets dazzled her still more. The host and hostess, who had been half an hour standing near the entrance and repeating over the same words of welcome, "Charmed to see you," met the Rostofs and Madame Peronski in the same way.

The two young girls, in their white gowns, each with a single rose in her dark locks, went in and curtsied exactly alike; but involuntarily the hostess let her glance rest longer on the slender little Natasha. She looked at her and smiled on her alone with a special graciousness; to the others she was only the hostess. As she looked at her, she perhaps remembered the golden days of her girlhood which would never more return, and her own first ball. The host also followed Natasha with his glance, and asked the count which of the two was his daughter.

"*Charmante!*" said he, kissing his finger tips.

In the ballroom the guests were crowded together near the entrance, awaiting the coming of the sovereign. The countess took her place in the front row of this group. Natasha had had her ears open, and was conscious that several had asked who she was and had looked at her. She knew she was making a pleasant impression on those whose attention she had attracted, and this fact somewhat calmed her agitation.

"There are some just like ourselves, and some not so good," she thought.

Madame Peronski was pointing out to the countess the most notable personages in the ballroom.

"There! that's the Dutch ambassador, see—that gray-haired man," said she, directing the countess' attention to a gentleman with abundant curly hair, silver-white. He was surrounded by ladies, whom he had just set to laughing by some remark.

"Ah! and there is the tsaritsa of Petersburg, Countess Bezukhof," she exclaimed, indicating Helene, who had just entered. "How handsome she is! She does not stand second even to Marya Antonovna. Just see how young and old stare after her. She's both handsome and intelligent. They say a royal prince has gone daft about her. And see those two, there! They are not pretty at all, but what a following they have!"

She indicated a lady and her extremely plain daughter who were just crossing the ballroom.

"That girl is the heiress to millions," said Madame Peronski; "and there are her suitors. That's Countess Bezukhof's brother, Anatol Kuragin," said she, calling attention to a handsome young cavalryman who was just then passing them, holding his head very high and not deigning to give the ladies any recognition. "How handsome he is! isn't he? They say he's going to marry this heiress; and your cousin, Drubetskoy, is also after her; they say she has millions. . . . Who? Oh! that is the French ambassador himself," she replied to the countess, who asked who Caulaincourt was. "Just see, he is like some tsar! And yet they are all so pleasant, so very pleasant, these French. Ah! and there she is! After all, there is no one who can be compared to our Marya Antonovna. And how simply she is dressed! Charming!—And the stout man over there, in spectacles, is the international Freemason," said she, pointing out Bezukhof. "Compare him with his wife! what a ridiculous creature!"

Pierre walked along, his stout form swaying, and pushed through the throng, bowing to the right and left carelessly and good-naturedly, as if he were making his way through the swarms of a market place. He passed along, evidently in search of someone.

Natasha was glad to see Pierre's well-known face, even if he was "a ridiculous creature," to use the words of Madame Peronski; and she knew it was her party, and herself in particular, that Pierre was looking for; Pierre had promised he would attend the ball and find partners for her.

But before he arrived where they stood, Pierre stopped near a short and very handsome dark-featured cavalryman in a white uniform: it was Bolkonsky, who seemed to her to have grown younger, gayer, and handsomer.

"There's another of our acquaintances—Bolkonsky—do you see him, mama?" asked Natasha, indicating Prince Andrei. "Do you remember? He spent a night with us at Otradnoye."

"Ah, indeed! so you know him, then?" asked Madame Peronski. "I cannot endure him. He's all the rage just now. There's no end to his pride. He's like his father. See how he treats the ladies! One just spoke to him, and he turned his back on her! I'd give him a lesson if he treated me as he did those ladies."

Suddenly there was a general stir: a whisper ran through the throng, which pressed forward and then divided again, making two rows. Between them came the sovereign, to the strains of the band, which just then began to play. He was followed by the host and hostess. The sovereign passed along, hastily bowing to the right and left, as if he were anxious to have done as soon as possible with these first formalities. The musicians played a polonaise then famous, on account of the words which had been set to it. These words began, "Alexander, Elizabeth, you enrapture us . . ."

The sovereign entered the drawing-room. The throng pushed toward the doors; several persons with anxious faces rushed hither and thither in great haste. The throng again moved away from the drawing-room door, where the sovereign made his appearance, engaged in conversation with the hostess. A young man with an expression of annoyance on his face came along and begged the ladies to step back. Several ladies, with eager faces, showing absolute disregard of all the conventional rules of good breeding, pushed forward, to the imminent risk of their toilets. The gentlemen began to select their partners and get into position for the polonaise.

Space was cleared; and the sovereign, with a smile, stepping out of time, passed into the ballroom, leading the lady of the house by the hand. They were followed by the host, with Marya Antonovna Narishkina; then ambassadors, ministers, and various generals, whom Madame Peronski indefatigably called by name. More than half the ladies had partners, and were already dancing or beginning to dance the polonaise. Natasha felt that she and Sonya, as well as her mother, were neglected, with that minority of ladies who lined the walls and were not invited to take part in the polonaise. She stood with her slender arms hanging by her sides; with her maidenly bosom, as yet scarcely defined, regularly rising and falling with long breaths; and she looked straight ahead with brilliant eyes full of alarm, indicating that she was ready for the greatest enjoyment or the greatest disappointment. She was not interested now in the sovereign or in any of those distinguished people whom Madame Peronski was calling to their attention; she had only one thought: "Isn't anyone coming to invite me? Can it be that

I am not going to be taken out for the first dance? Won't any of those men notice me?—of those men who now do not seem to see me; or, if they see me, look at me as much as to say, 'Oh, she's nothing—she's nothing to look at!' No, it cannot be!" said she to herself. "They must know that I am longing to dance, and how splendidly I dance, and how much they would enjoy it if they danced with me!"

The strains of the polonaise, which had now lasted some little time, began to have a melancholy cadence in Natasha's ears, as if connected with sad memories. She felt like having a good cry. Madame Peronski had left them; the count was at the other end of the ballroom; she and Sonya and the countess were as much alone in this throng of strangers as if they were in the woods; no one took any interest in them, or looked out for them. Prince Andrei passed them with a lady on his arm, and evidently did not recollect them. The handsome Anatol, smiling, said something to the lady with whom he was promenading, and looked into Natasha's face as one looks at a wall. Twice Boris passed them, and each time turned his head away. Berg and his wife, who were not dancing, joined them.

Natasha felt mortified to death at this family gathering, there, at the ball; as if they had no other place for family confidences than in a ballroom. She did not look at Vera, or listen to what she had to say about her emerald-green dress.

At last the sovereign sat down near his last partner—he had danced with three—and the music ceased. An officious aide bustled up to the Rostofs, begging them to move back a little more, and this although they almost touched the wall; and then from the gallery was heard the rhythmical, smooth, and enticing sound of the waltz.

The sovereign, with a smile, glanced down the ballroom. A moment passed, and no one had as yet begun. The aide, who acted as master of ceremonies, approached Countess Bezukhof, and asked her to dance. She accepted with a smile, and then, without looking at him, laid her hand on his shoulder. The aide, who was a master of his business, calmly, deliberately, and with all self-confidence, placing his arm firmly about her waist, at first started off with her in the glissade around the edge of the circle; then, when they reached the end of the ballroom, he took her right hand with his left, turned her around, and, while the sounds of the waltz grew more and more rapid, the clicking of the aide's spurs could be heard as his agile and skilful feet beat the time of the rhythm; while on the third beat, at every turn, his partner's velvet dress floated out and seemed to fly. Natasha gazed at them, and was ready to weep that it was not she herself who was leading this first waltz.

Prince Andrei, in the white uniform of a colonel of cavalry, in silk stockings and shoe buckles, stood, full of life and radiant with happiness, in the front row of the circle not far from the Rostofs. Baron Firhof was talking to him about the first meeting of the Imperial Council, which had been appointed for the next day. But Prince Andrei was not listening to what Firhof

was saying, and looked now at the sovereign and now at the various gentlemen who were all ready to dance but had not the necessary courage to take
the floor.

Prince Andrei was observing these gentlemen who showed such timidity
in the presence of their sovereign, and the ladies, whose hearts were sinking
within them with desire to be invited.

Pierre came up to Prince Andrei and took him by the arm.

"You are always ready for a dance. My protégée, the little Rostof girl, is
here; do invite her!" said he.

"Where?" asked Bolkonsky. "I beg your pardon," he added, turning to
the baron. "We will finish this conversation at another time; but at balls it is
our duty to dance."

He went in the direction indicated by Pierre. Natasha's despairing, sad
face attracted Prince Andrei's attention. He recognized her, and divined her
feeling; and, realizing that she was just "coming out," and remembering
her conversation, he went with a beaming countenance up to Countess
Rostof.

"Allow me to make you acquainted with my daughter," said the countess,
blushing.

"I have had the pleasure of meeting her before, but perhaps the countess
does not remember me," said Prince Andrei, with a low and respectful bow,
entirely belying Madame Peronski's spiteful observation about his rudeness. Approaching Natasha, he started to put his arm around her waist, even
before he had actually invited her to dance with him. Then he proposed
that they should take a turn of the waltz. Natasha's face, with its melancholy expression, ready to sink to despair or become radiant, was suddenly
lighted up with a happy, childlike smile of gratitude.

"I had been waiting long for you," this timid and radiant young girl
seemed to say by this smile, flashing out from under tears that had been
almost ready to start, as she put her hand on Prince Andrei's shoulder. They
were the second couple that ventured out upon the floor. Prince Andrei
was one of the best dancers of his time. Natasha danced exquisitely; her
dainty little feet, shod in her satin slippers, performed their duty with perfect ease and agility, independently of her volition; and her face beamed
with triumphant delight.

Her bare neck and arms were thin and far from pretty, compared with
Helene's charms. Her shoulders were slim, her figure undeveloped, her arms
slender, but Helene seemed to be already covered with an enamel left by the
thousand glances that had glided over her form, while Natasha seemed like
a girl appearing for the first time in a low-necked gown, and who would feel
very much mortified if she were not assured that it was the proper thing.

Prince Andrei liked to dance, and, as he wanted to escape as soon as
possible from the political and intellectual remarks with which all approached him, and to break up, as soon as possible, that tiresome circle of
people abashed by the presence of the sovereign, he was ready to dance; and

he chose Natasha because Pierre had suggested her, and because she happened to be the first among all the pretty women who attracted his attention. But as soon as he clasped her slender, supple form, and she began to move so close to him, and smiled up into his face, the wine of her fascination mounted to his head; he felt a renewed energy and fresh life when, having released her, he stopped and began to look at the other dancers.

VII

Following Prince Andrei's example, Boris came and invited Natasha to dance with him; also the master of ceremonies, who had opened the ball, and several other young men; and Natasha, turning her superfluity of partners over to Sonya, flushed and happy, did not miss a single dance throughout the rest of the evening.

She had eyes for nothing else, and she did not notice what had attracted the attention of everyone else at the ball. She did not once remark how the emperor had a long conversation with the French ambassador; or how he showed signal favor to a certain lady who was present; or how Prince So-and-So and So-and-So said and did this, that, and the other thing; or how Helene enjoyed a brilliant success and attracted the special attention of such-and-such a person: she did not even see the sovereign, and only noticed that he had withdrawn by the fact that, after his departure, the ball became livelier than ever.

Just before supper, Prince Andrei danced one of the liveliest cotillions with Natasha. He reminded her of their first meeting on the Otradnoye driveway, and how she could not go to sleep that moonlight night, and how he had involuntarily overheard what she said. Natasha blushed at this reminiscence, and tried to excuse herself, as if there were something of which she ought to be ashamed in the consciousness that Prince Andrei had accidentally overheard her.

Prince Andrei, like all men who had grown up in society, liked to meet anyone who was free from the stereotyped imprint of fashionable high life; and such a person was Natasha, with her admiration, her enjoyment, and her modesty, and even her mistakes in speaking French. He treated her and spoke to her with a peculiar delicacy and affectionate courtesy. As he sat next to her, talking on the simplest and most insignificant topics, Prince Andrei admired the merry gleam in her eyes, and her smile, answering not to what was said to her so much as to her inward happiness. If, by chance, Natasha was invited to dance, and got up with a smile and went dancing across the room, Prince Andrei found especial delight in watching her fawn-like grace. In the midst of the cotillion, Natasha, having just danced out one figure, came back to her place, still panting. A new partner again invited her out. She was tired and out of breath, and evidently at first inclined to refuse;

but instantly placed her hand on the cavalier's shoulder, and gave Prince Andrei a smile.

"I should like very much to get my breath, and sit with you—I am tired—but you see how I am in demand; and that pleases me, and I am happy, and I love you all, and you and I understand it all"; this, and much more besides, this smile of hers seemed to say. When her partner released her, Natasha glided across the room to choose two ladies for the figure.

"If she speaks to her cousin first, and then to the other lady, she will be my wife!" said Prince Andrei, unexpectedly even to himself, as he looked at her. She went to her cousin first!

"What nonsense sometimes enters one's head!" said Prince Andrei to himself. "But it is quite evident that this girl is so sweet, and so unlike anybody else, that she won't be kept dancing here for a month; she'll be engaged or married. . . . There's no one like her here!" he thought, as Natasha, smoothing out the crumpled petals of a rose in her corsage, came back and resumed her place next to him.

At the end of the cotillion the old count, in his blue coat, came up to the dancers. He invited Prince Andrei to call and see them, and he asked his daughter if she had been having a good time. Natasha at first did not reply, except by a smile which had a sort of reproach in it, as much as to say, "How can you ask such a question?"

"The loveliest time I ever had in my life," said she; and Prince Andrei noticed how she made a quick motion to raise her slender arms, as if to embrace her father, and instantly dropped them again. Natasha was happier than she had ever been in her life before; she had reached that lofty height of bliss when a person becomes perfectly good and lovely, and cannot believe in the existence or the possibility of wickedness, unhappiness, and sorrow.

At this ball, Pierre for the first time realized the humiliating position in which he was placed by the status occupied by his wife in court society. He was morose and absent-minded. A deep frown furrowed his brow; and, as he stood by the window, he glared through his spectacles and yet saw nothing.

Natasha, as she went down to supper, passed by him.

His gloomy, unhappy face struck her. She paused in front of him; she felt a desire to help him, to share with him the superfluity of her own happiness. "How gay it is, count," said she. "Isn't it?"

Pierre gave her a distracted smile, evidently not understanding what she said. "Yes, I am very glad," he replied.

"How can anyone be dissatisfied with anything?" wondered Natasha. "Especially such a good fellow as that Bezukhof."

In Natasha's eyes, all who were at the ball were alike good, sweet, lovely men, full of affection toward one another; hatred was out of the question, and therefore all ought to be happy.

VIII

Two DAYS LATER Prince Andrei went to make calls at several houses where he had not been as yet, among them the Rostofs', whose acquaintance he had renewed at the ball. Not only was he required by the laws of politeness to call at the Rostofs', but he also had a strong desire to see in her own home this unusual and lively young girl of whom he had such pleasant recollections.

Natasha was the first who came down to see him. She wore a simple blue morning dress, and it seemed to Prince Andrei that it was even more becoming to her than the one she had worn at the ball. She and the rest of the family received Prince Andrei simply and hospitably, as an old friend. The whole family, which he had at first been inclined to criticize severely, now seemed to him charming, simple-hearted and cordial people. The old count showed such genuine and unbounded hospitality, and his good nature was so contagious, especially there in Petersburg, that Prince Andrei could not with good grace refuse his invitation to dinner.

"Yes, they are excellent people," said Bolkonsky to himself. "Of course they cannot appreciate what a treasure they possess in Natasha; but they are good, kindly people, and they make a most admirable background against which to bring out all the charm of this wonderfully poetical young girl, so brimful with vivacity."

Prince Andrei sensed in Natasha a peculiar and unknown world, full of unrealized delights—that unknown world of which he had caught the first glimpse as he drove through the Otradnoye avenue, and then again at the window that moonlight night, when he had been so stirred by it.

Now this world no longer excited his curiosity, no longer was it a strange world; but, as he entered into it, he realized that new delight was awaiting him.

After dinner, Natasha, at the count's request, went to the clavichord and began to sing. Prince Andrei stood by the window and listened, occasionally exchanging words with the other ladies. In the middle of a sentence Prince Andrei stopped talking and, to his amazement, found that he was choked with tears, something he would not have believed possible for him. He looked at Natasha as she sang, and a new and joyous feeling arose in his heart. He was happy and at the same time sad. He had really nothing to weep about, but he was ready to burst into tears. For what? his former love? . . . For the little princess? . . . For his frustrated illusions? . . . For his hopes of the future? . . . Yes and no! The chief reason why he felt like weeping was the sudden awakening to that strange and vivid contradiction between the boundlessly immense and infinite that existed in him, and the narrow and limited world to which he felt that he himself, and even she, belonged. This contrast tormented and enthralled him while she was singing.

As soon as Natasha finished her song, she went to him and asked him frankly how he liked her voice. She asked the question, and was overwhelmed with confusion the moment she had spoken, realizing when it was too late that she ought not to have asked it. He smiled as he looked at her, and replied that he liked her singing just as he liked everything else she did.

It was late that evening before Prince Andrei left the Rostofs'. He went to bed as usual, but soon found that he had a sleepless night before him. Relighting his candle, he sat up in bed a little while; then he got up; then he lay down again; still, he was not in the least oppressed by this sleeplessness. His soul was so full of new and joyful sensations that it seemed to him as if he had just emerged from a stuffy room into God's free world. Nor did it once occur to him that he was in love with the young Countess Rostof; he did not think of her, he only imagined her; and the consequence of this was that his whole life presented itself to him in a new light.

"Why am I struggling, why am I toiling and moiling in this narrow, petty environment, when life, all of life, with all its pleasures, is open before me?" he asked himself.

And for the first time in many months he began to make cheerful plans for the future. He decided that it was his duty to undertake personally the education of his son, to find an instructor and put the child into his hands; then he would quit the service and travel abroad, and see England, Switzerland, and Italy.

"I must make the most of my freedom, since I feel myself so overflowing with strength and energy," said he to himself. "Pierre was right in saying that one ought to believe in the possibility of happiness, and now I believe it is so. Let the dead bury their dead; but, while we are alive, let us live," he thought.

I X

ONE MORNING Colonel Adolph Berg, with whom Pierre was acquainted, just as he was acquainted with everyone in Petersburg and Moscow, came to see him. He was dressed in an immaculate and brand-new uniform, with little pomaded lovelocks curling over his temples, just as the sovereign wore them.

"I have just come from calling on the countess, your wife, and I was so unfortunate in not being able to have my request granted! I hope, count, that I shall be more successful with you," said he, with a smile.

"What would you like, colonel? I am at your service."

"I am now completely settled in my new apartment, count," pursued Berg, evidently convinced in his own mind that this communication could not fail to be an agreeable piece of news. "And, consequently, I wanted to have a little reception for my friends and my wife's." He smiled more effusively than ever. "I wanted to ask the countess and yourself to do me the honor to come and take a cup of tea with us, and—and have supper."

Only Countess Elena, who considered the society of such people as the Bergs beneath her, could have had the heart to refuse such an invitation. Berg explained so clearly why he desired to gather around him a small and select company, and why it would be pleasant to him, and why he grudged money spent on cards and other disreputable occupations, but was willing to go to large outlay in entertaining good company, that Pierre could not think of refusing, and agreed to be present.

"Only don't come late, count, if I may be so bold as to beg of you; at ten minutes to eight, I beg of you. We will have cards; our general will come— he is very good to me. We will have a good supper, count. So please do me the favor."

Contrary to his usual habit of being late, Pierre that evening reached the Bergs' at a quarter to eight, five minutes before the appointed time.

The Bergs, having made every provision for the reception, were all ready and waiting for their guests to arrive.

Berg and his wife were sitting together in their library, all new and bright, and well provided with statuary and paintings and new furniture. Berg, in a nice new uniform, tightly buttoned up, was sitting near his wife explaining to her that it was always possible and proper to have acquaintances among people of high station, that being the only real advantage in having friends. "You can always find something to imitate, and can ask any sort of advice. You see, that's the way I have done ever since I was first promoted."—Berg did not reckon his life according to his years, but according to the various steps of promotion.—"My comrades are still of no account, but, at the first vacancy, I shall be made regimental commander; and then, I have the happiness of being your husband." He got up and kissed Vera's hand, but before he did so he straightened out the corner of a rug that was turned up. "And how have I accomplished all this? Principally by exercising a choice in my acquaintances. Of course, though, one has to be straightforward and punctual."

Berg smiled with the consciousness of his superiority over a weak woman, and relapsed into silence, saying to himself that his wife, lovely as she was, was nevertheless a feeble woman, unable to appreciate the full significance of the dignity of being a man. Vera at the same time smiled with a similar consciousness of her superiority over her good, worthy spouse; who nevertheless, like the rest of his sex, was quite mistaken, she thought, in his misunderstanding of the meaning of life. Berg, judging by his wife, considered that all women were weak and unintellectual. Vera, judging by her husband alone, and making wider generalizations, supposed that all men considered no one but themselves wise, and at the same time had no real understanding and were haughty and egotistical.

Berg got up, and, embracing his wife carefully—so as not to rumple her lace fichu, for which he had paid a high price—kissed her on the center of the lips.

"There is one thing—we must not begin to have children too soon," said he, by an unconscious correlation of ideas.

"Yes," replied Vera. "That's exactly what I do not want. We must live for society."

"Princess Yusupof has one exactly like this," said Berg, laying his finger on the lace fichu, with his honest, happy smile.

At this time Count Bezukhof was announced. The young couple exchanged congratulatory glances, each appropriating the honor of this visit.

"This is what comes of knowing how to make the right acquaintances," said Berg. "This comes of having tact!"

"Now, I beg of you, don't interrupt me when I am talking with guests," said Vera. "Because I know how to receive each one, and what to talk to them about."

Berg also smiled. "Of course; but sometimes, among men, there must be conversation for men," said he.

Pierre was shown into the new drawing-room, where one could not possibly take a seat without destroying the symmetry, neatness, and order that reigned there; and consequently, it was perfectly comprehensible and not to be wondered at that it required much magnanimity of Berg to allow this symmetry of chair or sofa to be disturbed for his beloved guest; or that, by reason of finding himself in a state of painful irresolution in regard to it, he should have allowed his guest to solve the problem in his own way. Pierre, accordingly, broke into the symmetry by pushing out a chair; and immediately after, Berg and Vera began their reception and began to talk, each interrupting the other, and trying to entertain their guest.

Vera, deciding in her own mind that Pierre would naturally be interested in the French embassy, immediately began to talk about it. Berg, deciding that a more virile subject must be chosen, broke into his wife's discourse by raising a question in regard to the war with Austria; and found himself involuntarily digressing from the abstract topic to various concrete proposals which had been laid before him in regard to taking part in the Austrian campaign, and the reasons which had led him to decline them.

Although the conversation was desultory, and Vera was indignant that this masculine element should have been introduced, both husband and wife had a feeling of satisfaction that, though as yet there was only one guest, still the evening had begun auspiciously, and that their reception was going to be like every other reception—with talk, tea, and brightly lighted candles —as like, in fact, as two drops of water.

Shortly after, Boris appeared, he having been Berg's former comrade. He treated Berg and Vera with a shade of superiority and condescension. Boris was followed by a colonel and his lady, then Berg's own general, then the Rostofs; and the reception by this time, without a shadow of a doubt, began to resemble all other receptions. Berg and Vera could not refrain from a blissful smile at the sight of this stir in the drawing-room, at the clatter of disconnected snatches of conversation, at the rustle of silken gowns, and the greetings. Everything was just as it would be everywhere else; especially so was the general, who could not find enough to say in praise of Berg's apartment, and patted him on the shoulder, and with fatherly authority arranged the disposition of the tables for boston-whist. The general then sat down by Count Rostof, as being, next to himself, the guest of the greatest importance. The old people gathered in groups by themselves, the young people by themselves; the hostess took her place at the tea table, which was laid out with exactly the same kind of macaroons in a silver cake basket as the Panins had had at their reception; in fact, everything was exactly the same as at all receptions.

X

Pierre, as one of the most distinguished guests of the evening, naturally had to play boston in the set with Count Rostof, the general, and the colonel. It happened that his place at the table brought him opposite Natasha, and he could not help being struck by the strange change that had come over her since the evening of the ball. She spoke scarcely a word, and was not so pretty as she had been at the ball; indeed, she would have looked plain, if it had not been for her sweet expression of resignation.

"What is the matter with her?" Pierre wondered, as he looked at her. She was sitting beside her sister at the tea table, and, with an air of utter indifference and without even looking at him, answered some remark that Boris had made to her. Having played out a whole suit and taken five tricks, greatly to his partner's satisfaction, Pierre, as he gathered up his cards, was again led to look at her by hearing complimentary greetings, and then the steps of someone entering the room.

"What has happened to her?" he asked himself, with even more wonder than before.

Prince Andrei, with an expression of protecting affection, was now standing in front of her and saying something to her. She had lifted her head and was gazing at him with flushed cheeks, and apparently striving to restrain her rapid breathing. And the brilliant light of a strange inner fire, till then suppressed, again flashed up in her. She was wholly transfigured: instead of being plain, she was as radiantly beautiful as she had been at the ball. Prince Andrei came toward Pierre, and Pierre noticed a new and youthful expression in his friend's face.

Pierre changed his seat several times during the game, sometimes being in front of Natasha, and sometimes behind; but during all the time of the six rubbers, he kept watching her and his friend.

"There is something very serious going on between them," said Pierre to himself; and a feeling of mingled joy and sadness stirred him, and made him forget his own grief.

After the sixth rubber the general got up, declaring that it was impossible to play in such a way, and Pierre regained his freedom. Natasha, on one side, was talking with Sonya and Boris; Vera, with a slight smile on her face, was talking to Prince Andrei about something or other.

Pierre joined his friend and, asking what secret they were discussing together, took a seat near them. Vera, having noticed Prince Andrei's attention to Natasha, had decided that that evening, that very evening, it was absolutely necessary for her to drop some shrewd insinuations in regard to the feelings; and so she took advantage of a moment when Prince Andrei was alone to begin to talk about sentiment in general, and about her sister in particular. With such a clever man as she knew Prince Andrei to be, she knew she must here use her diplomatic arts.

When Pierre joined them, he noticed that Vera was talking with great eloquence and self-satisfaction, while Prince Andrei seemed rather confused, which was a rare thing with him.

"What is your opinion?" asked Vera, with her slight smile. "You have such keen insight, prince, and are so quick to read people's characters: what do you think of Natasha? Would she be likely to be constant in her attachments? Would she be like other women"—Vera had herself in mind—"and love a man once, and remain forever faithful to him? That is what I call genuine love. What do you think, prince?"

"I have too slight an acquaintance with your sister," replied Prince Andrei, with a satirical smile under which he tried to hide his confusion, "to decide such a delicate question; and then, I have noticed that the less attractive a woman is, the more likely she is to be constant," he added, and looked at Pierre, who had just at that instant joined them.

"Yes, that is true, prince; in our days," pursued Vera—speaking of "our days" in a way affected by narrow-minded people who labor under the delusion that they are the only ones to discover and appreciate the peculiarities of their time, and that human nature changes with the changing years—"young girls have so much freedom that the pleasure of being wooed often stifles their true feelings. And Natasha, it must be confessed, is very susceptible to it."

This reference to Natasha again caused Prince Andrei to scowl disagreeably; he was about to rise, but Vera proceeded with a still more subtle smile:

"I think no one has ever been more courted than she," said Vera. "But no one had ever really seriously succeeded in pleasing her until very recently. You must know, count," said she, addressing Pierre, "even our dear Cousin Boris has, between ourselves, gone very, very far into the land of sentiment."

Prince Andrei, still scowling, said nothing.

"You and Boris are friends, are you not?" asked Vera.

"Yes, I know him."

"I suppose he has told you about his boyish love for Natasha?"

"Ah! so it was a boyish love, was it?" suddenly asked Prince Andrei, unexpectedly reddening.

"Yes! You know sometimes this intimacy between cousins leads to love; cousinhood is a risky neighborhood! That's true, isn't it?"

"Oh, yes, without doubt," said Prince Andrei; and suddenly, becoming unnaturally excited, he began to warn Pierre on his duty to be on his guard against any intimacy with his fifty-year-old cousins in Moscow; and then, right in the midst of his jesting talk, he got up, and taking Pierre by the arm, drew him aside.

"Well! what is it?" asked Pierre, amazed at his friend's strange excitement, and remarking the look which, as he got up, he threw in Natasha's direction.

"I must, I really must, have a talk with you," said Prince Andrei. "You know the gloves"—he referred to the Masonic gloves, which a newly initiated brother was to present to the lady of his love. "I . . . but no . . . I will talk with you about it by and by." And, with a strange light in his eyes and a restlessness in his motions, Prince Andrei crossed over to Natasha and sat down. Pierre saw how he asked her some question, and how she blushed as she answered him.

But just at that moment Berg came up to Pierre and urged him to take part in a discussion between the general and the colonel on Spanish affairs.

Berg was satisfied and happy. Not once did the smile of pleasure fade from his face. The reception had been a success, and exactly like other receptions he had attended. The similarity was complete. The nice little gossipy chats among the ladies; the cards, and the general raising his voice over the game; the samovar and the macaroons! One thing only was lacking, which he had always seen at receptions, and which he wished to imitate: That was a loud conversation among the men, and a discussion over some grave and momentous question. The general had begun this conversation, and now Berg carried Pierre off to take part in it.

XI

THE NEXT DAY Prince Andrei went to the Rostofs' to dinner and spent the whole evening there.

All in the house had an inkling of the reason for Prince Andrei's visits, and he made no secret of it, but tried to be in Natasha's company all the time.

Not only Natasha, in her heart of hearts frightened and yet blissful and full of enthusiasm, but all the household also, felt a sort of awe in the anticipation of a great and solemn event. The countess, with sad and gravely wistful eyes, gazed at Prince Andrei as he talked with Natasha, and with a sort of timidity tried to introduce some indifferent topic as soon as he turned to her. Sonya was afraid to leave Natasha, and equally afraid that she was in their way when she was with them. Natasha grew pale with fear and expectation if by chance she was left alone with him for a moment. Prince Andrei's timidity amazed her. She felt certain that he had something to say to her, but had not the courage to speak.

In the evening, when Prince Andrei had gone, the countess went to Natasha.

"Well?" said she, in a whisper.

"Mama, for pity's sake, don't ask me any questions now. It is impossible to tell."

Nevertheless, that night Natasha, at one moment full of excitement, at the next full of trepidation, lay for a long time in her mother's bed with eyes fixed on space. Now she would tell her mother how he praised her, and how he said he was going abroad, and how he asked her where the Rostofs were going to spend the summer, and how he had asked her about Boris.

"Well, it's so strange, so strange! . . . I never knew anything like it before," said she. "But I have such a feeling of terror when he is here; I always feel afraid when I am with him; what does it mean? Does it mean that it is really and truly . . . ? Mama, are you asleep?"

"No, my darling; I confess to the same feeling of terror," replied the mother. "Go, now!"

"I won't go to sleep, all the same. How silly it would be to go to sleep! Mama darling, nothing like it ever happened to me before," said she, in amazement and awe at the feeling which she was now experiencing. "How could we possibly have imagined . . ."

It seemed to Natasha that even as long ago as when Prince Andrei had come to Otradnoye she had fallen in love with him. She was terror-stricken, as it were, at that strange, unexpected happiness in meeting again with the very man whom she had—as she persuaded herself—chosen for her husband then, and feeling that he was not indifferent to her.

"And it had to be that he should come to Petersburg just at the time when we were here; and it had to be that we should meet at that ball. It was our fate. It is evident that it was our fate, that it all led to this—all this. Even when I saw him first, I felt something peculiar."

"What is it he has said to you? What were those verses? Repeat them to me," said the countess, trying to recall some verses Prince Andrei had written in Natasha's album.

"Mama, there's nothing to be ashamed of because he is a widower, is there?"

"Don't talk nonsense, Natasha. Pray to God! Marriages are made in heaven!"

"Sweetheart! mama darling! how I love you, how good you are!" cried Natasha, shedding tears of bliss and emotion, and hugging her mother.

At that same time, Prince Andrei was at Pierre's, telling him about his love for Natasha, and his firm intention of marrying her.

That same evening, the Countess Elena Bezukhof had given a reception. The French ambassador had been there; the foreign prince who for some time had been a frequent visitor at the countess' had been present; and a throng of brilliant ladies and gentlemen. Pierre had come down and wandered through the rooms, attracting general notice among the guests by his concentrated, distracted and gloomy looks.

Pierre, ever since the time of the ball, had been conscious that attacks of his old enemy, hypochondria, were imminent; and with the energy of despair, he had struggled to get the better of them. Since this prince had become the countess' acknowledged admirer, Pierre had unexpectedly been appointed one of the emperor's chamberlains; and from that time forth he began to feel a great burden and loathing for society, and his former gloomy, pessimistic thoughts, about the falsity of all things human, began to come back to him more and more frequently.

At this particular time his tendency to gloominess was accented by the discovery of the feeling existing between his little protégée Natasha and Prince Andrei, and by the contrast between his own position and his friend's. He vainly struggled to banish his thoughts about his wife, and about Natasha and Prince Andrei. But everything began once more to seem insignificant in comparison with eternity, and again the question arose, "To what end?" Night and day he compelled himself to toil over his Masonic labors, hoping to exorcise the evil demon that hovered near him.

At midnight, Pierre came from the countess' apartments to his own low-ceilinged room which smelled of stale tobacco, and had just sat down at the table in his soiled dressing gown and started to finish copying some original documents from Scotland, when someone came into the room.

It was Prince Andrei.

"Oh, it's you, is it?" said Pierre, in an abstracted and not overcordial manner.

"Here I am at work, you see," said he, pointing to his copybook, and his face showed that he was trying to find in it salvation from his troubles. Unhappy people always look at their work with that expression. Prince Andrei, his face radiant with enthusiasm and new life, came and stood in front of Pierre; and, not noticing his friend's unhappy face, smiled down on him with the egotism of happiness.

"Well, my dear fellow," said he, "last evening I wanted to tell you something, and now I have come for that purpose. It is something wholly unprecedented in my experience. I am in love, my friend."

Pierre suddenly drew a deep sigh and stretched his clumsy form out on the divan near Prince Andrei.

"With Natasha Rostof, I suppose?" said he.

"Yes, yes; who else could it be? I would never have believed it, but this feeling is stronger than I. Last evening I was tortured, I was miserable; but I would not exchange this agony for anything in the world. I have never lived till now. Only now do I live, and I cannot live without her. But can she love me? . . . I am too old for her. What do you say?"

"I? I? What *can* I say?" suddenly exclaimed Pierre, springing up and beginning to pace the room. "I have always thought . . . This girl is such a treasure, such a . . . she is a rare person . . . my dear fellow: I beseech you, don't reason about it, don't let doubts arise, but marry her, marry her, marry her . . . and I am convinced that you will be the happiest man alive!"

"But how about her?"

"She loves you!"

"Don't talk nonsense . . ." said Prince Andrei with a smile, and looking straight into Pierre's eyes.

"She loves you, I know she does," cried Pierre, bluntly.

"Now listen!" said Prince Andrei, holding him by his arm. "Do you know what a position I am in? I must tell someone all about it!"

"Well, well, go on, I am very glad," said Pierre, and in reality his face had changed; the frown had smoothed itself out, and he listened to Prince Andrei with joyous sympathy. Prince Andrei seemed, and really was, another and wholly new man. His melancholy, his contempt of life, all his disillusion had vanished. Pierre was the only man in whose presence he could speak with absolute frankness, and he poured out before him the fullness of his heart. Then fluently and boldly he made plans for the future, declaring that he could not think of sacrificing his happiness to his father's caprices, and expressing his hope that his father would consent to their marriage, and would come to love Natasha; then he expressed his amazement at the strange and uncontrollable feeling that dominated him.

"If anyone had predicted the possibility of my being so deeply in love, I wouldn't have believed it," said Prince Andrei. "It is an entirely different sentiment from the one I had formerly. The whole world is divided for me into two portions: The one is where she is, and there all happiness and hope and light are found; the other is where she is not, and there everything is gloom and darkness."

"Darkness and gloom," repeated Pierre. "Yes, yes, I appreciate that!"

"I cannot help loving light, and I am not to blame for it. And I am very happy. Do you understand me? I know you sympathize with my joy."

"Yes, indeed I do," said Pierre, earnestly, gazing at his friend with tender, melancholy eyes. Prince Andrei's fate seemed to him all the brighter from the vivid contrast with the darkness of his own.

XII

PRINCE ANDREI needed his father's sanction for his marriage, and the next day he set out for his home.

The old prince received his son's communication with external unconcern, but with wrath in his heart. As his own life was nearing its close, he could not understand how anyone could wish to make such a change in his life, to introduce into it such a new and unknown element.

"If only they would let me live out my life in my own way! then, when I am gone, they can do as they please," said the old man to himself. With his son, however, he made use of the diplomacy he employed in matters of serious import. Assuming a tranquil tone, he summed the whole matter up:

In the first place, the match was not brilliant as to the birth, fortune, or distinction of the bride's family. In the second place, Prince Andrei was not as young as he had once been, and his health was feeble—the old prince laid especial stress on this—and she was very young. In the third place, he had a son whom it would be a shame to give over to the mercy of a young stepmother.

"In the fourth place, finally," said the father, giving his son an ironical look, "I beg of you to postpone the affair for a year, go abroad, go through a course of treatment, find a good German tutor for Prince Nikolai; and then, if your love, passion, stubbornness, whatever you call it, is as strong as ever—why, marry her. And this is my last word, remember; absolutely my last word," concluded the old prince, in a tone that signified that nothing could ever change his mind.

Prince Andrei clearly saw that the old prince hoped that either his sentiments or his prospective bride's might not withstand the test of a year, or else that he himself—since he was an old man—might die in the meantime; he accordingly determined to obey his father's wishes, to offer himself, and then postpone the wedding for a year.

Three weeks after his last call at the Rostofs', Prince Andrei returned to Petersburg.

The day following her confidential talk with her mother, Natasha waited anxiously for Bolkonsky; but he did not come. The second day and the third day it was precisely the same. Pierre, also, failed to come; and Natasha, not knowing that the prince had gone to see his father, could not explain his absence.

Thus passed three weeks. Natasha had no desire to go anywhere, and she wandered like a languid and mournful shadow through the rooms; evenings, she hid herself away from the others and wept, and no longer came to her mother's bedchamber. She frequently flushed, and her temper grew peevish. She had an impression that everybody knew about her disappointment, and was laughing at her and pitying her. This grief, born of pride, added to her misery, all the more from the fact that it was hidden grief.

Once she went to the countess and tried to say something, but suddenly burst into tears. Her tears were like those of a child who had been punished without knowing for what reason. The countess tried to calm her; but Natasha, though she at first began to listen, suddenly interrupted her.

"Do stop, mama; I don't understand and I can't understand. He came, and then he stopped coming . . . he stopped coming . . ."

Her voice faltered, she almost wept; but she controlled herself and went on:

"I haven't any desire at all to be married; and I have been afraid of him all the time: I'm perfectly content now, perfectly content."

On the day following this conversation, Natasha put on an old gown for which she had an especially tender feeling, owing to the gay times she had enjoyed when wearing it in days past; and from that morning on, she resumed the occupations she had dropped since the time of the ball. After she had drunk her tea, she went into the ballroom, which she liked on account of its powerful resonance, and began to practice her solfeggios and other exercises. After she had finished her lesson, she stood in the middle of the room and repeated a single musical phrase which pleased her more than others. She joyfully listened to the charming and apparently unexpected way in which these notes reverberated through the empty spaces of the ballroom and slowly died away; and suddenly her heart grew lighter.

"What is the use of thinking so much about it all! It is good as it is." said she to herself, and she began to pace up and down the room, not content with simply walking along the echoing inlaid floor, but at every step—she wore her favorite new slippers—setting her little heels down first, and then her toes, and finding as much enjoyment in the regular clapping of the heel and the creaking of the toe, as in the sounds of her voice. As she passed by a mirror, she glanced into it.

"What a girl I am!" the expression of her face, as she caught sight of the reflection in the glass, seemed to say. "It's all good! I need no one."

A lackey was on the point of coming in to make some arrangements in the ballroom; but she sent him away, closing the door after him, and then continuing her walk. Now again, this morning, she resumed her former favorite habit of loving and admiring her own sweet self.

"How charming this Natasha is!" she was saying, as if the words were spoken by some third person, the man of her imagination. "Pretty, a good voice, young, and she does not interfere with anyone; only leave her in peace!"

But even if she had been left in peace, she could not have been calm; and of this she was immediately made aware.

The front door into the vestibule was opened, and someone asked: "Are they at home?" and then a man's steps were heard. Natasha was gazing into the mirror, but she did not see herself. She heard voices in the vestibule. When she looked in the mirror again her face was pale.

It was he! She was sure of it, though she could barely distinguish the voices through the closed doors.

Pale and frightened, Natasha ran into the drawing-room.

"Mama, Bolkonsky has come," she cried. "Mama! This is dreadful! This is unendurable! I will not be . . . tortured so! What shall I do?" . . .

Before the countess had time to answer her, Prince Andrei was shown in, his face grave and anxious. As soon as he caught sight of Natasha a flash of joy lighted it. He kissed the countess' hand, and Natasha's, and took a seat near the divan.

"It is a long time since we have had the pleasure . . ." the countess began to say, but Prince Andrei interrupted her. He answered her implied question, and was evidently anxious to speak what was on his mind as soon as possible.

"I have not been to see you all this time because I went to see my father; I had to confer with him regarding a very important matter. I returned only yesterday evening," he said, glancing at Natasha. "I should like to have a little conversation with you, countess," he added, after a moment's silence.

The countess, drawing a long sigh, dropped her eyes.

"I am at your service," she murmured.

Natasha knew that it was her duty to leave the room, but she found it impossible to stir; something choked her, and she stared at Prince Andrei almost rudely, with wide eyes.

"What! So soon? This very moment? . . . No, it cannot be!" she said to herself.

He again looked at her, and this glance told her beyond doubt that she was not deceived. "Yes, her fate was to be decided instantly, that moment, then and there!"

"Go, Natasha, I will send for you," whispered the countess.

Natasha, with startled, pleading eyes, looked at her mother, and at Prince Andrei, and left the room.

"I have come, countess, to ask your daughter's hand," said Prince Andrei.

The countess' face flushed, but she said nothing.

"Your proposal . . ." began the countess, gravely. Prince Andrei waited, and looked into her eyes. "Your proposal"—she grew confused—"is very pleasing to us, and . . . and I accept, accept your proposal, with pleasure. And my husband . . . I hope . . . but it will depend upon herself."

"I will ask her as soon as I receive your permission. Will you grant it?" said Prince Andrei.

"Yes," said the countess, and she offered him her hand; and, with a mixed feeling of alienation and affection, touched his brow with her lips as he bent over her hand. She was ready to love him as a son; but she was conscious that he held her at a distance; and he filled her with a sort of terror. "I am sure my husband will give his consent," said the countess; "but your father . . ."

"My father, to whom I have confided my plans, has consented, on the express stipulation that the wedding should not take place within a year; and this was the very thing that I wished to tell you," said Prince Andrei.

"It is true that Natasha is still young, but a year is so long."

"This cannot be otherwise," said Prince Andrei, with a sigh.

"I will send her to you," said the countess, and she left the room.

"Lord, have mercy upon us!" she repeated over and over, as she went in search of her daughter. Sonya said that Natasha was in her room. She found her sitting on her bed, pale, with dry eyes, gazing at the holy pictures and swiftly crossing herself, and whispering to herself. When she saw her mother, she jumped up and rushed to her.

"What? Mama? . . . What is it?"

"Go, go to him. He has proposed for your hand," said the countess, coldly, so it seemed to Natasha. "Go! . . . Go," repeated her mother, drawing a long sigh, and looking with sad, reproachful eyes after her daughter as she flew out of the room.

Natasha could not remember how she found herself in the drawing-room. But, as she went into the room and caught sight of him, she stopped short.

"Can it be that this stranger is now all in all to me?" she asked herself; and the reply came like a flash. "Yes! He alone is dearer to me than all in the world."

Prince Andrei went to her with downcast eyes. "I have loved you from the first moment I saw you. May I dare to hope?"

He looked at her, and the grave passion expressed in his face filled her with wonder.

Her eyes replied, "Why should you ask? Why should you doubt what you must surely know? Why should you speak, when it is impossible with words to express what you feel?"

She drew near to him, and paused. He took her hand, and kissed it: "Do you love me?"

"Yes, yes," exclaimed Natasha, with something that seemed almost like vexation; and, catching her breath more and more frequently, she began to sob.

"What is it? What is the matter?"

"Oh, I am so happy," she replied, smiling through her tears, and coming closer to him; she hesitated for a moment, as if asking if it were permissible, and then kissed him.

Prince Andrei held her hand and gazed into her eyes, and failed to find in his heart his former love for her. A sudden transformation seemed to have taken place in his soul: There was none of that former poetical and mysterious charm of longing; but there was a feeling akin to pity for her weakness, as a woman, as a child; there was a shade of fear, in presence of her utter self-renunciation and her fearless honesty; a solemn and, at the same time, blissful consciousness of the obligation which forever bound him to her. The present feeling, though it was not so bright and poetical as the former, was more deep and powerful.

"Has your mama told you that our marriage cannot be till a year has passed?" asked Prince Andrei, continuing to gaze into her eyes.

"Can it be that this is the little silly chit of a girl, as they all say of me?" mused Natasha. "Can it be that from this time forth, I am the wife, the equal, of this stranger, this gentle, learned man, whom even my father regards with admiration? Can it be true, can it be true that now, henceforth, life has become serious? That now I am grown up? That now I shall be responsible for every word and deed? . . . Yes, but what was that he asked me?

"No," she said aloud; but she did not know what he had asked her.

"Forgive me," said Prince Andrei. "But you are so young, and I have already had such long experience of life. I tremble for you. You do not know yourself!"

Natasha, with concentrated attention, listened to what he said, and did her best to take in the full meaning of his words; but it was impossible.

"How hard this year will be for me—deferring my happiness!" pursued Prince Andrei. "But during the time you will have made sure of your own heart. At the end of the year I shall ask you to make me happy; but you are free. Our betrothal shall remain a secret, and if you should discover that you do not love me, if you should love . . ." said Prince Andrei, with a forced and unnatural smile.

"Why do you say that?" asked Natasha, interrupting him. "You know that from that very first day you came to Otradnoye, I loved you," said she, firmly convinced that she was telling the truth.

"In a year you will have learned to know yourself."

"A whole year!" suddenly exclaimed Natasha, it now suddenly, for the first time, dawning upon her that the wedding was to be postponed. "And why a year?—Why a year?"

Prince Andrei began to explain the reasons for this postponement. Natasha refused to listen to him.

"And is there no other way?" she asked. Prince Andrei made no answer, but the expression of his face told her how unalterable his decision was.

"This is terrible! No, this is terrible, terrible!" suddenly exclaimed Natasha, and again she began to sob. "I shall die if I have to wait a year; it cannot be, it is dreadful."

She looked into her lover's face, and saw that it was full of sympathy and perplexity.

"No, no, I will do everything you wish," she said, suddenly ceasing to sob. "I am so happy."

Her father and mother came into the room and congratulated the affianced pair.

From that day forth, Prince Andrei began to visit the Rostofs as Natasha's accepted husband.

XIII

THERE WAS NO formal betrothal, and Bolkonsky's engagement to Natasha was not made public. Prince Andrei insisted on this point. He said that, as he was the cause of the postponement, he ought to bear the whole burden of it. He declared that he considered himself forever bound by his word; but he felt that he ought not to hold Natasha, and he granted her perfect freedom. If, within a half-year, she should discover that she did not love him, she should have complete right to break the engagement.

Of course, neither the parents nor Natasha would hear of this, but Prince Andrei pressed the matter. Prince Andrei was at the Rostofs' every day, but he did not treat Natasha with the familiarity of the betrothed: he always addressed her by the formal "you," and kissed only her hand.

Between Prince Andrei and Natasha, after the day of their betrothal, there came to be an entirely different relationship from before: one closer and more simple. At first the family felt a certain awkwardness in their relations toward Prince Andrei: he seemed like a man from another world, and it took Natasha a long time to train the others to feel at ease with him; and she felt a pride in assuring them all that it was only in appearance that Prince Andrei was so different, and that he was really like everyone else, and that she was not afraid of him, and that no one had any reason to fear him.

After some days the family became accustomed to him, and felt no awkwardness in going on in his presence with the ordinary routine of life, in which he also had a share.

That poetical melancholy and silence which always mark the presence of an engaged couple reigned in the house. Often when all were together no word would be said. Sometimes the rest would get up and leave the room, and even then the two young people, though by themselves, would sit in perfect silence, as before. They rarely spoke about their future; Prince Andrei avoided it from dread as well as from conscientious motives. Natasha shared his feelings, as, indeed, she shared all his feelings, which she was always quick to read.

Once Natasha began to ask him about his little boy; Prince Andrei flushed, as he was apt to do at that time—and Natasha particularly liked it in him—and replied that his son would not live with them.

"Why not?" asked Natasha, in alarm.

"I could not take him away from his grandfather; and, besides . . ."

"How I would love him!" exclaimed Natasha, instantly divining his thought. "But I understand; you are anxious to avoid any excuse for misunderstandings between us."

The old count sometimes came to Prince Andrei, kissed him, and asked him his advice in regard to Petya's education, or Nikolai's advancement in the army. The old countess would sigh as she looked at them. Sonya was always afraid she was in the way, and tried to invent excuses for leaving them alone, even when it was not necessary. When Prince Andrei talked— and he was very admirable in conversation—Natasha would listen to him with pride; when she herself spoke, she noticed, with fear and joy, that he listened to her with a tension and scrutinized her keenly. She would ask herself in perplexity:

"What is he searching for in me? What are his eyes trying to discover? Supposing he were not to find in me what he seeks to find?"

Occasionally she was attacked by one of those absurd fits of mirth peculiar to her, and then it was a delight for her to see and hear him laugh. He rarely laughed aloud, but when he did indulge in merriment he gave himself up entirely to it; and always after such an experience, she felt she had grown nearer to him. Natasha would have been perfectly happy if the thought of their parting, which was now near at hand, had not filled her with vague alarm—so much so that she grew pale and chill at the mere thought of it.

On the evening before his departure from Petersburg, Prince Andrei brought Pierre, who had not once called at the Rostofs' since the evening of the ball. Pierre seemed confused and out of spirits. He engaged in conversation with the countess. Natasha was sitting with Sonya at the checker table and asked Prince Andrei to join them. He did so.

"You have known Bezukhof for a long time, have you not?" he asked. "Do you like him?"

"Yes, he is a splendid man, but very absurd."

And, as was usually the case when speaking of Pierre, she began to relate anecdotes of his heedlessness, many of which had been invented about him.

"You know, I have told him our secret," said Prince Andrei. "I have known him since we were boys. His heart is true gold. I beg you, Natasha," said he, growing suddenly grave. "I am going away. God knows what may happen: you may cease to lo— . . . well, I know I ought not to speak of this. One thing, though: In case anything should happen, after I am gone . . ."

"What could happen?"

"If there should be any misfortune," pursued Prince Andrei, "I beg you, Mademoiselle Sonya, if anything should happen, go to him for help and counsel. He may be a most heedless and absurd man, but his heart is the truest gold."

Not Natasha's father, or mother, or Sonya, or Prince Andrei himself, could have foreseen what an effect parting from her lover would have upon Natasha. Flushed and excited, with burning eyes, she wandered all day long up and down the house, busying herself with the most insignificant things, as if she had no idea of what was going to happen. She did not shed a tear, even at the moment when he kissed her hand for the last time, and bade her farewell.

"Don't leave me," was all that she said; but these words were spoken in a voice that caused him to pause and consider whether it was really necessary for him to go away; and he remembered it long afterwards.

Even after he had gone, she did not weep; but she stayed in her room for many days, not shedding a tear, and she took no interest in anything, and only said from time to time:

"Oh, why did he go?"

But a fortnight after his departure, most unexpectedly to the household, she woke up out of this spiritual illness, and began to seem the same as formerly; except that her whole moral nature was changed, just as the faces of children change during protracted illness.

In the middle of the summer Princess Maria received a letter from her brother, from Switzerland, in which he confided the strange and surprising news of his engagement to Natasha. His whole letter breathed enthusiastic devotion for his "bride," and affectionate and trusting love for his sister. He wrote that he had never before loved as he loved now, and that only now did he realize and understand the meaning of life; he besought his sister to pardon him for not having said anything to her about this at his visit to Lisiya Gori, although he had confided his intention to his father. He had not told her because Princess Maria would have tried to persuade their father to grant his request; and if he had failed, it would have irritated her father and the whole weight of his displeasure would have come upon her.

> Moreover [he wrote], the matter was not so definitely settled as it is now. Then, my father had set a term of probation—a year; and now, already, six months have slipped away, half of the designated term, and I remain firmer than ever fixed in my determination. If the doctors had not detained me here at the springs, I would have been back before this, but now I must postpone my return for three months longer. You know me, and how I am situated with respect to my father; I really need nothing from him; I have been, and will always be, independent of him; but to act contrary to his wishes, to incur his anger, when perhaps he has so short a time to remain among us, would destroy half my happiness. I have just been writing him a letter about this, and I beg you, if you can find a favorable moment, give him this letter and inform me how he receives it, and whether there is any hope that he will consent to shorten the term by three months.

After a long period of indecision, doubting, and prayer, the princess handed the letter to her father. The day following, the old prince said to her, without any show of excitement:

"Write to your brother to wait till I'm dead. It won't be long. . . . He'll soon be free."

The princess tried to make some reply; but her father would not hear it, and his voice began to rise higher and higher.

"Marry, marry, my little dove! . . . Fine family! . . . Clever people, ha? . . . Rich? ha! Yes, a fine stepmother for the little Nikolusha she'll make. Write him that he may marry her tomorrow if he wishes. She'll make a fine stepmother for Nikolusha, and I'll marry Bourienne. Ha! ha! ha! So that *he* may have a stepmother too! There's one thing, though: There's no room for any more women here; let him marry, and go and live by himself. Perhaps you'd like to go and live with him?" said he, turning to Princess Maria. "Go, then, in God's name; through ice and snow, ice and snow—ice and snow!"

After this explosion, the old prince said nothing more on that score, but his restrained vexation at his son's weakness was expressed in his treatment of his daughter. And he now had new themes for his sarcasm, in addition to his old ones; namely, stepmothers, and his admiration for Mlle. Bourienne.

"Why shouldn't I marry her?" he asked his daughter. "She would make a splendid princess!"

And Princess Maria began to notice, with perplexity and amazement, that her father more and more tried to have the Frenchwoman about him as much as possible. Princess Maria wrote Prince Andrei how their father had received the letter, but she tried to comfort her brother, giving him to hope that their father might be dissuaded from this notion.

1810-1811

Napoleon is at the height of his power. By his marriage to Marie Louise of Austria in 1810 he has allied himself to the Hapsburg dynasty. The greatest king maker of all time, he has set his brothers and brothers-in-law on half-a-dozen European thrones. But the peace is not complete, for Britain continues to fight on the Iberian peninsula and the British fleet still rules the seas, preventing a return to normal trade conditions throughout Europe. In 1811 Russia, at peace with France, goes to war against Turkey to expand the empire of the Tsar; but it is a limited war, compared to the vital struggles with Napoleon: it engages few of Russia's forces and has little effect on the lives of the Russian nobility.

Part Seventh

NIKOLAI ROSTOF continued to serve in the Pavlograd regiment; he was now commander of the squadron of which Denisof had been deprived. Rostof had grown into a rather rough but kindly young fellow, whom his Moscow acquaintances would have found quite unconventional but who was loved and respected by his comrades, his subordinates as well as his superiors; and he was well satisfied with his existence. Lately, in 1809, in letters from home he had found more and more frequent complaints from his mother that their affairs were going from bad to worse, and that it would be a good idea for him to come home and give his old parents some joy and consolation.

In reading over these letters, Nikolai felt a sensation of alarm at the thought of being torn from a condition of life where he found himself so quiet and tranquil, far removed from the busy turmoil of society. He had a presentiment that sooner or later he would be dragged again into that whirlpool of life, with its wasteful expenditure and rearrangement of affairs; with its accounts to verify; with its quarrels, intrigues, obligations; with the demands of society, and with Sonya's love, and the necessity of an explanation. All this was terribly difficult and confused; and he answered his mother's letters with cold formality, beginning "Dear Mama," and concluding with "Your obedient son"; and studiously refrained from setting any time for his return home.

In 1810 he received a letter from his parents, who informed him of the engagement between Natasha and Bolkonsky, and that the wedding was put off for a year because the old prince had refused his sanction. This news grieved and disgusted Nikolai. In the first place he was pained at the thought of losing Natasha from the household, for he was fonder of her than of the other members of the family; in the second place, he was annoyed, from his point of view as a hussar, that he had not been on hand to make this Bolkonsky understand that this alliance was not a very great honor, and that if he loved Natasha, he might have married her, even without his scatterbrained father's consent. For a moment he almost made up his mind to ask for leave of absence, so as to see Natasha before she was married; but just then came the army maneuvers, he remembered Sonya and the various entanglements, and once more he postponed it.

But in the spring of that same year he received a letter from his mother, who wrote without the count's knowledge, and this letter prompted him to go. She wrote that if he did not come, and did not assume the management of their affairs, their whole property would have to be sold by auction, and they would all be thrown on the world. The count was so weak, he had such confidence in Mitenka, he was so good-natured and so easily cheated by everyone, that everything was going from bad to worse. "For God's sake, I beg of you, come immediately, unless you wish to make me and all the family unhappy," wrote the countess.

This letter had its effect upon Nikolai. He was possessed of the sound common sense of mediocrity, and it told him that this was his duty.

Now it was requisite that he should go either on leave of absence or on the retired list. He could not have explained why he had to go, but, after his siesta, he commanded his roan stallion Mars to be saddled—it had not been out for a long time, and was at any time a terribly fiery steed; and, when he brought it home all in a lather, he explained to Lavrushka—Denisof's man had stayed on with Rostof—and to his comrades who dropped in that afternoon, that he had obtained leave of absence and was going home.

How hard it was for him to realize that he was going to absent himself from army life—the only thing that especially interested him—and fail to find whether he had been promoted or granted the Order of St. George for the last maneuvers! How strange it was to think that he was going away before he had sold his three roans to the Polish Count Holuchowski, who had been negotiating for the horses, which Rostof had wagered would bring two thousand rubles! How impossible to realize that he would miss the ball which the hussars were going to give to the Pani Pscazdecska, in order to pique the Uhlans, who had given a ball to their Pani Borzjozowska! He knew that he must leave, go away from all this bright, pleasant existence, and go where everything was trouble and turmoil.

At the end of a week he was granted his leave of absence. His comrades of the hussars, not only of his regiment but of the whole brigade, gave him a dinner which cost them fifteen rubles a head; they had two bands to play and two choruses to sing for them. Rostof danced the *trépak* with Major Basof; the tipsy officers tossed him, embraced him, and deposited him on the ground again; the soldiers of the third squadron once more tossed him and cried hurrah. Then they carried him to his sleigh and escorted him as far as the first station.

As is usually the case, Rostof's thoughts during the first half of his journey, from Kremenchug to Kiev, were retrospective and connected with the affairs of his squadron; but, after he had gone halfway, he began to forget about the three roans and his quartermaster Dozhoiveik, and anxious questions began to arise in his mind as to what he would find at Otradnoye. The nearer he came to his home, the more powerfully he was affected by his forebodings. At the Otradnoye station he gave the driver three rubles for vodka, and, all out of breath, rushed like a schoolboy up the steps of the old home.

After the first enthusiastic greetings, and after that strange sense of vague disappointment at the reality falling short of expectation—"Everything is just the same; why, then, have I hastened so?"—Nikolai began to become accustomed to the old home life again. His father and mother were the same, except that they had grown a trifle older. He detected a peculiar restlessness about them, and sometimes a slight coldness between them, which was a new thing, and which Nikolai, as soon as he discovered it, attributed to the unfortunate condition of their affairs.

Sonya was now about twenty years old. She had reached the zenith of her beauty, and gave no promise that she would ever surpass what she already was; even thus, she was pretty enough. She simply breathed happiness and love from the moment that Nikolai came home, and this girl's faithful, unfaltering love for him had a delightful effect on him.

Nikolai was more than all surprised at Petya and Natasha. Petya had grown into a tall, handsome, frolicsome, intelligent lad of thirteen, whose voice was already beginning to break. It was long before Nikolai could get over his amazement at Natasha, and he said, laughing, as he gazed at her:

"You're not at all the same!"

"What! Have I changed for the worse?"

"Quite the contrary; but what dignity, princess!" said he in a whisper.

"Yes, yes, yes," exclaimed Natasha, gleefully.

Natasha told him of her romance with Prince Andrei, and about his visit to Otradnoye, and showed him her last letter from him.

"Tell me, aren't you glad for me?" she asked. "I am so calm, so happy now."

"Yes, very glad," replied Nikolai. "He is a splendid man. And are you very much in love with him?"

"How can I tell you?" replied Natasha. "I was in love with Boris, and with my teacher, and with Denisof, and—but this is not at all the same. My mind is serene and decided. I know that there is not a better man to be found, and so I feel perfectly calm and happy. It is entirely different from what it used to be . . . before . . ."

Nikolai expressed to Natasha his dissatisfaction that the wedding was to be postponed a year; but Natasha, with some show of exasperation, contended that it could not have been otherwise, that it would have been disgraceful to force her way into his family against his father's will, and that she herself had wished it.

"You don't in the least, in the least, understand," she said.

Nikolai said no more, and acquiesced. He often marveled as he looked at her. She was absolutely unlike a girl deeply in love and separated from her betrothed. Her temper was calm and even, and she was as merry as in days gone by. This was a surprise to Nikolai, and even made him look with some incredulity at her engagement to Bolkonsky. He could not make up his mind that her fate was as yet fully decided, the more so from the fact that he had not seen Prince Andrei with her. It seemed to him all the time that something was not as it should be in this proposed marriage.

"Why this postponement? Why are they not formally betrothed?" he asked himself. Once, when speaking with his mother about his sister, he found to his surprise, and to a certain degree his satisfaction, that his mother also did not in the depths of her heart feel any great confidence in the engagement.

"This is what he writes," said she, showing her son a letter she had received from Prince Andrei, with that secret feeling of discontent which a mother always has toward her daughter's future married happiness. "He writes that he will not be back before December. What do you suppose can detain him so? It must be he is ill. His health is very delicate. Don't say anything to Natasha. Don't be surprised that she is happy; these are the last days of her girlhood, and I know how it affects her whenever we get a letter from him. However, it is all in God's hands, and all will be well," she concluded; adding, as usual, "He is a splendid man."

II

THE FIRST DAYS after Nikolai's return he was grave and even depressed. He was tormented by the present necessity of making an investigation into the stupid details of the household economy, for which his mother had begged him to come home. On the third day after his return, in order to get this burden from his shoulders as soon as possible, he went, with contracted brows, sternly, and not giving himself time to decide what he was going to do, to the wing where Mitenka lived, and demanded of him the "accounts of everything." What he meant by the "accounts of everything," he had even less of an idea than Mitenka, who, nevertheless, was thrown into alarm and perplexity.

Mitenka's explanations about his accounts were soon finished. The manager of the estate, and the elder of the village, who were waiting in the anteroom, listened with terror and satisfaction at first, as the young count's voice began to grow fiercer and louder, while they could distinguish terrible words of abuse, following one upon another.

"You brigand, you ungrateful wretch! . . . I'll whip you like a dog! . . . You're not dealing with my old father now," and words of like import.

Then these men, with no less satisfaction and terror, saw the young count, all flushed, and with bloodshot eyes, dragging Mitenka by the collar, and reinforcing his efforts with very dexterous applications of his knees and feet whenever the pauses between his words gave him a convenient chance; while he cried at the top of his voice:

"Get out of here, you villain! Don't you ever show your face here again!"

Mitenka flew down the six steps head first, and landed in a bed of shrubbery. This shrubbery was a famous place of refuge for delinquents at Otradnoye. Mitenka himself, when he returned tipsy from town, used to hide in it; and many of the inhabitants of Otradnoye, trying to get out of Mitenka's way, knew the advantages of this place as a refuge.

Mitenka's wife and her sister, with terror-stricken faces, peered out of the door of the room where a polished samovar was bubbling, and where the high-post bedstead popular with overseers could be seen, covered with a patchwork quilt.

The young count, all out of breath, and giving them no attention, strode by them with resolute steps and went into the house.

The countess, who had heard from the maids all that had taken place in the wing, was in one sense delighted at the direction their affairs were now evidently going to take; and in another she was disquieted at the way in which her son had taken hold of the matter. She went several times on tiptoe to his door, and listened while he smoked one pipe after another.

The next day the old count called Nikolai to one side, and with a timid smile said:

"But do you know, my dear, you wasted your fire! Mitenka has told me all about it."

"I knew," thought Nikolai, "that I would never accomplish anything here, in this idiotic world."

"You were angry with him because he did not reckon in those seven hundred rubles. But, do you know, they were carried over, and you did not look on the other page."

"Dear papa, he is a scoundrel and a thief; I know he is! And what I have done, I have done. But if you don't wish it, I won't say anything more to him about it."

"No, my dear." The count was also confused. He was conscious that he himself had been a bad administrator of his wife's estate, and that he was to blame toward his children; but he did not know how to set things right. "No, I beg of you, take charge of our affairs; I am old, I . . ."

"No, papa, forgive me if I have done anything disagreeable to you; I am less able to attend to it than you are. . . . The devil take those peasants, and accounts, and carryings over," he said to himself. "I used to know well enough what quarter-stakes on a six at faro meant; but this carrying over to the next page, I don't know anything about it at all," said he to himself; and from that time forth he gave no more attention to their financial affairs.

Once, however, the countess called her son to her and told him that she had a note of hand given her by Anna Mikhailovna for two thousand rubles, and she asked Nikolai's advice as to what ought to be done about it.

"This is what I think," replied Niolai. "You have told me that I was to decide the question. Well, I don't like Anna Mikhailovna, and I don't like Boris; but they have been friends of ours, and they are poor. This is what we will do, then!" and he took the note and tore it in two; and this action made the old countess actually sob with delight.

After this, the young Rostof entirely forswore interference with their business matters, and entered with passionate enthusiasm into the delights of hunting with the hounds, for which the old count set him an example on a large scale.

I I I

COUNT ROSTOF had resigned his position as marshal of the district nobility because this office entailed too much expense. But still his finances showed no improvement. Often Natasha and Nikolai found their parents engaged in secret, anxious consultation; and they heard rumors about the sale of the magnificent ancestral home of the Rostofs, and their estate near Moscow. Now that the count was relieved from his office, it was not necessary for them to entertain so extensively, and life at Otradnoye went on more quietly than in former years; but the huge mansion and the wings were just as full of servants as ever, and more than twenty persons habitually sat down at table. And all these were the regular household who lived there, practically members of the family; or those who were obliged, for some reason or other, to live at the count's expense. Such, for instance, were Dimmler, the music master, and his wife; Vogel, the dancing master, and his whole family; then, an elderly lady of quality, named Bielova, who had her home there; and many others of the same sort: Petya's tutors, the young ladies' former governesses, and men and women who simply found it better, or more to their advantage, to live at the count's than at home.

They had not quite as much company as formerly; but the scale of living was practically the same, for the count and the countess found it impossible to adapt themselves to any other way of life. The hunting establishment was the same, it had even been increased by Nikolai: There were still fifty horses and fifteen coachmen in the stables; rich gifts on saint's-days were still given, and formal dinners to which all the neighborhood was invited; the count still had his whist and boston parties, from which, as he held his cards spread out so that everyone could see them, his neighbors were enabled to go away enriched to the extent of several hundred rubles every day, having come to regard it as their special prerogative to make up a table at which Count Rostof should serve as their chief source of income.

The count marched along through the monstrous tangle of his affairs, striving not to believe he was so involved, and at every step involving himself more and more, and feeling conscious that he had not the strength to rend the bonds that held him, or the zeal and patience required to unravel them.

The countess, with her loving heart, was conscious that their fortunes were going to rack and ruin; but she felt that the count was blameless; that he could not help being what he was; that he himself was suffering—though he tried to conceal it—from the consciousness of the ruin that faced him and his family, and was striving to devise means of rescue. From her woman's point of view, the only means that presented itself was to get Nikolai married to a wealthy heiress. She felt that this was their last hope; and that if Nikolai refused a certain match which she proposed to arrange for him, it would be necessary to bid a final farewell to every hope of restoring their fortunes. This match was with Julie Karagina, the daughter of most worthy and virtuous parents; a girl whom the Rostofs had known since she was a child, and who had lately come into a large fortune by the death of the last of her brothers.

The countess had written directly to Madame Karagina in Moscow, proposing a marriage between daughter and son; and she had received a most favorable response. Madame Karagina replied that she, for her part, was agreed, but that everything depended on her daughter's inclinations. Madame Karagina invited Nikolai to come to Moscow.

Several times the countess, with tears in her eyes, told her son that now, since both of her daughters were provided for, her sole desire was to see him married. She declared that she would go to her grave contented if this might be. Then she said that she happened to know of a very lovely young girl, and she wanted to know his ideas upon the subject. On other occasions, she openly praised Julie and advised Nikolai to go to Moscow and have a good time during the Christmas holidays. Nikolai was sharp enough to understand his mother's covert hints; and, during one of their talks, he managed to draw her out completely.

She told him that their sole hope of setting their affairs in order lay in his marriage to Julie Karagina.

"But what if I loved a girl who was poor, mama, would you insist upon my sacrificing my feelings and honor, for money?" he asked, not realizing the harshness of his question, and simply desiring to show his noble feelings.

"No, you don't understand me," said his mother, not knowing how to set herself straight. "You misunderstood me entirely, Nikolai dear. All I desire is your happiness," she added; and she had the consciousness that she had not spoken the truth, that she was getting beyond her depth. She burst into tears.

"Mama dear! don't cry; simply tell me that this is your real wish, and you know I would give my whole life—everything I have—to make you happy," said Nikolai. "I would sacrifice everything for you, even my dearest wishes."

But the countess had no desire to create a dilemma; she had no wish to demand a sacrifice from her son; she would have preferred herself to be the one to make the sacrifice.

"No, no, you did not understand me; we won't say anything more about it," said she, wiping away her tears.

"Yes, perhaps it is true that I am in love with a penniless girl," said Nikolai to himself. "Why should I sacrifice my sentiments and my honor, for the sake of wealth? I am amazed that mama should say such a thing to me! Is there any reason, because Sonya is poor, that I should not return her true, generous love? And, most certainly, I would be much happier with her than with such a doll as Julie! I can always sacrifice my feelings for my parents' good," said he to himself. "But to command my feelings is beyond my power. If I love Sonya, then my feeling is more powerful and above everything for me."

Nikolai did not go to Moscow. The countess did not renew her conversation with him about his marriage; but she saw with pain, and even with indignation, the signs of a constantly growing intimacy between her son and the dowerless Sonya. She reproached herself, but she found it impossible to resist heaping tasks upon Sonya, and finding fault with her; often unreasonably stopping her short, and addressing her with the formal "you" instead of by the usual tenderer epithets. What annoyed the worthy countess most of all was that this poor, dark-eyed niece of hers was so sweet, so gentle, so humbly grateful for all her kindnesses; and so genuinely, unchangeably, and self-sacrificingly in love with Nikolai, that it was impossible to find anything really to blame her for.

Nikolai stayed at home, waiting till his leave of absence expired.

A letter was received about this time from Natasha's lover, Prince Andrei, dated at Rome; it was his fourth. In it he wrote that he would long ago have been on the way home to Russia, had it not been that the warmth of the climate had unexpectedly caused his wound to re-open, which obliged him to postpone his journey till the beginning of the next year.

Natasha was deeply in love with her "bridegroom." Her character had been greatly modified by this love; at the same time, her nature was thoroughly open to all the joys of life; but toward the end of the fourth month of their separation, she began to suffer from attacks of melancholy which she found it impossible to resist. She was sick to death of herself; she grieved because all this time was slipping away so uselessly, while she felt that she was only too ready to love and to be loved. Life was far from cheerful at the Rostofs'.

IV

THE CHRISTMAS HOLIDAYS had come, and except for the High Mass, the formal and perfunctory congratulations of the neighbors and the household servants, and the new gowns that everyone had on, there was nothing that especially distinguished the season; though the perfectly still atmosphere, with the thermometer at thirteen degrees below zero, the sun shining dazzlingly all day long, and at night the wintry sky glittering with myriads of stars, seemed to imply that nature at least gave special distinction to the Christmastide.

After dinner on the third day of the holidays all the household had scattered to their respective rooms. It was the most tedious time of the day. Nikolai, who had been out in the morning making calls on the neighbors, was asleep in the sitting room. The old count was resting in the library. Sonya was sitting at the center table in the drawing-room copying some designs. The countess was laying out her game of patience.

Natasha came into the room and went directly up to Sonya, looked at what she was doing, then stepped across to her mother and stood by her without saying a word.

"Why are you wandering about like a homeless spirit?" asked her mother. "What do you want?"

"I want *him* . . . instantly! this very minute! I want *him*," said Natasha, with gleaming eyes, but without a trace of a smile.

The countess raised her head and gave her daughter a steady look.

"Don't look at me! Don't look at me, mama; I shall cry if you do!"

"Sit down, sit down with me here," said the countess.

"Mama, I must have him. Why am I perishing so, mama?"

Her voice broke; the tears started to her eyes, and in order to hide them she quickly turned away and left the room.

She went into the sitting room, stood there a moment lost in thought, and went to the maids' sitting room. There an elderly chambermaid was scolding a young girl who had just come in from out of doors all out of breath.

"You might play some other time," the old servant was saying. "There is a time for all things."

"Let her be, Kondratyevna," said Natasha. "Run, Mavrusha, run."

And having rescued Mavrusha, Natasha went through the ballroom into the anteroom. An old man and two young lackeys were playing cards. They stopped their game, and respectfully stood up as their young mistress came in.

"What shall I have them do?" wondered Natasha. "Yes, Nikita, please go . . . where shall I send him? oh, yes . . . go into the barnyard and get me a cock; yes, and you, Misha, bring me some oats."

"Do you wish a few oats?" asked Misha, with joyous readiness.

"Go, go, make haste," said the old man, imperiously.

"And you, Feodor, get me a piece of chalk."

As she went past the butler's pantry, she ordered the samovar to be got ready, although it was not anywhere near the time for it.

Foka, the butler, was the most morose man of all the household. Natasha took it into her head to try her power over him. He suspected that she was not in earnest, and began to ask her if she meant it.

"Oh, what a young lady she is!" said Foka, pretending to be very cross at Natasha.

No one in the house set so many feet flying, and no one gave the servants so much to do as Natasha. She could not have any peace of mind if she saw servants unless she sent them on some errand. It seemed as if she were making experiments whether she would not meet with angry answers or with grumbling on the part of some of them, but the servants obeyed no one so willingly as Natasha.

"Now, what shall I do? Where shall I go?" pondered the young countess, as she slowly passed along the corridor.

"My God! my God! it's this everlasting sameness! What shall I do with myself? Where can I find something to do?" and swiftly kicking her heels together, she ran upstairs to the quarters occupied by Vogel and his wife. Two governesses were sitting in the Vogels' room; on the table stood plates with raisins, walnuts, and almonds. The governesses were discussing whether it was cheaper to live in Moscow or Odessa.

Natasha sat down, listened to their conversation with a grave, thoughtful face, and then stood up.

"The Island of Madagascar!" she exclaimed. "Ma-da-gas-car," she repeated, laying a special emphasis on each syllable; and then, without replying to Madame Schoss, who asked her what she had said, she hastened from the room.

Petya, her brother, was also upstairs; he and his tutor were arranging for some fireworks they were going to set off that night.

"Petya! Petya!" she cried to him. "Carry me downstairs!"

Petya ran to her and bent his back. She jumped on and threw her arms around his neck, and he, with a hop, skip, and jump, started to run down with her.

"No, thank you! that will do! The Island of Madagascar!" she repeated, and jumping off, she flew downstairs.

Having made the tour of her dominions, as it were, having made trial of her power of command, and discovered that all were sufficiently obedient, but that everything was nevertheless utterly stupid, Natasha went into the ballroom, took the guitar, sat down in a dark corner behind a cabinet, and began to thrum the bass strings, practicing a theme she remembered from an opera she had heard at Petersburg with Prince Andrei. To those who were outside listening to her as she strummed on the guitar there seemed to be no sense to what she was playing, but in her imagination these sounds recalled from the dead past a whole series of memories. As she sat in the shadow of the cabinet, with her eyes fixed on the pencil of light that streamed from the door of the butler's pantry, she listened to herself and indulged in daydreams. She was in the mood for daydreaming.

Sonya, with a wineglass in her hand, passed through the ballroom on her way to the butler's pantry. Natasha looked at her, at the bright chink in the door; and it seemed to her that on some occasion, long before, she had seen the light streaming through the chink in the pantry door and Sonya crossing the room with a glass.

"Yes, and it was exactly the same!" said Natasha to herself. "What is this tune, Sonya?" she cried, moving her fingers over the bass strings.

"Ah! Are you here?" cried Sonya, startled at first, and then stopping to listen. "I don't know. Isn't it 'The Storm'?" she suggested timidly, for fear she was mistaken.

"Now, there! she gave a start in exactly the same way, she came up to me in exactly the same way, and her face wore the same timid smile when that took place," thought Natasha. "And in just the same way I felt that there was something lacking in her.—No! that is the chorus from 'The Water Carrier.' You ought to know!"

And Natasha hummed the air over to recall it to Sonya's memory.

"Where were you going?" asked Natasha.

"To change the water in this glass. I am just copying a sketch."

"You are always busy; and here am I, not good for anything," said Natasha. "Where is Nikolai?"

"Asleep, I think!"

"Sonya, do go and wake him up," urged Natasha. "Tell him I want him to sing."

She remained sitting there, and wondering why it was that this had happened so; but, as it did not disturb her very much that she could not solve this question, she once more relapsed into her recollections of the time when she was with *him* and he looked at her with loving eyes.

"Oh, I wish he would come! I am so afraid he won't come! But, worst of all, I'm growing old! that's a fact! Soon I shall not be what I am even now! But maybe he will come today. Maybe he is here now. Maybe he has come, and even now is sitting in the drawing-room. Maybe he came yesterday, and I have forgotten about it."

She got up, laid down the guitar, and went into the drawing-room. All the household—tutors, governesses and guests—were already gathered near the tea table. The men were standing around the table; but Prince Andrei was not among them, and everything was as usual.

"Ah! there she is," said Count Rostof, as he saw Natasha. "Come here and sit by me."

But Natasha remained standing near her mother, looking around as if she were in search of someone.

"Mama!" she murmured. "Give him back to me, mama, quick, quick!" and again she found it hard to keep from sobbing.

She sat down by the table and listened to the conversation of her elders and of Nikolai, who had also come to the table.

"My God! my God! the same faces, the same small talk! Even papa holds his cup and cools it with his breath just as he always does!" said Natasha, to her horror feeling a dislike rising in her against all the household because they were always the same.

After tea, Nikolai, Sonya and Natasha went into the sitting room, to their favorite corner, where they always held their most confidential conversations.

V

"Has it ever happened to you," asked Natasha of her brother, when they were comfortably settled in the sitting room, "has it ever happened to you that it seemed as if there were nothing, just nothing at all, left in the future for you? that all that was best was past, and that you were not so much bored as disgusted?"

"Hasn't it, indeed! Many a time, when everything was going well, and all were gay, it would come into my head that all was vanity and vexation of spirit, and that all of us would have to die."

"I know what you mean! I know! I know!" interrupted Natasha. "When I was a tiny bit of a girl it used to be that way with me. Do you remember I was punished once, on account of those cherries, and you were all dancing, while I had to sit alone in the classroom, and sobbed? I'll never forget how sad I felt, and how vexed with you all and with myself! Oh, yes, vexed with you all! all of you! And the worst of it was, I was not to blame," said Natasha; "do you remember?"

"I remember," replied Nikolai; "and I remember that I went to you and wanted to comfort you; and, do you know, I was ashamed to do it! We were terribly absurd! I had at that time a kind of toy, like a manikin, and I wanted to give it to you! Do you remember?"

"And do you remember," asked Natasha, with a thoughtful smile, "how once, a long, long time ago, when we were little tots, uncle took us into the library—that was in the old house and it was dark—and when we went in, suddenly there stood before us . . ."

"A Negro!" said Nikolai, taking the word from her mouth, and laughing merrily. "Of course I remember it! And now I can't tell for the life of me whether it was a Negro, or whether we saw it in a dream, or whether it was something that we were told!"

"He had gray hair, you remember, and white teeth, and he stood and stared at us . . ."

"Do you remember it, Sonya?" asked Nikolai.

"Yes, I have a dim recollection of something about it," timidly replied Sonya.

"I have asked both papa and mama about that Negro," said Natasha. "They declare that no Negro was ever here. But you see you remember about it!"

"Certainly I do! And now I recall his teeth very distinctly."

"How strange! Just as if it were in a dream! I like that!"

"And do you remember how we were rolling eggs in the dining room, and suddenly two little old women appeared and began to whirl around on the carpet? That was so, wasn't it? Do you remember how fine it was?"

"Yes; and do you remember how papa, in a blue coat, used to fire off his musket from the doorsteps?"

Thus, smiling with delight, they took turns in calling up, not the reminiscences of a gloomy old age, but the recollections of the sweet days of youth; impressions from the most distant past, dreams fused and confused with reality; and these happy recollections sometimes made them quietly laugh.

While they were still engaged in talking, Dimmler came into the sitting room and went to the harp which stood in one corner. As he took off the covering, the harp gave forth a discordant sound.

"Monsieur Dimmler, please play my favorite nocturne—that one by Monsieur Field," cried the old countess from the drawing-room.

Dimmler struck a chord, and turning to Natasha, Nikolai, and Sonya, said, "How quiet you young people are!"

"Yes, we are talking philosophy," said Natasha, looking up for an instant, and then pursuing the conversation. It now turned upon dreams.

Dimmler began to play. Natasha noiselessly went on tiptoe to the table, took the candle, and carried it out; then she came back and sat down quietly in her place.

In the room, especially that part where the divan was on which they were sitting, it was dark, but through the lofty windows the silver light of the full moon fell across the floor.

"Natasha! Now it is your turn. Sing me something!" said the countess' voice. "Why are you all sitting there like conspirators?"

"Mama! I don't feel like it," said Natasha; but nevertheless, she got up.

She had said she did not feel like singing; but it was long since she had sung as she sang that evening, and long before she sang so well again. Count Rostof listened to it from his library, where he was closeted with Mitenka; and, like a schoolboy in haste to go out to play as soon as his lessons are done, he stumbled over his words as he gave his instructions to his overseer, and finally stopped speaking; while Mitenka, also listening, stood silently in front of the count. Nikolai did not take his eyes from his sister, and even breathed when she did. Sonya, as she listened, thought what a wide gulf there was between her and her friend, and how impossible it would be to find anyone in the world so bewitchingly charming as her cousin. The old countess, with a smile of melancholy pleasure, and with tears in her eyes, sat occasionally shaking her head. She was thinking of Natasha, and of her own youthful days; and of that unnatural and terrible element that seemed to enter into this engagement of her daughter and Prince Andrei.

Dimmler, taking his seat next to the countess, and covering his eyes, listened.

"No, countess," said he, finally, "this talent of hers is European; she has nothing to learn; such smoothness, tenderness, power . . ."

"How I tremble for her, how worried I am!" said the countess, not realizing to whom she was speaking. Her maternal instinct told her that Natasha had more in her than ordinary girls, and that this would result in unhappiness for her.

Natasha had not quite finished her singing when fourteen-year-old Petya, all excitement, came running into the room with the news that some masqueraders had come.

Natasha abruptly stopped.

"Idiot!" she cried to her brother, and, running to a chair, flung herself into it and sobbed so that it was long before she could recover herself.

"It's nothing, mama; truly it's nothing; it was only that Petya startled me," she said, striving to smile; but her tears still flowed, and her throat was choked by her repressed sobs.

The house servants, who had dressed themselves up as bears, Turks, tavern keepers, fine ladies, monsters, old ogres, bringing in with them the outside cold and hilarity, at first shyly clustered together in the anteroom; but gradually, hiding one behind the other, they ventured into the ballroom; and at first timidly, but afterwards with ever-increasing fervor and zeal, began to perform songs, dances, and other Christmas games.

The countess, after she had recognized them and indulged in a hearty laugh at their antics, retired into the drawing-room. Count Rostof, with a radiant smile, took his seat in the ballroom, with approving glances at the masqueraders. Meantime, all the young people had mysteriously disappeared.

Within half an hour, the other masqueraders in the ballroom were joined by an elderly lady in a farthingale, and this was Nikolai; by a Turkish woman, and this was Petya; by a clown, Dimmler; by a hussar, Natasha; by a Circassian youth, Sonya. Both the girls had dark eyebrows and mustaches, contrived with the help of burnt cork.

After well-feigned surprise and pretended lack of recognition, as well as praise, from those who were not mumming, the young people decided that their costumes were too good to be wasted, and that they should go and exhibit them elsewhere.

Nikolai, who had a strong desire for a troika ride, the roads being in splendid condition, proposed that they should take with them the ten house serfs who were disguised, and that all should go and visit the "little uncle."

"No, you will disturb him," said the countess. "If you must go somewhere, then go to the Melyukofs."

Madame Melyukof was a widow who, with a host of children of various ages, and with tutors and governesses, lived about three miles from the Rostofs.

"There, my dear, a good idea!" cried the old count, becoming greatly excited. "Wait till I can get into a costume and I will go with you."

But the countess was not at all inclined to let the old count go, since for several days his leg had been troubling him. It was therefore decided that if Madame Schoss would act as chaperon, then the young ladies might also go to the Melyukofs.

Sonya, though generally very timid and shy, now was more urgent than all the others in her entreaties to Madame Schoss not to disappoint them.

Sonya's costume was the best of all. Her mustache and dark brows were extremely becoming to her. All assured her that she was very handsome, and she was keyed up to a state of energy and excitement quite out of her usual manner. Some inner voice told her that now or never her fate was to be decided; and now, in her masculine garb, she seemed like another person. Madame Schoss consented; and in less than half an hour four troikas, with jingling bells on the harness, swept, creaking and crunching over the frosty snow, up to the front steps.

Natasha was the first to catch the tone of Christmas festivity, and this jollity was infectious, growing more and more noisy, and reaching the highest pitch as they all came out into the frosty air, and with shouting and calling, and laughing and screaming, took their places in the sleighs.

Nikolai, in his old maid's costume, over which he threw his hussar's riding cloak, fastened with a belt, took his place in the middle of his sleigh and gathered up the reins. It was so light that he could see the metal of the harness plates shining in the moonbeams, and the horses' eyes, as they turned them anxiously toward the merry group gathered under the darkness of the porte-cochère.

In Nikolai's sleigh were packed Natasha, Sonya, Madame Schoss, and two of the maidservants; in the old count's went Dimmler with his wife and Petya; in the others, the rest of the household serfs were disposed.

"You lead the way, Zakhar!" cried Nikolai, to his father's coachman; he wished to have a chance to beat him on the road.

The old count's troika, with Dimmler and the other masqueraders, creaked as if its runners were frozen to the snow; and, with a jingling of its deeptoned bell, started forward. The side horses twitched at the shafts and kicked up the sugarlike gleaming crystals of the snow.

Nikolai followed Zakhar; behind them, with a creaking and crunching, came the others. At first they went rather gingerly along the narrow driveway. As they passed the park the shadows cast by the bare trees lay across the road and checkered the moonlight; but as soon as they got beyond the park enclosure, the snowy expanse—gleaming like diamonds with a deep blue phosphorescence, all drenched in moonlight, and motionless—opened out before them in every direction.

All at once, the foremost sleigh dipped into a cradle hole; in exactly the same way the one behind it went down and came up again, and then the next behind; and then, boldly breaking the iron-bound silence, the sleighs began to speed along the road one after the other.

"There's a hare track! Ever so many of them!" rang Natasha's voice through the frost-bound air.

"How light it is, Nikolai!" said Sonya's voice.

Nikolai glanced round, and bent over so as to get a closer look into her face. The pretty face, with an odd and entirely new expression caused by the black brows and mustache, glanced up at him from under the sables.

"That used to be Sonya," said Nikolai to himself. He gave her a closer look, and smiled.

"What is the matter, Nikolai?"

"Nothing," said he, and he again gave his attention to the horses.

Only by the increase of the wind that blew in their faces and by the straining of the side horses, which kept springing and galloping faster and more furiously, could it be told at what a pace the troika was flying. Nikolai glanced back. With shouts and whistling, with cracking of whips and encouraging words to the horses, the other troikas followed at a flying pace. Nikolai overtook the first troika. They glided down a little slope and came out upon a road wide enough for several teams to drive abreast, stretching along by the riverside.

Nikolai gave his horses rein; Zakhar, reaching out his arms, clucked his tongue, and also gave his horses free rein.

"Now, steady there, sir!" cried he.

Still swifter flew the two troikas, side by side; and swiftly the legs of the horses interwove as onward they sped.

Nikolai began gradually to forge ahead. Zakhar, not changing the position of his outstretched arms, kept the hand that held the reins a little higher.

"You can't make it, sir!" he cried to Nikolai. Nikolai urged all three of his horses to gallop, and sped past Zakhar. The horses kicked the fine dry snow into the faces of the party; the bells jingled together as they flew on, side by side; and the swiftly moving legs of the horses mingled together, while the shadows crossed and interlaced on the snow. The runners whizzed along the road, and the shouts and cries of the women were heard in each of the sleighs.

Once more reining in his horses, Nikolai glanced around him. Everywhere was the same magical expanse, flooded deep with the moonbeams, and with millions of stars scattered over it.

"Oh, see there! his mustache and eyelashes are all white," said one of the handsome young strangers, with delicate mustaches and eyebrows, who sat in the sledge.

"That, I think, must have been Natasha," said Nikolai to himself, "and that other is Madame Schoss; and, perhaps I am wrong, but that Circassian with the mustache I never saw before, but I love her all the same!"

VI

MADAME MELYUKOF, a very stout and energetic woman in spectacles, and wearing a loose-flowing dress, was sitting in the drawing-room surrounded by her daughters, whom she was doing her best to entertain. They were quietly molding wax, and looking at the shadows cast by passers-by, when the steps and voices of the visitors began to echo through the anteroom.

Hussars, high-born ladies, witches, clowns, bears, coughing and wiping their frost-bound faces, came into the ballroom, where the candelabras were hastily lighted. The clown (Dimmler), with the lady (Nikolai), opened the dance. Surrounded by gleefully shouting children, the masqueraders, hiding their faces and disguising their voices, made low bows before the mistress of the mansion and then scattered through the room.

"Oh, dear! it's impossible to tell! Ah, that's Natasha! Just see whom she looks like! Truly she reminds me of someone! And there's Monsieur Dimmler! How elegant! I wouldn't have known you. How elegantly he dances! And who is that Circassian? Indeed, it reminds me of Sonya! And who is that? Well, well! this is a kindness! Move out the tables, Nikita, Vanya. And we have been sitting here so solemnly."

"Ha! ha! ha!" . . . "What a hussar! What a hussar!" . . . "Just like a boy, and what legs!" . . . "I can't see!" . . . such were the remarks on every side.

After the Russian national dances, Madame Melyukof had all the serfs and the others together form into a great circle; a ring, a rope, and a ruble were brought, and they began to play various games.

By the end of an hour the costumes began to show signs of wear and tear. The charcoal mustaches and eyebrows began to disappear from the perspiring, heated, merry faces. Madame Melyukof began to recognize the masqueraders, and congratulate them on the skill with which they had made up their costumes, and tell them how very becoming they were to the young ladies, and she thanked them all for having entertained her so well. The guests were invited into the drawing-room, and refreshments were provided in the ballroom for the serfs.

"No, but what a terrible thing to read your fortune in a barn!" exclaimed an old maid, who lived with the Melyukofs.

"Why so?" asked the oldest daughter of the family.

They were now sitting down at supper.

"No, don't think of doing such a thing, it requires so much courage."

"I would just as lief," said Sonya.

"Now, what is the good of frightening them so!" protested Madame Melyukof.

"Mama, you yourself have had your fortune told that way," exclaimed one of the daughters.

"How is it fortunes are told in a granary?" asked Sonya.

"Well, this is the way of it: You go into the granary and listen. It depends on what you hear: If there is any knocking or tapping, it's a bad sign; but if the wheat drops, then it's for good, and it will come out all right."

"Mama, tell us what happened to you when you went to the granary." Madame Melyukof smiled.

"Oh, what's the use! and I have forgotten . . ." said she. "Besides, you wouldn't go, would you?"

"Yes, I would go, too; Madame Melyukof, do let me; I certainly will go," said Sonya.

"Very well, then, if you are not afraid."

While they were playing the games with the ring, the ruble, and the rope, and now, while they were talking, Nikolai had not left Sonya's side, and looked at her with wholly new eyes. It seemed to him that this evening, thanks to that charcoal mustache, he saw her for the first time as she really was. In reality, Sonya, that evening, was merrier, livelier, and prettier than Nikolai had ever seen her before.

"What a girl she is, and what an idiot I have been!" he said to himself, as he gazed into her gleaming eyes and saw her radiantly happy and enthusiastic smile dimpling her cheeks under her mustache, and that look which he had never seen before.

"I am not afraid of anything," said Sonya. "May I start now?"

She got up. She was told where the granary was, and how she must stand and listen, and make no noise. The servant brought her fur cloak. She flung it over her head, and glanced at Nikolai.

"How charming that girl is!" said he to himself. "And what have I been thinking about all this time?"

Sonya stepped out into the corridor on her way to the granary. Nikolai, making the excuse that he was too warm, hurried to the front steps. In fact, the crowd did make the air in the rooms close. Out of doors it was as cold and still as ever; the same moon was shining, only it was brighter than before. The brightness was so intense, and there were so many stars in the snow, that one had no desire to look at the sky; the real stars were insignificant. In the sky it was almost black and melancholy; on the earth it was gay.

"What an idiot I have been! what an idiot! Why have I waited so long?" mused Nikolai, and he sprang down the steps and turned the corner of the house by the path that led back to the rear entrance. He knew that

Sonya would come that way. Halfway along the path stood a great woodpile covered with snow, and casting a shadow; across it and beyond it fell the shadows of the lindens, bare and old, weaving patterns on the snow and the path. The path led to the granary. The timber walls of the granary and its roofs covered with snow shone in the moonlight like a palace made of precious stones. In the garden a tree creaked, and then everything became absolutely still again. It seemed to Nikolai that his lungs breathed in not common air, but the elixir of eternal youth and joy.

Feet were heard stamping on the steps of the servants' entrance. Someone was scraping the snow away from the lower step on which it had drifted, and then the voice of an old maid said:

"Straight ahead! straight ahead! right along this path, miss. Only you must not look round."

"I'm not afraid," replied Sonya's voice; and then toward Nikolai came Sonya's dainty feet, sliding and squeaking in her thin slippers.

Sonya came along, all muffled up in her cloak, and it was not till she was within two paces of him that she saw him. It seemed to her also that he was different from the Nikolai she had known before, and that he had nothing of what always made her a bit afraid of him. He was in his woman's dress, with clustering locks, and wearing a blissful smile such as Sonya had never seen before. She hurried swiftly to him.

"She's entirely different; not at all the same," thought Nikolai as he looked into her face, all kindled by the moonlight. He put his arms under her cloak, which encircled her head, strained her to his heart and kissed her lips, which still showed traces of the mustache, and had a faint odor of burnt cork. Sonya returned his kiss full on the lips, and putting up her slender hands laid them on his cheeks.

"Sonya!"

"Nikolai!"

That was all they said. They ran to the granary, and then went back into the house by the doors through which they had come.

VII

Shortly after Twelfth-night Nikolai announced to his mother his love for Sonya and his firm determination to make her his wife. The countess, who had long noticed what was going on between them and had been expecting this announcement, listened in silence, and then coldly informed him that he might marry anyone he pleased, but that neither she nor his father would countenance such a marriage. For the first time, Nikolai felt that his mother was offended with him; that, notwithstanding all her love for him, she would not yield to him in this matter. Coldly, not even looking at her son, she sent for her husband; and when he came, she tried in Nikolai's presence to tell him in a few chilling words what her son proposed to do.

But she had not the necessary self-control; tears of vexation sprang to her eyes and she was compelled to leave the room.

The old count tried feebly to reason with Nikolai, and begged him to give up his intention. Nikolai replied that he could not go back on his word; and the father, sighing, and evidently all upset, hastily ended his discourse and went to the countess.

In all his encounters with his son the count always was conscious of his own guilt toward him for having squandered his fortune; accordingly, he could not show his anger against his son for refusing to wed a rich wife, and for choosing the penniless Sonya. In all this affair, he remembered with keen sorrow that if only his estates had not been so ruined, it would be impossible for Nikolai to find a better wife; and that the only persons responsible for the wasting of this estate were himself and his Mitenka and their incorrigible habits.

The father and mother had nothing more to say to Nikolai about the matter; but a few days later the countess summoned Sonya, and with a bitterness which no one in the world would have expected of her, reproached her niece with having decoyed her son, and accused her of ingratitude. Sonya, in silence and with downcast eyes, listened to the countess' bitter words, and was at a loss to know what was required of her. She was ready for any sacrifice for all of them in return for their benefits. The thought of self-sacrifice was a delight to her; but in this affair she could not comprehend what she was required to sacrifice, or for whom. She could not help loving the countess and all the Rostof family; nor could she help loving Nikolai, or knowing that his happiness depended on her love for him. She therefore stood silent and sad, and had nothing to reply.

It seemed to Nikolai that he could no longer endure this state of things, and he went to his mother to have a final explanation. He first begged her to be reconciled with him and Sonya and consent to their marriage; then he threatened that, if they persecuted Sonya, he would instantly marry her secretly.

The countess, with a coldness her son had never experienced before, replied that he was of age, that Prince Andrei was going to marry without his father's sanction, and that he might do the same; but that she would never receive this schemer as her daughter.

Angry at her use of the term schemer, Nikolai raised his voice, and told his mother that he had never thought she would oblige him to sacrifice his noblest feelings; and that if this were so, then he would never . . .

But he did not finish uttering this rash vow, which his mother, judging by the expression of his face, awaited with horror, and which might have forever raised a cruel barrier between them. He did not utter it because Natasha, with a pale and solemn face, came into the room; she had been listening at the door.

"Nikolai, you don't know what you are saying; hush! hush! I tell you, hush!" she almost screamed, so as to drown his words. "Mama, darling, there's no sense in this at all, dear heart," said she, turning still paler and going to her mother, who felt that she was on the very edge of an abyss, and looked with horror at her son; and yet because of her stubbornness and the impulse of the quarrel, she would not, and could not, give in. "Nikolai, I beg you, go away; and you, sweetheart-mama, listen," Natasha entreated, turning again to her mother. Her words were incoherent; but they brought about the wished-for result.

The countess, deeply flushed, buried her face in her daughter's bosom; and Nikolai got up and, clasping his head between his hands, rushed out of the room.

Natasha acted the part of peacemaker so well that Nikolai received a promise from his mother that Sonya would not be annoyed; and he himself swore that he would never do anything without the knowledge of his parents.

With the firm intention to retire from the service as soon as he could wind up his connection with his regiment, and return and marry Sonya, Nikolai, sorrowful and grave, still in strained relations with his parents, but, as it seemed to him, passionately in love, rejoined his regiment early in January.

After his departure, life grew sadder than ever in the house of the Rostofs. The countess, owing to her mental tribulations, became seriously ill. Sonya was depressed because of her separation from Nikolai, and still more so on account of the unfriendly manner in which the countess, in spite of herself, treated her. The count was more than ever occupied by the wretched state of his affairs, which demanded of him the most heroic measures. It was absolutely necessary to dispose of their mansion in Moscow and their estate near Moscow; and in order to effect this sale it was essential to go to Moscow. But the countess' health caused him to postpone his departure from day to day.

Natasha, who had easily, and even cheerfully, borne the first weeks of separation from her lover, now every day grew more nervous and impatient. The thought constantly tortured her that she was wasting the best time of her life, when she might be spending it in loving sacrifice for him. His letters generally merely served to annoy her. It revolted her to think that when she was living only in the thought of him, he was living in the great world of action, seeing new places and new people who were full of interest to him. The more fascinating his letters were, the more they annoyed her.

Her letters to him gave her no consolation; they were nothing but tedious and hypocritical exercises. She was not able to write freely, because she felt that she could not express in a letter even the thousandth part of what she expressed with her voice, her smile, and her glance. She wrote him perfunctory and monotonous letters, the stupidity of which she herself acknowledged; while her mother corrected in the rough draft the mistakes she made in spelling.

The countess' health was still feeble; but it was now no longer possible to put off the return to Moscow. It was necessary to arrange for the marriage settlement, it was necessary to sell the mansion; moreover, Prince Andrei was now expected in Moscow, where his father was spending the winter; indeed, Natasha was certain that he had already arrived.

The countess remained in the country; but the count, taking Sonya and Natasha with him, went to Moscow toward the end of January.

1811

In 1811 there are murmurs against Napoleon in the European courts. His prohibition of trade with England is costly to everyone, including Russia, and the Tsar countenances the reception of British merchantmen at his ports. Napoleon is on the offensive in Spain, but cannot dislodge the British; he is harassed by Spanish and Portuguese guerillas; the expense of the war is weakening him, and as he loses in strength, the European nations gain courage to oppose him. Russia is apprehensive of Napoleon's continuing encroachments, particularly opposing French annexation of the Duchy of Oldenburg, domain of the Tsar's uncle. Napoleon is resentful of Russia's trade with Britain.

Part Eighth

AFTER the engagement of Prince Andrei and Natasha, Pierre suddenly, without any apparent reason, began to find it impossible to pursue his former mode of life. Firmly as he was convinced of the truths revealed by his benefactor, delightful as had been the first period of enthusiasm for the inward labor of self-improvement to which he had given himself with such zeal—all the charm of this former existence suddenly vanished after the betrothal of his friends and the death of Ossip Alekseyevitch Bazdeyef, news of which he received at about the same time. Nothing but the empty shell of life remained to him: his mansion, with his brilliant wife who was still enjoying the attentions of an influential personage; his acquaintance with all Petersburg; and his duties at court with all their tedious formalities. And this life suddenly began to fill Pierre with unexpected loathing; he ceased to write in his diary; he shunned the society of the brethren; he began once more to frequent the club and to drink heavily; he became intimate with the gay young bachelor set; and his behavior became such that Countess Elena found it necessary to give him a stern admonition.

Pierre felt that she was right; and in order not to compromise her, he decided to go to Moscow.

In Moscow, as soon as he set foot in his enormous house, with the dried-up and withered princesses and the swarm of menials; as soon as he went out into town and saw the Iverskaya Chapel with its innumerable tapers burning before the golden shrines, and the Square of the Kremlin with its wide expanse of snow, the sleigh drivers, and the hovels of the Sivtsef Vrazhek; when he saw the old men of Moscow, who, with never a desire or a quickening of the blood, lived out their days; the old ladies, the Muscovite girls, the Muscovite dances, the Muscovite ballrooms, and the Muscovite English Club—he felt himself at home in a refuge of quiet. Life in Moscow gave him a sensation of comfort and warmth and coziness, such as one has in a soiled old dressing gown.

Pierre was welcomed by all Moscow society, young and old, as a long-expected guest, whose place was always ready for him and never given to another. In the eyes of Moscow society, Pierre was most kindly, good-natured, intelligent, and benevolent, though eccentric; absent-minded, but cordial; a thoroughgoing Russian gentleman of the old brand. His purse was always empty because it was opened to all. Benefits, wretched pictures, statuary, benevolent societies, gypsies, schools, subscription dinners, drinking bouts, the Masons, churches, books—no one and nothing ever met with a refusal from him; and if it had not been for two friends of his, who had borrowed large sums of him and now took him under their guardianship, he would have had absolutely nothing left. At the club, no dinner or reception was complete without him. As soon as he took his place on the sofa after a couple of bottles of Margaux, the members would gather around him and vie with one another in all sorts of gossip, discussions, and clever stories. If discussions degenerated into quarrels, he would restore peace by his kindly smile alone, or by a clever jest. The Masonic meetings were tedious and dull if he was absent.

Often after dining with his bachelor friends he would yield with a genial and amiable smile to their entreaties, go with them where they went, and help the hilarious young fellows wake the echoes with their wild enthusiastic shouts. At the balls he would never refuse to dance if partners were scarce. Young matrons and young girls liked him because he was attentive, especially after dinner, to all alike, without making invidious distinctions. It was a common saying of him: "He is charming; he has no sex."

Pierre had become simply a retired court chamberlain, good-naturedly vegetating in Moscow like so many hundreds of others.

How horrified he would have been if, seven years before, when he was just back from abroad, someone had told him that it was idle for him to seek out or find a career; that the ruts in which he would move were long ago made for him, determined before the foundation of the world; and that in spite of all his struggles, he would be what everyone in his position was doomed to be. He could not have believed it.

Had he not with all his heart wished at one time that a republic might be established in Russia? then, that he might be a Napoleon? then, a philosopher? then, a general, the conqueror of Napoleon? Had he not seen the possibility, and passionately desired to take part in the mighty task, of regenerating depraved humanity, and of bringing himself to the highest degree of improvement? Had he not established schools and infirmaries, and emancipated his peasantry?

But instead of what he had dreamed, lo! here he was, the rich husband of an unfaithful wife; a court chamberlain retired; a gourmand and wine-bibber, and easily inclined to criticize the government; a member of the Moscow English Club; and a flattered member of Moscow society! It was long before he could reconcile himself to the thought that he himself was a court chamberlain living in Moscow, the very type he had so deeply despised seven years before.

Sometimes he comforted himself with the thought that this mode of life was only temporary; but then he would be terrified by another thought of how many people just like himself, with all their hair and their teeth still good, had entered temporarily into this mode of life and into this club, and were now passing from it, bald and toothless.

In moments of pride, when he thought over his position, it seemed to him that he was of an entirely different nature, distinct from these retired chamberlains whom he used to despise; that they were insipid and stupid, contented and satisfied with their position: "While I, on the contrary, am utterly dissatisfied; my sole desire is to do something for humanity," he would say to himself, in such moments of pride.

"But perhaps all these colleagues of mine are just like myself, and have been struggling and seeking to find some new and original path through life; and, like myself, have by sheer force of circumstances, by the conditions of society and birth—that elemental force against which man is powerless—been brought to the same condition as myself." This he would say to himself in moments of humility; and after he had lived in Moscow for some time he ceased to despise his colleagues, the retired courtiers, and began to like them, and to esteem them, and to pity them, as he did himself.

Pierre no longer suffered, as formerly, from moments of despair, hypochondria, and disgust of life; but the same disease, which formerly had been made manifest by occasional attacks, had struck inward, and not for a moment ceased its insidious working.

"For what end? Why? For what purpose were we created in the world?" he would ask himself in perplexity many times every day, in spite of himself beginning to reason out some explanation of life; but as he knew by experience that such questions as these must remain unanswerable, he would strive in all haste to put them out of his mind—taking up a book, or going over to the club, or calling on Apollon Nikolayevitch to talk over the gossip of the town.

"Helene, whom no one ever cared for except for her body's sake, and who is one of the stupidest women in the world," said Pierre to himself, "makes people believe that she is a woman of superior wit and refinement, and they bow down before her. Napoleon Bonaparte was despised by everyone until he became great; but since he has become a miserable comedian, the Emperor Franz is trying to make him take his daughter illegally for his wife. The Spaniards, through the Roman Catholic clergy, offered up prayers of thanksgiving to God for granting them a victory over the French on the twenty-sixth of June; while the French, through the medium of the same Catholic priesthood, offer up thanksgivings to the same God for having beaten the Spaniards on the twenty-sixth of June! My brethren, the Masons, solemnly swear that they will be ready to sacrifice all they possess for their neighbor; but when the box is passed around they do not contribute a single ruble for the poor. All of us profess the Christian law of forgiveness of injuries, and of love for our neighbor—a law in obedience to which we have erected, here in Moscow, our forty times forty churches; while yesterday a deserter was flogged with the knout, and the priest, the servant of this same law of love and forgiveness, presented the crucifix for the soldier to kiss before he received his punishment."

Thus mused Pierre; and this whole universal falsehood, acknowledged by everyone, amazed him every time he thought of it, just as if he were not used to it, as if it were some new thing.

"I understand this falsehood and confusion," he thought. "But how can I convince them of what I understand? I have made the experiment and have always found that they, in the depths of their hearts, understand it just as I do; but they strive not to see it. Of course, it must be so. But for me," Pierre asked himself, "what ought I to do?"

He was undergoing the unhappy experience of many people, especially Russians, who have not only the faculty of seeing and realizing the possibility of goodness and right, but of seeing too clearly the falsity and deception of life to feel able to take any serious part in it.

Every department of activity was, in his eyes, complicated with falsehood and deception. Whatever he had tried to be, whatever he had tried to accomplish, he always found himself impeded by this knavery and falsehood, with his path of activity completely blocked. But meanwhile it was necessary for him to live, to find occupation. It was too terrible for him to be crushed by the weight of these unsolvable problems of life; and so he gave himself up to the first temptation in order to forget them. He frequented the society of all sorts and conditions of men, he drank heavily, he purchased paintings, he built houses, and above all, he read.

He read, and read everything that came into his hands; he was such an omnivorous reader that even when, on his return home, his valet came in to undress him, he continued his reading, and, after reading till he was exhausted, he would fall asleep; and the next morning he would go to the club, or call on acquaintances and talk gossip, and from there go to some wanton carousal where wine and women served to occupy his mind; and thus, around the circle again, from orgy to reading, and then his idle gossip and his wine.

Strong drink was becoming for him constantly a greater and greater physical, and even spiritual, necessity. Although the doctors warned him that wine was dangerous to him because of his corpulency, he continued to drink heavily. He felt perfectly happy only when, without knowing or caring how, he had poured down his capacious throat several glasses of wine, and begun to experience the pleasant warmth spreading through his frame, and good will toward all the human race, and a mental readiness to touch superficially upon any question without pretending to penetrate deeply into its inner significance. Only after he had drunk a bottle or two of wine would he vaguely feel that this complicated, terrible coil of life, which had formerly appalled him, was now not so appalling as it had seemed. With a roaring in his ears, as he idly chatted, or listened to stories, or read his books after dinner or supper, he saw this tangle of doubts constantly besetting him on every side. But it was only under the influence of wine that he could say to himself, "This is nothing; I will put it away for the present, for I have an explanation all ready. But now is no time; I will think it all out by and by."

This "by and by" never came.

When his stomach was empty, the next morning, all the former questions arose, just as unsolvable and terrible; and Pierre hastened to seize his book and was delighted when anyone came to call on him.

Sometimes he remembered what he had heard of soldiers at war: that when they are lying idle under fire, they eagerly strive to invent some diversion, to forget more easily the threatening danger. And it seemed to Pierre that all men were similar soldiers, distracting themselves from life: some by ambition, some by cards, some by codifying laws, some by women, some by gambling, some by horses, some by politics, some by hunting, some by wine, some by statecraft.

"There is nothing insignificant, there is nothing of great importance; all is the same in the end; only how can I save myself from it?" thought Pierre. "Only by not seeing it, this terrible *it*."

II

EARLY IN THE winter Prince Nikolai Andreyitch Bolkonsky and his daughter took up their residence in Moscow. The fame of his past life, the keenness of his intellect, and his bold originality, immediately caused him to be regarded by the Muscovites with special admiration and respect; and, as the popular enthusiasm for the Emperor Alexander's management of affairs had notoriously cooled off and an anti-French and patriotic tendency was now the vogue in Moscow, he had become the center of the opposition to the government.

The prince had aged very considerably during the year past. He now began to manifest some of the acute symptoms of old age: unexpected naps, forgetfulness of recent events and vivid remembrance of those long past, and the childish vanity with which he accepted the rôle of chief of the Muscovite opposition. Nevertheless, when the old prince came down to evening tea, in his fur cloak and powdered wig, and at anyone's instigation began to tell his pithy anecdotes about the days gone by, or deliver his still pithier and harsher judgments on the present, he inspired in all his guests a unanimous feeling of sincere respect.

In the eyes of visitors, the old-fashioned house with its huge pier glasses, its anterevolutionary furniture and its powdered lackeys, presided over by this severe and intelligent old man of a past generation, with his gentle daughter, and the pretty Frenchwoman who treated him with such deference, presented an impressive but agreeable spectacle. But these visitors did not realize that, over and above the two or three hours when they saw the household, there were twenty-two more each day during which the inner life of the house went on unseen.

This inner life had recently, especially during their stay in Moscow, become exceedingly trying for Princess Maria. She did not go into society: everybody knew that her father would not allow her to go without him, and his health was too precarious to permit him to go out; consequently, she received no invitations to dinner parties or balls. She had renounced all hope of ever being married. She had too often witnessed the coldness and irritability with which her father received and dismissed young men who occasionally came to their house and who might have been her suitors.

Princess Maria had no friends: since her arrival in Moscow, her eyes had been opened in regard to the two who had been more intimate with her than all the rest. Mlle. Bourienne, in whom even in times past she could not feel perfect confidence, had now become positively disagreeable to her; and for several reasons she felt obliged to keep her at a distance. Julie, with whom she had kept up an uninterrupted correspondence for five years, was in Moscow, but she seemed like a stranger when they met again face to face. Julie was completely absorbed in the pleasures of fashionable society. Princess Maria, with a melancholy smile, remembered as each Thursday came around that now she had no one to write to, since Julie, whose presence gave her no delight, was in town and she could see her every week.

Princess Maria experienced a new and additional trial at this time in the lessons she gave her six-year-old nephew. In her treatment of little Nikolusha she recognized with dismay that she was liable to fits of irritability similar to her father's. No matter how many times she reproached herself for losing her temper during his lesson hours, almost every time, from her very desire to help him along as rapidly as possible, to make his tasks easy and to give the little fellow all the benefit of her own knowledge, the slightest inattention on his part would make her tremble with indignation, lose her patience, grow angry and raise her voice, and sometimes even seize him by the arm and stand him in the corner. After she had stood him in the corner, she would begin to shed tears over her hasty temper, her ugly nature; and the little boy, sobbing out of sympathy, would leave his corner without permission, run to her, pull her tear-wet hands from her face, and try to comfort her.

But by far the greatest trial of all was caused the princess by her father's irritability, which was always vented upon his daughter, and which had lately become even cruelty. If he had compelled her to do penance all night long with prayers and genuflections, if he had struck her, if he had compelled her to chop wood and carry water, it would never have occurred to her that her position was hard; but this loving tryant, all the more terrible from the very fact that he loved her, and therefore tormented both himself and her, took especial pains not only to insult and humiliate her, but to make her feel that she was always and forever in the wrong. And lately he had discovered a new whim that tormented Princess Maria more than all else put together. This was his constantly increasing intimacy with Mlle. Bourienne.

In Moscow, on one occasion when Princess Maria was present—it seemed to her that her father chose that time on purpose—the old prince kissed Mlle. Bourienne's hand, and, drawing her to him, embraced and fondled her. Princess Maria flushed with anger and left the room. After a few minutes Mlle. Bourienne rejoined her, smiling, and began to tell some entertaining story in her agreeable voice. Princess Maria hastily wiped away her tears, went with decided steps straight to Mlle. Bourienne, and, evidently not knowing what she was doing, began to shout at the Frenchwoman in furious haste and with explosive accents: "It is shameful, contemptible, beastly, to take advantage of a man's weakness . . ." She did not conclude her sentence. "Leave my room," she fairly screamed, and then burst into tears again.

The following day the prince said not a word to his daughter; but she observed that at dinner he ordered Mlle. Bourienne to be served in precedence of all others. At the end of the dinner when the butler, according to his usual custom, handed the coffee round, serving the princess first, the old prince suddenly flew into a passion, flung his cane at Filipp, and instantly gave orders that he should be sent off to the army.

"You didn't obey me! Twice I told you! You didn't obey me! . . . She's the first person in this house; she is my best friend," screamed the prince. "And if you," he added, in a perfect fury, for the first time addressing his daughter, "if you permit yourself, if you dare, another time, as you did this evening, to forget your duty before her, then I will show you who is master in this house. Away with you! Out of my sight! Here! Beg her pardon!"

Princess Maria begged Amélie Bourienne's pardon, and then interceded with her father for the butler Filipp.

At such moments there arose in Princess Maria's soul a feeling like the pride of an immolated martyr.

III

Boris HAD NOT succeeded in making a match with any of the rich Petersburg heiresses, and he had gone to Moscow with the same object in view. There he found himself undecided between two of the wealthiest girls in town, Julie and Princess Maria.

Although Princess Maria, in spite of her plain features, seemed to him more attractive than Julie Karagina, still there were difficulties in the way of paying court to Bolkonsky's daughter. Julie, on the other hand, received his attentions only too gladly, though in a way peculiar to herself alone.

Julie was twenty-seven. After the death of her brothers she had become very rich. She was now far from being a beauty; but she had conceived the idea that she was not only still pretty, but far more captivating than she ever had been before. In this illusion she was sustained by the fact that, in the first place, she had become a very rich heiress, and, in the second place, as she grew older and older, men found her less dangerous and were able to gather round her with more freedom, since they felt that they were not incurring any obligations. Men who ten years before would have thought a second time about going every day to a house where there was a young girl of seventeen, lest they should compromise her and get entangled themselves, now unhesitatingly appeared there daily, and treated her not as a marriageable damsel but as an acquaintance irrespective of sex.

The Karaginas' house that winter was the gayest and most hospitable in Moscow. Besides the formal receptions and state dinners, they entertained every day a numerous society, especially of men, who ate supper at midnight and departed only at three o'clock in the morning. Nor was Julie willing to miss a ball, an entertainment, or a new play at the theater. Her clothes were always in the height of the fashion. But nevertheless, Julie pretended to be disenchanted with life; she told everybody that she had no faith in friendship or in love, or in any of the pleasures of this world, and hoped for peace only "yonder." She affected the tone of a girl who has endured great disappointment—of one, for instance, who has been disappointed in the man she loved, or cruelly deceived in him. Although nothing of the sort had ever happened to her, it began to be thought that such was the case, and she herself came to believe that her sufferings in life had been grievous. This melancholia did not stand in the way of her enjoying herself, or prevent the young men who came to her house from having a delightful time there.

Julie played on her harp, for Boris, her most sentimental nocturnes. Boris read aloud to her "Poor Liza," and more than once had to pause in his reading because of the emotion that overmastered him. When they met in society, Julie and Boris exchanged glances to signify that they were the only people in the world capable of understanding and appreciating each other.

Anna Mikhailovna, who was a frequent visitor at the Karaginas', and always managed to be a partner with Julie's mother, took especial pains to procure all possible information in regard to Julie's fortune—which consisted of two estates in the vicinity of Penza, and forest lands near Nizhni-Novgorod. Anna Mikhailovna, with humble dependence on the will of Providence and with deep emotion, looked on the etherealized melancholy that served as a bond between her son and the wealthy Julie.

"Always charming and pensive, this dear Julie," she would say to the daughter.

"Boris says that here in your house he finds rest for his soul. He has suffered the loss of so many illusions, and he is so sensitive," she would say to the mother.

"Ah! My dear, I cannot tell you how devoted I have become to Julie," she would say to her son. "And who could help loving her? She is such a celestial creature! Ah! Boris! Boris!" She was silent for a minute. "And how sorry I am for her mama!" she went on to say. "Today she was showing me her accounts and letters from Penza, where they have colossal estates; and it is so trying for her to have no one to help her; they cheat her so!"

Boris' face wore an almost imperceptible smile as he listened to his mother's words. He was quietly amused at her transparent shrewdness; but he listened to her, and sometimes asked her questions in regard to these Penza and Nizh properties.

Julie had for some time been looking for a proposal from her melancholy-souled adorer, and she was ready to accept him. But some secret antipathy toward her, a distaste for her evident desire to get married, and of her affectations, and a feeling of horror at thus practically repudiating the bliss of true love, still kept Boris at a distance. His leave of absence was now drawing to a close. He spent long hours, and every Sunday, at the Karaginas'; and every day, when he came to think the matter over, he would decide that his proposal should take place on the morrow. But when he was in Julie's company, and saw her red face and chin, almost always dusted with powder, her moist eyes, and the expression of her face, which seemed ready at a moment's notice to fly from melancholy to the equally unnatural enthusiasm and rapture of wedded bliss, Boris could not bring himself to utter the decisive words; although in his imagination he had for some time regarded himself as the prospective master of the Karagina estates, and had many times overspent the income arising therefrom.

Julie noticed Boris' indecision, and it sometimes occurred to her that he had an antipathy for her; but her feminine vanity quickly restored her confidence, and she would assure herself that it was merely his love that made him so bashful. Her melancholia, however, was beginning to change into vexation; and shortly before the time of Boris' departure she was thinking of adopting some decisive plan.

Just before Boris' leave of absence drew to a close, Anatol Kuragin made his appearance in Moscow and, as a matter of course, in the Karaginas' drawing-room; and Julie, abruptly aroused from her depression, became very cheerful and manifested great friendliness toward Kuragin.

"My dear," said Anna Mikhailovna to her son, "I know on good authority that Prince Vasili has sent his son to Moscow to make a match with Julie. I am so fond of Julie that I should be very sorry for her. What do you think about it, my dear?" asked Anna Mikhailovna.

Boris was thoroughly humiliated at the thought of being left out in the cold and of having wasted this whole month in arduous, vaporous service to Julie, and of seeing another man—especially such an idiot as Anatol—having control of that income from the Penza estates, which he was already in his imagination enjoying and profiting by. He went to the Karaginas' with full determination to offer himself. Julie met him with a gay and careless mien, gave him a merry account of what a good time she had enjoyed at the ball the evening before, and asked him when he was going back.

In spite of the fact that Boris had come with the intention of confessing his love, and had, therefore, decided to be tenderly sentimental, he immediately began in a tone of irritation to complain of woman's inconstancy; pointing out how easy it was for women to shift from gloom to glee, and that their moods depended wholly on the one who happened to be dancing attendance upon them. Julie took offense at this, and declared that he was right; that women needed variety, and nothing was more annoying to anyone than to endure perpetual sameness.

"Then, I advise you . . ." began Boris, with the intention of winging a sharp retort; but at that instant came the humiliating thought that he was on the point of leaving Moscow without attaining his wished-for end, and at the cost of wasted labor—a thing to which he was unaccustomed. He paused in the middle of his sentence, dropped his eyes to avoid seeing the look of disagreeable annoyance and indecision on her face, and said:

"However, it was not at all for the purpose of quarreling with you that I came here. On the contrary . . ." He looked at her to see whether she would encourage him to proceed. All expression of annoyance had suddenly vanished, and her restless, imploring eyes were fixed on him with greedy expectation. "I can always manage to keep out of her way," thought Boris. "Here I am in for it; might as well finish."

He flushed crimson, raised his eyes to hers, and said:

"You know my sentiments toward you . . ."

There was no need of saying more; Julie's face had become radiant with triumph and satisfaction; but she compelled Boris to tell her all that it is customary to say in such circumstances, to tell her that he loved her, and that he had never loved anyone else so passionately. She knew that in exchange for her Penza estates and Nizh forests she had a right to exact this; and she obtained what she wished.

The young couple laid their plans for the future establishment of a magnificent home in Petersburg, made calls, and got everything ready for a brilliant wedding.

IV

COUNT ROSTOF, together with Natasha and Sonya, arrived in Moscow toward the end of January. The countess was still ailing and was unable to travel, but it was out of the question to wait for her recovery. Prince Andrei was expected in Moscow every day; besides, it was important to purchase Natasha's wedding outfit; it was necessary to sell the Moscow estate; and it was necessary to take advantage of the old prince's presence in Moscow to acquaint him with his future daughter-in-law.

The Rostofs' Moscow house had not been heated. Besides, they were to be in town for only a short time and the countess was not with them; accordingly, the count decided to accept the hospitality of Marya Dmitrievna Akhrosimova, who had long ago urged them to come to her.

Late one evening the four coaches on runners conveying the Rostofs drove into Marya Dmitrievna's courtyard an Old Konyushennaya Street.

Marya Dmitrievna lived alone. Her daughter was married. All her sons were in the government service. She was just as erect as ever; her words were as much to the point; she always expressed her opinion to everyone in a loud and decided voice, and her whole personality seemed to be a living reproach against all weaknesses, passions, and impulses, the necessity of which she utterly denied. From early morning, fully dressed, she gave personal attention to the domestic arrangements, and then went out for a drive; if it were a holy day, to Mass; and thence to the prisons and jails, where she had business that she never mentioned to anyone.

On ordinary days, on finishing her toilet, she received applicants of every rank and condition who chanced to come to her door. Her charities having been dispensed, she dined; and this abundant and well-ordered meal was always shared by three or four guests; after dinner she made up a table for boston. Late in the evening she had newspapers or some new book read aloud to her while she sat with her knitting. She rarely accepted invitations, and if she ever made any exceptions it was only in favor of the most important personages of the city.

She had not yet retired when the Rostofs arrived; as the door into the hall creaked on its hinges and admitted the travelers and their retinue of servants, together with a rush of cold air, Marya Dmitrievna, with her spectacles sitting on the end of her nose, came and stood in the doorway, her head erect, and gazed at the visitors with a stern and solemn face. One might have thought that she was really angry, and was about to turn the intruders out, if she had not been heard at that very instant giving the most urgent orders in regard to the disposition of her guests and their luggage.

When they had taken off their wraps and put themselves to rights after

317

their journey, they gathered around the tea table, and Marya Dmitrievna kissed them all in turn.

"I am very glad you have come, and that you will stay at my house," said she. "It's high time," she went on, giving Natasha a significant look. "The old man is here, and his son is expected from day to day. You must, you certainly must, make his acquaintance. Well, we'll talk about all this by and by," she added looking at Sonya as much as to say that she did not care to talk about this in her presence. "Now, listen!" said she, addressing the count. "What are your plans for tomorrow? Whom will you send for? Shinshin?" She doubled over one finger. "Then, that sniveling Anna Mikhailovna— Two. She and her son are here. Son's to be married. Then, Bezukhof, I suppose? He and his wife are here. He ran away from her, but she came traipsing after him. He dined with me on Wednesday. Well, then, and these?" she indicated the young ladies. "I will take them tomorrow to the Iverskaya Chapel, and then to Aubert-Chalme's. Of course, everything will have to be got new for them. Don't judge by me! Such sleeves they wear these days! Recently the young Princess Irena Vasilyevna came to call on me; she was a marvel to see; she had sleeves like two barrels on her arms. You see, there's some new fashion every day. And what business have you on hand?" she asked, turning sternly on the count.

"Everything in the quickest possible time," replied the count. "To buy the girls clothes, and to find a purchaser for my Moscow estate and town house. And so, if you will allow me, I will tear myself away for a little while and slip off to the estate for a day, and leave my girls with you."

"Very good, very good; they'll be safe with me. They couldn't be safer with the Orphans' Aid Society. I'll take them wherever they need to go, and scold them, and spoil them with flattery," said Marya Dmitrievna, stroking with her big hand the cheek of her favorite god-daughter, Natasha.

The following morning they went to pray before the Iverskaya Virgin, and to see Mademoiselle Aubert-Chalme, who stood in such awe of Marya Dmitrievna that, in order to get rid of her as soon as possible, she would always sell her goods at a positive loss. Marya Dmitrievna ordered there the larger part of the trousseau. On their return, she drove everybody else out of the room and called Natasha to her armchair.

"Now then, let us have a talk. I congratulate you on your choice. You have caught a fine young man. I am glad for you. I have known him ever since he was so high." She put her hand about thirty inches from the floor. Natasha colored with pleasure. "I am fond of him and of all his family. Now, listen! You know very well that the old Prince Nikolai is very averse to having his son marry. A whimsical old man! However, Prince Andrei is not a child, and his permission is not necessary; still, it is not pleasant to enter a family against their will. We must act quietly and with tact. You are clever; we will manage to bring him round where he ought to be. You must accomplish it by your sweetness and cleverness. That's all it requires, and it will come out all right."

Natasha made no reply—from shyness, Marya Dmitrievna supposed, but in reality because it was annoying to Natasha that anyone should meddle with her love affair with Prince Andrei; for it seemed to her so entirely above and beyond all ordinary human concerns that no one else, in her opinion, could understand it. She loved and admired Prince Andrei alone; he loved her, and was coming in a few days, and would make her his. That was all-sufficient.

"You see, I have known him for a long time, and Marie, also, your future sister-in-law. I am fond of her, in spite of the proverb about husband's sisters. She wouldn't hurt a fly. She asked me to introduce her to you. You and your father must go there tomorrow. Be sure to be very sweet to her, for you are younger than she is. Before your friend comes you will have already become acquainted with his sister and his father, and they will have grown fond of you. Am I not right? Isn't that best?"

"Yes," replied Natasha, without enthusiasm.

On the following day, on Marya Dmitrievna's advice, Count Rostof and Natasha went to call at Prince Bolkonsky's. The count made ready for this call in anything but a happy frame of mind; in fact, he felt terrible about it. He remembered too well his last encounter with the old prince at the time of the moblizing of the militia, when, in answer to his invitation to a dinner party, he had received an angry reprimand for not having furnished his full quota of men.

Natasha, however, having put on her best gown, was in the most radiant spirits. "They cannot help being fond of me," she said to herself. "Everyone likes me, and I am so willing to do for them all they could wish! I am so willing to love him because he is *his* father, and to love her because she is *his* sister, that they cannot fail to love me."

They drove up to the gloomy old house on Vozdvizhenka Street, and went into the vestibule.

"Well, God have mercy on us!" exclaimed the count, half in jest, half in earnest; but Natasha observed that her father was very much agitated as he hastened into the anteroom and asked in a timid, faltering voice if the prince and the princess were at home. After their names had been sent in, the prince's servants seemed to be thrown into great perplexity. The footman, who had hurried off to announce them, was stopped by another footman at the drawing-room door, and the two began to whisper together. A chambermaid came hurrying into the hall, and she also had something to say to them in reference to the princess. Finally, a stern-faced, elderly footman approached the Rostofs and announced that the old prince was unable to receive them but the princess would be glad to see them.

Mlle. Bourienne first came to receive the visitors. She met them with more than ordinary politeness, and conducted them to the princess. The princess, agitated and nervous, her face covered with crimson patches, hastened forward, stepping heavily and vainly endeavoring to appear calm and dignified.

At first sight Natasha did not please her. It seemed to her that she was too fashionably dressed, too frivolous, flighty, and conceited. Princess Maria did not realize that even before seeing her future sister-in-law she was prejudiced against her through an involuntary envy of her beauty, youth, and happiness, and jealousy of her brother's love for her. Over and above these obscure feelings of antipathy, Princess Maria was still more agitated from the fact that when the Rostofs were announced the prince had shouted at the top of his voice that he would not have anything to do with them; that Princess Maria might receive them if she so desired, but that they should not come into his presence. The princess determined to receive them, but she was afraid lest at any minute the prince might perform some act of rudeness, since he seemed greatly stirred up by the Rostofs' arrival.

"I have brought my little songstress, my dear princess," said the count, with a bow and a scrape, and looking round anxiously as if he were afraid the old prince might appear on the scene. "I am very anxious for you to become acquainted. . . . I am sorry, very sorry, that the prince is ill." And after making a few commonplace remarks, he got up, saying, "If you will excuse me, princess, I will leave my Natasha with you for a brief quarter of an hour while I slip out and call on Anna Semyonovna, who lives only a couple of steps from here. I will come back for her."

The count, as he afterwards told his daughter, conceived this master stroke of subtle diplomacy in order to give the future sisters-in-law a chance to get better acquainted; but he had another reason besides, which was that he might escape meeting the prince. This reason he did not confess to his daughter, but Natasha perceived this timidity and anxiety of her father's, and felt abused. She blushed for him, and was still more annoyed with herself for having blushed; and she looked straight at the princess with a defiant, challenging expression which seemed to imply that there was nothing she was afraid of. The princess told the count that he was excused, and only hoped that he would make his stay at Anna Semyonovna's as long as possible. Accordingly, he took his departure.

Mlle. Bourienne, in spite of the anxious, beseeching glances given her by Princess Maria, who was anxious to have a confidential talk with Natasha, did not see fit to leave the room and kept up a steady stream of chatter about the delights of Moscow and the theaters. Natasha was piqued by the confusion that had occurred in the reception room, by her father's cowardice, and by the unnatural tone affected by the princess, who, it seemed to her, felt that it was an act of condescension to receive her; consequently, everything gave her a disagreeable impression. Princess Maria displeased her; she thought the princess was very plain, stubborn, and unsympathetic. Natasha suddenly underwent a moral shrinking, as it were, and in spite of herself assumed such a reckless tone that Princess Maria was still further alienated from her.

After five minutes of a labored and artificial conversation, slippered feet were heard rapidly approaching. Into Princess Maria's face came a sudden look of dismay. The door opened, and the old prince came in, dressed in a white nightcap and dressing gown.

"Oh, countess!" he exclaimed; "countess—Countess Rostof, if I am not mistaken—I beg your pardon, I beg your pardon.—I did not know, 'fore God I did not know that you were honoring us with your presence. I was coming to see my daughter, which explains this costume. I beg you to pardon it—'fore God I did not know," he said for the second time, in such an unnatural tone, laying such a special stress on the "God," and speaking so disagreeably that Princess Maria got up and dropped her eyes, not daring to look either at her father or at Natasha. Natasha got up and then sat down again, and likewise did not know what to do. Only Mlle. Bourienne wore a pleasant smile.

"I beg your pardon. I beg your pardon. 'Fore God I did not know," grumbled the old prince, and after staring at Natasha from head to foot he left the room. Mlle. Bourienne was the first to recover self-possession after this apparition, and she began to talk about the prince's failing health. Natasha and the princess looked at each other without speaking, and the longer they looked at each other without expressing what they ought to have said, the more they were confirmed in their mutual dislike.

When the count returned, Natasha made an ill-mannered display of relief and immediately prepared to take her departure. At this moment she almost hated this dried-up old princess, who by her silence had put her in such an awkward position, and who, in half an hour's talk with her, had not once mentioned Prince Andrei. "Of course I can't be the first to speak of him in the presence of that Frenchwoman," said Natasha to herself.

Princess Maria, at the same time, was tormented by a similar compunction. She knew it was her duty to say something to Natasha; but she found it impossible, both because Mlle. Bourienne's presence embarrassed her, and because she herself did not know what made it so difficult to speak about the coming marriage. After the count had left the room, Princess Maria went to Natasha with hurried steps, seized her hand, and with a deep sigh said, "Wait a moment, I must . . ." Natasha gave her a satirical glance, though she could not have told what made her do so, and listened. "My dear Natasha," said Princess Maria, "you must know I am delighted my brother has found happiness . . ."

She paused with a consciousness that she was not telling the truth. Natasha noticed this pause, and suspected the cause of it.

"I think, princess, that it is not a propitious time to speak of this," said Natasha, with an appearance of outward dignity and hauteur, while the tears almost choked her.

"What have I said? what have I said?" she wondered, as soon as she left the room.

That day they waited for Natasha a long time at dinner. She was sitting in her room, sobbing like a child, blowing her nose, and then beginning to sob again. Sonya stood beside her, and kissed her on the hair.

"Natasha, what is there to cry about?" she asked. "Why should you care about them? It will all pass, Natasha."

"No; if you only knew how humiliating it was! I just . . ."

"Don't speak of it, Natasha. Of course you were not to blame, then why should you let it trouble you? Kiss me," said Sonya.

Natasha lifted her head and kissed her friend on the lips, laying her tear-wet face against Sonya's.

"I can't tell you; I don't know. No one is to blame," said Natasha. "If anyone is, I am. But all this is terribly painful. Oh, why doesn't he come?"

She went down to dinner with reddened eyes. Marya Dmitrievna, who had learned how the Rostofs had been received at the prince's, pretended to pay no attention to Natasha's disconsolate expression, and jested in loud and spirited tones with the count and her other guests.

V

THAT EVENING the Rostofs went to the opera, Marya Dmitrievna having obtained tickets for them. Natasha felt no desire to go, but it was impossible for her to refuse this kindness of her hostess, designed expressly for her pleasure. When, after she was dressed and had gone into the parlor to wait for her father, she surveyed herself in the great pier glass and saw how pretty, how very pretty, she was, she felt even more sorrowful than before, but her melancholy was mingled with a feeling of sweet and passionate love.

"Dear God! if he were only here I would not be so stupidly shy with him as I was before. I would throw my arms around him and cling close to him, and make him look at me with those deep, penetrating eyes of his, with which he has so often looked at me; and then I would make him laugh, as he laughed then, and his eyes . . . how plainly I can see his eyes even now," said Natasha to herself. "And what do I care for his father and his sister? I love him. I love him, him alone, with his dear face and eyes, with his smile, like that of a man and like that of a child too. . . . No, it is better not to think about it, to forget him, and to forget that time, too, absolutely. I cannot endure this suspense; I shall cry again" . . . and she turned away from the mirror, exercising all her self-control not to burst into tears. "And how can Sonya be so calm and unconcerned in her love for Nikolai, and wait so long and patiently?" she wondered, as she saw her cousin coming toward her, also in full dress, and with her fan in her hand. "No, she is entirely different from me. I can't behave as she does."

Natasha at that moment felt herself so full of passion and tenderness that it was not enough to love and to know that she was loved. What she wanted now, at this instant, was to throw her arms around her lover's neck, and speak to him, and hear him speak those words of love that filled her heart.

As she rode along in the carriage, sitting next to her father and dreamily looking at the lamplights that flashed through the frost-covered windows, she felt still deeper in love, and still more melancholy than ever, and she quite forgot with whom and where she was going.

Their carriage fell into the long line, and the wheels slowly creaked over the snow as they drew up to the entrance of the theater. The two girls gathered up their skirts and quickly jumped out; the count clambered down, supported by the footmen and, making their way through the throng of ladies and gentlemen and program venders, the three went into the corridor that led to their box. Already the sounds of music were audible through the closed doors.

"Natasha, your hair," whispered Sonya in French. The usher, hastening past the ladies, politely opened the door of their box. The music sounded louder; the brightly lighted rows of boxes occupied by ladies with bared shoulders and arms, and the orchestra seats filled with brilliant uniforms, dazzled their eyes. A lady who entered the adjoining box shot a glance of feminine envy at Natasha. The curtain was still down, and the orchestra was playing the overture.

Natasha, shaking out the train of her dress, went forward with Sonya and took her seat, glancing at the brightly lighted boxes on the opposite side of the house. The sensation, which she had not experienced for a long time, of having hundreds of eyes staring at her bare arms and neck, suddenly affected her both pleasantly and unpleasantly, and called up a whole swarm of recollections, desires, and emotions associated with that sensation.

Natasha and Sonya, both remarkably pretty girls, and Count Rostof, who had not been seen for a long time in Moscow, naturally attracted general attention. Moreover, everyone had a general notion that Natasha was engaged to marry Prince Andrei, and everybody knew that ever since the engagement the Rostofs had been living at their country estate; therefore they looked with much curiosity at the "bride" of one of the most desirable men in Russia.

Natasha's beauty, as everybody told her, had improved during their stay in the country, and that evening, owing to her excited state of mind, she was extraordinarily beautiful. No one could fail to be struck by her exuberance of life and beauty and her complete indifference to everything going on around her. Her dark eyes wandered over the throng, not seeking for anyone in particular, and her slender arm, bare above the elbow, leaned on the velvet rim of the box while, with evident unconsciousness of what she was doing, she crumpled her program, folding and unfolding it in time with the orchestra.

"Look, there's Alenina," said Sonya, "with her mother, I think."

"Saints! Mikhail Kirilitch has grown fat, though," exclaimed the old count.

"See, there's our Anna Mikhailovna. What kind of headdress does she have on?"

"There are the Karaginas, and Boris with them. Obviously an engaged couple. . . . Drubetskoy must have proposed."

"What! didn't you know it? It was announced today," said Shinshin, coming into their box.

Natasha looked in the same direction her father was, and saw Julie, who, with a string of pearls around her fat red neck—covered with powder, as Natasha well knew—sat beside her mother with a radiantly happy face. Behind them could be seen Boris' handsome head, with sleekly brushed hair. He was leaning over so that his ear was close to Julie's mouth, and as he looked askance at the Rostofs he was saying something to his "bride."

"They are talking about us—about me," thought Natasha, "and she's probably jealous of me, and he is trying to calm her. They needn't worry about it. If they only knew how little I care about them!"

Behind Julie and Boris sat Anna Mikhailovna, festive and blissful, and wearing her habitual expression of meek resignation to God's will. Their box was redolent of that atmosphere characteristic of a newly engaged couple, which Natasha knew and loved so well, She turned away, and suddenly all the humiliating circumstances of her morning visit recurred to her memory.

"What right has the old man to refuse to receive me as a relative? Oh, I'd better not think about it, at least not till he comes back," she said to herself, and she began to scan the faces of strangers or acquaintances in the orchestra seats.

In the front row, in the very middle of the house, leaning back against the railing, stood Dolokhof in Persian costume, with his curly hair combed back into a strange and enormous ridge. He was standing in full view of the whole theater, knowing that he was attracting the attention of everyone in the house, yet looking as unconcerned as if he were in the privacy of his own room. Around him were gathered a throng of the gilded youth of Moscow, and it was evident that he was their leader.

Count Rostof, with a smile, nudged the blushing Sonya, and called her attention to her former suitor.

"Did you recognize him? and where did he come from?" asked the count of Shinshin. "He had disappeared entirely, hadn't he?"

"Yes, completely," replied Shinshin. "While he was in the Caucasus he deserted, and they say he became minister to some reigning prince in Persia. After that he killed the Shah's brother, and now all the young ladies of Moscow have lost their wits over him. Now no one can do anything without Dolokhof. They swear by him. He appears at every party as if he were a sturgeon," said Shinshin. "Dolokhof and Anatol Kuragin have turned the heads of all our young ladies."

Just then a tall, handsome lady with a tremendous braid of hair entered the adjoining box. She displayed a great expanse of plump white shoulders

324

and neck, around which she wore a double string of large pearls. She was a long time in settling herself, with much rustling of her stiff silk dress. Natasha found herself involuntarily gazing at that neck, those shoulders and pearls, and that headdress, and she was amazed at their beauty. Just as Natasha was taking a second look at her, the lady glanced round and, fixing her eyes on Count Rostof, nodded her head and smiled. It was Countess Bezukhof, Pierre's wife.

Count Rostof, who knew everyone in society, leaned over and spoke with her.

"Have you been here long, countess?" he inquired. "I'm coming in, I'm coming in soon to kiss your hand. I'm in town on business, and have got my girls with me. They say Semyonova plays her part superbly," said the count. "I hope Count Bezukhof has not entirely forgotten us. Is he here?"

"Yes, he said he would come," said Helene, and she gave Natasha a scrutinizing look.

Count Rostof again sat back in his place. "Isn't she pretty, though?" asked he of Natasha.

"A perfect marvel," replied the latter. "I could understand falling in love with her."

By this time the last notes of the overture were heard, and the baton of the conductor rapped upon the stand. Those gentlemen who were late slipped down to their places, and the curtain rose.

As soon as the curtain went up silence reigned in the orchestra seats and the boxes, and all the gentlemen, young and old, whether in uniform or in civilian dress, and all the ladies, with precious stones glittering on their bare bosoms, turned their attention with eager expectation to the stage.

Natasha also did her best to look at the stage.

At one time, when there was perfect silence on the stage just before the beginning of an aria, a door that led to the orchestra seats creaked on its hinges, and a man who came in late was heard passing down to his seat. Countess Bezukhof turned her head and smiled at the newcomer. Natasha followed the direction of Countess Bezukhof's eyes, and saw an extraordinarily handsome aide, who, with an air of extreme self-confidence, but at the same time of good breeding, was just passing by their box.

This was Anatol Kuragin, whom she had seen and noticed some time before at a ball in Petersburg. He now wore his aide's uniform, with epaulet and shoulder knot. He advanced with a supreme air of youthful gallantry, which would have been ludicrous had he not been so good-looking, and had his handsome face not worn such an expression of cordial good humor and gaiety.

Although it was during the act, he sauntered along the carpeted corridor, slightly jingling his spurs, and holding his perfumed, graceful head high with easy grace. Glancing at Natasha, he joined his sister, laid his exquisitely gloved hand on the edge of her box, nodded to her, and bent over to ask some question in reference to Natasha.

325

"How charming!" said he, evidently referring to her. She understood less from hearing his words than from the motion of his lips.

During the second act every time Natasha looked down into the orchestra seats, she saw Anatol Kuragin, with his arm carelessly thrown across the back of his seat, gazing at her. It was pleasant for her to feel that she had so captivated him, and it never entered her head that in all this there was anything improper.

When the second act was over, Countess Bezukhof stood up, leaned over to the Rostofs' box—thereby exposing her whole bosom—and with her gloved finger beckoned the old count to come to her; and then, paying no heed to those who came to her box to pay her their homage, she began a smiling, confidential conversation with him.

"Now, my dear count, you must allow me to see something of your daughter. Though I don't expect to be here very long—you don't either, I believe—I will try to give them a good time. . . ." Then she proposed that, in order to become better acquainted, one of the young ladies should come over into her box for the rest of the performance, and Natasha went.

V I

DURING THE ENTR'ACTE a draft of cold air blew into Helene's box, the door was opened, and Anatol came in, bowing and trying not to disturb anyone.

"Allow me to present my brother," said Helene, uneasily glancing from Natasha to Anatol.

Natasha turned her pretty, graceful head toward the handsome young man, and smiled at him over her shoulder. Anatol, who was as good-looking near at hand as he was at a distance, sat down by her and said that he had long wished for the pleasure of her acquaintance—ever since the Narishkins' ball, where he had seen her, and never since forgotten her.

Kuragin was far cleverer and less affected with women than he was in the society of men. He spoke fluently and simply, and Natasha had a strange and agreeable feeling of ease in the company of this man about whom so many rumors were current. Not only was he not terrible, but his face even wore an innocent, gay and good-natured smile.

Kuragin asked her how she enjoyed the opera, and told her how Semyonova, at the last performance, had fallen while on the stage.

"Do you know, countess," said he, suddenly addressing her as if she were an old acquaintance, "we have been arranging a fancy-dress party. You ought to take part in it. It will be very gay. We are all to meet at the Karaginas'. Please come, won't you?" he insisted.

In saying this he did not once take his smiling eyes from her face, her neck, her naked arms. Natasha was left in no doubt of the fact that he admired her. This was agreeable, but somehow she felt constrained and troubled by his presence. When she was not looking at him, she was conscious that he was staring at her shoulders, and she involuntarily tried to catch his eyes, so that he might rather fix them on her face. But while she thus looked him in the eyes, she had a terrified consciousness that that barrier of modesty which she had always felt before, kept other men at a distance, was down between him and her. Without being in the least able to explain it, she was conscious within five minutes that she was on a dangerously intimate footing with this man. When she looked away from him, she feared he might put his hand on her bare arm, or kiss her on the neck. They talked about the simplest matters, and yet she felt that they were more intimate than she had ever been with any other man. She looked at Helene and at her father, as if asking them what all this meant; but Helene was busily engaged in conversation with some general, and paid no heed to her imploring look, and her father's said nothing more to her than what it always said: "Happy? Well, I am glad of it."

During one of those moments of constraint, while Anatol's prominent eyes were calmly and boldly surveying her, Natasha, in order to break the silence, asked him how he liked Moscow. Natasha asked the question, and blushed. It seemed to her all the time that she was doing something unbecoming in talking with him. Anatol smiled, as if to encourage her.

"At first I was not particularly charmed with Moscow, because what a city ought to have, to be agreeable, is pretty women; isn't that so? Well, now I like it very much," said he, giving her a significant look. "Will you come to our party, countess? Please do," said he; and, stretching out his hand toward her bouquet, and lowering his voice, he added in French, "You will be the prettiest. Come, my dear countess, and, as a pledge, give me that flower."

Natasha did not realize what he was saying any more than he did, but she had a consciousness that in his incomprehensible words there was an improper meaning. She did not know what reply to make, and turned away, pretending not to have heard him. But the instant she turned away, the thought came to her that he was there behind her, and so near.

"What is he doing now? Is he ashamed of himself? Is he angry? Is it my business to make amends?" she asked herself. She could not refrain from glancing round.

She looked straight into his eyes, and his nearness and self-possession, and the good-natured warmth of his smile, overcame her.

She gave him an answering smile and gazed straight into his eyes, and once more she realized, with a sensation of horror, that there was no barrier between them.

The curtain again went up. Anatol left the box, calm and serene. Natasha rejoined her father in her own box, but already she was under the dominion of this world into which she had entered. Everything that passed before her eyes now seemed to her perfectly natural, while all her former thoughts concerning her lover, and Princess Maria, and her life in the country, vanished from her mind as if all that had taken place long, long ago.

In the fourth act there was a strange kind of devil, who sang and gesticulated until a trap beneath him was opened, and he disappeared. This was all that Natasha noticed during the fourth act. Something agitated and disturbed her, and the cause of this vexation was Kuragin, at whom she could not help looking.

When they left the theater Anatol joined them, summoned their carriage, and helped them to get seated. As he was assisting Natasha, he squeezed her arm above the elbow. Startled and blushing, she looked at him. His brilliant eyes returned her gaze, and he gave her a tender smile.

Not until she reached home was Natasha able clearly to realize all that had taken place, and when she suddenly remembered Prince Andrei she was horrified; and as they all sat drinking tea she groaned aloud and, flushing scarlet, ran from the room.

"My God! I am lost," she said to herself. "How could I have let it go so far?" she wondered. For a long time she sat hiding her flushed face in her hands, striving to give herself a clear account of what had happened to her, and she could not do so, nor could she explain her emotions. Everything seemed to her dark, obscure, and terrible.

There in that huge, brilliant auditorium where Duport, with his bare legs and his spangled jacket, capered about on the dampened boards to the sounds of music, and the girls and the old men and Helene very décolleté, with her calm and haughty smile, were all applauding and enthusiastically shouting bravo—there, under the protection of this same Helene, everything was perfectly clear and simple; but now, alone by herself, it became incomprehensible.

"What does it mean? What is this fear that I experience in his presence? What mean these stings of conscience that I experience now?" she asked herself.

If only her mother had been there, Natasha would have confessed all her thoughts before going to bed that night. She knew that Sonya, with her strict and wholesome views, would either entirely fail to understand, or would be horrified by her confession. Natasha therefore tried, by her own unaided efforts, to settle the question that tormented her.

"Have I really forfeited Prince Andrei's love, or not?" she asked herself, and then, with a reassuring smile, she replied to her own question:

"What a fool I am to ask this! What has happened to me? Nothing. I have done nothing. I was not to blame for this. No one will know about it, and I shall not see him any more," said she to herself. "Of course it is evident no harm has been done; there's nothing to repent of, and no reason why Prince Andrei should not love me just as I am. But what do I mean by just as I am? Oh, my God! my God! why is he not here?"

Natasha grew calm for an instant, but then some instinct told her that, even though nothing had happened and no harm had been done, still the first purity of her love for Prince Andrei was destroyed.

And once more she let her imagination wander to her entire conversation with Kuragin, and she recalled his face and his gestures, and the tender smile that this handsome, impertinent man had given her while he was squeezing her arm.

VII

ANATOL KURAGIN was living in Moscow because his father had sent him there from Petersburg, where he had been spending more than twenty thousand rubles a year, and had accumulated heavy debts as well, which his creditors were trying to force his father to pay.

His father explained to him that he would, for the last time, pay one-half of his debts, but only on condition that Anatol would go to Moscow as aide to the governor-general of the city, an appointment which he obtained for him, and would at last try to win the hand of some rich heiress. He suggested Princess Maria or Julie Karagina.

Anatol consented and went to Moscow, where he took up his residence at Pierre's. At first Pierre received him with scant welcome, but at length became accustomed to him, and occasionally accompanied him on his jaunts, and, under the pretense of a loan, gave him money.

Anatol, as Shinshin correctly stated the case, had instantly turned the heads of all the young ladies in Moscow, and particularly because he neglected them, and openly neglected them, for gypsy girls and French actresses. The leading light of these, Mlle. Georges, was said to be on terms of close intimacy with Anatol. He never failed to be present at a single drinking bout given by Danilof or the other gay blades of Moscow; he could drink steadily from night till morning, outdrinking everyone else; moreover, he was always present at all the balls and receptions in the upper circles of society. Rumors were rife of various intrigues of his with married ladies in Moscow, and at the balls he always paid particular court to several.

But from young ladies, particularly those who were rich and in the marriage market—most of whom were excessively plain—Anatol kept at a respectful distance, and this arose from the fact, known only to a very few of his most intimate friends, that he had been married two years before. Two years before, while his regiment had been stationed in Poland, a Polish proprietor of a small estate had forced Anatol to marry his daughter.

Anatol had soon after abandoned his wife, and, after promising to send money periodically, he persuaded his father-in-law to let him still pass as a bachelor.

Anatol was always satisfied with his situation, with himself, and with other people. He was instinctively, by his whole nature, convinced that it was entirely impossible for him to live otherwise than as he was living, and that he had never in his life done anything wrong. He was unable to ponder on the effect that his behavior might have on others, or what might be the result of his behaving in this, that, or the other way. He was persuaded that, just as the duck was so created as always to be in the water, in the same way he was created by God for the purpose of living with an income of thirty thousand rubles a year, and of occupying the highest pinnacle of society. He was so firmly convinced of this that other people also, when they saw him, shared in his conviction, and never thought of refusing him either the foremost place in society, or the money which he took of anyone he met, without ever thinking of repaying it.

He was no gambler; at least, he never showed sordid love for gain. He was not ostentatious. It was a matter of complete indifference to him what men thought of him. Still less was he open to the charge of ambition. Many times he had annoyed his father by injuring his own prospects, and he always made sport of dignities. He was not stingy, and he never refused anyone who asked a favor of him. All that he cared for was "a good time" and women, and as, according to his opinion, there was nothing ignoble in these tastes, and he could not calculate the consequence for other people of the gratification of these tastes of his, he considered himself irreproachable, sincerely scorned ordinary scoundrels and base men, and held his head high with a tranquil conscience.

Debauchees, those male Magdalens, have a secret feeling of blamelessness, such as is peculiar to the frail sisterhood; and it is based on the same hope of forgiveness. "She shall be forgiven much, for she hath loved much; and he shall be forgiven much, because he hath enjoyed much."

Dolokhof, back again in Moscow, after his exile and his adventures in Persia, and once more leading a dissipated and luxurious life and playing high, naturally became intimate with his old Petersburg companion, Kuragin, and made use of him for his own ends.

Anatol really liked Dolokhof for his wit, intelligence, and audacity. Dolokhof, who found the name, the position and the connections of Anatol Kuragin an admirable decoy for attracting rich young fellows into his clutches, made use of him and got enjoyment out of him without letting him suspect it. Besides the financial purpose for which Anatol served him, the act itself of controlling the will of another was enjoyment, a habit and a necessity for Dolokhof.

Natasha had made a deep impression on Kuragin. At supper after the opera, with all the enthusiasm of a connoisseur, he praised to Dolokhof her arms, her shoulders, her ankles, and her hair, and he expressed his intention of making love to her. The possible consequences of such love-making Anatol did not stop to consider; nor was it in him to foresee them any more than in any other of his escapades.

"Yes, she's pretty, my dear fellow; but she's not for us," said Dolokhof.

"I am going to tell my sister to invite her to dinner. How's that?" suggested Anatol.

"You'd better wait till she's married."

"You know," said Anatol, "I adore young girls; you can turn their heads so quickly."

"You have already fallen into the hands of one young girl," said Dolokhof, who knew about Anatol's marriage. "See?"

"Well, I can't get caught a second time—hey?" replied Anatol, good-naturedly laughing.

VIII

THE NEXT DAY the Rostofs stayed at home, and no one came to see them. Marya Dmitrievna had a confidential conversation with Rostof, taking pains to keep it a secret from Natasha. Nevertheless Natasha suspected that they were discussing the old prince and concocting some scheme. It disquieted and humiliated her. She was every moment expecting Prince Andrei to come, and twice that day she sent the door man to the Bolkonskys' to learn if he had arrived. But he had not yet come.

She was having a more difficult time now than during the first days of his absence. Her impatience and melancholy thoughts about him were intensified by an unpleasant recollection of her interview with Princess Maria and the scene with the old prince, as well as by a vague and undefinable fear and uneasiness. She had a notion that either he would not come at all, or that before he came something would happen. She found it impossible, as before, to have calm and collected thoughts about him when alone by herself. As soon as her thoughts turned to him her recollections of him were confused by recollections of the old prince, of Princess Maria, of the operatic performance, and of Kuragin. Again the question arose whether she was to blame, whether her troth plighted to Prince Andrei was not already broken; and again she would picture to herself, even to the most trifling details, every word, every gesture, every slightest shadow in the play of expression on the face of that man who had succeeded in arousing in her such a terrible and inexplicable sensation.

In the eyes of the home circle, Natasha seemed livelier than usual, but she was far from being as calm and happy as she had been before.

On Sunday morning Marya Dmitrievna proposed to her guests to attend Mass at the parish chapel of Uspenie Mohiltsakh.

"I don't like these fashionable churches," said she, evidently priding herself on her independence. "God is everywhere One. We have an excellent priest, and deacon as well, and the service is well conducted. What kind of worship is it to have concerts given in the choir? I don't like it. It's dangerous nonsense."

Marya Dmitrievna liked Sundays, and insisted that they be observed as high festivals. Her house was thoroughly scrubbed and cleaned on Saturday; neither she nor the people within her gates did any work—they wore their best clothes, and all went to Mass. On Sunday she had an extra fine dinner prepared, and her servants were provided with vodka and a roasted goose or a suckling pig. But nothing in the whole house gave more decided evidence of its being a holiday than Marya Dmitrievna's broad, stern face, which on this occasion wore an unchangeable expression of solemn festivity.

After Mass, while they were drinking their coffee in the drawing-room, where the furniture covers had been removed, a servant announced to Marya Dmitrievna that the carriage was at the door. She drew a long face, and, putting on her best shawl, in which she always paid visits, she got up and announced that she was going to see Prince Nikolai Andreyevitch Bolkonsky, to have an understanding with him in regard to Natasha.

After Marya Dmitrievna had taken her departure, a modiste from Madame Chalme's came, and Natasha, retiring to the next room and shutting the door, occupied herself with trying on her new gowns and was very glad of the diversion.

Just as she had put on a hastily basted and still sleeveless waist, and was standing in front of the mirror, bending her head around to see how the back fitted, she heard in the drawing-room the lively tones of her father's voice, mingled with those of a woman, and it made her blush. It was Helene's voice.

Natasha had not time to take off the experimental waist before the door opened, and into the room came Countess Bezukhof, beaming with a good-natured and flattering smile, and wearing a dark purple velvet dress with a high collar.

"Ah, my delightful one!" she exclaimed to the blushing Natasha. "Charming! No, she is quite unlike anyone else, my dear count," said she, turning to the count, who followed her in. "The idea of living in Moscow and not going anywhere! No, I won't let you off. This evening Mlle. Georges is going to recite for me, and we will have a crowd, and if you don't bring your beauties, who are far better than Mlle. Georges, I will never forgive you. My husband is away, he has gone to Tver; otherwise I would have sent him to persuade you. Don't fail to come. Don't fail—at ten o'clock."

She nodded to the dressmaker, whom she knew, and received a most respectful curtsy, and then sat down in an armchair near the mirror, picturesquely disposing the folds of her velvet dress. She did not cease to chatter with good-natured and merry volubility, constantly saying pleasant, flattering things about Natasha's beauty. She examined her dresses and praised them, and also managed to say a good word for a new dress of her own, in metallic gauze, which she had just received from Paris, and advised Natasha to get one like it.

"Besides, it would be extremely becoming to you, my charmer," said she.

The smile of pleasure did not leave Natasha's face. She felt happy and exhilarated by the praise of this gracious Countess Bezukhof, who had heretofore seemed to her such an inaccessible, grand lady, and was now so cordial to her. Natasha's spirits rose, and she felt almost in love with this woman, who was so beautiful and so good-natured.

Helene, on her part, was sincerely enchanted by Natasha, and wanted her to have a good time. Anatol had urged her to foster his acquaintance with her, and it was for this purpose that she called on the Rostofs. The idea of helping her brother in such a flirtation was amusing to her. Although that winter in Petersburg she had felt a grudge against Natasha for alienating Boris from her, it had now entirely passed from her mind; and with all her heart she felt kindly disposed toward Natasha. As she was taking her departure, she called her protégée aside:

"Last evening my brother dined with me—we almost died of laughing—he eats just nothing at all, and can only sigh for you, my charmer! He is in love, madly in love with you, my dear."

Natasha flushed crimson on hearing those words.

"How she blushes! How she blushes, my delightful one," pursued Helene. "Don't fail to come. Even if you are in love, that is no reason for making a nun of yourself. Even if you are engaged, I am sure that your future husband would prefer to have you go into society, rather than die of tedium in his absence."

"Of course she knows that I am engaged; of course she and her husband, she and Pierre, that good, honest Pierre, have talked and laughed about this. And why shouldn't I have a good time?" said Natasha to herself, looking at Helene with wide eyes full of surprise.

Marya Dmitrievna returned in time for dinner, silent and solemn, having evidently suffered a rebuff at the old prince's. She was still laboring under too much excitement from her encounter to be able to give a calm account of it. To the count's question, she replied that everything would be all right, and she would tell him about it the next day.

When she was informed of Countess Bezukhof's visit, and the invitation for the evening, she said:

"I don't like the idea of your going to Bezukhof's and I would advise you not to; however, if you have already promised, go; perhaps you will have some fun," she added, addressing Natasha.

Count Rostof took his young ladies to Countess Bezukhof's.

The reception was fairly well attended, but most of the company were strangers to Natasha. Count Rostof saw with dissatisfaction that the large majority of those present consisted of men and women noted for their free and easy behavior.

Mlle. Georges stood in one corner of the drawing-room surrounded by young men. Count Rostof decided not to take a hand at the card table, or to leave the girls, but to take his departure as soon as Mlle. Georges had finished her recitation.

Anatol was at the door, evidently on the lookout for the Rostofs. As soon as he had exchanged greetings with the count, he joined Natasha, and followed her into the room. The moment she saw him she was assailed, just as she had been at the theater, by a mixed sense of gratified vanity that she pleased him and of fear because of the absence of moral barriers between her and him.

Helene received Natasha effusively, and was loud in praise of her beauty and her dress.

Soon after their arrival, Mlle. Georges retired from the room to change her costume. In the meantime, chairs were arranged in the drawing-room, and the guests began to take their seats. Anatol procured a chair for Natasha, and was just going to sit beside her; but the count, keeping a sharp eye on his daughter, took the seat next to her. Anatol sat behind.

Mlle. Georges, with plump and dimpled arms all bare, and with a red shawl flung across one shoulder, came out into the space around which the chairs were ranged, and assumed an unnatural pose. A murmur of admiration was heard.

Mlle. Georges threw a stern and gloomy glance around, and began to recite certain lines in French, in which the guilty love of a mother for her son is delineated. In places she raised her voice; then, again, she spoke in a whisper, triumphantly tossing her head; and in other places she broke off, or spoke in deep, hoarse tones, rolling her eyes.

"Adorable!" . . . "Divine!" . . . "Delightful!" were the encomiums heard on all sides.

Natasha's eyes were fastened on the stout actress, but she heard nothing, saw nothing, understood nothing, of what was going on before her; she felt that she was irrevocably drawn again into that strange, mad world, so far removed from the past world, where it was impossible to know what was right and what was wrong, what was reasonable and what was foolish. Behind her sat Anatol, and she was conscious of his nearness, and with terror awaited what might happen.

After the first monologue, the whole company arose and crowded around Mlle. Georges, expressing their enthusiasm.

"How beautiful she is!" said Natasha to her father, who had got up with the rest, and was starting to push his way through the throng toward the actress.

"I cannot think so when I look at you," said Anatol, sitting down beside Natasha. He spoke so that she only could hear what he said. "You are charming. . . . Since the first moment that I saw you, I have not ceased . . ."

"Come, let us go, Natasha," interrupted the count, returning to his daughter. "How pretty she is!"

Natasha, making no reply, followed her father, but gave Anatol a look of bewildered surprise.

After several more recitations, Mlle. Georges took her departure, and Countess Bezukhof invited her guests into the ballroom.

The count wanted to go home, but Helene begged him not to spoil her impromptu party. The Rostofs remained. Anatol took Natasha out for a waltz; and while they were on the floor, and he clasped her waist and hand, he told her that she was ravishing, and that he loved her.

During the *écossaise*, which she danced with Kuragin also, Anatol said nothing to her while they were by themselves, but merely gazed at her.

Natasha was in doubt whether she had not dreamed what he said to her during the waltz.

At the end of the first figure he again pressed her hand. Natasha lifted startled eyes to his; but his look and his smile had such an expression of self-confidence and flattering tenderness that she found it impossible to look at him and say to him what was on her tongue to say. She dropped her eyes.

"Do not say such things to me; I am betrothed—I love another," she hurriedly whispered.

She glanced at him. Anatol was not in the least confused or chagrined at what she said.

"Don't speak to me about that. What difference does it make to me?" he asked. "I tell you I am madly, madly in love with you. Am I to blame because you are bewitching? . . . It's our turn to lead."

Natasha, excited and anxious, looked around with wide, frightened eyes, and gave the impression of being gayer than usual. She remembered almost nothing of what took place that evening. While they were dancing the *écossaise* and the *grossvater*, her father came and urged her to go home with him, but she begged to stay a little longer.

Wherever she was, whoever engaged her in conversation, she was conscious all the time of his eyes upon her. Afterwards she remembered asking her father's permission to go to the dressing room to adjust her dress, and how Helene had followed her, and told her with a laugh that her brother was in love with her. She remembered how, in the little sitting room, she had again met Anatol, how Helene had suddenly disappeared, leaving her alone with him, and how Anatol, seizing her hand, had said, in a tender voice:

"I cannot call on you, but must I never see you? I love you madly, desperately! Can't I see you?" . . . And then, blocking her way, he had bent down his face close to her face.

His great, gleaming, masculine eyes were so near to her face that she could see nothing else except those eyes of his.

"Natasha?" she heard his voice whisper, with a questioning inflection, and her hand was squeezed almost painfully.

"Natasha?"

"I don't understand at all; I have nothing to say," said her glance.

His glowing lips approached her lips—but at that instant she felt that her deliverance had come, for the sound of Helene's footsteps and the rustle of her dress were heard in the room.

Natasha glanced at Helene; then, blushing and trembling, she gave him a terrified, questioning look, and started for the door.

"One word, only one, in God's name!" said Anatol.

She paused. She felt that it was imperative for her to hear that "single word," which would afford her an explanation of what had happened, and allow her something tangible to answer.

"Natasha, one word, only one," he kept repeating, evidently not knowing what to say; and he repeated it until Helene came close to him.

Helene and Natasha returned together to the drawing-room. Declining the invitation to stay to supper, the Rostofs went home.

That night Natasha could not sleep at all. She was tormented by the puzzling question, whom did she love, Anatol or Prince Andrei? She loved Prince Andrei—she had a very distinct remembrance of how warmly she loved him. But she loved Anatol also, there could be no doubt about that. "Otherwise, how could all this have taken place?" she asked herself. "If it was possible for me, on saying good-by to him, to answer his smiles with smiles—if I could permit myself to go so far, then of course I was in love with him at first sight. He certainly is good and noble and handsome, and it is impossible not to be in love with him. What can I do when I love him and love the other too?" she asked herself, and found no solution to the terrible problem.

I X

MORNING CAME, with its occupations and bustle. All arose, stirred about, engaged in talk; once more the modistes came; again Marya Dmitrievna appeared and summoned them to morning tea.

Natasha, with wide-open eyes, as if trying to anticipate and intercept every glance fixed upon her, looked anxiously about, and struggled to seem the same as usual.

After breakfast, which was her favorite meal, Marya Dmitrievna sat down in her easy-chair, and called Natasha and the old count to her.

"Well"—with strong emphasis on the word—"well, my friends, now I have thought the whole matter over, and this is my advice," she began. "Yesterday, as you know, I went to see Prince Nikolai. Well," again with strong emphasis, "I had an interview with him. He thought to shout me down, but I am not to be shouted down so easily. I had it all out with him." "Well, what did he do?" asked the count.

" 'What did he do?' He is a raving maniac. . . . won't listen to anything. Well, what's the use of talking? And, meanwhile, we are tormenting this poor girl so!" said Marya Dmitrievna. "And my advice to you is to transact your business, and go home . . . to Otradnoye . . . and there wait till . . ."

"Oh, no!" cried Natasha.

"Yes, you must go," maintained Marya Dmitrievna, "and wait there. If your betrothed should come here now, there would inevitably be a quarrel; but if he is left alone with the old man they will talk the whole thing over calmly, and then he will come for you."

The count approved of this plan, which instantly appealed to his good judgment. If the old prince was appeased, then they could rejoin him at

Moscow or Lisiya Gori; if not, as it would be contrary to his wishes, then the wedding could take place at Otradnoye.

"That is true as gospel," said he. "Only I am sorry that I went there and took her," said the old count.

"There's nothing to be sorry for. As long as you were here you couldn't help paying him that mark of respect. Well, if he does not approve, it is his affair," said Marya Dmitrievna, looking for something in her reticule. "Besides, the trousseau is all ready, so what have you to wait for? And what isn't ready I will send to you. Indeed, I am sorry about it, but you would be much better off to return—and God be with you!"

Having succeeded in finding what she was searching for, she handed it to Natasha. It was a letter from Princess Maria.

"She's written to you. How she torments herself, poor soul! She is afraid you will imagine she does not like you."

"Well, and she doesn't like me," said Natasha.

"Nonsense! Don't say such a thing!" cried Marya Dmitrievna.

"I take no one's opinion. I know she doesn't like me," said Natasha, boldly, snatching the letter, and her face assumed such an expression of hard and angry determination that it caused Marya Dmitrievna to look at her more closely, and frown.

"Don't you contradict me that way, my girl," said she. "What I tell you is the truth. Go and reply to her letter."

Natasha made no rejoinder, and retired to her own room to read Princess Maria's letter.

The princess wrote that she was in despair, owing to the misunderstanding that had arisen between them. Whatever were her father's feelings, she wrote, she besought Natasha to be assured that it was impossible for her not to love her, as the choice of her brother, for whose happiness she was ready to sacrifice everything.

"Moreover," she wrote, "do not imagine that my father was unkindly disposed toward you. He is old and feeble, and you must excuse him; but he is good and generous, and will not fail to love the one who can make his son happy."

Princess Maria further asked Natasha to appoint a time when they could have another meeting.

After reading the letter through, Natasha sat down at the writing desk to pen a reply.

"Dear princess," she wrote, hastily and mechanically, and paused. What more could she write, after all that had taken place the evening before?

"Yes, yes, all that is past, and now, already, everything is different," she said to herself, as she pondered over the letter thus begun. "Ought I to break our engagement? Is it really my duty? It is frightful!". . .

And, to escape from these terrible thoughts, she went to Sonya, and began to help her pick out her embroidery patterns.

After dinner Natasha again retired to her room, and took up Princess Maria's letter.

"Can it be that all is really over between us?" she mused. "Can it be that this has happened so quickly, and that all that is past is completely annihilated?"

She recalled, in all its intensity, her love for Prince Andrei, and yet, at the same time, she felt that she was in love with Kuragin. She vividly pictured herself as Prince Andrei's wife, and recalled those dreams of happiness with him which she had so many times enjoyed in imagination, and at the same time, fired with passionate emotions, she recalled every detail of her last meeting with Anatol.

"Why could it not be possible to love them both at once?" she more than once asked herself, in the depths of perplexity. "Then only could I be perfectly happy; but now I must choose, and I cannot be happy to be deprived of either of them. One thing is certain," she thought, "to tell Prince Andrei what has happened, or to hide it from him, is impossible. But as far as he is concerned no harm has been done. Can I break off forever, though, with that delicious love for Prince Andrei, to whom my life has been devoted so long?"

"Miss," said a maid, in a whisper, and coming into the room with a mysterious face, "a little man told me to give you this."

The maid handed her a note. "Only for Christ's sake . . ." she exclaimed, as Natasha, without thinking, mechanically broke the seal and began to read. It was a love letter from Anatol, and, while she did not comprehend a word of it, she comprehended enough to know that it was from him, from the man she loved. Yes, she loved him, else how could happen what had happened? How could she have in her hand a love letter from him?

With trembling hands Natasha held this passionate love letter, composed for Anatol by Dolokhof, and in reading it she found it contained what corresponded to everything she herself seemed to feel.

"Last evening decided my fate; you must love me or I die. I have no other alternative." So the letter began. Then he proceeded to say that he knew her parents would not consent to her marriage to him for various secret reasons which he could reveal to her alone, but that if she loved him, it was enough to say the little word yes, and no mortal power could suffice to destroy their bliss. Love conquers all. He would spirit her away, and fly with her to the ends of the earth.

"Yes, yes, I love him," mused Natasha, as she read the letter over for the twentieth time, and tried to discover some peculiarly deep meaning in every word.

That evening Marya Dmitrievna was going to the Arkharofs', and she invited the young ladies to accompany her. Natasha, under the pretext of a headache, remained at home.

338

X

Sonya, on her return late that evening, went to Natasha's room, and, to her amazement, found her still dressed and asleep on the divan. On the table near her lay Anatol's letter, wide open. Sonya picked the letter up, and began to read it.

She read it, and gazed at the sleeping Natasha, trying to discover in her face some key to the mystery of what she had read, and finding none. The expression of Natasha's face was calm, sweet, and happy.

Sonya, pale, and trembling with fright and emotion, clutching her breast lest she should choke, sat down in an easy-chair and began to weep.

"How is it I have seen nothing of this? How can this have gone so far? Is it possible she has ceased to love Prince Andrei? And how can she tolerate this Kuragin? He is a deceiver and a scoundrel—that is evident. What will Nikolai do, dear, noble Nikolai, when he learns of this? So this is what has caused her agitation and unnatural behavior for the last three days," said Sonya to herself. "But it is impossible that she is in love with him. Most likely she opened the letter without knowing from whom it came. In all probability she was offended. She couldn't have done such a thing knowingly."

Sonya wiped away her tears and went close to Natasha, and scrutinized her face.

"Natasha!" she murmured, almost inaudibly.

Natasha awoke and looked at Sonya. "Ah, are you back already?"

And in the impulse of the sudden awakening she gave her friend a warm and affectionate hug, but instantly noticing that Sonya's face was troubled, her face also became troubled and suspicious.

"Sonya, have you been reading that letter?" she asked.

"Yes," murmured Sonya.

Natasha smiled triumphantly.

"No, Sonya, it is impossible to remain silent any longer," said she. "I cannot hide it from you any more. You know, we love each other. Sonya, my darling, he has written me. . . . Sonya . . ."

Sonya, not believing her own ears, stared at Natasha with open eyes.

"But Bolkonsky!" she exclaimed.

"Ah, Sonya—ah! If you could only know how happy I am!" cried Natasha. "You can't imagine what such love is."

"But, Natasha, do you mean to say that the other is all at an end?"

Natasha gazed at Sonya with wide-open eyes, as if she did not understand her question.

"What, have you broken with Prince Andrei?" demanded Sonya.

"Oh, you can't comprehend it; don't talk nonsense. Listen to me," said Natasha, with a flash of ill temper.

"No, I cannot believe this," insisted Sonya. "I cannot understand it. How can you have loved one man a whole year, and then suddenly. . . . Why, you have only seen him three times! Natasha, I don't believe you. You are joking! In three days to forget everything? And so . . ."

"Three days!" interrupted Natasha. "It seems to me I have loved him a hundred years. It seems to me I have never loved anyone else before him. You cannot comprehend it. Sonya, wait; sit down!" Natasha threw her arms around her, and kissed her. "I have been told, and you have probably heard, that such love as this existed; but now for the first time I experience it. It is not like the one before. The moment I set eyes on him I felt that he was my master, that I was his slave, and that I could not help loving him. Yes, his slave! Whatever he commands me, I obey him. You can't understand that. What can I do? What can I do, Sonya?" pleaded Natasha, with a happy, frightened face.

"But just think what you are doing," insisted Sonya. "I cannot let this go on. This clandestine correspondence! How could you permit him to go so far?" she asked, with a horror and aversion which she tried in vain to hide.

"I've told you," replied Natasha, "that I have no will about it! Why can't you understand? I love him!"

"Then I will not let it go any further. I'll tell the whole story," cried Sonya, with a burst of tears.

"For God's sake . . . I beg of you . . . if you tell, you are my enemy!" exclaimed Natasha. "Do you want me to be unhappy? Do you want to separate us?"

Seeing how passionately excited Natasha was, Sonya shed tears of shame and regret for her friend.

"But what has passed between you?" she asked. "What has he said to you? Why doesn't he come to the house?"

Natasha made no reply to this question.

"For God's sake, Sonya, don't tell anyone, don't torment me," entreated Natasha. "Remember, it's never right to interfere in such matters. I have trusted you . . ."

"But why all this secrecy? Why doesn't he come to ask for your hand? You know Prince Andrei gave you absolute freedom, if such were the case; but I don't believe in this man. Natasha, have you considered what his secret reasons may be?"

Natasha gazed at Sonya with wondering eyes. Evidently this question had not occurred to her, and she did not know what answer to make.

"What reasons? I don't know. But of course there must be reasons."

Sonya sighed, and shook her head incredulously.

"If there were reasons . . ." she began; but Natasha, foreseeing her objections, with frightened eagerness interrupted her.

"Sonya, it is impossible to doubt him, impossible, wholly impossible, do you understand?" she cried.

"Does he love you?"

"Love me!" repeated Natasha, with a smile of contemptuous pity for her friend's incredulity. "You have read his letter, you have seen him, haven't you?"

"But if he were a dishonorable man?"

"He! A dishonorable man! If you knew him!" exclaimed Natasha.

"If he were an honorable man, then he ought either to explain his intentions, or else cease to see you; and if you are not willing to do this, then I will. I will write him, I will tell your papa," said Sonya, decidedly.

"But I can't live without him," cried Natasha.

"Natasha, I don't understand you! What are you saying? Think of your father, think of Nikolai."

"I want no one, I love no one but him! How dare you say he is dishonorable? Don't you know that I love him?" cried Natasha. "Sonya, go, I don't want to quarrel with you! Go away, for God's sake, go away! You see how tormented I am," she screamed in a voice of repressed anger and despair. Sonya began to sob, and rushed from the room.

Natasha went to her writing table and, without pausing a moment, wrote the letter to Princess Maria that she had not been able to write the morning before. In this letter she laconically informed the princess that all misunderstandings were at an end, that taking advantage of Prince Andrei's generosity in giving her perfect freedom, she begged her to forget all that had happened, and to forgive her if she had been to blame in respect to her; but that she could never be his wife. At that moment all seemed to her so easy, simple, and clear!

The Rostofs were to start for the country on Friday, and on Wednesday the count went with a prospective purchaser to his Moscow estate.

On the day of the count's trip, Sonya and Natasha were invited to a gala dinner at the Karaginas', and Marya Dmitrievna went as their chaperon.

At this dinner Natasha again met Anatol, and Sonya observed that Natasha had some mysterious conversation with him, which she evidently did not want to be overheard; and all during dinner she seemed to be more agitated than ever. On their return home, Natasha was the first to begin the explanation her friend was anxious to hear.

"There, Sonya, you have said all sorts of foolish things about him," Natasha began, in a cajoling tone, such as children use when they want to be flattered. "He and I came to a clear understanding today."

"Now, what do you mean? What did he say, Natasha? How glad I am that you are not angry with me! Tell me all, tell me the whole story. What did he say to you?"

Natasha pondered.

"Ah! Sonya, if you only knew him as I do. . . . He said . . . he asked me what sort of an engagement I had with Bolkonsky. He was delighted that it depended on me to break it off."

Sonya sighed mournfully.

"But you haven't broken your engagement with Bolkonsky, have you?"

"Well, perhaps I have broken my engagement with Bolkonsky! Perhaps it is all at an end! What makes you have such hard thoughts of me?"

"I have no hard thoughts of you; only I can't understand this . . ."

"Wait, Sonya, and you will understand the whole thing. You will learn what a man he is! But don't harbor hard thoughts of me, or of him either."

"I harbor no hard thoughts of anyone; I love you and I am sorry for you all. But what am I to do?"

Sonya, however, was not blinded by the affectionate manner in which Natasha treated her. The more gentle and insinuating Natasha's face grew, the more stern and serious became Sonya's face.

"Natasha," said she, "you yourself begged me not to say any more about this to you, and I have not; and now you reopen it yourself. Natasha, I have no faith in him. Why all this mystery?"

"There you begin again!" interposed Natasha.

"Natasha, I am afraid for you."

"Afraid of what?"

"I am afraid you are going to your ruin," said Sonya, in a resolute voice, frightened herself at what she said.

An angry look again came into Natasha's face.

"I will go to my ruin, I certainly will, and the faster the better. It's no affair of yours. It won't hurt you, even if it does hurt me. Leave me! leave! I hate you!"

"Natasha!" expostulated Sonya, in dismay.

"I hate you! I hate you! We can never be friends any more!"

Natasha rushed out of the room.

Natasha had nothing more to say to Sonya, and avoided her. With that peculiar expression of nervous preoccupation and guilt, she wandered up and down the rooms, trying one occupation after another, and instantly abandoning them.

Hard as this was for Sonya, she did not let Natasha out of her sight for a single moment, but followed her everywhere she went.

On the day before the count's return, Sonya observed that Natasha spent the whole morning at the parlor window, as if in expectation of someone, and that she made some sort of signal to an officer who drove by, and who Sonya thought must be Anatol. Sonya began to watch her friend still more closely, and remarked that all during dinner and throughout the evening, Natasha was in a strange and unnatural state of excitement, answering at random the questions that were asked her, beginning and not finishing sentences, and laughing at everything.

After tea, Sonya saw a timid chambermaid watching for her at Natasha's door. She let her enter, and listening at the keyhole discovered that she was the bearer of another letter.

And suddenly it became clear to Sonya that Natasha had some terrible plan on foot for that evening. Sonya knocked loudly at her door. Natasha refused to admit her.

"She is going to elope with him!" said Sonya to herself. "She is quite ready for anything. Her face today had a peculiarly pitiful and determined expression. She wept when she said good-by to her father," Sonya remembered. "Yes, it is evident that she is going to elope with him! What can I do about it?" she mused, recalling all the circumstances that now made her think Natasha had made some terrible resolution. "The count is away. What can I do? Write to Kuragin and demand an explanation? But who would make him reply to it? Write to Pierre, as Prince Andrei told me to do in case of misfortune? . . . But perhaps she has already broken with Bolkonsky! Certainly Natasha sent her letter to the princess last evening. . . . If her father were only here!"

It seemed terrible to tell Marya Dmitrievna, who had such confidence in Natasha. "But what else can I do?" mused Sonya, as she stood in the dark corridor. "Now or never is the time to show that I am grateful to this dear family, and that I love Nikolai. No! Even if I have to stay awake for three nights, I will not leave this corridor, and I will detain her by main force; and I will not allow any scandal to happen to this family," she said to herself.

X I

ANATOL HAD recently transferred his lodgings to Dolokhof's house. The plan of abducting the young countess had been suggested and arranged by Dolokhof some days before, and on that day when Sonya, listening at Natasha's door, had determined to protect her, this scheme was all ready to be carried into execution.

Natasha had agreed to meet Kuragin at ten o'clock that evening, at the back entrance. Kuragin was to put her into a troika which would be in waiting, and carry her forty miles to the village of Kamienko, where an unfrocked priest would be in readiness to perform a mock marriage ceremony. At Kamienko a relay would be ready to take them toward Warsaw, and thence by regular stages they would make their escape abroad.

Anatol had his passport and his order for post horses, and ten thousand rubles obtained from his sister, and ten thousand obtained through Dolokhof's mediation.

Two witnesses—Khvostikof, formerly a law clerk, who was now a creature of Dolokhof's, and Makarin, a hussar on the retired list, a weak and good-natured fellow who had an inordinate affection for Kuragin—were sitting in the front room over their tea.

In Dolokhof's large study, the walls of which were hung from floor to ceiling with Persian rugs, bearskins, and weapons, sat Dolokhof himself, in a traveling tunic and top boots, before an open desk on which lay bills and packages of money. Anatol, in his uniform, unbuttoned, came in from the room where the two witnesses were sitting, and was passing through the study into the adjoining room where his French valet and another servant were packing up the last remaining effects.

Dolokhof was making out the accounts and writing the amounts on a sheet of paper.

"Well!" said he, "you will have to give two thousand to Khvostikof."

"All right, give it to him!" said Anatol.

"Makarka"—this was an affectionate nickname for Makarin—"is so disinterested that he would go through fire and water for you. There now, the accounts are all made out," said Dolokhof, calling his attention to the paper. "Is that right?"

"Yes, of course it is," said Anatol, evidently not heeding what was said, and staring ahead with a dreamy expression and a smile that did not leave his face.

Dolokhof closed the desk with a bang, and turned to Kuragin with an amused smile.

"Listen here, now! You'd better give this up; there's still time," said he.

"Fool!" said Anatol, "stop talking nonsense. If you only knew! . . . But only the devil knows what this is to me!"

"Honestly!" said Dolokhof. "Drop the whole business. I'll tell you the honest truth. Do you imagine that this is a joke that you are getting into?"

"There you are upsetting me again. Go to the devil!" exclaimed Anatol, scowling. "I have no time to listen to your idiotic twaddle!"

And he started to leave the room.

Dolokhof smiled scornfully and condescendingly as Anatol turned away.

"Wait," he cried after him, "I'm not joking, I'm telling you the truth; come here, come here, I say!"

Anatol came back into the room again; and, trying to concentrate his attention, gazed at Dolokhof, apparently quite influenced by his vehemence.

"Listen to me, I speak for the last time. Why should I jest with you? Have I done anything to thwart you? Who is it that has made all the arrangements for you, who found your priest for you, who procured your passport, who got the money for you? Haven't I arranged the whole business?"

"Yes, and I thank you. Do you think I am not grateful?" Anatol sighed and embraced his friend.

"I have helped you; but it is my place to tell you the truth: this is a dangerous game, and if it misses fire a stupid one. Suppose you elope with her —well and good. What will be the next step? It will be discovered that you are married. You will be prosecuted as a criminal . . ."

"What nonsense! What stupid nonsense!" cried Anatol, frowning again. "Haven't I told you again and again? Hey?"

And Anatol, with that peculiar passion for argument characteristic of men of small intellects, when they want to show their wit, reiterated the considerations which he had laid before Dolokhof a hundred times.

"I have told you again and again; my mind is made up. If this marriage is invalid," said he, doubling over his finger, "of course I am not responsible

344

for it; well, then, suppose it is valid; it's just the same, and, when we are abroad, no one will know the difference; that's a fact, isn't it? So say no more, say no more, say no more!"

"But, really, forget about it! You will only get yourself into a scrape."

"Go to hell!" screamed Anatol, and, clutching his hair, he rushed into the next room; then he came back at once and sat down astride a chair in front of Dolokhof. "The devil only knows what this is to me! Hey? Just see, how it beats!" He took Dolokhof's hand and put it on his heart. "Ah! What an ankle! My dear, what eyes! She's a goddess!"

Dolokhof, smiling without sympathy, looked at him out of his handsome, impudent eyes, evidently feeling inclined to have a little more sport out of him.

"Well, but when your money is gone, what then?"

"What then? Hey?" repeated Anatol, with a touch of genuine distress at the thought of the future. "What then? I'm sure I don't know. But what's the use of talking nonsense?" He looked at his watch. "It's time."

Anatol went into the next room. "Hurry up, there! Aren't you almost ready? Why are you dawdling so?" he cried, addressing the servants.

Dolokhof put up the money, and, shouting to his man to have a basket of food and wine prepared for the travelers for their journey, he went into the room where Khvostikof and Makarin were waiting.

Anatol had flung himself down on the couch in the study, and, with his head resting on his hand, was dreamily smiling and whispering tender words.

"Come and have something to eat. Have a drink, then!" cried Dolokhof from the next room.

"I don't want anything," replied Anatol, still with the smile on his handsome lips.

"Come, Balaga is here!"

Anatol got up and went into the dining room. Balaga was a famous troika driver, who for half a dozen years had known Dolokhof and Anatol, and had furnished them with their troikas. More than once, when Anatol's regiment had been at Tver, he had started at nightfall from Tver, set him down in Moscow before daybreak, and brought him back by the following morning. More than once he had taken them out to drive with gypsies and damotchki —nice little dames—as Balaga called fast women. More than once at their instigation he had run down pedestrians and sleigh drivers in the Moscow streets, and always his "gentlemen," as he called them, had rescued him from the penalty. He had ruined more than one horse in their service. More than once he had been thrashed by them; many times had they given him champagne and Madeira, which he especially enjoyed, and he knew of escapades of theirs which would have condemned any ordinary man to Siberia.

During their orgies, they had often invited Balaga to take part, and made him drink and dance with the gypsies.

In service for them he had twenty times a year risked life and limb, and in accomplishing their deviltry he had killed more horses than their money would ever pay for. But he was fond of them; he was fond of that mad pace of twelve miles an hour; he was fond of upsetting some harmless coachman from his box, or running down some pedestrian on the street crossings, and of dashing at full tilt down the Moscow streets. He was fond of hearing behind him that wild cry of drunken voices, "Faster, faster!" when it was already a physical impossibility for his horses to carry them a step farther; he was fond of winding his whiplash around a peasant's neck, who shrank back more dead than alive as he passed by. "Real gentlemen," he called them!

Anatol and Dolokhof also were fond of Balaga because of his masterly skill in handling the reins, and because his tastes were similar to theirs. With others he drove hard bargains, charging twenty-five rubles for a two hours' outing, and he himself rarely condescended to drive others, but more frequently sent one of his subordinates. But with his "gentlemen," as he called them, he himself always went along, and never charged for his extra labor. Only when he learned through the valets that money was plentiful, he would come, after an interval of many months, and very soberly and obsequiously, bowing low, would ask to be helped out of his difficulties.

His "gentlemen" always made him take a seat.

"You will excuse me, your excellency," he would say, "I am entirely out of horses; I pray you to advance me enough to get more at the fair."

And Anatol and Dolokhof, if they happened to be in funds, would give him a thousand or so rubles.

Balaga was twenty-seven years old, a stocky, red-haired, snub-nosed peasant, with fiery red complexion, and still more fiery red neck, with glittering little eyes and a scrubby beard. He wore a fine blue silk-lined tunic, and over that a short sheepskin coat.

He crossed himself, turning to the shrine corner, as he came in, and advanced toward Dolokhof, holding out a small, dirty hand.

"Feodor Ivanovitch, your good health," he exclaimed, with a low bow. "How are you, brother? . . . There he is!"

"Good health, your excellency," said he, addressing Anatol, who came in at that moment, and offered him also his grimy hand.

"I ask you, Balaga," said Anatol, clapping his hand on his shoulder, "do you love me, or not, hey? Now there's a chance for you to prove it. . . . What horses have you come with, hey?"

"Those your man ordered, your own wild ones," said Balaga.

"Now see here, Balaga. No matter if you slaughter all three of your horses, provided you get us there within three hours. Hey?"

"If we slaughter them, how will we get there?" replied Balaga, with a wink.

"I'll smash your snout for you! And no joking!" cried Anatol, suddenly, with glaring eyes.

"Who's joking?" exclaimed the driver, with a laugh. "Do I ever grudge anything for my 'gentlemen'? Whatever my horses can show in the way of speed, that we will do."

"Ah!" grunted Anatol. "Sit down, then."

"Yes, why not sit down?" said Dolokhof.

"I will stand, Feodor Ivanovitch."

"Sit down, no nonsense. Have a drink," said Anatol, and poured him out a large glass of Madeira. The driver's eyes flashed at the sight of the wine. Refusing at first, for manners' sake, he drank it down and wiped his mouth with a red silk handkerchief which he kept in the top of his hat.

"Well, when shall we start, your excellency?"

"Let me see." Anatol glanced at his watch. "Start pretty soon now. See here, Balaga; you will get there on time?"

"Well, it depends on the start. If we get off luckily, then we'll be there in good time. I got you to Tver once—went there in seven hours. Don't you remember, your excellency?"

"Do you know, one Christmas we started from Tver," said Anatol, smiling at the remembrance and turning to Makarin, who was gazing affectionately at Kuragin with his heart in his eyes. "You wouldn't believe it, Makarka, we drove so that it quite took away my breath. We came upon a file of carts and jumped right over two of them. Hey?"

"What horses those were!" interposed Balaga, taking up the thread of the story. "At that time I put in two young side horses with the bay shaft horse," he said, turning to Dolokhof. "You would hardly believe it, Feodor Ivanovitch, those wild creatures actually flew for forty miles. It was impossible to hold them. My hands were numb, it was so cold. I threw down the reins. 'Look out for yourself, your excellency,' said I, and I rolled over backward into the sleigh. It was hopeless to control 'em, or even to stick to my seat. The devils got us there in three hours. Only the left off one was winded."

XII

ANATOL LEFT the room and after a few minutes came back in a sable coat, girdled with a silver-buckled leather belt, and wearing a sable cap, jauntily set on one side, and very becoming to his handsome face. Glancing into the mirror, and then taking the same posture before Dolokhof which the mirror had told him was most effective, he seized a glass of wine.

"Well, Fedya, good-by. Thank you for everything," said Anatol. "Well, comrades, friends"—he pondered a moment—"friends . . . of my . . . youth, farewell," he said, turning to Makarin and the others.

Although they were all going with him, Anatol evidently wanted to do something affecting and solemn on the occasion of this farewell. He spoke in a low, slow, deep voice, and throwing out his chest, he swayed a little as he rested his weight on one leg. "All of you take your glasses! You too, Balaga. Well, comrades . . . friends of my youth . . . we have had good times together, we have enjoyed life, we have been on many sprees, hey? Now, when will we meet again? I am going abroad; farewell . . . my boys. To your health! Hurrah!" he cried, draining his glass and smashing it on the floor.

"To your good health!" exclaimed Balaga, also draining his glass and wiping his mouth with his handkerchief. Makarin, with tears in his eyes, embraced Anatol.

"Eh! prince, how sad that we should have to part!" he exclaimed.

"Come, let us be off," cried Anatol.

Balaga was on the point of leaving the room.

"Hold on there, wait," said Anatol. "Shut the door. We must sit down first—there, that's the way."

They closed the door and sat down, in accordance with the superstition.

"Well, now be off with you, boys," said Anatol, getting up.

Anatol's valet, Joseph, gave him his purse and saber, and all crowded into the anteroom.

"But where is the cloak?" demanded Dolokhof. "Hey, Ignatka, go to Matriona Matveyevna, and ask her for the cloak—the sable cloak. I have heard how girls go off on such occasions," explained Dolokhof, with a wink. "She will come running out more dead than alive, dressed for staying in the house, and if you delay a moment too long, there will be tears, and 'Oh, papa dear!' and 'Oh, mama dear!' and she'll be cold, and back she'll go. So be sure you take this cloak with you, and have it all ready in the sleigh."

The valet brought a woman's cloak, lined with fox.

"You fool! I told you to get the sable. Hey, Matriona, bring the sable," he shouted, his voice ringing through the rooms.

A gypsy girl, handsome though thin and pale, with brilliant black eyes and curly, purplish black hair, with a red shawl over her shoulders, came hurrying out with the sable cloak over her arm.

"Why, I don't care; take it," said she, evidently afraid of her master, and yet regretting the cloak.

Dolokhof, without heeding her, took the fox-skin cloak, threw it over Matriona, and wrapped it around her.

"So," said Dolokhof; "and so," he repeated, as he pulled the collar up above her head, leaving only a small opening for her face.

"That's the way, do you see?" and he moved Anatol's head toward the opening left by the collar, where Matriona's brilliant smile could alone be seen.

"Well, good-by, Matriona," said Anatol, kissing her. "My follies here are ended. Give my regards to Stioshka. Good-by, Matriona. Wish me good luck."

"Well, then, prince, God grant you the best of luck," said Matriona, in her gypsy accent.

At the doorstep two troikas were waiting with two jaunty grooms in attendance. Balaga was on the box of the first sleigh, and, with his elbows held high, was carefully sorting the reins. Anatol and Dolokhof got in behind him; Makarin, Khvostikof and the valet took their places in the other troika.

"All ready?" inquired Balaga. "Let her go!" he cried, twisting the reins round his wrists, and the three horses flew like the wind down the Nikitsky Boulevard.

"Tproo! go! hey! . . . tproo!" rang out Balaga's shout and that of the groom sitting on the box. On the Arbatski Square the troika ran into a carriage; there was a crash, a shout was heard, and the troika flew down over the Arbat. After dashing down the Podnovinsky, Balaga began to draw rein, and, pulling up, halted the horses at the crossing of Staraya Konyushennaya.

The groom leaped down to hold the horses' heads by the curb, while Anatol and Dolokhof strode along the sidewalk. Coming to the gate, Dolokhof gave a low whistle. The whistle was returned, and immediately after a chambermaid came running out.

"Come into the court, else you will be seen; she'll be down presently," said she.

Dolokhof remained by the gate. Anatol followed the chambermaid into the courtyard, turned the corner, and ran up the steps.

Suddenly Gavrilo, Marya Dmitrievna's colossal footman, met Anatol.

"Be good enough to go to my mistress," said the footman, in a deep bass voice, as he blocked all retreat from the door.

"Who's your mistress? Who are you?" demanded Anatol, in a breathless whisper.

"If you please, I was ordered to show you . . ."

"Kuragin! back!" cried Dolokhof. "You are betrayed! back!"

Dolokhof, who had been left at the outside gate, was engaged in a tussle with the servant, who was trying to close it and prevent Anatol from escaping. Dolokhof, with a final spurt of force, overturned the servant, seized Anatol by the arm, pulled him through the gate, and ran together with him back to their troika.

Marya Dmitrievna, finding the weeping Sonya in the corridor, had obliged her to confess the whole story. Having obtained possession of Natasha's letter, and read it, Marya Dmitrievna took it and confronted Natasha with it.

"Wretched girl! shameless hussy!" said she to her. "I will not listen to a single word!"

Pushing away Natasha, who looked at her with wondering but tearless eyes, she shut her in under lock and key; then she ordered the servant to admit into the courtyard any who might come that evening, but not to let them out again, and she had ordered the footman to show such persons into her presence. Having made these arrangements, she took up her position in the drawing-room and waited for developments.

When Gavrilo came to inform Marya Dmitrievna that the abductors had escaped, she was very indignant; she got up, and for a long time paced up and down the room, with her hands clasped behind her back, deliberating on what she ought to do. At midnight, she got the key out from her pocket, and went to Natasha's room.

Sonya was still sitting in the corridor, sobbing, "Marya Dmitrievna, let me go to her, for God's sake," said she.

Marya Dmitrievna, giving her no reply, opened the door and went in. "Disgusting! abominable! . . . in my house! . . . Indecent, shameless wench! . . . Only I'm sorry for her father," said Marya Dmitrievna, trying to master her indignation. "Hard as it will be, I will bid them all hold their tongues, and I'll keep it from the count."

Marya Dmitrievna entered the chamber with a firm step. Natasha was lying on the sofa with her face hidden in her hands; she did not stir, but lay in the same position in which Marya Dmitrievna had left her. "Pretty conduct; pretty conduct, indeed!" exclaimed Marya Dmitrievna. "Making assignations with your lovers in my house! None of your hypocrisy! Listen when I speak to you!"

Marya Dmitrievna shook her by the arm.

"Listen when I speak to you! You have disgraced yourself, like any common wench! I'd settle this with you, but I have some pity for your father. I'll keep it from him."

Natasha did not change her position, but her whole body began to shake with the noiseless, convulsive sobs that choked her. Marya Dmitrievna glanced at Sonya, and sat down on the sofa near Natasha.

"Lucky for him he escaped me; but I'll find him," said she, in her harsh voice. "Do you hear what I am saying?" She put her big hand under Natasha's face, and turned it toward her. Both Marya Dmitrievna and Sonya were amazed when they saw her face. Her eyes were dry and glittering, her lips compressed, her cheeks hollow.

"Let . . . me . . . be! . . . What . . . do . . . I . . . care? I . . . shall die!" she murmured, turning away from Marya Dmitrievna with angry petulance, and hiding her face in her hands again.

"Natasha!" exclaimed Marya Dmitrievna, "I wish you well. Lie there . . . lie there if you wish; I won't touch you; but listen to me! I am not going to show you how guilty you have been. You know. But, don't you see, your father will be back tomorrow; what shall I say to him?"

Again Natasha's form was shaken by sobs.

"He will hear of it; and so will your brother, and so will your betrothed!"

"I have no betrothed; I have broken with him!" cried Natasha.

"That's immaterial," pursued Marya Dmitrievna. "Well, they will learn of it; do you think they will forgive it? There's your father, I know him— if he should challenge him, would it be a good thing? Ha?"

"Oh! leave me! why should you have interfered at all? Why? Why? Who asked you to?" screamed Natasha, sitting up straight on the sofa, and glaring angrily at Marya Dmitrievna.

350

"But what was your idea?" demanded Marya Dmitrievna, again losing her patience. "Were you kept locked up? Who on earth prevented him from coming to the house? Why must he needs carry you off like a gypsy wench? . . . Well, now suppose he had carried you off, do you suppose we wouldn't have found him? Either your father, or your brother, or your betrothed? Well, he's a scoundrel! a knave! that's what he is!"

"He's better than all of you put together," cried Natasha, sitting up very straight. "If you had not meddled! . . . My God, has it come to this, has it come to this? Sonya, what made you? . . . Go away!"

And she burst into a passion of tears, sobbing with desperation such as only those feel who know that they are responsible for their own woes. Marya Dmitrievna began to speak once more, but Natasha cried:

"Go away, go away! you all hate me! you all despise me!" And she threw herself on the sofa again.

Marya Dmitrievna continued for some time to give her advice, and assure her that this whole affair ought to be kept a secret from the count; that no one would know anything about it, if only Natasha would try to forget it all, and not betray in anyone's presence that anything had happened.

Natasha made no reply. She ceased to sob, but a fit of shivering and trembling came upon her. Marya Dmitrievna put a pillow under her head, covered her up with a couple of comforters, and herself brought her some tea; but Natasha had nothing to say to her.

"Now, let her go to sleep," said Marya Dmitrievna, and left the room, thinking that she would soon sleep.

But Natasha did not go to sleep, and with wide, staring eyes gazed into vacancy. She slept not at all that night, and she did not weep, and she did not speak to Sonya, who several times got up and went to her.

On the following day Count Rostof returned from his Moscow estate in time for breakfast, as he had promised. He was in a most genial frame of mind. He had come to a satisfactory arrangement with his purchaser, and now there was nothing to detain him in Moscow, and away from his countess, whom he was very anxious to see.

Marya Dmitrievna met him, and informed him that Natasha had been ill the day before, that they had sent for the doctor, and now she was better.

Natasha that morning did not leave her room. With set, cracked lips, with wide, dry eyes, she kept her place by the window, and anxiously gazed at the passers-by in the street, and turned anxiously toward those who entered her room. She was evidently expecting news from him—expecting that either he would himself come, or send her a letter.

When the count went to her she heard the sound of his heavy steps, and turned around nervously, and then her face assumed its former expression of hauteur, and even anger. She did not get up to meet him.

"What is the matter, my angel? Are you ill?" asked the count.

Natasha hesitated.

"Yes, I am ill," said she.

In reply to the count's anxious questions why she was so downcast, and whether anything had happened to her lover, she assured him that nothing had happened, and begged him not to be disturbed.

Marya Dmitrievna confirmed Natasha's statement that nothing had happened, but the count, judging from the imaginary illness, and by his daughter's absent-mindedness, by the troubled faces of Sonya and Marya Dmitrievna, saw clearly that during his absence something must have happened. It was so terrible, however, for him to think that anything disgraceful had happened to his beloved daughter, he was so happy in his buoyant good spirits, that he avoided asking any pointed questions, and tried hard to assure himself that nothing out of the way could have happened; and his only regret was that, on account of Natasha's indisposition, he was obliged to postpone their return to his country seat.

XIII

PIERRE, ON THE day of his wife's arrival in Moscow, had made up his mind to take a trip somewhere, so as to avoid being with her. Then, when the Rostofs came to Moscow, the impression produced upon him by Natasha made him hasten to carry out his intention. He went to Tver to see Bazdeyef's widow, who had some time since promised to put into his hands her husband's papers.

On Pierre's return to Moscow a letter was handed him from Marya Dmitrievna, who urged him to come and consult with her on some highly important business concerning Andrei Bolkonsky and his betrothed.

Pierre had avoided Natasha. It seemed to him that he felt for her a sentiment stronger than it was justifiable for a married man to harbor for his friend's betrothed, and some perverse fate was constantly throwing them together.

"What can have happened? and what can it have to do with me?" he wondered, while dressing to go to Marya Dmitrievna's. "It's high time for Prince Andrei to be back and marry her," thought Pierre, as he set out.

On the Tversky Boulevard someone hailed him.

"Pierre, been back long?" cried a well-known voice.

Pierre raised his head. It was Anatol and his inseparable companion, Makarin, dashing by in a double sleigh, drawn by two gray trotters, that sent the snow pelting over the dasher. Anatol sat bolt upright, in the classic pose of spirited warriors, with his neck muffled in a beaver collar, and bending his head a little. His face was fresh and ruddy; his hat, with a white plume, was set jauntily on one side, exposing his curled and pomaded hair, dusted with fine snow.

"Indeed, he's a real philosopher!" thought Pierre. "He sees nothing beyond the enjoyment of the present moment; nothing annoys him, and consequently he is always gay, self-satisfied, and calm. What wouldn't I give to be like him!" thought Pierre, with a feeling of envy.

In the anteroom of the Akhrasimov house, a footman, who relieved Pierre of his cloak, told him that Marya Dmitrievna would receive him in her own room. As he opened the door into the music room Pierre saw Natasha sitting by the window, with a pale, thin, angry face. She glanced at him and frowned, and, with an expression of chilling dignity, left the room.

"What has happened?" asked Pierre, on entering Marya Dmitrievna's room.

"Pretty state of affairs!" replied Marya Dmitrievna. "Fifty-eight years have I lived in this world, and I never saw anything so shameful."

And then, receiving Pierre's word of honor that he would keep secret what he should hear, Marya Dmitrievna confided to him that Natasha had broken her engagment with Prince Andrei without the knowledge of her parents; that the cause of this break was Anatol Kuragin, whom Pierre's wife had introduced to her, and with whom she had promised to elope during her father's absence, in order to enter into a clandestine marriage.

Pierre, with shoulders hunched and mouth open, listened to Marya Dmitrievna's story, not believing his own ears. That Prince Andrei's betrothed, that hitherto lovely Natasha, so passionately beloved, should give up Bolkonsky for that fool of an Anatol, who was a married man—for Pierre was in the secret of his marriage—and be so enamored of him as to consent to elope with him, Pierre could not comprehend and could not imagine.

Natasha's sweetness of character—he had known her since childhood—could not, in his mind, be associated with such baseness, folly, and cruelty in her. He remembered his own wife. "They are all alike," he said to himself, thinking that he was not the only one who had the misfortune to be in the toils of an unworthy woman; and at the same time he could have wept for his friend Prince Andrei, to whose pride this would be such a grievous blow. And the more he grieved for his friend, the greater scorn, and even aversion, he felt for this Natasha, who had just passed by him, with such an expression of haughty dignity, in the music room.

He did not know that Natasha's soul was full to overflowing of despair, shame, humiliation; and that she was not to blame for her expression, the result of despair, of cold dignity and disdain.

"But how could he marry her?" exclaimed Pierre, catching at Marya Dmitrievna's last word. "He could not marry her; he already has a wife."

"Worse and worse!" exclaimed Marya Dmitrievna. "Fine young man! . . . What a dastard he is! And she has been waiting here these two days for him to come! At any rate, she must cease expecting him; we must tell her."

When she learned from Pierre all the details of Anatol's marriage, and had poured out the vials of her wrath against Kuragin in abusive words, Marya Dmitrievna explained to Pierre why she had asked him to call upon her. She was afraid that the count or Bolkonsky—who was liable to return at any moment—might learn of the affair in spite of all her efforts to keep it a profound secret, and might challenge Kuragin to a duel; and, therefore, she besought him to add his influence to hers in getting Anatol to leave town and never show himself in her presence again.

Pierre willingly agreed to fulfil her wishes, since now he for the first time realized the danger threatening the old count and Nikolai and Prince Andrei.

Having made her request in short and precise terms, she took him back into the music room.

"Mind you! the count knows nothing of this. You must pretend that you also know nothing about it," said she. "And I am going this instant to tell her that she is to cease expecting him. And stay to dinner if you will," shouted back Marya Dmitrievna to Pierre.

Pierre met the old count. He was disturbed and annoyed. That morning Natasha had told him that she had broken her engagement with Bolkonsky.

"Too bad, too bad, my dear," he said to Pierre. "Too bad for these girls to be away from their mother; how sorry I am that I ever came at all. I am going to be frank with you: she has already broken her engagement, without telling any one of us about it. Now I will admit I have never been overpleased at this engagement; I will agree he's a fine man, and all that; but what could you expect? there would not be much happiness if the father was against the marriage; and Natasha does not lack chances of getting married. Still, the affair has gone on so long, and to take such a step without consulting her father or mother! And now she's sick, and God knows what's the matter. It's a bad thing, count, a bad thing, for daughters to be without their mother!"

Pierre perceived that the count was very much disturbed, and he tried to bring the conversation around to other topics; but the count kept returning to his grievance.

Sonya, with anxious face, came into the drawing-room.

"Natasha is not very well today; she is in her room, but she would like to see you. Marya Dmitrievna is with her, and would also like you to come."

"Yes, certainly, you and Bolkonsky were good friends; she probably wants to send some message," said the count. "Ah, my God! my God! How good it all was!" And, tearing at the locks of his gray hair, the count left the room.

Marya Dmitrievna had been explaining to Natasha that Anatol was married. Natasha refused to believe her, and insisted on having confirmation of it from Pierre himself. Sonya confided this to Pierre, as they passed along the corridor toward Natasha's room.

Natasha, pale and stern, was sitting next to Marya Dmitrievna. The moment Pierre entered the doorway, she met him with feverishly glittering, wildly imploring eyes. She did not smile, she did not even greet him with a nod, she only looked at him eagerly, and her eyes asked if he came as her friend, or, like all the rest, as her enemy, where Anatol was concerned. Pierre, in his own personality as Pierre, evidently did not exist for her.

"He knows all about it," said Marya Dmitrievna, indicating Pierre, and addressing Natasha. "Let him tell you if I am not speaking the truth."

Natasha, as a wounded animal at bay glares at the dogs and huntsmen approaching, looked first at the one and then at the other.

"Natasha," Pierre began, lowering his eyes, and experiencing a feeling of pity for her, and of aversion to the operation which he was obliged to perform, "it is true; but whether this is true or not true, as far as you are concerned, it cannot matter, because . . ."

"Then it is not true that he is married?"

"No, it is true."

"Has he been married for some time?" she asked. "On your word of honor!"

Pierre gave her his solemn word of honor.

"Is he still in town?" she asked hurriedly.

"Yes, I have just seen him."

The effort to say more was evidently too much for her, and she made them a sign with her hand to leave her alone.

XIV

PIERRE DID NOT stay for dinner, but immediately took his leave. He went out determined to find Anatol Kuragin, the mere thought of whom now made all his blood rush to his heart, and almost choked him. He sought him everywhere; at the ice hills, among the gypsies, at Comoneno's; but he was nowhere to be found.

Pierre went to the club. There everything was as usual; the members, who were assembling for dinner, formed little groups, and greeting Pierre, spoke of various items of city gossip.

One of Pierre's acquaintances, during some talk of the weather, asked him if he had heard of Kuragin's elopement with Natasha, about which the whole city was talking, and if it were true.

Pierre, with a laugh, said that it was all nonsense, because he had just come from the Rostofs'. He inquired of everyone if he had seen Anatol; one said he had not yet come, another that he would be there to dinner. It was strange for Pierre to look at this tranquil, indifferent throng of men, who had not the slightest inkling of what was passing in his mind. He sauntered through the hall till all had gone in to dinner; and then, giving up all hope of meeting Anatol, he did not go in to dinner, but went home.

Anatol, whom he was so anxious to find, dined that day with Dolokhof, and was discussing with him some plan of still carrying out their ill-fated enterprise. It seemed to him absolutely necessary to have an interview with Natasha. In the evening he went to his sister's, to arrange with her some means of procuring this interview.

When Pierre, who had vainly hunted all over Moscow, returned home, the footman informed him that Prince Anatol was with the countess. The countess' drawing-room was crowded with company.

Pierre, without greeting his wife, whom he had not seen since his return (never had she seemed to him more utterly detestable than at that moment), went into the drawing-room, and, catching sight of Anatol, went straight up to him.

"Ah, Pierre!" cried the countess, approaching her husband. "You don't know in what a position our Anatol . . ." She paused when she saw, in the forward thrust of her husband's head, in his flashing eyes and resolute manner, the same strange, terrible expression of frenzy and might which she had known and experienced after his duel with Dolokhof.

"Sin and lewdness are with you everywhere," said Pierre to his wife. "Anatol, come with me, I want a few words with you."

Anatol glanced at his sister and boldly rose, ready to follow Pierre. Pierre took him by the arm and hurried him out of the room.

"If you permit yourself in my salon to . . ." exclaimed Helene, in a whisper; but Pierre made no reply, and left the room. Anatol followed him with his usual jaunty gait, but there was a trace of anxiety on his face. When they reached Pierre's study, he shut the door, and addressed Anatol without looking at him.

"You promised to marry the Countess Rostof, and planned to elope with her?"

"My dear," replied Anatol in French, in which language indeed the whole conversation was carried on, "I consider myself under no obligation to answer questions asked in such a tone."

Pierre's face, white to begin with, was now distorted with rage. With his huge hand he seized Anatol by the collar of his uniform, and shook him from side to side until the young man's face expressed a sufficient degree of terror.

"When I tell you that I must have an answer from you?"

"Now, look here, this is stupid! Ha!" exclaimed Anatol, looking for a button that had been torn from his collar.

"You are a scoundrel and a blackguard, and I don't know what restrains me from the satisfaction of smashing your head with this," said Pierre, expressing himself with easy fluency because he spoke in French. He had taken into his hand a heavy paperweight, and he held it up menacingly, and then slowly laid it back in its place again.

"Did you promise to marry her?"

"I . . . I . . . I don't think so; besides, I couldn't have promised any such thing, be— because . . ."

Pierre interrupted him.

"Have you any of her letters?" he demanded, coming close to him.

Anatol gave him one look, and instantly put his hand into his pocket, and took out a wallet.

Pierre seized the letter Anatol handed to him, and violently pushing aside a chair that was in his way, he went to the couch and flung himself on it.

"I will not hurt you; have no fear," he said, in reply to Anatol's terrified gesture. "The letters . . . one thing," said Pierre, as if he were repeating a lesson for his own edification. "Secondly," he continued, after a moment's silence, getting to his feet again, and beginning to pace up and down the room, "you must leave Moscow tomorrow."

"But how can I?"

"Thirdly," pursued Pierre, not heeding him, "you must never breathe a word about what has taken place between you and the countess. This, I know, I cannot oblige you to do, but if you have a single spark of decency . . ."

Pierre walked in silence several times from one end of the room to the other. Anatol had sat down by the table, scowling and biting his lips.

"You must learn sometime that above and beyond your own pleasure the happiness and peace of others are to be considered, that you are ruining a whole life for the sake of having a little amusement. Trifle with women like my wife as much as you please—with such you have fair game; they know what you want of them. They are armed against you by their very experience in lust; but to promise a young girl to marry her . . . to deceive her . . . to rob her . . . why, don't you know that it is as cowardly as to strike an old man or a child?"

Pierre stopped speaking, and looked at Anatol inquiringly; his anger had vanished.

"I don't know, I'm sure," said Anatol, gaining confidence in proportion as Pierre's anger subsided. "I know nothing about it, and I don't want to know," said he, not looking at Pierre, while at the same time his lower jaw trembled slightly. "But you have spoken to me words so insulting that I as a man of honor cannot permit them."

Pierre looked at him in amazement, altogether unable to understand what was wanted of him.

"Though we have had no witnesses," continued Anatol, "still I cannot. . ."

"What! You wish satisfaction?" asked Pierre, scornfully.

"At least, you can retract what you said. Ha? That is, if you expect me to carry out your wishes. Ha?"

"I will! I'll take it back!" exclaimed Pierre. "And I beg you to forgive me." Pierre could not help looking at the torn button. "And money, if you need it for your journey."

Anatol smiled.

This contemptible, villainous smile, which he knew so well in his wife, stirred Pierre's indignation. "Oh! contemptible, heartless creatures!" he exclaimed, and left the room.

The next day Anatol started for Petersburg.

XV

PIERRE WENT to Marya Dmitrievna's to inform her how he had accomplished her wishes in regard to Anatol's expulsion from Moscow.

He found the whole house in terror and commotion. Natasha was very ill; and, as Marya Dmitrievna informed him, under seal of secrecy, the night after she had learned that Anatol Kuragin was married, she had poisoned herself with arsenic that she had managed surreptitiously to procure. Having swallowed a considerable quantity, she awakened Sonya and confessed what she had done. The proper antidotes to the poison had been given in time, and she was now out of danger, but she was still so weak that it was out of the question to think of taking her to the country, and the countess had been sent for. Pierre saw the troubled count and the weeping Sonya, but he was not allowed to see Natasha.

Pierre had that day dined at the club, and had heard on all sides gossip about the frustrated elopement; but he strenuously denied these rumors, assuring everyone that there was nothing in it, except that his brother-in-law had offered himself to Natasha and been refused. It seemed obvious to Pierre that it was his sacred duty to conceal the whole affair and save Natasha's reputation.

In the greatest anxiety he waited for Prince Andrei's return, and each day he went to the old prince's to inquire for news of him. Prince Nikolai had learned through Mlle. Bourienne of all this gossip flying through the city, and he read the letter to Princess Maria, in which Natasha broke off her engagement with Prince Andrei. He seemed in better spirits than usual, and with great impatience awaited his son's return. A few days after Anatol's departure, Pierre received a note from Prince Andrei announcing his arrival, and begging Pierre to come to see him.

When Prince Andrei arrived, his father immediately handed him Natasha's letter to his sister announcing the discontinuance of her engagement—this letter Mlle. Bourienne had purloined from the princess and given to the old prince—and told him, with elaborations, the various rumors current concerning the elopement.

Prince Andrei's arrival had been in the evening. Pierre went to see him the next morning. He expected to find him in almost the same state of mind as Natasha was, and, therefore, his amazement was great, when, on being shown into the drawing-room, he heard Prince Andrei, in the adjoining room, telling in a loud, animated manner of some Petersburg intrigue. He was occasionally interrupted by the old prince, and by a third person present.

Princess Maria came in to greet Pierre. She sighed as she turned her eyes toward the door of the room where her brother was, evidently anxious to give expression to her sympathy for his sorrow, but Pierre detected on her face evidences of her inward gratification at the turn affairs had taken, and at the manner in which her brother had received the news of Natasha's fickleness.

"He told me that he expected this," said she. "I know that his pride would not let him make any show of his feelings, but nevertheless he bears up under it better, far better, than I had any reason to expect. Of course, since it had to be so . . ."

"But do you mean to say it is all over between them?"

Princess Maria looked at him in amazement. She could not understand how anyone could even ask such a question.

Pierre went into the study. Prince Andrei, much altered, and apparently restored to perfect health, but with a new wrinkle between his brows, was standing, in civil dress, in front of his father and Prince Meshchersky, and was arguing eagerly, making energetic gestures.

"Well, how are you? Still stout!" he said in a lively tone, but the new frown on his brow grew still deeper. "Yes, I am well," he replied, in answer to Pierre's question, and laughed. Pierre saw clearly that this laugh was affected, and was simply equivalent to saying, "I am well, but who cares whether I am well?"

After exchanging a few words with Pierre in regard to the frightful road from the Polish frontier, and how he met in Switzerland a number of men who had known Pierre, and about Monsieur Dessalles, whom he had brought from abroad to be his son's tutor, Prince Andrei again, with feverish eagerness, returned to the conversation which the two men were still carrying on.

Pierre was aware that his friend was now laboring under that necessity, which he himself had only too often experienced, of getting thoroughly worked up and excited over some alien topic, simply for the purpose of dispelling thoughts too onerous to be endured.

When Prince Meshchersky had gone, Prince Andrei took Pierre's arm, and drew him into the room which had been prepared for him. In this room a bed had been hastily set up; trunks and boxes, opened, were scattered about. Prince Andrei went to one of these and took out a casket, and from the casket a packet wrapped in paper. All this he did silently and very swiftly. He straightened himself up and cleared his throat. His face was gloomy and his lips compressed.

"Forgive me if I trouble you . . ."

Pierre percieved that Prince Andrei was going to speak about Natasha, and his broad countenance expressed pity and sympathy. This expression on Pierre's face nettled Prince Andrei. He went on in a loud, decided, and disagreeable voice:

"I have received my dismissal from the Countess Rostof; and rumors have reached my ears that your brother-in-law offered himself to her, or something to that effect—is that true?"

"Whether true or false . . ." Pierre began, but Prince Andrei interrupted him.

"Here are her letters and her miniature."

He took the packet from the table and handed them to Pierre.

"Give this to the countess . . . if you happen to see her."

"She is very ill," said Pierre.

"So she is still here?" inquired Prince Andrei. "And Prince Kuragin?" he asked hastily.

"He left some time ago. She almost died . . ."

"I am very sorry for her illness," said Prince Andrei. He smiled coldly, evilly, disagreeably, like his father.

"But Prince Kuragin did not, then, honor the Countess Rostof with the offer of his hand?" asked Prince Andrei. He snorted several times.

"It is impossible for him to marry, for the reason that he is already married," said Pierre.

Prince Andrei gave a disagreeable laugh, again suggestive of his father.

"And where, pray, is your brother-in-law now to be found—may I ask?" said he.

"He has gone to Peters— However, I don't really know," said Pierre.

"Well, it's all the same to me," said Prince Andrei. "Assure the Countess Rostof that she has been, and is, perfectly free, and that I wish her all happiness."

Pierre took the package of letters. Prince Andrei, as if trying to make up his mind whether it was necessary for him to say something, or expecting Pierre to say something, looked at him keenly.

"Do you remember a discussion we once had in Petersburg? Do you remember . . ."

"Yes, I remember," said Prince Andrei, hurriedly. "I said that a fallen woman ought to be forgiven; but I did not say that in my own case I could forgive her. I cannot."

"But wherein is the comparison?" asked Pierre.

Prince Andrei interrupted him. His voice was loud and sharp.

"Yes, ask her hand again? Be magnanimous, and all that? Yes, that would be very noble, but I have no desire to follow in this gentleman's footsteps. . . . If you wish to continue my friend, never mention this to me again . . . not a word about it. Now, good-by. You will give that to her?"

Pierre left the room, and went to the old prince and Princess Maria.

The old prince seemed more animated than usual. Princess Maria was her ordinary self, but, back of her sympathy for her brother, Pierre could see that she was delighted at having the engagement broken. As Pierre looked at them, he realized how deep were the scorn and dislike they all felt for the Rostofs; he realized that it was quite hopeless even to mention

Natasha's name, though she might have had anyone else in the world in Prince Andrei's place.

At dinner the conversation turned on the war, which was unquestionably imminent. Prince Andrei kept up an unceasing stream of talk and discussion with his father, or with Monsieur Dessalles, his son's Swiss tutor, and he displayed more animation than usual; and Pierre knew only too well the true reason of this excitement.

XVI

THAT SAME EVENING Pierre went to call on the Rostofs to fulfil his commission.

Natasha was in bed, the count had gone to the club, and Pierre, having intrusted the letters into Sonya's hands, went to Marya Dmitrievna, who was greatly interested to know how Prince Andrei had received the news. Ten minutes later, Sonya appeared.

"Natasha is determined to see Count Bezukhof," said she.

"But how can he go to her room? Everything is in disorder there," said Marya Dmitrievna.

"But she is dressed, and has come down into the drawing-room," said Sonya.

Marya Dmitrievna merely shrugged her shoulders.

"If only the countess would come; this is a perfect torture to me. Now be careful, and don't tell her everything, Pierre," she added warningly. "It would break my heart if anything were said to hurt her; she is so to be pitied, so to be pitied!"

Natasha, grown decidedly thin, and with pale, set face—though not at all confused, as Pierre supposed she would be—stood in the middle of the drawing-room. When Pierre made his appearance in the door, she hesitated, evidently undecided whether to go to him or wait for him.

Pierre hastened forward. He supposed that she would, as usual, give him her hand. But she stood motionless, sighing deeply, and with her arms hanging lifelessly, in exactly the same pose that she always took when she went into the middle of the music room to sing, only with an entirely different expression.

"Count," she began, speaking very rapidly, "Prince Bolkonsky was your friend; and is still your friend," she added, as an afterthought; for it seemed to her that everything was past, and all things had changed. "He told me once to turn to you if . . ."

Pierre quietly blew his nose as he looked at her. Till that moment he had, in his heart, blamed her, and tried to despise her; but now she seemed to him so eminently deserving of pity, that there was no room in his heart for reproach.

"He is here now; please ask him to for— forgive . . ."

361

She paused, and breathed still faster, but she did not weep.

"Yes, I will tell him," said Pierre, "but . . ." He did not know what to say.

Natasha was evidently terrified by what Pierre might have thought she meant.

"Yes, I know all is over between us," said she, hurriedly. "No, it can never be. What tortures me is the wrong that I have done him. Only ask him to forgive, forgive, forgive me for all . . ."

Her whole frame trembled, and she sat down in a chair. Never before had Pierre experienced such a feeling of compassion as now came over him.

"I will tell him, I will certainly tell him all," said Pierre. "But . . . I would like to know one thing."

"What?" asked Natasha.

"I would like to ask if you loved . . ." Pierre did not know what term to use in speaking of Anatol, and reddened at the thought of him. "Did you love that vile man?"

"Don't call him vile," exclaimed Natasha. "But I . . . I don't know; I don't know at all." Then the tears came again. And a still more intense feeling of pity, affectionate compassion and love came over Pierre. He felt the tears welling out from under his spectacles and dropping, and he hoped they would not be noticed.

"Let us say no more about it, my dear," said Pierre.

Strange indeed suddenly seemed to Natasha the sound of his voice, so sweet, so tender, so sincere.

"Let us say no more about it, my dear, I will tell him all; but one thing I want to ask you: Consider me your friend, and if you need any help or advice, or simply if you need someone in whom you can confide—not now, but by and by, when everything is clear in your own mind, remember me." He took her hand and kissed it. "I will be happy if I am in the position to . . ."

Pierre grew confused.

"Don't speak to me so, I can't bear it!" cried Natasha, and she started to leave the room; but Pierre detained her by the hand. He knew that there was something more he must tell her. But when he had spoken it, he was amazed at his own words.

"Wait, wait! All the future is yours," said he.

"Mine! Only ruin is for me!" she exclaimed, in shame and self-reproach.

"Ruin!" he repeated. "If I were not myself, but the handsomest, wisest, and best man in the world, and were free, I would this very instant, on my knees, sue for your hand and your love."

Natasha, for the first time in many days, wept tears of gratitude and emotion; and, giving Pierre one look, she fled from the room. Pierre immediately afterwards almost ran out into the anteroom, and, restraining the tears of tenderness and happiness that choked him, he threw his cloak over his shoulders, but without putting his arms through the sleeves, and got into his sleigh.

"Where now?" asked the driver.

"Where?" repeated Pierre to himself. "Where can I go now? To the club, or to make some calls?"

All men, at this moment, seemed to him so contemptible, so mean, in comparison with the feeling of emotion and love that overmastered him—in comparison with that softened glance of gratitude which she had given him just now through her tears.

"Home," said Pierre, throwing back his bearskin cloak over his broad, joyfully throbbing chest, though the mercury marked ten degrees of frost.

It was cold and clear. Above the dirty, half-lighted streets, above the black roofs of the houses, stretched the dark, starry heavens. Only as Pierre gazed at the heavens above, he ceased to feel the humiliating pettiness of everything earthly in comparison with the height to which his soul aspired. As he drove out on the Argat Square, the mighty expanse of the dark, starry sky spread out before his eyes. Almost in the zenith of this sky—above the Pretchistensky Boulevard—convoyed and surrounded on every side by stars, but distinguished from all the rest by its nearness to the earth, and by its white light, and by its long, curling tail, stood the tremendous brilliant comet of 1812—the very comet that men thought presaged all manner of woes and the end of the world.

But in Pierre, this brilliant luminary, with its long train of light, awoke no terror. On the contrary, rapturously, his eyes wet with tears, he contemplated this glorious star which seemed to him to have come flying with inconceivable swiftness through measureless space, straight toward the earth, there to strike like an enormous arrow, and remain in that one predestined spot upon the dark sky; and, pausing, raise aloft with monstrous force its curling tail, flashing and sparkling with white light, amid the countless other twinkling stars. It seemed to Pierre that this star was the complete reply to all that was in his soul as it blossomed into new life, filled with tenderness and love.

1812

Growing ever bolder, the Tsar Alexander rejects the "Continental System," by which trade with England was forbidden; but, still fearful of Napoleon's power, tries to avoid war. It is too late; by the spring of 1812 Napoleon has advanced a huge army into the Duchy of War-saw. Confident of success in any cause of arms, and made more so by the signs of weakness revealed when the Tsar's government offers concession after concession to the French, Napoleon invades Russia late in June.

Part Ninth

TOWARD the end of the year 1811, a mobilization and concentration of forces began in Western Europe; and in 1812, these forces—millions of men, counting those who transported and fed them—were moved from west to east toward the borders of Russia, where the Russian forces were drawn up just as they had been the year before. On the twenty-fourth of June, the forces of Western Europe crossed the Russian frontier, and war began: In other words, an event took place opposed to human reason and human nature. Millions of men committed against one another a countless number of crimes, deceptions, treacheries, robberies, forgeries, issues of false money, depredations, incendiary fires, and murders, such as the annals of all the courts in all the world could not equal in the aggregate of centuries; and yet which, at that period, the perpetrators did not even regard as crimes. What brought about this extraordinary event? What were its causes?

The historians, with naive credulity, say that the causes are to be found in the affront offered to the Duke of Oldenburg, in the disregard of the Continental System, in Napoleon's ambition, Alexander's firmness, the mis-takes of diplomats, and so on.

Of course, in that case, to stop the war, Metternich, Rumyantsof, or Talleyrand, between a levee and a soirée, might merely have made a little effort and skilfully composed a state paper; or Napoleon might have written to Alexander: "Monsieur my brother, I consent to return the Duchy of Oldenburg to the duke."

It is easily understood that the matter presented itself in that light to the men of that day; but for us, posterity, who are far enough removed to contemplate the magnitude of the event from a wider perspective, and who seek to fathom its simple and terrible meaning, such reasons appear insufficient. To us it is incomprehensible that millions of Christian men killed and tortured each other because Napoleon was ambitious, Alexander firm, English policy astute, and the Duke of Oldenburg affronted.

If Napoleon had not been offended by the demand to retire his troops beyond the Vistula, and had not issued orders for them to give battle, there would have been no war; but if all the sergeants had refused to go into action, then also there would have been no war. And there would also have been no war if there had been no English intrigues, and no Prince Oldenburg; and if Alexander had not felt himself aggrieved; and if there had been no autocratic power in Russia; and if there had been no French Revolution, and no dictatorship and Empire following it; and nothing of all that led up to the Revolution, and so on. Had any one of these causes been missing, war could not have taken place. Consequently, all of them—billions of causes—must have coöperated to bring it about. And, as a corollary, there could have been no exclusive final cause for these events; and the great event was accomplished simply because it had to be accomplished.

Fatalism in history is unavoidable, if we would explain its preposterous phenomena (that is to say, those events for which the reason is beyond our comprehension). The more we strive by our reason to explain these phenomena in history, the more illogical and incomprehensible they become to us.

Every man has a twofold life: On one side is his personal life, which is free in proportion as its interests are abstract; the other is life as an element, as one bee in the swarm; and here a man has no chance of disregarding the laws imposed on him. The higher a man stands on the social ladder, the more men he is connected with, the greater the influence he exerts over others—the more evident is the predestined and unavoidable necessity of his every action.

The king is the slave of history. In the events of history, so-called great men are merely tags that supply a name to the event, and have quite as little connection with the event itself as the tag.

Every one of their actions, though apparently performed by their own free will, is, in its historical significance, out of the scope of volition, and is correlated with the whole trend of history; and is, consequently, preordained from all eternity.

On the tenth of June, Napoleon started from Dresden, where he had been for three weeks the center of a court composed of princes, dukes, kings, and at least one emperor.

Before his departure, Napoleon showed his favor to the princes, kings, and the emperor who deserved it; he turned a cold shoulder on the kings and princes who had incurred his displeasure; he gave the Empress of Austria pearls and diamonds which he called his own, though they had been stolen from other kings, and then tenderly embracing the *Empress* Maria Louisa, as the historian terms her, left her heartbroken by his absence, which seemed to her—now that she considered herself his consort, although he had another consort left behind in Paris—was too hard to be endured.

Although the diplomats stoutly maintained their belief in the possibility of peace and were working heartily for this end; although Napoleon himself wrote a letter to the Emperor Alexander, calling him monsieur my brother and sincerely assuring him that he had no desire for war, and that he would always love and respect him—still, he was off for the army, and at every station was issuing new orders to expedite the movement of the troops from west to east. He traveled in a calash drawn by six horses and accompanied by his pages, aides, and an escort, took the route through Posen, Thorn, Danzig, and Königsberg. The army was moving from the west to the east, and relays of fresh horses bore him in the same direction. On the twenty-second of June he overtook the army and spent the night in the Vilkovik forest on the estate of a Polish count, where quarters had been made ready for him.

On the following day, outstripping the army, he drove to the Niemen; and, for the purpose of reconnoitering the spot where the army was to cross, he put on a Polish uniform and went down to the banks of the river.

When he saw on the other side the Cossacks, and the wide-flung steppes, in the center of which was Moscow, the holy city, Napoleon unexpectedly gave orders for the advance, and on the next day the troops began to cross the Niemen.

Early on the morning of the twenty-fourth he emerged from his tent, which had been pitched on the steep left bank of the river, and looked through his field glass at the torrents of his troops pouring forth from the Vilkovik forest and streaming across the three bridges thrown over the Niemen. The troops were aware of the presence of the emperor; they searched for him with their eyes, and when they discovered him on the cliff, standing in front of his tent, and distinguished from his suite by his figure, in an overcoat and cocked hat, they threw their caps in the air and shouted, "Long live the emperor!" The faces of all bore one universal expression of delight at the beginning of the long-expected campaign, and of enthusiasm and devotion for the man in the gray overcoat standing on the hill.

On the twenty-fifth of June a small thoroughbred Arab steed was brought to Napoleon, and he mounted and set off at a gallop down to one of the bridges over the Niemen, greeted all the way by enthusiastic acclamations which he tolerated because it was impossible to prevent the men from expressing by these shouts their love for him. He rode across the bridge, which shook under his horse's hoofs, and on reaching the farther side turned abruptly to the left and galloped off in the direction of Kovno, preceded by his mounted guards. On reaching the broad river Vistula, he reined in his horse near a regiment of Polish Uhlans that was halted on the bank.

"Hurrah!" shouted the Poles enthusiastically, as they fell out of line, elbowing one another in their efforts to get a sight of him. Napoleon contemplated the river, then dismounted and sat down on a log which happened to be lying on the bank. At a mute signal, his telescope was handed him; he rested it on the shoulder of one of his pages who came forward beaming with delight, and he began to reconnoiter the other shore. Then he remained lost in study of a map spread out over the driftwood. Without lifting his head, he said something and two of his aides galloped off toward the Polish Uhlans.

The order was that they should find a ford and cross to the other side.

The Polish colonel who commanded the Uhlans, a handsome old man, flushing, and stumbling in his speech from excitement, asked the aide-de-camp whether he might be permitted to swim the river with his men, instead of trying to find the ford. He was evidently as apprehensive of receiving a refusal as a schoolboy who asks permission to ride on horseback; and what he craved was the chance to swim the river under his emperor's eyes.

The aide-de-camp replied that in all probability the emperor would not be displeased with this excess of zeal.

As soon as the aide-de-camp had said this, the old mustached officer, with beaming face and gleaming eyes, waved his sword and cried hurrah! And, ordering his Uhlans to follow him, he plunged spurs into his horse and dashed down to the river. The water was cold, and the swiftness of the current made the passage difficult. Hundreds of Uhlans galloped after him. The Uhlans clung to one another, in case they were dismounted from their horses. Several of the horses were drowned, and some of the men; others endeavored to swim, one clinging to his saddle, another to his horse's mane. Their endeavor was to swim to the farther side, and, although there was a ford only a few hundred yards below, they were proud of swimming and drowning in that river under the eye of a man who sat on the log and did not even notice what they were doing!

It was nothing new in his experience that his presence in any corner of the world, in the deserts of Africa as well as in the Muscovite steppes, was sufficient to stimulate and drive men into senseless self-sacrifice. He commanded a horse to be brought, and rode back to his bivouac.

Forty Uhlans were drowned in the river, although boats were sent to their aid. The majority gave up the task and returned to the side from which they had started. The colonel and a few of the men swam across the river, and with great difficulty crept up on the farther shore. But as soon as they were on the land, though their garments were streaming with water, they shouted hurrah! gazing with enthusiasm at the spot where Napoleon had been but from which he had vanished, and counting themselves fortunate.

In the afternoon, after making arrangements for procuring with all possible dispatch the counterfeit Russian money that had been prepared for use in Russia; and after issuing an order to shoot a certain Saxon, who, in a letter that had been intercepted, gave information in regard to the disposition of the French army; Napoleon, in still a third order, caused the Polish colonel who had quite needlessly flung himself into the river to be enrolled in the Legion of Honor, of which he himself was the head.

Quos vult perdere—dementat. (Whom God would destroy, he first makes mad.)

III

THE RUSSIAN EMPEROR, meantime, had now been for more than a month at Vilna, superintending reviews and maneuvers. Nothing was ready for the war, though all had foreseen that it was coming, and though the emperor had left Petersburg to prepare for it.

The longer the emperor stayed at Vilna, the less ready for the war were they who had grown weary of expecting it. The whole purpose of those who surrounded the sovereign seemed directed toward making him pass the time agreeably and forget about the impending conflict.

After a series of balls and festivities given by Polish magnates and by the emperor himself, one of the Polish adjutants general proposed in June that the imperial staff should give a banquet and ball in his majesty's honor. Count Benigsen, a landed proprietor of the Vilna government, tendered the use of his country house for the festivity.

On the very day when orders were given by Napoleon to cross the Niemen, and the vanguard of his army drove back the Cossacks and crossed the Russian frontier, Alexander was spending the evening at Count Benigsen's villa, at a ball given by his staff!

It was a gay, brilliant occasion. Connoisseurs in such matters declared that seldom had so many pretty women been gathered in one place. Countess Bezukhof, who with other Russian ladies had followed the sovereign from Petersburg to Vilna, was at this ball, her ample so-called Russian beauty quite putting into the shade the more refined and delicate Polish ladies. She attracted much attention, and the sovereign condescended to dance with her.

Boris Drubetskoy, having left his wife in Moscow, was also present at this ball, "as a bachelor"; and, although not an adjutant general, he was a participant in the festivities by virtue of having subscribed a large sum toward the expenses. Boris was now a rich man who had arrived at high honors and no longer required patronage, but stood on an equal footing with those of his own age, no matter how lofty their rank might be.

He met Helene at Vilna, not having seen her for some time; but he made no reference to the past. As Helene was "enjoying the favor" of a very influential individual, and Boris had not been long married, they met as good old friends.

At midnight they were still dancing. Helene, finding no partner to her taste, had herself proposed to Boris that they should dance the mazurka together. They were in the third set. Boris, with cool indifference glancing at Helene's dazzling bare shoulders, set off by a dark gauze dress shot with gold, was talking about old acquaintances; and, at the same time, neither she nor anyone else observed that not for a single second did he cease to watch the emperor, who was in the same hall. The emperor was not dancing; he was standing in the doorway, and addressing now to one and now to another those gracious words which he, of all men, alone had the art of speaking.

Just before the beginning of the mazurka, Boris noticed that Adjutant General Balashof, who stood on terms of special intimacy with the sovereign, approached him as he was talking with a Polish lady, and contrary to court etiquette stood waiting at a short distance from him. While still talking, the sovereign looked up inquiringly, and evidently perceiving that only weighty considerations would have caused Balashof to act thus, he gave the lady a slight bow and turned to Balashof.

At Balashof's very first words an expression like amazement came over the sovereign's face. He took Balashof's arm and crossed the ballroom with him, so absorbed that he did not notice how the company parted, making a sort of lane about seven yards wide through which he passed.

While Boris continued to perform the proper figures of the mazurka, he was continually tortured by the thought of what news Balashof had brought and how he might get hold of it before the others.

In the figure, when he had to choose a lady, he whispered to Helene that he wanted to get the Countess Potocka, who he believed had gone out on the balcony. Hastily crossing the parquet floor, he slipped out the open door into the garden; and there, perceiving the sovereign walking along the terrace in company with Balashof, he stepped to one side. The sovereign and Balashof were directing their steps toward the door. Boris, pretending that in spite of all his efforts he had not time to get out of the way, respectfully crowded up against the side of the door and bowed.

The sovereign, with the agitated face of a man personally offended, uttered these words:

"To make war against Russia without any declaration! I will never consent to peace so long as a single armed foe remains in my land!" It seemed to Boris tht the sovereign took a delight in uttering these words; he was satisfied with the form in which his thought was couched, but he was annoyed that Boris had overheard him. "Let not a word of this be known," he added, with a frown. Boris understood that this was a hint to him and, closing his eyes, he again bowed slightly. The sovereign returned to the ballroom and remained for about half an hour longer.

Boris was the first to learn the news that the French army had crossed the Niemen; and, turning his luck to good use, he made several important personages think that many things concealed from the others were known to him, and thereby succeeded in rising still higher in their estimation.

The next day, the following note was written to Napoleon:

> My Brother: I learned yesterday that, notwithstanding the fidelity with which I have adhered to my engagements toward your majesty, your troops have crossed the Russian frontier; and I have this moment received from Petersburg a note wherein Count Lauriston, in order to explain this aggression, announced that your majesty considered himself at war with me from the time that Prince Kurakin demanded his passports. . . . My ambassador was never authorized to take this step, as he himself explicitly declared; and, as soon as I was informed of it, I manifested the extent of my disapproval by ordering him to remain at his post. If your majesty is not obstinately bent upon shedding the blood of our peoples through a misunderstanding of this sort, and will consent to withdraw your troops from the Russian territory, I will regard what has passed as nonexistent, and we may arrive at some understanding. In the opposite case, your majesty, I shall be compelled to repulse an attack which I have done nothing to provoke. There is still a chance for your majesty to avoid the calamities of a new war.
>
> I am, etc.
> (Signed) Alexander.

IV

On the twenty-fifth of June at two o'clock in the morning, the sovereign, having summoned Balashof and read aloud his letter to Napoleon, ordered him to deliver it to the French emperor in person. In dispatching Balashof, the sovereign once more repeated what he had said about not making peace so long as a single armed foe remained on Russian soil, and he ordered him to quote these exact words to Napoleon. The sovereign did not incorporate this threat in his letter to Napoleon because his tact made him feel that they were inappropriate at a moment when last efforts were being made for reconciliation; but he strenuously commanded Balashof to repeat them to Napoleon verbally.

Balashof, accompanied by a bugler and two Cossacks, set off that very same night and by daybreak reached the village of Rykonty on the Russian side of the Niemen, where the French vanguard was stationed. He was brought to a halt by the French sentinels. A noncommissioned officer of hussars, in a crimson uniform and shaggy cap, challenged the approaching envoy and ordered him to halt. Balashof did not come instantly to a pause, but continued to advance at a footpace along the road.

The subaltern, scowling and muttering some abusive epithet, blocked Balashof's way with his horse and rudely shouted to the Russian general, asking if he were deaf, that he paid no attention to what was said to him. Balashof gave his name. The subaltern sent a soldier to the officer in command. Paying no further heed to Balashof, the noncommissioned officer began to talk with his comrades concerning their private affairs and did not even look at the Russian general.

It was an absolutely new experience for Balashof, accustomed to close proximity to the very fountainhead of power and might—having experienced, only three hours before, a personal conversation with his sovereign, and having been universally treated with respect—to find, here on Russian soil, this hostile and peculiarly disrespectful display of brutal insolence.

A French colonel of hussars, evidently just out of bed, came riding up from the village on a handsome, well-fed gray horse, accompanied by two hussars. The officer, the soldiers and their horses had an appearance of content and jauntiness.

The French colonel with difficulty overcame a fit of yawning, but he was courteous and evidently appreciated Balashof's high dignity. He conducted him past his soldiers inside the lines, and informed him that his desire to have a personal interview with the emperor would in all probability be immediately granted, since the imperial headquarters, he believed, were not far distant.

The sun had now risen, and was shining brightly on the vivid green of the fields. They had just passed a tavern on a hillside when they saw, coming up the hill to meet them, a little band of horsemen, in front of whom rode a tall man in a red cloak and a plumed hat, under which dark locks fell to his shoulders. He bestrode a coal-black horse whose trappings glittered in the sun, and his long legs were thrust forward in the fashion affected by French riders. This man came at a gallop toward Balashof, his plumes and gems and gold lace flashing in the bright June sun. Iulner, the French colonel, said in a deferential whisper, "The King of Naples."

This was indeed Murat, who was still called the King of Naples. Although it was wholly incomprehensible in what respect he was the King of Naples, still he bore that title; and he himself was convinced of its validity, and consequently assumed a more majestic and important aspect than ever before. But, though he firmly believed that he was King of Naples, and was grieved for the sorrow his faithful subjects must suffer in losing him, still when he was commanded to enter the military service again, and especially since his meeting with Napoleon at Danzig, when his august brother-in-law had said to him, "I made you king to reign in my way, not in yours," he had cheerfully taken up the business which he understood so well, and, like a carriage horse, driven but not overworked, feeling himself in harness, he was frisky even between the shafts and, decked out in the most gorgeous and costly manner possible, he galloped gaily and contentedly along the Polish highway, not knowing whither or wherefore.

As soon as he approached the Russian general he threw his head back in royal fashion, and solemnly, with his black curls flowing down over his shoulders, looked inquiringly at the French colonel. The colonel respectfully explained to his majesty Balashof's errand, though he could not pronounce his name.

"De Bal-ma-chève," said the king, his self-confidence helping him to overcome the difficulty that had floored the colonel. "Charmed to make your acquaintance, general," he added, with a royally gracious gesture.

The moment the king began to speak loud and rapidly all the kingly dignity instantly deserted him and, without his suspecting such a thing himself, changed into a tone of good-natured familiarity. He laid his hand on the withers of Balashof's horse.

"Well, general, everything looks like war, it seems," said he, as if he regretted a state of things concerning which he was in no position to judge.

"Sire," replied Balashof, "the emperor, my sovereign, has no desire for war, and, as your majesty sees," said Balashof, and thus he went on, with unavoidable affectation, repeating the title "your majesty" at every opportunity.

Murat's face glowed with stupid satisfaction while he listened to Monsieur de Balashof. But *royauté oblige;* and he felt that it was indispensable for him, as king and ally, to converse with Alexander's envoy, on matters of state. He dismounted, and taking Balashof's arm and drawing him a few paces aside, he began to walk up and down with him, trying to speak with great authority. He informed him that the Emperor Napoleon was offended by the demand made upon him to withdraw his forces from Prussia; especially as this demand was made publicly, and therefore was an insult to the dignity of France.

Balashof said that there was nothing insulting in this demand, "Because—"

Murat interrupted him.

"So then you do not consider the Emperor Alexander as the instigator of the war?" he asked suddenly, with a good-naturedly foolish smile.

Balashof explained why he really supposed that Napoleon was the aggressor.

"Ah, my dear general," again exclaimed Murat, interrupting him, "I desire, with all my heart, that the emperors should come to a mutual understanding, and that the war, begun in spite of me, should be brought to a termination as soon as possible," said he, in the tone of servants who wish to remain good friends, though their masters may quarrel. And he proceeded to make inquiries about the grand duke and the state of his health, and recalled the good times they had enjoyed together at Naples. Then suddenly, as if remembering his kingly dignity, Murat drew himself up haughtily, struck the same attitude in which he had stood during his coronation, and, waving his right hand, said: "I will not detain you longer, general; I wish you all success in your mission"; and then, with his embroidered red mantle and plumes fluttering, and his precious trinkets glittering in the sun, he rejoined his suite, which had been respectfully waiting for him.

Balashof went on his way, expecting, from what Murat said, to be very speedily presented to Napoleon himself. But instead of any such speedy meeting with Napoleon, the sentinels of Davoust's infantry corps detained him again at the next village—just as he had been halted at the outposts—until an aide of the corps commander, who was sent for, conducted him to Marshal Davoust in the village.

Davoust was the Emperor Napoleon's Arakcheyef—Arakcheyef except in cowardice: just as punctilious and cruel, and aware of no other way of manifesting his devotion than by cruelty.

In the mechanism of state, such men are necessary, just as wolves are necessary in the plan of nature; and they always exist and manifest themselves and maintain themselves, however incompatible their presence and proximity to the chief power may seem. Only this indispensability can explain how Arakcheyef—a cruel man, who personally pulled out the mustaches of grenadiers, and who because of weak nerves could not endure any danger, and was ill-bred and ungentlemanly—could maintain power and influence over a character so chivalrous, noble, and affectionate as Alexander's.

In the barn attached to a peasant's cottage, Balashof found Marshal Davoust, sitting on a keg and busily engaged in clerk's business (he was verifying accounts). An aide stood near him. He might have found better accommodations; but Marshal Davoust was one of those men who purposely made the conditions of life as disagreeable as possible for themselves, in order to have an excuse for being themselves disagreeable. He buried himself more deeply than ever in his work when the Russian general appeared. He glanced over his spectacles at Balashof's face, which was still glowing under the impression of the beautiful morning and the meeting with Murat, but he did not get up or even stir. He put on a still more portentous frown, and smiled sardonically.

Noticing the impression produced on Balashof by this reception, Davoust raised his head and chillingly demanded what he wanted.

Supposing that this insulting reception was given him because Davoust did not know that he was the Emperor Alexander's adjutant-general and what was more, his envoy to Napoleon, Balashof hastened to inform him of his name and mission. Contrary to his expectation, Davoust, after listening to Balashof's communication, became still more gruff and rude.

"Where is the letter?" he demanded. "Give it to me; I will send it to the emperor."

Balashof replied that he was ordered to give the package personally to the emperor.

"Your emperor's orders are carried out in your army; but here," said Davoust, "you must do as you are told."

Balashof took out the envelope containing the sovereign's note and laid it on the table—a table improvised of a door, with the torn hinges still protruding, laid on a couple of barrels. Davoust took the envelope and read the superscription.

"You have a perfect right to treat me with respect or not to treat me with respect," said Balashof. "But permit me to remark that I have the honor of being one of his majesty's aides."

Davoust gazed at him without saying a word; but a trace of annoyance and confusion betrayed in Balashof's face evidently afforded him gratification.

"All due respect will be shown you," said he; and, placing the envelope in his pocket, he left the barn.

A moment later the marshal's aide, Monsieur de Castrier, made his appearance and conducted Balashof to the lodgings made ready for him; Balashof dined that same day with the marshal, in the barn, the boards on the barrels serving as the table. Early in the morning of the following day Davoust came and, taking Balashof to one side, told him confidentially that he was requested to stay where he was; though if the baggage train received orders to advance, he was to advance with it, and not to communicate with anyone except with Monsieur de Castrier.

At the end of four days of solitude, of tedium, of consciousness of his helplessness and insignificance all the more palpable after the environment of power to which he had so recently been accustomed, after a number of transfers with the marshal's baggage and the French forces which occupied the whole region, Balashof was brought back to Vilna, now in possession of the French.

Napoleon received Balashof in the same house in Vilna from which Alexander had dispatched him.

V

THOUGH BALASHOF was accustomed to court magnificence, the sumptuousness and display of Napoleon's court surprised him. Count Turenne conducted him into the great drawing-room, where a throng of generals, chamberlains and Polish magnates, many of whom Balashof had seen at court during the sojourn of the Russian emperor, were in waiting. Duroc told the Russian general that the Emperor Napoleon would receive him before going out to ride.

At the end of some moments of expectation, the chamberlain on duty came into the great drawing-room, and, bowing courteously, invited Balashof to follow him.

Balshof passed into a small reception room which opened into the study —into the very same study where the Russian emperor had given his directions. Balashof stood two minutes waiting. Then quick steps were heard in the other room. The folding doors were hastily flung open. All was silent, and then firm, resolute steps were heard coming from the study; it was Napoleon. He had only just finished dressing for riding. He was in a blue uniform coat thrown open over a white waistcoat which covered the rotundity of his abdomen; he wore white chamois-skin breeches that fitted tightly over the stout thighs of his short legs, and Hessian boots. His short hair had evidently only just been brushed, but one lock of hair hung down over the center of his broad brow. His white, puffy neck was in sharp contrast with the dark collar of his uniform coat; he exhaled a strong odor of eau de Cologne. On his plump and youthful-looking face with its prominent chin was an expression of gracious, imperially majestic condescension.

He came in, giving little quick jerks as he walked along, and holding his head rather high. His whole figure, thickset and short, with his broad, stout shoulders and with the abdomen and breast involuntarily thrust forward, had that portly, stately carriage which men of forty who have lived in comfort are apt to have. Moreover, it was evident that on this particular day he was in excellent spirits.

He inclined his head in response to Balashof's low and respectful bow; and, approaching him, began immediately to speak like a man who values every moment of his time and does not condescend to make set speeches, but is convinced in his own mind that he always speaks well and to the point.

"How are you, general?" said he. "I have received the Emperor Alexander's letter which you brought, and I am very glad to see you."

He scrutinized Balashof's face with his large eyes and then immediately looked past him. It was evident that Balashof's personality did not interest him in the least. It was evident that only what came into his own mind had any interest for him. Everything outside of him had no consequence because, as it seemed to him, everything in the world depended on his will alone.

"I do not desire war, and I have not desired it," said he. "But I have been driven to it. Even now"—he laid a strong stress on the word—"I am ready to accept any explanation you can offer."

And he began clearly and explicitly to state the grounds for his dissatisfaction with the Russian government. Judging by the calm, moderate, and even friendly tone in which the French emperor spoke, Balashof was firmly convinced that he was anxious for peace and intended to enter into negotiations.

"Sire, the emperor my master—"

Balashof began his long-prepared speech when Napoleon, having finished what he had to say, looked inquringly at the Russian envoy; but the look in the emperor's eyes, fastened on him, confused him. *You are confused—regain your self-possession,* Napoleon seemed to say as he glanced with a hardly perceptible smile at Balashof's uniform and sword.

Having said all that he had been empowered to say, Balashof declared that the Emperor Alexander desired peace, but that he would not enter into negotiations except on condition that—here Balashof stopped short. He recollected the words that the Emperor Alexander had not incorporated in the letter but had strenuously insisted should be inserted in the order to Saltuikof and had commanded Balashof to repeat to Napoleon. Balashof remembered these words, "so long as an armed foe remains on Russian soil," but some complicated feeling restrained him. He found it impossible to repeat the words, in spite of his desire to do so.

He hesitated, and said, "On condition that the French troops retire beyond the Niemen."

Napoleon remarked Balashof's confusion as he said those last words. His face twitched; the calf of his left leg began to tremble nervously. Not stirring from the place where he was standing, he began to speak in a higher key and more rapidly than before.

"I desire peace no less than the Emperor Alexander," said he. "Have I not for eighteen months done everything to preserve it? I have been waiting eighteen months for an explanation. But what is demanded of me before negotiations can begin?" he asked, with a frown, and emphasizing his question with an energetic gesture of his little, white, plump hand.

"The withdrawal of the troops beyond the Niemen, sire," replied Balashof.

"Beyond the Niemen," repeated Napoleon. "So that is all that is wanted now, is it?—'beyond the Niemen,' merely beyond the Niemen," insisted Napoleon, looking straight at Balashof.

Balashof respectfully inclined his head.

"Four months ago the demand was to evacuate Pomerania, but now all that is required is to retire beyond the Niemen." Napoleon abruptly turned away and began to pace up and down the room. "You say that it is demanded of me to retire beyond the Niemen before there can be any attempt at negotiations; but in exactly the same way two months ago all that was required of me was to retire beyond the Oder and the Vistula, and yet you can still think of negotiating?"

He walked in silence from one corner of the room to the other, and then stopped in front of Balashof. Balashof noticed that his left leg trembled even faster than before, and his face seemed petrified in its sternness of expression. This trembling of his left calf Napoleon himself was aware of. He afterwards said, "The vibration of my left calf is a significant omen with me."

"Any propositions to abandon the Oder or the Vistula may be made to

376

the Prince of Baden, but not to me," Napoleon almost screamed, the words seeming to take him by surprise. "If you were to give me Petersburg and Moscow, I would not accept such conditions. You have said that I began this war. But who went to his army first? The Emperor Alexander, and not I. And you propose negotiations when I have spent millions, when you have made an alliance with England, and when your position is critical—you now offer to negotiate with me! But what is the object of your alliance with England? What has she given you?" he asked hurriedly, evidently now making no effort to show the advantages of concluding peace and discussing the possibility of it, but only to prove his own probity and power and Alexander's mistakes and blundering statecraft.

His first remarks were evidently intended to show the advantage of his position and to prove that, nevertheless, he would be willing to have negotiations opened again. But he was now fairly launched in his declaration, and the longer he spoke the less able he was to control the current of his discourse. The whole aim of his words now seemed to exalt himself and to humiliate Alexander, which was precisely what he least of all wished to do at the beginning of the interview.

"It is said you have concluded peace with the Turks?"

Balashof bent his head affirmatively. "Peace has been dec—" he began; but Napoleon gave him no chance to speak. It was plain that he wished to have the floor to himself, and he went on talking with that eloquence and unrestrained irritablity to which men who have been spoiled are so prone.

"Yes, I know that you have concluded peace with the Turks, and without securing Moldavia and Valakhia. But I would have given your sovereign these provinces, just as I gave him Finland! Yes," he went on to say, "I promised the Emperor Alexander the provinces of Moldavia and Valakhia, and I would have given them to him; but now he will not have those beautiful provinces. He could have annexed them, and in his reign alone he would have made Russia spread from the Gulf of Bothnia to the mouths of the Danube. Catherine the Great could not have done more," exclaimed Napoleon, growing more and more excited as he strode up and down the room, and repeating to Balashof almost the same words he had said to Alexander himself at Tilsit. "All this my friendship could have brought him! Oh, what a glorious reign! What a glorious reign!" he repeated several times. He paused and took out a gold snuffbox, and greedily sniffed at it. "What a glorious reign the Emperor Alexander's *might* have been!"

He gave Balashof a compassionate look, but as soon as the general started to make some remark, Napoleon hastened to interrupt him again.

"What could he have wished or sought for that he would not have secured through my friendship?" Napoleon asked, shrugging his shoulders in perplexity. "No; he preferred to surround himself with my enemies, and what enemies!" pursued Napoleon. "He has attached to himself Steins, Armfeldts, Benigsens, Winzengerodes! Stein, a traitor banished from his own country;

Armfeldt, a scoundrel and intriguer; Winzengerode, a fugitive French subject; Benigsen, a rather better soldier than the others, but still incapable, who had no idea how to act in 1807 . . . and what sort of part is your young sovereign playing in this abominable throng? They are compromising him and making him responsible for everything that takes place. A sovereign has no right to be with his army unless he is a general," said he, evidently intending these words to be taken as a direct challenge to the Russian emperor. Napoleon was well aware how desirous the Emperor Alexander was to be a military commander.

"The campaign is not a week old, and you could not defend Vilna. You are cut in two and driven out of the Polish provinces. Your army is already grumbling."

"On the contrary, your majesty," said Balashof, scarcely remembering what had been said to him, and finding it hard to follow this pyrotechnic of words, "the troops are full of zeal."

"I know all about it," said Napoleon, interrupting him. "I know the whole story; and I know the contingent of your battalions as well as I know my own. You have not two hundred thousand men; and I have three times as many. I give you my word of honor," said Napoleon, forgetting that his word of honor carried very little weight, "I give you my word of honor that I have five hundred and thirty thousand men on this side of the Vistula. The Turks will be no help to you; they are never of any use; and they have proved this by making peace with you. The Swedes—it is their fate to be ruled by madmen. Their king was crazy; they got rid of him, and chose another, Bernadotte, who instantly lost his wits; because it is sure proof of madness if a Swede enters into alliance with Russia."

Napoleon uttered this with a vicious sneer, and again carried the snuff-box to his nose.

To each of Napoleon's propositions Balashof was ready and willing to give an answer; he kept making the gestures of a man who had something to say; but Napoleon gave him no chance to speak.

"But what do I care for your allies?" demanded Napoleon. "I too have allies—these Poles, eighty thousand of them; they fight like lions, and there will be two hundred thousand of them."

And, probably still more excited by the fact that in making this statement he was uttering a palpable falsehood, and by Balashof standing there in silent submission to his fate, he abruptly turned back, came close to Balashof, and making rapid and energetic gestures with his white hands, he almost screamed:

"Understand! If you incite Prussia against me, I assure you, I will wipe her off the map of Europe," said he, his face pale and distorted with rage, and energetically striking one white hand against the other. "Yes, and I will drive you beyond the Dvina and the Dnieper; and I will again set up against you that barrier which Europe was stupid and blind enough to permit to be overthrown. That is what will become of you, that is what you

378

will have lost in alienating me," said he, and once more paced the room in silence a number of times, jerking his stout shoulders.

He replaced his snuffbox in his waistcoat pocket, took it out again, carried it to his nose several times, and halted directly in front of Balashof. He stood thus without speaking, and gazed directly into Balashof's eyes with a mocking expression; then he said, in a low tone:

"What a glorious reign your master *might* have had!"

Balashof, finding it imperative to make some answer, declared that affairs did not present themselves to the eyes of the Russians in so gloomy a light. Napoleon said nothing, but continued to look at him with the same mocking expression, and apparently had not heard what he said. Balashof declared that in Russia the highest hopes were entertained of the issue of the war. Napoleon nodded condescendingly, as much as to say, *I know it is your duty to say so, but you do not believe it; my arguments have convinced you.*

When Balashof had ended his speech, Napoleon once more raised his snuffbox, took a sniff from it, and then stamped twice on the floor as a signal. The door was flung open; a chamberlain, respectfully approaching, handed the emperor his hat and gloves; another brought him his handkerchief. Napoleon, not even looking at him, addressed Balashof:

"Assure the Emperor Alexander, in my name," said he, as he took his hat, "that I esteem him as warmly as before, I know him thoroughly, and I highly appreciate his lofty qualities. I will not detain you longer, general; you will receive my letter to the emperor."

And Napoleon swiftly disappeared through the door. All in the reception room hurried forward and down the stairs.

After all that Napoleon had said to him, after those explosions of wrath, and after those last words spoken so coldly, "I will not detain you longer, general; you will receive my letter to the emperor," Balashof was convinced that Napoleon not only would have no further desire to see him, but would rather avoid seeing him, a humiliated envoy, and, what was more, a witness of his undignified heat. But, to his amazement, he received through Duroc an invitation to dine that day with the emperor.

At dinner, Napoleon had Balashof seated next to himself, and treated him not only cordially, but even as if he considered him one of his own courtiers, one of those who sympathized with his plans and rejoiced in his successes. Among other topics of conversation he brought up Moscow, and began to ask Balashof about the Russian capital, not merely as an inquisitive traveler asks about a new place which he has in mind to visit, but as if he was convinced that Balashof, as a Russian, must be flattered by his curiosity.

"How many inhabitants are there in Moscow? How many houses? Is it a fact that Moscow is called 'Holy Moscow'? How many churches are there in Moscow?" he asked.

And when told that there were upward of two hundred, he asked:

"What is the good of such a flock of churches?"

"The Russians are very religious," replied Balashof.

"Nevertheless, a great number of monasteries and churches is always a sign that a people are backward," said Napoleon.

Balashof respectfully begged leave to differ from the French emperor's opinion. "Every country has its own customs," said he.

"But nowhere else in Europe is there anything like it," remarked Napoleon.

"I beg your majesty's pardon," replied Balashof. "In Spain as well as in Russia there are many monasteries and churches."

This reply of Balashof's, which hinted at the recent defeat of the French in Spain, was highly appreciated when Balashof repeated it at the Emperor Alexander's court; but it was very little appreciated at Napoleon's table, and passed unnoticed.

There is a familiar state of mind that comes over a man after dinner and, acting with greater force than all the dictates of mere reason, compels him to be satisfied with himself and to consider all men his friends. Napoleon was now in this comfortable mental condition. It seemed to him that he was surrounded by men who adored him. He was persuaded that even Balashof, after having eaten dinner with him, was his friend and worshiper. Napoleon addressed him with a pleasant and slightly satirical smile:

"This is the very room, I am informed, that the Emperor Alexander used. Strange, isn't it, general?" he asked, evidently not having any idea that such a remark could fail to be agreeable to his guest, as it insinuated that he, Napoleon, was superior to Alexander.

Balashof bowed and signified that he was anxious to withdraw, and that he listened simply because he could not help listening to what Napoleon said. But Napoleon paid no heed to this gesture; he addressed Balashof not as his enemy's envoy, but as a man who was for the time being entirely devoted to him and must needs rejoice in the humiliation of his former master.

"And why has the Emperor Alexander assumed the command of his forces? What is the reason of it? War is my trade, and his is to rule and not to command armies. Why has he taken upon him such responsibilities?"

Napoleon again took his snuffbox, silently strode several times from one end of the room to the other, and then suddenly and unexpectedly went straight up to Balashof, and with a slight smile he unhesitatingly, swiftly, simply—as if he were doing something not only important, but even rather agreeable to Balashof—put his hand into the Russian general's face and, taking hold of his ear, gave it a little pull, the smile being on his lips alone.

To have one's ear pulled by the emperor was considered the greatest honor and favor at the French court.

"Well, have you nothing to say, admirer and courtier of the Emperor Alexander?" asked Napoleon, as if it were an absurdity in his presence to be courtier and admirer of anyone except himself. "Are the horses ready for the general?" he added, slightly bending his head in answer to Balashof's bow. "Give him mine, he has far to go."

The letter intrusted to Balashof was the last that Napoleon ever wrote to Alexander. All the particulars of the interview were communicated to the Russian emperor, and the war began.

VI

AFTER HIS INTERVIEW with Pierre, Prince Andrei went to Petersburg on business, as he told his relatives, but in reality to find Prince Anatol Kuragin there, since he considered it his duty to fight him. But Kuragin, about whom he inquired as soon as he reached Petersburg, was no longer there. Pierre had sent word to his brother-in-law that Prince Andrei was in search of him. Anatol Kuragin had immediately secured an appointment from the minister of war and gone to the Moldavian army.

During this visit to Petersburg, Prince Andrei met Kutuzof, his former general, who was always well disposed to him, and Kutuzof proposed that he should go with him to the Moldavian army, of which the old general had been appointed commander-in-chief. Prince Andrei, having thereupon received his appointment as one of the commander's staff, started for Turkey.

Prince Andrei felt that it would not be becoming to write Kuragin and challenge him. Having no new pretext for a duel, he felt that a challenge from him would compromise Natasha, and therefore he sought for a personal interview with Kuragin, when he hoped he would be able to invent some new pretext for the duel. But in Turkey, too, he failed to meet Kuragin, who had returned to Russia as soon as he learned of Prince Andrei's arrival.

In a new country and under new conditions life began to seem easier to Prince Andrei. After the faithlessness of his betrothed, which had affected him all the more seriously because of his endeavor to conceal the grief it had caused him, the conditions of life in which he had found so much happiness had grown painful to him, and still more painful the very freedom and independence that he had so prized in the past. He now concerned himself solely with the narrowest and most practical interests, entirely disconnected with the past.

Of all the activities that offered themselves to his choice, the military service was the simplest and best known to him.

When in 1812 the news of the war with Napoleon reached Bucharest —where for two months Kutuzof had been living, spending his days and nights with his Wallachian mistress—Prince Andrei asked his permission to be transferred to the western army. Kutuzof, already weary of Bolkonsky's activity, which was a constant reproach to his own indolence, willingly granted the request and gave him a commission to Barclay de Tolly.

Before joining the army, which during the month of May was encamped at Drissa, Prince Andrei drove to Lisiya Gori, which was directly in his route, being only two miles from the Smolensk highway.

During the last three years of Prince Andrei's life there had been so many changes—he had thought so much, felt so much, seen so much, for he had traveled through both the East and the West—that he felt a sense of strangeness, of unexpected amazement, to find at Lisiya Gori the same old manner of life, even to the smallest details. As he entered the driveway and passed the stone gates that guarded his paternal home, it seemed as if it were an enchanted castle where everything was fast asleep. The same sobriety, the same neatness, the same quietude, reigned in the house; the same furniture, the same walls, the same sounds, the same odor, and the same timid faces, only grown a little older.

Princess Maria was the same timid, plain person, only grown into an old maid and living out the best years of her life in fear and eternal moral sufferings, without profit and without happiness. Bourienne was the same coquettish, self-satisfied creature, cheerfully getting profit out of every moment of her life, and consoling herself with the most exuberant hopes; only it seemed to Prince Andrei that she showed an increased self-assurance.

The tutor, Dessalles, whom Prince Andrei had brought from Switzerland, wore an overcoat of Russian cut; his unmanageable tongue involved itself in Russian speech with the servants, but otherwise he was the same pious and pedantic tutor of somewhat limited intelligence.

The only physical change in the old prince was a gap left in one corner of his mouth, caused by the loss of a tooth; in character, he was just the same as before, except for an accentuation of his ugly temper and his distrust in the genuineness of everything happening in the world.

Nikolusha, with his rosy cheeks and dark, curly hair, had been the one person to grow and change; and when he laughed and was merry he unconsciously lifted the upper lip of his pretty little mouth, just as the lamented princess, his mother, had done. He alone refused to obey the laws of immutability in this enchanted, sleeping castle.

But though externally everything remained as it had always been, the internal relations of all these people had altered since Prince Andrei had seen them. The members of the household were divided into two alien and hostile camps which made common cause now simply because he was there—for his sake changing the ordinary course of their lives. To the one party belonged the old prince, Bourienne, and the architect, to the other, Princess Maria, Dessalles, Nikolusha, and all the women of the establishment.

During his brief stay at Lisiya Gori, all the family dined together; but it was awkward for them all, and Prince Andrei felt that he was a guest for whose sake an exception was made, and that his presence was a constraint on them. At dinner the first day, Prince Andrei, instinctively feeling this, was taciturn; and the old prince, remarking the unnaturalness of his behavior, also relapsed into a moody silence and retired to his room immediately after dinner. When, later, Prince Andrei joined him there and, with the idea of entertaining him, began to tell him about the young Count Kamiensky's campaign, the old prince unexpectedly broke into a tirade against Princess Maria, blaming her for her superstition and for her dislike of Mlle. Bourienne, who, according to him, was the only person truly devoted to him.

The old prince attributed his feeble health entirely to Princess Maria, insisting that she continually annoyed and exasperated him; and that by her injudicious coddling and foolish talk she was spoiling the little Prince Nikolusha. The old prince was perfectly well aware that it was he who tormented his daughter and made her life exceedingly trying; but he was also convinced that he could not help tormenting her, and that she deserved it.

"Why does not Prince Andrei, who sees how things are, say anything to me about his sister?" wondered the old prince. "He thinks, I suppose, that I am a wicked monster, or an old idiot, who has unreasonably estranged himself from his daughter and taken a Frenchwoman in her place. He does not understand; and so I must explain to him, and he must listen to me," thought the old prince. And he began to expound the reasons that made it impossible to endure his daughter's absurd character.

"Since you ask my opinion," said Prince Andrei, not looking at his father —for he was condemning him for the first time in his life—"though I did not wish to talk about it; since you ask me, however, I will tell you frankly my opinion. If there is any misunderstanding and discord between you and Maria, I could never blame her for it, for I know how she loves and reveres you. And if you ask me further," pursued Prince Andrei, giving way to his irritation because of late he had become exceedingly prone to fits of irritation, "then I have one thing to say: If there is any such misunderstanding, the cause of it is that vulgar woman, who is unworthy to be my sister's companion."

The old man at first gazed at his son with staring eyes, and, by his forced smile, uncovered the new gap caused by the loss of the tooth, to which Prince Andrei could not accustom himself.

"What companion, my dear? Ha! Have you already been talking that over? Ha!"

"My dear father, I do not wish to judge you," said Prince Andrei, in a sharp and angry voice; "but you have driven me to it; and I have said, and always shall say, that Princess Maria is not to blame, the little Frenchwoman is to blame."

"Ha! you condemn me! you condemn me!" cried the old man, in a subdued voice, and with what seemed confusion to Prince Andrei; but then suddenly he sprang up, and screamed:

"Away! away with you! Don't dare to come here again!"

Prince Andrei intended to take his departure immediately; but Princess Maria begged him to stay another day. He did not meet his father that day; the old prince stayed in his room and admitted no one except Mlle. Bourienne and Tikhon; but he inquired several times whether his son had yet gone.

On the following day, just before dinner, Prince Andrei went to his little son's apartment. The blooming lad, with his curly hair just like his mother's, sat on his knee. Prince Andrei began to tell him the story of Bluebeard; but right in the midst of it he lost the thread and fell into a brown study. He did not give a thought to this pretty little lad, his son, while he held him on his knee, but he was thinking about himself. With a sense of horror, he sought and failed to find any remorse in the fact that he had exasperated his father, or any regret that he was about to leave him—after the first quarrel they had ever had. More serious than all else was his discovery that he did not feel the affection for his son which he hoped to arouse, as of old, by caressing the lad and taking him on his knee. "Well, go on, papa!" said the boy.

Prince Andrei, without responding, set him down from his knees and left the room. The moment Prince Andrei suspended his daily occupations, and especially the moment he encountered the former conditions of his life, in which he had been engaged in the old, happy days, the anguish of life took possession of him with fresh force; and he made all haste to leave the scene of these recollections and to find occupation as soon as possible.

"Are you really going, Andrei?" asked his sister.

"Thank God I can go," replied Prince Andrei. "I am very sorry that you cannot also."

"What makes you say that?" exclaimed his sister. "Why do you say that, now that you are going to this terrible war? and he is so old! Mlle. Bourienne told me that he had asked about you."

As soon as she recalled this subject, her lips trembled, and the tears rained down her cheeks. Prince Andrei turned away and began to pace up and down the room.

"Oh! my God! my God!" he cried. "And how can you believe that any-one—that such a contemptible creature can bring unhappiness to others!" he exclaimed, with such an outburst of anger that it frightened Princess Maria. She understood that in speaking of "such contemptible creatures" he had reference not alone to Mlle. Bourienne, who had caused him misery, but also to that man who had destroyed his happiness.

"Andrei! one thing I want to ask you; I beg of you," said she, lightly touching his elbow and gazing at him with her eyes shining through her tears. "I understand you." Princess Maria dropped her eyes. "Do not think that sorrow is caused by men. Men are His instruments." She gazed somewhat above her brother's head, with that confident look that people have who are accustomed to look at the place where they know a portrait hangs. "Sorrow is sent by Him, and comes not from men. Men are His instruments; they are not accountable. If it seems to you that anyone is culpable toward you, forget it and forgive. We have no right to punish. And you will find happiness in forgiving."

"If I were a woman I would, Maria! Forgiveness is a woman's virtue. But a man has no right and no power to forgive and forget," said he, and although he was not at that instant thinking of Kuragin, all his unsatisfied vengeance suddenly surged up in his heart. "If Princess Maria at this late day urges me to forgive, it is proof positive that I ought long ago to have punished," he said to himself. And not stopping to argue with his sister, he began to dream of the joyful moment of revenge when he would meet Kuragin, who (as he knew) had gone to the army.

Princess Maria urged her brother to delay his journey yet another day, assuring him how unhappy her father would be if Andrei went off without a reconciliation with him; but Prince Andrei replied that in all probability he would soon return from the army, that he would certainly write to his father, and that now the longer he stayed the more bitter this quarrel would become.

"Adieu, Andrei! remember that sorrows come from God, and that men are never accountable for them"; those were the last words his sister said as they bade each other farewell.

"Such is our fate!" said Prince Andrei to himself as he turned out of the avenue of the Lisiya Gori mansion. "She, poor innocent creature, is left to be devoured by this crazy old man. The old man is conscious that he is doing wrong, but he cannot change his nature. My little lad is growing up and enjoying life, though he will become like all the rest of us, deceivers or deceived. I am going to the army—for what purpose I myself do not know—and I am anxious to meet a man whom I despise, so as to give him a chance to kill me and exult over me."

In days gone by the same conditions of life had existed, but in some way everything was knit together; now everything was falling apart. Isolated, illogical thoughts, devoid of connection, arose one after another in Prince Andrei's mind.

VII

PRINCE ANDREI reached the army headquarters toward the first of July. The troops of the first division, commanded by the sovereign in person, were intrenched in a fortified camp on the Drissa; the troops of the second division were in retreat, though they were endeavoring to join the first, from which, as the report went, they had been cut off by a strong force of the French. All were dissatisfied with the general conduct of military affairs in the Russian army; but no one ever dreamed that any of the Russian provinces would be invaded, and no one supposed that the war would be carried beyond the western section of Poland.

Prince Andrei found Barclay de Tolly on the bank of the Drissa. He gave

Bolkonsky a dry and chilling welcome, and, speaking with a strong German accent, told him that he would have to send in his name to the sovereign for any definite assignment, but proposed that for the time being he should remain on his staff.

Anatol Kuragin, whom Prince Andrei expected to find with the army, was no longer there; he had gone to Petersburg, and this news was agreeable to Bolkonsky. He was absorbed in the interest of being at the very center of a mighty war which was just beginning, and he was glad to be for a short time freed from the provocation which the thought of Kuragin produced in him.

While the sovereign was still at Vilna, the troops had been divided into three armies: the first was placed under command of Barclay de Tolly; the second under the command of Bagration; the third under command of Tormasof.

The emperor was present with the first division, but not in his capacity as commander-in-chief. In the orders of the day it was simply announced that the sovereign would not take command, but would merely be present with the army. Moreover, the sovereign had no personal staff, as would have been the case had he been commander-in-chief, but only a staff appropriate to the imperial headquarters. Attached to him were the chief of the imperial staff, the General-Quartermaster Prince Volkonsky, generals, adjutants, diplomatic officials, and a great throng of foreigners; but these did not form a military staff. Besides these there were attached to his person, but without special functions, Arakcheyef, the ex-minister of war; Count Benigsen, with the rank of senior general; the grand duke and heir apparent, Konstantin Pavlovitch; Count Rumyantsef; the Chancellor Stein, who had been minister in Prussia; Armfeldt, a Swedish general; Pfuhl, the principal originator of the plan of the campaign; Paulucci, adjutant-general and a Sardinian refugee; Woltzogen and many others.

Although these individuals were present without any special military function, still by their peculiar position they wielded a powerful influence, and oftentimes the chief of the corps, and even the commander-in-chief, did not know whether such and such an order, couched in the form of a piece of advice, emanated from the speaker or the sovereign, and whether it was incumbent on him to carry it out.

Amid all the plans and voices in this tremendous, restless, brilliant, and haughty world, Prince Andrei distinguished the following sharply outlined subdivisions of tendencies and parties.

The first party consisted of Pfuhl and his followers, military theorists, who believed that there was a science of war, and that this science had its immutable laws—the laws for oblique movements for outflanking, and so on. Pfuhl and his followers insisted on retreating into the interior of the country, according to definite principles prescribed by the so-called science of war, and in every departure from this theory they saw nothing but barbarism, ignorance or evil intentions. To this party belong the German princes and Woltzogen, Winzengerode, and others—notably the Germans.

The second party was diametrically opposed to the first. And, as always happens, they went to quite opposite extremes. The men of this party were those who insisted on making Vilna the base of a diversion into Poland and demanded to be freed from all preconceived plans. Not only were the leaders of this party the representatives of the boldest activity, but at the same time they were also the representatives of nationalism, in consequence of which they showed all the more urgency in maintaining their side of the dispute. Such were the Russians Bagration, Yermolof—who was just beginning to come into prominence—and many others. It was at this time that Yermolof's famous jest was quoted extensively: It was said that he asked the emperor to grant him the favor of promoting him to be a German! The men of this party recalled Suvorof, and declared that there was no need to make plans or mark the map with pins, but to fight, to beat the foe, not to let him enter Russia, and not to let the army lose heart.

The third party, in which the sovereign placed the greatest confidence, consisted of those courtiers who tried to find a compromise between the two opposed schools. These men—for the most part civilians, and Arakcheyef was of their number—thought and talked as men usually talk who have no convictions but do not wish to show their opportunism. They declared that unquestionably the war, especially against such a genius as Bonaparte—they called him Bonaparte again—demanded the profoundest consideration and a thorough knowledge of the military science, and in this respect Pfuhl was endowed with genius; but, at the same time, it was necessary to acknowledge that theorists were often one-sided, and, therefore, it was impossible to have perfect confidence in them; it was best to heed also what Pfuhl's antagonists had to say, and also what was said by men who had had practical experience in military affairs, and then to balance the two.

The fourth group was the one of which the conspicuous representative was the grand duke, the Tsesarevitch Konstantin, heir apparent to the throne, who could not forget his disappointment at the Battle of Austerlitz—when he rode out at the head of his guards dressed in helmet and dress jacket as for a parade, expecting to drive the French valiantly before him, and unexpectedly finding himself at the very front—was involuntarily involved in the general confusion and rout. The men of this party showed in their opinions both sincerity and lack of sincerity. They were afraid of Napoleon; they saw that he was strong while they were weak, and they had no hesitation in saying so. They said:

"Nothing but misfortune, ignominy and defeat will come out of this. Here we have abandoned Vilna; we have abandoned Vitebsk; we must abandon the Drissa in like manner. The only reasonable thing left for us is to conclude peace, and as speedily as possible, before we are driven out of Petersburg."

A fifth party was formed by those who were partisans of Barclay de Tolly, not as a man but simply because he was minister of war and commander-in-chief. These said: "Whatever he is"—and that was the way they always began—"he is an honest, capable man, and he has no superior. Give him actual power, because the war can never come to any successful issue without someone in sole control, and then he will show what he can do, just as he proved it in Finland. If our army is well organized and powerful (and it made the retreat to the Drissa without suffering any loss), we owe it to this Barclay alone. If now Barclay is replaced by Benigsen, all will go to rack and ruin, because Benigsen made an exhibition of his incapacity in 1807."

A sixth party—the Benigsenists—claimed the contrary; that there was no one more capable and experienced than Benigsen, "and, however far they go out of his way, they'll have to return to him. Let them make their mistakes now!" And the men of this party argued that our whole retreat to the Drissa was a disgraceful defeat and an uninterrupted series of blunders.

The seventh party consisted of such men as always flourish around young monarchs—and the Emperor Alexander had a remarkable number of such—namely, generals and adjutants who were passionately devoted to their sovereign, not as an emperor but as a man whom they worshiped heartily and disinterestedly, just as Rostof had worshiped him in 1805, and who saw in him not only all virtues but all human qualities. These men, although they praised their sovereign's modesty in declining to assume the duties of commander-in-chief, still critized this excess of modesty, and had only one desire: That their adored monarch overcome his excessive lack of confidence in himself and openly announce that he would take his place at the head of his armies, gather around him the appropriate staff of a commander-in-chief, and while consulting in cases of necessity with theorists and practical men of experience, himself lead his troops, who by this mere fact would be roused to the highest pitch of enthusiasm.

The eighth and by all odds the largest group of men, which in comparison with the others all put together would rank as ninety-nine to one, consisted of men who desired neither peace nor war nor offensive operations, nor a defensive camp on the Drissa nor anywhere else, nor Barclay, nor the sovereign, nor Pfuhl, nor Benigsen, but simply wished one and the same essential thing: the utmost possible advancement and entertainment for themselves.

Just about the time Prince Andrei arrived at the army, still a ninth party was forming out of all these others, and beginning to let its voice be heard. This was the party of veteran statesmen, men of sound wisdom and experience, who shared in none of all these contradictory opinions and were able to look impartially upon all that was going on at headquarters and to devise means for escaping from this vagueness, indecision, confusion, and weakness.

The men of this party said and thought that nothing but mischief resulted preëminently from the presence of the sovereign with a military court at the front, introducing into the army that indeterminate, conditional and fluctuating irregularity of relations which, however useful at court, was ruinous to the troops; that it was the monarch's business to govern and not to direct the army; that the only cure for all these troubles was for the sovereign and his court to take their departure; that the mere fact of the emperor's presence paralyzed the movements of fifty thousand men who were required to protect him from personal peril; that the most incompetent general-in-chief, if he were independent, would be better than the best, hampered by the sovereign's presence.

While Prince Andrei was at Drissa without stated position, Shishkof, the imperial secretary, who was one of the chief members of this faction, wrote the sovereign a letter which Balashof and Arakcheyef agreed to sign. Taking advantage of the permission accorded him by the sovereign to make suggestions concerning the general course of events, he respectfully, and under the pretext that it was necessary for the sovereign to rouse the people of the capital to fresh enthusiasm for this war, proposed in the letter that he should leave the army.

The mission of fanning the enthusiasm of the people and of summoning them to defend the fatherland, the very thing that led to the ultimate triumph of Russia—and his personal presence in Moscow contributed largely to this end—was therefore offered to the emperor and accepted by him as a pretext for taking his departure from the army.

The earnest and absurdly opinionated Pfuhl aroused the most sympathy in Prince Andrei. He alone evidently sought no personal advantage, nor had he any hatred of anyone. He simply desired that his plan, elaborated from a theory he had deduced from his studies during long years, should be carried into execution. He was ridiculous; his use of sarcasm made him disagreeable; but at the same time he awakened involuntary respect by his boundless devotion to an idea.

Besides, all except Pfuhl had one common feature that had never been manifested in the council of war in the year 1805, and this was the secret but panic fear—dissembled—of Napoleon's genius; it showed itself in every argument. They took it for granted that Napoleon could do anything. They looked for him on every side, and by his terrible name each one of them demolished the proposals of the other. Pfuhl alone, it seemed, regarded even Napoleon as a barbarian, like all the other opponents of his theory.

Pfuhl awakened in Prince Andrei a feeling of pity as well as of respect. It was plain to see that the others knew, and he himself felt, that his fall was at hand. Although he did his best to dissimulate it under the guise of exasperation and scorn, he was in despair, because his only chance of showing his theory on a tremendous scale, and proving its value before all the world, was slipping from him.

Prince Andrei, listening to this polyglot debate and these propositions, plans and counterplans, and outcries, was amazed. The idea that had early and often suggested itself to him during the period of his former military service—that there was not, and could not be, any such thing as a military science, and consequently could not be any so-called military genius—now seemed to him a truth beyond doubt.

"How can there be any theory and science in a matter where the conditions and circumstances are unknown and cannot be determined—in which the force employed by those who make the war is still less capable of measurement? No one can possibly know what will be the position of our army and that of the enemy's a day from now, and no one can know what is the force of this or that division. Sometimes, when there is no coward in the front to cry, 'We are cut off!' and to start the panic, and there is a jovial, audacious man there to shout, 'Hurrah!' a division of five thousand is worth thirty thousand, as was the case at Schöngraben; and sometimes fifty thousand will fly before eight, as happened at Austerlitz. What science, then, can there be in such a business, and where nothing can be predetermined, as in any practical business, and where everything depends on numberless conditions, the resolving of which will come at some one moment, but *when*, no one can possibly foretell. Armfeldt says that our army is cut off, and Paulucci declares that we have got the French army between two fires. Michaud says that the uselessness of the camp on the Drissa consists in this, that the river is back of it; while Pfuhl declares that therein lies its strength. Toll proposes one plan, Armfeldt proposes another, and all are good and all are bad, and the advantages of each and every proposition can be proved only at the moment when the event occurs."

VIII

ROSTOF, BEFORE THE opening of the campaign, received a letter from his parents in which, after briefly announcing Natasha's illness and the rupture of the engagement with Prince Andrei—this rupture, they explained, was Natasha's own work—they again urged him to retire from the service and come home.

Nikolai, on receipt of this letter, made no attempt to secure either a furlough or permission to go upon the retired list, but wrote his parents that he was very sorry for Natasha's illness and breach with her fiancé, and that he would do all that he possibly could to fulfil their desires. He wrote a separate letter to Sonya.

"Adored friend of my heart," he wrote, "nothing except honor could keep me from returning home. But just now, at the opening of the campaign, I should consider myself disgraced not only before all my comrades but in my own eyes, if I were to prefer my pleasure to my duty, and my love to my country. But this is our last separation. Be assured that immediately after the war, if I am alive and you still love me, I will give up everything and fly to you to clasp you forever to my ardent heart!"

He was telling the truth—it was only the opening of the campaign that detained Nikolai and prevented him from fulfilling his promise by at once returning home and marrying Sonya. The autumn at Otradnoye, with its fun and games, and the winter with the Christmas holidays, and his love for Sonya, had opened up before him a whole perspective of the pleasures of a country nobleman and of domestic contentment which he had never known before and which now beckoned to him with their sweet allurements.

"A wonderful wife, children, a good pack of hunting dogs, a leash of ten or twenty spirited greyhounds, the management of the estate, the neighbors, and service at the elections," he said to himself. But now there was a war in prospect, and he was obliged to remain with his regiment. And, since this was a matter of necessity, Nikolai Rostof, in accordance with his character, was content with the life he led in the regiment, and had the skill to arrange it so that it was agreeable.

During his absence he had been promoted to captain of cavalry, and when the regiment was restored to a war footing, with increased complement, he was put in charge of his former squadron.

The troops evacuated Vilna for various complicated reasons—imperial, political, and tactical. At headquarters, every step of the retreat was accompanied by an intricate play of interests, arguments, and passions. For the hussars of the Pavlograd regiment, all this backward movement, in the best part of the summer, with abundance of provisions, was a simple and enjoyable affair. At headquarters men might lose heart and grow nervous and indulge in intrigues to their hearts' content; but in the ranks no one thought of asking where or wherefore they were moving. If they indulged in regrets at the retreat, it was simply because they were compelled to leave pleasant quarters and the pretty Polish women. If it occurred to anyone that affairs were going badly, then, as became a good soldier, the man who had such a thought would try to be jovial and not think at all of the general course of events, but only of what nearest concerned himself.

At first they were agreeably situated near Vilna, having jolly acquaintances among the Polish landed proprietors, and constantly expecting the sovereign and other commanders highest in station to review them, and as constantly being disappointed.

Then came the order to retire to Swienciany, and to destroy all provisions they could not carry away with them. Swienciany was memorable to the hussars simply because it was the "drunken camp," as the entire army called it from their stay at the place, and because many complaints had been made of the troops' having taken unfair advantage of the order to forage for provisions and had included under this head horses and carriages and rugs stolen from the Polish nobles. Rostof had a vivid remembrance of Swienciany, because on the first day of their arrival there he had dismissed a quartermaster, and had not been able to do anything with the men of his squadron, all of whom were tipsy, having without his knowledge brought away five barrels of old beer. From Swienciany they had retired farther, and then farther still, until they reached the Drissa; and then they had retired from the Drissa, all the time approaching the Russian frontier.

On the twenty-fifth of July, the Pavlograd regiment for the first time took part in a serious engagement.

On the twenty-fourth of July, the evening before the engagement, there was a severe thunderstorm, with rain and hail. That summer of the year 1812 was throughout remarkable for its thundershowers.

Two squadrons of the Pavlograd regiment had bivouacked in a field of rye, already eared but completely trampled down by the horses and cattle. It was raining in torrents, and Rostof, with a young officer named Ilyin who was his protégé, was sitting under the shelter of a sort of wigwam, extemporized at short notice.

This officer, a lad of only sixteen, had not been very long connected with the regiment, and was now in the same relation to Rostof that Rostof had borne toward Denisof seven years before. Ilyin had taken Rostof as his pattern in every respect, and was in love with him like a woman.

It was three o'clock in the morning, and no one had caught a wink of sleep, when the quartermaster made his appearance with orders to proceed to the little village of Ostrovno.

Within half an hour the squadron was drawn up on the road. The command was heard: "To saddle." The men crossed themselves and proceeded to mount. Rostof, taking the lead, gave the command, "March!" and, filing off four abreast, the hussars, with the sound of hoofs splashing in the pools, the clinking of sabers, and subdued conversation, started along the broad road lined with birch trees, following the infantry and artillery which had gone on ahead.

Rostof, during this campaign, had permitted himself to ride a Cossack horse instead of his regular horse of the line. Being both a connoisseur and a huntsman, he had recently selected a strong, mettlesome, dun-colored pony from the Don, which no one could think of matching in a race.

In days gone by, Rostof, on approaching an engagement, would have felt a pang of dismay; now he experienced not the slightest sensation of timidity. He was devoid of all fear, not because he was used to fire—it is impossible to become used to danger—but rather because he had learned to control his heart in the presence of danger. On going into an engagement he had trained himself to think about everything except the one thing that would have been most absorbing of all—the impending peril. In spite of all his efforts, in spite of all his self-reproaches for his cowardice, during the first term of his service, he had not been able to reach this point; but in the course of years it had come of itself. He rode now with Ilyin, side by side, between the birch trees, occasionally tearing off a leaf from a low-hanging branch, occasionally prodding the horse in the groin, occasionally, not even turning round, handing his exhausted pipe to the hussar just behind him, with such a calm and unconcerned appearance that one would have thought he was riding for pleasure.

He felt a pang of pity when he looked at Ilyin's excited face as he rode along, talking fast and nervously. He knew from experience that painful state of mind at the expectation of danger and death which the young officer was now experiencing, and he knew that nothing but time could cure him.

The squadron outstripped the infantry and artillery which were also hurrying forward, plunged down a hill, and, dashing through a village deserted by its inhabitants, galloped up a slope on the other side. The horses were all of a lather, the men were flushed.

"Halt! Dress ranks," rang out the command of the division leader at the front. "Guide left! Slow march!" again rang the command. And the hussars rode along the line of the troops toward the left flank of the position and drew rein just behind the Russian Uhlans, who were in the front rank. At the right stood the Russian infantry in a solid mass; they were the reserves; higher up on the slope could be seen in the clear, clear atmosphere our cannon shining in the slanting rays of the bright morning sun, on the very horizon.

Forward, beyond a ravine, were heard our infantry, already involved in the action and merrily exchanging shots with the enemy.

Rostof's heart beat high with joy as he heard these sounds which he had not heard for many a long day, and which now seemed like the notes of the jolliest music. Trap ta-ta-tap, several shots cracked, sometimes together, suddenly, then rapidly, one after another.

The hussars stood for about an hour in one place. The cannonade had also begun. Count Ostermann and his suite came riding up behind the squadron and, drawing rein, had a short conversation with the commander of the regiment, then rode off toward the cannon at the height.

As soon as Ostermann rode away, the Uhlans heard the command: "In column; make ready to charge!"

The infantry in front of them parted their ranks to let the cavalry pass. The Uhlans started away, the pennons on their lances waving gaily, and down the slope they dashed at a trot, toward the French cavalry which began to appear at the foot of the slope at the left.

As soon as the Uhlans started down the slope, the hussars were ordered to move forward and protect the battery on the height. While the hussars were stationed in the position before occupied by the Uhlans, bullets flew high over their heads, buzzing and humming through the air.

These sounds, which had not been heard by Rostof for long years, had a more pleasing and stimulating influence than the roar of musketry before. Straightening himself up in the saddle, he scrutinized the battlefield spread full before his eyes from the height where he was stationed, and his whole heart followed the Uhlans into the charge.

They had now flown almost down to the French dragoons; there was a collision in the smoke, and, at the end of five minutes, the Uhlans were being pressed back, not in the same place, indeed, but farther to the left. Mixed in with the orange-uniformed Uhlans on their chestnut horses, and behind them, in a compact mass, could be seen the blue French dragoons on their gray horses.

IX

ROSTOF, WITH HIS keen huntsman's eye, was one of the first to notice these French dragoons in blue pressing back our Uhlans. Nearer, nearer, in disorderly masses, came the Uhlans, and the French dragoons in pursuit of them.

Now all could see how these men, dwarfed by the distance, were jostling one another, driving one another, and brandishing their arms and their sabers.

Rostof looked down at what was going on as if he were present at a hunt. His instinct told him that, if the hussars could now add their impetus to that of the Uhlans, the French dragoons could not stand it; but if the blow was to be struck, it had to be done immediately, on the instant, otherwise it would be too late. He glanced around; a captain stationed near him likewise had his eyes fixed steadfastly on the cavalry contest below.

"Captain!" said Rostof, "see, we might crush them."

"That would be a dashing piece of work," said the captain, "but still . . ."

Rostof, not waiting to hear his answer, gave spurs to his horse, dashed along in front of his squadron, and, before he had even given the word for the advance, the whole squadron to a man, feeling exactly what he had, dashed after him.

Rostof himself did not know how and why he did this thing. The whole action was as instinctive, as unpremeditated, as if he had been out hunting. He saw that the dragoons were near at hand, that they were galloping forward in disorderly ranks. He knew that they would not withstand a sudden attack; he knew that it was a matter of a single moment that would not return if he let it go by. The bullets whizzed and whistled around him so stimulatingly, his horse dashed on ahead so hotly, that he could not but yield. He plunged the spurs still deeper into his horse's flanks, shouted his command, and, at that same instant, hearing behind him the hoof clatter of his squadron breaking into the charge at full trot, he gave his horse his head down the hill toward the dragoons. No sooner had they reached the bottom of the slope than their gait changed involuntarily from trot to gallop, growing ever swifter and swifter in proportion as they approached the Uhlans and the French dragoons who were driving them back.

The dragoons were close to them. The foremost, seeing the hussars, started to turn; those in the rear paused. Feeling as if he were galloping to cut off an escaping wolf, Rostof, urging his Don pony to his utmost, dashed on toward the disconcerted French dragoons. One of the Uhlans reined in his horse; one, who had been dismounted, threw himself on the ground to escape being crushed; a riderless steed dashed in among the hussars. Almost all the French dragoons were now in full retreat.

Rostof, selecting one of them mounted on a gray horse, started in pursuit of him. On the way he found himself rushing at a bush; his good horse, without hesitating, took it at a leap; and, almost before Rostof had settled himself in his saddle again, he saw that he should within a few seconds overtake the man whom he had selected as his objective. This Frenchman, evidently an officer by his uniform, bending forward, was urging on his gray horse, striking him with his saber. A second later Rostof's horse hit the other's rear with his chest, almost knocking him over; and, at the same instant, Rostof, not knowing why, raised his saber and struck at the Frenchman.

The instant he did so all Rostof's excitement suddenly vanished. The officer fell, not so much from the effect of the saber stroke, which had only scratched him slightly above the elbow, as from the collision of the horses and from panic. Rostof pulled up to look for his enemy and see whom he had vanquished. The French officer of dragoons was hopping along with one foot on the ground and the other entangled in the stirrup. His eyes squinting with fear as if he expected each instant to be struck down again, he was looking up at Rostof with an expression of horror. His pale face, covered with mud, fair and young, with dimpled chin and bright blue eyes, was not made for the battlefield—not the face of an enemy, but a simple home face.

Even before Rostof had made up his mind what to do with him, the officer cried: "I surrender." In spite of all his efforts he could not extricate his foot from the stirrup; and still, with frightened blue eyes, he kept gazing at Rostof. Some of the hussars who had come galloping up freed his foot for him and helped him to mount. The hussars were coming back in all directions with dragoons as prisoners: One was wounded, but, with his face all covered with blood, would not surrender his horse; another was seated on the crupper of a hussar's horse, with his arm around the man's waist; a third, assisted by a hussar, was clambering up on the horse's back.

In front the French infantry were in full retreat, firing as they went.

The hussars swiftly returned to their position with their prisoners. Rostof spurred back with the rest, a prey to a peculiarly disagreeable feeling that oppressed his heart. A certain vague perplexity, which he found it utterly impossible to explain, overcame him when he thought of the capture of the young French officer and the blow he had given him.

Count Ostermann-Tolstoy met the hussars on their return, summoned Rostof and thanked him, saying that he should report to the sovereign his gallant exploit and recommend him for the cross of St. George. When the summons to Count Ostermann came, Rostof remembered that the charge had been made without orders; and he was therefore fully persuaded that the commander called for him to punish him for his presumptuous action. Ostermann's flattering words and promise of a reward ought to have been all the more agreeable to Rostof; but the same vague, disagreeable feeling still tortured his mind.

"What can it be that troubles me so, I wonder?" he asked himself as he rode away from the interview. "Ilyin? No, he is safe and sound. Have I anything to be ashamed of? No, nothing of the sort at all"—it was an entirely different feeling, like remorse—"Yes, yes, that French officer with the dimple. And how distinctly I remember hesitating before I raised my arm."

Rostof saw the prisoners about to be led away, and he galloped up to them in order to have another look at the officer with the dimpled chin. He was sitting in his foreign uniform on a hussar's stallion, and was glancing around uneasily. The wound on his arm was scarcely deserving of the name. He gave Rostof a hypocritical smile and waved his hand, as a sort of salute. Rostof still had the feeling of awkwardness, and something seemed to weigh on his conscience.

All that day and the day following, Rostof's friends and comrades noticed that he was—not exactly gloomy or surly, but taciturn, thoughtful, and concentrated. He drank, as it were, under protest, tried to be alone, and evidently had something on his mind.

Rostof spent all the time thinking about his brilliant exploit, which, much to his amazement, had given him the cross of St. George, and had even given him the reputation of being a hero; and he found it utterly incomprehensible.

"And so they are still more afraid of us than we are of them!" he said to himself. "Is this all there is to what is called heroism? Did I do that for my country's sake? And wherein was he to blame, with his dimple and his blue eyes? And how frightened he was! He thought I was going to kill him! My hand trembled; but still they have given me St. George's cross. I don't understand it at all, not at all!"

But while Nikolai brooded over these questions in his own mind, and still failed to find any adequate solution of what was so confusing to him, the wheel of fortune, as so often happens in the military service, had been given a turn in his favor. He was promoted after the engagement at Ostrovno and given command of a battalion of hussars; and when there was any need to call on a daring officer, he was given the chance.

X

THE SYMPTOMS OF Natasha's illness were loss of appetite, sleeplessness, a cough, and a constant state of apathy. The doctors declared that it was impossible for her to dispense with medical treatment and consequently she was kept a prisoner in the sultry air of the city; so that during the summer of 1812 the Rostofs did not go to their country estate.

In spite of the immense quantity of pills, drops, and powders swallowed by Natasha, out of glass jars and gilt boxes of which Madame Schoss, who was a great lover of such things, had made a large collection; in spite of being deprived of her customary life in the country, youth at last got the upper hand: Natasha's sorrow began to disappear under the impressions of everyday life; it ceased to lie so painfully on her heart, it began to appear past and distant, and Natasha's physical health showed signs of improvement.

She scarcely ever went out of the house; and, of those who came to call, there was only one man whom she was glad to see, and that was Pierre.

It could not have been possible for anyone to show more tenderness and discretion, and, at the same time, more seriousness, in his treatment of her than did Count Bezukhof. Natasha unconsciously felt the spell of this affectionate tenderness and therefore took great delight in his society. But she was not really grateful to him for his kindness. Pierre's goodness seemed to her spontaneous. It seemed to her that it was so perfectly natural for Pierre to be kind to everyone that he deserved no credit for his goodness. Sometimes Natasha noticed his confusion and awkwardness in her presence, especially when he was anxious to do her some favor, or when he was apprehensive lest something in their talk might suggest disagreeable recollections. She noticed this and ascribed it to his innate kindness and shyness, which, in her opinion, as far as she knew, everyone experienced just as she did.

Since those ambiguous words, "If he were free, he would, on his knees, sue for her heart and her hand," spoken at a moment of such painful excitement on her part, Pierre had never made any allusion whatever to his feelings for Natasha; and as far as she was concerned, it was evident that those words, so consoling to her at the time, had had no more meaning to her than most thoughtless, unconsidered words spoken for the consolation of a weeping child. It never entered her head that her relations with Pierre might lead to love on her side—much less on his—or even to that form of tender, self-acknowledged, poetic friendship between a man and a woman, of which she had known several examples; and this was not because Pierre was a married man, but because Natasha was conscious that between him and her there existed a real barrier of moral obstacles, the absence of which she had realized in Kuragin.

During the first weeks of July more and more disquieting rumors about the progress of the war began to be circulated in Moscow: people talked about the sovereign's appeal to his people, and about the fact that he had left the army and was coming to Moscow. And as the manifesto and summons were not received in Moscow until the twenty-third of July, exaggerated reports about them and about the position of Russia were current. It was said that the sovereign was coming because the army was in a critical position; it was said that Smolensk had surrendered, that Napoleon had a million men, and that only a miracle could save Russia.

The manifesto was received on the twenty-third of July, on a Saturday, but as yet it had not been published; and Pierre, who was at the Rostofs', promised to come to dinner the next day, Sunday, and bring the manifesto and the proclamation, which he would get from Count Rostopchin.

From the day when Pierre left the Rostofs' with Natasha's look of gratitude still fresh in his mind, and gazed at the comet flaming across the sky and felt that he had made a new discovery, the eternally tormenting question as to the futility and folly of all things earthly had ceased to occupy his thoughts. This terrible question, *Why? Wherefore?* which formerly had come up before him amid every occupation, had now merged itself for him, not into another problem, and not into any answer to his question, but into her image.

Whether he listened or took the lead himself in trivial conversations, whether he read or heard about the baseness and absurdity of men, he no longer felt that sense of horror as before; he did not ask himself what caused men to struggle so when life was so short and incomprehensible, but he recalled how she looked when he saw her the last time, and all his doubts vanished, not because she had given the answer to his questions, but because her image instantly lifted him into another realm, serene and full of spiritual values, where there could be no question of right or wrong —the realm of beauty and love which alone makes life worth living. Whatever baseness in life might be brought to his attention, he would say to himself:

"Well, then, let so-and-so plunder the government and the Tsar, and let the government and the Tsar load him with honors; but *she* smiled on me last evening, and asked me to come again, and I love her, and no one shall ever know it!"

And his soul became calm and clear.

XI

THE ROSTOFS, as usual on Sundays, had some of their intimate friends to dine with them. Pierre went early, so as to find them alone.

Pierre had grown so stout this year that he would have seemed monstrous had he not been so tall, so broad-shouldered, and so strong that he carried his weight with evident ease.

Panting and muttering something to himself, he hurried upstairs. His coachman no longer thought of asking him whether he should wait for him. He knew by this time that when the count was at the Rostofs' he would stay till midnight. The Rostofs' lackeys cheerfully hastened forward to take his cloak and receive his hat and cane.

The first person he saw was Natasha. Even before he had caught sight of her, he heard her singing solfeggii in the music room.

He knew that she had not sung a note since her illness, and therefore the sound of her voice surprised and delighted him. He gently opened the door and saw Natasha in the lilac-colored dress in which she had been to Mass, pacing up and down the room and singing. She was walking with her back toward him when he opened the door, but when she turned quickly around and recognized his stout, amazed face, she blushed and came swiftly toward him.

"Count, tell me, is it wrong of me to be singing?" she asked, with a blush, but looking inquiringly into Pierre's face, without dropping her eyes.

"No! Why? On the contrary . . . but why did you ask me?"

"I am sure I don't know," replied Natasha, quickly; "but I did not wish to do anything that you would not approve. I have such perfect confidence in you! You don't know what you mean to me, how much you have done for me!" She spoke rapidly and did not notice how Pierre reddened at these words. "I saw that he . . . I mean Bolkonsky"—she spoke this name in a hurried whisper—"was mentioned in an order; so that he is in Russia and serving again. What do you think?" she asked, still speaking rapidly, evidently in haste to finish what she had to say, lest she should not have the strength necessary to do so. "Will he ever forgive me? Will he not always bear me ill will? What do you think about it? What do you think about it?"

"I think," Pierre began, "I think he has nothing to forgive. . . . If I were in his place . . ."

By the force of recollection Pierre was in an instant carried back in his imagination to that moment when, in order to comfort her, he had said that if he were the best man in the world, and free, he would, on his knees, ask for her hand; and now the same feeling of pity, tenderness, and love took possession of him, and the same words were on his lips. But she did not give him time to say them.

"Yes, you, *you*," said she, with a peculiar solemnity, repeating and dwelling on the pronoun—"you—that is another thing. I know no man who is kinder, nobler, better; and there could not be. If it had not been for you, then, and now too, I don't know what would have become of me, because . . ." the tears suddenly filled her eyes; she turned around, held her music before her face, and began to sing her scales, and started to walk up and down the room once more.

At this moment, Petya came running in from the drawing-room. Petya was now a handsome, ruddy lad of fifteen, with thick, red lips, and looked like Natasha. He was preparing for the university, but lately he and his comrade, Obolensky, had secretly resolved that they would enter the hussars.

He sprang forward to his namesake in order to speak with him about this. He had been begging him to find out whether he could be admitted to the hussars. Pierre went into the drawing-room, not heeding the lad.

Petya pulled him by the arm, to attract his attention.

"Now tell me, count, for heaven's sake, how is my business getting on? Is there any hope for us?" asked Petya.

"Oh, yes, your business. The hussars, is it? I will inquire about it; I will tell you about it, I will tell you the whole story this very day."

"Well, now, my dear fellow, have you brought the manifesto?" asked the old count. "The 'little countess' was at Mass at the Razumovskys', and heard the new prayer. Very fine, they say!"

"Yes, I have brought it," replied Pierre. "The sovereign will be here tomorrow. A special meeting of the nobility has been called, and they say there is to be a levy of ten out of every thousand. And I congratulate you!"

"Yes, yes, glory to God. Now tell me what is the news from the army?"

"We are still retreating. At Smolensk by this time, they say," replied Pierre.

"My God! My God!" exclaimed the count. "Where is the manifesto?"

"The proclamation? Oh, yes!"

Pierre began to search his pockets for the papers, but could not find them. While still rummaging through his pockets, he kissed the hand of the countess, who at that moment came in, and he looked around uneasily, evidently expecting to see Natasha, who had ceased to sing but had not as yet rejoined the others.

"On my word, I don't know what I have done with it!" he exclaimed.

"Well, you're always losing things," exclaimed the countess.

Natasha came in with a softened, agitated expression, and sat down, looking at Pierre without speaking. As soon as she appeared, Pierre's face, till then darkened with a frown, grew bright, and though he was still searching for the papers, he kept looking at her.

"By heaven! I must have left them at home. I will go after them. Most certainly . . ."

"But you will be late to dinner."

"Oh! And my coachman has gone too!"

Sonya, however, who had gone into the anteroom to look for the missing papers, found them in Pierre's hat, where he had carefully stuck them under the lining. Pierre wanted to read them immediately.

"No, not till after dinner," said the old count, evidently anticipating the greatest treat in this reading.

At dinner, during which they drank the health of the new knight of St. George in champagne, Shinshin related all the gossip of the town: about the illness of the old Princess of Gruzia, and how Metivier had disappeared from Moscow, and how they had arrested some German and brought him to Rostopchin, claiming that he was a "Frenchie." Count Rostopchin himself had told the story, and how Rostopchin had commanded them to let the Frenchie go, assuring the people that he was not a slick Frenchman, but simply an old German peasant.

"They'll catch it! They'll catch it!" said the count; "I have been telling the countess that she mustn't talk French so much. It is not the time to do it now."

"And have you heard?" proceeded Shinshin. "Prince Galitsin has taken a Russian tutor—to teach him Russian. It is beginning to be dangerous to speak French in the street."

"Well, count, if they are going to mobilize the landwehr, you'll have to get on horseback, won't you?" asked the old count, addressing Pierre.

Pierre was taciturn and thoughtful all during dinner. As if not comprehending, he gazed at the old count when thus addressed.

"Yes, yes, about the war," said he. "No! What kind of a soldier should I be? But, after all, how strange everything is! How strange! I can't understand it myself. I don't know; my tastes are so far from being military, but as things are now no one can answer for himself."

After dinner the count seated himself comfortably in his chair, and, with a grave face, asked Sonya, who was an accomplished reader, to read.

" 'To Moscow, our chief capital:

" 'The enemy has come with overwhelming force to invade the boundaries of Russia. He is here to destroy our beloved fatherland,' " read Sonya, in her clear voice. The count listened with his eyes shut, sighing heavily at certain passages.

Natasha, with strained attention, sat looking inquiringly now at her father and now at Pierre.

Pierre was conscious of her glance fastened on him, and strove not to look around. The countess shook her head sternly and disapprovingly at each enthusiastic expression contained in the manifesto, for everything made her see that the danger threatening her son would not soon pass by.

Shinshin, with his lips folded in a saturnine smile, was evidently making ready to turn into ridicule whatever first gave him a good opportunity: Sonya's reading, or what the count should say, or even the proclamation itself, if that offered him a suitable pretext.

Having read about the perils threatening Russia, the hopes which the sovereign placed in Moscow, and especially in its illustrious nobility, Sonya, with a trembling voice, which was caused principally by the fact that they were following her so closely, read the following words:

" 'We shall not be slow to take our place amidst our people in this capital, and in other cities of our empire, so as to lead in deliberations and to take the direction of all our troops, not only those which are at the present time blocking the way of the foe, but also those that are gathering to cause his defeat wherever he may show himself. And may the destruction in which he thinks to involve us react upon his own head, and may Europe, delivered from servitude, magnify the name of Russia!' "

"That's the talk!" cried the count, opening his moist eyes, and several times catching his breath with a noise as if a bottle of strong smelling salts had been put to his nose; he went on to say, "Only say the word, sire, and we will sacrifice everything without a regret!"

Shinshin had no time to utter the little joke which he had ready at the expense of the count's patriotism before Natasha sprang up from her place and ran to her father.

"How lovely he is—this papa of mine!" she exclaimed, giving him a kiss; and then she glanced at Pierre again with the same unconscious coquetry that had come back to her together with her animation.

"What an ardent little patriot she is!" cried Shinshin.

"Not ardent at all, but simply . . ." began Natasha, offended. "You turn everything into ridicule, but this is no joke."

"Jokes? Certainly not!" exclaimed the count. "Let him only say the word, and we will all follow . . . we are not Germans or . . ."

"And did you notice," said Pierre, "that it spoke about 'deliberations'?"

"Well, whatever he is here for . . ."

At that moment Petya, to whom no one had been paying any attention, came up to his father, and, all flushed, said, in that voice of his, which was now breaking, and was sometimes bass and sometimes treble:

"Now, then, papa, my mind is perfectly made up—and mama, too, if you please—I tell you both my mind is made up; you must let me go into the military service, because I cannot . . . and that's the end of it."

The countess raised her eyes to heaven in dismay, clasped her hands, and turned severely to her husband.

"Just think what he has said!"

But the count instantly recovered from his emotion.

"Well, well!" said he. "A fine soldier you are! What nonsense! You must study!"

"It is not nonsense, papa. Fedya Obolensky is younger than I am, and he is going; but, even if he weren't, I could never think of studying now when . . ." Petya hesitated, and flushed so that the perspiration stood out on his forehead, but still finished—"When the country is in danger."

"There! There! Enough of this nonsense!"

"But you yourself said we would sacrifice everything."

"Petya! I tell you hold your tongue!" cried the count, glancing at his wife, who had turned white, and was gazing with fixed eyes at her youngest son.

"But I tell you—and here is the count, who will speak about it."

"And I tell you it is all rubbish! The milk isn't dry on your lips yet; and here you are wanting to go into the army! Nonsense, I tell you!"

And the count, gathering up the papers, which he evidently intended to read over again in his study before going to bed, started to leave the room.

"Count, come and have a smoke."

Pierre was a state of confusion and uncertainty. Natasha's unnaturally brilliant and animated eyes fixed on him steadily rather than affectionately had brought him into this state.

"No, thank you, I think I will go home."

"What? Go home? I thought you were going to spend the evening with

us. And, besides, you don't come as often as you did. And this girl of mine
. . ." said the count, affectionately indicating Natasha, "is gay only when
you are here."

"Yes, but I had forgotten something. I must certainly go home. Some
business," said Pierre, hastily.

"Well, then, good-by," said the old count, and he left the room.

"Why must you go? Why are you so out of spirits? What is it?" asked
Natasha, looking inquiringly into Pierre's eyes.

"Because I love you!" was what was on his lips to say, but he did not
say it; he reddened till the tears came, and dropped his eyes.

"Because it is better for me not to be here so much . . . because . . . No,
simply because I have some business."

"What is it? No! Tell me," Natasha began resolutely, but suddenly
stopped. The two looked at each other in dismay and confusion. He tried
to smile, but it was a vain attempt; his smile expressed his suffering, and
he kissed her hand without speaking, and left the house.

Pierre had decided that he must not visit at the Rostofs' any more.

XII

ON THE MORNING of the twenty-seventh, three days later, a countless throng
of equipages was drawn up in the vicinity of the Slobodsky palace.

The halls were all crowded. In the front room were the nobles in their
uniforms; in the second room were the merchants, wearing medals, beards,
and blue caftans.

There was a bustle and movement in the room where the nobles were
gathered. Around a great table, over which hung a portrait of the sovereign,
sat the most distinguished dignitaries, in high-backed chairs; but the
majority of the nobles were walking up and down.

All the nobles—the very men whom Pierre was accustomed to see every
day at the club or at their own homes—were in uniforms; some dating from
Catherine's time, some from Paul's, some in the newer-fashioned ones that
had come in with Alexander, some in the ordinary garb of the Russian
nobility; and those who wore this characteristic uniform, young and old,
no matter how much they differed from one another in type or how well-
known they were, had something strange and fantastic about them. Especially noticeable were the old men, dull-eyed, toothless, bald, with flesh
turning to yellow fat, or wrinkled and thin. These, for the most part, sat in
their places and had nothing to say; and if they walked about and talked,
they addressed themselves to men their juniors. All their faces wore most
astoundingly contradictory expressions, the general expectation of some
solemn event, and the usual evening's routine: The card party, Petrusha
the cook, the exchange of greetings with Zinaida Dmitrievna, and things
of the sort.

Pierre, who since early morning had been pinched into an uncomfortable and too tightly fitting court uniform, was present. He was in a high state of excitement; a meeting extraordinary, not only of the nobility, but also of the merchant class—a legislative assembly, a parliament—had awakened in him a whole throng of ideas about the *contrat social* and the French Revolution—ideas he had long ago ceased to entertain, but which were, nevertheless, deeply engraved in his mind. The words of the proclamation which said that the sovereign was coming to the capital for the purpose of *deliberating* with his people, confirmed him in this opinion. And thus supposing that the important reform which he had long waited to see introduced would now be tried, he walked about, looked on, listened to the conversations, but nowhere found anyone expressing the ideas that occupied him.

The sovereign's manifesto was read, arousing great enthusiasm; and then the assembly broke up into groups, discussing affairs. Pierre heard men talking not only about matters of universal interest but also about such things as where the marshals of the nobility should stand when the sovereign came, when the ball should be given to his majesty, whether the division should be made by districts or taking the whole government, and other questions of the sort. But as soon as the war became a topic of conversation, or the object of calling the meeting of the nobility was mentioned, the discussions became vague and irresolute. All preferred to listen rather than to talk.

Count Rostopchin, in a general's uniform and with a broad ribbon across his shoulder, with his prominent chin and keen eyes, came into the room and swiftly passed through the throng of nobles, who made way for him.

"Our sovereign, the emperor, will be here immediately," said Rostopchin. "I have just come from there. I think that in the position in which we find ourselves there is very little room for debate. The sovereign has deigned to call us and the merchant class together," said Count Rostopchin. "They in there control millions"—he pointed to the hall where the merchants were—"and it is our business to arm the militia, and not to spare ourselves. That is the least that we can do!"

The secretary of the meeting was bidden to write that the Muscovites, in a meeting of the nobility, had unanimously resolved to follow the example of Smolensk and offer a levy of ten men out of every thousand, completely armed and equipped.

The gentlemen who had been sitting arose, as if freed from a heavy task, noisily pushed back their chairs, and stirred about the hall so as to stretch their legs, perhaps taking the arm of some acquaintance, and talking matters over.

"The sovereign! The sovereign!" was the cry suddenly shouted through the halls, and the whole throng rushed to the entrance.

Through a broad lane, between a wall of nobles, the sovereign entered the hall. All faces expressed a reverent and awesome curiosity. Pierre was standing at some little distance and could not fully catch all that the sovereign said in his address.

He comprehended only from what he heard that the sovereign spoke about the peril in which the country stood, and the hopes he placed in the Muscovite nobility. Someone spoke in response to the sovereign's address, and merely confirmed the resolution that had just before been adopted.

"Gentlemen," said the sovereign's trembling voice; a ripple of excitement ran through the throng, and then dead silence reigned again, and this time Pierre distinctly heard the sovereign's extremely agreeable voice, affected with genuine emotion, saying:

"I have never doubted the devotion of the Russian nobility. But this day it has exceeded my expectations. I thank you in the name of the fatherland. Gentlemen, let us act—time is more precious than anything."

. . . The sovereign ceased speaking; the throng gathered round him, and on every side were heard enthusiastic exclamations.

"Yes, precious indeed—the Tsar's word!" said Count Rostof, with a sob; he had heard nothing, but put his own interpretation on everything.

The sovereign passed from the hall where the nobles were, into that where the merchants were gathered. He remained there about ten minutes. Pierre and several others saw him on his way from their hall with tears of emotion in his eyes. As was learned afterwards, the sovereign had hardly begun his speech to the merchants before the tears had streamed from his eyes, and he had ended it in a voice broken with emotion. When Pierre saw him, he was coming out accompanied by two merchants. One was an acquaintance of Pierre's—a stout leaseholder; the other was the city provost, a man with a thin yellow face and a peaked beard. Both of them were in tears. The thin man wept, but the stout leaseholder was sobbing like a child, and kept saying:

"Take our lives and our all, your majesty!"

Pierre at this moment felt no other desire than to prove how little he treasured anything, and that he was ready to make any sacrifice. Learning that Count Mamonof had offered a regiment, he immediately announced to Count Rostopchin that he would give a thousand men and their maintenance.

Old Rostof could not refrain from tears when he told his wife what had been done, and he then and there granted Petya's request, and went himself to see that his name was enrolled.

The next day the sovereign took his departure. All the nobles who had assembled took off their uniforms, once more scattered to their homes and their clubs, and, groaning, gave orders to their overseers in regard to the militia, and marveled at what they had done.

1812

The invasion of Russia progresses with unexpected rapidity. At places the French are unopposed; where they meet opposition they overcome it with ease. Kutuzof makes a stand at Borodino; the result is disputed, but the Russian forces fall back on Moscow in September, 1812. The pleasant Russian summer lingers, the weather is comfortable but brisk.

Part Tenth

It is not plain to us what caused the destruction of the French army in the year 1812. No one will attempt to dispute that the cause of the destruction of Napoleon's French troops was, on the one hand, their plunging into the depths of Russia too late in the season, and without sufficient preparation; and, on the other hand, the character given to the war by the burning of the Russian cities, and the consequent awakening in the Russian people of hatred against the foe.

But at that time not only had no one any idea—though now it seems so evident—that an army of eight hundred thousand men, the best that the world had ever seen, and conducted by the greatest of leaders, could only in this way have met with its destruction in a collision with an army half its size, inexperienced, and led by inexperienced generals; *not only no one had any idea of such a thing,* but, moreover, all the exertions of the Russians were systematically directed toward preventing the only thing that could save Russia, and all the exertions of the French, in spite of Napoleon's experience and his so-called military genius, were directed toward reaching Moscow by the end of the summer—in other words, doing the very thing that was bound to prove his ruin.

Napoleon, having cut our armies asunder, moved on into the interior of the country, and neglected several opportunities for giving battle. In August he was at Smolensk, and his sole thought was how to advance into Russia, although, as we see now, this forward movement was certain to destroy him.

The facts prove that Napoleon did not foresee the risk of an advance on

Moscow, and that Alexander and the Russian generals had no idea at that time of decoying Napoleon, but quite the contrary.

The luring of Napoleon into the heart of the country was not in accordance with any plan—for no one believed in the possibility of such a plan—but came about from a complicated interplay of intrigues, desires, and ambitions of the men who took part in this war and had no conception of what was destined to be, or what would prove, the only salvation of Russia.

Everything proceeded in the most unexpected way. Our armies were divided at the opening of the campaign. We attempted to unite them, with the evident aim of giving battle and checking the invasion of the enemy; but in trying to effect this union our troops avoided battle because the enemy was stronger, and in our involuntary avoidance of them we formed an acute angle, and drew the French as far as Smolensk. But it is not enough to say that we gave way at an acute angle, because the French were moving between our two armies: The angle grew still more acute and we retreated still farther because Barclay de Tolly, an unpopular German, was odious to Bagration, who had to act under his command, and Bagration, the commander of the other army, tried as far as possible to delay the conjunction in order not to be under Barclay's orders.

At last, against the wishes of Bagration, the union of the two armies was effected at Smolensk.

Bagration drove in his carriage to the house occupied by Barclay. Barclay put on his scarf, came out to meet him, and saluted him as his superior in rank. Bagration, in this conflict of magnanimity, placed himself under Barclay's command, in spite of his superiority of rank, but though he took a subordinate position he was still less in agreement with him. Bagration, by the sovereign's express order, made direct reports.

He wrote to Arakcheyef:

My sovereign's will be done, but I can never work with the minister [Barclay]. For God's sake send me where you will, give me only a single regiment to command, but I cannot stay here. Headquarters are full of Germans, so that it is impossible for a Russian to breathe here, and there is no sense in anything. I thought that I was serving the sovereign and my country, but I am really serving Barclay. I confess this does not suit me.

The swarm of Brannitskys, of Winzengerodes, and others like them, still further poisoned the relations between the two chiefs, and united action became more and more impossible.

They prepared to attack the French at Smolensk. A general was sent to inspect the position. This general, hating Barclay, instead of obeying orders went to one of his friends, a corps commander, remained with him all day, and returned at night to Barclay to criticize at all points a field of battle which he had not even seen.

While quarrels and intrigues concerning the battlefield were in progress, while we were trying to find the French (of whose whereabouts we were ignorant) the French met Nevyerovsky's division and approached the very walls of Smolensk.

It was necessary to accept an unexpected battle at Smolensk in order to save our communications. The battle took place; thousands of men on both sides were killed.

Contrary to the wishes of the sovereign and the people, Smolensk was abandoned. But the inhabitants of Smolensk, betrayed by their governor, set fire to the city, and offering this example to other Russian towns, took refuge in Moscow, thinking only of their losses and kindling hatred against the enemy.

Napoleon advanced; we retreated, and the result was that the very measure necessary for defeating Napoleon was employed.

I I

On the day following his son's departure, Prince Nikolai Bolkonsky summoned Princess Maria.

"There, now, are you satisfied?" he demanded. "You have involved me in a quarrel with my son! Satisfied? That was what you wanted! Satisfied? This is painful, painful, to me. I am old and feeble, and this was what you wished. Well, take your pleasure in it, take your pleasure in it!"

And after that Princess Maria saw no more of her father for a whole week. He was ill and did not leave his room.

To her amazement, the princess noticed that during this illness the old prince did not permit even Mlle. Bourienne to come near him. Only Tikhon was admitted.

At the end of the week the prince emerged and began to lead his former life again, occupying himself with special zeal in his buildings and gardens, but discontinuing all his former relations with Mlle. Bourienne. His looks and his coolness toward Princess Maria seemed to say to her: *Here, you see, you have lied about me, you have slandered me to Prince Andrei in regard to my relations with this Frenchwoman, and you have made me quarrel with him; but, you see, I can get along without you or her either.*

Princess Maria had such thoughts about the war as women generally have regarding war. She trembled for her brother, who was in it; she was horror-stricken at the cruelty that led men to slaughter each other, though she had little comprehension of its reality; but she did not appreciate the significance of this particular war, which seemed to her exactly like the wars that had preceded it. The principal reason was that the old prince never said a word about it, never mentioned it, and at dinner often laughed at Dessalles, who would grow eloquent over it. The prince's tone was so calm and firm that Princess Maria believed in him without question.

All through the month of July the old prince was extraordinarily active and energetic. He set out another new orchard and put up a new building for the use of his household serfs. The only thing that disquieted Princess Maria was that he slept very little, and relinquishing his ordinary habit of sleeping in his study, he each day changed his sleeping room. One time he gave orders to have his camp bedstead set up in the gallery; then he would try the sofa, or the Voltair easy-chair in the drawing-room, and doze without undressing, while a lad—and not Mlle. Bourienne—read aloud to him; then, again, he would spend the night in the dining room.

In his first letter, which came soon after his departure for the army, Prince Andrei humbly begged his father's pardon for what he had permitted himself to say to him, and begged to be restored to favor. The old prince had replied to this in an affectionate letter, and shortly after that he gave up his intimacy with the Frenchwoman.

Lately, one of the prince's favorite occupations had been to arrange the papers which were to be left after his death, and which he called his "will." He had a sheet of paper on which were jotted down things he wanted done at Smolensk, and he summoned Alpatitch. As he paced back and forth through the room past the servant standing at the door, the prince delivered his instructions.

"First—do you hear?—letter paper like this specimen, gilt-edged—here's the pattern so as not to make any mistake—varnish—sealing-wax—" following the memorandum.

He paced up and down the room, and kept glancing at the list of purchases.

"Then be sure to give this letter about the deed to the governor in person."

Then he laid special stress on getting the bolts for his new building, which had to be of a special pattern invented by himself. It took more than two hours to charge Alpatitch with all the commissions, and still the prince did not let him go. He sat down, tried to think, and, closing his eyes, fell into a doze. Alpatitch stirred uneasily.

"Well, get you gone! Get you gone! If I need anything more I will send for you."

Alpatitch left the room. The prince went to the bureau again, glanced into it, touched the papers with his hand, closed the bureau again, and, going to his table, sat down to write his note to the governor.

It was already late when, having sealed the letter, he got up. He wanted to go to bed, but he knew that he would not sleep and that the most miserable thoughts would haunt him as soon as he lay down. He rang for Tikhon and went with him through the rooms, so as to select the place to set up the bed for the night. He went about measuring every corner.

There was no place that seemed to please him, but anything was better than his usual couch in his study. This couch was terrible to him, apparently because of the trying thoughts that passed through his mind as he lay on it. There was no place that satisfied him, but he was best of all pleased with the corner in the sitting room behind the piano; he had never before slept there.

Tikhon and a manservant brought in the bedstead and began to make the bed.

"Not that way! Not that way!" cried the prince, and with his own hand he pushed it an inch or two farther away from the corner, and then nearer again.

"Well, at last I have done everything; let me rest," thought the prince, and he commanded Tikhon to undress him.

Painfully scowling at the effort required to take off his caftan and pantaloons, the prince at last got undressed and let himself drop heavily on his bed, and then seemed lost in thought as he gazed scornfully at his yellow, shriveled legs. Thought, however, was absent; he was merely sluggish about undertaking the labor of lifting those same legs and getting them into bed.

"Oh! What a trial! Why must the end of these labors be so slow in coming! Why can't you leave me in peace?" he said to himself. Screwing up his lips, he made the effort for the twenty-thousandth time, and then lay down. But he was scarcely on his back before the whole bed suddenly began, with slow and regular motion, to rock backward and forward as if it were heavily breathing and tossing. This thing happened to him almost every night. He opened his eyes, which he had just closed.

"No repose! Curse it!" he exclaimed, full of fury against something. "Yes, yes! There must have been something else of importance, of very great importance, which I kept till I should go to bed. Was it the bolts? No, I told him about that. No, it was something that happened in the drawing-room. Princess Maria had some nonsense to repeat—Dessalles—that idiot!—made some remark. There was something in my pocket! I can't remember. . . . Hey, Tikhon! What were we talking about at dinner?"

"About Prince Mikhail . . ."

"Hold your tongue!"

The prince thumped his hand on the table. "Now I know . . . it was Prince Andrei's letter. Now I will read it."

He bade Tikhon fetch him the letter from his pocket and place a small table near the bed, with his lemonade and a wax taper, and, putting on his spectacles, he began to read. There, as he read the letter in the silence of the night by the feeble light of the candle under the green shade, he grasped its full meaning.

"The French at Vitebsk! In four marches they can reach Smolensk; maybe they are there now. Hey, Tikhon!"

Tikhon sprang forward. "No matter! Nothing! nothing!" he cried.

He slipped the letter under the candlestick and closed his eyes.

And there arose before him the Danube . . . a brilliant noonday . . . the rushes . . . the Russian camp and himself, a young general with not a single wrinkle on his face: hale and hearty, gay and ruddy, going into Potemkin's bright-colored tent, and the burning feeling of hatred against the "favorite" stirred in him now as violently as it did even then. And he recalled all the words which were spoken at his first interview with Potemkin. And his fancy brought up before him again a stout, short woman, with a fat, sallow face—the little mother empress—her smile, her words of flattery, when she for the first time gave him audience, and he remembered her face as it appeared on the bier, and then the quarrel with Zubof which took place over her coffin over the right to kiss her hand.

"Oh, would that those old times could return, and that the present would all come to an end soon . . . that I might at last find rest!"

III

LISIYA GORI, Prince Nikolai Bolkonsky's estate, was situated about forty miles from Smolensk and two miles from the Moscow highway.

That evening, while the prince was giving Alpatitch his commissions, Dessalles asked for a few moments' talk with Princess Maria, and told her that as the prince, her father, was not very well, and refused to adopt any measures for their safety, he respectfully advised her to send a letter by Alpatitch to the head of the government at Smolensk, asking him to let her know the real state of affairs, and the measure of danger to which Lisiya Gori was exposed. Dessalles wrote the letter for her to the governor, and she signed it, and it was put into Alpatitch's hands with strict injunctions to hand it to the governor, and in case the danger was urgent to return as soon as possible.

Having received all his instructions, Alpatitch, in a white beaver hat—a gift from the prince—with a walking stick exactly like that carried by the prince, went, escorted by all the servants, to get into the leather-hooded carriage to which three fat roan horses had been harnessed.

The bell on the carriage was tied up, and the little harness bells were stuffed with paper. The prince would not allow bells to be used at Lisiya Gori. But Alpatitch liked the sound of them on a long journey. His fellow servants, the communal scribe, the house clerk, the pastry cook, the scullery maid, two old women, a young groom, the coachman, and a number of other household serfs gathered to see him off.

His daughter stuffed back of the seat and under it some calico-covered down cushions. His wife's sister, an old woman, stealthily thrust in a small bundle. One of the coachmen helped him settle in his place.

"Well, well! women's fussiness! Oh, women, women!" he exclaimed, puffing and speaking in the same short, hurried way as the old prince did; and he took his place in the carriage.

Arriving on the evening of August sixteenth at Smolensk, Alpatitch put up at an inn kept by Ferapontof, across the Dnieper in the Gachensky suburb, where he had been accustomed to make his headquarters for the past thirty years. Ferapontof was standing at the street door of his shop in a bright cotton shirt and a waistcoat. Catching sight of Alpatitch, he came out to meet him.

"Welcome, Alpatitch. The people are leaving town, and here you are coming to town!" exclaimed the landlord.

"What do you mean? Leaving town?" asked Alpatitch.

"I mean what I say. The people are fools. They're all afraid of a Frenchman!"

"Woman's chatter! woman's chatter!" grumbled Alpatitch.

"That's my opinion, Alpatitch. I tell 'em there's orders not to let him in; so, of course, he won't get in. And yet those peasants ask three rubles for a horse and cart. It isn't Christian of 'em!"

Alpatitch paid little attention to what Ferapontof said. He asked for a samovar, and some hay for his horses, and, after he had sipped his tea, he went to bed.

All night long the troops went tramping by the tavern along the street. The next morning Alpatitch put on his fine waistcoat, which he wore only in town, and set out to do his errands. The morning was sunny, and at eight o'clock it was already hot. A fine day for harvesting the wheat, Alpatitch thought. Beyond the city the sounds of firing had been audible since early morning. About eight o'clock a heavy cannonading was heard in addition to the musketry.

The streets were crowded with people hurrying to and fro; there were many soldiers; but, just as usual, cabs were driving about, merchants were standing at their shop doors, and the morning service was going on in the churches.

Alpatitch did his errands at the shops, at the government offices, at the post office, and at the governor's. At the goverment offices, at the shops, at the post office, everywhere, everyone was talking of the war and the enemy, who was even now advancing on the city. Everyone was asking everyone else what was to be done, and everyone was trying to reassure everyone else.

At the governor's house, Alpatitch found a great throng of people, Cossacks, and a traveling carriage belonging to the governor. In the reception room were merchants, women, and officials, silently exchanging glances.

The governor summoned Alpatitch and said to him hurriedly:

"Inform the prince and the princess that I knew nothing about it at all. However, as the prince is ill, my advice to him is to go to Moscow. I am going there myself . . . immediately. Tell him . . ."

But the governor did not finish his sentence; an officer, breathless and sweating profusely, came rushing in, and hurriedly said something in French. An expression of horror crossed the governor's face.

"Go," said he, nodding to Alpatitch; and then he began to ply the officer with questions. Pitiful, frightened, helpless glances followed Alpatitch as he came out of the governor's cabinet. Involuntarily listening now to the cannonading, constantly growing nearer and more violent, Alpatitch hastened back to the inn.

People were roaming restlessly about the streets. Trucks, overflowing with domestic utensils, chairs, bureaus and furniture of every description, were coming out of the courtyard gates of the houses and proceeding along the streets. At the house next to Ferapontof's stood a number of teams, and the women were bidding one another good-by and exchanging parting gossip. The house dog barked and frisked around the heads of the horses.

Alpatitch picked up his purchases and gave them to the coachman, who came in; then he settled his account with the landlord. The sounds of carriage wheels, the trampling of the horses and the jingling of bells were heard outside the door as the carriage drove up.

By this time it was late in the afternoon. One side of the street was in shadow; the other was still brightly lighted by the sun. Alpatitch glanced out of the window and went to the door. Suddenly he heard the strange sound of a distant whizzing, and a thud, immediately followed by the long reverberating roar of a cannon, which made the windows rattle.

He went out into the street; a couple of men were running down toward the bridge. In various directions could be heard the whistling and crashing of round shot and the bursting of bombshells falling into the city. But these sounds attracted little attention among the citizens compared with the roar of the cannonading heard beyond the city. This was the bombardment that Napoleon commanded to be opened at five o'clock, from one hundred and thirty cannon. The people at first did not realize the significance of this bombardment. The crash of falling shells and cannonballs at first awakened only curiosity.

The cook and a shopkeeper came down to the gates. All looked with eager curiosity at the projectiles flying over their heads. Around the corner came several men, talking with great animation.

"Now, that was something. What force!" one was saying. "Smashed the roof and the ceiling all into kindling wood."

"And it threw up the ground just like a hog!" said another.

"It was a good shot! Lively work!" said he, with a laugh.

"You had to look sharp and jump, or it would have wiped you out!"

People gathered round these men. They stopped and told how shots had been falling into a house near them. Meantime other projectiles, now round shot with a pleasant whistling, now shells with a swift, melancholy hissing, kept flying over the heads of the people. But not a single projectile fell near them; all flew over and beyond. Alpatitch took his seat in his carriage. The landlord was standing at his gates.

"What are you gaping at?" he cried to the cook, who with sleeves rolled up above her bare elbows, and holding up her red skirt, had gone down to the corner to hear the news.

"But it was miraculous," she was just saying, but when she heard the sound of the landlord's voice she turned round and let her petticoat drop.

Once more, but very near this time, came something with a whistling sound, like a bird flying toward the ground; there was a flash of fire in the middle of the street, a loud, stunning crash, and the street was filled with smoke.

"You rascal, what did you do that for?" cried the landlord, rushing to the cook.

At the same instant the pitiful screaming of women was heard on various sides; a child wailed in terror, and the people, with pale faces, gathered in silence round the cook. Above all other sounds were heard the groans and exclamations of the cook. "Oh-h-h! my darlings! my dears! Don't let them kill me! My poor dears!"

Five minutes later not a soul was left in the street. The cook, whose thigh had been broken by a fragment of the bomb, was carried into the kitchen. Alpatitch, his coachman, and Ferapontof's wife and children and the house porter, were cowering in the cellar with ears alert. The roar of cannon, the whistle of projectiles, and the pitiful groans of the cook, which overpowered all other sounds, did not cease for a single instant.

Toward twilight the cannonade began to grow less violent. Alpatitch went out of the cellar and stood in the doorway. Now that the terrible roar of the cannon had ceased, silence fell upon the city, broken only by what seemed to be a constantly increasing rumble of hurrying steps, groans, distant shouts, and the crackling of flames. Soldiers in various uniforms, mixed all together, no longer in orderly ranks, but like ants from a demolished anthill, came running and walking from various directions down the street. It seemed to Alpatitch that some of them were making for Ferapontof's tavern. He went down to the courtyard gates. A regiment marching in serried ranks and hurrying along blocked the street from side to side.

"The city has surrendered! Get away! Get away!" cried an officer who noticed him, and then he turned to his soldiers: "Loot the houses if you want," he cried.

As Alpatitch drove out of the gates, he saw half a score of soldiers in Ferapontof's open shop, in loud discussion and busily filling bags and knapsacks with wheat flour and sunflower seeds. Just at that time Ferapontof himself happened to come into his shop from the street. When he saw the soldiers, he began to shout at them, but suddenly paused and, clutching his hair, broke into laughter that was like a lamentation.

"Take it all, boys. Don't leave any for those devils," he cried, grasping the bags himself and helping to fling them out into the street. Some of the soldiers, frightened, ran away; others still continued to fill their sacks. Seeing Alpatitch, Ferapontof called to him:

"It's all up with Russia," he shouted. "Alpatitch, it's all up with us! I myself helped set the fires. All ruined!"

Ferapontof ran into the courtyard.

The passing regiments so completely blocked the street that Alpatitch could not make his way along, and he had to wait. Ferapontof's wife and family also were seated in a cart, waiting for a chance to get away.

Night had now fallen. The sky was studded with stars, and occasionally the young moon gleamed from behind the billows of smoke. On the slope down toward the Dnieper, the teams of Alpatitch and the landlord, which had at last been slowly advancing amid the ranks of soldiers and other vehicles, were obliged to halt. A short distance from the crossroads where the teams had halted, a house and some shops were burning on a side street. The fire was burning itself out. The flame would die down and lose itself in black smoke, then suddenly flash forth brilliantly again, bringing out with strange distinctness the faces of the spectators standing at the crossroads. In front of the fire the dark forms of men were darting to and fro, and above the still audible crackling of the flames were heard shouts and cries. Alpatitch, dismounting from his carriage, saw that he would not be able to proceed for some time, and walked down the side street to look at the conflagration. Soldiers were constantly working on the fire, passing back and forth, and Alpatitch saw two of them, in company with another man in a rough coat, dragging some burning lumber from the fire across the street into the next yard; others were adding fagots of straw.

Alpatitch joined the great crowd standing in front of a tall warehouse that was one mass of roaring flames. The walls were all on fire, the back wall had fallen in, the timbered roof was giving way, the girders were blazing. The crowd was evidently waiting for the roof to cave in. At all events, that was what Alpatitch was waiting for.

"Alpatitch!"

A well-known voice suddenly called the old man by name.

"Dear God! your excellency!" replied Alpatitch, instantly recognizing the voice of his young prince.

Prince Andrei, in a riding cloak and mounted on a black horse, was stationed beyond the crowd and looking straight at Alpatitch.

"Why are you here?" he asked.

"Your . . . your excellency," stammered Alpatitch, and he sobbed. "Your —your . . . I—I . . . is . . . are we lost? Your father . . ."

"Why are you here?" demanded Prince Andrei a second time.

The flame blazed out again at that moment and revealed to Alpatitch his young master's pale, weary face. Alpatitch told how he had been sent and what difficulty he had met with in getting out of town.

"But tell me, your excellency, are we really lost?" he asked once more.

Prince Andrei, without replying, drew out a notebook, and, spreading it on his knee, hastily penciled a few lines on a torn leaf. He wrote his sister:

Smolensk is abandoned; Lisiya Gori will be occupied by the enemy inside of a week. Go immediately to Moscow. Send me word as soon as you start, by special messenger to Usviazh.

Having written this note and handed it to Alpatitch, he began to give him some verbal instructions about the arrangements for the journey of the prince and princess and his son and the tutor, and how and where to communicate with him immediately. He had not had time to finish these instructions when a mounted staff officer accompanied by a suite came galloping up to him.

"You, a colonel?" cried the staff officer in a German accent and a voice that Prince Andrei instantly recognized. "In your very presence they are setting houses on fire, and you allow it? What is the meaning of this? You shall answer for it!"

This was Berg, who had now the position of deputy chief of staff to the deputy chief of staff of the commander of the infantry corps of the left flank of the first division of the army—a place which was very agreeable and "on view," as Berg expressed it.

Prince Andrei glanced at him and without replying went on with his instructions to Alpatitch:

"Tell them that I shall expect an answer by the twenty-second, and that if by the twenty-second I do not get word that they have all gone, I myself shall be obliged to throw up everything and go to Lisiya Gori."

"I—prince, I only spoke as I did," exclaimed Berg as soon as he recognized Prince Andrei, "because . . . because it is my duty to carry out my orders, and I am always very scrupulous in carrying them out. I beg you to excuse me," said Berg, trying to apologize.

There was a crash in the burning building. The fire for an instant died down; volumes of black smoke rolled up from the roof. Again there was a strange crashing sound in the fire and something enormous fell in.

"Urrooroooroo!" yelled the crowd, with a roar rivaling that of the fallen barn, from which now came an odor like hot cakes caused by the burning flour. The flames darted up and sent a bright reflection over the spectators standing around the fire with gleefully excited or exhausted faces.

The man in the rough coat waved his arm and cried:

"Well done! She draws well now! Well done, boys!"

"That's the owner himself," various voices were heard saying.

"So then," said Prince Andrei, addressing Alpatitch, "give the message just as I have told you"; and, not saying a single word to Berg, who silently stood near, he set spurs to his horse and rode down the side street.

Prince Andrei was the commander of a regiment and deeply concerned in its organization and the well-being of his men, and the carrying out of the urgent orders which had to be given and received. The burning of Smolensk and its abandonment marked an epoch in his life. The new feeling of hatred against the enemy made him forget his own personal sorrow. He devoted himself exclusively to the affairs of his command; he was indefatigable in the service of his men and his subordinate officers, and was courteous to them. In the regiment they all called him "our prince"; they were proud of him and loved him.

But his kindness and affability were only for his own men—Timokhin and the like, men who were perfect strangers to him and his life, men who could not know him or recall his past; the moment he fell in with any of his former acquaintances, his fellow staff officers, he immediately bristled, grew fierce, sarcastic, and scornful. Everything that served as a connection with the past repelled him, and consequently in his relations with this former society he tried merely to be moderately just and to do his duty.

I V

AMONG THE numberless subdivisions that can be made of the phenomena of life, there is a category where substance predominates, and another where form predominates. A similar contrast may be observed between life in the country, in the village, in the small town, or even in Moscow; and that which can be seen in Petersburg, and especially in the Petersburg salons. This life goes on unchanging.

Since 1805 we had been quarreling and making up with Bonaparte; we had drafted constitutions and scrapped them; but Anna Pavlovna's salon and Helene's salon were exactly the same as they had been seven years before and five years before. Just exactly as before, at Anna Pavlovna's, they were amazed and perplexed at Bonaparte's successes, and detected not only in his successes but also in the subservience of the sovereigns of Europe a wicked conspiracy, the sole object of which was to discompose and alarm the courtly circle that regarded Anna Pavlovna as its representative.

And at Helene's, in 1812 as in 1808, they talked with enthusiasm of the "great nation" and the "great man," and regretted the rupture with the French, which in the opinion of the habitués of Helene's salon ought to end with peace.

Prince Vasili, who as always held important official posts, formed a bond of union between the two cliques. He was equally at home with "my good friend Anna Pavlovna" and in "the diplomatic salon of my daughter"; and frequently, owing to his constant visits from one camp to the other, he got confused, and said at Helene's what he should have said at Anna Pavlovna's, and vice versa.

Shortly after the sovereign's arrival, Prince Vasili was at Anna Pavlovna's conversing about the war, sharply criticizing Barclay de Tolly, and frankly confessing his doubt as to the fit person to call to the head of the armies.

One of the visitors, who was known as "the man of great merit," mentioning the fact that he had that day seen Kutuzof, the newly appointed chief of the Petersburg militia, at the Treasury Department enrolling volunteers, allowed himself cautiously to suggest that Kutuzof would be the man to satisfy all demands.

Anna Pavlovna smiled sadly and remarked that Kutuzof caused the sovereign nothing but unpleasantness.

"I have said, and I have said in the chamber of nobles," interrupted Prince Vasili, "but they would not heed me—I have said that his election as commandant of the militia would not please the sovereign. They would not listen to me. It is this everlasting mania for petty intrigue," pursued Prince Vasili. "And for what purpose? Simply because we want to ape that stupid Moscow enthusiasm," said Prince Vasili, becoming confused for a moment, and forgetting it was at Helene's that it was considered correct to make sport of Moscow enthusiasm, but the fashion to praise it at Anna Pavlovna's. But he instantly corrected himself.

"Now, then, is it fit for Count Kutuzof, Russia's oldest general, to be holding such sessions at the court? And that's as far as he will get. Is it possible to make a man commander-in-chief who cannot sit a horse, who dozes during council meetings—a man of the worst possible manners? He won a fine reputation for himself at Bucharest! And I have nothing to say about his qualities as a general; but is it possible, under present circumstances, to nominate to such a place a man who is decrepit and blind, simply blind? A blind general would be a fine thing! He can't see anything at all! He might play blindman's bluff—but, really, he can't see anything!"

No one raised any objection to this.

On the fifteenth of August this was perfectly correct. But five days later Kutuzof was made a prince. This advance in dignities might also signify that they wanted to shelve him, and therefore Prince Vasili's criticism would continue to be well received, although he was not so eager to deliver it. But on the twentieth of August, a committee was summoned composed of Field Marshal Saltikof, Arakcheyef, Viazmitinof, Lopukhin, and Kotchubey, to consider the conduct of the war. The committee decided that the failures were attributable to the division of command; and although the individuals composing the committee well knew the sovereign's dislike of Kutuzof, they determined after a brief deliberation to place him at the head of the armies. On that same day Kutuzof was made plenipotentiary commander-in-chief of the armies, and of the whole district occupied by the troops.

On the twenty-first Prince Vasili and "the man of great merit" met again at Anna Pavlovna's. "The man of great merit" was dancing attendance on Anna Pavlovna with the hope of securing the appointment of trustee to a woman's educational institute.

Prince Vasili entered the drawing-room with the air of a rejoicing conqueror who had reached the goal of all his ambitions.

"Well, you know the great news: Prince Kutuzof is appointed field marshal. All discords are at an end! I am so happy, so very happy!" exclaimed Prince Vasili. "There's a man for you!" he added, with significant emphasis, surveying all in the room with a stern glance.

"The man of great merit," in spite of his anxiety to obtain a fine position, could not refrain from reminding Prince Vasili of his former criticism. This was an act of discourtesy both toward Prince Vasili, in Anna Pavlovna's drawing-room, and toward Anna Pavlovna herself, who had also been greatly delighted with the news; but he could not refrain.

"But it is said that he is blind, prince," he suggested, quoting Prince Vasili's own words.

"Oh, nonsense! He sees well enough," replied Prince Vasili, in quick, deep tones, and clearing his throat—the same voice and the same clearing of the throat that he always used in getting himself out of an awkward situation. "Certainly he sees well enough," he repeated. "And what makes me happy," he went on to say, "is that the sovereign has given him full powers over all the forces and over the whole district—such powers as no commander-in-chief ever enjoyed before. This makes him the second autocrat," he said, in conclusion, with a triumphant smile.

"God grant it, God grant it," said Anna Pavlovna.

"The man of great merit," who was still somewhat of a novice in courtly circles, wishing to flatter Anna Pavlovna by taking the ground which she had formerly taken in regard to the same subject, said:

"They say it went against the sovereign's heart to allow these powers to Kutuzof. They say that Kutuzof blushed like a schoolgirl hearing *Jaconde* when the emperor said: 'The sovereign and your country confer this honor on you.'"

"Possibly his heart had nothing to do with it," said Anna Pavlovna.

"Oh, no, certainly not," hotly cried Prince Vasili, coming to his defense. He could not now allow anyone to surpass him in his zeal for Kutuzof. According to his idea at the present time, not only was Kutuzof himself the best of men, but everyone worshiped him. "No, that is impossible, because his majesty long ago appreciated his worth," said he.

"Only, God grant"—ejaculated Anna Pavlovna—"God grant that Prince Kutuzof may have actual power and will not allow *anyone* to put a spoke in his wheels."

Prince Vasili instantly understood whom she meant by anyone. He said in a whisper:

"I know for a certainty that Kutuzof demanded as an absolute condition that the heir apparent should not have anything to do with the army. You know what he said to the emperor?"—and Prince Vasili repeated the words that Kutuzof was supposed to have spoken to the sovereign—"'I cannot punish him if he does wrong, or reward him if he does well.' Oh! he is a shrewd man, that Prince Kutuzof—I have known him for a long time."

"But they do say," insisted "the man of great merit," not as yet having the tact required at court—"they do say that his serene highness made it a *sine qua non* that the sovereign himself should keep away from the army."

The moment he had spoken those words Prince Vasili and Anna Pavlovna simultaneously turned their backs on him and, with a sigh of pity for his simplicity, exchanged melancholy glances.

V

Princess Maria was not at Moscow and out of harm's way, as her brother supposed.

When Alpatitch returned from Smolensk, the old prince seemed suddenly to wake, as it were, from a dream. He ordered the peasantry from his villages to be enrolled in the militia and armed, and wrote a letter to the commander-in-chief informing him of his resolution to remain at Lisiya Gori and defend it to the last extremity, leaving it to his judgment whether or not to take measures for the defense of the place where one of the oldest of Russian generals proposed to be taken prisoner or to die. At the same time he announced to his household that he would remain at Lisiya Gori.

But while he was determined to remain at Lisiya Gori, he insisted that the princess with Dessalles and the young prince should go to Bogucharovo, and from there to Moscow. The princess, alarmed by her father's feverish, sleepless activity, which had so suddenly supplanted his former lethargy, could not bring herself to leave him alone, and for the first time in her life permitted herself to disobey him. She refused to leave, and this drew upon her a terrific storm of fury from the prince. He brought up against her everything he could find that was most unjust toward her. In his endeavors to incriminate her, he declared that she was a torment to him, that she had made him quarrel with his son, that she had harbored shameful suspicions of him, that she made it her purpose to poison his life; finally he drove her out of his study, saying that if he never set eyes on her again it would be all the same to him.

He declared that never would he allow her name to be mentioned in his hearing, and henceforth she might do what she pleased, but she was never to dare show herself to him again. The fact that in spite of Princess Maria's apprehensions he did not order her to be borne away by main force, but simply forbade her to come into his sight, was a comfort to her. She knew this proved that in the secret depths of his heart he was glad of her determination to stay at home and not forsake him.

On the morning of the day after Nikolusha's departure, the old prince put on his full uniform and prepared to visit the commander-in-chief. The carriage was already at the door. Princess Maria saw him as he left the house in his uniform with all his orders and went down into the park to review his peasantry and household serfs under arms. She sat at the window and listened to the tones of his voice echoing through the park. Suddenly a number of men came running from the avenue with frightened faces.

Princess Maria hastened down the steps, along the flower-bordered walk, and into the avenue. Here she was met by a great crowd of the militia and the household serfs, and saw in the center of this crowd several men carrying the poor little veteran in his uniform bedecked with all his orders.

Princess Maria ran up to him and, in the shifting play of the sunbeams which fell in little circles through the linden boughs and flecked the ground, she could not clearly make out what change had taken place in her father's face. The one thing she noticed was that the former stern and resolute expression of his face had changed into an expression of timidity and submission. When he caught sight of his daughter he moved his lips, but the words were unintelligible, and the only sound that came forth was a hoarse rattle. It was impossible to understand what he wished to say. They lifted him in their arms, carried him into his study, and laid him on the couch he had so dreaded of late. The doctor who was summoned that same night took blood from him and announced that paralysis had affected his right side.

As it grew more and more dangerous to remain at Lisiya Gori, the day after the stroke the prince was removed to Bogucharovo. The doctor went with him.

When they reached Bogucharovo, Dessalles and the little prince had already started for Moscow.

For three weeks the old prince, helpless with paralysis, lay in the same condition, neither better nor worse, in the new house his son had built at Bogucharovo. He was unconscious. He lay like a mutilated corpse. He kept muttering something with twitching brows and lips, but it was impossible to make out whether or not he realized what was going on around him. The only thing certain was that he felt an urgent impulse to say something; but no one could divine whether it was the whim of a sick and semidelirious man, or whether it referred to the general course of affairs, or whether it was in regard to the circumstances of the family.

The doctor insisted that there was no significance to be found in this restlessness, that it proceeded wholly from physical causes; but Princess Maria felt certain that he wished to say something to her, and the fact that her presence always increased his agitation confirmed her in this supposition.

He apparently suffered both physically and mentally. There was no hope of his recovery. It was impossible to move him. And what would happen if he died on the road?

"Would not the end, would not death, be far better?" Princess Maria sometimes asked herself. She sat by him night and day, almost denying herself sleep; and, terrible to say, she often watched him closely, not with the hope of discovering symptoms of improvement, but rather with the wish that she might discover the approaching end.

Strange as it was for the princess to confess to this feeling, still it was there. And what was still more horrible for her was that since the illness of her father—even if it were not earlier, at the time, say, when with some vague expectation she had elected to stay by him—all her long-forgotten hopes and desires seemed to wake and take possession of her once more. What she had long years ago ceased to think of—the thought of a life free from the terror of her father's tyranny, even the dream of love and possibility of family happiness—constantly arose in her imagination like the suggestions of the evil one.

No matter how strenuously she tried to put them all away, the thought would constantly arise in her mind how she would henceforth, after this was over, arrange her life. This was the devil's temptation, and Princess Maria knew it. She knew that the only weapon against *this* was prayer, and she tried to pray. She put herself into the attitude of prayer, she looked at the holy pictures, she read the words of the breviary, but she could not pray. She felt that now she would be brought into contact with life itself, hard and yet free activity, so different, so wholly opposed to that circumscribed world by which she had been hitherto surrounded, in which her best consolation had been prayer. She could not pray, could not weep, and the details of daily life occupied her.

It was becoming dangerous to remain at Bogucharovo. From every direction came rumors of the approach of the French, and in a village only ten miles from Bogucharovo a farmhouse had been pillaged by French marauders. The doctor insisted that it was necessary to get his patient farther away. The marshal of the nobility sent an officer to Princess Maria, urging her to get away as speedily as possible. The police inspector arrived in person at Bogucharovo and insisted on the same thing, declaring that the French were only some twenty-five miles off, that the French proclamations were circulating among the villages, and that if the princess did not get her father away by the twenty-seventh he would not answer for the consequences.

The princess resolved to start on the twenty-seventh. The work of preparation, the many orders she had to give, as everyone came to her for directions, kept her busy all day long. The night of the twenty-sixth she spent as usual, without undressing, in the room next to that occupied by the prince. Several times, aroused from a doze, she heard his hoarse breathing and muttering, the creaking of his bed, and the steps of Tikhon and the doctor as they turned him over. Several times she listened at the door, and it seemed to her that he muttered more distinctly than hitherto, and turned over more frequently. She could not sleep, and many times she went to the door and listened, wishing to go in and yet not having the courage to do so. Although he could not tell her so, still she had seen and she knew how much he was annoyed by every expression of solicitude on his account. She had observed how he impatiently avoided her eyes, which she sometimes fixed on him in spite of herself, full of anxiety. She knew that her intrusion at night, at such an unusual time, would annoy him.

But never before had she felt so sad, so terribly sad, at the thought of losing him. She recalled all her life with him and discovered the evidence of his love for her in his every word and every deed. Occasionally these recollections would be interrupted by those promptings of the devil, the thoughts of what would happen after he was gone, and how she would arrange her new life of freedom. But she dismissed such thoughts with loathing.

Toward morning he became quieter, and she fell into a sound sleep.

She awoke late. The clear-sightedness which accompanies our waking hours made her realize that her father's illness was the one predominant problem of her life. As she awoke she listened for what went on in the next room and, hearing his hoarse breathing, she said to herself with a sigh that there was no change.

"But why should there be? What is it that I wish? I am looking forward to his death," she told herself, revolted at the very thought.

She washed, changed her gown, said her prayers, and went out on the porch. In front of the door the carriages stood without horses; a number of things had been already packed.

The morning was warm and hazy. Princess Maria was standing on the steps, her mind still full of horror at the thought of her moral depravity, and striving to bring some order into her mental state before going to him. The doctor came downstairs and approached her.

"He is better today," said he. "I was looking for you. You may be able to understand something of what he says. His mind is clear. Come. He is calling for you."

Princess Maria's heart beat so violently at this news that she turned pale and leaned against the door lest she should fall. To see him, to speak with him, to come under the power of his eyes now when her soul had just been full of these terrible, criminal, sinful temptations was too painful a mixture of joy and horror.

"Come," said the doctor.

The princess went to her father's room and approached his bed. He was lying propped high up, with his small, bony hands with their network of knotted purple veins resting on the counterpane, his left eye straight as it always had been, and his right eye drawn down, though now his brows and lips were motionless. He was the same little, lean, wizened, pitiful old man. His face seemed shrunk up or shriveled, his features without character. Princess Maria approached him and kissed his hand. His left hand gave her hand a returning pressure which made it evident he had been expecting her for some time. He held her hand, and his brows and lips moved impatiently.

She looked at him in terror, striving to divine what he wanted of her. When she changed her position and moved so that he could see her face with his left eye, he seemed satisfied and for several seconds did not let her out of his sight. Then his brows and lips quivered; he uttered sounds and began to speak, looking at her timidly and supplicatingly, evidently apprehensive that she would not understand him.

Princess Maria, concentrating all her powers of attention, looked at him. The peculiar difficulty he had in managing his tongue caused her to drop her eyes and made it hard for her to choke down the sobs that rose in her throat. He said something, several times repeating his words. The Princess Maria could not understand them, but in her attempts to guess at what he said she uttered several sentences questioningly.

"Gaga . . . boi . . . boi . . ." he repeated several times. It was impossible to make any sense out of those sounds. The doctor thought that he had found the clue, and, trying to come the nearest to those sounds, asked: "Do you mean, is the princess afraid?"

He shook his head and again repeated the same sounds.

"His mind, his mind troubles him!" suggested the princess. He uttered a sort of roar by way of affirmation, seized her hand and pressed it here and there on his chest, as if trying to find a place suitable for it to rest.

"Think . . . all . . . the time . . . about . . . you," he then said far more distinctly than before—now that he was persuaded that they understood him. Princess Maria bowed her head down to his hand to hide her sobs and tears.

He smoothed her hair.

"I was calling you . . . all night," he went on.

"If I had only known," said she, through her tears. "I was afraid to come in."

He pressed her hand. "Were you not asleep?"

"No, I was not asleep," replied the princess, shaking her head. Involuntarily falling under the influence of her father's condition, she now, in spite of herself, had to speak, as he did, more by signs, and almost found it difficult to manage her tongue.

"Darling"—Or did he say little daughter?—She could not tell, but she was assured by his look that he had called her some affectionate, caressing name, which he had never done before—"why did you not come in?"

"And I was wishing him dead, wishing him dead," thought Princess Maria.

He lay silent.

"Thank you . . . daughter, dearest . . . for all . . . for everything. . . . Forgive . . . Thank you . . . Forgive . . . Thank you!"

And the tears trickled from his eyes.

"Call Andrei," he said suddenly, and as he made this request a childishly puzzled and distrustful expression came into his face. It seemed as if he himself knew that this request had no sense. So at least it seemed to Princess Maria.

"I have had a letter from him," replied Princess Maria. He gazed at her in puzzled amazement.

"Where is he?"

"He is with the army, father, at Smolensk."

He closed his eyes and remained silent for a long moment. Then he opened his eyes and nodded his head affirmatively as if in answer to his own doubts, as much as to say that now he understood and remembered everything.

"Yes," said he, in a low but distinct voice. "Russia is ruined, lost. They have ruined her!"

And again he sobbed and the tears rolled down his cheeks. Princess Maria could not longer contain herself, and she also wept as she looked into his face.

He again closed his eyes. His sobs ceased. He made a gesture toward his eyes with his hand, and Tikhon, understanding what he meant, wiped away the tears.

Then he opened his eyes and made some remark that no one understood for some time; at last Tikhon made out what he had said, and repeated after him. Princess Maria had been trying to connect the sense of his words with what he had just before been speaking about. She thought he might be speaking of Russia, or of Prince Andrei, or of herself, or of his grandson, or of his own death. And consequently she could not make it out.

"Put on your white dress; I like it," was what he had said.

On hearing this, Princess Maria sobbed still more violently; and the doctor, taking her by the arm, led her from the room out upon the terrace, telling her to calm herself and then finish the preparations for the departure. After his daughter had left him, the old prince again spoke about his son, about the war, about the sovereign, and scowled angrily, and tried to raise his hoarse voice; and then came the second and final stroke.

Under the supervision of Tikhon and the doctor, the women washed what had been the prince; they tied a handkerchief around his head, so that his jaw might not stiffen with the mouth open, and they bound together his legs with another handkerchief. Then they dressed him in his uniform, with his decorations, and laid out his little wizened body on a table. God knows under whose direction and at what time all this was accomplished, but everything seemed to be done of itself.

By night the candles were burning around the coffin, the pall was laid over it; juniper was strewn on the floor; a printed prayer scroll was placed under the wrinkled head of the dead, and in the room sat the deacon reading the psalms.

Just as horses shy and crowd together and neigh at the sight of a dead horse, so in the drawing-room, around the coffin of the dead prince, gathered a throng of strangers and the members of the household—the commander of the locality, and the elder of the village, and peasant women —and all, with terrified fixed eyes, crossed themselves and bowed low, and kissed the aged prince's cold, stiff hand.

VI

Until Prince Andrei settled at Bogucharovo, the place had always been an "absentee" estate where the peasantry bore an entirely different character from those of Lisiya Gori. They differed in speech and in dress and customs.

They called themselves "children of the steppe." Their crude manners had not been softened since Prince Andrei's last residence there, in spite of his dispensaries and schools, and his lightening of the taxes; on the contrary, those traits of character which the old prince called boorishness seemed to have been intensified. Strange, obscure rumors always found credence among them. At one time they got the notion that they were all to be enrolled as Cossacks; another time, it was a new religion which they were to be forced to accept; then, again, there was talk about certain imperial dispensations; then, at the time they took the oath of allegiance to Tsar Paul in 1797, they got the notion that their freedom had been granted them, but that their masters had deprived them of it.

Rumors of the war and of Napoleon and his invasion were connected in their minds with obscure ideas of Antichrist, the end of the world, and perfect freedom.

In the vicinity of Bogucharovo the lives of the peasantry were more noticeably and powerfully affected than elsewhere by those mysterious currents characteristic of the common people in Russia, the significance and causes of which are so inexplicable to contemporaries. A phenomenon which illustrates this had taken place a score of years before, when an exodus of the peasantry was made toward certain "warm rivers." Hundreds of peasants, including some from Bogucharovo, suddenly sold their cattle and set off with their families "somewhere" toward the southeast. Just as birds fly "somewhere" across the sea, so these men, with their wives and children, made every endeavor to reach that unknown southeast, where none of them had ever been before. They marched in caravans; here and there one bought his freedom; others ran away, and set forth in wagons or on foot for the "warm rivers"! Many were caught and punished; many were sent to Siberia; many perished of cold and starvation on the road; many returned of their own accord; and, at last, this migration died out of itself, just as it had begun—without any visible reason. But these underground currents never ceased to flow among these people, and they were gathering impetus for some new outbreak, likely to prove just as perplexing, as unexpected, and, at the same time, as simple, natural, and violent. In 1812 any man whose life brought him in contact with the people might have observed these hidden currents working with extraordinary energy, all ready for a new manifestation.

For thirty years, Dron, whom the old prince always called by the affectionate diminutive, Dronushka, had exercised the functions of bailiff at Bogucharovo.

Dron was one of those peasants—powerful, physically and morally—who as soon as they come to years of discretion, grow a beard and live on without change till they are sixty or seventy years old, without a gray hair or the loss of a tooth, just as erect and powerful at sixty as they were at thirty. During all the time of his service, Dron had never once been drunk or sick. Never, even after sleepless nights or after the most exhausting labors, was he known to show the slightest slothfulness, and, though he was illiterate, he never made any mistakes in his money accounts, or as to the number of pounds of flour that he carried in monstrous loads and sold, or as to the amount of a single rick of corn harvested in the fields of Bogucharovo.

Alpatitch, on his arrival from the devastated Lisiya Gori, summoned this Dron on the very day of the funeral, and ordered him to have ready a dozen horses for the princess' conveyance, and eighteen teams for the luggage she was to take with her from Bogucharovo. Although the peasantry paid taxes, Alpatitch never dreamed that there would be any difficulty in having this order carried out, since the villages contained two hundred and thirty taxable households, and the peasants were well-to-do.

But Dron, on receiving this order, dropped his eyes and made no answer. Alpatitch named certain peasants whom he knew, and ordered Dron to make the requisitions on them.

Dron replied that these men's horses were off on carrier duty. Alpatitch named still other peasants. And these men also, according to Dron, had no horses; some were off with the government trains; others were out of condition; still others had been lost through lack of forage. According to Dron's report it was impossible to secure horses for the carriages, to say nothing of those for the baggage wagons.

Alpatitch looked keenly at him and scowled. Just as Dron was a model of what a peasant leader should be, in the same way Alpatitch had not managed the prince's estates for nothing all those twenty years, and he also was a model overseer. He was in the highest degree qualified to understand the wants and instincts of the people with whom he dealt and this made him a surpassingly excellent overseer.

He knew from a single glance at Dron that Dron's answers were not the expression of Dron's individual opinions, but rather expressed the general wishes of the village council, to which the bailiff evidently belonged. But, at the same time, he knew that Dron, who had grown rich and was hated by the village, must necessarily waver between the two camps, the peasants' and the master's. This wavering he could detect in his eyes, and, therefore, Alpatitch, with a frown, drew near to Dron.

"Listen, you, Dron my friend!" said he. "You need not tell me idle tales. His excellency Prince Andrei himself gave me orders that all the peasantry should leave, and not remain behind with the enemy; and those are the Tsar's orders also. So anyone who stays is a traitor to the Tsar. Do you hear?"

"I hear," replied Dron, keeping his eyes lowered.

Alpatitch was not satisfied with this answer.

"Ah, Dron! ill will come of it!" exclaimed Alpatitch, shaking his head.

"You have the power," returned Dron, mournfully.

"Ah, Dron! give in!" exclaimed Alpatitch, taking his hand out from the breast of his coat, and with a solemn gesture pointing under Dron's feet. "Not only do I see through and through you, but I can see three yards under you; everything there is," said he, looking down at Dron's feet. Dron grew confused; he gave Alpatitch a fleeting glance and then dropped his eyes again.

"Stop all this nonsense and tell the people to get ready to leave for Moscow, and have the teams ready tomorrow morning for the princess, and mind you don't attend any more of their meetings! Do you hear?"

Dron suddenly threw himself at his feet.

"Alpatitch! Discharge me! Take the keys from me! Discharge me, for Christ's sake!"

"Stop!" said Alpatitch, sternly. "I can see three yards deep under you!" he repeated, knowing that his skill in going after bees, his knowledge of the times and seasons for sowing, and the fact that for a score of years he had succeeded in satisfying the old prince, had long ago given him the reputation of being a wizard, and that to wizards was attributed the power of seeing three yards under a man.

Dron got to his feet and tried to say something, but Alpatitch interrupted him.

"Come now! What is your idea in all this? Ha? What are you dreaming of? Ha?"

"What shall I do with the people?" asked Dron. "They are all stirred up! And, besides, I have told them . . ."

"Told them?" repeated Alpatitch. "Are they drunk?" he demanded laconically.

"All stirred up, Alpatitch! They have just brought another cask!"

"Now, then, listen! I will go to the police, and you hurry back to the people, and bid them quit all this sort of thing, and get ready the teams."

"I obey," replied Dron.

Alpatitch insisted on nothing more. He had been in control of the villages too long not to know that the best way to control them was by showing not the slightest doubt that they would become subordinate. Having wrung from Dron the submissive "I obey," Alpatitch contented himself with that, although he not merely suspected, but was even certain in his own mind, that without the assistance of a squad of militia nothing would be done.

And, in point of fact, there were no teams forthcoming, as he supposed. Another meeting of the peasantry was held at the village tavern; and this meeting voted to drive the horses out into the woods and not to furnish the teams. Saying nothing of all this to the princess, Alpatitch gave orders to unload the carts that had brought his own belongings from Lisiya Gori, and to have his horses put to Princess Maria's carriage; and he himself went to consult with the authorities.

VII

Princess Maria, after her father's funeral, shut herself up in her room and admitted no one. Her maid came to the door to say that Alpatitch

428

was there to learn her wishes in regard to the departure. (This was before his interview with Dron.) The princess sat up on the couch where she had been lying and spoke through the closed door, declaring that she would never go away anywhere, and asked to be left in peace.

She wanted, but she dared not, to pray; she dared not, in that state of mind in which she found herself, to turn to God in prayer. For a long time she lay in that position.

Someone, in a soft, affectionate voice, called her name from the park side of her window, and kissed her on the head. She looked up.

It was Mlle. Bourienne, in a black dress trimmed with white. She had softly approached Princess Maria, kissed her with a sigh, and immediately burst into tears. The princess looked at her. All her previous collisions with her, her jealousy of her, came back to her; she also remembered how *he* of late had changed toward Mlle. Bourienne, how he could not even bear to see her, and consequently how unjust had been the reproaches that Princess Maria had in her heart made against her.

"Yes, and can I, I who have wished for his death, can I judge anyone else?" she asked herself.

Princess Maria had a keen sense of Mlle. Bourienne's trying situation, held at a distance as she had recently been and yet at the same time dependent on her, and dwelling under a stranger's roof. And she began to feel pity for her. She looked at her with a sweet, questioning look, and stretched out her hand. Mlle. Bourienne immediately had a fresh paroxysm of tears, began to kiss the princess' hand and to speak of the sorrow that had come upon her, and claimed to share that sorrow. She declared that her only consolation was that the princess allowed her to share her sorrow. She said that all their previous misunderstandings ought to be forgotten in the presence of this terrible loss, that she felt that her conscience was clear before all men, and that *he* from above would bear witness to her love and gratitude.

The princess listened without comprehending, but looked at her from time to time and heard the sounds of her voice.

"Your position is doubly terrible, dear princess," said Mlle. Bourienne, after a short silence. "I understand how it is that you could not have thought . . . that you cannot think about yourself, but from the love I bear you, I am compelled to do so for you. Has Alpatitch been to see you? Has he said anything to you about going away?" she asked.

Princess Maria looked at her friend without comprehending what she was saying.

"Ah, if you could only know how little, how little I care now," said she. "Of course, I should never wish such a thing as to go away and leave *him*. . . . Alpatitch said something to me about going away. Talk it over with him; I cannot and I will not hear."

"I have spoken with him. He hopes that we will be able to get away tomorrow; but it is my opinion that we had better remain here now," said

Mlle. Bourienne. "Because—you must agree with me, dear Marie—to fall into the hands of the soldiers or insurgent peasants would be horrible."

Mlle. Bourienne drew forth from her reticule a proclamation—printed on paper different from that used generally in Russia—from the French General Rameau, in which the inhabitants were advised not to abandon their homes, since full protection would be given them by the French authorities. The princess, with the paper in her hand, got up from the window, and with a pale face left the room and went into Prince Andrei's study, which was the next room.

"What if Prince Andrei knew that I was under the protection of the French! That I, the daughter of Prince Nikolai Bolkonsky, had asked General Rameau to grant me his protection, and put myself under obligation for benefits received from him!"

The mere suggestion of such a thing filled her with horror, made her shudder, turn red, and feel still more violently than ever those impulses of anger and outraged pride. The demands of life, which she had felt were annihilated at the moment of her father's death, suddenly rose up before her with new violence never before experienced, and took possession of her.

Flushed with excitement, she walked up and down the room, summoning first Alpatitch, then Mikhail Ivanovitch, then Tikhon, then Dron. Alpatitch was not at home; he had gone to consult with the authorities. Mikhail Ivanovitch, the architect, on being summoned, came into Princess Maria's presence with sleepy eyes and could tell her nothing. Then the old valet Tikhon was called, and, with a downcast and impassive face, bearing all the marks of incurable woe, he replied to all her questions with "I obey," and could scarcely refrain from sobbing as he looked at her.

At last Dron came into the room, and, making her a low bow, stood respectfully at the threshold.

Princess Maria walked across the room and paused in front of him.

"Dear Dron!" said she, seeing in him a true friend, the same kind Dron who had always brought home pieces of gingerbread from his trips to the annual fair at Viazma, and presented them to her with a smile. "Dear Dron, now, since our sad loss . . ."

She began and then paused, unable to proceed.

"We are all in God's hands," said he, with a sigh. Neither spoke.

"Dron dear! Alpatitch has gone; I have no one to turn to; is it true, what I am told, that we cannot get away?"

"Not get away? Certainly you can get away, princess," said Dron.

"They tell me there is danger from the enemy. My friend, I am helpless, I don't understand anything about it, I am entirely alone. I decidedly wish to start tonight or tomorrow morning early."

Dron stood silent. He looked from under his brows at the princess.

"No horses," said he at last, "and I have told Alpatitch so."

"How is that?" asked the princess.

"It is God's punishment," said Dron; "what horses we had have been

430

taken by the troops, and the rest have perished. That's the way it is this year. It wouldn't so much matter about feeding the horses, if we ourselves weren't perishing of starvation. Often for three days at a time we go without a bite. We have nothing at all; we are utterly ruined."

Princess Maria listened attentively to what he said.

"The peasants are ruined? You mean they have no bread?" she asked.

"They are dying of starvation," said Dron. "And as for teams . . ."

"But why haven't you told me of this before, Dron? Can't they be helped? I will do all in my power . . ."

It was strange for Princess Maria to think that now, at this moment when her heart was filled with such sorrow, there could be poor men and rich, and that the rich did not help the poor. She had a general notion that when the masters had a reserve of grain it was distributed among the serfs. She knew also that neither her father nor her brother would refuse to help the peasantry in case of need; all she feared was that she might make some blunder in speaking about this distribution of grain which she was anxious to make. She was glad of some pretext for active work, something that would allow her without pangs of conscience to forget her own sorrow. She proceeded to question Dron in regard to the needs of the peasants and the store of reserve grain belonging to the estate at Bogucharovo.

"We have grain belonging to the estate, have we not, my friend?" she demanded.

"The master's grain is untouched," said Dron, with pride. "Our prince had not ordered it to be sold."

"Give that to the peasants; give them all they need. I grant it in my brother's name," said Princess Maria.

Dron made no reply, and drew a long sigh.

"You give them this grain, if there is enough for them. Give it all to them. I order it in my brother's name, and tell them: 'What is ours is always theirs. We shall not begrudge it.' Tell them so."

Dron looked steadily at the princess while she was saying this.

"Discharge me, my girl, for God's sake; order the keys to be taken from me," said he. "I have been in service for twenty-three years! I have never done anything dishonest; discharge me, for God's sake!"

Princess Maria could not understand what he wanted of her, or why he wished to be relieved of his office. She replied that she had never conceived a doubt of his devotion, and that she was always ready to do anything for him or for any of the peasants.

VIII

An hour later Dunyasha came to the princess with the news that Dron was there, and that all the peasants had collected at the granary in accordance with the princess' orders and wished to speak with their mistress.

"But I never called them," said Princess Maria; "I merely told old Dron to give them grain."

"Then, for God's sake, princess darling, order them to disperse and don't go to them. They are deceiving you," exclaimed Dunyasha. "But Alpatitch will soon be back, and then we will go . . . and don't you allow . . ."

"How are they deceiving me?" asked the princess in amazement.

"But I am certain of it! Only heed my words, for God's sake. Just ask nurse here. They declare they will not go away at your orders."

"You have it entirely wrong. Besides, I have never ordered them to go away," said the Princess Maria. "Fetch Dron."

Dron came in and confirmed what Dunyasha said: The peasants had assembled at the princess' orders.

"But I never summoned them," said the princess. "You did not give my message correctly. I only told you to give them grain."

Dron made no reply, but sighed.

"If you order it they will disperse," said he.

"No, no, I will go to them," said the princess.

In spite of the persuasion of Dunyasha and the old nurse, Princess Maria went down the steps. Dron, Dunyasha, the old nurse, and Mikhail Ivanovitch followed her.

"They apparently think that I give them the grain so that they should stay at home, while I myself am going away, abandoning them to the mercy of the French," thought Princess Maria. "But I will promise them rations and quarters at our Moscow estate; I am sure Andrei would do even more in my place," she said to herself as she went toward the crowd gathered in the twilight on the green near the granary.

The peasants showed some signs of confusion, and moved and swayed a little, and hats were quickly removed as she approached. Princess Maria, with downcast eyes, and getting her feet entangled in her dress, went toward them. So many different eyes from faces young and old were fixed on her, and so many different people were collected, that the princess did not distinguish any particular person; and, as she felt the necessity of addressing them all at once, she did not know how to set about it. But once more the consciousness that she was the representative of her father and brother gave her courage, and she boldly began to speak.

"I am very glad that you came," she began, not raising her eyes and conscious of her heart beating fast and strong. "Dron told me that you were ruined by the war. That is our common misfortune, and I shall spare no endeavor to help you. I myself am going away because it is dangerous here . . . and the enemy are near . . . because . . . I will give you everything, friends, and I beg of you to take all, all our grain, so that you may not suffer from want. And if you have been told that I distribute the grain among you so as to keep you here, that is a falsehood. On the contrary, I beg of you to go with all your possessions to our Moscow estate and I promise that you will not suffer. You will be given homes and provisions."

The princess paused. In the crowd sighs were heard, and that was all.

"Our misfortune is universal, and we will share everything together. All that is mine is yours," said she, gazing at the faces ranged in front of her.

All eyes were fixed on her with one expression, the significance of which she could not interpret. Whether it was curiosity, devotion, gratitude, fear, or distrust, that expression, whatever it was, was the same in all.

"Very grateful for your kindness, but we don't want to take the master's grain," said a voice in the rear of the crowd.

"Yes, but why not?" asked the princess.

No one replied, and Princess Maria, glancing around, observed that now all eyes that met hers immediately turned away.

"Why don't you speak?" demanded the princess, addressing an aged man, who, leaning on his cane, was standing in front of her. "Tell me if you think that anything else is needed. I will do everything for you," said she, as she caught his eye. But he, as if annoyed by this, hung his head and muttered:

"Why should we? We don't want your grain."

"What! Us abandon everything? We don't agree to it." . . . "We don't agree to it." . . . "Not with our consent." . . . "We are sorry, but it won't be done with our consent. Go off by yourself alone!" rang out from the mob on different sides.

And again all the faces of the throng had one and the same expression; but this time it was assuredly not curiosity or gratitude, but one of angry, obstinate resolution.

"Oh, but you have not understood me," exclaimed Princess Maria, smiling sadly. "Why are you unwilling to go? I promise to give you new homes and feed you. But if you stay here the enemy will ruin you."

But her voice was drowned by the voices of the mob.

"Not with our consent. Let him destroy us. We won't touch your grain. Not with our consent."

Princess Maria tried again to catch the eyes of some other person in the crowd; but not one was directed toward her; their eyes evidently avoided her. She felt strange, and ill at ease.

"There now! She's a shrewd one. Follow her to prison. They want to get our houses and make serfs of us again—the idea! We won't touch your grain," rang the various voices.

Princess Maria, hanging her head, left the crowd and went back to the house. Repeating her orders to Dron to have the horses ready for their departure the next day, she went to her room and remained alone with her thoughts.

IX

On the twenty-ninth of August, Rostof and Ilyin, accompanied only by Lavrushka and an orderly sergeant of hussars, set forth from their bivouac at Yankovo, ten miles from Bogucharovo, to try a new horse that Ilyin had recently purchased and to find whether there was any fodder in the villages roundabout. Rostof, like the thoughtful squadron commander that he was, conceived the notion of taking possession of the provisions at Bogucharovo before the French could get them.

Rostof and Ilyin were in the most jovial of moods on the way to Bogucharovo, the princely estate and farm where they hoped to find many domestics and pretty young girls. Rostof had not the slightest notion that this village where he was bound was the estate of that very same Bolkonsky who had been betrothed to his sister.

He and Ilyin, in trial of their horses, made a final spurt down the slope in front of Bogucharovo, and Rostof, outriding Ilyin, was the first to enter the street of the village.

They rode at a walk up to the granary, near which a great crowd of peasants were gathered. One of them came out of the crowd and approached Rostof.

"Which side are you from?" he asked.

"The French," replied Rostof, jokingly, with a smile. "And that's Napoleon himself," he added, pointing to Lavrushka.

"Of course you're Russians, aren't you?" asked the peasant.

"Is there a large party of you?" asked another, a little man, who also joined them.

"Ever so many," replied Rostof. "And what brings you all together here?" he added. "A holiday festival?"

"The elders have collected for village business," replied the peasant who had spoken first.

Alpatitch, who took off his hat some distance away, approached Rostof.

"I make bold to trouble your honor," said he, politely, but manifesting a certain scorn of the officer's youthful appearance, and placing his hand in the breast of his coat. "My mistress, the daughter of general-in-chief, the late Prince Nikolai Bolkonsky, who died on the twenty-seventh of this month, finds herself in difficulty on account of the insubordination and rudeness of these individuals here"—he pointed to the peasants. "And she begs you to confer with her—if it would not be asking too much," said Alpatitch, with a timid smile—"if you would come a few steps farther . . . and besides it is not so pleasant in the presence of . . ."

He indicated the two drunken peasants who were circling round them and in their rear like gadflies round a horse.

"Hey! Alpatitch—Hey!" . . . "Ser'ous shing! 'Scuse us! Ser'ous shing!"

. . . "'Scuse us, for Christ's sake! Hey!" said the peasants at him. Rostof looked at the drunken men and smiled.

"Or perhaps this pleases your excellency?" suggested Alpatitch, with a sedate look, and indicating the old men with his other hand—the one not in the breast of his coat.

"No, there's no pleasure in that," said Rostof, and started off. "What is the trouble?" he asked.

"I make bold to explain to your excellency that these coarse peasants here are not willing to have their mistress leave her estate, and they threaten to take her horses out; and though everything has been packed up since morning, her highness can't get away."

"Incredible!" cried Rostof.

"I have the honor of reporting to you the absolute truth," maintained Alpatitch.

Rostof dismounted and, throwing the reins to his orderly, went with Alpatitch to the house, questioning him on the state of affairs. In point of fact, the offer of grain which the princess had made to the peasants the evening before, her explanations to Dron and to the meeting, had made affairs so much worse that Dron had definitely laid down his keys, and taken sides with the peasantry, and had refused to obey Alpatitch's summons; and that morning, when the princess had ordered to have the horses harnessed for her departure, the peasants had gone in a regular mob to the granary, and sent a messenger declaring that they would not allow the princess to leave the village, that orders had come not to leave and they would unharness the horses.

Princess Maria, entirely bewildered and weak with fright, was sitting in the drawing-room when Rostof was brought in to her. When she saw his Russian face, and recognized by his manner and the first words he spoke that he was a man of her own class, she looked at him with her deep, radiant eyes, and began to speak in broken tones, her voice trembling with emotion.

Rostof immediately found something very romantic in this adventure. "An unprotected maiden, overwhelmed with grief, left alone at the mercy of rough, insurgent peasants! And what a strange fate has brought me here!" thought Rostof, as he listened to her and looked at her. "And what sweetness and gratitude in her features and her words!" he said to himself, as he listened to her faltering tale.

When she related all that had taken place on the day after her father's funeral, her voice trembled. She turned aside, and then, as if she were afraid Rostof would take her words to be an attempt to arouse his pity, she glanced at him with a timidly questioning look.

The tears stood in Rostof's eyes. Princess Maria observed this, and she looked gratefully at him with those brilliant eyes of hers which made one forget the plainness of her face.

"I cannot tell you, princess, how happy I am at the chance that brought

435

me here and puts me in a position to show you how ready I am to serve you," said Rostof, rising. "You can start immediately, and I pledge you my word of honor that no one shall dare cause you the slightest unpleasantness, if you will only permit me to serve as your escort"; and, making her a courtly bow such as are made to ladies of the imperial blood, he went to the door.

X

"WELL, NOW, PRETTY? Ah, brother, my pink one's a beauty, and her name is Dunyasha."

But as he glanced in Rostof's face Ilyin held his tongue. He saw that his hero and commander had come back in an entirely different frame of mind.

Rostof gave Ilyin a wrathful glance and without deigning to give him any answer strode swiftly down to the village.

"I will teach them! I will give it to those cutthroats," he muttered to himself.

Alpatitch, with a sort of swimming gait that was just short of running, found it hard to overtake him.

"What decision have you been pleased to come to?" he asked, at last catching up with him. Rostof halted and, doubling his fists, made a threatening movement toward Alpatitch suddenly.

"Decision? What decision? You old dotard!" cried he. "What are you staring at? Ha?—The peasants are in revolt and you can't bring them to terms? You yourself are a traitor! I know you. I'll take the hide off you, the whole of you." And, as if afraid of wasting the reserve fund of his righteous wrath, he left Alpatitch and hastened forward.

Alpatitch, evidently fighting down his sense of injured innocence, hastened after Rostof with that ambling gait of his, and continued to give him his opinions in regard to the matter. He declared that the peasants had got themselves into such a state of rebellion that at the present moment it would be imprudent to oppose them unless one had a squad of soldiers first.

"I'll give them a squad of soldiers . . . I'll show how to oppose them," replied Rostof, not knowing what he was saying, and breathing hard from his unreasoning, keen indignation and the necessity he felt of expressing this indignation. With no definite plan of action, he rushed with strong, resolute steps straight at the mob. And the nearer he approached it, the more firmly convinced grew Alpatitch that this imprudent action of his might lead to excellent results. The peasants felt the same thing as they saw his swift, unswerving movements and his resolute, scowling face.

After the hussars had entered the village and Rostof had gone to see the princess, a certain perplexity and division of opinion had prevailed among the peasantry. It began to be bruited among them that these visitors were

Russians, and some of them declared that the hussars would be angry because their young mistress was detained. Dron was of this opinion, but as soon as he had so expressed himself, the peasant Karp, and other peasants, who possessed great influence in the village, attacked their former bailiff.

"How many years have you been getting your belly full in this village?" cried Karp. "It's all the same to you. You'll dig up your pot of money and be off! What do you care whether they burn up our houses or not?"

As soon as Rostof, accompanied by Ilyin, Lavrushka, and Alpatitch, drew near the mob, Karp, thrusting his fingers in his belt and slightly smiling, came forward. Dron, on the contrary, got into the rear ranks, and the throng crowded closer together.

"Hey! Which of you is the elder here?" cried Rostof, coming up to the mob with swift strides.

"The elder? What do you want of him?" asked Karp.

But before he had a chance to utter another word his cap flew off, and he was sent reeling with a powerful blow.

"Hats off, you traitors!" cried Rostof, in a stentorian voice. "Where is the elder?" he thundered, in a voice of fury.

"The elder, he wants the elder . . . Dron, you!" was spoken by various officiously submissive voices, and every hat was doffed.

"We would never think of rebelling; we are keeping order," insisted Karp, and several voices in the rear suddenly shouted:

"It was what the village council ordered. We had to obey."

"Do you dare answer back? Mob! Cutthroats! Traitors!" yelled Rostof, beside himself with rage and in an unnatural voice, seizing Karp by the collar. "Tie him up! Tie him up!" he cried, though there was no one to execute his orders except Lavrushka and Alpatitch.

Lavrushka, however, sprang forward and seized Karp by the arms from behind.

"Do you wish us to call our boys from below?" he cried.

Alpatitch turned to the peasants, calling two by name, to bind Karp's arms. These peasants submissively stepped forth from the crowd and began to unfasten their belts.

"Where is the elder?" cried Rostof.

Dron, pale and scowling, stood forth.

"Are you the elder? Tie him up, Lavrushka," cried Rostof, as if it were impossible for this command to meet with resistance. And, in fact, two other peasants began to bind Dron, who in order to facilitate the operation took off his girdle and handed it to them.

"And see here . . . all of you obey me!"—Rostof had turned to the peasants —"Disperse to your homes instantly, and don't let me hear a word from one of you!"

"Come, now! We've done no harm!" . . . "We've only been acting silly." . . . "Made fools of ourselves, that's all." . . . "I said there wasn't no such orders," said various voices, reproaching one another.

437

"That's what I told you," said Alpatitch, resuming his rights. "It wasn't right of you, boys."

"Our foolishness, Alpatitch," replied the voices, and the crowd immediately began to break up and scatter to their homes.

The two peasants with their arms bound were taken to the master's house. Two drunken men followed.

"Now I get a good look at you!" said one of them, addressing Karp.

"How could you speak to your betters in that way? What were you thinking of? Idiot!" exclaimed the other. "Truly you were an idiot!"

Inside of two hours the teams were ready in the courtyard of the Bogucharovo mansion. The men were zealously lugging out and packing up the master's belongings, and Dron, at the princess' intercession, let out of the shed where he had been locked up, directed the peasants at their work, standing in the court.

Rostof, not wishing to impose himself on the princess, did not return to her, but remained in the village waiting for her to pass on her way. Having waited until Princess Maria's carriages had left the house he mounted and accompanied her on horseback along the highway occupied by our troops for a few miles.

At Yankovo, where his bivouac was, he politely took leave of her, and for the first time permitted himself the liberty of kissing her hand.

"But it was nothing—nothing," protested Rostof, reddening, as Princess Maria expressed her gratitude for his having saved her—for so she spoke of what he had done. "Any policeman would have done as much. If we had only peasants to fight with, we would not have let the enemy advance so far," said he, feeling a twinge of shame, and anxious to change the topic. "I am only delighted that this has given me a chance to make your acquaintance. Farewell, princess. I wish you all happiness and consolation, and I hope that we shall meet under more favorable circumstances. If you wish to spare my blushes, please do not thank me."

But the princess, if she did not thank him further in word, could not help expressing her gratitude in every feature of her face, which fairly beamed with acknowledgment and gentleness.

When she bade him farewell and was left alone, Princess Maria suddenly felt her eyes fill with tears, and then, it seemed not for the first time, the strange question came into her mind: *Did she love him?*

And it was fate that he should come to Bogucharovo, and at such a time! she thought. *And it was fate that his sister should jilt Prince Andrei!*

And in all this Princess Maria saw the workings of Providence.

The impression made on Rostof by Princess Maria was very agreeable. Whenever his thoughts returned to her, happiness filled his heart; and when his comrades, learning of his adventure at Bogucharovo, teased him because in going after hay, he had fallen in with one of the richest heiresses of Russia, Rostof lost his temper. He lost his temper for the very reason that the idea of marrying the princess, who had impressed him so pleasantly and who had such an enormous property, had more than once, against his will, occurred to him. As far as he personally was concerned, he could not wish a better wife than Princess Maria. To marry her would give great delight to the countess, his mother, and would help him to extricate his father's affairs from their wreck; and then, again—Nikolai felt this—it would be for Princess Maria's happiness.

But Sonya? And his plighted troth?

And that was the reason Rostof grew angry when they teased him about Princess Bolkonsky.

XI

HAVING ACCEPTED the command of the armies, Kutuzof remembered Prince Andrei and sent word to him to join him at headquarters.

Prince Andrei reached Tsarevo-Zaimishche and sat down to await his "serene highness," as everyone now called Kutuzof. Two of Kutuzof's servants—the courier and his house steward—stood near by.

A dark-complexioned little lieutenant colonel of hussars, with a heavy mustache and side whiskers, came riding up to the gates and, seeing Prince Andrei, asked if his serene highness lodged there.

Prince Andrei replied that he did not belong to his serene highness' staff, and had, likewise, only just arrived.

The lieutenant colonel turned to a spruce-looking orderly with the same question; and the chief commander's orderly answered him with that contemptuous indifference with which the servants of commanders-in-chief are apt to treat lower-ranking officers.

"What? His serene highness? Likely to be here before long. What do you want?"

The lieutenant colonel laughed in his mustaches at the orderly's tone, dismounted from his horse, gave the bridle to his orderly, and joined Bolkonsky, making him a stiff little bow. Bolkonsky made room for him on the bench. The lieutenant colonel of hussars sat down beside him.

"So you're waiting for the commander-in-chief, too, are you?" asked the lieutenant colonel. "He's weported to be vewy accessible! Thank God for that! That was the twouble with those sausage stuffers. There was some weason in Yermolof's asking to be weckoned as a German. Now pe'w'aps we Wussians will have something to say about things. The devil knows what they've been doing! Always wetweating—always wetweating! Have you been making the campaign?" he asked.

"I have had that pleasure," replied Prince Andrei. "Not only have I taken part in the retreat, but I have lost thereby all that I hold dear, to say nothing of my property and the home of my ancestors and my father, who died of grief. I am from Smolensk."

"Ah? Are you Pwince Bolkonsky? Vewy glad to make your acquaintance:

439

—Lieutenant Colonel Denisof, better known as Vaska," said Denisof, shaking hands with Prince Andrei and looking with a peculiarly gentle expression into his face. "Yes, I heard about it," said he sympathetically; and, after a short pause, he continued: "And so this is Scythian warfare. It's all vewy good except for those whose wibs are bwoken. And you are Pwince Andwei Bolkonsky?" He shook his head. "Vewy, vewy glad, pwince, vewy glad to make your acquaintance," he repeated for the second time, squeezing his hand.

Prince Andrei had known from Natasha that Denisof was her first suitor. This recollection, at once sweet and bitter, brought back to him those painful sensations which of late he had not allowed himself to harbor, but which were always in his heart. Recently so many other and more serious impressions—like the evacuation of Smolensk and the news of his father's death—and so many new sensations had been experienced by him, that it was some time since he had even thought of his disappointment, and now, when he was reminded of it, it seemed so long ago that it did not affect him with its former force.

For Denisof, too, the series of recollections conjured up in his mind by Bolkonsky's name belonged to a distant, poetic past, to that time when he, after the supper, and after Natasha had sung for him, himself not realizing what he was doing, offered himself to a maiden of fifteen! He smiled at his recollection of that time and of his love for Natasha, and immediately proceeded to the topic which at present passionately occupied him to the exclusion of everything else.

This was a plan of campaign which he had developed during the retreat, while on duty at the outposts. He had proposed this plan to Barclay de Tolly, and was now bent on proposing it to Kutuzof. The plan was based on the fact that the French line of operations was too widely spread out, and his idea was that instead of attacking them in front, or possibly in connection with offensive attacks at the front, so as to block their road, it was necessary to act against their communications. He began to outline this plan to Prince Andrei.

"They can't sustain such a long line. It is impossible! I'll pwomise to bweak thwough them; give me five hundred men and I'll cut my way thwough, twuly. A sort of system of guewillas."

Denisof had got up in his excitement, and as he laid his plan before Bolkonsky he gesticulated eagerly. In the midst of his exposition, the army was heard cheering, and the trampling of horses and shouts neared the village.

"Here he comes," shouted the Cossack guard.

"Hurrah! hurrah! hurrah!" The cheers rent the air behind him.

Kutuzof, since Prince Andrei had last seen him, had grown stouter than ever; he seemed flabby and bloated. But the whitened eye, and the scar, and that expression of lassitude in face and figure which Prince Andrei knew so well, were the same. He was dressed in a military long coat, a whip hung by a slender ribbon over his shoulder, and he wore his white cavalier-guard cap. Heavily sprawled out and swaying, he sat his little horse. His whistling breath could just be heard as he rode into the courtyard.

His face had that expression of relief which a man shows when he makes up his mind to have a rest after a public exhibition. He extricated his left leg from the stirrup, leaned back with his whole body, and, scowling with the exertion of getting his leg up over the saddle, rested with his knee a moment, and then with a whack like a duck he let himself down into the arms of the Cossacks and aides who were waiting to assist him.

He straightened himself up, looked around with blinking eyes, and, glancing at Prince Andrei but evidently failing to recognize him, he set out in his clumsy, plunging gait for the steps. *Fiu-fiu-fiu,* he puffed, and again he glanced at Prince Andrei. The impression made by Prince Andrei's face, though it was reached only after several seconds, at last connected itself with the recollection of who he was.

"Ah! How are you, prince, how are you, my good fellow? Come with me," he said wearily, glancing round, and beginning heavily to mount the steps, which groaned under his weight. Then he unbuttoned his uniform and sat down on the bench at the top of the steps.

"Well, how is your father?"

"Yesterday I received news of his death," said Prince Andrei abruptly.

Kutuzof looked at Prince Andrei with startled, wide-open eyes; then he took off his cap and crossed himself.

"The kingdom of heaven be his. God's will be done to us all."

He drew a deep, heavy sigh and was long silent. "I loved him dearly and I realized his worth, and I sympathize with you with all my heart."

He embraced Prince Andrei, pressed him to his fat chest, and held him there long. When at last he released him, Prince Andrei saw that his blubbery lips trembled, and that his eyes were full of tears. He sighed and took hold of the bench with both hands so as to rise.

"Come, come to my room and let us talk!" said he; but just at that instant Denisof, who was as little apt to quail before his superiors as before his enemies, strode with jingling spurs to the steps, in spite of the aides who with indignant whispers tried to stop him. Kutuzof, still clinging to the bench, gave him a displeased look.

Denisof, introducing himself, explained that he had something of the greatest importance for the good of the country to communicate to his serene highness. Kutuzof, with his weary look, continued to stare at Denisof, and with a gesture of annoyance released his hands and folded them on his belly, repeating: "For the good of the country? Well, what is it? Speak!"

Denisof reddened like a girl—it was so strange to see the blush on the veteran's mustached, bibulous face—and he began boldly to evolve his plan for breaking through the enemy's line between Smolensk and Viazma. Denisof's home was in this region, and he was well acquainted with every part of it. His plan seemed unquestionably excellent, especially owing to the force of conviction that he put into his words. Kutuzof regarded his own legs and occasionally looked over into the yard of the adjoining cottage, as if he were expecting something unpleasant to appear there. And sure enough, from the cottage at which he was looking during Denisof's speech, emerged a general with a portfolio under his arm.

"What?" exclaimed Kutuzof, interrupting Denisof in the midst of his exposition. "Ready so soon?"

"Yes, your serene highness," replied the general. Kutuzof shook his head as much as to say, "How can one man have time for all this?" and went on listening to Denisof.

"I give you my twuest word of honor as a Wussian officer," insisted Denisof, "that I will cut off Napoleon's communications."

"What! Is Quartermaster General Kirill Andreyevitch Denisof any relation of yours?" asked Kutuzof, interrupting him.

"My uncle, your sewene highness."

"Oh, we were good friends," exclaimed Kutuzof, jovially. "Very good, very good, my dear. Stay here at headquarters; we will talk it over tomorrow."

Nodding to Denisof, he turned away and stretched out his hand for the papers which Konovnitsin had brought him.

XII

IN HALF AN HOUR, Prince Andrei was again summoned to Kutuzof. Kutuzof was sprawled out in an easy-chair, with his uniform coat unbuttoned. He held a French book in his hand, and when Prince Andrei came in he laid it down, marking the place with a knife. This book, as Prince Andrei could see by the cover, was *Les Chevaliers du Cygne*, a work by Madame de Genlis.

"Well, now, sit down, sit down here," said Kutuzof. "It's sad, very sad. But remember, my boy, that I am a father to you—a second father."

Prince Andrei told Kutuzof all that he knew about his father's death.

"To what—to what have they brought us!" suddenly exclaimed Kutuzof in an agitated voice, evidently getting from Prince Andrei's story a clear notion of the state in which Russia found herself.

"Wait a bit! Wait a bit!" he added with a wrathful expression; and then, evidently not wishing to dwell on this agitating topic, he went on to say: "I have summoned you to keep you with me."

"I thank your serene highness," replied Prince Andrei. "But I fear that I am not good for staff service," he explained, with a smile which Kutuzof noticed. "And chiefly," added Prince Andrei, "I am used to my regiment. I have grown very fond of the officers, and the men, so far as I can judge, are fond of me. I should be sorry to leave my regiment. If I decline the honor of being on your staff, believe me, it is . . ."

A keen, good-natured, and at the same time shrewdly sarcastic expression flashed over Kutuzof's puffy face. He interrupted Bolkonsky.

"I am sorry. You might have been useful to me; but your are right, you are right. We don't need men here! There are everywhere plenty of advisers, but not of men. Our regiments would be very different if all the advice givers would serve in them as you do. I remember you at Austerlitz—I remember you, I remember you with the standard," said Kutuzof; and a flush of pleasure spread over Prince Andrei's face at this recollection. Kutuzof drew him close and stroked his cheek, and again Prince Andrei observed tears in his eyes. Though Prince Andrei knew that tears were Kutuzof's weak point, and that he was especially flattering to him, and was anxious to express his sympathy for his loss, still Prince Andrei felt particularly happy and gratified at this allusion to Austerlitz.

"Go, and God bless you! I know, your road is the road of honor."

He paused.

"I missed you sadly at Bucharest. I needed a messenger to send."

And, changing the conversation, Kutuzof began to talk about the Turkish war and the peace that had been concluded.

"Yes, they abused me not a little," said he, "both for the war and for the peace; but all came about in time. All things come to those who wait. There I had just as many advisers as I have here," he went on to say, turning to the counselors, who evidently were an annoyance to him. "Oh! These counselors, these counselors!" he exclaimed. "If their advice had been taken, we would still be in Turkey, and peace would not have been signed, and the war would not be over yet. Everything in haste, but 'more haste, less speed.' If Kamiensky had not died, he would have been ruined. He stormed a fortress with thirty thousand men. It is not hard to take a fortress; it's hard to gain a campaign. And to do that, not storm and attack, but patience and time are required. Kamiensky sent his soldiers against Rushchuk; and while I employed nothing but time and patience, I took more fortresses than Kamiensky ever did, and I made the Turks feed on horseflesh." He shook his head. "And the French will do the same. Take my word for it," he exclaimed, growing more animated, and pounding his chest, "if I have anything to do with it, they will be eating horseflesh too!"

And again his eyes overflowed with tears.

"Still, it will be necessary to accept a battle, won't it?" asked Prince Andrei.

"Certainly, if all demand it, there's no help for it. But trust me, my boy. There are no more powerful fighters than these two—time and patience; they do everything. But our advisers—they won't see it in that light, that's the trouble. Some are in favor, and some are opposed. What's to be done?" he asked, and waited for an answer. "Yes, what is it you advise doing?" he repeated, and his eyes gleamed with an expression of deep cunning. "I will tell you what is to be done, and I shall do it. When in doubt, my dear"—he hesitated—"don't. When in doubt, *don't*," he repeated, after an interval. "Well, good-by, my dear boy. Remember that I sympathize with all my

443

heart in your loss, and that to you I am not his serene highness nor prince nor commander-in-chief, but a father to you. If you want anything, apply directly to me. Good-by, my dear."

He again embraced and kissed him. And before Prince Andrei had actually reached the door, Kutuzof drew a long sigh of relief and had resumed his unfinished novel by Madame de Genlis, *Les Chevaliers du Cygne*.

Prince Andrei could not account to himself for the why or wherefore of it, but it was a fact that after this interview with Kutuzof he returned to his regiment much relieved as to the general course of affairs and as to the wisdom of intrusting them to this man whom he had just seen. The more he realized the utter absence of all self-seeking in this old man, who seemed to have outlived ordinary passions, and whose intellect—that is, the power of coördinating events and drawing conclusions—had resolved itself into the one faculty of calmly holding in check the course of events, the more assured Prince Andrei felt that everything would turn out as it should.

"There is nothing personal about him. He won't give way to his imaginations; he won't do anything rash," said Prince Andrei to himself, "but he will listen to all suggestions; he will remember everything; he will have everything in its place; he will hinder nothing that is useful, and permit nothing that is harmful; he will remember that there is something more powerful and more tremendous than his will—the inevitable course of events—and he will have the brains to see them; he will have the ability to realize their significance, and, in view of this significance, he will be sensible enough to see what a small part he himself and his own will have to play in them. But chief of all," thought Prince Andrei, "what makes me have confidence in him is that he is Russian, in spite of his French novel of Madame de Genlis, and his French phrases; because his voice trembled when he exclaimed, 'What have they brought us to!' and because he sobbed when he declared that he would make them eat horseflesh."

It was due to this feeling, which all felt more or less vaguely, that Kutuzof's selection as commander-in-chief, in spite of court cabals, met with such unanimous and general approval among the people.

XIII

After the sovereign's departure from Moscow, the life in the capital flowed on in its ordinary channels, and the current of this life was so commonplace that it was hard to recall those days of patriotic enthusiasms and impulses, and hard to believe that Russia was actually in peril, and that the members of the English Club were at the same time "Sons of the Fatherland," and had declared themselves prepared for any sacrifice.

The only thing that recalled the general spurt of patriotic enthusiasm that had taken place during the sovereign's recent visit to Moscow was the demand for men and money, which, coming now in legal, official form, had to be met, the sacrifice having once been offered.

Though the enemy was approaching Moscow, the Muscovites were not inclined to regard their situation with any greater degree of seriousness; on the contrary; the matter was treated with peculiar lightness, as is always the case with people who see a great catastrophe approaching. At such a time, two voices are always heard speaking loudly in the heart of man: the one, with perfect reasonableness, always preaches the reality of the peril and counsels him to seek for means of avoiding it; the other, with a still greater show of reason, declares that it is too painful and difficult to think about danger, since it is not in the power of man to foresee everything or to escape the inevitable course of events; and, therefore, it is better to shut the eyes to the disagreeable until it actually comes, and to think only of what is pleasant. When a man is alone, he generally gives himself up to the first voice, but in society, on the contrary, to the second. This was the case at the present time with the inhabitants of Moscow. Moscow had not been so gay for a long time as it was that year.

It was reported that Rostopchin had sent the French and, indeed, all other foreigners, out of Moscow. It was also reported that the courts of justice had been removed from the city, and here there was a chance given for repeating one of Shinshin's jests to the effect that for this, at least, Moscow ought to be grateful to Napoleon.

It was said that Mamonof's regiment would cost him eight hundred thousand rubles, that Bezukhof was spending still more on his warriors; but the best joke of all was that the count himself was going to buckle on his uniform and ride in front of his regiment, and those who would be in the front would not sell their chances to see this great sight for any money.

"You have no mercy on anyone," said Julie Drubetskoy, picking up and pressing together a bunch of picked lint between her slender fingers covered with rings.

Julie had determined to leave Moscow the next day, and she was giving her last reception. "Bezukhof is absurd, but he is so good, so kind! What is the pleasure to be so *caustique?*"

"Fined!" exclaimed a young man in a militia uniform, whom Julie called "My knight," and who was going to accompany her to Nizhni.

In Julie's set, as in many other sets of Moscow society, it had been agreed to speak only in Russian, and those who forgot themselves made use of French words in conversation had to pay a fine, which was turned over to the committee of public defense.

"That's a double fine, for a Gallicism," said a Russian author who was in the drawing-room. " 'Pleasure to be' is not good Russian."

"You show no mercy upon anyone," pursued Julie, paying heed to the author's criticism.

"For using the word *caustique*, I admit my guilt, and will pay my fine for it, and for the pleasure to tell you the truth, I am ready to pay another fine;

but for Gallicisms I am not to be held answerable," she said, turning to the author. "I have neither the money nor the time to hire a teacher and take Russian lessons, as Prince Galitsin is doing.

"Ah, there he is," exclaimed Julie. "*Quand on*—No, no," said she to the militiaman, "do not count that one, I'll say it in Russian: 'When we speak of the sun we see his rays,'" said the hostess, giving Pierre a fascinating smile—"we were just talking about you. We were saying that your regiment would be really much better than Mamonof's," said she, with one of those white lies so characteristic of society women.

"Don't speak to me about my regiment," replied Pierre, kissing the hostess's hand, and taking a chair near her. "I am tired to death of it."

"But surely you are going to take the command of it yourself?" asked Julie, shooting a glance of cunning and ridicule at the militiaman.

The militiaman in Pierre's presence was no longer so *caustique*, and his face expressed some perplexity at the meaning expressed in Julie's smile. In spite of his absent-mindedness and good humor, Pierre's personality immediately cut short all attempts to make a butt of him in his own presence.

"No," replied Pierre, with a glance down at his big, portly frame, "I would be too good a mark for the French, and I am afraid that I could not get on a horse."

Among those who came up as a subject for gossip in the course of the shifting conversation were the Rostofs.

"They say their affairs are in a very bad condition," remarked Julie. "And the count himself is so utterly lacking in common sense! The Razumovskys wanted to buy his house and his Moscow estate, and it is still in abeyance. He asks too much."

"No, I believe the sale was made a few days ago," said someone. "Though now it is nonsense for anyone to buy property in Moscow."

"What makes you go away?"

"I? That is an odd question. I am going because—well, I am going because everybody's going, and because I am not a Jeanne d'Arc and not an Amazon."

"There, now, give me some more rags."

"If he can only economize, he may be able to settle all his debts," pursued the militiaman, still speaking of Count Rostof.

"A good old man, but a very *pauvre sire*. And why have they been living here so long? They intended long ago to start for the country. Natasha, I believe, is perfectly restored to health? Isn't she?" asked Julie of Pierre, with a mischievous smile.

"They are waiting for their youngest son," replied Pierre. "He was enrolled among Obolensky's Cossacks and was sent to Byelaya Tserkov. The regiment was mobilizing there. But now he has been transferred to my regiment and is expected every day. The count wanted to start long ago, but the countess utterly refused to leave Moscow until her son came."

"I saw them three days ago at the Arkharofs'. Natasha has grown very pretty again and was very gay. She sang a romanza. How easy it is for some people to forget everything!"

"Forget what?" asked Pierre, impulsively.

Julie smiled.

"You know, count, that knights like you are to be found only in the romances of Madame de Souza."

"What sort of knights? Why, what do you mean?" asked Pierre, reddening.

"Oh, fie now! dear count, *c'est la fable de tout Moscou. Je vous admire, ma parole d'honneur!*"

"Fined! Fined!" exclaimed the militiaman.

"Very well, then! It's impossible to talk; how annoying!"

"What is the talk of all Moscow?" asked Pierre, angrily rising to his feet.

"Oh! fie! count. You know!"

"I don't know at all what you mean," said Pierre.

"I know that you and Natasha were good friends, and consequently . . . No, I always liked Vera better. *Cette chère Vera!*"

"*Non,* Madame," pursued Pierre, in a tone of annoyance. "I have never in the slightest degree taken upon myself to play the rôle of knight to the Countess Rostof, and I have not been at their house for almost a month. But I do not understand the cruelty . . ."

"*Qui s'excuse s'accuse,*" said Julie, smiling and waving the lint; and in order to have the last word herself, she abruptly changed the conversation. "What do you suppose I heard last night? Poor Maria Bolkonsky arrived in Moscow yesterday. Have you heard? She has lost her father!"

"Really? Where is she? I should like very much to see her," said Pierre.

"I spent last evening with her. She is going today or tomorrow morning with her little nephew to their estate near Moscow."

"But what about her? How is she?" insisted Pierre.

"Well, but sad. But do you know who rescued her? It's a perfect romance! Nikolai Rostof! Her people surrounded her; they would have killed her. She was already wounded. He rushed in and saved her."

"Lots of romances!" exclaimed the militiaman. "Really, this general stampede seems to have been made for providing husbands for all the old maids. Catherine is one, the Princess Bolkonsky two . . ."

"Do you know, really I think that she is *un petit peu amoureuse du jeune homme?*"

"Fined! Fined! Fined!"

"But really, how could one say that in Russian?"

XIV

WHEN PIERRE REACHED home he was handed two of Rostopchin's bulletins, which had been distributed that day.

In the first the count denied having forbidden anyone to leave Moscow, and declared that, on the contrary, he was delighted to have ladies of rank and merchants' wives leave town. "Less panic, less gossip!" said the bulletin. "But I'll answer for it with my life that the villain will never be in Moscow."

By these words Pierre was for the first time fairly convinced that the French would get to Moscow.

The second placard proclaimed that our headquarters were at Viazma, that Count Wittgenstein had beaten the French, but that, as very many of the inhabitants had expressed a desire to arm themselves, there were plenty of weapons for them at the arsenal: sabers, pistols, muskets, all of which the inhabitants might buy at the lowest prices.

"Shall I enter the military service and join the army, or shall I wait?" This question arose in his mind for the hundredth time. He took a pack of cards, which was lying on the table near him, and began to lay out a game of patience.

"If the game comes out," said he to himself, as he shuffled the cards, held them in his hand and looked up—"if it comes out right, then it means—What shall it mean?"

Before he had a time to decide on what it should mean, he heard at the door of his room the voice of the oldest princess, asking if she might come in.

"Well, it shall mean that I must join the army," said Pierre to himself. "Come in, come in," he added, replying to the princess.

Only the oldest of the three princesses—the one with the long waist—continued to make her home at Pierre's; the two younger ones were married.

"Forgive me, cousin, for disturbing you," said she, in an agitated voice. "But you see it is high time to reach some decision. What is going to be the outcome of this? Everyone is leaving Moscow, and the people are riotous. Why do we stay?"

"On the contrary, everything looks very propitious, cousin," said Pierre, in that bantering tone which, in order to hide his confusion at having to play the part of benefactor before the princess, he always adopted in his dealings with her.

"Yes, everything is propitious! . . . Certainly a fine state of affairs! This very day Varvara Ivanovna was telling me how our armies had distinguished themselves. It brings them the greatest possible honor. But still the servants are exceedingly refractory; they won't obey at all; my maid—why, she was positively insolent! And before we know it they will be massacring us. It is impossible to go into the streets. But worst of all the French are liable to be here today or tomorrow! Why should we wait for them? I ask for only one favor, cousin," pleaded the princess. "Give orders to have me taken to Petersburg. Whatever I am, I cannot endure to live under the rule of Bonaparte! If you do not wish to do this for me . . ."

"Yes, I will do it. I will give orders immediately."

The princess was evidently annoyed that she had no one to quarrel with. She sat on the edge of her chair, muttering to herself.

"Nevertheless, this has been reported to you all wrong," said Pierre. "All is quiet in the city, and there is not the slightest danger. Here, I am just this moment reading . . ." Pierre showed the princess Rostopchin's placards.

"Oh, this count of yours," exclaimed the princess, angrily. "He's a hypocrite, a rascal who has himself been exciting the people to sedition. Varvara Ivanovna told me that the mob almost killed her because she spoke French."

"Well, there's something in that. But you take everything too much to heart," said Pierre, and he began to lay out his game of patience.

The game of patience came out correctly, and yet Pierre did not join the army but remained in deserted Moscow in the same fever of anxiety and indecision and fear, and, at the same time, joy, though he was expecting something horrible.

Toward evening of the following day the princess took her departure, and Pierre's head overseer came to him with the report that the money required by him for the equipment of his regiment could not possibly be raised except by selling one of his estates. The head overseer explained to him that such expensive caprices as fitting out regiments would be his ruin. Pierre, with difficulty repressing a smile, listened to the man's despair.

"Well, sell it, then," he replied. "There's no help for it now. I cannot go back on my promise now."

The worse the situation of affairs in general, and his own in particular, the more agreeable it was to Pierre; the more evident it seemed to him that the long-expected catastrophe was drawing near. Already almost none of his acquaintances remained in town. Julie had gone; Princess Maria had gone. Of near acquaintances only the Rostofs were left; but Pierre stayed away from their house.

On the fifth of September foul weather was followed by fair, and that day after dinner Pierre left Moscow. In the evening while stopping to change horses at Perkhushkovo, Pierre learned that a great battle had been fought that afternoon. He was told that there at Perkhushkovo the cannon had shaken the ground; but when Pierre inquired who had been victorious, no one could give him any information.

This was the Battle of Shevardino, which was fought on the fifth of September.

Cossacks, infantry, cavalry, baggage wagons, caissons, were to be seen on all sides. Pierre made all haste to reach the front, and the farther he went from Moscow, and the deeper he penetrated into this sea of troops, the more he was overcome by anxiety, disquietude, and a feeling of joy such as he had never before experienced. It was somewhat akin to that which he had experienced at the Slobodsky palace at the time of the sovereign's visit—a feeling that it was indispensable to do something and make some sacrifice.

He now felt the pleasant consciousness that all that constitutes the happiness of men—the comforts of life, wealth, even life itself—was rubbish, which it was a delight to renounce in favor of something else.

Still Pierre could not account to himself, and indeed he made no attempt to decide, for whom or for what the sacrifice of everything, which gave him such a sense of charm, was made. He did not trouble himself to ask inquiry for what he wished to sacrifice himself; the mere act of sacrifice constituted for him a new and joyful feeling.

X V

On the fifth of September was fought the battle at the redoubt of Shevardino; on the sixth not a single shot was fired on either side; on the seventh came the Battle of Borodino.

Why was the Battle of Borodino fought? Neither for the French nor for the Russians had it the slightest sense. The most immediate result for the Russians—and it was inevitable—was an onward step toward the destruction of Moscow, a thing that we dreaded more than anything else in the world; and for the French an onward step toward the destruction of their entire army—a thing they dreaded more than anything else in the world. This result was even then perfectly obvious, and yet Napoleon offered battle and Kutuzof accepted it.

Up to the Battle of Borodino our forces were to the French in the approximate proportion of five to six, but after the battle, of one to two. That is, before the battle we had 100,000 to every 120,000; but after the battle 50,000 to every 100,000. And yet the wise and experienced Kutuzof accepted battle. Napoleon, also, the leader of genius, as he was called, offered battle, losing a fourth of his army, and still further extending his line. The historians of Napoleon themselves admit that he was anxious to call a halt at Smolensk; that he knew the risk he ran in his extended position, and knew that the capture of Moscow would not be the end of the campaign, because he had seen, by the example of Smolensk, in what a state the Russian cities would be left to him, and he did not receive a single response to his repeated offers to negotiate.

After the loss of the Shevardino redoubt on the morning of the sixth, we were left without any position on our left flank, and were reduced to the necessity of straightening our left wing and of making all haste to fortify it as best we could. The Battle of Borodino did not take place on a selected and fortified position, or with forces only slightly disproportioned; but the battle, in consequence of the loss of the Shevardino redoubt, was accepted by the Russians at an exposed and almost unfortified position, with doubly strong forces opposed to them—in other words, under conditions whereby it was not only unfeasible to fight ten hours and then leave the contest doubtful, but unfeasible to keep the army even for three hours from absolute confusion and flight.

Pierre left Mozhaisk on the morning of the seventh.

On the monstrously steep and precipitous hillside down which winds the road from the city, just beyond the cathedral that crowns the hill on the right, where service was going on and the bells were pealing, Pierre dismounted from his carriage and proceeded on foot.

Behind him, laboriously proceeding downhill, came a regiment of cavalry led by its singers.

A train of carts full of men, wounded in the last evening's engagement, met him on its way up the hill. The peasant drivers, shouting at their horses and lashing them with their knouts, ran from one side to the other. The carts, on which lay or sat three or four wounded soldiers, bumped over the rough stones which were scattered about and did duty as a causeway on the steep road. The soldiers, bandaged with rags, pale, and with compressed lips and knit brows, clung to the sides as they were bounced and jolted in the carts. Nearly all of them looked with naive, childlike curiosity at Pierre's white beaver hat and green coat.

The strange thought struck Pierre that out of all the thousands of living, healthy men, young and old, who had looked at his white hat with such jovial curiosity, probably twenty thousand were doomed to suffer wounds and death—very possibly among them the very men he saw that moment.

"They, very possibly, will be dead men tomorrow; how, then, can they be thinking of anything besides death?"

Pierre drove on farther, to Gorki. Mounting the hill, and passing beyond the narrow street of the village, he saw for the first time the peasant militia, with crosses on their caps and in white shirts, working with a will, with boisterous talk and laughter at something, on a high, grass-grown mound to the right of the road.

Pierre left his equipage, and, passing by the laboring militia, he directed his steps to the mound, from which the whole battlefield was visible.

It was eleven o'clock in the morning. The sun stood a trifle to Pierre's left and rear, and sent its beams down through the pure, rarefied atmosphere, brilliantly lighting up the immense panorama of hill and vale that spread before him as in an amphitheater.

All that Pierre saw was so confused that he found nothing that in any degree fulfilled his expectations. Nowhere could he find any such field of battle as he had counted on seeing, but only fields, clearings, troops, woodland, bivouac fires, villages, hills, brooks; and in spite of all his efforts he could not make out any definite position in this varied landscape, nor could he even distinguish our troops from the enemy's.

"I must ask someone who knows," he said to himself, and he addressed himself to one of the officers, who was looking inquisitively at his huge, unmilitary figure.

"May I ask," said Pierre, turning to this officer, "what that village is yonder?"

"Burdino, isn't it?" replied the officer, referring to his comrade.

"Borodino," said the other, correcting him.

The officer, evidently pleased to have a chance to talk, approached Pierre.

"Are those our men yonder?" asked Pierre.

"Yes, and still farther are the French," said the officer. "There they are, there. Can you see?"

"Where? where?" asked Pierre.

"You can see them with the naked eye. See there."

The officer pointed at the columns of smoke rising at the left, on the far side of the river, and his face assumed that stern and grave expression which Pierre had noticed on many faces he had lately seen.

"Ah! Are those the French? But who are yonder?" . . .

Pierre indicated a mound at the left, where troops were also visible.

"Those are ours."

"Oh, ours! But there? . . ."

Pierre pointed to another hill in the distance, where there was a tall tree near a village showing up in a valley, and with smoking bivouac fires and something black.

"That is them again," explained the officer (this was the Shevardino redoubt). "Yesterday it was ours, but now it's theirs. And who are you? One of the doctors, are you?"

"No, I was merely looking."

And Pierre again descended the hill, past the militiamen.

Extricating himself from the crowd, Pierre looked around.

"Count Bezukhof! How did you get here?" cried a voice. Pierre looked round. Boris Drubetskoy came up to him, smiling. Boris was elegantly attired, with just a shade of the wear and tear of having been on service. He wore a long frock coat and a whip over his shoulder in imitation of Kutuzof.

Kutuzof, meantime, had reached the village and sat down in the shadow cast by the adjoining house, on a bench brought out in all haste by a Cossack, while another had covered it with a rug. A large and brilliant suite gathered about him.

Pierre, engaged in talking with Boris, remained standing about thirty paces from Kutuzof. He was explaining his intention of being present at the battle, and of reconnoitering the position.

"This is what you must do," said Boris. "I will do you the honors of the camp. The best thing is for you to see the whole affair from where Count Benigsen will be. You see, I am with him. I will propose it to him. And if you would like to ride around the position we will do it together. And when we return I will beg you to do me the favor of spending the night with me, and we will get up a party."

"Yes, yes. But where is Prince Bolkonsky's regiment? Can't you show me?" demanded Pierre.

"Andrei's? We shall ride directly past it; I will take you to him."

Kutuzof caught sight of Pierre's figure and the group that had gathered round him.

"Bring him to me," said Kutuzof. An aide communicated his serene highness' message, and Pierre started for the place where he was sitting. But before he got there, a private of militia approached Kutuzof.

It was Dolokhof.

"How comes this man here?" asked Pierre.

"He's such a beast! He's sneaking in everywhere!" was the answer. "He has been cashiered. Now he must climb up again. He has all sorts of schemes, and one night he crept up as far as the enemy's picket lines . . . he's brave."

Pierre, taking off his hat, bowed respectfully to Kutuzof.

"I had an idea that if I made this report to your serene highness, you might order me off, or tell me that what I had to say was already known to you, and then all would be up with me . . ." Dolokhof was saying.

"Very true, very true!"

"And if your serene highness needs a man who would not care if he came out with a whole skin or not, then please remember me . . . maybe I might be of use to your serene highness."

"Very true, very true!" said Kutuzof for the third time, looking at Pierre with his one eye squinted up, and smiling.

At this instant Boris, with his usual adroitness, came up in line with Pierre close to the chief, and, in the most natural manner in the world, said to Pierre in his ordinary tone of voice, as if he were pursuing what he had already begun to say:

"The militia have put on clean white shirts, so as to be ready for death. What heroism, count!"

Boris said this to Pierre evidently for the sake of being overheard by his serene highness. He knew that Kutuzof would be attracted by these words, and, in fact, his serene highness turned to him.

"What did you say about the militia?" he asked of Boris.

"I said, your serene highness, that they had put on white shirts for tomorrow, as a preparation for death."

"Ah! They are a marvelous, incomparable people!" exclaimed Kutuzof, and, closing his eyes, he shook his head. "An incomparable people," he repeated, with a sigh. "So you wish to smell gunpowder?" he asked, addressing Pierre. "Well, it's a pleasant odor. I have the honor of being one of your wife's admirers; is she well? My quarters are at your service."

When Pierre left Kutuzof, Dolokhof approached and took him by the arm.

"Very glad to meet you here, count," said he in a loud tone and with peculiar resolution and solemnity, not abashed by the presence of strangers. "On the eve of a day when God knows which of us may quit this life, I am glad of the opportunity to tell you that I am sorry for the misunderstandings which have existed between us, and that I hope you bear me no grudge. I beg you to pardon me."

Pierre, smiling, gazed at Dolokhof, not knowing what answer to make.

Dolokhof, with tears in his eyes, threw his arms around Pierre and kissed him.

XVI

PRINCE ANDREI, that bright September afternoon of the sixth, was stretched out with his head leaning on his hand, in a dilapidated barn in the village of Kniazkovo, at the end of the position occupied by his regiment. Through a hole in the broken wall he was gazing at a row of thirty-year-old birches with their lower limbs trimmed off, which ran along the edge of the inclosure, and at a plowed field over which were scattered sheaves of oats, and at the wood where the smoke of bivouac fires was rising and where the soldiers were cooking their suppers.

Narrow and useless and sad as Prince Andrei's life now seemed to him, he felt excited and irritable on the eve of the battle, just as he had seven years before at Austerlitz.

The orders for the next day's battle were given and received by him. There was nothing further left for him to do. But his thoughts, the simplest, clearest, and therefore most terrible thoughts, would not give him respite. He was aware that tomorrow's engagement would be the most formidable of all in which he had ever taken part, and the possibility of death, for the first time in his life without reference to any worldly aspect, without consideration as to the effect it might produce upon others, but in its relation to himself, to his own soul, confronted him with vividness, almost with certainty, in all its grim reality. And from the height of this consideration, all that which hitherto tormented and preoccupied him was suddenly illumined by a cold white light, without shadow, without perspective, without distinction of outline.

All his life appeared to him as in a magic lantern, into which he had long been looking through a glass and by artificial light. Now he could suddenly see without a glass, by the clear light of day, these wretchedly painted pictures.

"Yes, yes, here are those false images which have excited and enraptured and deceived me," said he to himself, as he passed in review, in his imagination, the principal pictures of his magic-lantern life, now looking at them in this cold white light of day—the vivid thought of death.

"Here they are, these coarsely painted figures which pretended to represent something beautiful and mysterious. Glory, social advantages, woman's love, the country itself—how great seemed to me these pictures, what deep significance they seemed to possess. And now it all seems so simple, so cheap and tawdry, in the cold white light of that morning which I am convinced will dawn for me tomorrow."

The three chief sorrows of his life especially arrested his attention—his love for a woman, the death of his father, and the French invasion that was engulfing half of Russia.

"Love! . . . That young girl seemed to me endowed with mysterious powers. How was it? I loved her, I dreamed poetic dreams of love and happiness with her. What a foolish boy!" he cried aloud savagely. "How was it? I had faith in an ideal love that would keep her faithful to me during the whole year of my absence. Like the tender dove of the fable, she should have pined away while separated from me. But the reality was vastly more simple. . . . It was all horribly simple, disgusting!

"My father was building at Lisiya Gori and supposing that it was his place, his land, his air, his peasants; but Napoleon came, and, not even knowing of his existence, swept him aside like a chip from the road, and his Lisiya Gori was swallowed up, and his life with it. But Princess Maria says that this is a discipline sent from above. For whom is it a discipline, since he is no more and will never be again? He will never be seen again. He is no more. Then to whom is it a discipline?

"The fatherland, the destruction of Moscow! But tomorrow I shall be killed—perhaps not even by the French, but by one of our own men, just as I might have been yesterday when a soldier discharged his musket near my head—and the French will come, will take me by the legs and shoulders and fling me into a pit, so that I may not become a stench in their nostrils, and new conditions of existence will spring up, to which other men will grow just as accustomed, and I shall not know about them, for I shall be no more!"

He gazed at the row of birches shining in the sun, with their motionless yellow, green and white boles.

"I must die; suppose I am killed tomorrow, suppose it is the end of me, the end of all, and I no longer exist!"

He vividly pictured the world, and himself not in it. The birches, with the light and shade, and the billowing clouds, and the smoke of the bivouac fires—all suddenly underwent a change and became for him terrible and threatening. A cold chill ran down his back. Quickly leaping to his feet, he began to walk up and down.

Voices were heard behind the shed.

"Who is there?" asked Prince Andrei.

"What the devil!" exclaimed the voice of a man, as he tripped over something.

Prince Andrei, peering out of the shed, saw advancing toward him his friend Pierre, who had just succeeded in stumbling and almost falling flat over a pole that was lying on the ground. As a general thing it was disagreeable for Prince Andrei to see men from his own rank in life, and especially to see Pierre, who brought back to his remembrance all the trying moments which he had experienced during his last visit to Moscow.

"Well, well!" he exclaimed. "What chance brings you here? I was not expecting you."

While he was saying these words his eyes and his whole face expressed something more than mere coolness—it was rather an unfriendliness, which Pierre instantly noticed. He had approached the shed in the most cheerful frame of mind, but when he saw Prince Andrei's face he felt suddenly embarrassed and awkward.

"I came . . . well . . . you know . . . I came . . . it was interesting to me," stammered Pierre, who had already used the word "interesting" no one knows how many times during the course of that day. "I wanted to see a battle."

"So, so, but what does your brotherhood of Masons say about war? How can it be prevented?" asked Prince Andrei, ironically. "Well, how is Moscow? How are my family? Have they got to Moscow at last?" he asked gravely.

"Yes, they got there. Julie Drubetskoy told me. I went to call upon them, and failed to find them. They had gone to your estate near Moscow."

XVII

THE OFFICERS WERE going to take their leave, but Prince Andrei, apparently not wishing to be left alone with his friend, invited them to sit down and take tea. Stools and tea were brought. The officers, not without amazement, gazed at Pierre's enormously stout figure and listened to his stories of Moscow and the position of our troops which he had chanced to visit.

"So you understood all the arrangement of our forces, did you?" suddenly interrupted Prince Andrei.

"Yes—that is, to a certain extent," said Pierre; "so far as a civilian can. I don't absolutely, but still I understood the general arrangements."

"Then you are ahead of anyone else!" said Prince Andrei.

"Ha?" exclaimed Pierre, looking in perplexity over his glasses at Prince Andrei. "Well, what do you think about the appointment of Kutuzof?" he asked.

"I was very much pleased with it; that is all I can say about it," replied Prince Andrei.

"Now, then, please tell me your opinion of Barclay de Tolly. They are saying all sorts of things about him in Moscow. What is your judgment of him?"

"He is good for nothing now, for the very reason that he lays out all his plans beforehand very judiciously and punctiliously, as it is natural for every German to do. How can I make it clear? See here! Your father has a German lackey, and he is an excellent lackey, and he serves him in all respects better than you could do, and so you let him do his work; but if your father is sick unto death, you send the lackey off, and with your own unaccustomed, unskilful hands, you look after your father, and you are more of a comfort to him than the skilful hand of a foreigner would be. And that is the case with Barclay. As long as Russia was well, a stranger could serve her and was an excellent servant; but as soon as she was in danger, she needs a man of her own blood. Well, you have accused him at the club of being a traitor. The only effect of traducing him as a traitor will be that afterwards, becoming ashamed of such a false accusation, the same men will suddenly make a hero or a genius of him, and that will be still more unjust. He is an honorable and very punctilious German."

"At all events, they say he is a skilful commander," interposed Pierre.

"I don't know what is meant by a skilful commander," said Prince Andrei, with a sneer.

"A skilful commander," explained Pierre, "well, is one who foresees all contingencies, reads his enemy's intentions."

"Well, that is impossible," said Prince Andrei, as if the matter had been settled long ago.

Pierre looked at him in amazement.

"Certainly," said he, "it has been said that war is like a game of chess."

"Yes," replied Prince Andrei; "only with this slight difference: that in chess you can think over each move as long as you wish, for you are freed from conditions of time; and there is this difference also, that the knight is always stronger than the pawn, and two pawns are always stronger than one, while in war a single battalion is sometimes stronger than a division, and sometimes weaker than a company. The relative strength of opposing armies can never be predicted. Believe me," said he, "if it depended on the dispositions made by the staff officers, then I would have remained on the staff and made my dispositions; while as it is, instead, I have the honor of serving here in the regiment with these gentlemen, and I take it that, in reality, the affair of tomorrow will depend on us, and not on them. Success never has depended, and never will depend, either on position or on armament or on numbers, and least of all on position."

Contrary to his ordinary silent self-restraint, Prince Andrei seemed now excited. Evidently he could not refrain from expressing the thoughts that had unexpectedly occurred to him.

"The battle will be won by the side that is resolutely bent on winning it. Why did we lose the Battle of Austerlitz? Our loss was not much greater than that of the French, but we said to ourselves very early in the engagement that we would lose it, and we did lose it. And we said this because there was no reason for being in a battle there, and we were anxious to get away from the battlefield as soon as possible. 'We have lost, so let us run,' and we did run. If we had not said this till evening, God knows what would have happened. But tomorrow we shall not say that. You may say our position, the left flank, is weak, the right flank too much extended," he pursued, "but that is all nonsense. It is not so at all. For what is before us tomorrow? A hundred millions of the most various possibilities, which will be decided instantaneously: the fact that either they, or our men, will start to run; this one or that one will be killed. All that is being done now, though, is mere child's play. The fact is, those with whom you rode around inspecting the position, instead of promoting the general course of events, rather hinder it. They are occupied only with their own petty interests."

"At such a moment?" asked Pierre, reproachfully.

"Yes, even at such a moment," repeated Prince Andrei. "For them this is only a propitious time to oust a rival or win an extra cross or ribbon. I will tell you what I think tomorrow means. A hundred thousand Russian and a hundred thousand French soldiers meet in battle tomorrow, and the result will be that when these two hundred thousand soldiers have fought, the side will win that fights most desperately and is least sparing of itself. And, if you like, I will tell you this: Whatever happens, whatever disagreements there may be in the upper circles, *we* will win the battle tomorrow. Tomorrow, whatever happens, we will win."

"So you think we will win a victory tomorrow?" asked Pierre.

"Certainly I do," replied Prince Andrei, absently. "One thing I would have done if I could," he began, after a short pause; "I would have allowed no prisoners to be taken. What is the taking of prisoners? It is chivalry. The French have destroyed my home, and they are coming to destroy Moscow; they have insulted me, and they go on insulting me every second. They are my enemies, they are in my opinion criminals. And that expresses the feeling of the whole army. They must be punished. If they are my enemies, they cannot be my friends, whatever may have been said at Tilsit."

"Yes, you are right," assented Pierre, glancing at Prince Andrei with shining eyes. "I entirely agree with you."

The question which had been troubling Pierre ever since he had been on the hillside of Mozhaisk, and all that long day, now became to him perfectly clear and settled beyond question. He now comprehended all the meaning and significance of this war and of the impending battle. All he had seen that day, all the stern thoughtful faces of which he had caught a cursory glimpse, now were illuminated with a new light for him. He comprehended that latent heat of patriotism—to use a term of physics— which was hidden in all the men he had seen, and this explained to him why it was all these men were so calm and, as it were, heedless in their readiness for death.

"Let no quarter be given," pursued Prince Andrei. "That alone would change all war, and would really make it less cruel. But, as it is, we play at making war. That's the wretchedness of it; we are magnanimous and all that sort of thing. This magnanimity and sensibility—it is like the magnanimity and sensibility of a high-born lady, who is offended if by chance she sees a calf killed; she is so good that she cannot see the blood, but she eats the same calf with good appetite when it is served with gravy. They prate to us about the laws of warfare, chivalry, flags of truce, humanity to the wounded, and the like. It's all nonsense. I saw what chivalry, what our 'parliamentarism' was in 1805; they duped us, we duped them. They pillage our homes, they issue counterfeit money, and worst of all, they kill our children and our fathers, and then talk about the laws of warfare and generosity to our enemies. Give no quarter, but kill and be killed! Whoever has reached this conclusion, as I have, by suffering . . ."

Prince Andrei, who had believed that it was a matter of indifference to him whether Moscow were taken or not taken—just as Smolensk had been —suddenly stopped short in the middle of his argument, owing to an unexpected cramp that took him in the throat. He walked up and down a few times in silence; but his eyes shone fiercely and his lip trembled when he again resumed the thread of his discourse.

"If there were none of this magnanimity in warfare, then we would only undertake it when, as now, it was a matter for which it was worth while to meet one's death. Then there would not be war because Pavel Ivanitch had insulted Mikhail Ivanitch. But if there must be war like the present one, let it be war. Then the zeal and intensity of the troops would always be like what it is now. Then all these Westphalians and Hessians whom Napoleon has brought with him would not have come against us to Russia, and we would never have gone to fight in Austria and Prussia without knowing why. War is not sweetness and light, but the dirtiest thing in the world, and it is necessary to understand it as such and not to play at war. It is necessary to take this frightful necessity sternly and seriously. This is the core of the matter; avoid falsehood, let war be war, and not sport. For otherwise war becomes a favorite pastime for idle and frivolous men. The military are the most honored of any class.

"But what is war, and what is necessary for its success, and what are the laws of military society? The end and aim of war is murder; the weapons of war are espionage, and treachery and the encouragement of treachery, the ruin of the inhabitants, and pillage and robbery of their possessions for the maintenance of the troops; deception and lies which pass under the name of military finesse. The privileges of the military class are the lack of freedom, that is, discipline, idleness, ignorance, rudeness, debauchery, drunkenness. And yet this is the highest caste in society, respected by all. All rulers except the Emperor of China wear military uniforms, and the one who has killed the greatest number of men gets the greatest reward.

"Tens of thousands of men meet, just as they will tomorrow, to murder one another; they will massacre and maim; and afterwards thanksgiving Te Deums will be celebrated, because many men have been killed—the number is always exaggerated—and victory will be proclaimed on the supposition that the more men killed, the greater the credit. Think of God looking down and listening to them!" exclaimed Prince Andrei, in his sharp, piping voice. "Ah! my dear fellow, of late life has been a heavy burden. I see I have obtained too deep an insight into things. It is not for man to taste of the knowledge of good and of evil—well, it is not for long, now," he added. "However, it is your bedtime; and it is time for me to turn in too. Go back to Gorki!" suddenly exclaimed Prince Andrei.

"Oh, no," cried Pierre, looking at Prince Andrei with frightened, sympathetic eyes.

"Go, go; before an engagement one must get some sleep," insisted Prince

Andrei. He came swiftly up to Pierre, threw his arms around him, and kissed him. "Good-by; go now," he cried. "We may not meet again . . . no" . . . and, hurriedly turning his back on his friend, he went into the barn.

It was already dark, and Pierre could not make out the expression of Prince Andrei's face, whether it was angry or tender.

Pierre stood for some time in silence, deliberating whether to follow him or go to his lodgings.

"No, he does not want me," Pierre decided, "and I know that this is our last meeting."

He drew a deep sigh and went back to Gorki.

Prince Andrei, retiring into the barn, threw himself down on a blanket, but he could not sleep.

He closed his eyes. One picture after another rose before him. One in particular held him long in rapt, joyous attention. He had a vivid remembrance of an evening at Petersburg. Natasha, with her eager, vivacious face, was telling him how, the summer before, while she was out gathering mushrooms, she had lost her way in the great forest. She gave him a disconnected description of the darkness of the woods, and her sensations, and her conversation with a bee hunter whom she had met; and every little while she had interrupted her story and said: "No, I can't tell you, you won't understand," although Prince Andrei had tried to calm her by assuring her that he understood; and in reality he had understood all that she wanted to say.

Natasha had been dissatisfied with her own words; she felt that she could not express the passionately poetical sensation she had felt that day, and which she desired to express in words.

"The old man was so charming, and it was so dark in the forest . . . and he had such good . . . but, oh dear, I can't describe it," she had said, blushing and becoming agitated.

Prince Andrei smiled even now the same joyous smile he had smiled then as he looked into her eyes.

"I understood her," said he to himself; "not only did I understand her, but I loved that spiritual power of hers, that frankness, that perfect honesty of soul—yes, her soul itself, which seemed to dominate her body—her soul itself I loved—so powerfully, so happily I loved . . ."

And suddenly he recalled what it was that had put an end to his love.

"*He* needed nothing of the sort. *He* saw nothing, understood nothing, of all this. All he saw was a very pretty and innocent young girl, with whom he did not even think it worth his while to join his fate. But I? . . . and he is still alive and enjoying life!"

Prince Andrei, as if something had seared him, sprang up and once more began to pace up and down in front of the barn.

XVIII

On the sixth of September, the day before the Battle of Borodino, M. de Beausset, grand chamberlain to the emperor of the French, and Colonel Fabvier arrived, the first from Paris, the other from Madrid, with dispatches to the Emperor Napoleon at his camp at Valyevo.

After M. de Beausset had put on his court uniform, he ordered a packet he had brought to be taken in, and he entered the outer division of Napoleon's tent, where, while talking with Napoleon's aides-de-camp who crowded round him, he busied himself with undoing the wrapper of the case.

Fabvier, not entering the tent, paused at the entrance, and entered into conversation with generals of his acquaintance.

The Emperor Napoleon had not yet left his bedroom, where he was engaged in making his toilet. Sniffing and grunting, he was turning first his stout back, then his fat chest, to the valet who was plying the brush. A second valet, holding his fingers over the bottle, was sprinkling the emperor's neatly arrayed person with eau de cologne, his expression intimating that he was the only one who knew how much cologne to use, and where it should be applied. Napoleon's short hair was wet and pasted down on his forehead. But his face, though puffy and sallow, expressed physical satisfaction. "Brush harder . . . put more energy in it," he was saying to the valet, as he shrugged his shoulders and grunted.

One of his aides-de-camp, who had been admitted into his bedroom to submit a report to the emperor as to the number of prisoners taken during the engagement of the preceding day, having accomplished his errand, was standing by the door, awaiting permission to retire. Napoleon scowled and glared at the aide from under his brows.

"No prisoners," said he, repeating the aide-de-camp's words. "They compel us to annihilate them. So much the worse for the Russian army. Go on, more energy!" he exclaimed, hunching up his back and offering his plump shoulders. "That'll do. Show in M. de Beausset, and Fabvier as well."

"Yes, sire," and the aide-de-camp disappeared through the door of the tent.

The two valets de chambre quickly dressed his majesty, and, in the blue uniform of the Guards, he entered the anteroom with firm, swift steps. Beausset was at that instant engaged in placing the gift which he had brought from the empress on two chairs directly in front of the entrance. But the emperor had dressed·and come out with such unexpected promptness that he had not time to get the surprise arranged to his satisfaction.

Napoleon instantly noticed what he was doing, and conjectured that they were not quite ready for him. He did not want to spoil their pleasure in surprising him. He pretended not to see Beausset, and addressed himself to Fabvier.

With a deep frown and without speaking, Napoleon listened to what Fabvier said about the bravery and devotion of his troops who had been fighting at Salamanca, at the other end of Europe, and who had only one thought—to be worthy of their emperor; and one fear—that of not satisfying him.

The result of the engagement had been disastrous. Napoleon, during Fabvier's report, made ironical observations, giving to understand that the affair could not have resulted differently, he being absent.

"I must regulate this in Moscow," said Napoleon. "Good-by for now," he added, and approached de Beausset, who by this time had succeeded in getting his surprise ready—some object covered with a cloth having been placed on the chairs.

De Beausset bowed low with that courtly French bow which only the old servants of the Bourbons could even pretend to execute, and advancing, he handed Napoleon an envelope.

Napoleon approached him and playfully took him by the ear.

"You have made good time; I am very glad. Well, what have they to say in Paris?" he asked, suddenly changing his former stern expression into one of great amiability.

"Sire, all Paris regrets your absence," replied de Beausset, as in duty bound.

But though Napoleon knew that de Beausset was bound to say this, or something to the same effect, though in his lucid intervals he knew it was not true, it was agreeable to him to hear this from de Beausset. He again did him the honor of taking him by the ear.

"I am sorry to have caused you to make such a long journey," said he.

"Sire, I expected nothing less than to find you at the gates of Moscow," said Beausset.

Napoleon smiled and, heedlessly raising his head, he glanced to the right. An aide-de-camp with a gliding gait apporached with a gold snuffbox and presented it. Napoleon took it.

"Yes, it has turned out luckily for you," he said, putting the open snuffbox to his nose. "You enjoy traveling; in three days you will see Moscow. You really could not have expected to see the Asiatic capital. You will have had a pleasant journey."

Beausset made a low bow to express his gratitude for this discovery of his proclivity for traveling, till now unknown to him.

"Ah, what is that?" exclaimed Napoleon, noticing that all the courtiers were glancing at the *something* hidden by a covering.

Beausset, with courtierlike dexterity, not turning his back on his sovereign, took two steps around and at the same time snatched off the covering, saying: "A gift to your majesty, from the empress."

This was Gerard's portrait in vivid colors of the little lad born to Napoleon and the Austrian emperor's daughter—the child whom all, for some reason, called the King of Rome.

The lovely, curly-haired boy, with a face like the face of the child in the Sistine Madonna, was represented playing cup-and-ball. The ball represented the earth, and the cup in his other hand represented a scepter. Although it was not perfectly clear why the artist wished to represent the so-called King of Rome impaling the earth-ball with a stick, still this allegory seemed perfectly clear to all who saw the picture in Paris, as well as to Napoleon, and greatly delighted them.

"King of Rome!" he exclaimed, with a graceful gesture pointing to the portrait. "Admirable." With that facility, characteristic of Italians, of changing at will the expression of his countenance, he approached the portrait and assumed a look of thoughtful tenderness.

He was conscious that what he was saying and doing at that moment was history. And it seemed to him that the best thing he could do now was to display the simplest paternal affection, as being most in contrast to that majesty whose consequence was that his son played cup-and-ball with the earth for the ball.

His eyes grew dim; he drew near it, he looked around for a chair—the chair sprang forward and placed itself under him—and he sat down in front of the portrait. He waved his hand, and all retired on their tiptoes, leaving the great man to himself and his feelings.

After sitting there for some time and letting his attention, he knew not why, be attracted to the rough texture of the paints, he got up and again beckoned to Beausset and the aide on duty.

He gave orders to have the portrait carried out in front of his tent so that his Old Guard, who were stationed around his tent, might not be deprived of the bliss of seeing the King of Rome, the son and heir of their beloved monarch. As he anticipated, while he was eating breakfast with Beausset, on whom he conferred this honor, he heard the enthusiastic shouts of the officers and soldiers of the Old Guard, who came to view the portrait.

"Long live the emperor! Long live the King of Rome! Long live the emperor!" shouted the enthusiastic voices.

After breakfast, Napoleon, in Beausset's presence, dictated his address to the army.

"Short and to the point!" exclaimed Napoleon as he read aloud the proclamation which had been written down word for word as he dictated it, without a change. The proclamation said:

"Soldiers! the battle which you have so eagerly desired is at hand. Victory depends on you, but victory is indispensable for us; it will give you all that you need, comfortable quarters, and a speedy return to your native land. Behave as you behaved at Austerlitz, Friedland, Vitebsk, and Smolensk. Let your remotest posterity recall with pride your exploits of this day. And it will be said of each one of you, 'He was present at the great battle of Moscow.'"

"De la Moskowa," repeated Napoleon, and taking with him M. de Beausset, who was so fond of traveling, he left the tent and mounted his horse, which was waiting already saddled.

463

"Your majesty is too kind," said Beausset, in reply to the emperor's invitation to accompany him on his ride; he would have preferred to go to sleep, and he did not like, nay, he even feared, to ride on horseback.

But Napoleon nodded his head to the traveler, and Beausset had to go.

When Napoleon left the tent the cheers of his guards in front of his son's portrait were more eager than ever. Napoleon frowned.

"Take it away," said he, pointing to the portrait with a graceful and imperious gesture. "He is too young yet to see a battle."

Beausset, closing his eyes and bending his head, drew a deep sigh, signifying thereby how able he was to appreciate and prize his emperor's words.

XIX

THE PRINCIPAL ACTION in the Battle of Borodino took place on a space of seven thousand feet, between Borodino and Bagration's earthworks.

Outside of this space there had occurred about noon, on one side, a demonstration on the part of Uvarof's Russian cavalry; on the other, beyond Utitsa, the skirmish between Poniatowski and Tutchkof had taken place; but these were two distinct engagements and insignificant in comparison with what went on in the middle of the battlefield.

On this field, between Borodino and the fortifications, near the forest, on an open tract visible from both sides, the principal action of the battle was fought in the simplest, most artless manner imaginable.

The action began with a cannonade on both sides from several hundred cannon.

Then, when the smoke had settled down on the whole field, forward through it, on the side of the French, at the right, moved the two divisions of Dessaix and Campan against the earthworks, and at the left moved the viceroy's regiments against Borodino.

From the Shevardino redoubt, where Napoleon had taken up his position, the distance to Bagration's fortifications was about two-thirds of a mile, while Borodino was more than a mile distant in a straight line, and, consequently, Napoleon could not see what was going on there—all the more because the smoke, mingling with the mist, covered the whole locality.

The soldiers of Dessaix's division, as they moved against the fortifications, were visible only until they began to descend the ravine that separated them from the earthworks. As soon as they descended into the ravine, the smoke of the cannon and musketry from the earthworks was so dense that it completely masked everything on the farther side of the ravine.

Through the smoke, here and there, gleamed some black object, apparently a body of men, and from time to time the glittering of bayonets. But whether they were moving or standing still, whether they were French or Russians, it was impossible to distinguish from the Shevardino redoubt.

The sun came out bright and shone with its slanting rays full into Napoleon's face, as he looked from under the shade of his hand toward the fortifications.

The smoke hung like a curtain in front of them, and sometimes it seemed that the smoke was in motion, sometimes that the troops were in motion. Occasionally, above the noises of the musketry, the shouts of men could be heard; but it was impossible to know what they were doing.

Napoleon, standing on the knoll, gazed through his field glass, and in the small circlet of the instrument he could see smoke and men, sometimes his own, sometimes Russians; but when he came to use his naked eye, he could not find even where he had been looking the moment before.

He went down from the redoubt, and began to pace back and forth in front of it.

Occasionally he paused and listened to the firing, or strained his sight to see the battlefield.

Not only from that lower ground where he was standing, not only from the mound on which some of his generals were left, but likewise from the fortifications themselves—where, now together and now alternately, Russians and French were in the fore, crowded with soldiers, dead and wounded, panic-stricken or frenzied—it was impossible to make out what was going on in that place.

For several hours, amid the incessant firing of musketry and cannon, now the Russians appeared in the ascendant, and now the French; now the infantry, and now the cavalry; they showed themselves, they fell, they fired, they struggled hand to hand; not knowing what they were doing to one another, they shouted and they retreated.

Napoleon's aides and his marshals' orderlies kept galloping up from the battlefield with reports as to the progress of affairs; but all these reports were false for the reason that, in the heat of the engagement, it was impossible to say what was taking place at a given moment; and for the reason that many of the aides did not reach the actual place of conflict, but reported what they had heard from others; and again for the reason that, while some aide was traversing the mile or so which separated his starting point from Napoleon, the circumstances might have changed and the tidings become false.

Thus the viceroy sent an aide posthaste with the report that Borodino had been captured and the bridge over the Kalotcha was in the hands of the French. The aide asked Napoleon whether he would command the troops to make a flank movement.

Napoleon commanded them to be drawn up into line on the other side of the river and to wait, but at the time when Napoleon issued this command —in fact, even before the aide had fairly left Borodino—the bridge was recaptured and burned by the Russians.

Another aide, galloping up from the fortifications with frightened face, reported to Napoleon that the charge had been repulsed, and that Campan was wounded and Davoust killed; but, in reality, the fortifications had been recaptured by another division of the troops at the very moment that the aide was told that the French were defeated, and Davoust was alive and suffering only from a slight contusion.

Drawing his own conclusions from such unavoidably false reports, Napoleon made his dispositions, which either were already fulfilled before he had made them, or else could not be, and never were, fulfilled.

The marshals and generals, who were in closer touch with the battlefield, but who, nevertheless, just like Napoleon, did not actually take part in the battle itself, and only rarely came actually under fire, did not ask Napoleon, but made their dispositions and gave their orders as to where and whence to fire, and when to have the cavalry charge and the infantry take to the double-quick.

But even their dispositions, exactly like Napoleon's, were only partly and rarely carried out. For the most part exactly the opposite of what they ordered was carried into effect. Soldiers commanded to advance would be exposed to a fire of grape, and retreat; soldiers commanded to hold their ground, suddenly seeing an unexpected body of Russians coming against them, would sometimes rush on to meet them, and the cavalry without orders would gallop off to cut down the fleeing Russians.

All dispositions as to where and when cannon were to be unlimbered, when the infantry were to be sent forward, when to fire, when the cavalry were to hammer down the Russian infantry—all these dispositions were made on their own responsibility by the subordinate officers who were close at hand, in the ranks, and they did not stop to consult with either Ney or Davoust or Murat, and certainly not with Napoleon.

X X

NAPOLEON'S GENERALS—Davoust, Ney, and Murat—finding themselves near to this terrain of fire, and sometimes even riding up into it, more than once led into it enormous and well-ordered masses of troops. But, contrary to what had invariably happened in all their former engagements, instead of the expected report that the enemy were fleeing, these well-ordered masses of troops returned in disorderly, panic-stricken mobs.

Then again the generals would collect them, but each time in diminished numbers. In the afternoon Murat sent his aide to Napoleon for reënforcements.

Napoleon was sitting at the foot of the mound, drinking punch, when Murat's aide-de-camp came galloping up with the report that the Russians would be defeated if his majesty would send one more division.

"Reënforcements?" exclaimed Napoleon, in grim amazement, as if not realizing the meaning of his words, and looking at the handsome young aide, who wore his dark hair in long curls just as Murat wore his. "Reënforcements!" muttered Napoleon. "How can they ask for reënforcements when they already have in their hands half of the army to throw against the weak, unfortified Russian flank! . . . Tell the King of Naples," said Napoleon, sternly, "tell the King of Naples that it is not noon, and that I do not yet see clearly on my chessboard. Go!"

The handsome young aide-de-camp with the long hair, not removing his hand from his hat, heaved a deep sigh, and galloped back again to the place where they were slaughtering men.

Napoleon got up and, calling Caulaincourt and Berthier, began to discuss with them matters that had nothing to do with the battle.

In the midst of this conversation, which began to engross Napoleon, Berthier's eyes were attracted to a general with a suite who came galloping up to the mound on a sweaty horse.

This was Belliard. Throwing himself from his horse, he approached the emperor with swift strides, and boldly, in a loud voice, began to argue the imperative necessity of reënforcements.

He swore on his honor that the Russians were beaten if the emperor would only give them one division more.

Napoleon shrugged his shoulders and without making any reply kept on pacing back and forth. Belliard began to talk loud and earnestly with the generals of the suite gathered round him.

"You are very hot-headed, Belliard," exclaimed Napoleon, again approaching the general who had brought the message. "It is easy to make a mistake in the thick of battle. Go back and look again, and then return to me."

Hardly had Belliard time to disappear from sight when, from the other side, a new messenger came hastening up from the battlefield.

"Well, what is it?" demanded Napoleon in the tone of a man annoyed by importunate difficulties.

"Sire, the prince . . ." began the aide-de-camp.

"Wants reënforcements?" said Napoleon with a furious gesture, taking the words out of his mouth. The aide-de-camp bowed his head affirmatively, and began to make his report; but the emperor turned away, took a couple steps, paused, turned back, and addressed Berthier.

"We must give them the reserves," said he, slightly throwing out his hands. "Which should we send?" he asked, addressing Berthier, "that gosling which I made into an eagle," as he was of late in the habit of calling him.

"Sire, send Claparède's division," suggested Berthier, who knew by heart every division, regiment, and battalion.

Napoleon nodded approval.

The aide-de-camp dashed off to Claparède's division, and within a few minutes the Young Guard, who were drawn up back of the mound, were on the way. Napoleon looked on in silence at this movement.

"No," he cried, suddenly turning to Berthier, "I cannot send Claparède. Send Friant's division," said he.

Although there was no advantage in sending Friant's division rather than Claparède's, and the delay caused by recalling Claparède and sending Friant was unfortunate, still this order was carried out to the letter. Napoleon did not see that in thus treating his forces he was playing the part of a doctor who, by his very remedies, hinders recovery—a part which he thoroughly appreciated and criticized.

Friant's division, like the others, also vanished in the smoke that hung over the battlefield. From all sides aides kept galloping up with reports, and all, as if by previous agreement, had one and the same story to tell. All asked for reënforcements, all declared that the Russians were holding desperately to their positions and that they were returning an infernal fire—a hellfire—under which the French troops were melting away.

Napoleon, in deep thought, sat down on a camp chair.

M. de Beausset, who was so fond of traveling, and had been fasting since early morning came up to the emperor and permitted himself the boldness of respectfully proposing to his majesty to eat some breakfast.

"I hope that I am not premature in congratulating your majesty on a victory," said he.

Napoleon silently shook his head. M. de Beausset, taking it for granted that this negation was a disclaimer of victory and did not refer to breakfast, permitted himself in a playfully respectful manner to remark that there was no reason on earth why they should not have some breakfast when they could have some.

"Go away!" suddenly cried Napoleon, gruffly, and turned his back on him. A beatific smile of pity, regret, and enthusiasm irradiated M. Beausset's face, and with a swaggering gait he rejoined the other generals.

Napoleon was under the sway of a gloomy feeling like that experienced by a universally fortunate gambler who has senselessly staked his money because he is always sure of winning, and suddenly, just at the moment when he has calculated all the chances of the game, realizes that the more he puzzles over its course, the more surely will he lose.

The troops were the same, the generals were the same, the preparations were the same, the same disposition, the same proclamation short and to the point; he himself was the same—he knew it; he knew that he had vastly more experience and skill than ever before; even the enemy were the same as at Austerlitz and Friedland—but the magnificent crushing swing of his hand fell powerless as if magic interfered.

All those former measures which had invariably been crowned with success—the concentration of all the batteries on one spot, and the attack of the reserves to crush the lines, and the charge of the cavalry, his men of iron—all these measures had already been employed, and not only there was no victory, but from all sides came the same reports of generals killed and wounded, of the necessity of reënforcements, of the impossibility of defeating the Russians, and of the demoralization of the troops.

Hitherto, after two or three moves, two or three hasty orders, marshals and aides-de-camp would come galloping up with congratulations and joyous faces, announcing whole corps of prisoners as trophies, sheaves of standards and eagles taken from the foe, and cannon, and provision trains; and Murat would only ask for permission to let the cavalry set forth to gather in the booty. This was the case at Lodi, Marengo, Arcole, Jena, Austerlitz, Wagram, and so on, and so on. But now, something strange had happened to his warriors!

Notwithstanding the report that the fortifications had been captured, Napoleon saw that this success was different, entirely different, from what had occurred in all his other battles. He saw that his feeling was also felt by all the men around him who were familiar with military affairs. All faces were gloomy, all eyes were averted. Beausset alone failed to understand the significance of what was happening.

Napoleon, after his long experience of war, well knew what it meant that, after eight hours' steady fighting, after the expenditure of such efforts, victory had not crowned the attacking columns. He knew that it was almost a defeat, and that the slightest mischance might now, at this critical apex on which the battle teetered, ruin him and his army.

When he passed in review all this strange Russian campaign, in which not one victory had been won—in which for two months not a standard, not a cannon, not a squad of men had been captured; when he looked at the openly dejected faces of those around him, and heard the reports that the Russians still stood their ground—a terrible feeling like that experienced in nightmares seized him, and all the unfortunate circumstances that might ruin him came into his mind.

The Russians might fall on his left wing, might break through his center, a random projectile might even kill him! All this was possible. In his previous battles he had reckoned only with the chances of success; now, an infinite number of possible mischances confronted him, and he expected them all. Yes, this was just as in a dream, when a man imagines that a murderer is attacking him, and the man, in his dream, swings his arms and strikes his assailant a tremendous blow which he knows must annihilate him, and then feels that his arm falls weak and limp as a rag, and the horror of inevitable destruction, because he is helpless, seizes him.

The report that the Russians were really charging the left flank of the French army awoke in Napoleon this horror. He sat in silence at the foot of the mound, on his camp chair, with his head bent and his elbows on his knees. Berthier came to him and proposed to him to ride around the line, so as to assure himself how affairs really stood.

"What? What did you say?" asked Napoleon. "Yes, have my horse brought." He mounted, and rode toward Semenovskoye.

In the slowly dissipating gunpowder smoke that spread all over this terrain where Napoleon rode, in the pools of blood, lay horses and men, singly and in heaps. Such a horror, such a collection of slaughtered men, neither Napoleon nor any of his generals had ever seen in so small a place. The thunder of the cannon, which had not ceased rolling for ten hours, and had become a torment to the ear, gave a peculiar significance to this spectacle (as music does to pageants).

Napoleon rode to the height over Semenovskoye, and through the smoke he could see ranks of men in uniforms of unfamiliar colors. They were the Russians.

The Russians, in dense rows, were posted behind Semenovskoye and the mound, and their cannon all along the line roared incessantly, filling the air with smoke. This was not a battle. It was wholesale butchery, incapable of bringing any advantage to either the Russians or the French.

Napoleon reined in his horse, and again fell into a fit of musing like that from which Berthier had aroused him. He could not stop this show that was going on in front of him and all around him. A show supposedly directed by him and dependent on his will; a show that now, for the first time, because of its failure, appeared to him as pointless and horrible.

One of the generals who came galloping up to Napoleon permitted himself to propose that the Old Guard should be sent into the battle. Ney and Berthier, who were standing near Napoleon, exchanged glances and smiled scornfully at this general's senseless proposal.

Napoleon let his head sink on his breast, and was long silent.

"We are eight hundred leagues from France, and I will not have my Guard destroyed!" said he; and, turning his horse, he rode back to Shevardino.

XXI

Kutuzof, with his grey head lowered and his heavy body sprawled out on a rug-covered bench, was sitting in the same place where Pierre had seen him that morning. He gave no definite orders, but merely approved or disapproved of what was reported to him.

"Yes, yes, do so," he would answer to the various suggestions. "Yes, yes, go, my boy, go and see!" he would say to one or another of those near him; or, "No, it is not necessary, we had better wait," he would say.

He listened to the reports brought to him, gave his commands when his subordinates expected them; but even while he was listening to what was said to him, he was apparently not interested in the sense of the words so much as in the expression of the faces, in the tones of voice, of those who brought the reports. Long experience in war had taught him, and his old man's wisdom made him realize, that it is impossible for one man to direct a hundred thousand men engaged in a death struggle, and he knew that the issue of a battle is determined, not by the plans of the commander-in-chief, not by the place where the troops are stationed, not by the number of the cannon or the multitude of the slain, but by that imponderable force called the spirit of the army; and he made use of this force, and directed it, as far as it was in his power.

The general expression of Kutuzof's face was one of calm concentrated attention and energy, barely able to overcome the weariness of his old and feeble frame.

At eleven o'clock in the morning he was informed that the fortifications captured by the French had been retaken, but that Prince Bagration was wounded. Kutuzof groaned and shook his head.

"Go to Prince Bagration, and learn the particulars, what and how," said he to one of his aides; and immediately after he turned to the Prince of Würtemberg, who was standing just back of him:

"Would not your highness like to take command of the first division?"

Soon after the prince's departure, so soon, in fact, that he could not have reached Semenovskoye, the prince's aide came back and informed his serene highness that the prince desired more troops.

Kutuzof frowned and sent word to Dokhturof to take command of the first division, and begged the prince to return to him, as, so he said, he could not do without him at this important crisis.

When the report was brought that Murat was taken prisoner, and the staff hastened to congratulate Kutuzof, he smiled.

"Wait, gentlemen," said he. "There is nothing extraordinary in the victory being won, and Murat being a prisoner. But it is best to postpone our elation."

Nevertheless, he sent one of his aides to ride along the lines and announce this news to the troops.

When Shcherbinin came spurring up from the left flank to report that the French had captured the fortifications and Semenovskoye, Kutuzof, judging from the sounds on the battlefield and by Shcherbinin's face that he was bringing bad news, got up, as if to stretch his legs, and, taking Shcherbinin by the arm, he led him to one side.

"Go, my dear," said he to Yermolof, "go and see if it is possible to do anything."

Kutuzof was at Gorki, the center of the position of the Russian troops. The assaults on our left flank, directed by Napoleon, had been several times repulsed. At the center the French had not pushed beyond Borodino. On the right Uvarof's cavalry had put the French to flight.

At three o'clock the French attack began to slacken in violence. On the faces of all who came from the battlefield and of all who stood around him, Kutuzof read an expression of the most intense excitement. Kutuzof was satisfied with the success of the day, which surpassed his expectations. But the old man's physical strength began to desert him. Several times his head sank forward as if out of his control, and he dozed. They brought him something to eat.

Adjutant General Woltzogen came riding up while Kutuzof was eating his dinner. Woltzogen came from Barclay with a report as to the course of affairs on the left wing. The prudent Barclay de Tolly, seeing the throngs of wounded hastening to the rear, and the ragged ranks of the army, and taking

471

all circumstances into consideration, decided that the battle was lost, and sent his favorite with his news to the general-in-chief.

Kutuzof laboriously chewed a piece of roasted chicken and gazed at Woltzogen with squinting, jocose eyes.

Woltzogen, stretching his legs negligently, with a half-scornful smile on his lips, came to Kutuzof, barely lifting his hand to his vizor. He behaved to his serene highness with a certain affectation of indifference which was intended to show that he, as a highly cultured military man, permitted the Russians to make an idol of this good-for-nothing old man, but that *he* knew with whom he was dealing. "*Der alte Herr*—the old gentleman," as Kutuzof was called by the Germans in his circle—"is taking things very easy," said Woltzogen to himself; and, casting a stern glance at the platter set in front of Kutuzof, he proceeded to report to the old gentleman the position of affairs on the left flank, as Barclay had told him to do, and as he himself had seen and understood them.

"All the points of our position are in the enemy's hands, and we cannot regain them, because we have no troops; they are in full retreat, and there is no possibility of stopping them," was his report.

Kutuzof, ceasing to chew, stared at Woltzogen in amazement, as if he did not comprehend what was said to him.

Woltzogen, observing the *alter Herr's* excitement, said with a smile, "I did not feel that it was right to conceal from your serene highness what I have been witnessing. The troops are wholly demoralized."

"You have seen it? You have seen it?" screamed Kutuzof, scowling and leaping to his feet, and swiftly approaching Woltzogen. "How . . . how dare you?" and he made a threatening gesture with his palsied hands, and, choking, he cried: "How dare you, dear sir, say this *to me?* You know nothing about it. Tell General Barclay from me that his observations are inaccurate, and that the actual course of the battle is better known to me, the commander-in-chief, than it is to him!"

Woltzogen was about to make some remark, but Kutuzof cut him short:

"The enemy are beaten on the left and crushed on the right. If you saw things wrong, my dear sir, you should not permit yourself to talk of what you know nothing about. Be good enough to go to General Barclay and tell him that it is my absolute intention to attack the enemy tomorrow," said Kutuzof, sternly.

Everyone was silent, and all that could be heard was the heavy breathing of the excited old general.

"They are beaten all along the line, thank God and the gallantry of the Russian army for that! The enemy are crushed, and tomorrow we will drive them from the sacred soil of Russia," said Kutuzof, crossing himself, and suddenly the tears sprang to his eyes and he sobbed.

Woltzogen, shrugging his shoulders, and pursing his lips, silently went to one side, expressing his amazement at the old gentleman's conceited stubbornness.

"Ah, here comes my hero," exclaimed Kutuzof, to a stalwart, handsome, dark-haired general, who at this moment approached the mound.

This was Rayevsky, who had been all that day at the critical point of the field of Borodino.

Rayevsky reported that the troops were unmoved in their positions, and that the French did not dare to attack them any more.

On hearing this, Kutuzof said in French, "Then you do not think, *as some others do,* that we are forced to withdraw?"

"On the contrary, your highness, in drawn battles it is always the most stubborn who can be called victorious," replied Rayevsky, "and my opinion . . ."

"Kaisarof!" cried Kutuzof, summoning his adjutant. "Sit down and write an order for tomorrow. And you," he said, addressing another, "hasten down the lines and have them understand that we attack tomorrow."

While Kutuzof was talking to Rayevsky and dictating his order of the day, Woltzogen came back from Barclay and announced that General Barclay de Tolly would like a written confirmation of the order which the field marshal had delivered to him.

Kutuzof, not looking at Woltzogen, commanded his aides to write out the order, which the former commander-in-chief desired to have to relieve him completely of personal responsibility.

And by that intangible, mysterious connection which communicates throughout a whole army one and the same disposition, the so-called esprit de corps, and constitutes the chief sinew of an army, Kutuzof's words and his order for renewing the battle on the following day were known simultaneously from one end of the force to the other.

The exact words or the absolute form of the order was not indeed carried to the utmost limits of this organization; in the stories that were repeated in the widely separated ends of the lines there was probably nothing like what Kutuzof really said; but the gist of his words was conveyed everywhere, for the reason that what Kutuzof said sprang not from logical reasoning, but was the genuine outcome of the sentiment that was in the heart of the commander-in-chief, and to which every Russian heart responded.

And when they knew that on the next day they were to attack the enemy, and heard from the upper circles of the army the confirmation of what they wished to believe, these men, tortured by doubt, were comforted and encouraged.

XXII

PRINCE ANDREI's regiment was among the reserves, which had been stationed until two o'clock behind Semenovskoye, remaining inactive under the severe fire of the artillery. At two o'clock the regiment, which had already lost more than two hundred men, was moved forward upon the trampled field of oats, on that space between Semenovskoye and the "Kurgan" battery where thousands of men were killed that day, and on which was now concentrated a tremendous fire from several hundred enemy guns.

Without stirring from that spot, and not themselves replying with a single shot, the regiment lost here two-thirds of its effectives. In front and especially at the right-hand side, amid the perpetual smoke, the cannons boomed, and from that mysterious domain of smoke that shrouded all the space in front, the projectiles constantly flew with a quick hissing whistle, and the more deliberate shells sputtered. Sometimes, as if to give a respite, a quarter-hour would pass during which all the shot and shells would fly overhead, but then, again, several men would be struck down in the course of a moment, and they were constantly engaged in dragging the dead to one side, and carrying the wounded to the rear.

With each new casualty the chances of life were diminished for those who were as yet unscathed. The regiment was posted in battalion columns at intervals of three hundred paces, but nevertheless all the men were under the influence of the same mood. The men of the regiment, without exception, were silent and melancholy. Once in a while a few words were spoken in the ranks, but this conversation was always abruptly cut short when the thud of a falling missile was heard, and the cry of "Stretchers!" The larger part of the time, the men of the regiment, by their chief's orders, lay low on the ground.

Prince Andrei, anxious and pallid, like all the other men in his regiment, paced back and forth along the meadow next to the oat field, from one end to the other, with his arms behind his back and with bent head. There was nothing for him to do or to order. Everything went like clockwork. The dead were dragged to one side, away from the front; the wounded were carried to the rear; the ranks were closed up. If the soldiers stood aside, they instantly hastened back to their places again.

At first Prince Andrei, considering it his duty to encourage his men and to set them an example of gallantry, kept walking up and down along the ranks; but afterwards he became convinced that they had nothing to learn from him. With all the energy of his soul—and this was true also of every one of the soldiers—he unconsciously tried to blind himself to the horrors of their situation.

He marched along the meadow, dragging his feet, trampling down the grass and contemplating the dust that covered his boots; then again with long strides he would try to step from ridge to ridge left by the mowers' scythes along the meadow; or, counting his steps, he would calculate how many times he must go from one boundary to the other in order to make a mile. He would pluck up the wormwood growing on the edge of the field and rub the flowers between his palms, and sniff the powerful, penetrating bitterness of their odor.

Nothing remained of the fabric of thought that he had so painfully elaborated the evening before. He thought of nothing at all. He listened with weary ears to that perpetual repetition of sounds, distinguishing the whistling of the missiles above the roar of the musketry. He gazed at the indifferent faces of the men in the first battalion, and waited.

"Here she comes! That's one for us," he would say to himself as he caught the approaching screech of something from that hidden realm of smoke. "One, a second! There's another! It struck!"

He paused, and looked along the ranks. "No, it went over. Ah! But that one struck!"

And once more he would take up his promenade, trying to measure long steps, so as to reach the boundary in sixteen strides.

A screech, and a thud! Within half a dozen steps from him a projectile flung up the dry soil and buried itself. An involuntary chill ran down his back. Once more he looked along the ranks: evidently many had been struck down; a great crowd had come together in the second battalion.

"Mr. Adjutant," he cried, "tell those men not to stand so close together."

The aide, having delivered the order, returned to Prince Andrei. From the other side the battalion commander rode up on horseback.

"Look out!" cried a soldier in a terrified voice; and, like a bird whistling in its swift flight and settling earthward, a shell came plunging down—not noisily—within two paces of Prince Andrei, and near the battalion commander's horse.

The horse, not pausing to consider whether it was well or ill to manifest fear, snorted, shied, and darted off, almost unseating the major. The horse's panic was shared by the men.

"Lie down!" cried the aide, throwing himself on the ground.

Prince Andrei stood undecided. The shell, with its fuse smoking, was spinning like a top between him and the aide, on the very edge between the plowed land and the meadow, near the clump of wormwood.

"Can this be death?" wondered Prince Andrei, casting a fleeting glance full of a newly born envy at the grass, the wormwood, and the thread of smoke that escaped from the whirling black ball. "I cannot, I will not die; I love life, I love this grass, the earth, the air . . ."

All this flashed through his mind, and at the same time he remembered that they were looking at him. "For shame, Mr. Officer!" he started to say to the aide. "Any . . ."

He did not finish. There came simultaneously a crash, a whizzing of fragments as of broken glass, a powerful odor of gunpowder smoke, and Prince Andrei was struck in the side, and, throwing his arms up, he fell on his face.

Several officers hastened to him. From the right side of his abdomen a great gush of blood stained the grass.

The stretcher-bearers came up and stood behind the officers. Prince Andrei lay with his face buried in the grass, gasping painfully.

"Now, then, what are you waiting for? Come on!"

The peasants came close and lifted him by the shoulders and legs; but he groaned piteously, and the men, exchanging glances, laid him down again.

"Give us a hand there! Up with him! It's all the same!" cried someone's voice. Once more they took him by the shoulders and laid him on the stretcher.

"Ah! My God! My God! What?" . . . "In the belly? That finishes him!" . . . "Oh, my God!" exclaimed various officers.

"Na! A fragment whizzed past my ear," said the aide.

The militiamen carried Prince Andrei to the forest, where the wagons were sheltered and where the field hospital had been established. This field hospital consisted of three tents with upturned flaps, pitched on the edge of the birch grove. Within the grove stood the wagons and horses. The horses were munching oats in haversacks, and the sparrows were pouncing down and carrying off the scattered grains; crows, scenting blood and impatiently cawing, were flying about over the treetops.

Around the tents, occupying more than five acres of ground, lay and sat and stood blood-stained men in various attire.

Around the wounded stood a throng of stretcher-bearers, soldiers, with sad but interested faces, whom the officers, attempting to carry out orders, found it impossible to keep away. Not heeding the officers, the soldiers stood leaning on the stretchers and gazed steadily as if trying to grasp the meaning of the terrible spectacle before their eyes.

From the tents could be heard, now loud, fierce sobs, then pitiful groans. Occasionally assistants would come hurrying out after water and indicate the next ones to be brought in. The wounded by the tents, waiting their turn, hoarsely cried, groaned, wept, screamed, cursed, clamored for vodka. Some were delirious.

Prince Andrei, as regimental commander, was carried through this throng of unbandaged sufferers close to one of the tents, and there his bearers waited for further orders. He opened his eyes, and it was some time before he could comprehend what was going on around him. The meadow, the wormwood, the plowed field, the black whirling ball, and that passionate throb of love for life, occurred to his recollection.

Two paces from him, talking loudly and attracting general attention, stood a tall, handsome, black-haired, noncommissioned officer with a bandaged head, leaning against a dead tree. He had been wounded in the head and leg with bullets. Around him, attracted by his talk, were gathered a throng of wounded and of stretcher-bearers.

"We gave it to him so hot that they dropped everything; they even left the king," cried the soldier, snapping his fiery black eyes and glancing around. "If only the reserves had been sent up just at that time, I tell you, brother, there would not have been left a show of him, because I am sure . . ."

Prince Andrei, like all the circle gathered around the speaker, gazed at him with gleaming eyes, and felt a sense of consolation. "But why is it not a matter of indifference to me now?" he asked himself. "What is going to happen, and what does it mean? Why do I have such regret in leaving life? There was in this life something I have not understood, and which I still fail to understand."

XXIII

ONE OF THE surgeons, with blood-soaked apron and with his small hands covered with gore, holding a cigar between thumb and little finger so as not to besmear it, came out of the tent. This doctor lifted his head and proceeded to look on all sides, but beyond the wounded. He was evidently anxious to get a little rest. Having for some time looked toward the right and then toward the left, he drew a long sigh and dropped his eyes.

"In a moment now," said he in reply to his assistant, who called his attention to Prince Andrei, and he gave orders for him to be carried into the tent.

The wounded who had been waiting were disposed to grumble. "In this world it seems only 'gentlemen' are permitted to live!" exclaimed one.

Prince Andrei was taken in and deposited on a table that had just been vacated. The assistant was that instant engaged in rinsing something from it. Prince Andrei could not distinctly make out what there was in the tent. The pitiful groans on all sides, the excruciating agony in his ribs, his belly, and his back, distracted him. All that he saw around him was confused for him in one general impression of naked, blood-stained human flesh, filling all the lower part of the tent.

There were three tables in this tent. Two were occupied. Prince Andrei was laid on the third. He was left to himself for some little time, and he could not help seeing what was doing at the other two tables. On the one nearest lay a Tartar—a Cossack to judge by his uniform, which was thrown down beside him. Four soldiers held him down. A surgeon in spectacles was cutting into his cinnamon-colored, muscular back.

"Ukh! Ukh! Ukh!" The Tartar grunted like a pig, and suddenly turned up his swarthy face with its wide cheekbones and squat nose, and unsheathing his white teeth, he began to tug and to struggle, and set up a long, shrill, penetrating screech.

On the other table, around which were gathered a number of people, a large, stout man lay on his back with his head thrown back. His streaming hair, its color, and the shape of the head seemed strangely familiar to Prince Andrei.

Several of the assistants were leaning on this man's chest, and holding him down. His large, stout, white leg was subject to an incessant and rapid trembling, as if it had the ague. This man was convulsively sobbing and choking. Two surgeons—one was pale and trembling, were silently doing something to this man's other handsome leg.

Having finished with the Tartar, over whom they threw his cloak, the spectacled surgeon, wiping his hands, came to Prince Andrei. He looked into Prince Andrei's face and hastily turned away.

"Undress him. What are you dawdling for?" he cried severely to his assistants.

Prince Andrei's very earliest and most distant childhood occurred to him as the assistant, with hasty hands, began to unbutton his clothes and remove them. The surgeon bent down low over the wound, probed it, and drew a heavy sigh. Then he made a sign to someone.

The exquisite agony which Prince Andrei felt within his abdomen caused him to lose consciousness.

When he came to himself, the broken splinters of his thighbone had been removed, and torn clots of flesh cut away, and the wound was dressed. They were dashing water into his face. As soon as Prince Andrei opened his eyes, the surgeon bent silently down to him, kissed him on the lips, and hastened away.

After the agony he had endured, Prince Andrei was conscious of a well-being such as he had not experienced for a long time.

All the best and happiest moments of his life, especially his earliest childhood, when they used to undress him and put him to bed, when his old nurse used to lull him to sleep with her songs, when as he buried his head in the pillows he had felt himself happy in the mere consciousness of being alive: all recurred to his imagination, no longer as something long past, but as actuality.

Around that wounded man whose features seemed familiar to Prince Andrei the doctors were still busy, lifting him and trying to calm him.

"Show it to me . . . Ooooo! O! Ooooo!" he groaned, his voice broken by frightened sobs, subdued by suffering.

Prince Andrei, hearing these groans, felt like weeping himself: either because he was dying without fame, or because he regretted being torn from life, or because of these recollections of a childhood never to return, or because he sympathized in the sufferings of others and this man was groaning so piteously near him; but, at any rate, he felt like weeping good, childlike, almost happy tears.

The wounded man was shown the amputated leg, still in its boot, which was full of blood.

"O! Ooooo!" and he sobbed like a woman. The surgeon, who had been standing in front of the patient and preventing his face from being seen, stepped to one side.

"My God! What does this mean? Why is *he* here?" Prince Andrei wondered.

In this wretched, sobbing, exhausted man whose leg had just been taken off, he recognized Anatol Kuragin. They lifted Anatol's head and gave him water in a glass; but his trembling, swollen lips could not close over the edge of the glass. Anatol was still sobbing bitterly.

"Yes, it is he! Yes, this man who has somehow been so closely, so painfully, connected with my life!" said Prince Andrei to himself, not as yet realizing clearly all the circumstances. "What has been the link that connects this man with my childhood, with my life?" he asked himself, and could not find the answer to his question. And suddenly a new and unexpected remembrance from that world of the childlike, pure and lovely past arose before Prince Andrei. He recalled Natasha just as he had seen her at the ball in 1810, with her slender neck and arms, with her timid, happy face so easily wakened to enthusiasm, and his love and tenderness for her arose more keenly and powerfully in his soul than ever before. He remembered now the connection between him and this man, who, through the tears that suffused his swollen eyes, was gazing at him with such an expression of agony. Prince Andrei remembered everything, and a solemn pity and love for this man welled up in his happy heart.

Prince Andrei could no longer restrain himself, and he wept tears of compassionate love and tenderness over other men and over himself, over their errors and his own.

"Sympathy, love for one's brothers, for those who love us, love for those who hate us, love for our enemies, yes, the love that God preached on earth, which Princess Maria taught me and which I have not understood—that is what made me feel regret for life; that is what would have remained for me if my life had been spared. But now it is too late, I know it."

XXIV

Tens of thousands of men lay dead in various positions and uniforms on the fields and meadows belonging to Mr. Davidof and certain crown serfs, on those fields and meadows where for centuries the peasants of Borodino, Gorki, Shevardino and Semenovskoye had together harvested their crops and pastured their cattle.

Around the field hospitals, for several acres, the grass and ground were soaked with blood. Thousands of men, wounded and not wounded, belonging to various commands, from the one side fell back to Mozhaisk, from the other to Valuyevo. Other thousands, weary and hungry, led by their chiefs, moved onward to the front. Still others stood in their places and went on firing.

Over the entire field where, in the morning, the sun had shone on glittering bayonets and wreaths of smoke, now hung a pall of fog and smoke, and the air was foul with a strange reek of nitrous fumes and blood.

Clouds had gathered, and the raindrops began to fall on the dead, on the wounded, on the panic-stricken and the weary and the despairing. It seemed to say to them:

"Enough! Enough, ye men! Cease! . . . Remember! What are ye doing?"

The men on either side, utterly weary, without food and without rest, began alike to question whether it was any advantage for them longer to exterminate one another, and hesitation could be seen in every face, and in every mind the question arose:

"Why, wherefore are ye killing and being killed? Kill whomever ye please, do whatever ye please, but as for me I want no more of it!"

This thought, toward late afternoon, burned with equal force in every heart. At any moment all these men might suddenly manifest their horror at what they had been doing, give it all up, and fly anywhere at all.

But although toward the end of the struggle the men began to feel all the horror of their actions, although they would have been glad to cease, some strange, incomprehensible, mysterious power still continued to direct them; and the surviving gunners—one out of every three—covered with sweat, grimed with powder and stained with blood, staggered and panting with weariness, still dragged the projectiles, charged the guns, sighted them and applied the fuses, and the shot flew just as swiftly and viciously from the one side and the other, and crushed human forms, and still that strange affair went on which was accomplished, not by the will of men, but by the will of Him who rules men and worlds.

Anyone who had looked at the vanishing remnants of the Russian army would have said that all the French needed to do would be to make one small last effort and the Russian army would vanish; and anyone who had looked at the remnants of the French would have said that all the Russians had to do was to make one small last effort and the French would be destroyed. But neither the French nor the Russians made this last effort, and the flame of the conflict slowly flickered out.

The Russian failure to make this effort was in not charging the French. At the beginning of the battle they merely stood on the road to Moscow, disputing it, and they continued to stand at the end of the battle as they had stood at the beginning. But if the aim of the Russians had been to defeat the French, they could not put forth this last effort because all the Russian troops had been defeated, there was not a single division of their army that had not suffered in the engagement, and, though the Russians still held their own, they had lost *half* their troops.

The French, with the recollections of all their fifteen years of past victories, with their confidence in Napoleon's invincibility, with the consciousness that they had gained possession of a portion of the battlefield, that their loss was only a quarter of their contingent, and that they had still twenty thousand in reserve, not counting the Guard, might easily have made the effort. The French, who were attacking the Russian army with the intention of defeating it, ought to have made the effort because as long as the Russians disputed the road to Moscow, as they did before the battle began, the aim of the French was not attained and all their efforts and losses were thrown away.

But the French did not make the effort.

Certain historians assert that Napoleon had only to send forward his Old Guard, who were still fresh, and the battle would have been won. To say what would have happened if Napoleon had sent forward the Guard is just the same as to say what would happen if autumn turned into spring.

It was an impossibility.

Napoleon did not sent forward his Guard, not because he did not want to do it, but because it was impossible for him to do it. All the generals, all the officers and the soldiers of the French army knew that it was impossible to do this, because the dejected spirit of the army would not allow it.

Napoleon was not the only one to experience that nightmare feeling that the terrible blow of the arm was falling in vain, but all his generals, all the soldiers of the French army who took part or who did not take part, after all their experiences in former battles, when, after exerting a tenth as much force as now, the enemy would be vanquished, now experienced alike a feeling of awe at that enemy who, having lost *half* his troops, still stood just as threateningly at the end as he had stood at the beginning of the engagement.

The moral force of the French attacking army was exhausted.

Victory is not something signalized by the fastening of certain strips of cloth called flags to poles, nor by the space on which troops have stood or are standing; victory is moral, when the one side has been persuaded as to the moral superiority of the other and of its own weakness; and such a victory was won by the Russians over the French at Borodino.

The invading army, like an exasperated beast of prey, having received as it ran a mortal wound, became conscious that it was doomed; but it could not halt any more than the Russian army, which was not half so strong, could help giving way. After the shock that had been received, the French army was still able to crawl to Moscow; but there, without any new efforts on the part of the Russian troops, it was doomed to perish, bleeding to death from the mortal wound received at Borodino.

The direct consequence of the Battle of Borodino was Napoleon's causeless flight from Moscow, the return along the old Smolensk highway, the ruin of the five hundred thousand men of the invading army, and the destruction of Napoleonic France, on which at Borodino for the first time fell the hand of an opponent stronger by force of spirit!

1812

Warfare between Napoleon and Russia with its vast population is the signal for the European satellites of France to rise against their foreign master. On the peninsula Wellington is now on the offensive; a rejuvenated Prussia gives lip service to its French alliance, while actually preparing to take the side of the Russians and British; Austria is openly hostile and awaits only the proper moment to enter the war. Now is joined a contest in which Napoleon must conquer or lose all. The key is Russia; he keeps his place with his invading army and takes Moscow.

Part Eleventh

THE Russians retreated eighty miles, beyond Moscow; the French advanced as far as Moscow, and there came to a standstill.

During the five weeks that followed there was not a single battle. The French did not stir.

Like a mortally wounded beast, which licks its profusely bleeding wounds, the French remained for five weeks at Moscow, making no attempts to do anything. Then, suddenly, without new reason, they fled back; they took the road to Kaluga, and, after one victory, since the field of Malo-Yaroslavets was theirs, they retreated still more rapidly, without risking any important battle, to Smolensk, beyond Smolensk, beyond Vilna, beyond the Berezina, and so on.

On the night of September 7 Kutuzof and the whole Russian army were convinced that they had won the Battle of Borodino. Kutuzof even thus reported a victory to his sovereign.

Kutuzof gave orders to prepare for another battle to finish the enemy, not because he wanted to deceive anyone, but because he knew that the enemy had been beaten; and this fact was likewise known to all the participants in the battle.

But that night, and the next day, reports one after another began to come in, of the unprecedented losses sustained, showing that the army had been reduced to one-half; and another battle now seemed physically impossible.

It was impossible to give battle when their condition was as yet unknown, their wounded uncared for, their dead uncounted, fresh missiles not furnished, new officers lacking to replace those killed, and the men unrefreshed by food and sleep. Moreover, the morning after the battle, the French army, its impetus increasing by the law of momentum, had already begun to move of itself against the Russian army.

Kutuzof wanted to renew the attack on the following day, and all his army desired this. But the desire to make an attack is not enough. There must also be the opportunity to make one; and in this case opportunity was lacking.

It was impossible to prevent a one day's retreat; in the same way, it was impossible to prevent retreating a second day's march, then a third; and finally, when on September 13 the army neared Moscow, notwithstanding all the sentiment aroused in the ranks of the Russian army, force of circumstance obliged them to retire beyond the city. Thus they made a last retrograde movement and abandoned Moscow to the enemy.

Yermolof, who had been sent by Kutuzof to reconnoiter a position, came back to the field marshal and said it was impossible to fight in that position and they must retreat.

Kutuzof looked at him in silence.

"Give me your hand," said he; and, turning it round so as to feel his pulse, he said:

"You are sick, my dear! Think what you are saying."

Not even then could Kutuzof comprehend that it was possible to retire beyond Moscow without a battle. Kutuzof got out of his carriage on the Paklonnaya Hill and sat down on a bench at the edge of the road. A portentous array of generals gathered around him. Count Rostopchin, who had driven out from Moscow, joined them. All this brilliant society, dividing itself into little circles, was discussing the advantages and disadvantages of the position, the condition of the forces, the various plans proposed, the state of Moscow, and military matters in general.

The commander-in-chief listened, and occasionally asked for a repetition of what was said around him; but he did not himself take part in the conversation, and he expressed no opinion. For the most part, after listening to what was said in any little group, he would turn abruptly away with a look of disgust, as if what they said was not all what he wanted to hear.

Some talked about the position chosen, criticizing not the position so much as they did the intelligence of those who had selected it. Others tried to prove that a mistake had been made before, that they should have accepted battle two days earlier; still others were talking about the Battle of Salamanca, which a Frenchman named Crossart, who had just arrived in a Spanish uniform, described to them.

In a fourth group, Count Rostopchin declared that he, together with the

483

Moscow city troop, was ready to perish under the walls of the capital, but that he could not help regretting the uncertainty in which he had been left, and that if he had only known about this before, things would have been different.

A fifth group, making a display of the profundity of their strategical calculations, talked about the route our troops should have taken.

A sixth group talked sheer nonsense.

Kutuzof's face grew more and more troubled and melancholy.

Benigsen, having selected a position, hotly insisted on the defense of Moscow, thereby making a show of his Russian patriotism. Kutuzof, as he listened to him, could not restrain a frown. Benigsen's motive was as clear as day to him: In case of disaster and failure he would lay the blame on Kutuzof, who had led the troops without a battle to the Sparrow Hills; while in the event of success he would claim all the credit for himself; but if Kutuzof refused to make the attempt, Benigsen would wash his hands of the crime of abandoning Moscow.

But the old man was not at present occupied with this intrigue. One single, terrible question occupied him. And from no one could he obtain an answer to this question. The question was now merely this:

"Have I allowed Napoleon to reach Moscow, and when did I do it? When was this decided? Was it yesterday, when I sent the order to Platof to retreat, or was it the day before yesterday, in the evening, when I was sleepy, and ordered Benigsen to make his own dispositions? Or was it before that? But when, when was this terrific deed decided? Moscow to be abandoned! The troops must retire, and I must give this order!"

To issue this terrible order seemed to him tantamount to resigning the command of the army. But, besides the fact that he loved power and was accustomed to it, he was also deeply convinced that the salvation of Russia was predestined to be accomplished by him; and that it was only for this reason, against the sovereign's will but in accordance with the will of the people, he had been placed in supreme command. He was convinced that he alone could in these trying circumstances remain at the head of the army; that he was the only one in all the world who was able to view without terror the invincible Napoleon as his opponent, so that he was overwhelmed at the mere thought of the command he would have to give. But it was essential to come to some decision; it was essential to cut short these discussions around him, which were beginning to grow altogether too unrestrained.

He called to him the senior generals:

"Ma tête, fut elle bonne ou mauvaise, n'a qu'à s'aider d'elle-même— whether my judgment is good or bad I have no other in which I can put faith," said he, as he rose from the bench; and he drove to Fili, where his horses were stabled.

A council was convened at two o'clock in the largest and best room of the peasant Andrei Savostyanof's cottage. The men, women and children belonging to the peasant's large household were huddled together in the living room across the entry. Only Andrei's granddaughter, Malasha, a little girl of six, whom his serene highness had petted and to whom he had given a lump of sugar while he was drinking tea, remained in a corner of the large room, on a broad shelf above the stove. Malasha coyly and gleefully looked down on the faces, uniforms and crosses of the generals who came one after the other into the room and took their places on the wide benches in the "best corner," under the holy pictures.

The "little grandfather" himself, as Malasha secretly called Kutuzof, sat apart from the rest in the dark corner behind the stove. He sat far back on a camp chair, and kept grumbling and pulling at his coat collar, which, though it was turned back, seemed to choke him.

The men as they came in one at a time paid their respects to the field marshal. He shook hands with some of them; he nodded to others. Adjutant Kaisarof was about to draw aside the curtain at the window facing Kutuzof, but the general fiercely waved his hand at him; Kaisarof understood that his serene highness did not wish his face to be seen. Around the peasant's pine table, on which lay maps, plans, pencils, and sheets of paper, were gathered so many men that the orderlies had to bring in still another bench and set it down near the table.

On this bench sat the late comers: Yermolof, Kaisarof, and Toll. Under the icons, in the place of honor, sat Barclay de Tolly, with the St. George Cross round his neck, with his pale, sickly face and lofty brow, between which and the bald head there was no dividing line. For two days he had been suffering from an attack of ague, and at this very moment he was chilled and shaking with fever.

Next him sat Uvarof, who in a low tone of voice (and they all spoke that way) was making some statement accompanied by quick gestures.

The little rotund Dokhturof, arching his brows and with folded hands on his paunch, was listening attentively.

On the other side sat Count Ostermann-Tolstoy, with bold features and gleaming eyes, leaning his big head on his hand, and seemingly lost in thought.

Rayevsky, a look of impatience on his face, was as usual engaged in twisting his black curls forward into lovelocks, and gazed now at Kutuzof, now at the front door.

Konovnitsin's reliable, handsome, good face was lighted by a shrewd and friendly smile. He was trying to catch Malasha's eyes, and was winking at her and making the little one smile.

All were waiting for Benigsen, who had used the pretext of once more checking the position so he could eat his sumptuous dinner in peace. They waited for him from four o'clock till six; and during that time they refrained from any deliberation, talking in undertones exclusively about irrelevant matters. Only when Benigsen entered did Kutuzof leave his corner and approach the table, but even then he took care that the candles placed there should not light up his face.

Benigsen opened the council with the question:

"Shall the holy and ancient capital of Russia be deserted without a blow being struck, or shall it be defended?"

A long, general silence followed. Faces grew grave, and in the silence could be heard Kutuzof's angry grunting and coughing. All eyes were fixed on him. Malasha also gazed at the "little grandfather." She was nearer to him than any of the others and could see how his face contracted; he seemed ready to burst into tears. But this did not last long.

"The holy, ancient capital of Russia!" he suddenly repeated in an angry voice, repeating Benigsen's words and underlining the false note in these words. "Permit me to tell you, your excellency, that this question makes no sense to a Russian." He leaned forward with his heavy body. "It is impossible to put such a question, and such a question has no sense. The problem I have convened these gentlemen to consider is a military one. This problem is as follows: The salvation of Russia is her army. Would it be more to our advantage to risk the loss of the army, and of Moscow as well, by accepting battle; or to abandon Moscow without a battle? It is on this matter that I wish to know your mind."

He threw himself back into his chair again.

The discussion began.

Benigsen refused to believe that the game was already lost. Granting the opinion of Barclay and the others that it was impossible to accept a defensive battle at Fili, he, being thoroughly imbued with Russian patriotism and love for Moscow, proposed to lead the troops during the night over from the right to the left flank, and on the next day to strike a blow at the right wing of the French.

Opinions were divided; discussion waxed hot over the pros and cons of this movement. Yermolof, Dokhturof and Rayevsky concurred with Benigsen's views. Whether they were dominated by a sense that some sacrifice was necessary before the capital was abandoned, or whether personal considerations influenced them, still all these generals seemed unable to comprehend that no advice could alter the inevitable course of events, and that Moscow was already practically abandoned.

The other generals understood this and, setting aside the question of Moscow, they merely discussed the route which the army should take in its retreat.

Malasha gazed with steady eyes at what went on before her, and understood the significance of this council in an entirely different way. It seemed to her that the trouble was merely a personal quarrel between the "little grandfather" and "long-coat," as she called Benigsen. She saw that they became excited when they talked together, and in her heart she was on the side of the "little grandfather."

In the midst of the discussion she noticed the keen, shrewd glance he cast upon Benigsen, and immediately after, much to her delight, she noticed that the "little grandfather," in saying something to "long-coat," offended him. Benigsen suddenly flushed and angrily walked across the room. The words which had such an effect upon Benigsen were spoken in a calm, low tone, and merely expressed Kutuzof's opinion of Benigsen's suggestion.

"Gentlemen!" said Kutuzof, "I cannot approve of the count's plan. Transfers of troops in the immediate proximity of the enemy are always dangerous, and military history confirms this view. Thus, for example"—Kutuzof paused as if he were trying to recall the desired example, and gave Benigsen a bright, naive look—"yes, suppose we should take the Battle of Friedland, which I presume the count remembers was . . . well . . . about as good as given away simply for the reason that our troops attempted to cross from one flank to the other while the enemy were too near." . . .

A silence followed, lasting for a minute, but seeming an age to all present.

The discussion was resumed; but there were frequent interruptions, and there was a general feeling that nothing more could be said.

During one of these lulls in the conversation Kutuzof drew a long sigh, as if he were preparing to speak.

All looked at him.

"*Eh bien, Messieurs, je vois que c'est moi qui payerai les pots cassés*— I see that I must bear the brunt of it," said he. And slowly getting to his feet he approached the table: "Gentlemen, I have listened to your views. Some of you will be dissatisfied with me. But"—he hesitated—"I, by virtue of the power confided to me by the sovereign and the country, I command that we retreat."

Immediately after this the generals began to disperse with that solemn and silent circumspection which people observe after a funeral. Several of the generals, in low voices but in an entirely different key from that in which they had spoken during the council, conferred briefly with the commander-in-chief.

Malasha, who had long since been expected at the supper table, cautiously let herself down backwards from the shelf above the stove, clinging with her little bare toes to the projections of the stove; and, slipping between the legs of the officers, darted out the door.

Having dismissed the generals, Kutuzof sat for a long time with his elbows on the table and pondered over the same dread question:

"When was it, when was it, that it finally became inevitable that Moscow must be abandoned? What was it that forced the decision? And who is to blame for it?"

"I did not expect this, I did not expect it," said he aloud to his aide, Schneider, who came to him late that night. "I did not expect this. I did not dream of such a thing!"

"You must get some rest, your serene highness," said Schneider.

"It's not finished yet! They shall choke on horseflesh yet like the Turks," cried Kutuzof, not heeding him and thumping his fat fists on the table. "They shall . . . as soon as . . ."

I I

HELENE, WHO HAD returned with the court from Vilna to Petersburg, found herself in a trying and delicate situation.

At Petersburg, Helene enjoyed the special protection of a grandee who held one of the most important offices in the empire. But at Vilna she had become intimate with a young foreign prince. When she returned to Petersburg, the prince and the grandee were both in town; both claimed their rights, and Helene found that she had to face a new problem in her career: to preserve her intimacy with both without offending either.

What would have seemed difficult and even impossible for any other woman did not cause Countess Bezukhof even a moment's hesitation, thereby proving that she deserved her reputation of being a very clever woman. If she had tried to hide her actions, to employ subterfuge in escaping from an awkward position, she would by that very method have spoiled her game by admitting her guilt. Instead, Helene, openly, after the manner of a truly great man who can do anything he pleases, assumed that she was in the right, as she really believed, and that all the rest of the world was in the wrong.

The first time the young foreign princeling permitted himself to reproach her, she, proudly holding high her beautiful head and looking at him over her shoulder, said steadily:

"Here is an example of man's egotism and cruelty! I might have expected it. A woman sacrifices herself for you, and this is her reward! What right have you, monseigneur, to hold me to account for my friendships, for my affections? This man has been more than a father to me."

The princeling began to make some answer. Helene interrupted him:

"Well, then, granted," said she. "Perhaps he has for me other sentiments than those of a father; but that is no reason why I should shut the door to him. I am not a man that I should be ungrateful. I would have you understand, monseigneur, that in all that touches my private sentiments, I am accountable only to God and my conscience," said she in conclusion, and pressed her hand to her beautiful, heaving bosom, with a glance toward heaven.

"But, for God's sake, listen to me."

"Marry me and I will be your slave."

"But it is impossible."

"You are too proud to stoop to marriage with me, you . . ." said Helene, bursting into tears.

The princeling tried to console her. Helene, through her tears, declared (as if she had forgotten herself) that no one could prevent her from marrying; that there were examples—at that time there were few examples, but she mentioned Napoleon and other men of high degree; that she had never been to her husband what the name of wife implies; and that she had been led to the altar as a sacrifice.

"But laws, religion . . ." murmured the princeling, beginning to yield.

"Laws, religion! . . . Why were they ever invented, if they could not help in such a case as this?"

The exalted personage was amazed that such a simple line of reasoning had never entered his mind, and he applied for advice to the holy brethren of the Society of Jesus, with whom he stood in intimate relationship.

A few days later, at one of the enchanting fêtes which Helene gave at her suburban residence on the Kamennoi Ostrow, M. de Jobert, a Jesuit, but a lay brother, a fascinating man, no longer young, with hair as white as snow and with dark, glittering eyes, was presented to her; and for a long time, as they sat in the garden in the brilliant light of the illuminations, listening to the music, he conversed with her about love of God, of Christ, of the Sacred Heart of Mary, and about the consolations vouchsafed in this life and the life to come by the one true Catholic religion.

Helene was touched, and several times the tears stood in the eyes of both of them, and her voice trembled.

The dance for which a partner came to claim Helene interrupted her interview with her future religious adviser; but on the evening of the following day M. de Jobert came alone to Helene's, and from that time he was frequently at her house.

One day he took the countess to the Catholic church, and there she remained on her knees before the altar to which she was brought.

The elderly, fascinating Frenchman laid his hands on her head, and, as she herself afterwards declared, she became conscious of something like a cool breeze entering her soul.

Then an abbé heard her confession and granted her absolution from her sins.

After a few days Helene, to her satisfaction, learned that she had now entered the true Catholic Church, and that shortly the Pope would be informed of the matter, and would send her a certain document.

All that happened at this time around her and within her; all the attention lavished on her by so many clever men, and expressed in such agreeable, refined forms; and the dovelike purity in which she dwelt—during these days she constantly wore white gowns with white ribbons—all this afforded her great satisfaction, but she did not for a moment allow this satisfaction to prevent her from the attainment of her ambitions. During one of her interviews with her spiritual guide, she strenuously insisted on his answering her question, how far was she bound by her marriage?

They were sitting in the drawing-room by the window. It was twilight. Through the window drifted the fragrance of flowers. Helene wore a transparent white gown which barely veiled her bosom and shoulders. The abbé, well-fed, with a plump face smooth-shaven, a pleasant, determined mouth, and white hands folded on his knees, sat close to Helene, and, with a slight smile on his lips and eyes, decorously devouring her beauty, was looking from time to time into her face and explaining his views on the question that occupied them.

Helene, with an uneasy smile, looked at his flowing locks, his smooth-shaven, dark-shaded, plump cheeks, and each moment expected some new turn to the conversation. But the abbé, though he evidently appreciated his companion's beauty, was carried away by the skill he used in his arguments. The course of his reasoning was as follows:

"In your ignorance of the significance of what you took upon yourself, you plighted your troth to a man who, on his side, by entering into marriage without believing in the religious sacrament of marriage, committed sacrilege. This marriage had not the complete significance it should have. But, nevertheless, your vow binds you. You have broken it. What have you committed thereby, a venial sin, or a mortal one? Venial sin, because what you have done has been without evil intent. If you now, for the sake of having children, should enter into a marriage bond, your sin might be forgiven you. But this question resolves itself into two: first—"

"But I think," said Helene, suddenly losing patience and turning her fascinating smile on him, "I think that now that I have entered into the faith, I cannot remain bound by what was imposed on me by a false religion."

The spiritual guide was astonished at this solution, which had all the simplicity of Columbus' egg. He was delighted by the unexpected rapidity with which his teachings had met with success, but he could not refrain from following out the train of thought which he had elaborated with so much effort.

"Let us understand each other, countess," he said with a smile, and he proceeded to refute his spiritual daughter's reasoning.

III

HELENE CONSIDERED the matter very simple and easy from the religious standpoint, but she saw that her spiritual directors held out against her solution simply because they were apprehensive of the way it might strike the temporal powers.

Consequently, she resolved that it was necessary for society to be prepared for this eventuality. She aroused the old grandee's jealousy and told him exactly what she had said to her first suitor; in other words, she made him understand that the only way of establishing his rights over her was to marry her.

The aged personage at first was just as much astonished as the young princeling had been at this proposal of marrying during the husband's lifetime. But Helene's imperturbable assurance that this was as simple and natural as the marriage of a virgin had its effect even on him. If he had noticed the slightest symptom of vacillation, shame, or underhandedness on Helene's part, her game would have undoubtedly been lost; but, on the contrary, with simple and good-natured innocence, she told her closest friends (and that was all Petersburg) that both the grandee and the prince had proposed to her, and that she was in love with both of them and afraid of paining either.

The rumor was instantly bruited through Petersburg—not that Helene desired to obtain a divorce from her husband; if this report had been current, very many would have protested against such a lawless proceeding—that the unhappy, fascinating Helene was in perplexity as to which of the two men she should marry.

The question was not at all how far this was permissible, but which alliance was the most desirable, and how the court looked on it. There were, to be sure, a few obdurate people who were unable to rise to the height of this question, and who saw in this project a profanation of the marriage sacrament; but such people were few and they held their peace, while the majority were merely interested in which Helene would choose, and which choice would be the better. As to the question whether it were right or wrong to marry a second time during the lifetime of the first husband, nothing was said, because this question had evidently been settled by people "who were wiser than you and me" (so they said), and to express any doubt of the correctness of such a settlement was to run the risk of showing one's stupidity and one's ignorance of society.

Marya Dmitrievna Akhrasimova, who had gone that summer to Petersburg to visit one of her sons, was the only one who permitted herself frankly to express her opinion, though it was in direct contravention to that of society in general. Meeting Helene one time at a ball, Marya Dmitrievna stopped her in the middle of the ballroom, and in her loud voice which rang through the silence, she said:

"So you propose to marry again while your husband is alive! Perhaps you think you have discovered something new! . . . You have been forestalled, my girl. This way of behaving was invented long ago. In all the brothels they do the same thing."

And with these words Marya Dmitrievna, with that characteristic, threatening gesture of hers, turned back her flowing sleeves and, glancing sternly around, passed through the room.

Marya Dmitrievna, although she was feared, was regarded in Petersburg as a joke, so everyone merely took notice of her use of the coarse word, and repeated it in a whisper, supposing that therein lay all the sting of her remark.

Prince Vasili, who of late had grown peculiarly absent-minded and repeated himself a hundred times, said to his daughter whenever he chanced to see her:

"Helene, I have a word to say to you"; and he would draw her to one side and give her hand a tug. "I have heard rumors of certain projects concerning —you know who. Well, my dear child, you know that my paternal heart would rejoice to feel . . . you have had so much to endure. . . . But, dear child . . . consult only your own heart. That is all I have to say."

And, hiding the emotion that always overmastered him, he would press his cheek to his daughter's and go away.

Bilibin had not lost his reputation of being a clever man, and as he had been a disinterested friend of Helene's, one of those friends whom brilliant women always manage to attach to themselves—men who may be relied on never to change from friend to lover—he once, in an intimate talk, gave Helene the benefit of his views in regard to all this business.

"Listen, Bilibin," said Helene, who always called all such friends as Bilibin by their last names—and she laid her white hand, blazing with rings, on his coat sleeve; "tell me as you would a sister, what ought I to do? Which one of the two?"

Bilibin knitted his brows and sat reflecting with a smile on his lips.

"You do not take me by surprise, you know," said he. "As a true friend I have thought and thought about your affairs. You see, if you marry the prince" (that was the young man)—he bent down a finger—"you lose forever your chance of marrying the other one, and, besides, you offend the court. As you are aware, there is some sort of relationship. But if you marry the old count, you will make his *last* days happy, and then as the widow of the great man . . . the prince will not make a misalliance in contracting a marriage with you."

"Here is a true friend!" cried Helene, radiantly, and once more laying her hand on Bilibin's sleeve. "But the trouble is that I love both of them; I should not wish to pain either of them. I would sacrifice my life to make both of them happy," said she.

Bilibin shrugged his shoulders as much as to say that even he himself could not endure such a grievous thing.

"A mistress-wife! That is what is called stating the question squarely. She would like to have all three as husbands at once!" thought Bilibin. "But tell me how your husband is going to look on this matter," he asked, trusting to the solid foundation of his reputation, and therefore having no fear of hurting himself by such an artless question. "Will he consent?"

"Ah! He loves me so!" cried Helene, who had somehow conceived the notion that Pierre also loved her! "He will do anything for me!"

Bilibin again puckered his forehead, so as to give intimation of the approaching *mot*. "Even unto divorce?" he asked.

Helene laughed.

Among those who permitted themselves to doubt the legality of the proposed marriage was Helene's mother, the Princess Kuragin. She was constantly tortured by jealousy of her daughter, and now when the object that especially aroused this jealousy was the one dearest to the princess' heart, she could not even endure the thought of it. She consulted with a Russian priest in regard to how far divorce and marriage during the life of the husband was permissible, and the priest informed her that this was impossible, and to her delight pointed out to her the Gospel text where it is strictly forbidden to marry again during the life of a husband.

Armed with these arguments, which seemed to her irrefutable, the princess drove to her daughter's early one morning, so as to find her alone.

After listening to her mother's objections, Helene smiled a sweet but satirical smile. "Here it is said in so many words," said the old princess. "He who ever shall marry her who is put away . . ."

"Ah, mama, don't talk nonsense. You do not understand at all. In my position I have duties," interrupted Helene, changing the conversation into French, since it always seemed to her that the Russian brought out a certain lack of definiteness in this transaction of hers.

"But, my dear . . ."

"Ah, mama! Can't you understand that the Holy Father, who has the right to grant dispensations . . ."

At this instant the lady companion who lived at Helene's came in to announce that his highness was in the drawing-room and wished to see her.

"No, tell him that I do not wish to see him, that I am furious with him because he has broken his word!"

"Countess, there is a pardon for every sin!" said a fair young man with a long face and long nose, who came into the room.

The old princess arose most respectfully and curtsied; the young man who came in paid no attention whatever to her. The princess nodded to her daughter and sailed out.

"Yes, she is right," mused the old princess, all of whose convictions were dissipated by the sight of his highness. "She is right. But how was it we did not know this in those days which will never return, when we were young? And it is such a simple thing," mused the old princess, as she settled herself in her carriage.

Toward the beginning of August Helene's affairs were entirely settled, and she wrote her husband—who was so fond of her, as she thought—informing him of her intention of marrying So and So, and that she had embraced the one true religion, and begging him to fulfil all the indispensable formalities of the divorce, in regard to which the bearer of her letter would give due particulars:

And so I pray God, my dear, to have you in His holy and mighty protection.

Your friend,
HELENE.

This letter was brought to Pierre's house at the very time when he was on the field of Borodino.

I V

On the tenth of September Pierre arrived at Moscow. Near the city gates he was met by one of Count Rostopchin's aides.

"Well, we have been searching for you everywhere," said the aide. "The count wants very much to see you. He begs that you will come to him immediately on very important business."

Pierre, without even going first to his own house, called a cab and drove to the governor-general's.

Just as he entered the reception room, a courier from the army left the count's room. The courier made a despairing gesture in answer to the questions showered on him, and passed through the room. Pierre, with weary eyes, gazed at the various officials, old and young, military and civil, who were waiting in the room. All seemed anxious and ill at ease.

Pierre joined one group among whom he saw an acquaintance. After exchanging greetings with Pierre they went on with their conversation.

"Whether they exile him or let him come back, there's no telling; you can't answer for anything in such a state of affairs."

"Well, here is what he writes," said another, calling attention to a printed broadside in his hand.

"That's another thing. That's necessary for the people," said the first speaker.

"What is that?" asked Pierre.

"This is the new placard."

Pierre took it and read as follows:

His serene highness, the Prince, in order to effect a junction as soon as possible with the troops coming to meet him, has passed through Mozhaisk and occupied a strong position where the enemy will not find it easy to reach him. Forty-eight cannon, with ammunition, have been sent to him from here, and his serene highness declares that he will shed the last drop of his blood in defense of Moscow, and that he is ready to fight even in the streets. Brothers, do not be surprised that the courts of justice have ceased to transact business; it was best to send them to a place of safety, but the evil-doer shall have a taste of the law all the same. When the crisis comes, I shall want some gallant fellows, from both town and country. I shall utter my call a day or two before, but it is not necessary yet. I hold my peace. An ax is a good weapon; a boarspear is not bad, but best of all is a three-tined pitchfork; a Frenchman is no heavier than a sheaf of rye. Tomorrow, after dinner, I shall take the Iverskayaicon to the Yekaterininsky Hospital, to the wounded. There we will bless the water; they will get well all the sooner and I now am well; I have had a bad eye, but now I see out of both.

494

"But military men," said Pierre, "have told me that it was perfectly impossible to fight in the city, and that the position . . ."

"Yes, yes, that is just what we were talking about," interrupted the first official.

"But what does he mean by saying: 'I have had a bad eye, but now I see out of both'?" asked Pierre.

"The count has had a sty," replied the aide, with a smile, "and he was very much disturbed when I told him that people were calling to ask what was the matter with him. And how is everything with you, count?" said the aide abruptly, addressing Pierre, with a smile. "We have heard the rumor that you have some domestic tribulations . . . that the countess, your wife . . ."

"I have heard nothing," replied Pierre, indifferently; "what have you heard?"

"Oh, well, you know, stories are often invented. I am only saying what I heard."

"But what have you heard?"

"Well, they say," replied the aide, with the same smile, "that the countess, your wife, is about to go abroad. Of course, it is all nonsense . . ."

"Perhaps so," said Pierre, carelessly glancing around. "And who is that?" he asked, referring to a short old man in a clean blue coat, and with an enormous beard as white as snow, eyebrows the same, and a florid complexion.

"He? That's a merchant: that is, he is the tavern keeper Vereshchagin. . . . Perhaps you have heard that story about the proclamation?"

"Ah! and so that is Vereshchagin," exclaimed Pierre, gazing into the old merchant's calm, self-reliant face, and trying to discover in it any characteristics of a traitor.

"Yes, that is the very man. That is, he is the father of the one who wrote the proclamation," said the aide. "The young man is in jail, and it looks as if it would go hard with him."

A little old man with a star, and another official, a German with a cross suspended around his neck, joined the group.

"You see," proceeded the aide with his story, "it is a puzzling piece of business. This proclamation appeared a couple of months back. It was brought to the count. He ordered it investigated. Gavrilo Ivanitch here looked into it; this proclamation passed through as many as sixty-three hands. We go to a certain man: 'Whom did you have this from?' . . . 'From so-and-so.' . . . We go to the next man: 'Whom did you get this from?' and so on, till it was traced to Vereshchagin—an ignorant little merchant. We ask him: 'Whom did you have this from?' And here you must understand that we know whom he got it from; from no one else than the director of posts. There had been connivance between them for some time. But he says: 'I didn't get it from anyone. I wrote it myself.' We threatened and entreated; he stuck to it—wrote it himself. Well, now, you know the count," said the aide, with a proud, gay smile. "He flew into a terrible rage, but just think of it—'such cunning, falsehood, and stubbornness'!" . . .

"Ah! the count wanted them to implicate Kliucharef, I understand," said Pierre.

"Not at all," said the aide, startled. "They had sins enough to lay against Kliucharef without this; that was why he was sent away. But the truth of the matter was that the count was very indignant . . . 'How could you have written it?' asked the count. He picked up from the table this Hamburg paper. 'Here it is. You did not write it, but you translated it, and you translated it atrociously, because even in French you are an idiot, don't you know? . . . Now, what do you think?' . . . 'No,' says he, 'I have never read any papers, I composed it.' . . . 'Well, if that is so, you are a traitor and I will have you tried and hanged. Confess! From whom did you receive it?' . . . 'I have never seen any papers. I composed it myself!' . . . And so it hung fire. The count called the father also. He stood by his own. And they handed the son over to the court, and he was condemned to penal labor. Now the father has come to intercede for him. But what a wretched creature! You know the kind . . . these merchants' sons, a regular dude. A seducer! learned a few things, and thinks himself a shade better than anyone else. That's the kind of fellow he is. And his father keeps an inn there by the Kamennoi Bridge . . . you know, there's a big picture of Almighty God, who is represented with a scepter in one hand and the imperial globe in the other . . . well, he took this picture home for a few days, and what do you think he did? He found a scoundrelly artist who . . ."

In the midst of this new anecdote, Pierre was summoned to the governor-general.

Pierre went into Count Rostopchin's room. Rostopchin, scowling, was rubbing his forehead and eyes with his hand as Pierre entered. A short man was saying something, but as Pierre approached he stopped and left the room.

"Well, how are you, mighty warrior?" exclaimed Rostopchin, as soon as this man had gone. "But that is not the point just now. My dear, *entre nous*, are you a Mason?" asked Count Rostopchin in a stern tone, as if there were something wrong in that, but that he was ready to grant his forgiveness.

Pierre made no reply.

"My dear, I have been told, but I know that there are Masons and Masons, and I hope that you don't belong to that set which, under the guise of saving the human race, are doing their utmost to ruin Russia."

"Yes, I am a Mason," replied Pierre.

"Well, then, look here, my dear boy, I think you are not ignorant of the fact that Messrs. Speransky and Magnitsky have been sent somewhere into exile; the same thing has happened to Mr. Kliucharef, and the same thing has happened to others besides, who, under the pretext of erecting Solomon's Temple, have been trying to overturn the temple of their country. You can understand that there are reasons for this and that I could not have sent off the local director of posts if he had not been a dangerous man. Now I am informed that you provided him with a carriage to take him from the city, and also that you received from him papers for safekeeping. I like you and I do not wish you ill, and, as I am more than twice your age, I advise you as a father to cut short all dealings with people of this sort, and to leave Moscow as speedily as possible."

"But of what, count, was Kliucharef guilty?" asked Pierre.

"That is my business to know, and not yours to ask me," cried Rostopchin.

"He was accused of having circulated Napoleon's proclamation, but it was not proved against him," said Pierre, not looking at Rostopchin; "and Vereshchagin . . ."

"That is just the point," interrupted Rostopchin, suddenly scowling, and speaking much louder than before. "Vereshchagin is a traitor and a renegade, who has received the punishment he richly deserves," said Rostopchin, with that heat and venom characteristic of men at the recollection of an insult. "I did not summon you to criticize my actions, but to give you some advice, or a command if you prefer that term. I beg of you to cut short your dealings with such gentlemen as Kliucharef and to leave town. I'll knock the nonsense out of anyone, no matter who it is"; but, apparently discovering that he was almost shouting at Bezukhof, who was not as yet in any way to blame, he added in a mixture of French and Russian, cordially seizing Pierre's hand: "We are on the eve of a public disaster, and I have no time to make civil speeches to all who come to see me. My head is sometimes in a whirl. . . . Now then, my dear boy, what are you doing . . . you personally?"

"Nothing at all," replied Pierre, not lifting his eyes and not altering the expression of his thoughtful face.

The count frowned.

"Take the advice of a friend, my dear boy. Leave town, and as soon as possible; that is all I have to say to you. Fortunate is he who has ears to hear. Good-by, my dear. Oh, wait," he shouted, as Pierre was about to leave the room. "Is it true that the countess has fallen into the clutches of the Jesuits?"

Pierre made no reply, and scowling and angry as he had never been seen before, he left Rostopchin's.

When he reached home it was already dark. Eight different people came to see him that evening—the secretary of a committee, the colonel of his battalion, his overseer, his major-domo, and several petitioners. All had business with Pierre which he was obliged to settle. Pierre could not understand at all, he was not interested in such matters, and he gave only such replies to all questions as would soonest rid him of these people.

At last, when he was left alone, he broke the seal of his wife's letter, and read it.

When he awoke the next morning, his major-domo came to inform him that a police officer had come directly from Count Rostopchin to find whether Count Bezukhof had left or was leaving.

A dozen persons who had business with Pierre were waiting for him in the drawing-room. Pierre dressed hurriedly, but instead of going down to those who were waiting for him he went out by the back steps and thence through the gates.

From that time forth until after the burning of Moscow, no one of Bezukhof's household, in spite of all their search for him, saw anything more of Pierre or knew what had become of him.

V

The Rostofs remained in the city up to the thirteenth of September, the day before the enemy entered Moscow.

After Petya had joined Obolensky's Cossack regiment and gone to Byelaya Tserkov, where this regiment was recruiting, a great fear came upon the countess. The thought that both her sons had gone to the war, that both had left the shelter of her wing, that today or tomorrow either one of them, or perhaps even both of them, might be killed, as had been the case with the three sons of a friend of hers, for the first time recurred with cruel vividness to her mind during this summer. The countess could not sleep nights, and even when she dozed she saw in her dreams her sons slain.

After many plans and discussions, the count at last found a means of consoling the countess' apprehensions. He had Petya transferred from Obolensky's regiment to Bezukhof's, which was mobilizing near Moscow. Although Petya remained in the military service, still the countess by this transfer had the consolation of having one of her sons at least partly under her wing, and she cherished the hope of arranging matters so that he would not be sent away any more, and would always be assigned to such places in the service where he would not be exposed in battle.

As long as Nikolai alone was in danger, it seemed to the countess—and it even caused her a pang of remorse—that she loved her eldest more than her other children; but when her youngest, the mischievous, spoiled Petya, who was forever breaking things in the house, who was always in everybody's way, this snub-nosed Petya with his merry dark eyes, his fresh ruddy complexion, and the down just beginning to cloud his cheeks, went off yonder, to mingle with terrible, coarse, grown-up men who were fighting, and finding a real pleasure in doing such things—then it seemed to the mother that she loved him more, far more than all her children. The nearer the time came for her rapturously awaited Petya to return to Moscow, the more the countess' uneasiness increased; she even began to imagine that she would never live to experience the happiness of his return. The presence not only of Sonya, but even of her beloved Natasha, even her husband's presence, irritated the countess.

"What do I care for them? I want no one but Petya," she would say to herself.

Although almost all of the Rostofs' acquaintances had left Moscow, even as early as the first of September, and although they all tried to persuade the countess to start as soon as possible, she would not hear of going until her treasure, her idolized Petya, returned.

Petya came on the ninth of September. The sixteen-year-old officer was not pleased by the morbidly passionate affection with which his mother welcomed him. He treated her coldly, avoided her, and during his stay in Moscow devoted himself exclusively to Natasha, for whom he had always cherished a peculiarly tender brotherly affection, almost as chivalrous as a lover's.

When the ninth of September arrived, thanks to the count's characteristic unconcern, nothing was yet ready for the journey, and the carts they expected from their estates at Riazan and Moscow, to carry all their movable property from the city, did not arrive until the twelfth.

From the ninth until the twelfth of September, all Moscow was in a turmoil and ferment of excitement. Each day thousands of wounded from Borodino poured through the Diagomilov barrier and scattered through the city, and thousands of teams, laden with the inhabitants and their belongings, passed out through the other barriers.

In spite of Rostopchin's placards, or independently of them, or as a direct result of them, the strangest and most contradictory rumors were current throughout the city. The chief of the family, Count Rostof, was constantly rushing around the city, picking up on all sides the flying rumors, and when at home making inadequate and hurried arrangements to speed their departure.

The countess superintended the packing, but she was in a sad state of dissatisfaction with everyone, and kept tagging after Petya, who avoided her; and she was devoured by jealousy of Natasha, with whom he spent all his time.

Sonya was the only one who looked after the practical side of affairs: the packing of their effects. But Sonya had been strangely melancholy and silent of late. The letter in which Nikolai had spoken of Princess Maria had caused the countess to express in her presence the most joyful auguries: she declared that in the meeting of Nikolai and Princess Maria she saw God's providence.

"I never felt happy at all," said the countess, "when Bolkonsky was engaged to Natasha, but I always wished that Nikolai might marry the princess, and I had a presentiment that it would turn out so. And how wonderful that would be!"

Sonya felt that this was true, that the only possibility of retrieving the fortunes of the Rostofs was for Nikolai "to make a rich marriage," and that the princess was an excellent match. Still it was very bitter to her. But in spite of her grief, or possibly because of it, she took upon herself all the difficult labor of arranging the packing and loading, and was busy from morning till night.

The count and countess turned to her when they had any orders to give.

Petya and Natasha, on the other hand, not only did not help their parents, but for the most part were a hindrance and a burden to all in the house. And almost all day long the house echoed with their dancing footsteps, their loud talk and merry laughter. They laughed and enjoyed themselves, not because there was any reason for laughter, but because their hearts were full of life and joy, and because everything they heard seemed to them a reason for laughter and gaiety.

Petya was gay because, having left home a lad, he returned—as everyone told him—a gallant young hero; he was happy because he was at home, because he had left Byelaya Tserkov, where there had been not even a remote prospect of taking part in a battle, and had come to Moscow, where any day they might have fighting; and above all he was gay because Natasha, to whose moods he was always very responsive, was gay also.

Natasha was gay because she had been sad too long, and now nothing reminded her of the reason for her previous sadness, and she was cured! Moreover, she was happy because there was someone who admired her —admiration was an absolutely essential lubricant if her ego was to function with perfect harmony, and Petya admired her.

Chiefly they were gay because the war had come to the very gates of Moscow, because there was a possibility of fighting at the barriers, because they were handing out guns, because there was much commotion, because some great event was in the very air and this is always provocative of good spirits in people, especially in the young.

V I

On Saturday the eleventh of September, everything in the Rostofs' house seemed topsy-turvy. All the doors were open, all the furniture was being carried out or displaced, mirrors and paintings were taken down. The rooms were full of packing boxes and littered with hay, wrapping paper, and pieces of twine. Peasants and household serfs trod over the parquet floors with heavy steps as they hauled the furniture. In the yard stood a throng of peasants' carts, some already loaded and corded up, and some still empty.

Natasha was sitting on the floor in her own dismantled room amid a heap of dresses, laces, and ribbons, and holding lifelessly in her hands an old ball dress, the very one—how out of style it was!—which she had worn to her first Petersburg ball. She was aroused from the daydream into which she had fallen by the chatter of the maids in the adjoining room, and by the sounds of their hurried steps as they ran from this room toward the rear of the house. Natasha got up and looked out the window.

An enormous train of wounded men had come to a halt in the street.

The maids, the lackeys, the housekeeper, the old nurse, the cooks, the coachmen, the postilions, the scullions, all were standing at the gates, gazing at the wounded.

Natasha, throwing a white handkerchief over her hair and holding the ends with both hands, ran down into the street.

The former housekeeper, old Mavra Kuzminishna, broke through the crowd collected at the gates and, going up to a covered cart, entered into conversation with a pale young officer who was stretched out on it. Natasha advanced a few steps and stood timidly, still holding her handkerchief and listening to what the old housekeeper said.

"Well, I suppose you haven't any kith or kin in Moscow, have you?" asked Mavra Kuzminishna. "You would be so much more comfortable in a room somewhere . . . here, for instance, in our house. The folks are going off."

"I don't know that it would be permitted," replied the officer, in a feeble voice. "There's our commander over there—you see?" and he indicated a stout major who was walking back along the street, past the line of carts.

Natasha, with startled eyes, looked into the wounded officer's face, and immediately went to meet the major.

"Can some of the wounded be taken into our house?" she asked.

The major, with a smile, raised his hand to his visor.

"What would you like, mamzel?" he asked, squinting his eyes, and smiling.

Natasha calmly repeated her question, and her face and her whole manner, although she still kept hold of the ends of the handkerchief, were so serious, that the major ceased to smile; and, after first stopping to consider, as if he were asking himself whether this could be permitted, at last gave her an affirmative answer.

"Oh, yes, certainly they can," said he.

Natasha bowed slightly and returned with swift steps to Mavra Kuzminishna, who was still standing by the officer and talking with him compassionately.

"They can, he said they could," whispered Natasha.

The covered cart in which the officer was lying was driven into the Rostofs' yard, and a dozen carts with their loads of wounded, by invitation of the householders, were taken in at different yards and driven up to the steps of the houses on the Povarskaya Street.

Natasha was evidently pleased with having something to do with new people, remote from the ordinary conditions of life. She and Mavra Kuzminishna made as many more of the wounded come into the yard as possible.

"Still, we must ask your papa," Mavra Kuzminishna said.

"Not at all, not at all; what difference can it possibly make? Just for one night, we could sleep in the drawing-room. We can let them have all our rooms."

"What queer notions you do have, young lady! Even if we gave them the wing and the unfinished rooms, we would have to ask permission!"

"Well, I will go and ask."

Natasha ran into the house, and on tiptoe passed through the half-open door of the sitting room, where there was a strong scent of vinegar and Hoffmann's drops.

"Are you asleep, mama?"

"Oh! how can I sleep?" said the countess, waking from a doze into which she had fallen.

"Mama, darling," said Natasha, kneeling beside her and leaning her cheek close to her mother's, "I am sorry; forgive me for waking you up, I will never do it again. Mavra Kuzminishna sent me . . . some wounded men have been brought here, some officers. Will you let them come in? They don't know where to take them; I know you will let them in," said she hurriedly, without stopping to breathe.

"What officers? Who has been brought here? I don't understand at all!" said the countess.

Natasha began to laugh; the countess responded with a feeble smile.

"I knew that you would let them come . . . well, then, I will go and tell them," and Natasha, kissing her mother, jumped up and hurried off.

In the hall she met her father, who had come home with bad tidings.

"Here we are still!" cried the count, with involuntary vexation. "The club is already closed, and the police are going."

"Papa, it does not make any difference, does it? I have invited some wounded men to be brought in?" asked Natasha.

"Why, of course not," said the count, distractedly. "But that's not the trouble. I beg of you that no one will waste time. All must help get packed up, so we can go, go, go tomorrow."

And the count proceeded to give the major-domo and all the servants the same order.

After dinner all the household of the Rostofs, in a frenzy of zeal, set themselves to the task of packing up their effects and preparing for the departure. The old count, suddenly taking a hand in affairs, from dinnertime forth trotted back and forth between the yard and the house, incoherently shouting to the hurrying servants and urging them to still greater haste. Petya remained in the yard, giving orders there. Sonya did not know what to do under the count's contradictory orders, and entirely lost her head. The men, shouting, scolding, and making a fearful racket, hastened through the rooms and bustled about in the courtyard.

Natasha, and that zeal that was characteristic of her, suddenly also put her hand to the work. At first her interference with the task of packing was resented. All that was ever expected of her was quips, and now they were in no mood for such things; but she was so earnest and eager in claiming their submission to her will, she was so grave, and came so near weeping because they would not listen to her, that at last she won the victory and their confidence.

Her first achievement, which cost her enormous efforts and gave her power, was the packing of the rugs. The count had in his house some precious Gobelins and Persian carpets. When Natasha first put her hand to the work two great chests stood open in the ballroom; one was filled almost to the top with china, the other with rugs. There was still a great quantity of china standing about on the tables, and they were bringing still more from the storerooms. It was necessary to begin still a third fresh packing case, and some of the men had been sent after one.

"Sonya, wait, we can get it all in as it is," said Natasha.

"Impossible, miss! We've tried it already," said the butler.

"No, wait and see, please."

And Natasha began rapidly to take out of the packing case the plates and dishes wrapped up in paper.

"The platters must be put in there with the rugs," said she.

"But there are rugs enough as it is for all three of the boxes!" exclaimed the butler.

"Now wait, please." And Natasha began swiftly and skilfully to unpack. "Those are not needed," she said of some Kief-ware plates. "But those are to be put in with the rugs," she said of some Dresden dishes.

"There, now, let it alone, Natasha; there, that'll do, we'll get it packed!" exclaimed Sonya, reproachfully.

"Ah, Miss!" exclaimed the major-domo. But Natasha would not yield; she took out everything and proceeded rapidly to pack again, deciding that there was no need at all of taking the cheap, ordinary carpets and the superfluous tableware.

When everything was taken out they began to pack up again. And in fact, after the removal of everything it was not worth while to take with them, all that had any value could be put into the two packing cases. But it was impossible to close the lid of the box that held the rugs. It could be done by taking out one or two things, but Natasha was bound to have it done in her own way. She arranged the things, and rearranged them, pressed them down, and compelled the butler and Petya, whom she called in to help her pack, to sit on the lid, and she herself put forth all her strength with the energy of despair.

"There, that's enough, Natasha," said Sonya; "I see you are right, only take out the top one."

"I don't want to," cried Natasha, with one hand pushing back her disheveled locks from her perspiring face and pressing down the rugs with the other. "Now press down, Petya, push! Vasilyitch, keep pressing down!" cried she.

The rugs gave way and the cover was shut.

Natasha, clapping her hands, actually squealed with delight, and the tears gushed from her eyes. But this lasted only a second. She immediately applied herself to something else, and by this time they had begun to have implicit confidence in her; even the count was not indignant when he was informed that Natasha had countermanded some order of his, and the household serfs came to her to ask: Should they cord up the loads or not, or was not the team full enough? Thanks to Natasha's clever management great progress was made in the work; articles of little account were left out, and the most precious things were packed in the most practical form possible.

But in spite of the efforts of all the people, the labor of packing was not completed that night, though they worked till late. The countess went to bed, and the count, deferring the start till morning, also retired.

Sonya and Natasha, without undressing, went to sleep in the sitting room.

That night another wounded man was brought through the Povarskaya, and Mavra Kuzminishna, who happened to be standing near the gates, had him brought into the Rostof house. This wounded man, according to Mavra Kuzminishna, was evidently a man of great distinction. He was carried in a two-wheel carriage entirely covered with the apron and with the hood let down. On the box with the driver sat a very dignified old valet. The carriage was followed by a team with the doctor and two soldiers.

"Come into our house, come in. The folks are all going; the whole house will be deserted," said the old woman, addressing the aged servant.

"Well," said the valet, sighing, "we did not know where to take him. We have our own house in Moscow, but it's far off and no one in it."

"We beg it as a favor; our folks have always a houseful, so please come," said Mavra Kuzminishna. "What! is he very bad?" she added.

The valet spread open his hands.

"We did not know whether we could get him here. I must ask the doctor." And the valet sprang down from the box and went to the other team.

"Very good," said the doctor.

The valet returned to the carriage, looked into it, shook his head, bade the driver turn into the yard, and he himself remained standing by Mavra Kuzminishna.

"Merciful Saviour!" she exclaimed.

Mavra Kuzminishna invited them to carry the wounded man into the house.

"The folks won't say anything," she went on. But it was necessary to avoid carrying him upstairs, and therefore the wounded man was taken into the wing and placed in the rooms formerly occupied by Madame Schoss.

The wounded officer was Prince Andrei Bolkonsky!

VII

T<small>HE</small> <small>LAST</small> <small>DAY</small> of Moscow dawned.

It was clear, brisk autumn weather. It was Sunday. Just as on ordinary Sundays, the bells of all the churches rang for Mass. It seemed as if even now no one realized what was coming upon Moscow.

In the dignified old house of the Rostofs, the disintegration of the former way of life showed very little. As far as the servants were concerned, the only indication was that during the night three servants, out of all the enormous retinue, ran away; but nothing was stolen, and the prices of things were clearly indicated by the fact that the thirty teams brought from the country represented an enormous fortune which many men coveted and for which tremendous offers were made to the Rostofs.

Although great sums of money were offered for these teams, nevertheless, during the evening of the twelfth and on the morning of the thirteenth of September, there was a constant stream of orderlies and other servants sent by wounded officers, as well as the wounded men themselves who had been accommodated at the Rostofs' and at neighboring houses, begging the Rostofs' servants to obtain these teams for them so they could escape from Moscow.

The major-domo, to whom these men applied with such petitions, although he pitied the wounded, gave a decided refusal, declaring that he would not dare propose such a thing to the count. However hard it was to leave the wounded behind, it was self-evident that if one team were given up, there would be no reason for refusing another, and another, and finally all their teams and even their private carriages. Thirty teams would not save all the wounded, and in the universal calamity it was out of the question that each person should not think of himself and his family first. Thus the major-domo reasoned in the interests of his master.

On waking on the morning of the thirteenth, Count Rostof softly left his chamber so as not to arouse the countess, who had fallen asleep only toward morning, and in his lilac-colored silk dressing gown went down to the front steps.

The teams, loaded and ready, stood in the yard. The traveling carriages were at the door. The major-domo was standing by the entrance, conversing with an elderly orderly and a pale young officer with his arm in a sling. The major-domo, seeing the count, made a stern and significant sign to the officer and the man that they should go.

"Well, is everything ready, Vasilyitch?" asked the count, rubbing his bald spot and looking good-naturedly at the officer and the man, and nodding to them. The count was fond of new faces.

"About ready to hitch up, your excellency."

"Well, that is fine! The countess will soon be awake, and then God speed us. Well, sir?" said he, turning to the officer. "You will make yourself at home in my house, I hope."

The officer drew nearer. His pale face suddenly flushed a brilliant crimson.

"Count, do me the favor . . . allow me . . . for God's sake . . . let me creep into one of your wagons. I have no luggage with me here. . . . I would as soon go in the cart. . . ."

The officer had not finished speaking before an orderly came up to the count to make the same request in behalf of his master.

"Oh, yes, yes, yes," cried the count, hastily. "I am very, very glad. Vasil-yitch, you make the arrangements; have one or two of the carts unloaded . . . say, that one yonder . . . well . . . any one that seems most advisable . . ." said the count, giving his orders in vague phrases.

At nine o'clock the countess awoke, and Matriona Timofyevna, her former lady's maid who now exercised in the countess' behalf the duties of chief of police, came to inform her old mistress that Madame Schoss was greatly incensed, and that it was quite impossible for the young ladies' summer dresses to be left behind!

When the countess made inquiries, it appeared that Madame Schoss' trunk had been taken from the cart, and that they were unloading all the teams; that they were making ready to take on and carry away with them the wounded whom the count, in his simple-hearted kindness, had promised to rescue.

The countess had her husband summoned.

"What does this mean, my love? I hear they are unloading the things again."

"You see, my dear . . . I was going to tell you, my dear . . . the officer came to me . . . and begged me to let them have a few of the teams for the wounded. Of course, this is all worth a good deal, but how could we leave them behind? Just think! . . . It's a fact, they're in our yard . . . we invited them in. . . . You see, I think . . . we really ought, my dear . . . so now, my dear . . . let them go with us . . . what is the hurry, anyway?" . . .

The count spoke timidly, as he always did when there was any money transaction under discussion. The countess was accustomed to this tone, which always preceded any project that was going to eat up his children's fortunes, as for instance starting a picture gallery, new hothouses, the arrangement of private theatrical performances, or music; and she was accustomed, and had long considered it her duty, to oppose anything that was suggested in this tone of voice.

She assumed her obstinate, tearful expression, and said to her husband:

"Listen, count; you have brought things to such a pass that we aren't worth anything, and now all our property—our children's—all that's left—you want to make away with. Why, you yourself said that what was in the house was worth a hundred thousand! I will not consent, my love, I will not consent. Do as you please! It's for the government to look after the wounded. They

506

know it. Look across the street there at the Lopukhins'; everything was carted off three days ago. That's the way other people do! We alone are idiots! If you don't have any pity on me, at least remember your children!"

The count made a gesture with his hands, and saying nothing further, left the room.

"Papa! what is the matter?" asked Natasha, who had followed him to her mother's room.

"Nothing! none of your concern!" replied the count angrily.

"No, but I heard what you were saying," said Natasha. "Why isn't mama willing?"

"What business is it of yours?" cried the count.

Petya was standing on the steps, busy issuing arms to the men who were to escort the family from Moscow. In the yard the teams still stood ready to leave. Two of them had been unloaded, and in one the young officer had already taken his place, assisted by his orderly.

"Do you know what the trouble was?" asked Petya of Natasha. Natasha understood that Petya referred to the dispute between their father and mother. She made no reply.

"Because papa wanted to give up all the teams to the wounded!" said Petya. "Vasilyitch told me. In my opinion . . ."

"In my opinion," suddenly interrupted Natasha, almost screaming and turning her wrathful face full upon Petya—"in my opinion, this is so mean, so shameful, so . . . so . . . I can't express it! Are we miserable Germans?"

Her throat swelled with convulsive sobs, and, fearing lest she should break down and waste the ammunition of her wrath, she turned on her heel and flew impetuously upstairs.

The count, with his pipe in his hand, was striding up and down, when Natasha, her face distorted with indignation, dashed into the room, and hurried to her mother with rapid steps.

"This is shameful! This is abominable!" she cried. "It cannot be that you have given such an order."

The countess looked at her in fear and bewilderment. The count paused by the window, and listened.

"Mama dear, it must not be! See what they are doing in the yard!" she cried. "They are to be left!"

"What is the matter? Who are to be left? What do you want?"

"The wounded men, that's who! It must not be, mama! This is not like you at all! No, mama darling, dearest! Mama! What do we want with all those things? only look out into the yard! . . . Mama! . . . This must not, cannot be." . . .

The count still stood by the window without turning his face away, as he listened to Natasha's words.

Suddenly he blew his nose and leaned over toward the window.

The countess gazed at her daughter, saw her face tinged with shame for her mother's sake, saw her agitation, understood now why it was her husband would not look at her, and then glanced around her with a troubled face.

"Oh, you may do as you please! Am I interfering with anyone?" she exclaimed, not willing even yet to give in suddenly.

"Mama, dearest, forgive me!" But the countess pushed her daughter away and went over to the count.

"My dear, you give what orders are necessary. You see, I know nothing about this at all!" said she, guiltily dropping her eyes.

"The eggs . . . the eggs are teaching the old hen," exclaimed the count through his happy tears, and he embraced his wife, who was glad to hide her face, crimson with shame, against his heart.

"Papa, mama love! Shall I give the orders? May I?" . . . asked Natasha. "We will still take all we really need," said Natasha.

The count nodded assent, and Natasha, with the same swift steps with which she ran when she used to play tag, flew across the room into the anteroom, and downstairs into the courtyard.

The men gathered around Natasha, and they would not put any faith in the strange command which she gave them until the old count himself came down, and, in the name of his wife, ordered them to give up all the wagons to the wounded and to carry the boxes and trunks back to the storerooms.

After they had understood the meaning of the order, the men with joyful eagerness addressed themselves to the new task. This no longer seemed strange to the servants, but, on the contrary, it seemed to them that it could not be ordered otherwise; just the same as, a quarter of an hour before, it did not seem strange to anyone that the wounded men were to be left and the things carried away.

All the household, as if grieved because they had not got at this work sooner, took hold of it with a will, and made place for the wounded. The wounded men dragged themselves down from their rooms, and their pale faces lighted up with joy as they gathered around the teams.

The rumor spread to the adjoining houses that the teams were going to start from the Rostofs', and still more of the wounded came crowding into the Rostofs' yard from the other houses.

Many of the wounded begged them not to remove all the things, but simply to let them sit on top. But the work of unloading having once begun, it could not stop. It was a matter of indifference whether all the things were left or only half of them. The courtyard was littered up with chests and boxes full of china, bronzes, paintings, mirrors, which had been so carefully packed up the night before, and still the work went on of taking off this thing and that, and giving up one team after another.

"We can take four more," said the overseer. "Here, I will give up my team! But then, what should I do with them?"

"Well, give them the one that has my trunks," said the countess; "Dunyasha can sit with me in the carriage."

So they gave up also the wardrobe wagon, and let the wounded from two neighboring houses have the use of it. All the household and the servants were full of happy excitement. Natasha had risen to such a state of enthusiastically happy emotion as she had not experienced for a long time.

"How shall we tie this on?" asked some of the men, who were trying to fasten a chest on the narrow footboard of one of the carriages. "We ought to give up a whole team to it!"

"What does it contain?" asked Natasha.

"The count's books."

"Leave it, Vasilyitch will take care of it. We don't need them."

The carriage was full; there was some question where Petya was to sit.

"He can sit on the coachman's box. Get up there on the box!" cried Natasha.

Sonya was also indefatigably at work, but the object of her labors was diametrically opposed to the object of Natasha's. She was looking out for the things that had to be left behind, labeling them by the countess' desire, and doing her best to have as much taken as possible.

VIII

By two o'clock the four equipages of the Rostofs, loaded and packed, stood at the door. The teams with the wounded, one after the other, filed out of the gate.

The count, Petya, Madame Schoss, Mavra Kuzminishna, and Vasilyitch came into the room, and, shutting the door, all sat down, and remained for some seconds in silence, not exchanging glances.

The count was the first to rise, and, drawing a loud sigh, he began to cross himself before the holy pictures. All did likewise. Then the count began to embrace Mavra Kuzminishna and Vasilyitch, who were to be left in Moscow, and while they fondled his hand and kissed him on the shoulder, he lightly patted them on the back, muttering some vague, affectionately consoling phrases.

The countess went to the oratory, and Sonya found her there on her knees in front of the icons, which were left there and here on the wall. The most precious icons, as family heirlooms, had been taken down and carried off.

On the stairs and in the yard, the men who were to accompany the teams, furnished with daggers and sabers delivered to them by Petya, and with their trousers tucked into their boots and their coats tightly belted around them, were exchanging farewells with those who were to stay behind.

The old coachman, Yefim, with whom alone the countess would consent to travel, sitting high on his box, did not even deign to glance around at what was going on behind him. He knew from thirty years' experience that it would be still some time before they said to him their "God bless us— Let us be off"—and that, even after the order to start was given, he would still be stopped two or three times while they sent back for things forgotten; and that even then he would be stopped again, and the countess herself would thrust her head out of the window and ask him in the name of Christ the Lord to drive more cautiously down the slopes. He knew this, and therefore, with even greater patience than his horses—especially more than the off chestnut, Hawk, which stood pawing with his hoofs, and champing his bit—he waited for what would be.

At last all were in their places; the carriage steps were folded up, the door shut with a bang, a forgotten box sent for, the countess put her head out and made the stereotyped remark. Then Yefim deliberately removed his hat from his head and proceeded to cross himself. The postilion and all the people did the same. "God with us," cried Yefim, as he put on his cap. "Off we go!"

Natasha had rarely known such a feeling of keen delight as she experienced now, sitting in the coach beside the countess and gazing out at the walls of abandoned, turbulent Moscow slowly moving past. From time to time she put her head out of the window and gazed forward and back at the long string of wagons, containing the wounded, accompanying them. Almost at the very front of the line she could see Prince Andrei's covered carriage. She did not know who was in it, and yet every time she surveyed their train her eyes turned instinctively to this carriage. She knew that it was in the lead.

A number of carriage trains like the Rostofs' had turned into Kudrina Street, and when they reached the Sadovaya there was already a double row of vehicles and trains moving along.

As they passed the Sukharef tower, Natasha, glancing with curiosity at the throng of people coming and going, suddenly uttered an exclamation of delight and amazement.

"My goodness! Mama! Sonya! look, there he is!"

"Who? who?"

"Look! for heaven's sake, Bezukhof!" exclaimed Natasha, putting her head out of the carriage window, and staring at a tall, stout man in a coachman's coat—evidently a gentleman in disguise, to judge by his gait and carriage —who was walking along with a sallow, beardless little old man in a rough woolen cloak under the arch of the Sukharef tower.

"Indeed, it's Bezukhof, in the coachman's coat, walking with a little old man! Indeed it is!" exclaimed Natasha. "Look! look!"

"Why, no! It can't be. How can you say such absurd things!"

"Mama!" cried Natasha. "I'll wager my head that it is he. I assure you it is. Stop! stop!" she cried to the coachman. But the coachman could not stop because a whole file of wagons and vehicles came in from Meshchanskaya, and shouted to the Rostofs to drive on and not delay the others.

But, although he was now at a much greater distance from them all, the Rostofs now recognized Pierre, or the man in the coachman's coat who looked like Pierre, pacing along the street with dejected head and solemn face, side by side with the little beardless man who had the appearance of a footman. This little old man noticed the face thrust forth from the carriage window and trying to attract their attention, and he respectfully nudged Pierre's elbow and said something to him, pointing to the carriage.

It was sometime before Pierre realized what he said, he seemed to be so deeply sunk in thought. At last, when his attention was roused, he looked in the indicated direction, and, recognizing Natasha, gave himself up for a second to the first impression and ran nimbly over to the carriage.

But, after taking a dozen steps, some thought apparently struck him, and he paused.

Natasha put her head out of the window and beamed with a sort of quizzical affectionateness.

"Count, count, come here! You see, we recognized you. This is marvelous!" she cried, giving him her hand. "What does this mean? Why are you dressed this way?"

Pierre took the proffered hand, and, as he walked along—for the carriage was still moving—he awkwardly kissed it. "What is the matter with you, count?" asked the countess, in a voice expressing amazement and sympathy.

"I . . . I . . . Why? . . . don't ask me," said Pierre, and he glanced at Natasha, whose eyes, beaming with delight—he felt them even though he did not look into them—overwhelmed him with their charm.

"What are you going to do? Stay behind in Moscow?"

Pierre made no reply.

"In Moscow?" he repeated questioningly. "Yes, in Moscow. Farewell."

"Oh! I wish I were a man, I would certainly stay behind with you. How wonderful that would be!" exclaimed Natasha. "Mama, if you will let me, I will stay."

Pierre gave Natasha an absent look, and was about to say something, but the countess interrupted him.

"We heard you were in the battle."

"Yes, I was," replied Pierre. "Tomorrow, there is to be another battle . . ." he began to say, but Natasha interrupted him.

"What is the matter with you, count? You aren't like yourself."

"Oh, don't, don't ask me, don't ask me, I myself don't know. Tomorrow . . . but no! Farewell, farewell," he went on. "Terrible times!" and, moving away from the carriage, he passed along on the sidewalk.

Natasha for a long while still kept her head out of the window, beaming on him with an affectionate and somewhat quizzical smile of joy.

I X

DURING THE TWO days since his disappearance from home, Pierre had been living in the late Bazdeyef's deserted rooms.

This was how it happened.

On waking up the morning after his return to Moscow and his interview with Count Rostopchin, it was a long time before Pierre could realize where he was and what was required of him. When he was informed that among those waiting to see him in his reception room there was the Frenchman who had brought him the letter from his wife, the Countess Elena, suddenly he experienced that feeling of embarrassment and helplessness to which he was peculiarly prone.

All at once he realized that everything was now at an end, that ruin and destruction were at hand, that there was no distinction between right and wrong, that there was no future, and that there was no escape from this condition of things. With an unnatural smile on his lips, and muttering unintelligible words, he first sat for a while on his couch; then he got up, went to the door, and looked through the crack into the reception room; then, making a fierce gesture, he tiptoed back and took up a book. The major-domo came for the second time to tell Pierre that the Frenchman was very anxious to see him, "if only for a little minute," and that a messenger had come from I. A. Bazdeyef's widow to get his late master's books and papers, as Madame Bazdeyef had herself gone to the country.

"Oh, yes, immediately . . . wait . . . or no, no . . . go and say that I will come immediately," said Pierre to the major-domo.

But, as soon as the major-domo had gone, Pierre took his hat, which lay on the table, and left his room by the back door. From the landing where he stood, another flight of stairs led to the rear entrance. Pierre went down this and came out into the yard. No one had seen him.

Of all the business that faced Pierre that morning, the business of assorting Bazdeyef's books and papers seemed to him most urgent. He took the first cab that happened to come along, and ordered him to drive to the Patriarch's Pools, where the widow Bazdeyef lived.

On reaching the Patriarch's Pools, Pierre had to search for Bazdeyef's house, as he had not been there for some time. He approached the gate. Gerasim, the same sallow, beardless little old man whom Pierre had seen five years before at Torzhok with Bazdeyef, came out at his summons.

"Anyone at home?" asked Pierre.

"Owing to present circumstances, Madame Bazdeyef and her children went yesterday to their Torzhok estate, your excellency."

"Nevertheless, I will come in; I must sort the books," said Pierre.

"Please come in, I beg of you," said the old servant.

Pierre went into the gloomy study. It was dusty, and had not been touched since Bazdeyef's death; it was gloomier than ever. Pierre crossed the floor, went to one of the bookcases in which manuscripts were kept, and took out one of the most important of the documents of the order at that time. He took a seat at the dusty writing table and spread the manuscripts in front of him, opened them, then shut them, folded them up, and finally, pushing them away, rested his head on his hands and fell into deep thought.

Several times Gerasim cautiously came and looked into the library and found Pierre still in the same attitude. More than two hours passed, while Pierre still sat at the desk. Gerasim permitted himself to make a little stir at the door so as to attract his attention; Pierre did not hear him.

"Do you wish me to send away the driver?"

"Oh, yes," said Pierre, starting from his reverie and hastily jumping to his feet. "Listen," he added, taking Gerasim by his coat button and looking down on the little old man with glittering, humid eyes, full of enthusiasm. "I beg of you not to tell anyone who I am. And do what I tell you."

"I will obey," replied Gerasim. "Do you want something to eat?"

"No, but I want something else. I want a peasant's clothes and a pistol," said Pierre, unexpectedly reddening.

"I will obey," said Gerasim, after turning this over in his mind.

All the rest of the day Pierre spent alone in the Benefactor's library, and Gerasim could hear him restlessly pacing from one corner of the room to the other and sometimes talking to himself; and he spent the night in a bed made ready for him there.

Gerasim, with the equanimity of a servant who has seen many strange things in his day, accepted Pierre's residence without amazement and seemed well satisfied to have someone to wait on. That same evening, without even asking himself what was the reason for the request, he procured for Pierre a coachman's coat and hat, and promised on the following day to get the pistol.

Pierre, dressed in his coachman's coat, refitted for him by Gerasim, and accompanied by the old man, was on his way to get the pistol at the Sukharef tower when he met the Rostofs.

The Russian troops poured through Moscow from two o'clock in the morning until two o'clock in the afternoon, and they took with them the last fleeing inhabitants and the wounded.

While they were flowing in two streams around the Kremlin and over the Stone and Moscow River bridges, a tremendous mob of soldiers, taking advantage of the delay and crush, ran back from the bridge, and stealthily and noiselessly sneaked into the city to the Red Square, where they knew by their keen scent that they might without much difficulty lay their hands on what did not belong to them.

A similar throng of men, as if in search of cheap bargains, also thronged the Gostinyi Dvor—Moscow's great bazaar—in all its alleys and passageways. But absent were the persistent, softly wheedling voices of the shopkeepers; absent the peddlers and the variegated throng of women customers. Nothing was to be seen but uniforms and the cloaks of unarmed soldiers, silently entering without burdens and returning to the ranks laden with spoil.

Merchants and bazaar men—a few of them—ran about among the soldiers like crazy men, opening and closing their shops and themselves helping the gallant soldier lads to carry off their wares.

On the square in front of the bazaar stood drummers beating to arms, but the rattle of the drums did not call back the soldier plunderers, but on the contrary drove them to run farther and farther from its signal.

Two officers, one with a scarf over his uniform and riding a lean, dark-gray horse, the other in a cloak and on foot, stood at the corner of Ilyinka Street engaged in conversation. A third officer dashed up to them.

"The general has given orders that they be all driven out instantly at any cost. Why, there never has been anything like this before! Half of the men have left the ranks.—Where are you going?—And you, too?" he cried, first to one and then to three infantry soldiers who, without weapons and holding up the tails of their overcoats, were sneaking past him to rejoin their ranks. "Halt, you dogs!"

"Try and catch them," replied the other officer. "You can't do it! The only way is to march more rapidly, and then the ones in the rear can't drop out, that's all."

"But how move faster, or move at all, when there's a halt and a jam at the bridge? Why not post sentinels and keep them from breaking ranks?"

"Forward and drive them out!" cried the senior officer.

The officer in the scarf dismounted, beckoned to the drummer, and went with him under the arched gallery of the bazaar. A number of soldiers started away on the run. A merchant with red pimples around his nose, and with an expression of cool, calculating composure on his oily face, came to the officer with all the haste compatible with his elegant dignity, and wringing his hands.

"Your honor," said he, "do me a favor; give me your protection. As far as any small trifles go we shall be only too glad to accommodate you, you know . . . if you please I will bring you some cloth instantly . . . glad enough to give a gentleman a couple of rolls, it's a pleasure to us because we feel . . . but this, this is out-and-out robbery! Please! If they had only set a guard, or at any rate let us know in time to shut up."

A number of merchants gathered around the officer.

"Ah, it's a waste of breath to whine like that!" said one of them, a lean man with a grave face. "Men with their heads off don't weep for their hair! Let 'em have what they want!"

And he made an energetic gesture and came to the officer's side.

"It's fine talk for you, Ivan Sidoritch!" exclaimed the first merchant, angrily. "I beg of you, your honor!"

"Fine talk!" echoed the lean man. "I have three shops over there, and a hundred thousand worth of goods. How can we have protection when the troops are gone? 'God's powers are not ours.'"

"I beg of you, your honor," persisted the first merchant, making a low bow. The officer stood in uncertainty, and his face showed his irresolution.

"But, after all, what business is it of mine?" he suddenly cried, and went with swift strides toward the front of the line.

X

THE CITY PROPER, meantime, was deserted. Almost no one was on the streets. The house gates and shops were all locked up. Here and there in the vicinity of taverns could be heard occasional shouts of revelry or drunken singing. Not a carriage passed along, and the steps of pedestrians were rarely heard.

All that night Rostopchin gave out instructions to all who came for them from every part of Moscow. His intimates had never seen the count so gloomy and irascible.

"Your excellency, a messenger from the Chancery Department: the director asks instructions" . . . "from the Consistory" . . . "from the Senate" . . . "from the University" . . . "from the Foundling Asylum" . . . "the suffragan has sent to" . . . "wants to know" . . . "What orders are to be given to the fire brigade?" . . . "the superintendent of the prison" . . . "the director of the Lunatic Asylum."

Thus all night long without cessation men came to the count for their orders. To all these queries the count gave curt and surly answers, indicating that any regulations of his were now unnecessary, that all his preparations, so carefully elaborated, someone had now rendered useless, and that this *someone* would have to shoulder all the responsibility for what was now taking place.

"Well, tell that blockhead that it is his business to guard his papers," he replied to the query from the Chancery Department. "Well, now, what is that nonsense about the fire brigade? If they have horses, let 'em go to Vladimir!" . . . "Don't leave them for the French."

"Your excellency, the overseer of the Lunatic Asylum is here; what orders for him?"

"What orders? Let 'em all out, that's all . . . let the lunatics loose in the city. When lunatics are at the head of our armies, God means for these to be out!"

When asked what to do with the convicts in the jail, the count wrathfully shouted to the inspector: "What? Did you expect me to give you a couple of battalions as escort, when there aren't any to be had? Let 'em out; that's all."

"Your excellency, there are the political prisoners, Mieskhof and Vereshchagin."

"Vereshchagin! Hasn't he been hanged yet?" cried Rostopchin. "Bring him to me."

By nine o'clock in the morning, when the troops were already on the way across Moscow, no one came any more to ask the count for orders. All who could leave had left on their own responsibility; those who remained behind decided for themselves what they should do.

The count commanded his horses to be brought round to take him to Sokolniki. He sat waiting in his study with folded arms, scowling, sallow, and taciturn. The chief of police, who had been stopped on his way by a mob, came just when the count's aide brought word that the horses were ready. Both were pale; and the chief of police informed the count that in the courtyard was a vast crowd of people anxious to see him.

Rostopchin went to the balcony door.

"Now what do they want?" he asked the chief of police.

"Your excellency, they declare that they have come on your orders, ready to go out against the French; they are shouting something about treason! It is a riotous mob, your excellency. I barely escaped alive. Your excellency, may I be bold enough to suggest . . ."

"Be good enough to withdraw; I know what to do without your advice," cried Rostopchin, savagely. He stood by the balcony door, looking down at the crowd. "This is what they have brought Russia to! This is how they have treated me!" brooded Rostopchin, feeling uncontrollable rage rising in his heart against whoever might be the cause of what had taken place. As often happens with hot-tempered men, he was overmastered by rage, but he was still looking for some scapegoat on whom to vent it.

"Look at that populace, the dregs of the people," he said to himself in French, as he gazed down at the mob. "The plebs stirred up by their folly! They must have a victim," he thought. And this idea came into his head precisely for the reason that he himself wanted a victim, an object for his wrath.

"Carriage ready?" he demanded.

"It is, your excellency. What orders do you wish to give in regard to Vereshchagin? He is waiting on the stairs," replied the aide.

"Ah!" cried Rostopchin, as if struck by an unexpected thought.

And, quickly throwing open the door, he went with resolute steps out on the balcony. The murmur of the crowd suddenly ceased; hats and caps were doffed, and all eyes were turned on the count.

"Good morning, boys!" cried the count, hurriedly, and in a loud voice. "Thank you for coming. I will be down directly, but, first of all, we must settle accounts with a villain. We must punish the villain who is the cause of Moscow's ruin. Wait for me!"

And the count retired from view, slamming the door behind him.

An approving roar of satisfaction ran through the throng.

"Of course he'll settle with all villains!" . . . "You talk about the French!" . . . "He'll put things straight!" said the people, as if reproaching each other for their lack of faith.

In a few minutes an officer came hastily out of the rear door, gave some order, and a line of dragoons was formed. The mob eagerly rushed from the balcony toward the steps. Rostopchin, coming out on the porch with swift steps, looked around him angrily as if searching for someone.

"Where is he?" asked the count.

And, at the instant the words left his mouth, he saw coming around the corner of the house, between two dragoons, a young man with a long, thin neck, and with one-half of his head shaven, though the hair had begun to grow again. He was dressed in a short, blue cloth coat lined with foxskins, which had once been a stylish garment, and dirty, cotton peasant trousers, stuffed into fine boots covered with mud and run down at the heels. On his slender, weak legs he dragged along heavy iron shackles, which made his gait difficult and stumbling.

"Ah!" exclaimed Rostopchin, hastily turning his eyes away from the young man in the foxskin jacket and pointing to the lower step of the porch. "Stand him there!"

The young man, with chains clanking, heavily dragged himself to the spot indicated; and, after pulling with his finger at his jacket collar, which was too tight, and twice stretching out his long neck and sighing, he submissively folded his slender hands, which were those of a man unaccustomed to work.

Silence prevailed for several seconds, until the young man had taken his position on the steps. In the rear of the crowd, where people were trying to press forward, there were grunts and groans and jostling and the shuffling of moving feet.

Rostopchin waited until the prisoner was in the designated place, then frowned and passed his hand over his face.

"Boys!" cried he in a voice ringing out with metallic clearness, "this man, Vereshchagin, is the scoundrel who has lost us Moscow!"

The young man in the foxskin-lined jacket stood in a submissive stooping attitude, with his wrists crossed on his abdomen. He hung his shaven head; his thin young face wore a hopeless expression. At the first words spoken by the count he slowly raised his head and glanced at the count as if wishing to say something, or, at least, to get his eye. But Rostopchin did not look at him. On the young man's long, slender neck, behind his ear, a vein stood out like a whipcord, tense and bluish, and his face suddenly flushed.

All eyes were fastened on him. He returned the gaze of the crowd and, as if he found some cause for hope in the expression of the faces, he gave a timid and pitiful smile, and, again dropping his head, shifted his feet on the step.

"He is a traitor to his Tsar and his country; he has sold himself to Bonaparte; he alone of all Russians has shamed the name of Russian, and by him Moscow has been destroyed," cried Rostopchin in a steady, sharp voice; but suddenly he gave a swift glance at Vereshchagin, who continued to stand in the same submissive attitude. This glance seemed to infuriate the count. Raising his hand, he shouted, stepping almost down to the crowd:

"Take the law into your own hands! I give him over to you!"

The mob made no answer, and merely pressed together more and more densely. To be crushed together, to breathe in that infected atmosphere, to be unable to stir, and to expect something unknown, incomprehensible and terrible, was above human endurance. The men standing in the front row, who saw and heard all that was taking place before them with startled, wide-staring eyes and gaping mouths, exerted all their force and resisted with their backs the forward thrust and pressure of the rear ranks.

"Kill him! . . . let the traitor perish and not shame the name of a Russian!" yelled Rostopchin. "Kill him! I order it!"

The mob, understanding only the venomous sound of Rostopchin's voice, without hearing the actual words, groaned and moved forward, then instantly stood still again.

"Count!" exclaimed Vereshchagin's timid but at the same time theatrical voice, amid the momentary silence that had fallen—"Count, there is one God over us," said Vereshchagin, lifting his head; and again the thick vein on his slender neck throbbed, and the red flush spread over his face and receded. He had not said what he meant to say.

"Kill him! I order it!" shouted Rostopchin, suddenly growing as pale as Vereshchagin.

"Draw sabers!" commanded the officer to the dragoons, himself unsheathing his saber.

Another and still more violent wave of emotion rolled through the crowd. Reaching those in the front rows, it seemed to lift them, and, reeling, broke against the very steps of the porch.

"Cut him down!" came the whispered command of the officer to the dragoons; and suddenly, one of the dragoons, his face distorted with rage, gave Vereshchagin a blow on the head with his dull broadsword.

"Ah!" cried Vereshchagin, in amazement, and looked around in terror as if he could not understand why this was done to him. The same groan of amazement as before ran through the crowd. "O Lord—O Lord!" exclaimed some voice.

But instantly following his cry of amazement, Vereshchagin gave a piteous shriek of pain, and that shriek was his undoing.

The tense barrier of humane feeling which had held back the mob suddenly broke. The crime was begun, and it had to be accomplished. The lugubrious groan of reproach was swallowed up in the fierce and maddened roar of the mob. Like the seventh and last wave which wrecks the ship, this final irresistible billow, impelled from the rear, was borne through to those in front, overwhelmed them, and swallowed up everything.

The dragoon who had used his sword was about to repeat the blow. Vereshchagin, with a cry of horror, warded off the stroke with his arm, leaped among the people. The tall young fellow against whom he struck grasped his slender neck with his hands, and with a savage yell fell together with him under the trampling feet of the frenzied crowd.

Some beat and mangled Vereshchagin; others, the tall young fellow. And the cries and yells of the surging multitude and of the men who were trying to rescue the tall young fellow only increased the fury of the mob. It was long before the dragoons were able to extricate the tall factory hand, who was half beaten to death and covered with blood. And it was long, in spite of all the haste with which the mob strove to finish the work they had begun, before those men who were beating, trampling, and mangling Vereshchagin were able to kill him; but the crowd pressed them on every hand, and at the center it was like a solid mass rocking and swaying from side to side, giving them no chance either to finish with him or to let him go.

"Finish him with an ax, hey?" . . . "They've crushed him well." . . . "The traitor! He sold Christ." . . . "Is he alive yet?" . . . "He's a tough one!" . . . "He gets his deserts." . . . "Try it with a bar!" . . . "Isn't he dead yet?"

Only when the victim ceased to struggle and his shrieks gave way to the measured, long death rattle, did the mob begin hastily to avoid the spot where lay the bleeding corpse. Each one came up, gave a look at what had been done and, full of horror, remorse and amazement, pressed back.

"O Lord, men are like wild beasts! Wonder anyone was spared!" exclaimed some voice in the crowd.

"And a young fellow too!" . . . "Must be a merchant's son." . . . "What a mob!" . . . "They say he's the wrong one." . . . "What do you mean . . . the wrong one?" . . . "O Lord!" . . . "Someone else was beaten to death too!" . . . "They say he just escaped with his life!" . . . "Oh, what people!" . . . "Not afraid to commit any sin."

Those remarks were made by the same men who had attacked Vereshchagin. They looked now with bewildered pain at the dead body, the face smeared with blood and begrimed with dust, and the long, slender neck half hacked off.

A zealous police official, thinking it unbecoming to have a corpse encumbering his excellency's yard, ordered the dragoons to drag it forth into the street. Two dragoons seized the body by the mutilated legs and hauled it out. The blood-stained, dust-begrimed, dead shaven head, rolling on the long neck, was dragged along thumping on the ground. The mob surged away from the corpse.

At the moment that Vereshchagin fell and the mob with a savage yell burst forward and rushed over him, Rostopchin turned suddenly pale, and, instead of going to the rear stairs where his horses were waiting for him, he started with sunken head and swift steps, without knowing where or why, along the corridor that led to the rooms on the ground floor. His face was pallid, and he could not keep his lower jaw from trembling, as if he had an ague.

"Your excellency, this way . . . where are you going? . . . This way, if you please!" exclaimed a shaking, frightened voice behind him.

Count Rostopchin was in no condition to answer, and obediently wheeling about, he went in the direction indicated. At the rear entrance stood his carriage. Even here the distant roar of the excited mob reached his ears. Count Rostopchin hastily sprang into the carriage and ordered the coachman to drive to his suburban house at Sokolniki.

When they reached the Miasnitakaya and the yells of the mob were no longer audible, the count began to feel qualms of conscience. He now remembered with dissatisfaction the excitement and terror he had displayed before his subordinates. "The populace is terrible; it is frightful," he said to himself. "They are like wolves, which can be appeased only with flesh."

"Count, there is one God over us!"

Vereshchagin's words suddenly recurred to him, and a disagreeable chill ran down his back. But this feeling was only momentary, and Count Rostopchin smiled a scornful smile at himself.

"I had other obligations," he said to himself. "The people had to be appeased. Many other victims have perished, and are perishing, for the public good."

Not only did he not reproach himself for what he had done, he even found reason to congratulate himself that he had so happily succeeded in taking advantage of this fortuitous circumstance for punishing a criminal and at the same time pacifying the mob.

"Vereshchagin was tried and condemned to death," said Rostopchin to himself, though Vereshchagin had been condemned only to hard labor. "He was a spy and a traitor; I could not leave him unpunished, and, besides, I killed two birds with one stone. I offered a victim to pacify the people, and I punished an evildoer."

By the time he reached his suburban house and began to make his domestic arrangements, he had become perfectly calm.

At the end of half an hour the count was driving behind swift horses across the Sokolniki meadow, no longer remembering what had happened, thinking only of events to come. He was on his way now to the Yauzsky Bridge, where he had been told Kutuzof was to be found.

Count Rostopchin was preparing mentally the angry and caustic reproaches he intended to hurl at Kutuzof for so deceiving him.

The troops were still crowding the bridge over the Yauza. It was hot. Kutuzof, frowning and depressed, sat on the bench near the bridge, playing with his whip in the sand, when a carriage drove up in hot haste. A man wearing a general's uniform and a plumed hat, with wandering eyes expressing a mixture of wrath and terror, got out and, approaching Kutuzof, began to say something to him in French.

This was Count Rostopchin.

He told Kutuzof that he had come because Moscow and the capital were no more, and the army was all that was left.

"It would have been different if your serene highness had not told me you would not abandon Moscow without giving battle; then this would not have happened at all," said he.

Kutuzof glanced at Rostopchin and, apparently not taking in the full significance of the words, seemed to exert all his energies to read the peculiar expression that was written in the face of the man addressing him.

Rostopchin grew confused and stopped speaking. Kutuzof shook his head slightly and, with his inquisitive glance still fixed on Rostopchin's face, he said in a low tone:

"No, we are not giving up Moscow without a struggle!"

Whether Kutuzof was thinking of something entirely irrelevant when he said those words, or said them on purpose, knowing their absurdity, at all events Rostopchin made no reply and hastily turned away from him. And— strangely enough—the governor-general of Moscow, the haughty Count Rostopchin, seizing a whip, went to the bridge and began to shout and hurry along the teams that were blocked together there.

XI

At four o'clock in the afternoon, the troops under Murat entered Moscow. In front rode a detachment of Wurtemberg hussars; next followed the King of Naples in person, mounted, and surrounded by a large suite.

The bells began to ring for vespers in the Kremlin, and this sound confused the French. They supposed that it was an alarm. Several of the infantry soldiers ran toward the Kutafya gates, which were barricaded with beams and planks. Two musket shots rang sharply out from behind the gates as soon as the officer and his detachment started to approach. The general, standing by the cannon, shouted some command to the officer, and the officer and one of the soldiers hastened back to him. The cannon were pointed. The artillerists breathed on their lighted fuses. The officer gave the command: Fire! And two hissing sounds of canister shot followed one after the other. The grape clattered on the stones of the gateway, on the beams and the barricade, and two puffs of smoke floated away over the square.

A few seconds later, when the echoes of the reports had died out along the stone walls of the Kremlin, a strange noise was heard over the heads of the French. An enormous flock of jackdaws arose above the walls and circled around in the air, cawing and flapping their countless wings. At the same instant a single human yell was heard from the gates, and through the smoke appeared the figure of a hatless man in a peasant's coat. He held a musket, and aimed it at the French. "Fire!" cried the artillery officer a second time, and at exactly the same instant rang out one musket shot and two cannon shots.

Smoke again concealed the gates.

Behind the barricade no one any longer moved, and the French infantry soldiers and their officers again approached the gates. At the gates lay three men wounded and four dead. Two men in peasant coats were in full flight down along the walls.

Murat was informed that the way was clear. The French poured through the gates, and began to set up their camp in the Senate Square. The soldiers flung chairs out of the windows of the Senate House into the square, and used them as fuel for their fires.

Other divisions crossed through the Kremlin and took up their stations. Finding nowhere any hospitality, the French settled down, not in "quarters," as they usually would in a city, but as it were in a camp pitched inside the city limits.

The French, though ragged, hungry, weary, and reduced to one-third of their original numbers, entered Moscow in regular military order. It was a jaded, exhausted but still martial and redoubtable army.

But it was such only until the moment when the soldiers of that army were distributed in their billets. As soon as the men of the various regiments began to scatter among the rich and deserted mansions, then the martial quality disappeared forever, and the men were neither citizens nor soldiers, but were changed into something betwixt and between, called marauders.

When, five weeks later, these same men marched out of Moscow, they were no longer troops. They were a throng of marauders, each one of whom brought or carried away with him a quantity of articles which seemed to him valuable or necessary.

The object of each of these men as they left Moscow was not, as formerly, to conquer, but merely to keep what they had obtained. Like the monkey which has thrust its paw into the narrow neck of a jar and grasped a handful of nuts, and will not open its fist lest it lose its prize—thus destroying itself—the French, on leaving Moscow, were evidently doomed to perish in consequence of dragging their plunder with them, since to relinquish what they had taken as plunder was as impossible as it was impossible for the monkey to let go its handful of nuts.

On the day the French entered Moscow, order after order was issued by the French commanders with the object of preventing the troops from scattering about through the city—sternly forbidding violence to the inhabitants or looting, and insisting on a general roll call—that same evening; but in spite of such precautions, the men, who just before had constituted an army, wandered about through the rich, deserted city, which still abounded in comforts and enjoyments. As a famished herd of cattle go huddled together over a barren field, but become uncontrollable and scatter as soon as they come into rich pasture lands, so did this army separate and scatter irreclaimably through the opulent city.

The French attributed the burning of Moscow to the fierce patriotism of Rostopchin; the Russians, to the savagery of the French. Actually, responsibility for the burning of Moscow was not due and cannot be attributed to any one person or to any group of persons. A timber-built city, which has its conflagrations almost daily in summer in spite of the police and in spite of proprietors who are careful of their houses, could not fail to burn when the inhabitants were gone and their places taken by soldiers who smoked their pipes, made campfires of senators' chairs in the Senate Square, and cooked their meals there twice a day.

Even if there were incendiaries (which is very doubtful, since there was no reason for setting fires, and to do such a thing would have been difficult and risky), they could not be considered as the cause of the conflagration, since it would have taken place without them.

Moscow was burned by its citizens—that is true; not, however, by the citizens who remained, but by those who went away.

Moscow, occupied by the enemy, did not remain intact like Berlin, Vienna, and other cities, simply because the inhabitants did not come forth to offer the French the bread and salt of hospitality, and the keys of the city, but left it.

The infiltration of the French into Moscow, spreading out starwise, did not reach the quarter where Pierre was now living until the evening of September 14.

After the two days Pierre had spent alone and in such an unusual manner, he had fallen into a state of mind that bordered on insanity. His whole being was possessed by one importunate idea. He himself did not know how or when it came about, but this idea had such a hold on him that he remembered nothing of the past, had no comprehension of the present, and what he saw and heard seemed as if it had happened in a dream. It was his duty, he felt, to remain in Moscow incognito, to fire at Napoleon and to kill him; either he must perish himself, or put an end to the misery which afflicted all Europe and was caused, as Pierre reasoned, by Napoleon alone.

Pierre knew all the particulars of the German student's attempts on Bonaparte's life in Vienna in 1809, and he was aware that the student had been shot. And the danger to which he was about to expose his life, in carrying out his purpose, filled him with still greater zeal.

Pierre's physical condition, as was always the case, corresponded with his mental state. The coarse, unusual food, the vodka he had been drinking those days, the abstinence from wine and cigars, the dirty, unchanged linen, the two almost sleepless nights he spent on the short, pillowless couch, all this had reduced him to a state not far removed from insanity.

It was already two o'clock in the afternoon; the French had already entered Moscow. Pierre knew it; but instead of acting, he thought only of his enterprise, considering all its minutest details. In his wishful dream

Pierre did not picture the act itself of firing the shot, or the death of Napoleon; but he imagined with extraordinary vividness and with a melancholy delight his own ruin and his heroic courage.

"Yes, one for all! I must accomplish it or perish!" he said to himself. "Yes, I will go up to him . . . and then suddenly . . . with a pistol . . . or would not a dagger be better?"—mused Pierre—"However, it is immaterial. 'Not I, but the hand of Providence strikes you!' I will exclaim." Pierre was rehearsing the words he would utter as he killed Napoleon—" 'Well, then, take, punish me,' " Pierre went on to say, still further imagining the scene, and drooping his head with a sad but determined expression.

XII

PIERRE, DECIDING for himself that until the time came for the fulfilment of his project it was best not to disclose his identity or his knowledge of French, stood in the half-open door leading into the corridor, intending instantly to go and hide himself as soon as the French entered. But the French came in, and Pierre had not stirred from the door; an overwhelming curiosity held him there.

There were two of them. One was an officer, tall, gallant-looking, and handsome; the other, evidently a soldier, or his servant, was short and crabbed, lean and sunburned, with sunken cheeks and stupid expression of face. The officer, resting his weight on a cane and limping a little, came forward. Having advanced a few steps, he halted as if deciding that the rooms were good; and turning to some soldiers who appeared in the doorway, in a tone of command shouted to them to put up their horses. Having attended to this, the officer, with a swagger, raised his elbow, twisted his mustache and then touched his cap.

"*Bonjour la compagnie!*" he cried cheerily, glancing around with a smile. No one made any answer.

"*Vous êtes le bourgeois?* [Are you the master of the house?]" asked the officer, addressing Gerasim. Gerasim, with a scared, questioning look, stared at the officer.

"Quartee, quartee—*logement!*" exclaimed the officer, surveying the little man from top to toe with a condescending and benevolent smile. "*A ça! Dites donc, on ne parle donc français dans cette boutique?* [Tell me, isn't French spoken in this establishment?]" he added, glancing around and catching Pierre's eyes. Pierre slunk aside from the door.

The officer again addressed himself to Gerasim. He tried to make the old man show him the rooms in the house.

"The master is gone—no understand! . . . my . . . you . . . your . . ." stammered Gerasim, striving to make his words more comprehensible by speaking in broken Russian.

The French officer, with a smile, waved his hands in front of Gerasim's nose to indicate that he did not understand him, and he limped again to the door where Pierre was standing. Pierre started to go away in order to hide from him, but just at that instant he saw through the open door of the kitchen Makar Alekseyitch, Bazdeyef's half-witted brother, peering out, with a pistol in his hand. With the cunning of a madman, Makar Alekseyitch gazed at the Frenchman, and, raising the pistol, aimed.

Before Pierre had time to seize and throw up the pistol, Makar Alekseyitch got his fingers on the cock and a sharp report rang out, deafening them all and filling the passage with gunpowder smoke. The Frenchman turned pale and sprang back to the door.

Pierre seized the pistol, flung it away and ran after the officer; then (forgetting his intention to conceal his knowledge of French) began to speak with him in French.

"You are not wounded?" he asked, with solicitude.

"I think not," replied the officer, examining himself. "But I had a narrow escape that time," he added, pointing at the broken plastering on the wall. "Who is that man?" he demanded, giving Pierre a stern look.

"I am really greatly distressed at what has just happened," said Pierre, speaking fluently, and entirely forgetting the part he was going to play. "He is crazy, an unfortunate man who did not know what he was doing."

The officer turned to Makar Alekseyitch and seized him by the collar. Makar, thrusting out his lips, swayed as if he were sleepy, and stood leaning against the wall.

"Brigand! You shall answer for this!" said the Frenchman, letting go of Makar. "It's in our nature to be merciful after victory, but we do not forgive traitors," he added, with a look of gloomy solemnity on his face.

Pierre continued in French to urge the officer not to be too hard on this half-witted drunkard. The Frenchman listened in silence, without a change in his scowling face, then suddenly turned to Pierre with a smile. He looked at him for a few seconds without speaking. His handsome face assumed a tragically sentimental expression, and he held out his hand:

"You have saved my life. You are French. You ask me to pardon him. I will. Take this man away!" exclaimed the French officer, rapidly and energetically, and, linking his arm with Pierre's he went with him into the house.

The soldiers who had been in the courtyard hastened into the entry when they heard the pistol shot, asking what was up and expressing their readiness to punish the offenders; but the officer sternly repressed them.

"You will be summoned when you are needed," said he.

The soldiers flocked out. The man who had meantime explored the larder came back to the officer and reported finding soup and roast mutton, and asked if he should bring it.

"Yes, and bring some wine!" said the captain.

At Pierre's assertion that he was not a Frenchman, the captain, evidently not comprehending how it could enter the heart of man to refuse such a flattering designation, shrugged his shoulders and declared that if Pierre were resolutely bent on passing for Russian he might do so, but still, nevertheless, he was eternally grateful to Pierre for saving his life. If this man had been gifted with the slightest capacity for entering into the feelings of others, and had guessed Pierre's sentiments, Pierre would undoubtedly have left him; but the captain's insensibility to everything except his own personality quite won Pierre.

"French, or a Russian prince in disguise," said the Frenchman, scrutinizing Pierre's fine but soiled linen and the ring on his finger, "I owe you my life, and I offer you my friendship. A Frenchman never forgets an insult or a favor. That is all I have to say."

In the tones of this officer's voice, in the expression of his face, in his gestures, there was so much genuine friendliness and good breeding (in the French use of the terms), that Pierre, giving back unconsciously smile for smile, pressed the proffered hand. "Captain Ramball of the 13th light artillery, decorated for action in the September battle," he went on to say, introducing himself, with a smile of exuberant self-satisfaction curling his lips under his mustaches. "Will you not tell me, now, with whom I have the honor of conversing so agreeably instead of being in the ambulance with that madman's pistol shot in me?"

Pierre replied that he could not tell him his name, and reddened as he tried to think of some name, to invent some reason for not giving his own; but the Frenchman hastily interrupted him.

"I beg of you!" said he. "I appreciate your scruples; you are an officer . . . an officer of rank, perhaps. You have borne arms against us . . . it is not my affair. I owe my life to you. That is enough for me. I am wholly at your service. You are a gentleman," he added, with just a shade of question. Pierre nodded assent.

"Your given name, please; I ask nothing more. Monsieur Pierre, you say . . . excellent! That is all that I wish to know."

When the mutton and omelet, the samovar, vodka, and wine which the French had obtained from a Russian cellar and brought with them, had been set on the table, Ramball invited Pierre to share in this repast; and instantly he himself fell to, ravenously and hastily attacking the viands like a healthy, hungry man, chewing lustily with his sound, strong teeth, constantly smacking his lips, and exclaiming, "Excellent, delicious!" His face grew flushed and moist. Pierre was hungry, and participated with great satisfaction in this dinner. Morel, the servant, brought a saucepan full of warm water, and set in it a bottle of red wine.

The captain wrapped the bottle up to the neck in a napkin and poured the wine out for himself and Pierre. Hunger alleviated and the wine enlivened the captain more and more, and throughout the meal he chattered without cessation.

"On my word of honor, without reference to my gratitude to you, I feel a genuine friendship for you. Can I do anything for you? I am entirely at your service. It is for life or for death! I tell you this with my hand on my heart!" said he, slapping himself on the chest.

"No, thank you," said Pierre.

The captain kept his eyes on him, and his face suddenly beamed.

"Ah! In that case, I drink to our friendship," he gaily cried, pouring out two glasses of wine.

Pierre took his, and drained it. Ramball drank his, again pressed Pierre's hand, and then leaned his elbows on the table in thoughtful, melancholy pose: "Yes, my dear friend, see the caprices of fortune!" he began. "Who would ever have said that I was going to be a soldier and captain of dragoons in the service of Bonaparte, as we called him a little while ago! And yet, here I am in Moscow with him. I must tell you, my dear fellow," he continued, in the solemn and measured voice of a man who is getting ready to spin a long yarn: "I must tell you our name is one of the most ancient in France . . ."

And, with the easygoing and simple frankness of a Frenchman, the captain told Pierre the story of his ancestors, his childhood, youth, and manhood, giving all the particulars of his ancestry, his estates, and his relationships. "My poor mother," of course, played an important rôle in this story.

"But all that is only the stage setting of life; the real thing is love. Love! Isn't that so, Monsieur Pierre?" said he, growing more animated. "Have another glass."

Pierre drank it up, and poured himself still a third glass.

"Oh, les femmes, les femmes!" and the captain with shining eyes, gazing at Pierre, began to talk about love and about his gallant adventures. He had enjoyed a very great number of them, as it was easy to believe from a glance at his handsome, self-satisfied face and the enthusiastic eagerness with which he talked about women.

Although all of Ramball's adventures had that sensuality in which the French find the exclusive charm and poetry of love, still the captain told his stories with the honest conviction that he was the only one who had ever experienced and understood all the delights of love, and he gave such alluring descriptions of women that Pierre listened to him with curiosity.

It was evident that l'amour which the Frenchman so loved was not that low and simple sensual passion which Pierre had once experienced for his wife, nor yet that romantic flame which was kindled in his heart by Natasha—both of which kinds of love Ramball held in equal contempt—one being, according to him, carter's love; the other, booby's love; l'amour which the Frenchman worshiped consisted preëminently in unnatural relations toward women, and in combinations of incongruities which gave the chief charm to the passion.

Thus the captain related a touching story of his love for a bewitching marquise of thirty-five, and, at the same time, for a charming innocent maiden of seventeen, the daughter of the bewitching marquise. The struggle of magnanimity between mother and daughter, ending with the mother sacrificing herself and proposing that the daughter should become her lover's wife, even now, though it was a recollection brought up from a long-buried past, moved the captain.

Then he related an episode in which the husband played the lover's part, while he—the lover—played the part of husband; and then several comical episodes from his German adventures, where husbands eat sauerkraut, and where the young girls are too blond!

Finally, his latest episode in Poland, which was still fresh in the captain's recollections, for he told it with eager gestures and a flushed face, consisted in his having saved a Pole's life (as a general thing, in the captain's narrations, lifesaving was an important feature), and this Pole had intrusted to him his most fascinating, bewitching wife, while he himself entered the French service. The captain was fortunate, the bewitching Polish lady wanted to run away with him, but, moved by generosity, he had restored the wife to the husband, saying: "I saved your life, now I save your honor!" In pronouncing these words the captain rubbed his eyes and gave himself a little shake as if to drive away his weakness at such a touching recollection.

While listening to the captain's yarns, Pierre, as was apt to be the case, late in the evening and under the influence of the wine, took in all that the captain had to say, comprehended it all, and, at the same time, connected it with a whole series of personal recollections which somehow suddenly began to rise up in his mind. As he listened to these stories of love, his own love for Natasha occurred to him with unexpected suddenness, and as he unrolled, in his imagination, the pictures of this love, he mentally compared them with Ramball's.

Thus, when he followed that story of the struggle between love and duty, he saw with wonderful vividness in all its details, his last meeting with the object of his love near the Sukharef tower. At that time the meeting had not made any special impression upon him; he had not once since thought of it. But now it seemed to him that this casual meeting had something very significant and poetic.

"Count! Come here! I recognized you!"

He now heard her saying those words; he had before him a vision of her eyes, her smile, her traveling hood, a lock of hair escaping from it— and something very touching and tender interwove itself with the whole scene.

Having finished his tale about the bewitching Polish lady, the captain asked Pierre if he had ever experienced anything like self-sacrifice for love, or jealousy of a woman's husband.

Aroused by this question, Pierre raised his head and felt that he must pour out the thoughts that filled his mind. He began to explain in what a different manner he understood love for a woman. He declared that in all his life he had loved and would love only one woman, and that this woman could never be his.

"You don't say!" exclaimed the captain.

Pierre explained that he had loved this woman when he was very young; but he did not then dare to aspire to her because she was too young, while he was an illegitimate son without name. Afterwards, when he had received a name and fortune, he could not think of her, because he loved her too much, regarded her too far above all the world, and accordingly too far above himself.

When he reached this part of his confession, Pierre turned to the captain and asked him if he understood.

The captain made a gesture, as much as to say that if he did not understand him, he would still like to hear the rest of it: "Platonic love is a mirage," he muttered.

Either from the wine he had drunk, or from the need that he felt of pouring out his heart, or from the thought that this man would never know any of the people in his story, or from everything combined, Pierre's tongue became unloosened. So with thick utterance and bleary eyes looking into space, he related his whole story; about his marriage, and the story of Natasha's love for his best friend, and the change that had taken place in her, and all his simple relations with her. And, after a little prodding from Ramball, he disclosed what at first he had concealed, his position in society, and even disclosed his name.

What amazed the captain more than anything else was the fact that Pierre was very rich, that he had two palaces in Moscow, and that he had given up everything and, instead of fleeing from Moscow, had remained in the city, concealing his name and rank.

It was very late when they went out into the street. The night was mild and bright. To the left of the house gleamed the ruddy glare of the first fire, that on the Petrovka. It was the beginning of the conflagration of Moscow.

At the right, high up in the sky, hung the young, slender sickle of the moon, and over against the moon could be seen that brilliant comet which was connected in Pierre's mind with his love.

Gerasim, the valet, stood near the gates with two Frenchmen, laughing and talking, each in a language incomprehensible to the other. They were gazing at the ruddy glow which could be seen across the city. There was nothing terrible in a small fire at a distance in the vast city.

As he looked up at the distant, star-studded sky, at the moon, at the comet, and at the glare of the conflagration, Pierre experienced an agreeable emotion.

"How beautiful this is! What more can man need?" he asked himself.

And suddenly, when he remembered his decision, he grew giddy, he felt so dizzy that he had to cling to the fence not to fall.

Without saying good-night to his new friend, Pierre, with tottering steps, left the gates and, returning to his room, lay down on his couch and instantly fell asleep.

XIII

THE GLARE of the first fire that broke out, on the fourteenth of September, was witnessed from various roads and with various feelings by the escaping and departing citizens and the retreating troops.

The Rostofs were spending that night at Mitishchi, about fourteen miles from Moscow. They had started so late on the thirteenth, the road was so encumbered with trains and troops, so many things had been forgotten for which men had to be sent back, that they decided to spend the night at a place three miles from Moscow.

On the next morning they awoke late, and again there were so many delays that they got no farther than Bolshiya Mitishchi. At ten o'clock the Rostof family and the wounded men they had brought with them were all quartered among the houses and cottages of the great village. The servants, the Rostofs' drivers, and the orderlies of the wounded men, having arranged for their comfort, had eaten their suppers and fed their horses, and had come out on the steps.

The night was dark, and one of the servants had noticed, from behind the high body of a carriage standing near the gate, the small glare of a second conflagration. One had already been noticed some time before, and all knew it had been the village of Maliya Mitishchi, set on fire by Mamonof's Cossacks.

"Look at that, boys! Another fire!" said an orderly. The attention of all was attracted to the glare.

"Oh, yes, they say Maliya Mitishchi has been set on fire by Mamonof's Cossacks."

"They? No! That's not Mitishchi; it's farther off. See there! That must be Moscow!"

An old man, the count's valet as they called him, Danilo Terentyitch, came out to the crowd and shouted to his subordinate Mishka:

"What are you staring at, you fool?—The count is calling, and no one there; go put his clothes away."

"I only came out after some water," said Mishka.

"Now, what do you think, Danilo Terentyitch—it looks like Moscow is burning," said one of the lackeys.

Danilo Terentyitch made no reply, and again they all stood silent for a long time.

The glare spread and flickered over a wider and wider expanse of the horizon.

"God have mercy! The wind and the drought!" said a voice at last.

"Just look! How far it has gone! O Lord! I think I can see the jackdaws! Lord, have mercy on us sinners!"

"They'll put it out, never fear!"

"Who's to put it out?" Danilo Terentyitch's voice was heard asking. He had not spoken till then. His tone was calm and deliberate. "Yes, that is Moscow, boys," said he. "Our white-walled mother-city . . ."

His voice broke, and he sobbed like an old man.

And as if all had been waiting for his words, before they could realize the significance of the blaze they saw, sighs were heard, and fragments of prayers, and the old valet's sobs.

The valet returned to the house and informed the count that Moscow was in flames. The count put on his dressing gown and went out to look. With him went Sonya and Madame Schoss, who had not yet undressed.

"Oh, how horrible!" exclaimed Sonya, coming in from the stoop, chilled and scared. "I think all Moscow is on fire; it's a terrible blaze! Natasha, come here and look. You can see it now from this window!" she exclaimed, evidently wishing to rouse her cousin from her thoughts.

But Natasha looked at her as if not comprehending what she wanted, and again she turned her eyes toward the stove.

Natasha had been in a state of stupor since early that morning, from the moment when Sonya, to the amazement and annoyance of the countess, without any reason for doing so, had felt obliged to tell Natasha that Prince Andrei was wounded and was with them in their train. The countess was more angry with Sonya than she had ever been before. Sonya had wept and begged for forgiveness, and now, as if she were striving to atone for her error, she was assiduous in waiting on her cousin.

"Look, Natasha! What a terrible fire it is!" said Sonya.

"What fire?" asked Natasha. "Oh, you mean Moscow?"

And, not wishing to offend Sonya by refusing, in simple acquiescence she turned her head to the window and glanced out in such a way that she evidently saw nothing, and immediately resumed her former position.

"But you didn't see, did you?"

"Yes, truly, I did!" exclaimed Natasha in a tone that implied her desire to be left in peace.

Both the countess and Sonya understood that for Natasha, Moscow, or the burning of Moscow, or anything else, in fact, had no significance.

The count had gone back to bed. The countess went to Natasha, smoothed her head with the back of her hand, as she used to do when her daughter was ill, then touched her forehead with her lips to see whether she was feverish, and kissed her.

"Are you cold? You are all a-tremble! You had better go to bed!" said she.

"Go to bed? Oh, yes, all right! I will go to bed. I will in a moment," said Natasha.

"Natasha, undress! Come, darling, get into bed with me." (The countess was the only one who had a regular bed; Madame Schoss and the two young ladies slept on the floor, on straw.)

"No, mama, I will lie here on the floor!" said Natasha irritably, and, going to the window, she threw it open. She thrust her head out into the damp night air, and the countess saw how her slender neck was swollen with her repressed sobs and throbbed against the window frame. She knew that Prince Andrei was in the same row of cottages where they were, in the next cottage, with only a wall between. The countess exchanged glances with Sonya.

"Go to bed, darling, go to bed, sweetheart!" said the countess, giving Natasha a gentle touch on the shoulder. "Go to bed now."

"Oh, yes . . . yes, I will go to bed at once . . . at once," said Natasha, hastily beginning to undress, and breaking the strings of her petticoats.

The countess, Madame Schoss and Sonya hastily undressed and went to bed. The night lamp alone was left burning in the room. But outside it was light as day from the fire at Maliya Mitishchi, a mile and a half distant; and from across the street at the tavern, which Mamonof's Cossacks were rifling, came the drunken shouts of men, and the aide's groans were incessant.

Natasha listened for a long time to all of these sounds without and within, and did not stir. At first she heard her mother's muttered prayer and sighs, the creaking of the bed as she moved, Madame Schoss' well-known piping snore, Sonya's gentle breathing. Then the countess spoke to Natasha. Natasha made no reply.

"I think she's asleep, mama," softly replied Sonya.

The countess, after a little interval of silence, spoke again, but this time no one answered her.

Soon after, Natasha heard her mother's measured breathing.

Natasha did not move, though her little bare foot, thrust out from under the bed covering, was chilled by the uncarpeted floor.

"Sonya, are you asleep? . . . mama?" she whispered.

No one answered.

Natasha slowly and cautiously arose, crossed herself, carefully set her light, slender, bare foot on the cold, dirty floor. The boards creaked. She ran nimbly as a kitten for a few steps, and took hold of the cold latch of the door. It seemed to her as if something heavy were knocking with regular blows on all the walls of the cottage. It was her heart beating and almost bursting with terror and love.

She opened the door, crossed the threshold, and set foot on the damp, cold earth of the passageway. The all-enveloping coolness refreshed her. She touched a sleeping man with her bare foot, stepped over him, and opened the door into the cottage where Prince Andrei was lying. It was dark in this room. On a bench in the corner, just back of the bed on which something lay, stood a tallow candle which in burning had taken the form of a great mushroom.

Natasha, ever since that morning, when she learned about Prince Andrei's wound and that he was with them, had made up her mind that she must see him. She did not know why this was necessary, but she knew the interview would be painful and therefore she was all the more certain that it was inevitable. All that day she had lived in the hope of being able to see him that night. But now, when the moment had actually come, she was filled with horror at the thought of what she was going to see. How was he mutilated? How much of him was left?

When she caught sight of an ill-defined mass in the corner, and took his knees thrust up under the bedclothes for his shoulders, she imagined some horrible body, and in her terror she paused. But an irresistible force compelled her to go forward. She cautiously took one step, then another, and found herself in the middle of the small room filled with luggage. On the bench in the corner under the holy pictures lay another man—this was Timokhin; and on the floor lay two other men—these were the doctor and the valet.

The valet sat up and whispered something. Timokhin, suffering from pain in his wounded leg, was not asleep, and stared with wide-open eyes at this strange apparition of a young girl in her white nightgown, dressing gown and nightcap.

The sleepy and startled words of the valet, "What do you want? Who is it?" merely caused Natasha to move the more quickly to what was lying in the corner. However incongruously unlike the form of man that body was, she still must see it. She passed by the valet; the candle flared up and she clearly saw Prince Andrei with his arms stretched out over the spread, and looking just as she had always known him.

He was the same as ever. But the flushed face, his gleaming eyes gazing at her with ecstasy, and especially his delicate, boyish throat, relieved by the opened shirt collar, gave him a peculiarly innocent, childlike appearance that she had never before seen in him.

She went to him and threw herself on her knees with the swift, pliant grace of youth.

He smiled, and stretched out his hand to her.

XIV

A WEEK HAD passed since Prince Andrei had come to himself in the field hospital of Borodino. Almost all this time he had been in a state of unconsciousness. His feverish condition and the inflammation of his intestines, which had suffered a lesion, were, in the opinion of the surgeon who attended him, destined to finish him off. But on the seventh day he ate a morsel of bread and drank some tea with appetite, and the doctor noticed that his fever had diminished.

Prince Andrei had regained consciousness in the morning. The first night after they left Moscow had been quite warm, and Prince Andrei had not been moved from his carriage; but at Mitishchi he himself had asked to be taken into a house and given some tea. The anguish caused by moving him into the cottage caused Prince Andrei to groan aloud and to lose consciousness again. When they had placed him on the camp bed, he lay for a long time motionless, with closed eyes. Then he had opened them, and asked in a whisper:

"May I have tea?"

Such a memory for the small details of life had amazed the surgeon. He felt of Prince Andrei's pulse, and to his surprise and regret discovered that it was better. (The doctor noticed it with regret because from his experience he was certain that Prince Andrei could not live, and if he were to live on he would only have to die a little later in terrible agony.)

The red-nosed major of Prince Andrei's regiment, Timokhin, had been brought to Moscow with him, wounded in the leg in the same Battle of Borodino. They were accompanied by the surgeon, the prince's valet, his coachman, and two orderlies.

They had handed Prince Andrei his tea. He drank it eagerly, looking with feverish eyes straight ahead at the door, apparently trying to understand and remember something.

"I don't want any more. Is Timokhin there?" he asked. Timokhin crept along on the bench toward him.

"I am here, your excellency."

"How is the wound?"

"Mine? It's all right. But you?"

Prince Andrei again lay thinking, as if trying to remember something.

"Can't you get me the book?" he asked.

"What book?"

"The New Testament."

"The New Testament? I haven't one."

The doctor promised to get one for him, and began to inquire of the prince how he felt. Prince Andrei replied reluctantly but intelligibly to all the doctor's questions, and then said he would like a bolster, for he felt uncomfortable, and his wound was very painful. The doctor and valet took off the cloak that covered him, and scowling at the putrid odor of the gangrene spreading through the wound, began to examine the terrible place. The surgeon found the state of things very unsatisfactory, made some different disposition of the bandages, and turned the wounded man over, making him groan again; and the agony caused in turning him back again caused him to lose consciousness; he became delirious. He kept insisting that they should fetch, as quickly as possible, the book he wanted, and place it in such and such a place.

"What would it cost you?" he asked. "I haven't one—please get me one!— let me have it for just a minute!" he had pleaded, in a pitiful voice.

The doctor went into the vestibule to wash his hands.

"Ah! it's terrible, truly!" he said to the valet, who was pouring water over his hands. "Only look at him for a moment. Why, it's such agony I'm amazed that he endures it."

534

"Well, we have to take what is sent us! O Lord Jesus Christ!" ejaculated the valet.

Prince Andrei for the first time had realized where he was and what was the matter with him, and remembered that he had been wounded, and how, when the carriage stopped at Mitishchi, he had asked to be taken into the cottage. His mind grew confused again from the pain, but he had come to himself, for a second time, in the cottage, as he was drinking the tea; and then once more, as he recalled all his experiences, he recalled more vividly than anything else that moment in the field hospital when, at sight of the sufferings of the man he so hated, new thoughts that gave promise of happiness came to him. And these thoughts, though obscure and vague, had now again taken possession of his mind.

"Yes, a new happiness, not to be taken from man, was revealed to me," he said to himself, as he lay in the semiobscurity of the quiet hut, and looked up with feverishly wide-open and fixed eyes. "A happiness to be found outside of material forces, outside of exterior, material influences, the happiness of the spirit alone, of love. Every man can understand it, but God alone can adjudge it and prescribe it. But how does God prescribe this law? Why did the Son . . . ?"

And suddenly the course of his thoughts was broken off, and Prince Andrei heard—but he could not tell whether he really heard it or whether it was his delirium—he heard a low lisping voice constantly rehearsing in measured rhythm: "*i piti - piti - piti*"—and then again "*i ti-ti*," and then "*i piti-piti-piti*," and then once more "*i ti-ti*."

At the same time, while this whispered music was echoing, Prince Andrei felt that over his face, over the very center of it, was rising a strange sort of airy edifice of delicate little needles or splinters. He felt—but this was trying to him—that it was necessary for him to keep in perfect equilibrium, so that the growing edifice might not crumble; but nevertheless it collapsed, and then slowly rose again to the sounds of this whispered, rhythmic music.

"It is growing, it is growing! It is stretching up and growing!" said Prince Andrei to himself. "But why does that structure rise up and stretch out so, and that *piti-piti-piti i ti-ti i piti—piti—piti?*—That is enough . . . please stop," begged Prince Andrei, as if addressing someone. And suddenly again his thoughts and feeling became extraordinarily clear and distinct.

"Yes, love," he thought, with perfect clarity, "but not that love which loves for a purpose, for a personal end, but that love which I for the first time experienced, when, dying, I saw my enemy and could still love him. I experienced the feeling of love which is the very essence of the soul, and which needs no object. And even now I experience that blessed feeling. To love one's neighbors, to love one's enemies. Always to love—to love God in all His manifestations. To love one's friends is human love, but to love one's enemies is divine. And this is what made me experience such bliss when I felt I loved that man! What has become of him? Is he living, or—

535

"Love in its human form may change into hate; but divine love cannot change. Nothing, not even death, can destroy it. It is the very essence of the soul. But how many people have I hated in my life! And none have I ever loved more warmly or hated more bitterly than her!"

And he vividly pictured Natasha, not as she had formerly appealed to his imagination, through her charming personality alone; but, for the first time, in her spiritual nature. And he understood her feelings, her suffering, her shame, and her repentance. Now for the first time he realized all the cruelty of his renunciation, saw the cruelty of his break with her.

"If I might only see her once again . . . once again look into her eyes, and tell her. . ."

"*I piti - piti - piti - i ti-ti i piti - piti - bumm!*" went the fly. And his attention was suddenly diverted to that other world of delirious activity in which such strange things took place.

"Oh! how trying this incessant hallucination is!" said Prince Andrei to himself, striving to banish this vision from his imagination. But the face still appeared before him in all the vividness of reality; this face even approached him.

Prince Andrei was anxious to return to the former world of pure thought, but he could not, and delirium held him in thraldom. The low whispering voice continued its rhythmic lisping, something like a weight oppressed him, and the strange vision stood in front of him. Prince Andrei summoned all his energies, so as to become master of himself; he moved, and suddenly in his ears there was a humming, his eyes grew clouded, and, like a man plunged in water, he lost consciousness. When he came to his senses, Natasha, the veritable living Natasha, whom of all people in the world he had been most anxious to love with that new, pure, divine love just revealed to him, was before him, on her knees! He realized that this was the living, actual Natasha; and he felt no surprise, but only a gentle sense of gladness.

Natasha, on her knees before him, restrained her sobs and gazed at him timidly but intently; she could not stir. Her face was pale and motionless; only the lips quivered slightly.

Prince Andrei drew a sigh of relief, smiled, and stretched out his hand.

"You?" he asked. "What happiness!"

Natasha, still on her knees, with swift but cautious movement bent over to him, and, cautiously taking his hand, bent her face down to it and began to kiss it, scarcely touching it with her lips.

"Forgive me!" she murmured, lifting her head and gazing at him. "Forgive me!"

"I love you!" said Prince Andrei.

"Forgive . . ."

"What have I to forgive?" asked Prince Andrei.

"For . . . give me for . . . what I . . . did!" continued Natasha, almost inaudibly, in a broken whisper, and she began to kiss his hand more rapidly than before, scarcely touching it with her lips.

"I love you better, more dearly than ever," said Prince Andrei, lifting her face with his hand so that he might look into her eyes.

Those eyes, overflowing with happy tears, looked at him timidly, compassionately, and with the ecstasy of love. Natasha's face was thin and pale, the lips swollen; was now more than ugly, it was ghastly. But Prince Andrei did not notice that; he saw her shining eyes, and they were beautiful.

Voices sounded behind them. Peter, the prince's valet, now thoroughly awake, aroused the doctor. Timokhin, who had not been asleep at all because of the pain in his leg, had not noticed what was going on, and, after carefully covering himself, curled up on the bench.

"What does this mean?" asked the doctor, sitting up. "Please go, young lady!"

At the same time the maid sent by the countess to fetch her daughter knocked at the door.

Like a sleepwalker awakened in the midst of a dream, Natasha left the room, and, returning to her own cottage, fell sobbing on her bed.

From that day forth, during all the rest of the Rostofs' journey, at all their halts and resting places, Natasha sat by the wounded Bolkonsky's side, and the doctor was forced to confess that he had never expected to see in a young girl such constancy or such skill in nursing a wounded man.

Terrible as it seemed to the countess to think that the prince might (or, as the doctor said, probably would) die during the journey, in her daughter's arms, she had not the heart to refuse Natasha.

Though, in consequence of the now reëstablished relationship between the wounded prince and Natasha, it occurred to them that in case he recovered, the engagement might be renewed, no one—Natasha and Prince Andrei least of all—spoke about it.

The undecided question of life and death which hung over not Bolkonsky alone, but over Russia as well, kept all other considerations in the background.

XV

Pierre awoke late on the fifteenth of September. His head ached; his clothes, in which he had slept without undressing, hung heavy on him, and his mind was burdened by a dull consciousness of something shameful he had done the night before.

This shameful act was his talk with Captain Ramball.

It was eleven o'clock by his watch, but it seemed peculiarly dark out of doors. Pierre got up, rubbed his eyes, and, seeing the pistol with its carved handle, which Gerasim had replaced on the writing table, he remembered where he was, and what was before him on that day.

"But am I not too late?" he queried. "No, probably *he* would not make his entrance into Moscow before twelve o'clock."

Pierre did not allow himself to think what was before him, but he made all the greater haste to act.

Having adjusted his attire, Pierre took up the pistol and made ready to go. But then for the first time he wondered how he should carry his weapon through the street otherwise than in his hand. It was hard to hide the great pistol even under the flowing coachman's coat. Nor was it possible to keep it out of sight in his belt or under his arm. Moreover, the pistol had been discharged and Pierre had not had time to reload it.

"Well, the dagger is just as good," said he to himself, though more than once while deliberating over the accomplishment of his undertaking, he had come to the conclusion that the chief mistake made by the student in 1809 consisted in his attempt to kill Napoleon with a dagger.

But Pierre's chief end consisted not so much in carrying out his scheme as it did in proving to himself that he had not renounced his purpose and was doing everything to fulfil it. He hastily seized the blunt and notched dagger in its green sheath, which he had bought together with the pistol at the Sukharef tower, and concealed it under his waistcoat.

Having belted up his coat and pulled his hat down over his eyes, Pierre, trying to make no noise and to avoid the captain, crept along the corridor and went into the street.

The fire, which he had looked at so indifferently the evening before, had noticeably increased during the night. Moscow was burning at various points. Most of the houses had their doors and shutters nailed up. The streets and alleys were deserted. The air was full of smoke and the smell of burning. Occasionally he met Russians with anxiously timid faces, and Frenchmen of uncitified, military aspect, who walked in the middle of the street. All looked with amazement at Pierre. The Russians were impressed not only by his great height and stoutness, but by the strange, gloomily concentrated and martyrlike expression of his face and figure, and they stared at him because they could not make out to what rank of life he belonged. The French followed him in amazement because Pierre, unlike the other Russians, paid absolutely no attention to them, instead of looking at them in trepidation or curiosity.

He heard nothing and saw nothing of what was going on around him. With a sense of nervous haste and horror, he took with him, like something terrible and alien to him, that project of his; and he feared—taught by his experience of the night before—that something would distract him. But it was not Pierre's fate to reach his destination in the same frame of mind. Moreover, even if nothing had occurred to detain him, his project could not now have been carried out, for the reason that Napoleon already was seated, in the gloomiest frame of mind, in the imperial study of the Kremlin palace, issuing detailed and urgent orders in regard to the measures to be taken at once for extinguishing the fires, preventing pillage, and reassuring the inhabitants.

But Pierre knew nothing about this; wholly absorbed in the present, he was tormenting himself as men do who recognize that their undertaking is impossible, not because of its difficulties but because it is so entirely unsuited to their nature. He was tormented by his fear that at the decisive moment he might weaken, and consequently lose his self-respect.

Although he saw nothing and heard nothing, he instinctively took the right road. But as Pierre approached the Povarskaya the smoke grew denser and denser, and he even began to feel the heat from the fire. Occasionally, he could see tongues of flame behind the roofs of the houses. More people were found on the streets, and these people were more excited and anxious. But Pierre, though he was conscious that something extraordinary was going on around him, did not realize that he was approaching the conflagration.

As he followed along a footpath that skirted a large open space bordered on one side by the Povarskaya, on the other by the park attached to Prince Gruzinsky's mansion, Pierre suddenly heard near him the pitiful shrieks of a woman. He stopped as if wakened out of a dream, and raised his head.

On one side of the footpath, on the dry, dusty grass, was piled up a heap of household furniture: feather bed, samovar, icons, and trunks. On the ground next to the trunks sat a lean, elderly woman, with long, projecting upper teeth. She was dressed in a black cloak and a cap. This woman rocked herself to and fro, and was muttering as she wept and sobbed. Two little girls, ten or twelve years old, dressed in short, dirty skirts and little cloaks, gazed at their mother with an expression of perplexity on their pale, frightened faces. A little boy of seven, in a coat and cap altogether too big for him, was weeping in his old nurse's arms. A dirty, barelegged servant girl was sitting on a trunk, and, having let down her pale blond plait, was pulling out the scorched hairs, smelling of them as she did so. The husband of the family, a short, round-shouldered little man in undress uniform, with wheel-like little side whiskers and lovelocks brushed smoothly from under his cap, with impassive face, was sorting the trunks piled one on top of the other, and trying to get some clothes out.

The woman almost threw herself at Pierre's feet when she saw him.

"Oh, good father! Oh, orthodox Christian! Help, save her! . . . Oh, dear sir! . . . Whoever you are, help!" she cried, through her sobs. "My little daughter! . . . my daughter! . . . My youngest daughter has been left behind! . . . She is burning up! Oh! oh! oh! oh, why did I nurse her? . . . Oh! oh! oh!"

"There! that'll do, Marya Nikolayevna," expostulated her husband in a mild voice, but evidently merely so as to make a good impression on the stranger. "Sister must have got her. If not, it's all over with her by this time," he added.

"Monster! Villain!" angrily screamed the woman, suddenly ceasing to weep. "There's no heart in you! You have no pity for your own child! Any other man would have snatched her from the fire. But you are a monster . . . and not a man, and not a father. . . . But you, sir, you are noble!" cried the woman, addressing Pierre, speaking rapidly, and sobbing. "The row was on fire; ours caught. The girl cried: 'We are on fire.' We tried to save what we could. Whatever we could lay our hands on, we carried out. This here is what we saved. . . . The holy picture and our wedding bed—all the rest was lost. We got the children, all but Katitchka! Oh! oh! oh! oh, Lord!" and again she burst into tears. "My darling little one! she's burnt up! she's burnt up!"

"But where was it, where was she left?" asked Pierre.

By the expression of his excited face, the woman realized that this man might help her.

"Father!" she cried, clasping him around the legs. "Benefactor! set my heart at ease! . . . Aniska, go, you nasty hussy! show him the way," she cried to the girl, and angrily opened her mouth, still more exposing her long teeth.

"Lead the way, lead the way . . . I . . . I . . . I will do what I can," stammered Pierre, in a panting voice.

The dirty-looking girl came out from behind the trunk, put up her braid, and, with a sigh, started off down the footpath, with her stubbed, bare feet.

Pierre had, as it were, wakened suddenly to life after a heavy swoon. He raised his head higher, his eyes were filled with the spark of life, and with rapid strides he followed the girl, passed her, and hurried along the Povarskaya. The whole street was shrouded in clouds of black smoke. Tongues of flame here and there darted out from it. A great crowd of people were packed together in front of the fire. In the middle of the street stood a French general saying something to those around him. Pierre, accompanied by the girl, was going toward the place where the general stood, but French soldiers halted him.

"You cannot pass!" cried a voice.

"This way, uncle," cried the girl; "we'll go around by this side street, through Nikulini."

Pierre turned back and almost ran as he hastened in her footsteps so as to overtake her. The girl scurried along, turned down a cross street at the left, and, passing by three houses, turned into the gates of a house at the right.

"There it is . . . right there!" cried the girl, and, running across the yard, she opened a wicket door in the deal fence, and, stepping back a step, pointed out to Pierre a small wooden "wing" where the flames were burning bright and hot. One side was already fallen in; the other was burning, and the flames were bursting out from the broken windows and from under the roof.

When Pierre reached the wicket he was suffocated by the heat, and involuntarily drew back.

"Which . . . which is your house?" he asked.

"Oh! oh! oh!" howled the girl, as she pointed to the wing. "That one there; that was our home."

"Are you burnt up, O Katitchka! our treasure! my darling little mistress! Oh! oh!" howled the girl at the sight of the fire, feeling it necessary for her also to express her feelings.

Pierre edged toward the burning wing, but the heat was so powerful that he was obliged to make a wide circle around the building, and he came out next to a large house which was as yet burning only on one side of the roof. A great crowd of Frenchmen were swarming around it.

Pierre could not at first understand what these Frenchmen, who appeared to be dragging something, were doing; but when he saw one of them strike a peasant with the flat of his saber, and take away from him a foxskin coat, Pierre had a dim idea that pillaging was going on there; still the idea merely flashed through his mind.

The noise of the crackling and the crash of falling walls and ceilings, the hissing and snapping of the flames, and the excited cries of the people, the spectacle of billowing, whirling clouds of smoke now thick and black, now dotted with gleaming sparks, now lighted up with solid, sheaf-shaped red and golden-scaled flames lapping the walls, the sense of the heat and the smoke, and the swiftness of motion, all served to produce upon Pierre the usual exciting effect of fires. This effect was peculiarly powerful upon him, because suddenly, at the sight of this fire, he felt himself liberated from the oppression of his thoughts. He felt young, gay, agile, and resolute. He ran around the wing from the burning house, and tried to force his way into that part of it that was still standing, when suddenly he heard, over his very head, several voices shouting, immediately followed by the rush and metallic ring of some heavy body falling near him.

Pierre looked around and saw in the windows of the house some Frenchmen who had just flung out a chest of drawers full of some metallic articles. Other French soldiers, standing below, were running to the chest of drawers.

"Well, what does this fellow want here?" cried one of the Frenchmen, seeing Pierre.

"A child in this house? Haven't you seen a child?" asked Pierre, in French.

"Wait! What's he babbling about? Go to the devil!" replied a voice; and one of the soldiers, evidently fearing that it was Pierre's intention to rob them of the silver and bronzes that were in the drawers, came up to him in a threatening manner.

"A child?" cried the Frenchman from above, "I heard something squealing in the garden. Perhaps it was the poor man's little brat. Must be humane, you know."

"Where is it? Where is it?" asked Pierre.

"There! There!" cried the Frenchman from the window, pointing to the garden behind the house. "Wait, I'm coming right down." And, in fact, in a moment the Frenchman, a black-eyed fellow with a spot on his cheek, and in his shirt sleeves, sprang from the window of the first story, and, giving

Pierre a slap on the shoulder, ran with him down into the garden. "Hurry up, boys," he cried to his comrades. "Beginning to grow warm."

Running behind the house, on the sand-strewn path, the Frenchman gave Pierre's arm a pull and pointed to a round open space. On a bench sat a little girl of three years, in a pink dress.

"There's your brat. Ah! a little girl! So much the better," said the Frenchman. "Good-by, old fellow. Must be humane. We are all mortal, you know." And the Frenchman with the spot on his cheek hurried back to his comrades.

Pierre, choking with delight, started toward the girl, and was going to pick her up in his arms. But the little one, pale like her mother, and scrofulous—an unpleasant-looking child—seeing the strange man, set up a screech and tried to run away. Pierre, however, seized her, and took her in his arms. She screamed in a desperately angry voice, and with her slender little arms struggled to tear herself away from Pierre and to bite him with her slobbery mouth. Pierre was seized by a feeling of horror and revulsion such as he would have felt at contact with any nasty little animal. But he forced himself not to abandon the child, and hastened with her back to the great house. He found it impossible to return the same way; the servant girl had disappeared, and Pierre, with a feeling of pity and disgust, holding to his heart as tenderly as he could the miserably sobbing and wet little girl, ran through the garden to find another exit.

XVI

WHEN PIERRE, making his way around by yards and alleys, brought his burden back to Prince Gruzinsky's garden, on the corner of the Povarskaya, he did not at first recognize the place he had left when he went after the child—it was so swarming with people and with household furniture. Besides the Russian families taking refuge here with their treasures, there were also many French soldiers, in various garb.

Pierre paid no attention to them. He was in haste to find the official's family, so as to restore the little girl to her mother, and then go and rescue someone else. It seemed to him that he still had very much to do, and as speedily as possible. Heated with the fire and his exertion in running, Pierre at that moment experienced more keenly than ever that feeling of youth, energy, and resolution which had taken possession of him when he started to rescue the child.

The little girl was calmer now, and, clinging to Pierre's coat, she sat on his arm and like a little wild animal gazed around her.

Pierre occasionally looked down at her and smiled. It seemed to him that he saw something touchingly innocent in that scared and sickly little face.

Neither the official nor his wife was to be seen in the place where they had been before. Pierre, with rapid strides, wandered round among the people, scrutinizing the various faces.

His attention was accidentally attracted to a Georgian or Armenian family, consisting of a handsome man of very advanced age with a face of Oriental type and dressed in a new sheepskin coat and new boots, an old woman of the same type, and a young woman. This very young woman seemed to Pierre the perfection of Oriental beauty, with her dark brows delicately arched, and her long face of remarkable freshness of complexion and genuine but expressionless beauty. Amid the indiscriminate heap of the household articles on the green, she, in her rich satin mantle and bright lilac kerchief covering her head, reminded one of a delicate hothouse flower flung out into the snow. She sat on a parcel behind the old woman, and with her motionless, big, dark, long eyes, shaded by long lashes, looked at the ground.

Evidently she was conscious of her beauty, and it filled her with alarm. This face struck Pierre, and, in spite of his haste as he passed along the fence, several times he glanced around at her.

On reaching the fence and still not finding those of whom he was in search, Pierre paused and looked around. His figure, with the child in his arms, was now even more noticeable than before, and a number of Russians, both men and women, gathered around him.

"Have you lost anyone, dear man?" . . . "You are a noble, aren't you?" . . . "Whose child is that?" were among the questions put to him.

Pierre explained that the child belonged to a woman in a black mantle, who had been sitting in that very spot with her children; and he asked if no one knew who she was, and where she had gone.

"It must be the Anferofs," said an old deacon, addressing a pock-marked woman. "Lord, have mercy! Lord, have mercy!" he added, in his usual bass.

"Where are the Anferofs?" asked the woman. "The Anferofs started early this morning. This may be Marya Nikolayevna's or the Ivanofs'."

"He said a woman, but Marya Nikolayevna is a lady," said a household serf.

"Surely you must know her—long teeth, a thin woman," said Pierre.

"Certainly, it's Marya Nikolayevna. They went into the garden as soon as these wolves came down on us," said the peasant woman, pointing to the French soldiers.

"O Lord, have mercy!" again ejaculated the deacon.

"Go down yonder, then. You'll find them. She's there. She was all tired out; she was crying," said the peasant woman. "She is over there. You'll find her."

But Pierre did not hear what the woman said. For several seconds he had been watching anxiously what was going on a few steps away. He was looking at the Armenian family and a couple of French soldiers who had approached them. One of these soldiers, a little, nimble man, wore a blue overcoat belted with a rope. He had a nightcap on his head and was barefooted.

The second, who especially attracted Pierre's attention, was a long, lank, round-shouldered, white-haired man, slow in his movements, and with an idiotic expression of countenance. He was clad in a rough wool cloak, with blue trousers, and Hessian boots which were full of holes.

The little bootless Frenchman in the blue overcoat had gone up to the Armenians, and, after making some remark, had seized the old man by the legs, and the old man had immediately begun to pull off his boots in great haste.

The other one had taken up his position in front of the pretty Armenian girl, and, with his hands thrust deep in his pockets, was staring at her in perfect silence, without moving.

"Take it, take the child!" exclaimed Pierre, addressing the peasant woman in imperative tones, holding out the little girl. "Take her and give her back to them!" he cried, and set the screaming child on the ground, and then turned once more to look at the Frenchman and the Armenian family.

The old man was, by this time, barefooted. The little Frenchman had appropriated his second boot, and was knocking the two together. The old man with a sob made some remark, but Pierre merely glanced at him; his whole attention was attracted to the Frenchman in the cloak, who, slowly swaggering, had by this time approached the young woman, and, drawing his hands from his pockets, was just taking her by the neck.

The beautiful Armenian girl continued sitting in the same impassive posture, with her long lashes drooping, and apparently neither saw nor felt what the soldier was doing to her.

By the time Pierre had taken the several steps that separated him from the Frenchmen, the lank marauder had already snatched a necklace from the Armenian girl's neck, and the young woman, clasping her hands around her throat, uttered a piercing shriek.

"Let this woman alone!" roared Pierre in a furious voice, clutching the lank, stooping soldier by the shoulder, and flinging him off. The soldier fell flat, picked himself up, and ran away. But his comrade, throwing down his booty of boots, drew his cutlass, and advanced threateningly against Pierre. "See here! None of your nonsense!" he cried.

Pierre was in that rapt state of fury which, when it came upon him, made him oblivious of everything, and multiplied his strength tenfold. He threw himself upon the barefooted Frenchman, and, before the fellow had time to use his cutlass, he had knocked him over and was beating him with his fists.

The people gathered around with an approving yell, but just at that instant appeared around the corner a mounted squad of French Uhlans. The Uhlans came up to Pierre and the Frenchman at a trot, and surrounded them. Pierre remembered nothing of what followed. He only remembered that he was pounding someone, that he himself was pounded, and that, finally, he became conscious that his arms were bound; that a crowd of French soldiers were standing around him and searching his clothes.

"He has a dagger, Lieutenant," were the first words that Pierre comprehended.

"Aha, armed!" said the officer, and he turned to the barefooted soldier who had been taken at the same time with Pierre.

"Very good; you shall tell all this at the court-martial," said the officer. And immediately he turned to Pierre.

"*Parlez-vous français, vous?*"

Pierre glared around him with bloodshot eyes, and made no reply. Evidently his face must have seemed very terrible, because the officer gave a whispered order and four other Uhlans detached themselves from the squad and stationed themselves on each side of Pierre.

"*Parlez-vous français?*" asked the officer a second time, keeping at a respectful distance from him. "Bring the interpreter."

A little man in the dress of a Russian civilian came forth from the ranks. Pierre instantly knew by his attire and his accent that he was a Frenchman from some Moscow shop.

"He does not look like a man of the common people," said the interpreter, eyeing Pierre.

"Oh, ho! it seems to me he has the appearance of being one of the incendiaries," said the officer. "Ask him who he is," he added.

"Who are you?" demanded the interpreter. "You should reply to the authorities," said he.

"I will not tell you who I am. I am your prisoner. Take me away," suddenly exclaimed Pierre, speaking in French.

"Aha!" exclaimed the officer, scowling. "Come on."

A crowd had gathered around the Uhlans. Closest of all to Pierre stood the pockmarked peasant woman with the little girl. When the squad started she sprang forward.

"Where are they taking you, my good friend?" she demanded. "The little girl! What shall I do with the little girl if she isn't theirs?" insisted the woman.

"What does this woman want?" asked the officer.

Pierre was like one drunk. His exalted state of mind was still more intensified at the sight of the little girl whom he had saved.

"What does she want?" he exclaimed. "She has brought my daughter, whom I just saved from the flames," he explained. "Adieu!" and he himself, not knowing why he should have told this aimless falsehood, marched off with resolute, enthusiastic steps, surrounded by the Frenchmen.

This patrol of French horsemen was one of those sent out to put a stop to pillaging and especially to apprehend the incendiaries who, according to the general impression prevalent that day among the French, were the cause of the conflagrations. After riding up and down several streets, the squad had gathered in some half-dozen Russians—a shopkeeper, two students, a peasant, and a manservant, and a few marauders.

But of all the suspects the most suspicious of all seemed to be Pierre. When they were all taken to the place of detention—a great mansion on the Zubovsky Val—where the guardhouse was established, Pierre was given a special, separate room, under a strong guard.

1812

The Russians, fighting for the first time in history a strategically planned "defense in depth," have burned Moscow. Napoleon, while meeting no opposition of arms, faces a Russian winter without food and fuel for half a million men. To escape disaster he must retrieve his communications with the home country, retreat to where distance does not preclude the maintenance of supply lines. He leaves Moscow.

Part Twelfth

PETERSBURG life went on in its old channels—tranquil, sumptuous, engrossed only in phantoms and reflections of life; and anyone in the current of this life needed to exercise great energy to recognize the peril and the difficult position in which the Russian nation was placed. There were the same levees and balls, the same French theater, the same court interests, the same official interests, and the same intrigues.

Only in the very highest circles were any efforts made to realize the difficulties of the actual situation.

On the seventh of September, the same day as the Battle of Borodino, Anna Pavlovna gave a reception. The chief item of news that day in Petersburg was Countess Bezukhof's illness. The countess had been unexpectedly taken ill several days before; she had missed several assemblies of which she was the adornment, and rumor had it that she received no one, and that, instead of the famous Petersburg doctors who had usually prescribed for her, she had intrusted her case to an Italian doctor, who was treating her by some new and extraordinary method.

All knew perfectly well that the charming countess' illness arose from the difficulty of marrying two husbands at once, and that the Italian's treatment consisted in the removal of these difficulties; but in Anna Pavlovna's presence no one even dared think about this; it was as if it were not known by anyone.

"They say the poor countess is very ill. The doctor says it is angina pectoris."

"Angina? Oh, that is a terrible illness."

"They say the rivals are reconciled, thanks to this angina." The word "angina" was pronounced with great unction.

"The old count, I am told, is very pathetic. He wept like a child when the doctor told him it was a dangerous case."

"Oh, it would be a terrible loss! She's a bewitching creature!"

"You were speaking of the poor countess," said Anna Pavlovna, joining the group. "I sent to hear how she was. They informed me that she was a little better. Oh, unquestionably she is the most charming woman in the world," said Anna Pavlovna, with a smile at her own enthusiasm. "We belong to different camps, but that does not prevent me from esteeming her as she deserves. She is very unhappy," added Anna Pavlovna.

Supposing that Anna Pavlovna by these words slightly lifted the veil of mystery that shrouded the countess' illness, one indiscreet young man allowed himself to express his amazement that physicians of repute had not been called, but that a charlatan, who might very easily administer dangerous remedies, was treating the countess.

"You may be better informed than I am," suddenly said Anna Pavlovna in a cutting tone to the inexperienced young man. "But I have been told on very good authority that this doctor is a very learned and very skilful man. He is private physician to the Queen of Spain."

And having thus annihilated the young man, Anna Pavlovna turned to Bilibin, who, in another circle, having wrinkled up his face and evidently made ready to smooth it out again preliminary to getting off a witticism, was speaking about the Austrians.

"I find it charming," said he, referring to a diplomatic document which had been sent to accompany some Austrian standards captured by Wittgenstein—the hero of Petrolpolis, as he was called in Petersburg.

"What, what is that?" said Anna Pavlovna, turning to him with a view to causing a silence, so that the witticism, which she had already heard, might be more effective.

And Bilibin repeated the following authentic words of the diplomatic dispatch, which he himself had drawn up.

" 'The emperor returns the Austrian flags,' " said Bilibin, " 'friendly flags gone astray, which he found off the usual route.' "

"Delightful, delightful!" exclaimed Prince Vasili.

"You will see," exclaimed Anna Pavlovna. "We shall have news tomorrow; it's the sovereign's birthday. I have a happy presentiment."

Anna Pavlovna's presentiment was in fact justified.

On the following day, during the Te Deum chanted at the palace in honor of the emperor's birthday, Prince Volkonsky was called out from the chapel and handed an envelope from Prince Kutuzof. This contained Kutuzof's report written from Tatarinovo on the day of the battle. Kutuzof wrote that the Russians had not fallen back a step, that the French had lost far more than we had, that he made his report in all haste from the field of battle, without having had time, as yet, to receive all details.

Of course it was a victory. And instantly, without dismissing the audience, a thanksgiving was sung to the Creator for His aid and for the victory.

Anna Pavlovna's presentiment was justified; and throughout the city there reigned, all that morning, joyful and festive enthusiasm. All considered the victory complete, and many went so far as to talk about Napoleon himself being a prisoner, and of his overthrow and the choice of a new sovereign for France.

"What did I tell you about Kutuzof?" now exclaimed Prince Vasili, with the pride of a prophet. "I always said he was the only one capable of beating Napoleon."

But on the following day no news was received from the army, and the general voice began to be anxious. The courtiers suffered from the painful state of ignorance in which the sovereign was left.

"What a position for the sovereign!" said the courtiers; and before the third day had passed they already began to pass judgment on Kutuzof, who was regarded as the cause of the sovereign's uneasiness.

Prince Vasili on that day ceased to boast of his *protégé* Kutuzof, and maintained a discreet silence when the commander-in-chief was mentioned.

Moreover, on the evening of this same day, as if all things conspired together to alarm and disquiet the inhabitants of Petersburg, another terrible piece of news was announced. Countess Elena Bezukhof suddenly died of that terrible disease which her friends found it so pleasant to name.

Officially, in all the great coterie it was declared that the Countess Bezukhof had died of a terrible attack of angina pectoris, but in select circles details were forthcoming: how the private physician of the Queen of Spain had prescribed for Helene small doses of some medicine so as to bring about certain effects; and how Helene, worried because the old count had some suspicion of her, and because her husband, to whom she had written (that miserable, depraved Pierre), did not reply to her, suddenly took an overdose of the drug prescribed, and died in agony before help could be got to her. It was said that Prince Vasili and the old count had at first blamed the Italian; but the Italian had showed them such letters from the late unfortunate countess that they had instantly let him go.

On the third day after Kutuzof's dispatch had been received, a landed proprietor arrived at Petersburg from Moscow, and soon the whole city was ringing with the news that Moscow was abandoned to the French.

This was terrible! In what a position it placed the sovereign! Kutuzof was a traitor, and Prince Vasili, while receiving visits of condolence on the death of his daughter, speaking of that same Kutuzof whom he had but shortly been praising (it was pardonable that in his grief he should forget what he said before), declared that it was idle to expect anything else from a blind and lewd old man.

"I am only amazed that the fate of Russia should have been intrusted to such a man!"

I I

Nine days after the abandonment of Moscow, a messenger from Kutuzof arrived in Petersburg with the official confirmation of the abandonment of Moscow. This courier was the Frenchman Michaud, but, though a foreigner, yet a Russian in heart and soul—as he himself declared.

Though the source of Monsieur Michaud's chagrin must have been very different from that from which the grief of the Russian people proceeded, Michaud drew such a melancholy face as he was ushered into the sovereign's study, that the sovereign instantly asked him:

"Are you bringing me bad news, colonel?"

"Very bad, sire," replied Michaud, with a sigh, and dropping his eyes, "the abandonment of Moscow!"

"Can they have surrendered my ancient capital without a battle?" exclaimed the emperor, an angry flush suddenly rising in his face.

Michaud respectfully delivered the message with which he had been intrusted by Kutuzof; namely, that it was a sheer impossibility to accept an engagement at Moscow, and that as but one choice was left, to lose both the army and Moscow, or Moscow alone, the field marshal had felt it his duty to choose the latter alternative.

The sovereign listened in silence, not looking at Michaud.

"Has the enemy entered the city?" he demanded.

"Yes, your majesty, and it is a heap of ashes by this time. When I left it, it was all on fire," said Michaud, resolutely; but when he glanced at the emperor, Michaud was horror-struck at what he had said. The sovereign was breathing with quick labored respirations; his lower lip trembled and his handsome blue eyes for an instant overflowed with tears.

But this lasted only a moment. The sovereign suddenly scowled as if he were annoyed at himself for his weakness. And, raising his head, he turned to Michaud, with a steady voice:

"I see, colonel, from all that is happening to us," said he, "that Providence demands great sacrifices of us. . . . I am ready to submit to His will; but tell me, Michaud, how did you leave the army which saw my ancient capital thus abandoned without striking a blow? Did you see no signs of discouragement?"

Michaud, seeing this calmness of his "very gracious sovereign," instantly recovered his own presence of mind; but he was not yet ready to reply to the emperor's straightforward and unequivocal question which demanded a straightforward answer.

"Your majesty, will you allow me to speak freely, as a loyal soldier?" he asked, for the sake of gaining time.

"Colonel, that is what I always demand," said the emperor. "Conceal nothing from me; I wish to know absolutely how matters stand."

"Your majesty," said Michaud, with a shrewd but scarcely perceptible smile on his lips, having now collected himself sufficiently to formulate his answer in a graceful and respectful play of words: "Your majesty, I left the whole army, from the chiefs down to the last soldier, without exception, in a state of terrible, desperate fear . . ."

"How is that?" interrupted the sovereign, frowning darkly. "Will my Russians allow themselves to be cast down by misfortune? . . . Never!"

This was all that Michaud wished so as to complete his play of words.

"Your majesty," said he, with a sprightly but respectful expression, "their only fear is that your majesty, through kindness of heart, will be persuaded to make peace. They are burning to fight," said the accredited representative of the Russian people, "and to prove to your majesty by the sacrifice of their lives how devoted they are."

"Ah!" said the sovereign, reassured; and with an affectionate gleam flashing from his eyes, he tapped Michaud on the shoulder. "You relieve me, colonel."

The sovereign then dropped his head and remained for some time lost in thought.

"Very well! Return to the army," said he, drawing himself up to his full height and turning to Michaud with a gentle but majestic gesture. "And tell our brave men, tell all my good subjects everywhere you go, that when I have no soldiers left, I will place myself at the head of my beloved nobles and of my worthy peasants, and thus I will exhaust the last resources of my empire. It will furnish me yet with more than my enemies think," said the sovereign, growing more and more moved. "But if ever it were written in the decrees of Divine Providence," he went on to say, raising to heaven his beautiful, kindly eyes, gleaming with emotion, "that my family should cease to reign on the throne of my ancestors, then, after having exhausted all the means that are in my power, I will allow my beard to grow to here" —the sovereign placed his hand halfway down his chest—"and I will go and eat potatoes with the humblest of my peasants sooner than sign the shame of my country and of my beloved nation, whose sacrifices I can appreciate."

Having said these words in a voice full of emotion, the sovereign suddenly turned round, evidently to hide from Michaud the tears that filled his eyes, and walked to the end of his study. After standing there a few moments he came back to Michaud with long strides, and gave his arm a powerful squeeze below the elbow. His handsome, kindly face was flushed, and his eyes flashed with decision and wrath:

"Colonel Michaud, do not forget what I have said to you here; perhaps some day we will recall it with pleasure—either Napoleon or I," said the sovereign, laying his hand on his chest. "We can no longer reign together. I have learned to know him; he will never deceive me again!"

And the sovereign, with a frown, relapsed into silence.

Michaud, though a foreigner, yet a Russian in heart and soul, felt at that solemn moment enraptured by all that he had just heard (as he said afterwards), and in the expressions that followed, he uttered not only his own feelings but also the feelings of the Russian people, whose representative he considered himself.

"Sire!" said he, "your majesty at this moment seals the glory of the nation and the safety of Europe."

The sovereign with an inclination of the head dismissed Michaud.

III

AT THE TIME when Russia was half conquered and the inhabitants of Moscow were fleeing to distant provinces, and levy after levy of the militia was rising for the defense of the fatherland, we, who were not alive at the time, involuntarily imagine that all the men of Russia, from small to great, were solely occupied in sacrificing themselves, in saving the country, or in bewailing its ruin. Stories and descriptions of that period, all without exception, speak of self-sacrifice, love for the fatherland, the desperation, sorrow, and heroism of the Russians. In reality this was not so at all. The majority of the men of that time paid no attention to the general course of events, and were merely guided by the personal interests of their day. And those very men were the most important factors of the time.

The significance of the event which was at that time taking place in Russia was proportionately incomprehensible according to the part which any man took in it. In Petersburg and the provinces remote from Moscow, ladies and men in militia uniforms mourned over Russia and the capital and talked about self-sacrifice and other such things; but in the army which was retreating from Moscow almost nothing was said or thought about Moscow; and as they looked at the conflagration no one dreamed of wreaking vengeance on the French, but they thought of the next quarter's pay, about the next halting place, about Matrioshka the canteen wench, and the like.

Nikolai Rostof, without any pretense of self-sacrifice, but casually, the war having surprised him while he was still in the service, took a genuine and continuous part in the defense of his country, and accordingly looked without despair and without somber forebodings on what was then happening in Russia. If anyone had asked him what he thought about the condition of Russia at the time, he would have replied that it was not for him to think about it, that Kutuzof and the others were for that, but he had heard that more regiments were mobilizing, and that there would be still more fighting, and that if nothing happened it would not be astonishing if in a couple of years he were given command of a regiment.

It was because he took this view of affairs that he not only felt no regret at being deprived of participation in the last engagement, having received word that he was appointed commander of a remount expedition to Voronezh after horses for his division, but was even perfectly delighted, and took no pains to hide it from his comrades, who were generous enough to sympathize with him.

In the most jovial frame of mind, Nikolai reached Voronezh in the evening, put up at the inn, ordered all that he had so long been in need of at the front, and on the next day, after getting a clean shave and putting on his long unused dress uniform, he went to pay his respects to the city officials.

The governor was a lively little man, very friendly and simple-hearted. He told Nikolai of several establishments where he might obtain horses, recommended to him a horse dealer in the city and a landed proprietor fourteen miles from the city who kept good horses, and he promised him every kind of coöperation.

"Are you Count Ilya Rostof's son? My wife used to be very good friends with your mother. On Thursdays I always have a reception: today is Thursday; do me the favor of coming informally," said the governor, as Nikolai took his leave.

Provincial life in 1812 was pretty much the same as ever, with only this difference, that it was unusually gay in the little city owing to the presence of a number of wealthy families from Moscow and to the fact that, as in everything that was done in Russia at this time, there was unprecedented luxury observable (the sea being but knee-deep to drunken men), while the small talk which is a necessity among people, and which hitherto had been concerned merely with the weather and petty gossip, now turned on the state of Moscow, the war, and Napoleon.

The society which met at the governor's was the best society of Voronezh.

There were any number of ladies, there were several of Nikolai's Moscow acquaintances; but there was not a man who could in any way compare with the gallant hussar, decorated with the highest St. George's cross, the good-natured, well-bred Count Rostof!

Among the men was an Italian who had been an officer in the French army and was now a prisoner, and Nikolai felt that this prisoner's presence still further enhanced his importance as a Russian hero. It was a kind of trophy! Nikolai felt this, and it seemed to him that this was the way they all regarded the Italian, and so he treated him cordially, but with a certain dignity and reserve.

As soon as Nikolai entered the room in his hussar's uniform, diffusing around him an odor of perfumes and of wine, he became the center of the gathering; all eyes were fixed on him, and he immediately felt that the position of general favorite which he had taken in the province was exceedingly appropriate to him, and pleasant, and, after such long deprivation, really intoxicating in its agreeableness. Not only at the post stations and the taverns were the servants maids flattered by his attentions, but here, at the governor's reception, it seemed to Nikolai that there was an inexhaustible array of young married women and pretty girls who were impatient to have him give them a share of his attention. The ladies and young girls flirted with him, and the old people, from the very first moment, took it on themselves to find a wife for this madcap young hussar and make him settle down. Among the latter was the governor's wife herself, who received Rostof like a near relative, and called him "Nikolai."

All that evening Nikolai devoted most of his attentions to a blue-eyed, plump and pretty little blonde, the wife of one of the government officials. With that naive conviction with which young men flatter themselves that other men's wives were created especially for their diversion, Rostof stayed by this lady, and treated her husband in a friendly, somewhat conspiratorial way, as if it were to be quite taken for granted, though as yet nothing had been said about it, that they would get along splendidly—that is, Nikolai with this man's wife! The husband, however, did not seem to share in this conviction and did his best to treat Rostof with marked coldness. But Nikolai's unaffected frankness was so unbounded that more than once the husband was obliged, in spite of himself, to give way to Nikolai's geniality. Toward the end of the evening, however, in proportion as his wife's face grew more and more flushed and excited, her husband's face grew more and more set and melancholy, as if there were a common fund of vivacity shared by the two so that in proportion as it increased in the wife, it decreased in the husband.

Nikolai, with a beaming smile on his lips, sat in his armchair, leaning over as near as possible to the pretty blonde, whispering flowery compliments into her ear. Briskly shifting his legs in their tight riding trousers, exhaling the odor of perfumes, and contemplating his lady and himself, and the handsome shape of his calves under his top boots, Nikolai was telling the pretty blonde that it was his plan, while he was there at Voronezh, to run away with a certain lady.

"Who is she?"

"Charming, divine! Her eyes"—Nikolai looked closely at his neighbor—"are blue; her lips, coral; her white skin"—he gave a significant look at her shoulders—"her form, Diana's!"

The husband joined them and asked his wife gloomily what she was talking about.

"Ah! Nikita Ivanovitch," exclaimed Nikolai, politely rising. And, as if he were anxious for Nikita Ivanovitch to share in his jokes, he confided to him his intention of eloping with a certain pretty blonde.

The husband smiled chillingly, the wife rapturously. The governor's worthy wife came up to them with a disapproving look on her face.

"Anna Ignatyevna is anxious to talk to you, Nikolai," said she, and by her tone Rostof instantly realized that Anna Ignatyevna was a very important individual. "Come, let us go, Nikolai. You permit me to call you so, don't you?"

554

"Oh, yes, aunt. But who is she?"

"Anna Ignatyevna Malvintsev. She has heard of you through her niece . . . how you rescued her! . . . Can you guess?"

"But was she the only one I rescued there?" said Nikolai.

"Her niece, the Princess Bolkonsky. She is here with her aunt in Voronezh. Oho! how he blushes! What does that mean, now?"

"I could not imagine, . . . there, there, aunt."

"Pretty good, pretty good! Oh, what a boy you are!"

The governor's wife led him to a tall and very stately old lady with a blue toque, who had just finished a hand at cards with the most consequential personages of the city. This was Madame Malvintsev, Princess Maria's aunt on her mother's side, a rich, childless widow who had always lived in Voronezh. She stood settling her card account when Rostof was brought to her. She blinked her eyes with a stern and important expression, glanced at Nikolai, and went on berating the general who had won her money.

"Very glad to see you, my dear," said she, extending her hand. "Pray come and see me."

After speaking a few words about Princess Maria and her late father, whom, evidently, Madame Malvintsev had not loved, and asking a few questions as to what news Nikolai had to give about Prince Andrei, who also seemed not to enjoy her good graces, she dismissed him, repeating her invitation to visit her.

Nikolai promised, and again flushed as he took leave of the widow.

At the remembrance of Princess Maria, Rostof experienced a feeling of bashfulness, even of fear, which he could not understand.

After leaving Madame Malvintsev, Rostof intended to return to the dancing again, but the little wife of the governor laid her plump little hand on his sleeve, saying that she wanted to have a talk with him; and she led him into the sitting room, which was instantly evacuated by those who were in it and who did not want to be in her way.

"You must know, my dear," said the governor's wife, with a serious expression on her good little face, "I have found exactly the right wife for you; do you want me to arrange the match?"

"Who is it, aunt?" asked Nikolai.

"I propose the princess. What do you say? I am sure your mama would be very thankful. Truly, she is a charming girl, and, after all, she is not so very plain!"

"Indeed, she isn't!" exclaimed Nikolai in an injured tone. "As for myself, aunt, I do as a soldier should; I never offer myself, and I never refuse anything," said Nikolai, before he had time to think what he was saying.

"But remember! This is no joke."

"What is no joke?"

"Yes, yes," said the governor's wife, as if speaking to herself. "And see here, my dear, you are quite too attentive to that other lady, the blonde. Really, her husband is to be pitied."

"Oh, no; he and I are very good friends," replied Nikolai, who in his simplicity of soul never once dreamed that such a gay way of whiling away time could be anything else than gay to anyone.

"What foolish nonsense did I speak to the governor's wife?" Nikolai suddenly asked himself while at supper. "She is trying to make a match . . . but Sonya . . . ?"

And on bidding the governor's wife good night, when she with a smile said to him, "Now remember . . ." he drew her to one side.

"Aunt, I have something which I really ought to tell you . . ."

"What can it be, my boy? Come in, and let us sit down here."

Nikolai suddenly felt a desire and an irresistible impulse to confide to this woman, who was almost a stranger, all his private thoughts—thoughts he would never have told his mother, his sister, his friend. Afterwards, when he remembered this outburst of needless, inexplicable frankness, which nevertheless had very important consequences, it seemed to him as it always seems to people—that he had acted very foolishly; this outburst of frankness, together with other trivial circumstances, had for him and for his whole family portentous results.

"This is what I mean, aunt. Mama has for a long time been anxious for me to marry a rich young lady. But the idea of marrying for money has always been extremely repugnant."

"Oh, yes, I understand," assented the governor's wife.

"But Princess Bolkonsky; that is another thing. In the first place, I will tell you honestly, she pleases me very much; I like her extremely. And besides, after meeting her in such a way, in such a terrible position, the thought has often occurred to me that it was fate. You may remember, mama long, long ago thought about this, before I ever happened to meet her, and somehow it happened that we never met. And then when my sister Natasha was engaged to her brother, why, of course, then it became out of the question to think of marrying her. And now, just as Natasha's engagement is broken off, it must needs happen that I meet her; well, it's all . . . this is the trouble. . . . I have never told anyone about this, and I shall never speak of it again. Only to you."

The governor's wife gave his elbow an encouraging pressure.

"You know Sonya, my cousin. I love her, and I have promised to marry her, and I shall marry her. . . . And so you see there is nothing to be said about this other matter," explained Nikolai, disconnectedly and reddening.

"My dear! My dear! How can you have such ideas? Why, you know Sonya has nothing, and you yourself have told me that your papa's affairs are in a wretched state. And your mama? This would kill her, surely! Then Sonya, if she is a girl with any heart, what a life it would be for her! Your mother in despair, your property all dissipated! . . . No, my dear, you and Sonya must see things as they are."

Nikolai made no reply. It was pleasant for him to hear this reasoning.

"Still, aunt, this cannot be," said he, with a sigh, after some little silence. "Then, do you suppose the princess would marry me? And besides, she is in mourning. How can such a thing be thought of?"

"What? Do you suppose I would have you marry her instantly? There are ways and ways!" said the governor's wife.

"What a matchmaker, aunt!" said Nikolai, kissing her plump hand.

IV

WHEN, ON THE day following her reception, the governor's wife went to call upon Madame Malvintsev, after a private conversation with her in regard to her scheme (making the reservation that, though under present circumstances it was impossible to think of a formal courtship, still the young people might be brought together and made acquainted); and when, after receiving the aunt's approval, the governor's wife spoke in Princess Maria's presence of Rostof, praised him, and told how he had reddened at the mere mention of the princess' name, Princess Maria experienced a feeling not of pleasure but of pain; her inward calm had entirely vanished, and again arose her desires, doubts, self-reproaches, and hopes.

During the two days that intervened between hearing this news and her interview with Rostof, Princess Maria did not cease to think how she ought to behave toward him. At one moment she made up her mind that she would not go into the drawing-room when he came to call on her aunt, that it was not becoming for her to receive callers when she was in deep mourning; then again she thought that it would be rude after all that he had done for her; then it occurred to her that the governor's wife and her aunt must have some designs on her and Rostof—their glances, and certain words they had dropped, it seemed to her, confirmed this supposition—then she said to herself that nothing but her inborn wickedness made her have such thoughts; the others could not help remembering that in her situation, while she had not yet taken off her "deep mourning," such a wooing would be an insult to her as well as to her father's memory.

Assuming that she should go down to meet him, Princess Maria tried to imagine what words he would say to her and she should say to him, and at one moment these words seemed to possess too great significance. More than all else she was apprehensive that on meeting him she would show her bashfulness, that it would take possession of her and betray her as soon as she saw him. But when on Sunday, after Mass, the footman announced at the drawing-room door that Count Rostof had come, the princess showed no symptoms of confusion; only a faint tinge of color suffused her cheeks, and her eyes shone with a new, luminous light.

"You have seen him, auntie?" asked Princess Maria in a tranquil voice, surprised herself that she could be outwardly so calm and natural.

When Rostof entered the room the princess let her head droop for a moment, as if for the purpose of allowing the guest time to exchange greetings with her aunt; then, at the very moment that Nikolai came toward her, she raised her head and with radiant eyes met his glance. With a movement full of grace and dignity, she arose with a joyful smile, offered him her slender, delicate hand, and spoke to him in a voice which for the first time vibrated with new, deep, womanly tones.

Mlle. Bourienne, who was in the drawing-room, looked at Princess Maria in wonder and perplexity. She herself, though a most accomplished coquette, could not have maneuvered better on meeting a man she wished to fascinate.

"Either black is becoming to her, or really she has grown pretty; I certainly never noticed it before," said Mlle. Bourienne to herself.

If Princess Maria had been in a position to think at that moment, she would have been even more amazed than was Mlle. Bourienne. From the instant that she saw that kind face, so beloved, a new power of life took possession of her and compelled her, irrespective of her own will, to speak and act. Her face was suddenly transformed, just as the complicated artistic work on the sides of a painted or carved lamp shade comes out with sudden and unexpected details of beauty when a light is lighted in it. For the first time all her pure, spiritual, inward travail of so many years was laid open to the light. Her suffering, her yearnings after the right, her submission, love, self-sacrifice—all shone forth in her luminous eyes, in her gentle smile, in every feature of her tender face.

Rostof saw all this so clearly that it seemed to him he had known her all his life. He felt that the being before him was different, was better, than all he had met before, and, what was more important, was better than himself.

Their conversation was extremely simple and insignificant. They talked about the war, involuntarily, like everyone else, exaggerating their grief at the event; they talked about their last meeting, whereupon Nikolai tried to turn the conversation to something else; they talked about the governor's good wife, about their parents.

Princess Maria did not speak of her brother, deflecting the subject to another topic as soon as her aunt mentioned Andrei. It was evident that, while there might be some pretense in her expressions of grief in the miseries of Russia, her brother was an object too near to her heart, and she would not and could not talk about him. Nikolai noticed this, for, with a keenness of observation that was not at all characteristic of him, he noticed all the little shades of the princess' nature, with the effect of greatly intensifying his conviction that she was a being entirely out of the common.

Nikolai, exactly the same as the princess, had changed color and become confused when her name was mentioned in his presence, and even when he thought about her; but in her presence he felt perfectly unhampered, and by no means confined himself to the set speeches he had made ready in advance, but spoke whatever came into his head.

After his meeting with Princess Maria, although his manner of life continued to be the same outwardly, still he lost zest for his former pleasures. He frequently found himself thinking of her, but never as he had always, without exception, thought of the various young ladies he had met in society, nor even as he had thought of Sonya.

Like almost every decent young man, when he had thought about any young lady as his possible wife he had tried to make her fit the conditions of marital existence, as he imagined it—the white dressing gown, the wife behind the samovar, his wife's carriage, wee bits of children, mama and papa, their relations to her, and so forth, and so forth; and these visions of the future had given him pleasure. But when he thought about Princess Maria, who was being proposed to him as a wife, he could not make the visions of his future married life in any way concrete. Even when he tried, everything seemed incoherent and false. All that remained in his mind was a kind of dread.

V

THE TERRIBLE NEWS of the Battle of Borodino, of our losses in dead and wounded, and the still more terrible tidings of the loss of Moscow, were received in Voronezh toward the end of September.

Princess Maria, learning from the bulletin only that her brother was wounded, and having no definite information about him, determined to go in search of him. This was what Nikolai heard. He himself had not seen her again.

On learning of the Battle of Borodino and the abandonment of Moscow, Nilolai, while not giving himself up to despair, anger, or desire for vengeance or the like, still suddenly began to feel bored and out of place at Voronezh; his conscience almost reproached him, and he felt awkward. All the talk that he heard seemed to him hypocritical; he did not know what judgment to pass on events, and he was conscious that not until he returned to his regiment would things become clear to him again. He made haste to accomplish his purchase of horses, and often without any just cause became impatient with his servant and the quartermaster.

Several days before Rostof's departure a solemn service was held in the cathedral in honor of the victory that had been won by the Russian troops, and Nikolai was present. He was standing a little behind the governor, and though his gravity was worthy of the occasion, he was thinking of the most varied subjects even while he listened to the service. When the Te Deum was ended, the governor's wife called him to her.

"Have you seen the princess?" she asked, with her head indicating a lady in black who stood behind the choir.

Nikolai instantly recognized Princess Maria, not so much by her profile, a glimpse of which could be seen under her hat, as by that feeling of shyness, fear and pity which instantly came over him. Princess Maria, evidently absorbed in her thoughts, was crossing herself for the last time before leaving the church.

Without waiting for the governor's wife to advise him to join her, without asking himself whether it was right or proper for him to address her there in the church, he instantly went to her and said that he had heard of her sorrow and that he sympathized with her with all his heart. She had hardly caught the first sound of his voice when suddenly a bright light flashed into her face, showing at the same time her sorrow and her joy.

"I only wanted to tell you this, princess," said Rostof; "that if Prince Andrei were not alive, it would be instantly announced in the bulletins, since he is a regimental commander."

The princess looked at him, not comprehending his words, but delighting in the expression of sympathy and sorrow in his face.

"And I have known so many cases where a wound caused by a splinter (in the bulletins it said by a shell) was either fatal immediately, or, if not, very trifling," said Nikolai. "You must hope for the best, and I am certain . . ."

Princess Maria interrupted him:

"Oh, this would be so hor . . ." she began, but her emotion overmastered her, and, without completing the word, she bent her head with a graceful motion (like everything that she did in his presence), and, giving him a grateful look, rejoined her aunt.

That evening Nikolai accepted no engagements out, but remained at his lodgings in order to square up certain accounts with the horse dealers.

When he completed his business it was too late to go anywhere, but too early to retire for the night. For a long time he walked up and down his solitary room, thinking over his life, which was an unusual thing for him to do.

"She must be a marvelous girl! A real angel!" said he to himself. "Why am I not free? Why was I in such haste with Sonya?"

And involuntarily he began to compare the two: the poverty in one, the abundance in the other, of those spiritual gifts which Nikolai himself had not, and which therefore he prized so highly.

He tried to imagine what would be if he had been free. How he would have made his proposal to her, and how she would become his wife! But no, he could not imagine it.

A strange feeling of dread came over him, and nothing clear presented itself to his imagination. He had long ago drawn the picture of his future with Sonya, and it was all clear and simple because it had been thought out and he knew all that was in Sonya; but it was impossible to formulate any scheme of life with Princess Maria, because he did not understand her, but only loved her.

"Why cannot I pray for what I need?" he asked himself. "What do I need? My freedom, to be released from Sonya. She said what was true"—he was recalling the words of the governor's wife—" 'Nothing but misfortune would

560

come of my marrying her.' Confusion, grief to mama . . . terrible confusion! Yes, and I don't love her. I don't love her as I ought. My God! Save me from this terrible inextricable state of things!" he began, trying to offer a prayer. "Yes, prayer moves the mountain, but faith is needful, and one should not pray as Natasha and I used to pray when we were children, that the snow would change to sugar, and then run outdoors to see whether our prayers were answered. No, but I cannot pray about trifles now," said he, as he laid his pipe down in the corner; and, folding his hands, he stood in front of the holy pictures. Touched by his recollection of Princess Maria, he began to pray as he had not prayed for a long, long time. The tears were standing in his eyes and swelling his throat when Lavrushka suddenly came in with documents in his hand. "Idiot!—why do you come sneaking in when you weren't called?" exclaimed Nikolai, abruptly changing his position.

"From the governor," said Lavrushka, in a sleepy voice; "a courier came; letter for you."

"All right, thanks! Now go!"

Nikolai had two letters. One was from his mother, the other from Sonya. He recognized them by their handwriting, and he opened Sonya's first. He had only read a few lines when his face grew pale and his eyes opened wide in terror and delight.

"No, it cannot be!" he exclaimed aloud. He could not sit still, but with the letter in his hand began to pace the room. He glanced through the letter, then read it, once and a second time, and, shrugging his shoulders and throwing out his hands, he stood still in the middle of the room with open mouth and set eyes.

The very thing he had just been praying for, with the faith that God would fulfil his prayer, was granted; but Nikolai was amazed by this, as if it had come, not by the will of God, to whom he had offered his petition, but from ordinary chance.

The apparently unsolvable knot that hampered Rostof's freedom was cut by this letter from Sonya—so unexpected (as it seemed to Nikolai) and unsolicited. She wrote that the recent unfortunate events, the loss of almost all the Rostofs' property in Moscow, and the countess' desire, more than once expressed, that Nikolai should marry Princess Bolkonsky, and his own silence and coldness of late, all taken together had caused her to decide to release him from his promise and give him perfect freedom. She wrote:

> It was too painful for me to think I might be a source of sorrow or dissension in a family which has loaded me with benefits, and my love has for its one single aim the happiness of those whom I love. And therefore I beseech you, Nikolai, to consider yourself perfectly free, and to know that, in spite of all, no one could love you more truly than your Sonya.

The second letter was from the countess. In this there was given a full description of the last days in Moscow, their departure, the fire, and the loss of all their property. In this letter also, among other things, the countess wrote that Prince Andrei was among the wounded whom they had brought away with them. His condition was very critical, but now the doctor declared that there was more hope. Sonya and Natasha were nursing him as watchers.

On the following day, Nikolai took this letter, and went to see Princess Maria. Neither Nikolai nor the princess said a word as to the significance of the fact that Natasha was attending Andrei; but, thanks to this letter, Nikolai felt drawn closer to the princess, almost as if he were a relative.

On the next day, Rostof escorted Princess Maria to Yaroslavl, and not long after rejoined his regiment.

VI

SONYA'S LETTER to Nikolai, coming so opportunely in answer to his prayer, had been written from Troitsa. This was the way it happened:

The old countess had become more and more occupied with the idea of Nikolai's marrying a rich wife. She knew that Sonya was the chief obstacle in the way of this. And Sonya's life in the countess' home had been made more and more trying of late, especially since Nikolai wrote of meeting Princess Maria at Bogucharovo. The countess lost no opportunity to make insulting or cruel insinuations to Sonya.

A few days before their departure from Moscow, however, the countess, moved and excited by all that was happening, had called Sonya to her, and, instead of loading her with reproaches and demands, had begged her with tears in her eyes to have pity, and, as a return for all that had been done for her, to release Nikolai from his engagement.

"I shall never be content until you have given me this promise."

Sonya sobbed hysterically, promised through her sobs that she would do anything, that she was ready for any sacrifice; but she did not give the promise in so many words, and in her heart she found it impossible to consent.

It was necessary for her to sacrifice herself for the happiness of the family that had sheltered and educated her. To sacrifice herself for the happiness of others was second nature to Sonya. Her position in the household was such that only through sacrifice could she show her worth, and she was accustomed to sacrifice herself, and loved to do so. But hitherto she had enjoyed the pleasant consciousness that in sacrificing herself she was enhancing her value in her own eyes and the eyes of others, and was becoming more worthy of Nikolai whom she loved above all else in the world. Now her sacrifice was to consist in renouncing all that had promised to be the reward of her sacrifice, the whole meaning of life. And for the first time in her life she had bitter feelings against those very people who had loaded her with benefits only to torment her the more. She began to hate Natasha, who had never been required to sacrifice herself, but who had obliged others to sacrifice themselves for her, and yet was loved by all.

And for the first time she felt that her gentle, pure love for Nikolai was growing into a passion which was mightier than law and virtue and religion. Under the influence of this feeling, Sonya, who had been involuntarily taught by her life of dependence to be reserved, replied to the countess in general, indefinite terms, avoided saying more, and made up her mind to wait until she should see Nikolai again, with the idea, not of giving him his freedom, but, on the contrary, of binding him to her forever.

The labors and terror incident to those last days that the Rostofs spent in Moscow put out of mind the gloomy thoughts that had been weighing her down. She was glad to find an escape from them in practical activity. But when she learned of Prince Andrei's presence in the house, notwithstanding her genuine pity felt for him and for Natasha, she was seized by a blithe and superstitious presentiment that God did not wish her to be separated from Nikolai.

She knew that Natasha had never loved anyone but Prince Andrei, and that she still loved him. She knew that, now being brought together in such terrible circumstances, they would renew their mutual affection, and that it would then be impossible for Nikolai to marry Princess Maria because of the relationship. Notwithstanding the horror of all that had taken place during the last days in Moscow and during the early part of their journey, this feeling, this consciousness of the interference of Providence in her personal affairs, had rejoiced Sonya's heart.

The Rostofs made their first halt at the Troitsa, or Trinity, Monastery.

At the hostelry of the monastery the Rostofs were assigned three large rooms, one of which was taken by Prince Andrei. The wounded man was much better that day. Natasha had been sitting with him. In the adjoining room the count and countess were engaged in a polite conversation with the Father Superior, who had come to pay his respects to his old acquaintances and benefactors. Sonya was also sitting with them, and was tormented by curiosity as to what Prince Andrei and Natasha were talking about, for she could hear the sounds of their voices. The door of Prince Andrei's room had been left open.

Natasha, with agitated face, came running out, and not heeding the monk, who rose to meet her and offered her his right hand under his flowing sleeves, went straight to Sonya and took her by the arm.

"Natasha! What is the matter? Come here!" said the countess.

Natasha submitted to the priest's blessing, and the Father Superior advised her to go for help to God and his saint.

As soon as the Father Superior was gone, Natasha took her cousin's hand, and drew her into the empty room.

"Sonya! Is he going to live? Say yes!" said she. "Sonya! How happy I am, and how unhappy! Sonya darling, it is all just as it used to be. If only he would live! . . . He can't get well . . . because . . . be . . . cause . . ."

And Natasha burst into tears

"Yes! He will. I have been sure of it! Glory to God! He will get well!"

Sonya was no less agitated than Natasha, not only because of her friend's suffering and sorrow, but also because of her own private thoughts, which she shared with no one. Sobbing, she kissed Natasha, and tried to soothe her.

"If only he would get well!" she said to herself.

There happened to be on that day an opportunity to send letters to the army, and the countess was writing to her son.

"Sonya," said the countess, lifting her head from her letter as her niece passed her, "Sonya, won't you write Nikolai?" She asked in a gentle, trembling voice; and by the look in her weary eyes, gazing at her over her spectacles, Sonya knew what she meant by those words. In that look was expressed a prayer, and fear of a refusal, and shame that she was obliged to ask such a thing, and readiness for implacable hatred in case of refusal.

Sonya went to the countess, and, kneeling down beside her, kissed her hand.

"I will write," said she.

Now, when she knew that, in case Natasha's engagement to Prince Andrei was renewed, Nikolai could not marry Princess Maria, she had a sense of joy in the return of this condition of self-sacrifice which was her habit. And with tears in her eyes and blissful consciousness of having accomplished a magnanimous action, though several times interrupted by the tears that clouded her velvety dark eyes, she wrote the touching letter, the receipt of which had so amazed Nikolai.

VII

ALL THE RUSSIANS locked in with Pierre were men of the very lowest station. And all of them, recognizing that Pierre was a gentleman, shunned him, and all the more from the fact that he spoke French. Pierre with a certain sadness listened to their sarcasms at his expense.

On the following evening Pierre learned that all these prisoners (and apparently he himself in the number) were to be tried for incendiarism. On the third day Pierre and the rest were conducted to a house where were a French general with a white mustache, two colonels, and several other Frenchmen with chevrons on their sleeves. Pierre, just as the others, was subjected to a series of questions put with that shrewdness and precision that affect to be superior to all human weaknesses and are characteristic of all ordinary dealings with prisoners at the bar. Who was he? Where had he been? For what purpose? And so forth.

These questions, putting aside the essence of the vital fact and excluding the possibility of getting at the truth, were like all questions put at legal examinations, having for their object the laying down of a sort of gutter in which examiners wish the answers of the victim to trickle so that he may be brought to the desired point; namely, incrimination! Moreover, Pierre experienced what is always experienced by men on trial: a sense of perplexity, of wonder why all these questions were asked. It was evident that all his answers were taken as proof of his guilt.

To the question as to what he was doing when he was arrested, Pierre replied with a certain tragic force that he was restoring to its parents a child he had rescued from the flames.

Why had he fought with the marauder? Pierre replied that he was protecting a woman, that the defense of an insulted woman was the duty of every man, that . . .

They interrupted him; this was irrelevant.

Why had he been in the yard of the burning building where the witnesses had seen him?

He replied that he had gone out to see what was happening in Moscow.

He was again interrupted; he had not been asked where he was going, but why he was in the vicinity of the fire.

Who was he? they asked, reiterating their first question; he replied once more that he could not tell them that.

"Write that down; it looks bad. Very bad," sternly said the white-mustached general with the florid complexion.

Pierre and thirteen others were removed to the Krimsky Brod, or Crimean Ford, and placed in the barn of a merchant's mansion. As they marched along the streets Pierre was suffocated by the smoke, which seemed to him to have settled down over the entire city. In various directions fires could be seen.

On the twentieth of September an officer of very great importance, to judge by the respect the guards showed him, came into the barn to see the prisoners. This officer, who apparently belonged to Napoleon's staff, had a list in his hand, and called a roll of all the Russians, designating Pierre as "the man who refuses to give his name." Surveying the prisoners with a look of lazy indifference, he ordered the officer of the guard to see that they were decently clad and tidy before they were brought into the marshal's presence. Within an hour, a file of soldiers appeared, and Pierre and thirteen others were taken out to the Virgin's Field.

No flames were visible, but on all sides arose columns of smoke, and all Moscow, as far as Pierre could see, was one conflagration.

Pierre and the other prisoners were conducted to the right-hand side of the Virgin's Field, to a large white house with an immense garden not far from the monastery. This was Prince Shcherbatof's house, which Pierre had often been in, and which now, as he ascertained from the talk of the soldiers, was occupied by the marshal, the Prince d'Eckmühl (Davoust). They were taken to the porch, and led into the house one at a time. Pierre was the sixth. Through the glass gallery, the entry, the anteroom, rooms all well known to Pierre, he was led into a long, low study at the door of which stood an aide-de-camp.

Davoust, with his spectacles on his nose, sat by a table at one end of the room. Pierre came close to him. Davoust consulted a document placed in front of him. Without even raising his eyes, he asked in a low voice: "Who are you?"

Pierre said nothing, for the reason that he had not the power to utter a word. Davoust, in Pierre's eyes, was not simply a French general; for Pierre, Davoust was a man notorious for his cruelty. As he looked into that icy face, like that of a stern teacher who is willing to be patient for a time and wait for a reply, Pierre felt that every second of delay might cost him his life, but he did not know what to say. He could not make up his mind to repeat what he had said at the first examination; to divulge his name and station was at once dangerous and shameful.

Pierre said nothing.

But before he had time to come to any decision Davoust raised his head, pushed his spectacles up on his forehead, squinted his eyes, and gave Pierre a fixed stare.

"I know this man," said he, in an icy tone, evidently meant to alarm Pierre. The chill which before had been running up and down Pierre's back clutched his head as in a vise.

"General, you cannot possibly know me; I have never seen you . . ."

"He is a Russian spy," interrupted Davoust, turning to another general who happened to be in the room and had not before been observed by Pierre. And Davoust looked away.

With an unexpected rumbling in his voice, Pierre suddenly began to speak rapidly.

"No, monseigneur," said he, unexpectedly remembering that Davoust was a duke. "No, monseigneur, you cannot have known me. I am an officer of militia, and I have not been out of Moscow."

"Your name?" demanded Davoust.

"Bezukhof."

"Who will prove that you are not lying?"

"Monseigneur!" cried Pierre, in a tone that betrayed not offense but expostulation.

Davoust raised his eyes and stared at Pierre. For several seconds they looked into each other's eyes, and this look was what saved Pierre. In this look there was established between these two men, above and beyond all the conditions of war and the courtroom, the relations of a common humanity. Both of them at that one moment became confusedly conscious of an infinite number of things, and realized that they both were children of humanity—that they were brothers.

For Davoust, who had only just raised his head from the list where the acts and lives of men were represented by numbers, Pierre at first glance was only an incident, and Davoust would have had him shot without his conscience regarding it as a wicked deed; but now he began to see that he was a man. He deliberated for an instant.

"How will you prove the truth of what you tell me?" asked Davoust, coldly.

Pierre remembered Ramball, and mentioned his regiment and name and the street where his lodgings would be found.

"You are not what you say you are," reiterated Davoust.

Pierre, in a trembling, broken voice, began to adduce proofs of the correctness of his representation.

But at this instant an aide entered and made some report to Davoust. Davoust suddenly grew radiant at the news communicated by the aide-de-camp, and began to button up his coat. He had evidently forgotten Pierre's existence.

When the aide reminded him of the prisoner, he frowned and nodded in Pierre's direction, and ordered him to be led away. But where was he to be led? Pierre had no idea, whether back to the barn or to the place prepared for the execution, which, as he had crossed the Virgin's Field, his comrades had pointed out to him.

Pierre had no idea how long he was kept walking or where he was taken. In a condition of absolute stupor and abstraction, conscious of nothing around him, he mechanically moved his legs together with the others until they were all halted, and then he also halted.

During all this time one thought filled his mind. This thought was: Who had in the last analysis condemned him to be executed? It was not the same men who had examined him at the court-martial; there was not one man among them who would have been willing, or, in all probability, could have done so. It was not Davoust, who had looked at him with such a human look. One instant more and Davoust would have understood that they were making a mistake, but that moment was disturbed by the aide who had come in. And this aide evidently would not willingly have done anything wrong, but he could not help it. Who, then, was it that was the final cause of his being punished, killed, deprived of life—he, Pierre, with all his recollections, yearnings, hopes, ideas? Who was doing this?

And Pierre felt that it was no one.

It was the order of things, the chain of circumstances.

This order of things was somehow killing him—Pierre—depriving him of life, destroying him.

From Prince Shcherbatof's house, the prisoners were conducted directly down along the Virgin's Field, to the left of the monastery, and were brought into a kitchen garden where stood an upright post. Back of the post a great pit had been dug, the fresh earth was piled up at one side, and around the pit and the pillar, in a semicircle, stood a great crowd of people, consisting of a few Russians and a great number of Napoleonic troops out of military rank; Prussians, Italians, and French, in various uniforms. At the right and left of the post stood files of French troops in blue uniforms with red epaulets, in gaiters and shakoes.

The condemned were stationed in the same order as they had occupied on the list—Pierre was number six—and they were brought up to the post. A number of drums were beaten suddenly on two sides, and Pierre felt that at these sounds a part of his very soul was torn from him. He lost the faculty of thinking and considering. He could only see and hear. He had only one desire left—that the terrible thing that had to be done should be done as speedily as possible. Pierre glanced at his comrades and observed them.

Two men at the end were shaven-headed convicts. One was tall, thin; the other, dark, hirsute, muscular, with a flattened nose. Number three was a domestic serf, forty-five years old, with grayish hair and a plump, well-fed body. The fourth was a very handsome peasant with a bushy, reddish beard, and dark eyes. Number five was a factory hand, a sallow, lean fellow of eighteen, who wore a loose coat.

Pierre listened to the French soldiers asking how the men should be shot: one at a time or two at a time.

"Two at a time," replied the senior officer, in a tone of cool composure.

A stir ran through the rank and file of the soldiery, and it was plain to see that all were making ready, and making ready not as men who make haste to do something that all comprehend, but rather as men make haste to finish some unusual task that must be done, yet is unpleasant and incomprehensible.

A French official wearing a scarf came up to the right-hand side of the file of the condemned, and read the sentence in Russian and in French.

Then two couples of the French soldiers advanced to the prisoners, and, by direction of the officer, pinioned the two convicts who stood at the end. The convicts were halted at the post, and while the death caps were being brought looked silently around them, as a disabled wild beast at bay glares at the approaching hunter.

One kept crossing himself, the other scratched his back and tried to force his lips to smile. The soldiers, with hasty hands, began to bind their eyes, to put on the death caps, and fasten the men to the post.

A dozen musketeers with their guns in their hands stepped forth with firm measured steps, and came to a halt eight paces from the post.

Pierre looked away so as not to see what was going to happen. Suddenly came a crash and a rattle which seemed to Pierre louder than the most terrific thunderclap, and he looked around. There was smoke, and some Frenchmen, with pale faces and trembling hands, were doing something at the pit.

Two others were led out. In the same way, with the same eyes, these two also gazed at them all, vainly, with their eyes alone—for their lips were silent—begging for help, and evidently not comprehending and not realizing what was going to be. They could not believe, because they alone knew what life meant to them, and therefore they neither understood nor believed that it could be taken from them.

Pierre wished not to look, and again turned his head away; but again his ears were assailed as by a terrible explosion, and, at the same time, he saw the smoke, the blood of someone, and the pale, frightened faces of the Frenchmen again occupied with something near the post—with trembling hands jostling one another.

Pierre, breathing heavily, glanced around him, as if to ask, "What is the meaning of this?"

The same question was expressed in all the eyes that met Pierre's.

On all the faces of the Russians, on the faces of the French soldiers and officers, all without exception, he read the same fear, horror and struggle that were in his heart.

"Yes, who is really doing this? They all suffer just exactly as I do. Who is it? Who?" Such was the question that flashed through Pierre's mind.

"Squad of the 86th, forward," someone commanded.

The man who was fifth on the list, and stood next to Pierre, was led out—alone!

Pierre did not comprehend that he was saved; that he and all the others had been brought out simply to be witnesses of the execution. With ever-increasing horror, but with no sense either of joy or of relief, he watched what was going on.

The fifth man was the factory workman in the loose coat. The moment they laid their hands on him he seemed overwhelmed with terror, and clung to Pierre.

Pierre shuddered and shook him off.

The factory hand could not walk. He was seized under the arms and dragged away, yelling something. When they brought him to the post he suddenly became quiet. An idea suddenly seemed to occur to him. Whether he realized that it was idle to scream, or felt that it was impossible that these men really meant to kill him, at all events he stood by the post waiting for his eyes to be bandaged, just as the others had done, and like the wild beast at bay glared around him with flashing eyes.

Some command must have been given; the command must have been followed by the reports of eight muskets. But Pierre, in spite of all his subsequent efforts to remember, heard not the slightest report from the firearms. He only saw how the factory hand for some reason suddenly leaned with all his weight on the ropes, how blood showed in two spots, and how the ropes themselves gave way from the weight of the suspended body, and the factory hand, unnaturally lolling his head, and with his legs doubling under him, sat down.

Pierre ran up to the post. No one detained him. The terror-stricken men were doing something or other about the factory hand. One old, mustached French soldier, as he untied the ropes, could not prevent his lower jaw from trembling. The body was laid on the ground. The soldiers clumsily and in all haste dragged it behind the post, and proceeded to push it into the pit. They all, evidently, were well assured that these men were criminals, and that it was necessary as quickly as possible to put out of sight all traces of their crime.

"This'll teach 'em to set fires," said one of the Frenchmen.

VIII

AFTER THE EXECUTION Pierre was separated from the others and placed by himself in a small, dilapidated and filthy church.

Just before evening a noncommissioned officer of the guard, accompanied by two soldiers, came into the church and explained to Pierre that he was reprieved and was to be put into the barracks of the prisoners of war.

Without comprehending what was said to him, Pierre got up and went with the soldiers. He was conducted to some huts at the upper part of the field, constructed of charred planks, beams, and scantling, and placed in one of them. He found himself in the dark, surrounded by a score of various men. He looked at these men, without comprehending who they were, why they were there, or what they wanted of him. He looked at the faces and forms, and they all alike seemed to him meaningless.

From the moment that Pierre had looked on that horrible massacre perpetrated by men who did not wish to do it, the mainspring by which everything had been coördinated and kept alive in his mind seemed to have been torn away, and everything had crumbled into a heap of meaningless rubble. Although he made no attempt to explain how it happened, his faith in the beneficent ordering of the universe, in the human soul, including his own, and in God, was destroyed.

He sat motionless and silent on the straw against the wall, now opening and now closing his eyes. But as soon as he closed his eyes he saw before him the factory workman's face, terrible, especially terrible, from its very simplicity, and the still more terrible faces of the reluctant executioners, with their anxious looks. And he would again open his eyes and stare unseeing into the darkness around him.

Beside him sat a little man all doubled up, of whose presence Pierre was made aware from the very first by the strong odor of sweat which emanated from him every time he moved.

"Well, have you seen pretty hard times, sir? Huh?" suddenly asked the little man.

And there was such an expression of gentleness and simplehearted goodness in his singsong voice that Pierre would have instantly replied, but his jaw trembled and tears came into his eyes. The little man at the same second, not giving Pierre time to betray his confusion, went on in the same pleasant voice:

"Ah, my dear friend, don't fret," said he, in that gentle, singsong, affectionate tone with which old Russian peasant women talk, "don't fret, my friend. An hour to suffer, but an age to live! That's the way it is, my dear!

But we live here, thank God, without offense. There's bad men and there's good men as well," said he, and, while still speaking, he got up on his knees with an agile motion, arose, and, coughing, went somewhere.

"Here, you little rascal, you've come, have you!" Pierre heard the same caressing voice at the other end of the hut, saying, "You remembered me, did you? There, there! That'll do!"

And the soldier, pushing off a puppy that was jumping up on him, returned to his place and sat down. He carried in his hand something wrapped up in a rag.

"Here's something to eat, sir," said he, returning to his former respectful tone, and unwrapping the bundle, he gave Pierre several baked potatoes. "We had thin soup for dinner. But potatoes are excellent."

Pierre had eaten nothing all day, and the smell of the potatoes seemed to him extraordinarily good. He thanked the soldier and began to eat.

"Well, how is it?" asked the soldier, with a smile, and taking one of the potatoes—"do you relish it?" He got out his jackknife, laid the potato on his palm and cut it into halves, sprinkled salt on from the rag, and offered it to Pierre. "Potatoes are supergood," he repeated. "Eat it that way!"

It seemed to Pierre that he had never eaten anything that tasted better.

"No, it makes no difference to me, one way or the other," said Pierre. "But why did they shoot those poor wretches? . . . The last one wasn't twenty."

"*Tts! tts!*" . . . said the little man. "A sin! A sin!" he quickly added; and as if words were always ready to his lips, winged to fly away very unexpectedly from them, he added:

"How was it, sir, that you stayed in Moscow?"

"I did not think they would come so soon. It was by accident I stayed," replied Pierre.

"And how came they to take you? Was it from your own house, my dear?"

"No; I was going to the fire, and then they seized me and tried me as an incendiary."

"Where the tribunal is, there is injustice," said the little man, sententiously.

"Have you been long here?" asked Pierre, as he munched the last potato.

"I? Since Sunday. I was taken from the hospital in Moscow."

"So you were a soldier, were you?"

"One of Apsheron's regiment. I was dying of fever. No one had ever told us anything about it. There were twenty of us lying there. We had no idea of such a thing . . . didn't dream of it!"

"Well, are you bored at being here?"

"How can I help being, my dear? My name is Platon; surname, Karatayef," he added, evidently so as to make Pierre's intercourse with him less formal. "They always called me 'the hawk' in the army. How can one help being bored, my dear? Moscow is the mother of our cities! How can one look on and see her destruction and not be sad? 'The worm gnaws the cabbage, but perishes before it'; that's the old folks' saying," he added quickly.

"How, how did you say that?" asked Pierre.

"I?" asked Karatayef. "Oh, I say, 'Not by our wit, but as God sees fit,'" said he, thinking he was repeating the former proverb. And immediately he went on:

"And you have property, haven't you, sir? And a house? Your cup must be full. And have a wife? And old folks alive?" he asked.

And Pierre, though he could not see because it was so dark, still knew that the soldier's lips were curved in a respectful smile of friendliness as he asked these questions.

He was evidently grieved to learn that Pierre had no parents, especially no mother.

"A wife for advice, a wife's mother for a welcome, but nothing sweeter than one's own little mother!" said he. "But have you any children?" he proceeded to inquire. Pierre's negative reply again evidently grieved him, and he hastened to add: "Well, you are young yet; God may give them. Only you should live in good understanding . . ."

"It's all the same to me now," said Pierre, involuntarily.

"Eh! My dear man!" exclaimed Platon. "There's no getting rid of the beggar's sack nor of the prison cell!" He got into a more comfortable attitude, cleared his throat, and was evidently preparing to spin a long yarn. "This was the way, my dear friend, I lived when I was at home," he began. "We had a rich estate . . . much land . . . peasants lived well, and we in the house too, glory to thee, O God! My own dad would go out and mow. Lived well, as *Christians* should! But it happened . . ."

And Platon Karatayef related a long story about how he went into another man's grove after firewood, and the watchman had caught him; how he had been flogged, tried, and sent off as a soldier.

"Well, my dear friend," said he, his voice altered by his smile, "it seemed a misfortune; on the contrary, good thing! My brother would have had to go if it hadn't been for my sin. But my younger brother had five children, while, you see, I had only a wife to leave. I had a little girl once, but God took her back before I went soldiering. I went home on leave once. I will tell you about it. I see they live better than they did before. Yard full of livestock; women at home; two brothers off at work. Only Mikhailo, the youngest, at home. And my dad, he says, says he, 'All my children are alike to me; no matter which finger you pinch, it hurts just the same. And if they had not taken Platon, Mikhailo would have had to go.' He took us all in front of the 'images'—would you believe it?—and made us stand there. 'Mikhailo,' says he, 'come here. Bow down to the ground before him; and you, woman, bow down; and you, little ones, bow down, all of you! Have you understood?' says he. And that's the way it is, my dear friend. 'No escaping Fate.' And we are always declaring, 'This is not good, or this is all wrong.' But our happiness is like water in a net; put it in, and it's full; take it out, and it's empty! That's the way it is."

And Platon shifted his seat on his straw.

After a short silence Platon arose: "Well, I suppose you'd like to go to sleep?" said he, and he began to cross himself, muttering, "Lord Jesus Christ! Saint Nikola! Frol and Lavra! Lord Jesus Christ, Saint Nikola! Frol and Lavra, Lord Jesus Christ—have mercy upon us and save us!" he said in conclusion, then bowed down to the very ground, got up, drew a deep sigh, and lay down on his straw. "Now, O God! Let me 'sleep like a stone and rise like a loaf,'" he exclaimed, and lay down, covering himself with his soldier's coat.

"What was that prayer you were repeating?" asked Pierre.

"Heh?" said Platon. He was already dozing. "Repeated what? I was praying to God. Don't you say your prayers?"

"Certainly I say my prayers," replied Pierre. "But what was that about Frol and Lavra?"

"Why," swiftly replied Platon, "that's the horses' saints. For we must have pity on the cattle," said Karatayef. "Oh, you rascal! You have come back, have you? You want to get warm, do you, you nice little bitch?" said he, fondling the puppy at his feet, and, turning over again, instantly fell asleep.

Outside in the distance were heard the sounds of wailing and yells, and through the cracks in the hut the glare of the fire could be seen, but within it was dark and still. It was long before Pierre could go to sleep; and he lay in his place in the darkness with wide-open eyes, listening to Platon's measured snoring as he lay near him, and feeling that that formerly ruined world was now arising again in his soul, in new beauty and with new and steadfast foundations.

The hut where Pierre was confined, and where he spent four weeks, contained twenty-three soldiers, three officers, and two civilian officials—all prisoners.

Afterwards all of them seemed to be misty memories to Pierre; but Platon Karatayef forever remained in his mind as a most powerful and precious recollection, the very embodiment of all that was good and worthy and truly Russian.

When on the following day, at dawn, Pierre saw his neighbor, the first impression of something rotund was fully confirmed; Platon's whole figure, in his French overcoat belted with a rope, in his forage cap and birch-bark shoes, was rotund. His head was perfectly round; his back, his chest, his shoulders, even his arms, which he always carried as if he were ready to throw them around something, were round; his pleasant smile and his large, thick brows and his gentle eyes were round.

Platon Karatayef must have been more than fifty, to judge by his stories of campaigns in which he had taken part as a soldier. He himself had no idea and could never have told with any accuracy how old he was. But his teeth, brilliantly white and strong, were always displayed in two unbroken rows whenever he laughed—which he often did—and not one was not good and sound. There was no trace of gray in beard or hair, and his whole frame had the appearance of agility and especially of sturdiness and endurance.

His face, in spite of a multitude of delicate round wrinkles, gave the impression of innocence and youth; his voice was agreeable in its melodious singsong. But the chief peculiarity of his speech consisted in its spontaneity and shrewdness. He evidently never thought of what he said or what he was going to say. And from this arose the irresistible persuasiveness that was found in the rapidity and certainty of his intonations.

His physical powers and activity were so great during the early part of their term of captivity that it seemed as if he did not know what weariness or ill-health meant. Every morning and evening, as he lay on his couch of straw, he would say, "Lord, let me 'sleep like a stone and rise like a loaf.'"

When he got up in the morning he always shrugged his shoulders in a certain way and said, "Turn over when you lie down, shake yourself when you get up."

And, in point of fact, all he had to do was to lie down and instantly he would be sound asleep; and all he had to do was to shake himself and without a second's delay he would be ready to take up anything, just as children, when they are once up, take to their toys.

He was a jack-of-all-trades, but neither very good nor very bad at any. He could bake, cook, sew, cut hair, cobble boots. He was always busy, and only when it came night did he allow himself social converse, though he enjoyed it, and to sing. He sang his songs, not as singers usually sing, knowing that they will be heard; but he sang as the birds sing, evidently because it was just as much a necessity for him as it was for him to stretch himself or to walk. And these sounds were always gentle, soft, almost like a woman's, plaintive, and his face while he was singing was very grave.

The proverbs of which he made so much use were not that generally coarse and vulgar slang which soldiers are apt to employ, but were genuine popular "saws," which seem quite insignificant when taken out of context, but which suddenly acquire a meaning of deep wisdom when applied appositely.

Special attachments, friendships, loves, as Pierre understood them, Karatayef had none; but he liked all men, and lived in a loving way with all with whom his life brought him into contact, and especially with men— not any particular men—but with such as were in his sight. He loved his dog; he loved his comrades and the French; he loved Pierre, who was his companion; but Pierre felt that Karatayef, in spite of all the affectionate spirit he manifested toward him—and which he could not help giving as a tribute to Pierre's spiritual life—would not for one moment grieve over separation. And Pierre began to have the same feeling toward Karatayef.

Platon Karatayef was, in the eyes of all the other prisoners, a most ordinary soldier. They called him "little hawk," good-naturedly quizzed him, made him do odd jobs for them.

But for Pierre he remained forever what he had seemed to him the first

574

night—the incomprehensible, "all around" and eternal personification of the spirit of simplicity and truth.

Every word Platon spoke and everything he did was the manifestation of that, to him, incomprehensible activity, his life. But his life, as he himself looked at it, had no sense as a separate existence. It had sense only as it was a part of the great whole of which he was constantly conscious. His words and deeds flowed from him as regularly, unavoidably, and spontaneously as the fragrance exhales from a flower. He could not comprehend either the object or the significance of words or deeds taken separately.

IX

PRINCESS MARIA, having learned from Nikolai that her brother was with the Rostofs at Yaroslavl, immediately, in spite of her aunt's dissuasion, made arrangements to join him, not alone, but with her nephew.

Her outfit consisted of the vast, princely coach in which she had made the journey to Voronezh, a small carriage, and a baggage wagon. She was accompanied by Mlle. Bourienne, Nikolusha with his tutor, the old nurse, three maids, Tikhon, a young footman, and a courier whom her aunt sent with her.

During this trying journey, Mlle. Bourienne, Dessalles, and Princess Maria's servants were amazed at her determination and activity. She was the last of all to retire, she was the first of all to rise, and no difficulties sufficed to daunt her. Thanks to her activity and energy, which inspired her companions, at the end of the second week they reached Yaroslavl.

During the latter part of her stay in Voronezh, Princess Maria had experienced the keenest joy of her life. Her love for Rostof no longer tormented her or excited her. This love filled her whole soul and became an inseparable part of her being, and she no longer struggled against it. Of late, she had persuaded herself—though she never said this in so many words even to herself—that she loved, and was loved in return.

Nikolai had not intimated by a single word that now, in case of Prince Andrei's restoration to health, the former relations between him and Natasha would be renewed, but Princess Maria saw by Nikolai's face that he knew it was possible and had thought of it.

The heavy carriage, rumbling, jolting, and swaying, stopped. The steps were let down with a clatter. The door was thrown open. At the left was water—the great river; at the right a doorstep; on the doorstep were servants and a young, ruddy-faced girl with a long, dark plait of hair, who wore what seemed to Princess Maria a disagreeably hypocritical smile. This was Sonya.

The princess got out and mounted the steps; the hypocritically smiling young girl said, "This way, this way"; and the princess found herself in the anteroom, in the presence of an elderly woman with an Eastern type of face, who, with a flurried expression, came swiftly to meet her. This was the old countess.

She threw her arms around Princess Maria and began to kiss her.

"My child!" she exclaimed, "I love you, and I have known you for a long time."

In spite of all her agitation the princess realized that this was the countess, and that she must say something to her. She, without knowing how she did it, murmured a few polite words in French, in the same tone in which those spoken to her were said, and then she asked:

"How is he?"

"The doctor says that there is no danger," said the countess; but even while she made that remark she sighed and raised her eyes to heaven, and in this action contradicted what she had just said.

"Where is he? May I see him? May I?" asked the princess.

"Directly, princess, directly, dear friend! Is this his son?" she asked, turning to Nikolusha, who had come in with Dessalles. "There will be room enough for us all. It is a large house. . . . oh, what a lovely little boy!"

The countess took the princess into the drawing-room. Sonya engaged in conversation with Mlle. Bourienne. The countess fondled the boy. The old count came into the room to pay his respects to the princess.

The old count had completely altered since the princess had seen him the last time. Then he was a lively, jovial, self-confident little old man; now he seemed like a melancholy wreck of himself. As he talked with the countess he kept looking around, as if he were asking all present whether he was doing the proper thing.

"This is my niece," said the count, introducing Sonya. "You have not met her, have you, princess?"

The princess turned to her, and, trying to overmaster the feeling of hostility which this young lady caused in her heart, she kissed her. But it was hard for her because of the want of harmony between all these people and what was in her own heart.

"Where is he?" she asked again, addressing no one in particular.

"He is downstairs. Natasha is with him," replied Sonya, coloring. "They've sent word to him. I think you must be tired, princess."

Tears of vexation came to the princess' eyes. She turned away, and was going once more to ask the countess how she could go to him, when light, impetuous, one might almost say gay, steps were heard in the adjoining room. The princess glanced round and saw Natasha almost running—that same Natasha who, when she had last seen her in Moscow, had so completely failed to please her.

The princess had scarcely glanced into the face of this Natasha before she perceived that this was a genuine sympathizer in her grief, and hence her friend. She went to meet her, and, throwing her arms around her, melted into tears on her neck.

As soon as Natasha, who had been sitting by Prince Andrei's bedside, learned of the princess' arrival, she had quietly left the room, and with the same swift, and, as it seemed to the Princess Maria, gay steps, hurried to meet her.

On her agitated face there was only one expression when she came into the room—the expression of love, unbounded love for him, for his sister, for everything that was near and dear to this beloved man, the expression of pity, of sympathy for others, and a passionate desire to give herself completely to the task of helping him in any way. It was evident that at that moment there was no room in Natasha's soul for thoughts about herself, or about her relations toward him.

The sensitive Princess Maria, at the first glance into Natasha's face, realized all this, and, with a bitter sweetness, she wept on her neck.

"Let us go to him; come, Maria!" exclaimed Natasha, leading her into the next room.

Princess Maria looked up, wiped her eyes, and was about to ask Natasha a question. She felt that from her she could ask and learn all she wanted to know.

"How . . ." she began to ask, but suddenly paused. She felt that her question could not be asked or answered in words. Natasha's face and eyes would tell her everything more clearly and with deeper meaning.

Natasha looked at her, but it seemed she was in too great fear or doubt either to tell or not to tell all she knew; she seemed to feel that, in the presence of those lucid eyes, searching the very depths of her soul, it was impossible not to tell the whole truth, everything as she herself saw it. Natasha's lip suddenly trembled, the ugly wrinkles grew more pronounced around her mouth, and she burst into tears and hid her face in her hands.

Princess Maria understood all. But still she hoped, and she asked in words in which she had no faith:

"But how is his wound? What is his general condition?"

"You . . . you . . . will see for yourself," was all that Natasha could manage to say.

The two waited for some time downstairs next to his room, so as to finish crying and to go to him with composed faces.

"How has his whole illness gone? Has the change for the worse been of recent occurrence? When did *this* take place?" asked Princess Maria.

Natasha had told her that during the first part of the time there was danger from his fever and suffering, but that at Troitsa this had passed off and the doctor had only feared gangrene. But even this danger of mortification had been avoided. When they reached Yaroslavl, the wound began to suppurate (Natasha understood all about suppuration and such things), and the doctor said that the suppuration might take its normal course. There had been some fever. The doctor declared that this fever was not ominous. "But two days ago," Natasha said, "*this* suddenly came upon him."—She restrained her sobs.—"I don't know why, but you will see how he is."

"Has he grown weaker? Has he grown thin?" . . . asked the princess.

"No, not exactly, but thinner. You will see. Ah, Marie! he is too good; he cannot, cannot live . . . because . . ."

When Natasha, with her ordinary composure, opened the door of his room, allowing the princess to enter before her, Princess Maria felt that the sobs were already swelling her throat. In spite of her preparations, her endeavors to compose herself, she knew that she would not be able to see him without tears.

Princess Maria comprehended what Natasha meant by the phrase, *"Two days ago this suddenly came upon him."* She realized what it meant that he had suddenly grown gentle; this sweetness and humility were the symptons of death. As she entered the doorway, she already saw in her fancy the face of her darling Andrei as she had known it in childhood, gentle, sweet, full of feeling, sensitive in a way which in later days had rarely shown itself, and which had, therefore, always made such a vivid impression on her. She knew he would speak to her those subdued, affectionate words such as her father had spoken just before he died, and that she would not be able to endure it and would burst into tears before him.

But sooner or later it had to be, and she entered the room. The sobs rose higher and higher in her throat, as, with greater and greater distinctness, with her nearsighted eyes, she distinguished his form and searched his features, and then saw his face and met his eyes.

He lay on a couch, propped up with pillows, and wrapped in a squirrel-skin dressing gown. He was thin and pale. One thin, transparently white hand held his handkerchief; with the other he was, by a gentle motion of the fingers, caressing his soft whiskers, which had been allowed to grow. His eyes were turned toward the visitors.

When Princess Maria saw his face and her eyes met his, she suddenly modified the haste of her steps, and felt that her tears were suddenly dried and her sobs relieved. As she caught the expression of his face and eyes she suddenly grew awestruck, and felt that she was guilty.

"But what am I guilty of?" she asked herself.

"Because thou art alive, and art thinking of the future, while I?"—was the reply of his cold, stern look.

In that look of his, not outward from within, but turned inward upon himself, there was almost an expression of hostility as he slowly turned his eyes on his sister and Natasha. He exchanged kisses with his sister and shook hands as usual.

"How are you, Maria? How did you get here?" he asked, but his voice had the same monotonous and alien sound that was in his look. If he had uttered a desperate cry, this cry would have filled Princess Maria with less horror than the sound of his voice. "And have you brought Nikolusha?" he asked, in the same slow, indifferent way, and evidently finding it hard to recollect.

"How are you now?" inquired Princess Maria, amazed, herself, at her question.

"That you must ask the doctor," he replied; and evidently collecting his strength, so as to be more gracious, he said with his lips alone (it was evident that he did not think at all of what he was saying), "Thank you for coming!"

Princess Maria pressed his hand. He almost noticeably frowned at the pressure of her hand. He was silent, and she did not know what to say. She now understood what had come over him two days before. In his words, in his tone, especially in this glance of his, this cold, almost hostile look, could be perceived that alienation from all that is of this world, that is so terrible for a living man to witness. He evidently found it difficult to understand the interests of life, but at the same time one could feel that this was so, not because he was deprived of the power of remembrance, but because his mind was turned to something else, which the living do not and cannot comprehend, and which was absorbing him entirely.

X

PRINCE ANDREI not only knew he was going to die, but also felt that he was dying, that he was already halfway toward death.

He experienced a consciousness of alienation from everything earthly, and a strange beatific exhilaration of being. Without impatience and without anxiety, he waited for what was before him.

That ominous Eternal Presence, unknown and far away, which had never once ceased, throughout all his life, to haunt his senses, was now near at hand, and, by reason of his strange exhilaration, was almost comprehensible and palpable.

Before, he had feared the end. Twice he had experienced that terribly tormenting sense of the fear of death, of the end, and now he did not realize it.

The first time he had experienced that feeling was when the shell was spinning like a top before him, and he looked at the stubble field, at the shrubbery, at the sky, and knew that death was before him.

When he waked to consciousness after his wound, and in his soul, for an instant freed from the burden of life that crushed him, there had sprung up that flower of love eternal, unbounded, independent of all life, he no longer feared death, and thought no more of it.

During the tormenting hours of loneliness and half-delirium he had spent since he was wounded, the more he pondered over this new-found source of eternal love, the more he became alienated from the earthly life, though the process was an unconscious one. To love everything, all men, always to sacrifice self for love's sake, meant to love no one in particular, meant not to live this mundane life. And the more he imbued himself with this source of love, the more he let go of life, and the more absolutely he broke down that terrible impediment which, if love is absent, holds between life and death.

When, during this first period, he remembered that he must die, he said to himself, "Well, then, so much the better."

But after that night at Mitishchi, when in his semidelirium she whom he had longed for appeared before him, and when he, pressing his lips to her hand, had wept gentle tears of joy, then love for one woman imperceptibly took possession of his heart and again attached it to life. And joyful but anxious thoughts began to recur to him. As he remembered the moment at the field station, when he had seen Kuragin, he could not now renew that former feeling; he was tortured by the question: "Is he alive?" But he dared not make the inquiry.

His illness had followed its physical course, but what Natasha had spoken of as *having come over him* happened two days before the Princess Maria's arrival. This was the last moral combat between life and death, and death had been victorious. It was the unexpected discovery that he still prized his life, which presented itself in the guise of his love for Natasha, and the last victorious attack of horror before the unknown.

It was evening. As was usually the case after dinner, he had been in a slightly feverish condition, and his mind was unnaturally acute. Sonya was sitting by the table. Suddenly, a sense of bliss took possession of him.

"Ah! she has come!" he said to himself.

In point of fact, Sonya's place was occupied by Natasha, who had just come in with noiseless steps.

Ever since the time when she had begun to be his nurse, he had always experienced this physical sense of her presence.

She sat in the armchair, with her side toward him, shading his eyes from the candlelight, and knitting stockings. (She had learned to knit stockings because once Prince Andrei had told her that no one made such admirable nurses for the sick as old nurses who are always knitting stockings, because there is something very soothing about the process of knitting.) Her slender fingers swiftly plied the occasionally clicking needles, and the pensive profile of her bent head was full in his sight. She moved—the ball of yarn rolled from her lap. She started, glanced at him, and, shading the candle with her hand, with a cautious, lithe and graceful movement, she bent over, picked up the ball, and resumed her former position.

He looked at her without stirring, and noticed that after she had picked up the ball she had wanted to draw a long breath, with her full bosom, but had refrained from doing so and had cautiously masked her sigh.

At the Troitsa Monastery they had talked over the past, and he had told her that in case he lived he should eternally thank God for his wound, which had brought him back to her; but from that time they had not spoken of the future.

"Can it possibly be?" he was now musing, as he looked at her and listened to the slight metallic click of her knitting needles, "can it be that Fate has so strangely brought us together again only that I may die? . . . Can it be that the true meaning of life was revealed to me only that I might live in a lie? I love her more than all else in the world. But what can I do if I love her?" he asked himself, and he suddenly, in spite of himself, groaned, as he often did, from habit acquired while he had been suffering.

Hearing this sound, Natasha laid down her stocking, bent nearer to him, and, suddenly noticing his beaming eyes, she went over to him and bent down to him.

"Haven't you been asleep?"

"No; I have been looking at you for a long time. I knew by instinct when you came in. No one except you gives me such a sense of gentle restfulness . . . such light! I feel like weeping from very joy."

Natasha moved still closer to him. Her face was radiant with solemn delight.

"Natasha, I love you too dearly! More than all in the world!"

"And I?" She turned away for an instant. "Why 'too dearly'?" she asked.

"Why too dearly? . . . Well, tell me what you think—what you think in your heart, in the depths of your heart! Will I get well? How does it seem to you?"

"I am sure of it, sure of it," Natasha almost screamed, with a passionate motion seizing both his hands.

He was silent.

"How good it would be!" And, taking her hand, he kissed it.

Natasha was happy and agitated; and instantly she remembered that this was all wrong, that he needed to be kept perfectly quiet.

"But now you have not been asleep," said she, calming her delight. "Try to get a nap. . . . Please."

He had relinquished her hand, after pressing it once again, and she had gone back to the candle and resumed her former position. Twice she had looked at him; his eyes had met hers. She had set herself a stint on the stocking and resolved that she would not look up until she had finished it.

In point of fact, soon after this he had closed his eyes and gone to sleep. He had not slept long, but had awakened suddenly in a cold perspiration.

During his nap, his mind had still been occupied with the constant subject of his thoughts of late—life and death. And more than anything else of death. He felt that it was near.

"Love? What is love?" he asked himself.

"Love stands in the way of death. Love is life. All, all that I understand, I understand solely because I love. All is, all exists, simply and solely because I love. All is summed up in this alone. Love is God; and death for me, a tiny particle of love, means returning into the universal and eternal source of love."

These thoughts had seemed consoling to him. But they were only thoughts. There was something lacking in them, something that was exclusive and personal—there was no basis of reality. And he was a prey to the same restlessness and lack of clearness.

He had fallen asleep.

It had seemed to him, in his dream, that he was lying in the same room in which he was actually lying, but that he was not wounded, but quite well. Many persons, insignificant, indifferent, appeared before him. He was talking with them, discussing something of no earthly consequence. They were preparing to go somewhere. He dimly comprehended that all this was a mere waste of time, and that he had something of real importance to accomplish, but still he went on talking, filling them with amazement at his words, which were witty but devoid of sense. Gradually, but imperceptibly, all these persons began to disappear, and his attention was wholly occupied by the question of a closed door. He got up and went to the door, with the intention of pushing the bolt and closing it. *Everything* depended on whether or not he succeeded in closing it. He started, he tried to make haste, but his legs refused to move, and he knew he would not have time to close the door, but still he morbidly put forth all his energies. And a painful anguish of fear seized him. And this fear was the fear of death: Behind the door *It* was standing.

But by the time that he feebly, awkwardly dragged himself to the door, this *something* horrible, pushing its way from the other side, broke through. Something that was not human—Death—was pushing the door open, and he must keep it shut. He clutched the door, exerted his final energies—not indeed to shut it, for that was impossible, but to hold it; his energies, however, were weak and maladroit, and, crushing him with its horror, the door opened and closed again.

Once more the pressure came from without. His last, superhuman energies were vain, and both wings of the door noiselessly swung open. *It* came in, and it was Death.

And Prince Andrei was dying.

But at the very instant that he was dying, Prince Andrei remembered that he was asleep, and at the very instant that he was dying, he made one last effort and awoke.

"Yes, that was *death*. I died—I woke up. Yes, death is an awakening."

This thought had suddenly flashed through his soul, and the veil which till then had covered the unknown was lifted from before his spiritual eyes. He felt as it were a deliverance from the bonds which before had fastened him down, and that strange buoyancy which from that time forth did not forsake him.

When he had awakened in a cold sweat and stirred on his couch, Natasha had gone to him and asked him what was the matter. He had made no reply, and, not understanding what she had said, had given her a strange look.

This was what had taken place two days before Princess Maria's arrival. From that day, as the doctor said, his wasting fever had taken a turn for the worse, but Natasha had no need to depend on what the doctor said; she could see for herself those terrible symptoms which no longer allowed room for doubt.

From that time forth had begun for Prince Andrei, simultaneously with the awakening from his dream, the awakening from life. And, considering the length of life, this seemed to him no slower than the awakening from the dream when compared to the length of his nap.

There was nothing terrible and nothing cruel in this relatively slow awakening.

The last days and hours glided away peacefully and simply. Both Princess Maria and Natasha, who stayed constantly by his side, felt this. They did not weep or tremble, and the last part of the time, as they themselves realized, they were watching, not the man himself—for he was no more; he had gone from them—but simply the most immediate remembrance of him, simply his body. The feelings of both were so strong that the external, terrible side of death had no effect on them, and they found it unnecessary to give vent to their grief. They wept neither in his presence nor when away from him, and they never talked about him together. They felt they could not express in words what was real to their understandings. They both saw how he was sinking, deeper and deeper, slowly and peacefully, away from them into the *whither*, and they both knew that this was inevitable and that it was well. He was confessed and partook of the sacrament. All came to bid him farewell.

When his little son was brought, he kissed him and turned away, not because his heart was sore and filled with pity (Princess Maria and Natasha understood this), but simply because he supposed it was all that was required of him. When he was told he should give his son his blessing, he did what was required of him, and looked around as if to ask whether it was necessary to do anything more.

When the last gentle spasm shook the body, as it was deserted by the spirit, the princess and Natasha were present.

"It is over!" said Princess Maria, after his body had lain motionless and growing cold for several moments. Natasha came to the couch, looked into his dead eyes, and made haste to close them. She closed them and did not kiss them, but reverently touched that which had been the most immediate remembrance of him.

"Where has he gone? Where is he now?"

When the mortal frame, washed and clad, lay in the coffin on the table, they all went in to say farewell, and all shed tears.

Nikolusha wept from the tormenting perplexity that tore his young heart.

The countess and Sonya wept from sympathy for Natasha, and because he was no more.

The old count wept because very soon, as it seemed to him, he also would have to take this terrible step.

Natasha and the princess also wept now, but they wept not because of their own personal sorrow; they wept from a reverent emotion which took possession of their souls in presence of the simple and solemn mystery of death, which had been accomplished before their eyes.

1812

France is threatened everywhere; the European nations are rising against Napoleon, the grande armée *is harried by the stubborn Russian defenders and is in serious danger of annihilation by cold and hunger. Napoleon's vast empire is crumbling, though he does not know it yet.*

Part Thirteenth

THE Russian army, which had been rolling, like a ball, in the direction given it by a blow, all through the campaign and especially at the Battle of Borodino, assumed its natural position of stable equilibrium as soon as the force of the blows diminished and no new ones fell.

Kutuzof's merit lay not in what is called "a stroke of genius" in making a strategical maneuver, but simply in the fact that he was the only one who understood the meaning of what was taking place about him.

He alone understood what the inactivity of the French army signified, he alone persisted in declaring that the Battle of Borodino was a victory for the Russians. He alone—the very man who, it would seem, from his position as commander-in-chief, ought to have been disposed to favor aggressive measures—used all his power to restrain the Russian army from undertaking useless battles.

The beast wounded at Borodino lay where it had been left by the escaping huntsman; but whether it was alive, or whether it still had strength left, or whether it was hiding itself, the huntsman knew not.

Suddenly was heard this wild beast's cry.

The cry of this wounded beast—the French army—the premonition of its approaching doom, was the sending of Lauriston to Kutuzof's camp with a request for peace.

Napoleon, with his conviction that whatever it occurred to him to do was as right as right could be, wrote to Kutuzof the first words that entered his mind. They had no sense whatever.

Prince Kutuzof (he wrote), I send you one of my general aides to discuss with you on various matters of interest. I wish your highness to repose confidence in what he will say, especially when he expresses the sentiments of esteem and respect which I have long felt for you personally. This letter having no other purpose, I pray God, prince, that He have you in His holy and beneficent care.

(Signed) NAPOLEON.

Moscow, October 30, 1812.

"I should be cursed by posterity if I were regarded as the first to move toward any compromise. Such is the present spirit of our people," replied Kutuzof, and he continued to put forth all his energies to keep his troops from a battle.

During the month spent by the French army in the pillage of Moscow and by the Russian army in tranquil recuperation at Tarutino, a change had taken place in the relative strength of the two armies—their spirit and effectives—in consequence of which a preponderance of strength began to show itself on the side of the Russians. Although the condition of the French army and its effectives were unknown to the Russians, yet, as soon as the relative position was changed, the inevitability of an attack was shown by a multitude of symptoms.

These symptoms were the sending of Lauriston; and the abundance of provisions at Tarutino; and the reports coming in from all sides of the inactivity and disorderliness of the French; and the replenishing of our regiments with recruits; and the fine weather, and the long rest accorded to the Russian soldiers; and the general impatience caused among the troops by the long rest, and their desire to finish the work for which they had been brought together; and the curiosity about what was going on in the French army, which had been lost from sight so long; and the audacity with which now the Russian outposts skirmished around the French stationed at Tarutino; and the news of easy victories over the French won by Russian peasants and "partisans," and the jealousy aroused by this; and the desire of vengeance kindled in every man's soul from the moment that the French occupied Moscow; and, above all, the indefinite but genuine consciousness, which filled the heart of every soldier, that the relative positions were reversed and the superiority was on our side.

The material relations were changed, and the attack was becoming inevitable. And instantly, just as the chime of bells in the clock begin to strike and to play when the hand has accomplished its full circuit of the hour, so in the higher circles, by the correspondingly essential correlation of forces, the increased motion was effectuated—the whizzing of wheels and the playing of the chimes.

THE RUSSIAN ARMY was directed by Kutuzof and his staff, and by the sovereign, who was at Petersburg.

Even before news of the abandonment of Moscow had reached Petersburg, a circumstantial plan of the whole war had been drawn up and sent to Kutuzof for his guidance. Although the plan was made with the presupposition that Moscow was still in our hands, it was approved by Kutuzof's staff and accepted as the basis of action.

Kutuzof merely wrote that plans made at a distance were always hard to carry out. And then further instructions, meant to solve the difficulties that might arise, were sent, and individuals were charged to watch Kutuzof's movements and to send back reports.

On October 14 the sovereign wrote the following letter, which was received by Kutuzof after the Battle of Tarutino:

Prince Mikhail Ilarionovitch!

Since September 14, Moscow has been in the hands of the enemy. Your latest reports are dated October 2; and in all this time not only has nothing been done in the way of a demonstration against the enemy and to deliver the first capital, but according to your last reports you have been retreating again. Serpukhof is already occupied by a detachment of the enemy, and Tula, with its famous arsenal so indispensable to the army, is in peril.

From General Winzengerode's report, I see that a body of the enemy, of ten thousand men, is moving along the Petersburg road. Another of several thousand men is marching upon Dmitrovo. A third is advancing on the road to Vladimir. A fourth, of considerable size, is between Ruza and Mozhaisk. Napoleon himself, on the seventh, was at Moscow.

Since, according to all this information, the enemy has scattered his forces in strong detachments, since Napoleon himself is still at Moscow with his Guard, is it possible that the strength of the enemy before you has been so great as to prevent you from taking the offensive?

One might assume, on the contrary, with certainty, that he would pursue you with detachments, or at least by an army corps far weaker than the army which you command.

It seems as if, profiting by these circumstances, you might with advantage have attacked an enemy weaker than yourself and exterminated him, or, at least, by obliging him to retire, have regained a great part of the province now occupied by the enemy, and at the same time have averted the peril of Tula and our other cities of the interior.

Responsibility will rest on you if the enemy send a considerable body of troops to Petersburg to threaten this capital, which is almost destitute of troops; for, with the army confided to you, if you act with firmness and celerity, you have all the means needed to avert this new misfortune.

Bear in mind that you are still bound to answer before an insulted country for the loss of Moscow!

You have already had proof of my readiness to reward you. This good will shall not grow less, but I and Russia have a right to demand from you all the zeal, fortitude, and success that your intellect, your military talents, and the gallantry of the troops under your command assure us.

But while this letter, which shows how the state of things was regarded in Petersburg, was on its way, Kutuzof could no longer restrain the army which he commanded from taking the offensive, and the battle had already been fought.

On October 14, a Cossack, Shapovalof, while on patrol duty, killed one hare and shot at another. In pursuing the wounded hare, Shapovalof struck into the forest at some distance and stumbled upon the left flank of Murat's army, which was encamped without outposts.

The Cossack laughingly told his comrades how he had almost fallen into the hands of the French. A cadet who heard this tale told it to his commander.

The Cossack was sent for and questioned. The Cossack chiefs wished to profit by this chance to get horses; but one of them, who was acquainted at headquarters, told a staff general what had occurred.

Lately the relations of the army staff had been strained to the last degree. Yermolof, several days before, had gone to Benigsen and implored him to use all his influence with the commander-in-chief in favor of assuming the offensive.

"If I did not know you," replied Benigsen, "I should think that you did not want what you were asking for. I have only to advise anything and his serene highness will do exactly the contrary."

The news brought in by the Cossacks being confirmed by scouts sent out, it became evident that the time was ripe for action.

The strained cord broke, and the clock whizzed and the chimes began to play. Notwithstanding all his supposed power, his intellect, his experience, and his knowledge of men, Kutuzof—taking into consideration Benigsen's report sent directly to the sovereign, and the one desire expressed by all of his generals, and the sovereign's supposed wishes, and the information brought by the Cossacks—could no longer restrain a movement that was inevitable, and gave the order for something that he regarded as useless and harmful; consented to an accomplished fact!

The plan of attack drawn up by Toll was very admirable. Just as for the Battle of Austerlitz it had been laid down in the "disposition": "the first column marches this way and that way, the second column marches this way and that way"; so here also, only not in German, it was prescribed where the first column and the second column should march.

And all these columns, on paper, were to unite at a designated time and at a designated place, and annihilate the enemy. Everything was beautifully foreseen and provided for as in all "dispositions," and as in all "dispositions," not a single column was in its place at the right time.

Several of the columns halted, stacking their arms, and threw themselves down on the cold ground, supposing that they had reached their destinations; others—the majority—marched the whole night, and came to places which were obviously not their destinations.

Count Orlof-Denisof with his Cossacks—the smallest detachment of all—was the only one who reached the right place and at the right time. This detachment was halted at the very edge of the forest, on the narrow footpath that led between the villages of Stromilova and Dmitrovskoye.

Before dawn, Count Orlof, who had fallen asleep, was aroused. A deserter from the French camp had been brought in. This was a Polish noncommissioned officer from Poniatowsky's corps. He explained in Polish that he had deserted because he had been insulted in the French service, that he ought long before to have been promoted to be an officer, that he was the bravest of them all, and therefore he had given them up, and was anxious to have his revenge on them. He declared that Murat was spending the night only two-thirds of a mile from there, and that if they would give him an escort of a hundred men he would take him alive.

Count Orlof-Denisof consulted with his comrades. The proposal was too attractive to be refused. All offered to go; all advised to make the attempt. After many discussions and calculations, Major General Grekof, with two regiments of Cossacks, decided to go with the noncommissioned officer.

"Now mark my word," said Count Orlof-Denisof to the Pole, as he dismissed him, "in case you have lied, I will have you hanged like a dog; but if you have told the truth—a hundred gold pieces!"

The noncommissioned officer, with a resolute face, made no reply to these words, leaped into the saddle, and rode off with Grekof, who had swiftly mustered his men. They vanished in the forest.

Count Orlof, pinched by the coolness of the morning which was now beginning to break, excited and made anxious by the responsibility of letting Grekof go, went out a little from the forest and began to reconnoiter the enemy's camp, which could now be seen dimly in the light of the dawn and the dying watch fires.

At Count Orlof's right, on an open declivity, our columns were to show themselves. Count Orlof glanced in that direction; but, although they would have been visible for a long distance, these columns were not in sight. But in the French camp, it seemed to Count Orlof-Denisof, who also put great confidence in what his clear-sighted aide said, there were signs of life.

"Ah! too late!" said Count Orlof, as he gazed at the camp.

Just as often happens when a man in whom we have reposed confidence is no longer under our eyes, it suddenly seemed to him clear and beyond question that the Polish noncommissioned officer was a traitor, that he had deceived them, and the whole attack was going to be spoiled by the absence of the two regiments which this man had led off no one knew where. How could they possibly seize the commander-in-chief from among such a mass of troops? "Of course he lied, that scoundrel!" exclaimed the count.

"We can call them back," said one of the suite, who, exactly like Count Orlof-Denisof, felt a distrust in the enemy on seeing the camp.

"Ha? So? . . . What do you think? Shall we let them go on, or not?" "Do you order them recalled?"

"Yes, recall them, recall them," cried Count Orlof, coming to a sudden decision, and looking at his watch. "It would be too late; it's quite light."

And the adjutant galloped off through the forest after Grekof. When Grekof returned, Count Orlof-Denisof, excited both by the failure of this enterprise and by his disappointment at the nonarrival of the infantry columns, which had not even yet showed up, and by the proximity of the enemy—all the men of his division experienced the same thing—decided to attack.

He gave the whispered command: "To horse!"

They fell into their places. They crossed themselves.—"God be with us! . . . Away!"

"Hurra-a-a-ah!" rang through the forest, and the Cossack companies, one after another, as if they were poured out of a sack, flew with lances poised across the brook and against the camp.

One desperate, startled yell from the first Frenchman who saw the Cossacks, and all in the camp, suddenly awakened from their dreams, fled undressed in all directions, abandoning their artillery, their muskets, and their horses.

If the Cossacks had followed the French without heeding what was back of them and around them, they would have captured Murat and his whole force. This was what the officers wanted. But it was an impossibility to make the Cossacks stir when once they had begun to occupy themselves with the booty and their prisoners. No one would heed the word of command.

Fifteen hundred prisoners were captured, thirty-eight cannons, flags, and—what was more important for the Cossacks—horses, saddles, blankets, and various articles. They must needs oversee all this, secure the prisoners and the cannon, divide the spoils, shout, and even quarrel among themselves; with all this the Cossacks were busying themselves.

The French, finding that they were no longer pursued, came to their senses, formed their lines, and began to fire. Orlof-Denisof was all the time expecting the infantry columns, and refrained from further offensive action.

The whole battle was summed up in what Orlof-Denisof's Cossacks did;

the rest of the troops simply lost several hundred men absolutely uselessly.

In consequence of this battle, Kutuzof received a diamond order; Benigsen, also, some diamonds and a hundred thousand rubles; the others, according to their ranks, also received many agreeable tokens, and after this battle some further changes were made in the staff.

The Battle of Tarutino evidently failed of attaining the object which Toll had in mind—to lead the troops into the battle in proper order according to the "disposition"; or the object which Count Orlof may have had in mind—to take Murat prisoner; or that which Benigsen and many others may have had—of destroying the whole corps at a single blow; or the object of the officer who wished to fall in the battle and distinguish himself; or that of the Cossack who was desirous of getting more booty than he got, and so on.

But if the object of the battle was what actually resulted, and which, at that time, was the chief desire of all the Russians—the driving of the French from Russia and the destruction of their army—then it is perfectly clear that the Battle of Tarutino, precisely in consequence of its absurdity, was the very thing that was necessary at that period of the campaign.

With the very slightest effort, in spite of the most extraordinary confusion, with the most insignificant loss, the most important results of the whole campaign were attained; a change from retreat to advance was made, the weakness of the French was manifested, and to the Napoleonic army was communicated the impulse which alone was needed to make them begin their retreat.

III

PIERRE'S COSTUME now consisted of a torn and dirty shirt—the only remains of his former dress—soldier's trousers, by Karatayef's advice tied with string around the ankles for the sake of greater warmth, a coachman's coat, and his peasant's cap.

Physically, during this time Pierre had greatly changed. He no longer seemed portly, although he still retained that appearance of rotundity and strength which in their nature are hereditary. His beard and mustache had grown and covered the lower part of his face. His long hair, all in a tangle on his head and full of lice, fell in tangled locks from under his cap. The expression of his eyes was firm, steadfast, calm, and full of an alertness which had never before been characteristic of him. His old-time indolence, manifested even in his eyes, had now given place to an energetic spirit which was ready for activity and resistance. His feet were bare.

Pierre looked now at the field along which, that morning, teams and mounted men were moving; now far off across the river; now at the puppy, which was pretending that she was going to bite him in real earnest; and now at his bare feet, which, for the sport of the thing, he was placing in various attitudes, wagging his dirty thick toes. And every time he looked at his bare feet a smile of lively satisfaction illumined his face. The sight of those bare feet reminded him of all that he had been through and had learned to understand in that time, and this recollection was agreeable to him.

The weather for several days had been mild and bright, with light frosts in the morning—the so-called "woman's summer." In the sun the air felt warm; and this warmth, together with the invigorating freshness of the morning frost, which left its influence in the air, was very pleasant.

A French corporal in undress uniform, in his nightcap, with a short pipe between his teeth, came from behind the corner of the hut, and, with a friendly wink, joined Pierre.

"What sunshine, Monsieur Kiril!" (for that was what all the French called Pierre), "you'd think it was springtime."

And the corporal leaned up against the doorpost and offered Pierre his pipe, although whenever he offered it Pierre always declined it.

"If we started marching in such weather as this . . ." he began.

Pierre asked what the news was in regard to a retreat, and the corporal told him that almost all the troops were beginning to move, and that the order regarding the prisoners was to be issued that day.

In the hut in which Pierre was confined, a soldier named Sokolof was dying, and Pierre told the corporal that something ought to be done about this soldier.

The corporal replied that Pierre might be easy on that score, that there were permanent and movable hospitals, and that the sick would be cared for, and that the authorities had provided for all emergencies.

"And besides, Monsieur Kiril, you have only to say a single word to the captain, you know. Oh, he is a—he never forgets anything! Tell the captain when he makes his tour of inspection, and he will do anything for you."

The captain of whom the corporal was speaking had often talked with Pierre and had shown him all manner of condescension.

" 'Do you see, St. Thomas,' says he to me the other day, 'Kiril is a man of education who speaks French; he is a Russian seigneur who has been unfortunate, but he's a man! And he knows what . . . if he asks for anything,' says he, 'let him tell me; I couldn't refuse him. When one has been studying, you see, you like education and the right kind of people.' It's for your sake I tell you this, Monsieur Kiril. In that affair the other day, if it hadn't been for you, it might have come out pretty bad!" The "affair" was a squabble, a few days before, between the prisoners and the French, in which Pierre had assumed the rôle of peacemaker.

Four weeks had passed since Pierre had been taken prisoner. Although the French had proposed to transfer him from the privates' hut to the officers', he still remained in the one where he had been placed on the first day.

In burned and plundered Moscow, Pierre experienced almost the utmost privations which man can endure; but, owing to his vigorous constitution and health—a blessing which he had never appreciated till then—and especially owing to the fact that these privations had come on him so imperceptibly that it was impossible to say when they began, he not only bore them easily but even cheerfully.

And at this very time he began to feel a calmness and contentment that he had before vainly striven to attain. He had sought it in philanthropy, in Freemasonry, in the diversions of fashionable life, in wine, in the heroic effort of self-sacrifice, in his romantic love for Natasha. He had sought it in the path of thought, and all these efforts and experiments had disappointed him. And now without any effort or thought he had discovered this calmness and contentment only by the horror of death, by privations, and by what he had found in Karatayef.

He no longer thought about Russia, or the war, or politics, or Napoleon. It was evident to him that none of this concerned him, that he was not called on to decide and therefore could not judge. His indignation against his wife, and his anxiety that his name should not be disgraced, seemed to him now not only insignificant, but even ludicrous. What difference did it make to him if this woman led the life that best pleased her, and where? Whose business was it and what difference did it make to him whether it were known or not known to the French that their prisoner was Count Bezukhof?

The gratification of desires—good food, cleanliness, independence—now that he was deprived of them all, seemed to Pierre perfect happiness; and the choice of occupation—that is, life—now when this choice was so limited, seemed to him such an easy matter that he forgot that the freedom which in his case was given him by his culture, his wealth, his position in society, is exactly what makes a choice of occupations hopelessly difficult and destroys the very desire and possibility of occupation.

All Pierre's thoughts of the future were directed toward the time when he would be free. But nevertheless, afterwards, and all his life long, Pierre thought and spoke with enthusiasm of that month of imprisonment, of those strong and pleasurable sensations which would never return again, and above all of that utter spiritual peace, of that perfect inward freedom, which he had experienced only at that time.

IV

THE FRENCH TROOPS started to retreat on the night of the eighteenth of October. Kitchens and huts were dismantled; wagons were loaded; and the troops and trains set forth.

At seven o'clock in the morning, in marching trim, in shakoes, with muskets, knapsacks, and huge bundles, the convoy of the French stood in front of the huts, and a lively interchange of French talk, interspersed with oaths, rolled along the whole line.

In the hut all were ready, clothed, belted, shod, and only awaiting the word of command to start.

The sick soldier, Sokolof, pale and thin, with livid circles under his eyes, was the only one unshod and unclad. He lay in his place, and his eyes, bulging from his very leanness looked questioningly at his comrades, who paid no heed to him or his low and regular groans. Evidently it was not so much his sufferings—he was ill with dysentery—as it was fear and grief at being left alone that caused him to groan.

Pierre, with his feet shod in slippers fabricated for him by Karatayef out of remnants of goatskin which a Frenchman had brought him to make into inner soles for his boots, and belted with a rope, came to the sick man and squatted down beside him on his heels.

"Now, see here, Sokolof, they're not absolutely all going away. They're going to have a hospital here. Maybe you'll be better off than the rest of us," said Pierre.

"Oh, Lord, oh! The death of me! Oh, Lord!" groaned the soldier, louder than ever.

"There, I'll go directly and ask them," said Pierre, and, getting up, he went to the door of the hut.

Just as Pierre reached the door, the very corporal who the day before had offered Pierre his pipe appeared with two soldiers. The corporal and the two soldiers also were in marching trim, with knapsacks, and wore shakoes with chin straps. This gave a new appearance to their well-known faces. The corporal approached the door for the purpose of locking it, according to the order of the authorities. Before letting out the prisoners they had to call the roll.

"Corporal, what is to be done with the sick man?" . . . Pierre began to say; but the instant he said this, the doubt arose in his mind whether this was the corporal he had known, or an entirely different man—the corporal was so unlike himself at that instant. Moreover, at the instant Pierre spoke, on two sides the rolling of drums was suddenly heard.

The corporal scowled at Pierre's words, and, uttering a meaningless oath, he slammed the door.

In the hut there was semidarkness; on two sides the sharp rattle of the drums drowned the sick man's groans.

"Here it is! . . . here it is again!" said Pierre to himself, and an involuntary chill ran down his back.

In the changed face of the corporal, in the tone of his voice, in the exciting and deafening rattle of the drums, Pierre recognized that mysterious, unsympathetic power which compels men against their wills to murder their kind, that power he had seen at work during the executions.

To fear this power, to try to escape it, to address with petitions or with reproaches the men who served as its instruments, was idle. Pierre now realized this. It was necessary to wait and have patience. He did not go

594

back to the sick man, or even look in his direction. Silent, scowling, he stood at the door of the hut.

When the doors of the hut were thrown open and the prisoners, crowding against each other, came flocking out, Pierre threw himself in front of them and went to the very captain who, according to the corporal's account, was ready to do anything for him.

This captain was in marching trim, and from his cold face looked forth that same "it" which Pierre had recognized in the corporal's words and in the rattle of the drums.

"Carry on, carry on—on with you!" commanded the captain, frowning sternly as he looked at the prisoners crowding past him. Pierre knew beforehand that his effort would be wasted, but still he went up to him.

"Well, what do you want?" asked the officer, coldly, scanning Pierre as if he did not recognize him.

Pierre told him about the wounded.

"He can walk, the devil take him!" replied the captain. "Carry on, carry on!" he went on saying, not looking at Pierre.

"No, but he is dying," began Pierre.

"Go to the devil!" cried the captain, scowling wrathfully.

Dram da-da-dam-dam-dam went the rattle of the drums. And Pierre realized that this mysterious force was already in full possession of these men, and that to say anything now was useless.

The officers among the prisoners were separated from the privates and ordered to go forward. The officers, including Pierre, numbered thirty, the privates three hundred.

On the streets that crossed Khamovniki, the prisoners marched along with their convoy and the wagons and teams that belonged to the soldiers composing it, and followed behind them; but when they reached a storehouse of provisions, they found themselves in the midst of a vast detachment of artillery, moving in close order, which had got mixed up with a number of private conveyances.

On the bridge itself all halted, and waited for those in front to move on. From the bridge the prisoners could see before them and behind them endless lines of moving vehicles. In every direction was heard the incessant roar of carriages like the tumult of the sea, and trampling of feet and incessant angry shouts and curses. Pierre stood crushed up against the wall of a house which had been exposed to the flames, and listened to this uproar, which blended in his imagination with the rattle of the drum.

Several of the officers in the group of prisoners, in order to get a better view, climbed up on the wall of the burned house next to which Pierre was standing.

"What crowds of people! Oh, what crowds!" . . . "They're even riding on the guns! See the furs!" they exclaimed. "Oh, the carrion eaters! what thieves!" . . . "Look yonder, on that cart!" . . . "Do you see that, they've got an icon, by God!"

"Those must be Germans." . . . "And our peasants, by God!"

"Oh, the scoundrels!" . . . "See how they're loaded down, as much as they can do to get along! And there's one's got a cab—they stole even that!" . . .

"See! he's sitting on the trunks! Ye saints!" . . . "There, they're having a fight." . . .

"See! He hit him in the snout, right in the snout!"

"At this rate they won't get through till night!" . . .

"Look! Just look! Those must be Napoleon's! See what fine horses! With monogram and crown!"

"This was a fine house!" . . . "See, he's dropped a bag and didn't notice it!" . . .

"There! they're fighting again!" . . .

"There's a woman with a baby! Not so bad looking either!" . . .

"See! There's no end to it. Russian wenches! There's the wenches for you, by God!" . . .

"They're having an easy time in that carriage there, hey!"

The wave of general curiosity drove all the prisoners into the street; and Pierre, thanks to his stature, could see over the heads of the others what had so awakened the curiosity of the prisoners: in three calashes, jammed in among some artillery caissons, rode several women, sitting close together, adorned with bright colors, painted, and shouting at the top of their shrill voices.

Since the moment Pierre had recognized the reappearance of that mysterious power, nothing seemed to him strange or terrible: neither these women hastening no one knew where, nor the conflagration that had destroyed Moscow. All that he now saw produced scarcely any impression on him—as if his soul, preparing for a hard struggle, refused to submit to any impressions that might render it weaker.

Sometime before nightfall the leader of the convoy mustered his command, and with shouts and disputes marched them in among the teams, and the prisoners, guarded on every side, emerged onto the Kaluga road.

They proceeded very rapidly, without stopping to rest, and only halted at sunset. The teams ran into one another, and the men prepared for their night encampment. All seemed angry and dissatisfied. It was long before the curses and shouts and blows ceased on all sides. A private carriage, which had been following the prisoners' guard, came up against one of the wagons belonging to the same, and the pole ran into it. Several soldiers ran up from various sides; some struck the heads of the horses that drew the private carriage, and tried to turn them aside; others squabbled among themselves, and Pierre saw a German severely wounded in the head with a short saber.

During this halt the soldiers in charge of the prisoners treated them even worse than they had during the march. At this halt horseflesh was for the first time issued to the prisoners.

From officers down to humblest soldiers, all seemed alike to feel a personal sense of anger against each one of the prisoners, all the more noticeable because of the unexpected change from their former friendliness. This ill will grew more and more pronounced, when, at roll call of the prisoners, it was found that during the bustle attendant on leaving Moscow a Russian soldier, feigning to be ill with colic, had escaped. Pierre saw a Frenchman strike a Russian soldier for having strayed away from the road too far; and he heard the captain, his friend, reprimand a noncommissioned officer for the escape of the Russian soldier, and threaten him with court-martial. At the corporal's excuse that the soldier was ill and could not march, the officer replied that the orders were to shoot those who had to be left.

The evening was over, but the night had not fairly begun. Pierre left his new comrades, and, stepping among the watch fires, started to cross to the other side of the road, where he had been told the privates of the prisoner party were encamped. He wanted to have a talk with them. But a sentinel halted him on the road and ordered him back.

Pierre returned, but not to the watch fire, to his companions, but to an unharnessed wagon where there was no one. Doubling up his legs and dropping his head, he sat down on the cold ground by the wagon wheel, and remained there for a long time, motionless, thinking.

More than an hour passed in that way. No one disturbed him.

Suddenly he burst into a loud and rich peal of jovial laughter, so loud that men gathered around from various directions in amazement, to see what caused this strange and solitary fit of laughter.

"Ha! ha! ha!" roared Pierre, and he went on talking aloud to himself. "The soldier would not let me pass. I was caught, I was shut up. They still keep me as their prisoner. Who am I? I? I? . . . my immortal soul! Ha! ha! ha!" and he laughed until the tears ran down his cheeks.

Someone got up and came over to see what this strange big man found to laugh at, all alone by himself. Pierre ceased to laugh, got up, went off to some distance from the inquisitive man, and glanced around him.

The huge, endless bivouac, which shortly before had been noisy with the crackling of campfires and the voices of men, was now silent; the ruddy fires were dying down and paling. High in the bright sky stood the full moon. Forest and field, before invisible beyond the confines of the bivouac, could now be seen stretching far away. And still farther beyond these forests and fields the eye followed the bright, quivering, alluring, infinite distance.

Pierre gazed up into the sky, into the depths of the marching host of twinkling stars.

"And all that is mine, and all that is in me, and all that is *me*," thought Pierre. "And they took all that and shut it in a hut made of boards!" He smiled and went back to his comrades, and lay down to sleep.

V

TOWARD THE middle of October a messenger came to Kutuzof with still another letter from Napoleon and a proposal for peace. It was deceitfully dated from Moscow, since at that time Napoleon was not far in advance of Kutuzof on the old Kaluga highway.

Kutuzof replied to this letter exactly as he had replied to the first one, with which Lauriston had been sent: He declared there could be no question of peace.

Shortly after this, word was received that the enemy had appeared in Fominskoye, that these troops consisted of Broussier's division, and that this division, being separated from the rest of the army, might easily be destroyed. Soldiers and officers again demanded offensive operations. Kutuzof considered it unnecessary to make any attack. A middle course was adopted: a small detachment was sent to Fominskoye, charged to attack Broussier.

This operation—most difficult and most important, as it turned out, in its consequences—was intrusted to Dokhturof.

On the twenty-second of October, the same day on which Dokhturof traversed halfway toward Fominskoye, and halted in the village of Aristovo, preparing himself accurately to carry out the orders that had been given him, the whole French army, in its spasmodic motion moving down as far as Murat's position, as if for the purpose of giving battle, suddenly, without any reason, swerved to the left to the new Kaluga highway, and moved toward Fominskoye, where shortly before only Broussier had been.

Dokhturof at this time had under his command, with the exception of some partisans, only the two small divisions of Figner and Seslavin.

On the afternoon of October twenty-third, Seslavin came to the commander at Aristovo with a French guardsman who had been taken prisoner. The prisoner said that the troops which had that day occupied Fominskoye consisted of the vanguard of the main army, that Napoleon was there, that the whole army had left Moscow five days ago.

That same evening a domestic serf who had come from Borovsko declared that he had seen an enormous host entering the town.

The partisans brought word that they had seen the French guard marching along the road to Borovsko.

From all these rumors it was evident that where they had expected to find a single division was now the whole army of the French, which had marched out of Moscow in an unexpected route—along the old Kaluga highway.

Dokhturof was loath to make any demonstration, since it was not now at all clear to him what it was his duty to do. He had been commanded to attack Fominskoye.

But where, before, Broussier had been alone in Fominskoye, now there was the whole French army.

Yermolof wanted to act on his own judgment, but Dokhturof insisted that it was necessary to have orders from his serene highness. It was determined to send a messenger back to headquarters.

For this duty was chosen a highly intelligent officer, Bolkhovitinof, who, in addition to the written report, was to give a verbal report of the whole matter. At midnight Bolkhovitinof, having received the envelope and the verbal message, galloped off, accompanied by a Cossack with extra horses, to headquarters.

Kutuzof, like all old people, slept little at night. In the daytime he frequently dozed at unexpected times; but at night, throwing himself, still dressed, down on his couch, he would lie awake and think.

Thus it was at this time. He was lying on his bed, leaning his heavy, big, scarred head on his fat hand, and thinking, his one eye staring out into the darkness.

Since Benigsen, who was in correspondence with the sovereign and had more influence with the staff than anyone else, had kept out of his way, Kutuzof was less troubled by the thought that he would be forced to send his troops to take part in useless offensive actions. The lesson of the Battle of Tarutino and of the day before it, ever memorable to Kutuzof, must have had its effect, he thought.

"They must understand that it can only be a losing game with us to act on the offensive. Patience and time, they are my invincible warriors," said Kutuzof to himself.

He knew that it is not good to pluck the apple while it is green. It will fall of itself when it is ripe; but if you pluck it green, then it spoils the apple and the tree, and sets your teeth on edge as well.

Like an experienced huntsman, he knew that the wild beast was wounded —wounded as only the whole force of Russia could wound; but whether or not the wound was mortal was as yet an undecided question.

Now, by the sending of Lauriston and Berthémi, and from the reports of the guerrillas, Kutuzof was almost certain that the wound was mortal. But proofs were still needed; it was necessary to wait.

"They want to rush forward and see how they have killed him. Wait, and you'll see. Always 'maneuvers,' always 'offensive movements'!" he said to himself. "What for? So as to gain distinction. One would think there was something jolly in this fighting. They are just like children, from whom you can't expect reason, for the truth is that they all want to prove how well they can fight. But that is not the way now. And what fine maneuvers they are always proposing to me! It seems to them that when they have devised two or three chances"—he was thinking about the general plan sent from Petersburg—"they have exhausted the list, but there's no end to them."

The more he thought about them, the more abundantly they arose before him. He imagined every kind of diversion the Napoleonic army might make, whether as a whole, or in divisions, against Petersburg, against himself, against his flank. There was one contingency he dreaded more than any other: It was that Napoleon might turn against him his own weapon—that he might settle down in Moscow and wait for him. But the one thing that he could not have forseen was the very thing that happened—that senseless, cautious doubling to and fro of Napoleon's army during the first eleven days after it left Moscow; that indecision which rendered possible what Kutuzof had not till then dared even to think about—namely, the absolute destruction of the French.

The information imparted by the partisans in regard to the distress of Napoleon's army, the rumors of preparation for evacuating Moscow, all taken together confirmed the presumption that the French army was worsted and was preparing to flee. But these presumptions appealed to the younger men only, not to Kutuzof.

He, with his sixty years' experience, knew how much dependence was to be put on hearsay, knew how prone men who wished anything were to group all the indications in such a way as to conform with their desire, and he knew how in such a case as this they are glad to overlook anything that may seem opposed to it.

And the more Kutuzof desired to believe, the less he permitted himself to put any trust in the rumors. This question engaged all the energies of his mind. Everything else was for him merely the ordinary business of life. And such subordinate business of life included his conversation with his staff officers, his letters to Madame Stahl written from Tarutino, the reading of novels, the granting of rewards, his correspondence with Petersburg, and the like.

But the destruction of the French, which he had been the only one to foresee, was the only real desire of his soul.

On the night of the twenty-third of October he was lying down, his head resting on his hand, and was thinking about this.

There was a commotion in the next room, and the steps of Toll, Konovnitsin and Bolkhovitinof were heard.

"Eh! Who is there? Come in, come in! What news?" cried the field marshal to them.

While the servant was lighting a candle, Toll told the gist of the news.

Kutuzof sat down, stretching out one leg on the bed, and resting his huge paunch on the other, which he doubled up. He blinked his sound eye to get a better sight of the messenger, as if he expected in his features to read the answer to what was occupying him.

"Go on, tell us about it, friend," said he to Bolkhovitinof, in his low, senile voice, pulling his shirt, which had fallen open, over his chest. "Come here, come nearer. What is this bit of news you have brought me? What! Napoleon left Moscow? And his army too? Ha?"

Bolkhovitinof gave him a detailed account, from the very beginning, of all that had been intrusted to him.

"Speak faster, faster; don't torment my very soul," exclaimed Kutuzof, interrupting him.

Bolkhovitnof told the whole story and then remained silent, awaiting orders.

Toll began to make some remark, but Kutuzof interrupted him. He wished to say something, but suddenly his face wrinkled and frowned. Waving his hand to Toll, he walked across the room, to the "red corner" of the cottage, dark with many icons.

"Lord, my Creator! Thou hast heard our prayer . . ." said he, in a trembling voice, folding his hands. "Saviour of Russia! I thank thee, O Lord." And he burst into tears.

V I

From the time that this news came until the end of the campaign, all Kutuzof's activity was confined to exercising his power, shrewdness, and persuasion to prevent his troops from useless attacks, maneuvers, and encounters with an enemy already doomed.

Kutuzof fell back; but the enemy, not waiting for his retreat, took to flight in the opposite direction.

When the retreat of the French army took the definite shape of flight along the Smolensk road, all the superior generals of the army wished to distinguish themselves, to cut the French off, to take them prisoners, to set upon them; and all demanded offensive operations.

Kutuzof alone employed all his powers—the powers of any commanding general are very small—to resist offensive operations.

He could not say what we can say today—why fight battles, why dispute the road, why lose your own men, and why inhumanly kill unfortunate wretches? Why do all this, when from Moscow to Viazma, without any combat whatever, a third of this army has disappeared? But drawing from his wisdom what they might have understood, he told them about "the golden bridge" ("Let them cross the golden bridge"; that is, "Give them every chance of self-destruction."); and they mocked him, slandered him, and hurled themselves on the dying beast to rend it and cut it in pieces.

At Viazma, Yermolof, Miloradovitch, Platof and others, finding themselves near the French, could not restrain themselves from cutting off and destroying two French army corps. Kutuzof they derided by sending him a sheet of blank paper in an envelope, instead of a report of their undertaking.

And, in spite of all Kutuzof's efforts to restrain our troops, the troops assailed the French and endeavored to dispute their way. Regiments of infantry, we are told, with music and drums, boldly advanced to the attack, and killed and lost thousands of men.

But they could not cut off the fugitives or exterminate the enemy. And the French army, drawing its ranks more closely together because of the danger, and regularly melting away, advanced along this—its fatal road to Smolensk.

1812

The Russian winter is on. The grande armée, retreating, is attacked by Russia's armies and harassed by guerrillas. In France the morale is poor, internal forces opposing Napoleon are strengthened. Under these circumstances the only hope is to get the army out of Russia intact.

Part Fourteenth

ONE of the most obvious and advantageous infractions of the so-called rules of war is the action of isolated individuals against troops crowded together into a mass. This sort of activity is always seen in wars which assume a popular character. In this form of warfare, instead of one compact body meeting another compact body, men disperse, attack separately, instantly retire when threatened by superior forces, and then reappear at the first favorable opportunity. Thus did the guerrillas in Spain, thus did the mountaineers in the Caucasus, thus did the Russians in 1812.

Warfare of this sort is called "partisan" warfare, and people suppose that when it is thus named its meaning is explained. Such warfare, however, not only fails to come under any rules, but is directly opposed to a well-known law of tactics regarded as infallible. This law demands that the assailant shall concentrate his troops so as to be, at the moment of combat, stronger than his enemy.

Partisan warfare (always successful, as history proves) is directly opposed to that law.

This contradiction arises from the fact that military science takes the strength of armies to be identical with their numbers. Military science says: The more troops, the greater the strength. Great battalions are always right: "God is on the side of the heavier battalions." In making this assertion, military science is like the science of mechanics, which, considering the momenta of moving bodies only in relation to their masses, affirms that these forces will be equal or unequal as their masses are equal or unequal.

Momentum (quantity of movement) is the product of the mass and the velocity.

In war the momentum of troops is likewise the product of the mass multiplied by some unknown quantity, x.

This x is the spirit of the army; in other words, the more or less intense desire of all the men composing the army to fight and expose themselves to perils, independently of whether they are under the command of men of genius or otherwise, whether they fight in three or two ranks, whether they are armed with clubs or with guns delivering thirty shots a minute.

Men who have the most intense desire to fight always put themselves in the most advantageous position for fighting.

The rule of tactics commanding troops to act in masses during an attack, and separately in a retreat, is an unconscious expression of the truth that the strength of troops depends on their spirit. Better discipline is required to lead men into fire then to induce them to defend themselves against assailants, and is obtained exclusively by movements in masses. But this rule, which takes no account of the spirit of the troops, constantly proves fallacious and particularly opposed to the reality, when there is an increased or diminished spirit among the troops—in all popular wars.

The French, in retreating in 1812, though according to tactics they should have defended themselves separately, drew into closer masses because the spirit of the troops had fallen so low that the army could be maintained only by holding the men in mass.

The Russians, on the contrary, should according to tactics have attacked in mass; instead, they scattered their forces, because the spirit of their troops had risen so high that isolated men attacked the French without waiting for orders, and there was no need of pressure to induce them to expose themselves to fatigues and perils.

The so-called partisan or guerrilla war began with the arrival of the French at Smolensk.

Before this guerrilla warfare was officially recognized by our government, thousands of the hostile army—marauders left behind and foraging parties—had been exterminated by Cossacks and peasants, who killed these men as instinctively as dogs worry to death a mad dog that has run astray.

The partisans demolished the "Grand Army" in detachments. They trampled down the fallen leaves that fell from the dried tree—the French army—and now and again shook the tree itself. In October, when the French were on their way back to Smolensk, there were hundreds of these bands, of various sizes and characters.

On the fourth of November, Denisof, who was one of these partisan leaders, found himself, with his band, in the very center of partisan excitement. Since morning, he and his band had been on the march. All day long, keeping under shelter of the forest that skirted the highway, he had been following a large French convoy of cavalry baggage and Russian prisoners, isolated from the other troops and under a powerful escort, on its way to Smolensk, as was known from scouts and prisoners.

The existence of this train was known not only to Denisof and

Dolokhof—who was also a partisan leader with a small band, and was advancing close by—but to the heads of several large bands, with their staffs. All knew about this train and, as Denisof expressed it, "were whetting their teeth for it." Two of these large bands, one commanded by a Pole, the other by a German, almost simultaneously sent to Denisof to join forces, each inviting him to help them attack the "transport."

"No, thank you, bwother, I gwow my own whiskers," said Denisof as he read their letters; and he replied to the German that, in spite of the heartfelt desire which he had of serving under the command of such a valiant and distinguished general, he should have to deprive himself of that pleasure because he had already joined the command of the Polish general. And to the Polish general he wrote the same thing, assuring him that he had already joined the command of the German.

Having thus disposed of these matters, Denisof made his plans, without reference to these high officials, to join with Dolokhof and attack and capture this train with the small force at their command.

The "transport" mustered fifteen hundred men. Denisof had two hundred, and Dolokhof had perhaps as many. But the preponderance of numbers did not deter Denisof. The only thing that he cared now to know was what sort of men composed these troops, and, with this end in view, Denisof wanted to capture a "tongue"—that is, a man from the enemy's ranks. To make a descent, Denisof considered, would be at the risk of arousing the whole column, and therefore he sent forward to Shamsheva the peasant Tikhon Shcherbatof, one of his band, to pick up, if possible, one of the French quartermasters who might be there in advance.

I I

It was a mild, rainy, autumn day. The sky and the earth blended in the same hue, like that of muddied water. At one moment a sort of fog descended; at the next, round, slanting drops of rain would suddenly fall.

Denisof, in his felt cloak and Cossack cap, from which the water was streaming, was riding along on a lean thoroughbred, with tightened girths. Like his horse, he kept his head bent and ears alert, and, scowling at the slanting rain, peered anxiously ahead. His face was somewhat thinner than formerly and, with its growth of thick, short black beard, looked fierce. Abreast of Denisof, also in cloak and Cossack cap, on a plump, coarse-limbed Don pony, rode a Cossack captain, Denisof's ally.

A third, Captain Lovaiski, likewise in cloak and Cossack cap, was a long-limbed, light-complexioned man, as flat as a plank, with narrow bright eyes and a calmly self-confident expression of both face and pose. It was evident at a glance, first at the captain and then at Denisof, that Denisof was wet and uncomfortable, that Denisof was a man who merely rode his horse; while the captain was as comfortable and confident as he always was, and was not a man who merely rode the horse, but a man who was one being with his horse and thus possessed of double strength.

A short distance ahead of them walked their guide, a little peasant in a gray coat and a white cap, wet to the skin.

A little behind them, on a small, lean Kirghiz pony with a huge tail and mane and torn, bloody lips, rode a young officer in a blue French cape.

Next to him rode a hussar who had taken up behind him, on his horse's crupper, a lad in a torn French uniform and blue cap. This lad clung to the hussar with hands red with cold, rubbed his bare feet together to warm them, and gazed around him in amazement with uplifted brows. This was a French drummer boy whom they had taken prisoner that morning.

Behind them, three and four deep, the line of hussars stretched along the narrow, winding and well-worn forest path; then came Cossacks, some in felt cloaks, some in French capes, some with horsecloths thrown over their heads. Their horses, whether roan or bay, seemed all black as coal in the rain that was streaming from them. The horses' necks seemed strangely slender from their soaked manes. From the horses rose steam. The clothes and the saddles and the bridles—everything was wet, slippery, and limp, just like the ground and the fallen leaves that covered the path. The men sat with scowling faces, trying not to move, so as to warm the water that had trickled down their backs, and not to allow any fresh invasion of cold water under their saddles, on their knees, or down their necks.

In the midst of the long train of Cossacks the two wagons drawn by French and Cossack horses (the latter harnessed in with their saddles on) rattled over the stumps and roots and splashed through the ruts full of water. Denisof's horse, avoiding a puddle which covered the road, sprang to one side and struck his knee against a tree.

"Oh, the devil!" cried Denisof wrathfully, and, showing his teeth, he gave the horse three blows with the whip, spattering himself and his comrades with mud. Denisof was not in good spirits, owing to the rain and his hunger—he had eaten nothing since morning—and principally because nothing had been heard from Dolokhof, and because the man sent to capture the "tongue" had not returned.

"We won't be likely to find another chance like today's to stwike the twansport twain. To attack them alone is too much of a wisk; and to wait till another day—some of those big bands of pa'tisans will be sure to snatch it away from under our vewy noses," said Denisof, who kept his eyes constantly toward the front, thinking he might see the expected messenger from Dolokhof.

On coming out into a vista where there was a clear view extending to some distance toward the right, Denisof reined in.

"Someone's coming," said he.

The captain looked in the direction indicated by Denisof.

"There are two of them—an officer and Cossack. Only you don't suppose it is the sublieutenant himself, do you?" said the captain.

The riders coming toward them were lost from sight, and after a little while reappeared again. The officer, with disheveled hair, wet to the skin, and with his trousers worked up above his knees, came riding in advance at a weary gallop, urging his horse with his whip. Behind him, standing up in his stirrups, trotted his Cossack. This officer, a very young lad with a broad, rosy face and alert, merry eyes, galloped up to Denisof and handed him a wet envelope.

"From the general," said the officer. "Excuse its not being perfectly dry."

Denisof, frowning, took the envelope and started to break the seal.

"Now they all said it was dangerous . . . dangerous," said the young officer, turning to the captain while Denisof was reading the letter. "However, Komarof"—he pointed to the Cossack—"Komarof and I made all our plans. We each had two pist—but who is that?" he asked, breaking off in the middle of the word on catching sight of the French drummer boy. "A prisoner? Have you had a fight? May I speak with him?"

"Wostof! Petya!" cried Denisof, at that instant having run through the letter that had been given him. "Why didn't you say who you were?" and Denisof, smiling and turning around, gave the young officer his hand.

The young officer was Petya Rostof!

All the way Petya had been revolving in his mind how he should behave toward Denisof as became a full-fledged officer, and not give a hint of their former acquaintance.

But as soon as Denisof smiled on him Petya immediately became radiant, flushed with delight, forgot the formality he had stored up against the occasion, and began to tell him how he had galloped past the French, and how glad he was that such a commission had been intrusted to him, and how he had been in the battle near Viazma, where a certain hussar greatly distinguished himself.

"Well, I'm wight glad to see you," said Denisof, interrupting him, and then his face assumed again its anxious expression. "Captain," said he, turning to the captain, "you see this is fwom the German again. He insists on our joining him."

And Denisof proceeded to explain to the captain that the contents of the letter just received constituted another request from the German general to unite with him in an attack on the transport train. "If we don't get at it tomowwow, he will certainly take it away fwom under our vewy noses," he said in conclusion.

While Denisof was talking with the captain, Petya, abashed by Denisof's chilling tone and supposing that the reason for it might be the state of his trousers, strove to pull them down under shelter of his cloak, so that no one would notice him, and did his best to assume as military an aspect as possible.

"Will there be any order from your excellency?" he asked of Denisof, raising his hand to his visor, and again returning to the little comedy of general and aide for which he had rehearsed himself. "Or should I remain with your excellency?"

"Orders?" repeated Denisof, thoughtfully. "Can you wemain till to-mowwow?"

"Ah! Please let me. . . . May I stay with you?" cried Petya.

"I suppose your orders fwom the genewal were to wetuan immediately —weren't they?" asked Denisof.

Petya reddened. "He said nothing at all about it; I think I can," he replied, somewhat doubtfully.

"Well, all wight!" said Denisof.

And, turning to his subordinates, he made various arrangements for the party to make their way to the place of rendezvous, at the watchhouse in the forest, that had been agreed upon; and for the officer on the Kirghiz horse—this officer performed the duties of aide—to ride off in search of Dolokhof, and find out whether or not he would come that evening.

Denisof himself determined to ride down with the captain and Petya to the edge of the forest nearest Shamsheva to reconnoiter the position of the French, and find the best place for making their attack on the following day.

"And now, gwaybeard," said he, turning to the peasant who was serving as their guide, "take us to Shamsheva."

Denisof, Petya, and the captain, accompanied by a few Cossacks and the hussar who had charge of the prisoner, rode off to the left, through the ravine, toward the edge of the forest.

III

It HAD STOPPED raining; there was merely a drizzling mist, and drops of water fell from the branches of the trees. Denisof, the captain and Petya rode silently behind the guide, who, lightly and noiselessly plodding along in his plaited shoes of wood fiber over the roots and wet leaves, led them to the edge of the wood.

On reaching the crest of a slope, the guide paused, glanced around, and strode toward where the wall of trees was thinner. Under a great oak which had not yet shed its leaves he paused and mysteriously beckoned with his hand.

Denisof and Petya rode up to him. From where the guide was standing, the French could be seen. Immediately back of the forest, occupying the lower half of the slope, spread a field of spring corn. At the right, beyond a steep ravine, could be seen a small village and the manor house with dilapidated roofs. In this hamlet, and around the manor house, and over the whole hillside, and in the garden, around the well and the pond, and along the whole road up from the bridge to the village, which was hardly a quarter of a mile, masses of men could be seen in the rolling mist. Their non-Russian cries to the horses that were dragging the teams up the hill, and their calls to one another, could be heard distinctly.

"Bwing the pwisoner here," said Denisof in a low tone, not taking his eyes from the French.

A Cossack dismounted, helped the lad down, and came with him to Denisof. Denisof, pointing to the French, asked what troops such and such divisions were. The little drummer, stuffing his benumbed hands into his pockets and lifting his brows, gazed at Denisof in fright and, in spite of his evident anxiety to tell all that he knew, got confused in his replies and merely said yes to everything that Denisof asked him. Denisof, scowling, turned from him, and addressed the captain, to whom he communicated his impression.

Petya, moving his head with quick gestures, looked now at the little drummer boy, now at Denisof, and from him to the captain, then at the French in the village, and did his best not to miss anything of importance that was going on.

"Whether Dolokhof comes or does not come, we must make the attempt, hey?" said Denisof, his eyes flashing with animation.

"An excellent place," replied the captain.

"We'll attack the infantwy on the lowland, the swamp," pursued Denisof. "They'll escape into the garden. You and the Cossacks will set on them fwom that side." Denisof pointed to the woods beyond the village. "And I fwom this, with my hussars. And when a gun is fired . . ."

"You won't be able to cross the ravine; there's a quagmire," said the captain. "The horses would be mired. You'll have to strike farther to the left."

While they were thus talking in an undertone, there rang out below them, in the hollow where the pond was, a single shot; a white puff of smoke rolled away, then another, and they heard friendly, almost jolly, shouts from hundreds of the French on the hillside.

At first both Denisof and the captain drew back. They were so near, it seemed to them that they were what had occasioned those shots and shouts. But the shots and shouts had no connection with them. Below them a man in something red was running across the swamp. Evidently the French had shot and were shouting at this man.

"Ha! that's our Tikhon," said the captain.

"So it is, so it is."

"Oh! the wascal!" exclaimed Denisof.

"He'll escape 'em!" said the captain, blinking his eyes.

The man they called Tikhon ran down to the creek and plunged into it, spattering the water in every direction. Disappearing for a moment, he crawled out on all fours, and, black with water, dashed off once more. The French who had started in pursuit paused.

"Cleverly done!" exclaimed the captain.

"What a creature!" snarled Denisof, with the same expression of vexation as before. "And what has he been up to all this time?"

"Who is it?" asked Petya.

"Our scout. We sent him to catch a 'tongue.'"

"Oh, yes," said Petya at Denisof's first word, nodding his head as if he understood, although really he did not comprehend a single word.

Tikhon was one of the most useful men of the band.

He was a peasant from Pokrovskoye. When Denisof, near the beginning of his enterprise, reached Pokrovskoye, according to his usual custom he summoned the village elder and asked him what news they had about the French. The elder had replied—as all elders always reply as if called to account for some mischief—that they had not seen or heard anything.

But when Denisof explained to him that his aim was to beat the French, then the elder told him that marauders had only just been there, but that Tikhon was the only man in their village who troubled himself about such things.

Denisof ordered Tikhon to be summoned, and, after praising him for his activity, spoke to him, in the elder's presence, a few words about that fidelity to the Tsar and the fatherland, and that hatred toward the French, which the sons of the fatherland were in duty bound to manifest.

"We haven't done any harm to the French," said Tikhon, evidently confused by this speech of Denisof's. "We only amused ourselves, as you might say, with the boys. We killed a few dozen of the marauders, that was all; but we haven't done them any harm."

On the next day, when Denisof, who had entirely forgotten about this peasant, was starting away from Pokrovskoye, he was informed that Tikhon had joined the band and asked permission to stay. Denisof gave orders to keep him.

Tikhon, who at first was given the "dirty work" of making campfires, fetching water, and currying horses, quickly displayed great willingness and aptitude for partisan warfare. He would go out at night after booty, and every time he would return with French clothes and arms, and when told to do so he would even bring in prisoners.

Denisof then relieved Tikhon of drudgery, began to take him along on raids, and enrolled him among the Cossacks.

Tikhon was not fond of riding horseback, and always traveled on foot, but he never let the cavalry get ahead of him. His weapons consisted of a musket, which he carried as a joke, a lance, and a hatchet, which he used as a wolf uses his teeth, with equal facility chasing a flea out of his hair, or crashing stout bones. Tikhon, with absolute certainty, would split a skull with his hatchet at any distance, and, taking it by the butt, he would cut out dainty ornaments, or carve spoons.

In Denisof's band Tikhon enjoyed an exclusive and exceptional position. When there was need of doing anything especially difficult and obnoxious —to put a shoulder to a team stuck in the mud, or to pull a horse from the bog by its tail, or act as butcher, or make his way into the very midst of the French, or travel thirty-five miles a day—all laughed and gave the job to Tikhon.

"What harm will it do him, the devil? He's tough as a horse!" they would say of him.

One time a Frenchman whom Tikhon had taken prisoner fired his pistol at him and wounded him in the buttocks. This wound, which Tikhon treated with nothing but vodka, taken internally and externally, was the object of the merriest jokes in the whole division, and Tikhon put up with them with a very good grace.

"Well, brother, how's it coming on? Does it double you up?" the Cossacks would ask mockingly; and Tikhon, entering into the fun of the thing, would make up a face and, pretending to be angry, would abuse the French with the most absurd objurgations. The only impression the affair made on Tikhon was that, after his wound, he was chary of bringing in prisoners.

Tikhon was the most useful and the bravest man in the band. No one was quicker than he was in discovering the prospects of a raid; no one had conquered and killed more of the French; and, consequently, he was the buffoon of the whole band, and he willingly accommodated himself to this standing.

Tikhon had now been sent by Denisof the evening before to Shamsheva to capture a "tongue." But either because he had not been satisfied with a single Frenchman, or because he had slept that night, during daylight he had crept among the bushes in the very midst of the French, and, as Denisof had seen from the brow of the ravine, had been discovered by them.

IV

AFTER TALKING with the captain for some little time longer about the morrow's raid, which Denisof, it seemed, having got a view of the French near at hand, was determined to make, he turned his horse and rode back.

"Well, bwother, now we'll go and dwy ourselves," said he to Petya.

As they rode up to the forest watchman's cottage, Denisof reined in and gazed into the woods. Along the forest, among the trees, came, at a great swinging gait, a long-legged, long-armed man, in a felt cloak, plaited shoes of wood fiber, and a Kazan cap, with a musket over his shoulder and a hatchet in his belt. On catching sight of Denisof, this man hastily threw something into the thicket and, removing his wet cap with its pendant brim, he approached his leader.

This was Tikhon.

His face, pitted with smallpox and covered with wrinkles, and his little, narrow eyes, fairly beamed with self-satisfied jollity. He lifted his head high; and, as if trying to refrain from laughing, looked at Denisof.

"Where have you been all this time?" asked Denisof.

"Where have I been? I went after the French," replied Tikhon, boldly and hastily, in a hoarse but singsong bass.

"Why did you keep out of sight all day? Donkey! Well, why didn't you bring him?"

"I brought what I brought," said Tikhon.

"Where is he?"

"Well, I got him, in the first place, before sunrise," pursued Tikhon, setting his legs, high-wrapped in wood-fiber shoes, wide apart. "And I lugged him into the woods. But I see he's no good. I thinks to myself, 'I'll try it again; I'll have better luck with another.'"

"Oh, you wascal! What a man he is!" exclaimed Denisof, turning to the captain. "Why didn't you bwing him?"

"Yes, why didn't I bring him!" exclaimed Tikhon, angrily. "No good! Don't I know what kind you want?"

"What a son-of-a! . . . Well?"

"I went after another one," resumed Tikhon. "I crept this way into the woods, lying flat!" Tikhon here unexpectedly and abruptly threw himself on his belly, watching their faces while he did so. "Suddenly one shows up," he went on to say; "I collar him . . . this way." Tikhon swiftly, lithely leaped to his feet. "'Come along,' says I to the colonel. What a racket he made! And there were four of 'em! They sprang on me with their little swords. And I at 'em, like this, with my hatchet: 'What's the matter with you! Christ be with you!' says I," cried Tikhon, waving his arms and, putting on a frightful scowl, swelling his chest.

"Yes, we just saw from the hill what a tussle you had with 'em, and how you went through the swamp!" exclaimed the captain, screwing up his glistening eyes.

Petya felt a strong inclination to laugh, but he saw that all the others kept perfectly sober. He swiftly ran his eyes from Tikhon's face to the captain's and Denisof's, not understanding what all this meant.

"Stop acting like a fool!" cried Denisof, angrily coughing. "Why didn't you bwing in the first one?"

Tikhon began to scratch his back with one hand and his head with the other, and suddenly his whole mouth parted in a radiant, stupid smile, which exposed the lack of a tooth. Denisof smiled, and Petya indulged in a hearty laugh, in which Tikhon himself joined.

"Oh, well, he was no good at all!" said Tikhon. "His clothes were wretched, or I'd have brought him. And besides he was surly, your excellency. Says he, 'I am an admiral's son,' says he, 'and I won't come,' says he."

"What a bwute!" exclaimed Denisof. "I wanted to question him. . . ."

"Well, I questioned him," said Tikhon. "'Hard to talk by signs!' says he. 'Lots of us,' says he, 'but a poor lot. Only,' says he, 'they are all the same kind. Groan a little louder,' says he, 'you'll get 'em all,'" said Tikhon in conclusion, looking gaily and resolutely into Denisof's eyes.

"I'll have you thwashed with a hot hundwed, and then perhaps you'll stop acting like a fool," said Denisof severely.

"What's there to get mad about?" asked Tikhon. "Because I didn't see your Frenchmen? Wait till after dark, and then, if you want some, I'll bring in three of them."

"Well, come on," said Denisof; and he rode away, angrily scowling, and did not utter a word until he reached the watchman's cottage.

Tikhon followed, and Petya heard the Cossacks laughing with him and at him about the pair of boots he had flung into the bushes. When he had recovered from the fit of laughing that overcame him on account of Tikhon's words and queer smile, and he understood in a flash that Tikhon had killed a man, Petya felt uncomfortable.

He glanced at the little drummer, and something wrung his very heart. But this sense of awkwardness lasted only for a second. He felt that he must lift his head again and pluck up his courage; and he asked the captain, with an air of great importance, about the next day's enterprise, so as to be worthy of the company in which he found himself.

The officer who had been sent to find Dolokhof met Denisof on the road with the report that Dolokhof would be there immediately, and that, as far as he was concerned, all was favorable.

Denisof suddenly recovered his spirits and beckoned to Petya.

"Now, tell me all about yourself," said he.

Petya, on leaving Moscow and bidding farewell to his parents, had joined his regiment, and soon after had been appointed orderly to a general who had a large detachment under his command.

Since the time of his promotion to the rank of officer, and especially since his transfer into the active army, with which he had taken part in the Battle of Viazma, Petya had been in a chronic state of excitement and delight because he was now "grown up," and full of enthusiastic eagerness to snatch at the slightest opportunity where heroism could be displayed.

He was much delighted with what he saw and experienced in the army, but, at the same time, it seemed to him that all the chances of heroism developed not where he was, but where he was not. And he was crazy to be on the move all the time.

When, on November second, his general expressed the desire to send someone to Denisof's division, Petya pleaded so earnestly to be sent that the general could not refuse. But—remembering Petya's reckless escapade in the Battle of Viazma, when, instead of taking the road that had been indicated to him, he galloped off in front of the lines and under the French fire, shooting his pistol twice as he rode—the general now permitted Petya to go only after expressly forbidding him to take part in any of Denisof's enterprises.

That was why Petya had flushed and become confused when Denisof asked whether he could stay.

Until he reached the edge of the forest, Petya had promised himself that he would immediately return, strictly fulfilling his duty as he should. But when he saw the French, when he saw Tikhon, and learned that during the night there would certainly be a raid, with the swift changeableness of youth he decided in his own mind that his general, whom till then he had highly respected, was a rubbishy German, that Denisof was a hero, that the captain was a hero, that Tikhon was a hero, and that it would be shameful of him to desert them at such a critical moment.

It was twilight by the time Denisof, with Petya and the captain, reached the forest watchman's cottage. Through the twilight could be seen saddled horses, Cossacks, hussars, shelter huts set up on the clearing, and the scattered glow of fires built in the forest ravine so that the smoke might not betray them to the French. In the entry of the little hovel, a Cossack with sleeves rolled up was cutting up mutton. In the cottage itself were three officers of Denisof's band constructing a table out of a door. Petya pulled off his wet clothing, giving it to be dried, and immediately offered his services in helping to set the dinner table.

Within ten minutes the table was ready, spread with a cloth and loaded with vodka, a bottle of rum, white bread, and roasted mutton and salt.

Sitting down with the officers at the table, tearing the fat, fragrant mutton with their hands dripping with grease, Petya found himself in an enthusiastic, childlike state of affectionate love for all men, and consequently assured that all men felt the same love toward him.

"Say, what do you think, Vasili Feodorovitch," he asked, turning to Denisof, "would I get into trouble if I stayed with you for a single little day?" And, without waiting for an answer, he went on answering himself, "For you see I was ordered to find out, and I will. Only you must send me into the most . . . into the chief . . . I don't want any reward . . . but I want. . ."

Petya set his teeth together and lifting his head glanced around and waved his hand.

"Into the chief. . . ?" repeated Denisof, smiling.

"Only please let me have a company; let me command it myself," pursued Petya. "Now, what difference will it make to you? Ah! would you like a knife?" he asked, turning to an officer who was trying to dissect the mutton. And he handed him his case knife.

The officer praised the knife.

"Pray keep it. I have several like it," said Petya, blushing. "Ye saints! I forgot all about it," he suddenly cried. "I have some splendid raisins, quite without seeds, you know. We had a new sutler, and he brought some magnificent things. I bought ten pounds. I like something sweet. Would you like them?" . . . And Petya ran into the entry where his Cossack was and brought back a basket containing five pounds of raisins. "Take them, gentlemen, take them. I wonder if you need a coffeepot?" he asked, addressing the captain. "I bought a splendid one of our sutler. He had magnificent things. And he was very honest. That is the main thing. I will send it to you without fail. And perhaps you are out of flints? Do you need some? I've got some here"—he pointed to his basket. "A hundred flints. I bought them very cheap. Take them, I beg of you, as many as you need, take them all . . ."

And, suddenly scared lest he was talking too much, Petya stopped short and colored.

V

FROM THE DRUMMER, who by Denisof's order was served vodka and mutton and dressed in a Russian coat so that he might remain with Denisof's men and not be sent off with other prisoners, Petya's attention was diverted by Dolokhof's arrival. He had heard many stories in the army about Dolokhof's phenomenal courage and tough treatment of the French, and so from the moment that Dolokhof came in, Petya gazed at him continuously and held his head high, so as to be worthy of such society.

Dolokhof's outward appearance struck Petya strangely by its very simplicity. While Denisof was dressed in a Cossack coat, wore a beard, and on his chest an image of St. Nicholas the Miracle-worker, and in his manner of speech, in all his ways, emphasized his special position, Dolokhof, on the contrary, who had before worn a Persian costume in Moscow, now looked like a most correct officer of the Guards. His face was smooth-shaven, he wore the wadded uniform coat of the Guards, with the order of St. George in the buttonhole, and his forage cap was set straight. He removed his wet cloak in the corner, and, going directly to Denisof without exchanging greetings with anyone, immediately proceeded to inquire about the business in hand.

Denisof told him about the plans of the large detachments of troops to attack the transport train, and about the message Petya had brought, and how he had replied to the two generals. Then Denisof related all he knew about the position of the French escort.

"So far, so good; but we must know what sort of troops and how many they are," said Dolokhof. "We will have to go over there and get more information. If we don't know exactly how many of them there are, it's no use to attempt this enterprise. I like to do such business in good style. Here, I wonder if any of these gentlemen will go with me into their camp. I have an extra uniform with me."

"I . . . I . . . I will go with you!" cried Petya.

"You are pwecisely the one who shall not go," said Denisof; and, turning to Dolokhof, "I would not let him go on any account."

"That's just fine!" cried Petya. "Why can't I go?"

"Why, because there's no weason why you should."

"Well, now, you will excuse me because . . . because . . . but I will go; that's all there is to it!—You will take me, won't you?" he asked, addressing Dolokhof.

"Why not?" replied Dolokhof, absent-mindedly, staring into the face of the French drummer.

"Have you had this young lad long?" he asked of Denisof.

"Took him today, but he knows nothing; I kept him with me."

"Well, now, what did you do with the others?" asked Dolokhof.

"What should I do? I sent them in and got a weceipt," replied Denisof, suddenly reddening. "And I'll tell you fwankly, that I have not a single man on my conscience. What's the matter with sending thirty or thwee hundwed under escort to the city? I tell you honestly it's better than to stain the honor of a soldier."

"Let this little sixteen-year-old count have such fine notions," said Dolokhof, with icy ridicule, "but it's time you gave them up."

"Well, I say nothing of the sort, I only say that I am certainly going with you," timidly interrupted Petya.

"Yes, it's high time you and I, brother, gave up these fine notions," insisted Dolokhof, as if he found especial delight in dwelling on this point which was annoying to Denisof. "Now, for instance, why did you keep this one?" he asked, shaking his head. "Why, it was because you pitied him, wasn't it? We know well enough what your receipts amount to! You will send a hundred men, and thirty'll get there! They'll die of starvation or be killed. So why isn't it just as well not to take any?"

The captain, snapping his bright eyes, nodded his head in approval.

"It's all wight; no need of weasoning about it here. I don't care to take the wesponsibility on my soul. You say they die on the woad. Well and good. Only it isn't my fault."

Dolokhof laughed. "Haven't they been told twenty times to take me? And if they should . . . or you, either, with all your chivalry, it would be an even game . . . a rope and the aspen tree!" He paused. "However, we must get to work. Have my man bring in my pack. I have two French uniforms. So you are going with me, are you?" he asked of Petya.

"I? I? Yes, certainly!" cried Petya, reddening till the tears came, and glancing at Denisof.

Having donned the French uniforms and shakoes, Petya and Dolokhof rode to the gap in the forest, and, emerging from the forest in absolute darkness, made their way down into the ravine. On reaching the bottom, Dolokhof ordered the Cossack who accompanied them to wait for them there, and started off at a round trot along the road to the bridge; Petya, his heart in his mouth with excitement, rode by his side.

"If we fall into their clutches, I won't give myself up alive; I have a pistol," whispered Petya.

"Don't speak in Russian!" exclaimed Dolokhof, in a quick whisper, and, at that instant, they heard in the darkness the challenge "Who goes there?" and the click of the musket.

The blood rushed into Petya's face, and he grasped his pistol.

"Lancers of the Sixth," cried Dolokhof in French, neither hastening nor checking his horse's pace.

The dark figure of the sentinel stood out upon the bridge.

"Password!"

Dolokhof reined in his horse, and rode at a footpace.

"Tell me, is Colonel Gerard here?" he demanded.

"The countersign," insisted the sentinel, not answering the question, and blocking the way.

"When an officer is making his round, the sentinels do not ask the countersign," cried Dolokhof, suddenly losing his temper, and spurring his horse against the sentinel. "I ask you if the colonel is here?"

And, without waiting for an answer from the sentinel, whom he shouldered out of the way, Dolokhof rode up the slope at a footpace.

Perceiving the dark figure of a man crossing the road, Dolokhof halted him and asked where the commander and the officers were. This man, who had a basket on his shoulder, paused, came close to Dolokhof's horse, laid his arm on her, and told in a simple, friendly way, that the commander and the officers were higher up on the hill, at the righthand side, at the "farm," as he called the estate.

After riding along the road, on both sides of which were the bivouac fires, where they could hear the sounds of men talking in French, Dolokhof turned into the yard of the manor house. On reaching the gates, he slid off his horse and went up to a great blazing campfire around which sat a number of men talking loudly. In a kettle at the edge of it something was cooking, and a soldier in a cap and blue cape was on his knees in front of it, his face brightly lighted by the flames, and was stirring it with his ramrod. "It's a tough one to cook!" cried one of the officers who were sitting in the shadow on the opposite side.

"He'll make the rabbits fly," said another, with a laugh. Both relapsed into silence and looked out into the darkness at the sounds of Dolokhof and Petya's footsteps as they came up to the fire, leading their horses.

"Good evening, gentlemen," cried Dolokhof, in a loud tone, saluting the officers politely. The officers made a little stir in the shadow by the watch fire, and a tall man with a long neck, coming around the fire, approached Dolokhof.

"Is it you, Clement?" he began. "Where the deuce?"—but he did not finish his question, recognizing his mistake; and, slightly frowning, he exchanged greetings with Dolokhof as with a stranger, asking him in what way he might serve him.

Dolokhof replied that he and his comrade were in search of their regiment, and, addressing the officers in general, he asked if they knew anything about the sixth regiment.

No one knew anything about it, and it seemed to Petya that the officers began to look suspiciously and with animosity at him and Dolokhof.

For several seconds all were silent.

"You are too late if you expect soup this evening," said a voice from behind the fire, with a suppressed laugh.

Dolokhof explained that they were not hungry, and that they had to go still farther that night. He handed over his horse to the soldier who had been busy over the stew, and squatted down on his heels by the fire, next to the long-necked officer. This officer stared at Dolokhof, without taking his eyes from him, and asked him for a second time what regiment he belonged to.

Dolokhof made no reply, affecting not to hear his question; and, as he puffed at the short French pipe which he took from his pocket, he inquired of the officers how far the road in front of them was free from danger of the Cossacks.

"The brigands are everywhere!" replied an officer from the other side of the campfire.

Dolokhof remarked that the Cossacks were dangerous only for those who were alone, as he and his companion were, but that certainly they would not venture to attack a large detachment—"Would they?" he added dubiously.

All the time Petya, who was standing in front of the fire and listening to the conversation, kept saying to himself, "Now surely he will leave."

But Dolokhof took up the thread of the conversation that had been dropped, and began again to ask without hesitation how many men there were in their battalion, how many battalions, how many prisoners. And while asking his questions about the Russian prisoners, Dolokhof said:

"Wretched business to drag these corpses around with us. We'd much better shoot such trash," and he laughed aloud with such a strange laugh that it seemed to Petya as if the French would then and there discover the imposition, and he involuntarily took a step away from the fire.

No one responded to Dolokhof's remark or his laugh, and a French officer who till then had not showed himself (he had been lying down wrapped up in his cape) raised himself up and whispered something to his comrade. Dolokhof got up and beckoned to the soldier who held his horse.

"Will they let us have the horses or not?" wondered Petya, involuntarily moving nearer to Dolokhof.

The horses were brought.

"Good night, gentlemen," said Dolokhof.

Petya wanted to say "Good night" too, but he could not pronounce a word. The officers said something among themselves in a whisper. Dolokhof sat for some time on his horse, which was restive; then he rode out of the gates at a footpace. Petya rode after him, wishing, but not daring, to glance around to see if the French were following.

On striking the road, Dolokhof did not ride back into the fields, but along the village street.

In one place he stopped and listened.

"Listen!" said he.

Petya recognized the sound of Russian voices, and saw by the watch fires the shadowy forms of the Russian prisoners. On reaching the bridge again, Petya and Dolokhof rode past the sentinel, who, not saying a word, was moodily pacing back and forth across the bridge; and then they plunged into the ravine, where their Cossacks were waiting for them.

"Well, good-by for now. Tell Denisof: at daybreak, at the sound of the first shot," said Dolokhof, and he started to ride away; but Petya seized him by the arm.

"Oh," he cried, "you are such a hero! Oh, how splendid! how glorious! How I like you!"

"All right, all right!" said Dolokhof, but Petya did not let go of him, and in the darkness Dolokhof could just make out that Petya was leaning over toward him. He wanted to kiss him. Dolokhof kissed him laughingly, and, turning his horse, disappeared in the darkness.

VI

FROM THE watchman's cottage came Denisof, who, nodding to Petya, gave orders to get ready. In the half-light of dawn the horses were speedily brought out, saddle girths were tightened, and the men fell into line.

Denisof stood by the cottage, giving the final directions. The infantry detachment, with their hundreds of feet splashing at once, marched ahead along the road and were soon hidden from sight among the trees in the morning mist.

The captain gave some command to his Cossacks. Petya held his horse by the bridle, impatiently awaiting the signal to mount. His face, which he had splashed with cold water, and especially his eyes, glowed with fire; a cold shiver ran down his back, and his whole body shook with a rapid, nervous trembling.

"Well, are you all weady?" asked Denisof. "Bwing the horses!"

The horses were brought out. Denisof scolded his Cossack because his saddle girth was loose, and, after tightening it, he mounted. Petya put his foot in the stirrup. His horse, as always, tried to bite his leg; but Petya, not conscious of his weight, quickly sprang into the saddle, and, looking at the long line of hussars stretching away into the darkness, rode up to Denisof.

"Vasili Feodorovitch, you'll give me some assignment, won't you? Please—for God's sake!" he said.

Denisof seemed to have forgotten about Petya's existence. He glanced at him.

"I'll ask you one thing," said he, severely, "to obey me and to mind your own business."

During all the march Denisof said not a word further to Petya, and rode in silence.

When they reached the edge of the forest the morning light was spreading over the fields. Denisof held a whispered consultation with the captain, as the Cossacks rode past Petya and him. When they had all filed by, Denisof turned his horse and rode down the slope. The horses, sitting back on their haunches and sliding, let themselves and their riders down into the ravine. Petya rode by Denisof's side. The trembling of his whole body kept increasing.

It was growing lighter and lighter. Only distant objects were still concealed in the fog. On reaching the bottom, Denisof, after glancing back, nodded to a Cossack standing near him.

"The signal," he cried.

The Cossack raised his hand. A shot rang out, and at the same instant they heard the trampling hoofs of the horses simultaneously dashing forward, and yells from different directions, and more cries.

At the instant that the first sounds of the trampling hoofs and the yells broke upon the silence, Petya, giving a cut to his horse, and letting him have full rein, galloped forward, not heeding Denisof, who called him back.

It seemed to Petya that at the moment he heard the musket shot it suddenly became perfectly light, like midday. He galloped up to the bridge. In front of him, along the road, the Cossacks were dashing ahead. On the bridge he collided with a Cossack who had been left behind, but still he galloped on. In front of him he saw some men—they must be the French—running from the right side of the road to the left. One fell in the mud under the feet of Petya's horse.

Around one hut a throng of Cossacks were gathered doing something. From the midst of the throng arose a terrible shriek. Petya galloped up to this throng, and the first thing he saw was a Frenchman's white face, his lower jaw trembling. He was clutching the shaft of a lance directed at his breast.

"Hurrah! boys . . . Ours!" yelled Petya, and giving free rein to his excited horse, he streaked up the street.

Ahead he heard shots. Cossacks, hussars, and tattered Russian prisoners, running from both sides of the road, were incoherently shouting something at the top of their voices. A youthful Frenchman in a blue cape, without his cap, and with a red, scowling face, was defending himself with his bayonet against the hussars.

When Petya reached him he had already fallen.

"Too late again!" flashed through Petya's head, and he dashed off to where the shots were heard most frequently. This was in the yard of the manor house where he had been the night before with Dolokhof. The French had intrenched themselves behind the hedge and in the park, where the bushes grew dense and wild, and they were firing at the Cossacks clustered around the gates. On reaching the gates, Petya, through the gunpowder smoke, saw Dolokhof, with a pale greenish face, shouting something to his men.

"At their flank! Wait for the infantry!" he was yelling, just as Petya rode up.

"Wait? . . . Hurra-a-a-a-ah!" yelled Petya; and without pausing a single instant he rode up to the very place where the shots were heard, and where the gunpowder smoke was densest. A volley rang out; the bullets fell thick and fast, and did their work. The Cossacks and Dolokhof followed Petya through the gates. The Frenchmen could be seen through the thick, billowing smoke, some throwing down their arms and coming out from behind the bushes to meet the Cossacks, others running down the slope to the pond.

Petya still rode his horse at a gallop around the manor-house yard, but instead of guiding him by the bridle, he was waving both his hands in the strangest, wildest manner, and was leaning more and more to one side of the saddle. His horse, coming on the campfire, which was smoldering in the morning light, stopped short, and Petya fell heavily on the wet ground. The Cossacks saw his arms and legs twitch, although his head was motionless. A bullet had struck him in the head.

Dolokhof, after a moment's conversation with an old French officer who came out of the house with a handkerchief on his sword, and explained that they surrendered, dismounted and went to Petya, lying there motionless, with outstretched arms.

"Done for," he said, scowling; and he went to the gates to meet Denisof, who was coming toward him.

"Killed!" cried Denisof, seeing, while still at a distance, the unquestionably hopeless position, only too well known to him, in which Petya's body lay.

"Done for," repeated Dolokhof, as if the repetition of this word gave him some satisfaction; and he hastened to the prisoners around whom the Cossacks were crowding. "We can't take him," he called back to Denisof.

Denisof made no reply. He rode up to Petya, dismounted, and with trembling hands turned Petya over; he looked at his face, already turned pale, and stained with blood and mud.

"I like something sweet. Splendid raisins, take them all," echoed in his mind. And the Cossacks, with amazement, looked around as they heard the sound, like the barking of a dog, with which Denisof quickly turned away, went to the hedge, and clutched it.

Among the Russian prisoners released by Denisof and Dolokhof was Pierre Bezukhof.

VII

THE FRENCH COMMANDERS had given no new orders concerning the party of prisoners to which Pierre belonged at the time of the general exodus from Moscow.

On the third of November this party found itself with a different escort and with a different train of wagons from the ones with which they had left Moscow.

One-half of the provision train, which had followed them during the first stages of the march, had been captured by the Cossacks; the other half had gone on ahead. The cavalrymen without horses, who had marched in the van, had all disappeared; not one was left.

The number of prisoners had melted away more than any of those in the three divisions. Out of three hundred and thirty men who had left Moscow, there now remained less than one hundred. The order which had been observed on the departure from Moscow, of keeping officers separate from the other prisoners, had for some time been disregarded; all those who could march went together, and Pierre after the third march was again brought into the company of Karatayef and the gray bow-legged dog which had chosen Karatayef as her master.

Karatayef, on the third day out from Moscow, had a relapse of the same fever from which he had suffered in the Moscow hospital, and as he grew worse Pierre avoided him. He did not know why it was, but from the time that Karatayef began to fail, Pierre could not approach him without exercising great self-control. And when he did, and heard the muted groans that Karatayef emitted when he stretched out to rest, and smelled the odor that now more powerfully than ever emanated from Karatayef, Pierre avoided him as much as possible, and kept him out of his mind.

During his imprisonment in the barn, Pierre was made aware, not by logic but by his whole being, by life itself, that man is created for happiness, that happiness lies in himself, in the satisfaction of the simple needs of living, and that all unhappiness arises not from lack but from superfluity. Now, during these last three weeks of the march, he learned still another new and consoling truth—that there is nothing fearsome in the world. He learned that just as there is no condition in which a man can be happy and absolutely free, so also there is no condition in which a man can be completely unhappy and unfree.

He learned that suffering has its limits, and freedom has its limits, and these limits are very close together; that the man who suffers because one petal on his bed of roses is crumpled, suffers just as much as he now suffered sleeping on the cold, damp ground, one side roasting from the campfire, the other freezing; that when he wore dancing pumps that were too tight, he suffered just as much as he suffered now going barefoot—his shoes were completely worn out—with his feet covered with sores.

He learned that when he seemingly, of his own free will, married his wife, he was not really any more free than now, when he was shut up for the night in a stable.

Of all that he afterwards called suffering, but scarcely felt at the time, the worst was from his bare, bruised feet covered with sores. The horseflesh was palatable and nourishing; the saltpeter odor of the gun-powder, which they used instead of salt, was even pleasant; the weather was not very cold— in the daytime while marching it was even warm, and at night they had bivouac fires; the vermin which fed upon him warmed his body. The one thing hardest to bear was the state of his feet.

On the second day of the retreat, Pierre, examining his sores by the fire, felt that it was impossible to take another step; but when all got up, he hobbled along, and later, when he had warmed up, he walked without pain, though when evening came it was more terrible than ever to look at his feet. But he did not look at them, and turned his thoughts to other things.

Now for the first time Pierre realized all man's power of vitality, and the saving force of diverting the attention, which, like the safety valve in the steam engine, lets off the excess of steam as soon as the pressure exceeds the normal.

He neither saw nor heard how the prisoners who fell behind were shot down, although more than a hundred perished in this way. He did not think of Karatayef, who grew weaker every day, and was evidently fated to suffer the same lot. Still less did Pierre think of himself. The more painful his position, the more appalling the future, the more did thoughts come to him, joyful and consoling memories, and visions which had no connection with his present misery.

At noon of November third Pierre was climbing up a muddy, slippery hill, looking at his feet and at the roughness of the road.

Occasionally his eyes glanced at the familiar throng around him, and then back to his feet again. Both the one and the other were peculiarly connected with his individual impressions.

The gray bow-legged Sieri was frolicking by the side of the road, occasionally lifting up her hind leg as a sign of her agility and jollity, flying along on three legs, and then again on all four darting off to bark at the crows which were feasting on carrion. Sieri was more frolicsome and in better condition than she had been in Moscow. On all sides lay the flesh of various animals—men as well as horses—in various degrees of putrefaction, and the constant passing of people did not permit the wolves to approach, so that Sieri was able to get all she wanted to eat.

It had been raining since morning, and if for a moment it seemed that it was passing over and the skies were going to clear, instantly after a short respite the downpour would be heavier than ever. The road was completely soaked and could not absorb any more water, and little brooks ran along the ruts.

Pierre plodded along, looking at one side, counting his steps by threes, and doubling down his fingers. Apostrophizing the rain, he kept repeating mentally, "Rain, rain, please don't come again."

"To your places!" suddenly cried a voice.

A happy commotion and expectation of something good and solemn stirred among the prisoners and convoy. On all sides were heard shouts of command, and at the left suddenly appeared well-dressed cavalrymen, trotting by the prisoners on handsome horses. All faces wore that expression of tension which is usually seen in the neighborhood of important personages.

The prisoners were collected and pushed off the road; the soldiers formed in line.

"The emperor! the emperor! the marshal! the duke!"—and as soon as the plump horses of the mounted escort had dashed by, a coach drawn by six gray horses thundered past. Pierre caught a glimpse of the calm, handsome, plump but pale face of a man in a three-cornered hat. This was one of the marshals.

The marshal's eye rested on Pierre's rotund, noticeable figure, and the expression with which the marshal scowled and turned away his face made it evident to Pierre that he felt sympathy and wanted to hide it.

The general in charge of the division, with a red, frightened face, galloped after the carriage, spurring on his lean horse. Several officers gathered together; the soldiers pressed around them. All faces wore an expression of excitement and tension.

"What did he say? What did he say?" Pierre heard them asking.

While the marshal had been passing, the prisoners had gathered in a bunch, and Pierre noticed Karatayef, whom he had not seen since early that morning. Karatayef in his short coat was leaning up against a birch tree. His face was lighted by an expression of gentle solemnity. He looked at Pierre out of his kindly round eyes, which were now full of tears, and he seemed to be calling to him, as if he wanted to say something. But Pierre was too absorbed in his own trouble. He pretended not to see him, and hastened away.

When the prisoners started on their march again, Pierre glanced back. Karatayef was sitting by the edge of the road, under the birch tree, and two Frenchmen were arguing about something over him. Pierre did not look longer. He went on his way, limping up the hill.

From the place where Karatayef had been left behind, the report of a musket shot was heard. Pierre distinctly heard this report, but at the instant he heard it he recollected that he had not finished his calculation of how many stages there were to Smolensk, a calculation in which he had been interrupted by the arrival of the marshal. And he proceeded with his counting.

The two French soldiers, one of whom held the smoking musket which he had just discharged, ran past Pierre. Both of them were pale, and in the expression of their faces—one of them looked timidly at Pierre—there was something that reminded him of the young soldier who had been executed. Pierre looked at this soldier, and remembered how this private, a few days before they had started, had scorched his shirt as he was drying himself by the campfire, and how they had made sport of him.

The dog stayed behind, and was howling around the place where Karatayef was left.

"What a fool! what is she barking about?" Pierre exclaimed inwardly.

The soldiers, Pierre's comrades, walking in file with him, did not look back either to the place whence first the shot and then the howl of the dog came, but a stern expression settled on all their faces.

VIII

THE PROVISION TRAIN and the prisoners and the marshal's baggage wagons halted at the village of Shamsheva. All gathered in groups around the bivouac fires. Pierre went to a campfire, and, after eating some roasted horse-flesh, lay down with his back to the fire and instantly fell asleep.

And suddenly there seemed to be standing before Pierre, as if alive, a weak little old man, long forgotten, who in Switzerland had taught Pierre geography.

"Wait," said the little man. And he showed Pierre a globe. This globe was a living, vibrating ball, and had no natural divisions. The whole surface of the globe consisted of drops closely packed together. And these drops were all in motion, changing about, sometimes several coalescing into one, sometimes one breaking up into many. Each drop tried to expand, to occupy as much space as possible; but others, striving for the same end, crushed it, sometimes annihilated it, sometimes coalesced with it.

"Such is life," said the little old teacher.

"How simple and how clear," thought Pierre. "Why is it I never knew this before?"

"In the center is God, and each drop strives to spread out, to expand, so as to reflect Him in the largest possible proportions. And each expands, and coalesces, and is pressed down, and is to all outward appearance annihilated, and sinks into the depths and comes out again."

"That was what happened to Karatayef; he overflowed and vanished."

"You understand now, my boy!" said the teacher. "You understand? The devil take you!" cried a voice, and Pierre awoke.

He sat up. Squatting on his heels by the campfire sat a Frenchman who had just been pushing away a Russian soldier, and was now broiling a piece of meat stuck on a ramrod. His muscular red hand, short-fingered, covered with hair, was skilfully twirling the ramrod. His cinnamon-colored, scowling face and knitted brows could be clearly seen in the light of the embers.

"It's all the same to him," he growled, addressing the soldier standing near him. "Brigand! Go!" And the soldier, twirling the ramrod, glared gloomily at Pierre. Pierre turned away and gazed into the darkness.

A Russian soldier, one of the prisoners—the same one the Frenchman had pushed away—was sitting by the fire and was patting something with his hand. Looking closer, Pierre recognized the little bow-legged gray dog, which was wagging its tail as it crouched down beside the soldier.

"Ah! She's come, has she?" said Pierre, "but Plat—" he began, but did not finish the name.

Before sunrise he was awakened by loud and frequent firing and yells. The French were rushing past him.

"The Cossacks!" cried one of them, and in a moment Pierre was surrounded by a crowd of Russians.

It was some time before Pierre could realize what had happened to him. On all sides he heard the joyful exclamations of his comrades. "Brothers! comrades! friends!" shouted old soldiers, and burst into tears as they embraced Cossacks and hussars. Cossacks and hussars surrounded the prisoners and made haste to offer them clothes, shoes, bread.

Pierre stood in the midst of them, sobbing, and could not speak a word. He threw his arms around the first soldier he met, and kissed him, weeping.

Dolokhof stood at the gates of the dilapidated mansion, watching the disarmed French file past him. The Frenchmen, excited by all that had occurred, were talking loudly among themselves; but when they passed Dolokhof, who stood lightly flicking his boots with his short whip, and watching them with his cool, glassy glance that boded them nothing good, their voices were hushed. On the other side stood Dolokhof's Cossack, counting the prisoners, scoring them in hundreds on the gate with a bit of chalk.

"How many?" asked Dolokhof of the Cossack who was counting the prisoners.

"Into the second hundred," replied the Cossack.

"Move on, move on!" exclaimed Dolokhof in French; and as his eyes met those of the prisoners who filed past, they lighted with a cruel gleam.

Denisof, with a gloomy face, walked bareheaded behind the Cossacks who were carrying the body of Petya Rostof to a grave which they had dug in the garden.

IX

AFTER THE NINTH of November, when hard frosts began, the flight of the French assumed a still more tragic character because of the many who perished of cold or were burned to death at the campfires, while the emperor, kings and dukes continued to pursue their homeward route wrapped in furs and riding in carriages, and carrying the treasure that they had stolen.

But in its real essence, the process of flight and disintegration of the army had not really changed.

From Moscow to Viazma the seventy-three thousand composing the French army, not counting the Guard—which throughout the whole war had done nothing except pillage—the seventy-three thousand of the army were reduced to thirty-six thousand. Out of the number lost, not more than five thousand perished in battle. This is the first term of a progression whereby, with mathematical accuracy, the succeeding terms are determined.

The French army melted away and was destroyed in the same proportion from Moscow to Viazma, from Viazma to Smolensk, from Smolensk to the Beresina, from the Beresina to Vilna, independently of the greater or less degree of cold, the pursuit of the Russians, the obstruction of the road, and all other conditions taken singly.

After Viazma, the French armies, instead of marching in three columns, went in one crowd, and thus proceeded to the end.

Berthier wrote to his sovereign (it is well known how far commanders allow themselves to depart from the truth in describing the position of their armies)—he wrote:

> I think it my duty to acquaint your majesty with the condition of the troops in the different army corps that I have observed during these last three days in the various stages. They are almost disbanded. Less than a fourth of the soldiers, at most, remain under the standards. This proportion holds in nearly all the regiments. The others are straggling off by themselves in different directions, trying to find provisions and to escape from discipline. All of them look to Smolensk as the place where they will retrieve themselves. During the last few days many soldiers have been noticed throwing away their cartridges and muskets. In this condition of things, the interests of your majesty's service require that, whatever your ultimate plans may be, the army should be rallied at Smolensk, and rid of noncombatants, of unmounted cavalrymen, of superfluous baggage, and a portion of the artillery, since it is no longer in proportion to the other forces. Moreover, the soldiers require some days of rest and supplies of food, for they are worn out by hunger and fatigue; many in the last few days have died on the road or in bivouac. This state of things is constantly growing worse, and there is danger that, if remedies are not promptly applied, the troops could not be controlled in case of battle.—November 9, at twenty miles from Smolensk.

Rushing into Smolensk, which was to them like the Promised Land, the French fought with one another for food, pillaged their own stores, and, when everything had been plundered, hurried on.

All fled, not knowing whither or why; and Napoleon, with all his genius, knew less than others why they did so, for no one ordered him to fly.

But, nevertheless, he and those around him observed their old habits:

wrote orders, letters, reports, Orders of the Day; and they addressed one another as Sire, My Cousin, Prince d'Eckmühl, King of Naples, etc.

But these orders and reports were only on paper; nothing was done according to them, because they could no longer be carried out; and though they continued to call each other Majesty, Highness, and Cousin, they all felt that they were miserable wretches who had done much evil, and that expiation had begun. And, though they pretended to be very solicitous about the army, each of them thought only of himself and how he might get off and escape as speedily as possible.

1812-1813

The grande armée is lost; France itself totters as the Prussians, Austrians, Italians join in the kill. Napoleon leaves his army and returns to France to raise new forces, with a view to defending his country from invasion. However, it is too late. In little more than a year Paris will have fallen; Napoleon will abdicate and will be exiled.

Part Fifteenth

WHEN a man sees a dying animal, horror seizes him; what he himself is—his own essence—is evidently perishing before his very eyes, ceasing to exist.

But when the dying one is a human being, and a person beloved and tenderly cherished, then, over and above the horror at the cessation of the life, the soul itself is torn and wounded. This wound, like a physical wound, sometimes kills, sometimes heals, but it is always painful, and shrinks from any external, irritating touch.

After Prince Andrei's death, Natasha and Princess Maria both felt this. Their souls had quailed and bowed under the threatening cloud of death that hung over them, and they dared not look into the face of life. They were extremely cautious not to expose their wounds to humiliating, painful contact.

Everything—a swiftly passing carriage on the street, the announcement of dinner, the maid's question as to what gowns she would prepare for them; still worse, a word of perfunctory, feeble sympathy—made the wound throb painfully, seemed an affront, and profaned that urgent silence in which they both were striving to listen to that stern, terrible choir which ceased not, in their imagination, to chant, and prevented them from looking into those mysterious, infinite distances which, for an instant, opened out before them.

Only when they were together alone, they felt no sense of pain and humiliation. They talked together very little. When they talked, it was on the most insignificant topics. And both of them alike avoided all reference to anything concerning the future.

To recognize the possibility of a future seemed to them an offense to his memory. All the more sedulously they avoided in their talk everything that had reference to Prince Andrei. It seemed to them that what they experienced and felt could not be expressed in words. It seemed to them that every verbal reference to the separate events of his life disturbed the majesty and sacredness of the mystery which had been accomplished before their eyes.

Their continual self-restraint, their constant, strenuous avoidance of all that might lead to mention of him, these halting places that stood in the way of every possible approach to the subject which they had tacitly agreed to leave untouched, brought up before their imaginations with all the greater clearness and distinctness that which they felt.

But pure, unmitigated grief is as impossible as pure and unmitigated joy.

Princess Maria, by her position as sole and independent mistress of her fate, as guardian and instructor of her nephew, was the first to be brought, by the exigencies of real life, forth from that world of tribulation in which she had been living for the past fortnight. She received letters from her relatives, and they had to be answered; the room that Nikolusha occupied was damp, and he began to have a cough. Alpatitch came from Yaroslavl with his accounts to be checked, and with his proposal and advice for her to go back to Moscow, to her house on the Vozdvizhenka, which had remained intact and needed only minor repairs.

Life would not stand still, and it was necessary to live.

Hard as it was for Princess Maria to emerge from that world of solitary contemplation in which she had been living till then, sorry as she was, and almost conscience-stricken, to leave Natasha alone, the labors of life demanded her participation, and she, in spite of herself, had to give way. She verified Alpatitch's accounts, consulted with Dessalles in regard to her nephew, and made arrangements and preparations for her journey to Moscow.

Natasha was left to herself, and, since Princess Maria had begun to get ready for her departure, avoided even her. Princess Maria asked the countess to let Natasha go to Moscow with her, and both father and mother gladly consented, since each day they noticed a decline in their daughter's physical vigor, and hoped that a change of scene would do her good and that the physicians of Moscow would help her.

"I will go nowhere," replied Natasha, when this matter was proposed to her. "All I ask is to be left in peace," said she, and she hastened from the room, scarcely able to restrain her tears—tears not so much of grief as of vexation and anger.

About the beginning of January, Natasha, thin and pale, and dressed in a black woolen dress, with her braid carelessly knotted up in a pug, was sitting with her feet up on the couch, nervously crumpling and unfolding the ends of her sash, and gazing with her eyes fixed on the door.

She was looking at the place to which he had vanished, at that side of life. And that side of life, of which she had never thought in days gone by, which before had always seemed so distant and unreal, was now nearer and more familiar, more comprehensible, than the ordinary side of life, where everything was either emptiness and decay or suffering and humiliation.

She looked at the place where she knew he had been, but she could not convince herself that he was not the same. She saw him once more as he had been at Mitishchi, at Troitsa, at Yaroslavl. She saw his face, heard his voice, repeated his words and the words that she had said to him, and sometimes imagined words which they might have spoken.

There he is lying in the easy-chair, in his velvet cloak, with his head leaning on his thin white hand. His chest is terribly sunken and his shoulders raised. His lips are firmly set, his eyes are gleaming, and on his pallid brow a wrinkle comes and goes. One leg trembles almost imperceptibly with a rapid motion.

Natasha knows he is struggling with tormenting pain. "What is that pain like? Why that pain? How does he feel? How does it pain him?" she wondered.

He noticed her fixed gaze, he raised his eyes, and without a trace of a smile began to speak:

"There is one thing which is terrible," said he; "to be bound forever to a suffering man. This is eternal torment!"

And he looked at her with a scrutinizing glance. Natasha replied then, as she always did, before she had time to think what she should reply. She said: "This cannot continue so, it will not be so always; you will get well—entirely well."

She now saw him as he had been from the first, and lived over in her memory all she had then experienced. She recalled that long, melancholy, stern look which he had given her at those words, and she realized the significance of the reproach and despair expressed in this protracted look.

"I agreed with him," said Natasha to herself, "that it would be terrible if he should remain always suffering so. I said this at that time, simply because I meant that for him it would be terrible, but he understood it in a different way. He thought it would be terrible for me. At that time he was still anxious to live, was afraid to die. And I said this so crudely, so stupidly! I did not think of that. I meant something entirely different. If I had said what I meant, I would have said: 'If he were to perish by a living death before my eyes, I would be happy in comparison with what I feel now.' Now there is no one, nothing! Could he have known this? No! He did not know it, and he will never know! And now it is too late, too late to set this right."

And once more he said to her those same words, but this time Natasha, in her imagination, answered him in a different way. She stopped him and said: "Terrible for you, but not for me. You know that for me life without you would be nothing, and to suffer with you is the dearest happiness."

And he seized her hand and pressed it just as he had pressed it that terrible evening four days before he died. And in her imagination she spoke to him still other tender, loving words which she might have uttered then, but did not, and which now she could and did say: "I love you! . . . I love you. . . . I love, I love!" she repeated, convulsively wringing her hands, clenching her teeth, with fierce determination.

And the bitter sweetness of grief took possession of her, and her eyes filled with tears, but suddenly she asked herself to whom she was saying that. "Where is he and what is he now?" And once more everything grew dark with hard and cruel doubt; and once more contracting her brows into a frown, she looked at the place where he had been. And now, now it seemed to her that she was going to fathom the mystery. . . .

But at the very instant when it seemed to her that the incomprehensible was already about to reveal itself to her, a loud rattling of the doorknob painfully struck upon her ears. With hasty, incautious steps, with a frightened expression never before seen on her face, Dunyasha the maid came running into the room.

"Please come to your papa as quick as possible," said Dunyasha, with that peculiar and excited look. "Bad news . . . about Count Petya . . . a letter," she cried, with a sob.

II

BESIDES HER general feeling of aversion for all people, Natasha at this time experienced a peculiar feeling of aversion for the members of her own family. All her relatives—father, mother, Sonya—were so near to her, so familiar, so everyday, that all their words, their sentiments, seemed to her a disrespect to that world in which she had been living lately, and she looked upon them not only with indifferent but even with hostile eyes. She heard Dunyasha's words about Petya, about bad news, but she did not take them in. "What misfortune can have happened to them? What bad news can it be? Everything with them goes on calmly, as it always has," said Natasha mentally.

As she went into the hall her father was coming hastily out of the countess' room. His face was wrinkled and wet with tears. He was evidently hastening from her room so as to give free course to the affliction that overmastered him. When he saw Natasha he waved his hands in despair, and burst into painfully convulsive sobs, which distorted his round, placid face.

"Pet—Petya . . . go to her, go . . . she . . . she is . . . calling for you . . ."

And crying like a child, swiftly shuffling along on his feeble legs, he went to a chair and almost fell into it, burying his face in his hands.

Suddenly something like an electric shock ran over Natasha's whole being. A terribly acute pain struck her heart. She experienced a cruel agony. It seemed to her that something within her snapped and that she was dying. But immediately succeeding this agony there came a sense of deliverance from the torpor that had been weighing down her life. Seeing her father, and hearing her mother's terrible agonized cry in the next room, she instantly forgot herself and her own sorrow. She ran up to her father, but he, feebly waving his arm, pointed to her mother's door.

Princess Maria, pale and with her lower jaw trembling, came out of the room, and taking Natasha by the hand, said something to her. Natasha neither saw her nor heard her. With swift steps she passed through the door, paused for an instant, as if struggling with her own emotion, and ran to her mother.

The countess lay in her easy-chair, in a strangely awkward and stiff position, and was beating her head against the wall. Sonya and the maids were holding her by the arms.

"Call Natasha! Natasha!" cried the countess. "It is false! False! . . . He lies! . . . Call Natasha!" she cried, trying to tear herself away from those holding her. "Go away, all of you. It is false! . . . Killed? . . . Ha! ha! ha! . . . It is false!"

Natasha leaned her knee on the chair, bent over her mother, threw her arms around her, lifted her up with unexpected strength, turned her face around, and pressed her cheeks against hers.

"Mama! . . . Darling! . . . I am here, dearest! Mama!" she kept whispering, without a second's intermission.

She kept her arms firmly around her mother, gently struggled with her, called for cushions and water, and unbuttoned and began to take off her mother's gown.

"Darling, dearest . . . mama, dearest heart!" she kept whispering, while she kissed her head, hands, and face, and felt how her tears, like rivulets, tickling her nose and her cheeks, kept flowing.

The countess pressed her daughter's hand, closed her eyes, and was calm for an instant. Then suddenly, with unnatural swiftness, she raised herself up, glared around wildly, and, seeing Natasha, pressed her head with all her might. Then she turned toward her Natasha's face, convulsed with the pain, and long scrutinized it.

"Natasha, you love me," she said, in a low, confidential whisper. "Natasha, you would not deceive me? Tell me the whole truth."

Natasha looked at her with eyes brimming with tears, and her face expressed only a prayer for forgiveness and love.

"Dearest, mama," she repeated, exerting all the energies of her love, in order to take upon herself some of the excess of woe that had become too heavy for her mother to bear. And again, in the unequal struggle against the reality, the mother, refusing to believe that she could still exist when her darling boy, treasured far more than life, was killed, she relapsed from the reality into the world of unreason.

Natasha could not have told how that first day passed, that night, the following day, and the following night. She did not sleep, and did not leave her mother's side. Natasha's love, faithful and patient, seemed to wrap itself around the countess every second; not with consolation, not with explanation, but with something like a summons back to life.

On the third night the countess grew calm for several minutes, and Natasha closed her eyes and rested her head on the arm of the chair. The bed creaked; Natasha opened her eyes. The countess was sitting up in bed, and speaking in a low tone:

"How glad I am that you have come! You are tired; wouldn't you like some tea?"

Natasha went to her.

"You have grown handsome and strong!" continued the countess, taking her daughter's hand.

"Mama, what are you saying?"

"Natasha! He is dead, he is dead!" And, throwing her arms around her daughter, the countess for the first time began to weep.

Princess Maria postponed her departure.

Sonya and the count tried to take Natasha's place, but they found it impossible. They saw that she alone could keep her mother from wild despair. For three weeks Natasha lived constantly by her mother's side, slept in a chair in her room, gave her food and drink, and talked to her unceasingly, talked because her tender, caressing voice was the only thing that calmed the countess.

A wound in the heart of a mother cannot heal. Petya's death had torn away half of her life. At the end of a month, after the news of Petya's death had arrived, though it had found her a fresh and well-preserved woman of fifty, she crept out of her room an old woman, half dead, and no longer taking any interest in life. But the same wound which had half killed the countess—this new wound brought Natasha back to life.

A spiritual wound, arising from the laceration of the spiritual body, exactly like a physical wound, strange as it may seem, after the deep wound has cicatrized, and its edges have come together—the spiritual wound, like the physical one, heals only through the inward working of the forces of life. Thus healed Natasha's wound. She had thought that life for her was finished. But suddenly her love for her mother proved to her that the essence of her life—love—was still alive within her. Love awoke and life awoke.

Prince Andrei's last days had brought Natasha and Princess Maria close together. This new misfortune still more united them. Princess Maria postponed her departure, and for three weeks tended Natasha like an ailing child. The weeks spent by her in her mother's room had been a severe drain on her physical energies.

Neither of them liked to speak of him, for fear they might in words desecrate what seemed to them those lofty heights of feeling which were in their hearts; but this reticence concerning him was causing them, little by little—though they would not have believed it—to forget him.

Natasha grew thin and pale, and feeble physically, so that they kept talking about her health; but this was agreeable to her. But sometimes, unexpectedly, there came over her not so much a fear of death as a fear of pain, weakness, loss of beauty; and, in spite of herself, she sometimes attentively contemplated her bare arm, marveling at its thinness, or in the morning she gazed into the mirror at her pinched and, as it seemed to her, ugly face. It seemed to her that this was unavoidable, and at the same time it was terrible and sad to her.

One time she ran quickly upstairs, and found herself breathing hard. The next moment she involuntarily invented some excuse to go down again, and then once more ran upstairs to test her strength and experiment on herself.

Another time she called Dunyasha, and her voice sounded weak. She tried it once more; she called her, although she heard her coming—called her in those chest tones which she used to use in singing, and listened to them.

She did not know it, she would not have believed it, but under what seemed to her an impenetrable layer of mold that buried her soul, the delicate, tender young shoots of grass were already germinating, were inevitably growing; and thus, by their life-giving, victorious force, would hide from sight the sorrow she had suffered, so that it would soon be forgotten. The wound was healing inwardly.

Toward the beginning of February, Princess Maria went to Moscow, and the count insisted on Natasha's going with her, so as to consult with the doctors.

III

After the encounter at Viazma, where Kutuzof could not restrain his troops from the desire to overthrow, to cut off, the enemy, the further movement of the fleeing French and the pursuing Russians took place without a battle until they reached Krasnoye.

The flight of the French was so rapid that the pursuing Russians could not catch up with them, the horses in the cavalry and artillery came to a standstill, and information in regard to the movements of the French was always untrustworthy.

The men of the Russian army were so worn out by these uninterrupted marches of almost thirty miles a day that they could not move onward any faster. To appreciate the degree of exhaustion from which the Russian army suffered, it is only necessary to realize the significance of the fact that while the Russian army, on leaving Tarutino, had a hundred thousand men, and lost during the whole march not more than five thousand in killed and wounded and less than a hundred taken prisoners, they had only fifty thousand men when they got to Krasnoye.

The principal cause of the diminution of Napoleon's army was the rapidity of its flight, and indubitable proof of this is furnished by the corresponding diminution of the Russian troops.

All Kutuzof's efforts, just as at Tarutino and at Viazma, were directed—as far as lay in his power—solely to the prevention of interference with the destructive movement of the French (though this was contrary to desires expressed in Petersburg and in the Russian army by his own generals), and to cooperation with it which would facilitate the movement of his own troops.

But it seemed to the other generals, especially those who were not Russian —being anxious to distinguish themselves, to astonish the world, for some reason or other to take some duke or king prisoner—it seemed to these generals that now, when any battle was abominable and absurd, it was the very time to give battle and conquer someone.

Kutuzof merely shrugged his shoulders when, one after another, they laid before him their plans for maneuvers to be accomplished by these badly shod, half-famished soldiers, without heavy winter coats, who during a month had been reduced one-half though they had not fought a battle, and who must still go to the frontier—a distance greater than that already traversed.

At Krasnoye they took twenty-six thousand prisoners and captured hundreds of cannon and a kind of a stick that they called "the marshal's baton"; and they quarreled as to which had distinguished themselves, and they were contented with this, but much regretted that they had not captured Napoleon or some hero, some one of the marshals, and they blamed one another, and especially Kutuzof.

In 1812-1813, Kutuzof was openly accused of serious mistakes. The sovereign was displeased with him; and in the history of the campaign, written not long since, by imperial orders, it is declared that Kutuzof was a crafty court liar, who trembled at the name of Napoleon, and who, by his blunders at Krasnoye and the Beresina, deprived the Russian troops of the glory of a complete victory over the French.

And yet it is hard to conceive a historical personage whose activity was so faithfully and so constantly devoted to a single aim. It is hard to imagine an aim more worthy or more consistent with the will of a whole people. Still more difficult would it be to discover another example in history where an aim set by a historical personage was so completely realized as the aim to which Kutuzof devoted his whole activity in 1812.

Kutuzof never talked about the forty centuries that looked down from the Pyramids, of the sacrifices he had made for his country, of what he intended to accomplish or had already accomplished. As a general thing, he spoke little of himself, never played any part, seemed always a most simple and ordinary man, and said only the most simple and the most ordinary things.

When Count Rostopchin galloped across the Yauza bridge up to Kutuzof, and loaded him with personal reproaches for the loss of Moscow, and said, "How was it that you promised not to give up Moscow without a battle?" Kutuzof replied, "I will not give up Moscow without a battle."

And yet Moscow was already abandoned.

When Arakcheyef came to him from the sovereign and said that Yermolof must be appointed chief of artillery, Kutuzof replied: "Yes. I was just now proposing that myself."

And yet, a few moments before, he had expressed himself quite differently.

What was it to him, who alone amid the foolish throng about him understood all the mighty significance of the event, what was it to him whether Count Rostopchin attributed to him or to anyone else the abandonment of the capital? Still less could he be concerned with the question who should be named chief of artillery.

But this same man, who scorned speech, never once, throughout the whole period of his activity, uttered a single word that would not have agreed with the one object toward which he moved throughout the course of the war. With evident reluctance, with a painful assurance that he would not be understood, again and again in the most varied circumstances he expressed his thought.

From the time of the Battle of Borodino, when his quarrel with those around him began, he alone declared that the Battle of Borodino was a victory. He alone declared that the loss of Moscow was not the loss of Russia. He, in reply to Lauriston's offer of peace, said that peace could not be made because such was not the will of the people. He alone, during the retreat of the French, declared that all our maneuvers were useless, that everything would come out of itself better than we could wish, that it was only necessary to give the enemy the "golden bridge"; that neither the Battle of Tarutino, nor that of Krasnoye, nor that of Viazma, was necessary; that, to reach the frontier, troops were needed; that he would not sacrifice a single Russian soldier for ten Frenchmen.

And he alone, this deceitful courtier, as he is represented to us, this man who to please his sovereign lied to Arakcheyef, he alone, this courtier, at the risk of winning his sovereign's ill will, declared, at Vilna, that war prolonged beyond the frontier would be dangerous and useless.

He, this Kutuzof, the temporizer, whose device was "patience and time," the enemy of decisive actions, he gave battle at Borodino, clothing the preparation for it with unexampled solemnity.

He, this Kutuzof, who at Austerlitz, before the battle began, declared that it would be lost; and at Borodino, in spite of the conviction of the generals that it was a defeat, protested up to the time of his death that the Battle of Borodino was a victory, though the example of an army that had won a victory being obliged to retreat was unheard of in history—he alone, during all the time of the retreat, insisted on refraining from further battles, since they were now useless—from beginning a new war, and from crossing the frontier.

It is easy at the present time to comprehend the significance of the event, provided we do not concern ourselves with the mass of plans fermenting in the heads of a dozen men, since the whole event, with all its consequences, lies before us. But how, at that time, could this old man alone, against the opinions of many, divine so accurately the significance of the national impression of the event; why did he not once prove false to it?

This extraordinary power of insight had its source in that national senti-ment which he carried in his heart in all its purity and vigor. Only the recognition of this sentiment in Kutuzof compelled the people by such strange paths to choose this old man, in disgrace as he was, and against the will of the Tsar, to be their representative in the national war. And only this sentiment elevated Kutuzof to the high pinnacle of humanity from which he, the general-in-chief, employed all his efforts, not to kill and ex-terminate men, but to save and have pity on them.

This simple, modest, and therefore truly majestic figure could not be cast in the counterfeit mold employed by history to describe the European hero, supposed to be a ruler of the nations.

For the valet there can be no great man, because the valet has his own conception of greatness.

I V

THE SEVENTEENTH of November was the first day of the so-called Battle of Krasnoye. Before dark, when after many disputes and blunders caused by generals who did not reach the places where they should have been, after much galloping about of aides with commands and counter-commands, when it was already self-evident that the enemy were everywhere running away and that a battle could not and would not take place, Kutuzof set forth from Krasnoye and rode to Dobroye, where the headquarters had been established for that day.

The day was clear and frosty. Kutuzof, with a big suite of generals, most of whom were dissatisfied with him and were whispering behind his back, rode to Dobroye mounted on his stout white cob. The road all along was crowded with French prisoners captured that day, seven thousand of them had been taken, who were trying to warm themselves around the bivouac fires.

Not far from Dobroye a huge crowd of ragged prisoners, wearing what-ever they happened to have laid their hands on, were loudly talking as they stood in the road near a long row of unlimbered French cannon. As the commander-in-chief approached, the talking quieted down and all eyes were fixed on Kutuzof, who in his white fur cap with a red top, and wadded cloak hunched upon his stooping shoulders, slowly moved along the road. One of the generals was reporting to Kutuzof where the prisoners and can-non had been captured.

Kutuzof semed preoccupied and did not hear the general's words. He blinked his eyes with displeasure and kept gazing attentively and fixedly at the figures of the prisoners, who presented a particularly sad spectacle. Most of the French soldiers were maimed, with frostbitten noses and cheeks, and almost all of them had red, swollen, festering eyes.

One group of the French was near the roadside, and two soldiers—the face of one was covered with scars—were tearing a piece of raw meat. There was something terrible and bestial in the wild glances they cast on the new-comers and in the ugly expression with which the scarred soldier, after gazing at Kutuzof, immediately turned away and went on with his occupation.

Kutuzof gazed long and attentively at these two soldiers; frowning still more portentously, he blinked his eyes and thoughtfully shook his head.

In another place he observed a Russian soldier, who, with a laugh, gave a Frenchman a slap on the shoulder and made some friendly remark to him. Kutuzof, again with the same expression, shook his head.

"What were you saying?" he asked of the general, who had gone on with his report and was calling the commander-in-chief's attention to the captured French colors which were bunched in front of the Preobrazhensky regiment.

"Oh, the colors," said Kutuzof, evidently finding it hard to turn his mind from the object that occupied his thoughts. He looked around absent-mindedly. Thousands of eyes from every side looked at him, expecting his reply.

He reined in his horse in front of the Preobrazhensky regiment, drew a heavy sigh, and closed his eyes. One of the suite made a signal to the soldiers who had charge of the standards to advance and group the flag-staffs around the commander-in-chief.

Kutuzof said nothing for some seconds, and then, with evident reluctance yielding to the necessity of his position, raised his head and began to speak. The officers gathered around him. With an attentive glance he surveyed the circle of officers, some of whom he recognized.

"I thank you all," he said, addressing the soldiers and then the officers again. In the silence that reigned around him his slowly spoken words were perfectly distinct. "I thank you all for your hard and faithful service. The victory is complete, and Russia will not forget you. Your glory will be eternal." He was silent and looked around.

"Bend down, bend down its head!" said he to the soldier who held the French eagle and had unexpectedly inclined it toward the Preobrazhensky standard. "Lower, lower still—that's the way. Hurrah, boys!" he cried, with a quick movement of his chin, turning to his soldiers.

"Hurrah, rah-rah!" roared forth from thousands of voices.

While the soldiers were cheering, Kutuzof bent down to his saddle, inclined his head, and his eyes gleamed with a gentle, perceptibly ironical gleam.

"Well, boys!" he began when the cheering had ceased.

And suddenly his voice and the expression of his face changed; no longer the commander-in-chief spoke, but a simple old man who evidently had something of importance to communicate to his comrades.

Through the crowd of officers and the ranks of the soldiers ran a stir, as they pressed forward to hear more distinctly what he would now have to say:

"Well, boys! I know it's hard for you, but what's to be done? Have patience; it is not for long. When we have escorted our guests out of the country we will rest. The Tsar will not forget your labors, will not forget you. It is hard for you, but you are at home all this time, while they—see what they have come to," said he, indicating the prisoners, "worse than the lowest beggars. While they were strong we had no pity on them, but now we may pity them. They, too, are men. Isn't that so, boys?"

He glanced around him, and in the earnest, respectfully perplexed glances fixed on him he read their sympathy with what he had said. His face was constantly more and more illumined by the benevolent smile of old age, by the starlike lines irradiating from the corners of his mouth and eyes. He remained silent for a little, and in apparent perplexity dropped his head.

"Of course it may be said, who invited them to come to us? They deserve it, the damned sons of bitches," said he, suddenly raising his head. And, cracking his whip, he rode off at a gallop, for the first time in the whole campaign followed by roars of laughter and a bellowing hurrah ringing down the long lines of the soldiers as they broke ranks.

The words spoken by Kutuzof could scarcely have been understood by the troops. No one could have been able to report accurately either the solemn words which the field marshal had spoken first, or the kindly simplicity of the old man's words at the last; but not only was the tone of sincerity that rang through the whole speech comprehensible, but that peculiar sense of majestic solemnity in union with compassion for their enemies, and with the feeling of the righteousness of their cause—expressed, if in nothing else, in that old-fashioned, good-natured execration—this feeling found an echo in every man's breast, and found utterance in that joyful, long-sustained cheer.

When afterwards one of the generals came and asked Kutuzof if he would not prefer to ride in his carriage, when he replied he unexpectedly broke into sobs, evidently overcome by profound emotion.

V

THE FRENCH TROOPS melted away in a regular mathematical progression. Even that crossing of the Beresina River, about which so much has been written, was only one of the intermediate steps in the destruction of the French army, and not at all a decisive episode of the campaign. If so much has been written and still is written about the Beresina, it is, so far as it concerns the French, simply because the misfortunes that the French army had up to that time endured steadily, here suddenly accumulated in one moment at the broken bridge on the river—one tragic disaster, which remained in the memory of all.

On the part of the Russians so much has been said and written about the Beresina simply because at Petersburg, far away from the theater of war, a plan was made (by Pfuhl) for drawing Napoleon into a strategical snare on the river Beresina. All were persuaded that everything would be carried out in conformity with the plan, and therefore they insisted that the crossing of the Beresina was the destruction of the French. In reality, the results of the crossing of the Beresina were far less disastrous to the French in loss of artillery and prisoners than the Battle of Krasnoye, as is proved by statistics.

The farther the French fled and the more pitiable the condition of their remnants became, especially after the Beresina—on which, in consequence of the Petersburg plan, especial hopes had rested—the more frenetically waxed the passions of the Russian generals, who indulged in recriminations of each other and especially of Kutuzof.

Kutuzof knew this, and, sighing, simply shrugged his shoulders. But one time—after the Beresina—he lost his temper and wrote the following note to Wittgenstein, who had made a special report to the sovereign:

> Owing to your severe attacks of illness, your excellency will be kind enough on receipt of this to retire to Kaluga, where you will await his imperial majesty's further commands and orders.

But after the retirement of Benigsen came the Grand Duke Konstantin Pavlovitch, who had been present at the beginning of the campaign and had been removed from Kutuzof's army. The grand duke, as soon as he reached the army, assured Kutuzof of his majesty the emperor's dissatisfaction at the insufficient successes of our troops and the slowness of our movements, and informed him that his majesty the emperor himself intended shortly to be present with the army.

This old man, who was no less experienced in the affairs of courts than in affairs military, this Kutuzof who had been appointed commander-in-chief the previous August against the sovereign's will, this man who sent the heir apparent and the grand duke away from the army, who by the power invested in him had signed the abandonment of Moscow, this same Kutuzof now instantly realized that his time was come, that his part was played, and that the semblance of power which he had held was his no more.

And not by his court instinct alone did he realize this. On the one hand he saw that the war in which he had played his part was ended, and he felt that his mission was fulfilled. On the other hand, at the same time, he began to feel physical weariness in his old frame and the absolute need of physical rest.

Kutuzof, on the eleventh of December, arrived at Vilna—"his good Vilna," as he called it. Twice during his career Kutuzof had been governor of Vilna. In the rich city, which had not suffered from the devastation of war, Kutuzof found, besides the amenities of life, of which he had been deprived so long, old friends and pleasant recollections. And suddenly, casting off all military and governmental cares, he plunged into this calm, equable life as far as he was allowed to do so by the passions seething around him, as if all that was occurring and about to occur in the historical was no concern of his.

When, on the twenty-third of December, the sovereign with his suite—Count Tolstoy, Prince Volkonsky, Arakcheyef, and others—after a four days' journey from Petersburg reached Vilna, he drove in his traveling sleigh directly to the castle. In spite of the severe cold, a hundred generals and staff officers in full-dress uniform, and the guard of honor of the Semyonovsky regiment, were waiting at the castle.

A courier, dashing up to the castle in a sleigh drawn by three sweaty horses, cried, "He's coming!" Konovnitsin hurried into the vestibule to inform Kutuzof, who was expecting him in the doorman's little room.

In a moment the old general's stout, portly form, in full-dress uniform, his full regalia covering his chest, and with a scarf tied around his abdomen, came tottering and swaying to the head of the stairs. Kutuzof put his three-cornered hat on, point to the front, took his gloves in his hand, and, letting himself painfully, toilsomely sidewise down the stairs, stepped forth holding in his hand the report which had been prepared to give to the sovereign.

There was a running to and fro, a sound of hurried talking; more horses came unexpectedly dashing by, and all eyes were fixed on a sleigh which came flying up. In it could be seen the figures of the sovereign and Volkonsky.

All this had its physically exciting effect on the old general, though he had been used to it for half a century. With a hasty, nervous movement he adjusted his decorations and straightened his hat, and the instant that the sovereign, stepping out of the sleigh, raised his eyes to him, taking courage and lifting himself up to his full height, he handed him the report and began to speak in his measured, ingratiating voice.

The sovereign with a swift glance measured Kutuzof from head to foot, frowned for an instant, but, instantly mastering himself, stepped forward and, stretching out his arms, embraced the old general.

Once more, owing to the old familiar impression and to the thoughts that came surging into his mind, this embrace had its usual effect upon Kutuzof: he sobbed.

The sovereign greeted the officers and the Semyonovsky Guard, and, having once more shaken hands with the old general, he went with him into the castle.

After the sovereign was left alone with his field marshal, he freely expressed his dissatisfaction with the slowness of the pursuit, with the mistakes made at Krasnoye and on the Beresina, and gave him his ideas as to what should be the coming campaign beyond the frontier. Kutuzof made no reply or remark. That same submissive and stupid expression with which seven years before he had listened to his sovereign's comments on the field of Austerlitz settled now on his face.

When Kutuzof left the study and was passing along the hall with his heavy, plunging gait and with sunken head, someone's voice called him back.

"Your serene highness," cried someone.

Kutuzof raised his head and looked long into the eyes of Count Tolstoy, who, with a small trinket on a silver platter, stood before him. Apparently Kutuzof did not know what was wanted of him. Suddenly he came to himself; a scarcely perceptible smile flashed across his pudgy face, and, making a low and respectful bow, he took the object lying on the platter.

It was the St. George decoration of the first degree.

When, on the following morning, the sovereign said to the officers who came to pay their respects to him, "You have saved not Russia alone; you have saved all Europe," everyone understood perfectly that the war was not ended.

Kutuzof was the only one who would not see this, and he openly expressed his opinion that a new war could not improve the position or increase the glory of Russia, but could only weaken her position and diminish the already lofty pinnacle of her glory on which Russia, in his opinion, now stood. He endeavored to show the sovereign the impossibility of recruiting fresh armies; he spoke about the difficult position of the inhabitants, and hinted at the possibility of failure and the like. Having such ideas, the field marshal naturally became only a hindrance and a stumblingblock in the path of the coming war.

A convenient way of avoiding collisions with the old man presented itself. This was just what it had been at Austerlitz, and at the beginning of the campaign when Barclay was commander-in-chief—namely, to snatch the props of power which upheld him, without disturbing him or even letting him realize the change, and to transfer them to the sovereign himself. With this end in view, the staff was gradually reorganized and all that constituted the strength of Kutuzof's staff was destroyed or transferred to the sovereign's.

Just as naturally and simply and gradually as Kutuzof had been summoned from Turkey to Petersburg, to take charge of the militia and afterwards of the army, so now when it was necessary it came about just as naturally, gradually, and simply, when Kutuzof's part had been played to the end, that his place should be filled by the new actor who was needed.

The war of 1812, besides accomplishing the national object so dear to every Russian heart, was destined to have another significance still—a European one. The movements of the nations from west to east were to be followed by a movement from east to west, and for this new war a new actor was needed, who had other qualities and views from those of Kutuzof, and was moved by other impulses.

Alexander the First was as necessary to move the nations from east to west and to establish the boundaries of the nations as Kutuzof had been for the salvation and glory of Russia.

Kutuzof had no notion of the meaning of Europe, the balance of power, Napoleon. He could not understand this. For the representative of the Russian people, after the enemy had been annihilated, Russia saved and established on the highest pinnacle of glory—for him, a Russian, as a Russian, there was nothing left to do. For the representative of the national war there was nothing left except death.

And he died.

VI

Pierre, as is generally the case, felt the whole burden of his physical deprivations and the long strain to which he had been subjected while a prisoner, only when the strain and the privations were at an end.

After his liberation he went to Orel; and on the second day after his arrival, just as he was about to start for Kiev, he fell ill, and remained in Orel for three months.

He had what the doctors called bilious fever. The doctors treated him, bled him, and make him swallow drugs; nevertheless he recovered.

During his convalescence, Pierre only gradually got rid of the impressions that the preceding months had made on him, and accustomed himself to the thought that no one would drive him forth the next morning; that no one would dispossess him of his warm bed; and that he was certain to have dinner and tea and supper. But in his dreams he still, for a long time, continued to see himself in the same conditions of captivity.

In the same way Pierre gradually realized the significance of the news he had heard on the day of his liberation: Prince Andrei's death, the death of his wife, the annihilation of the French.

The joyous feeling of freedom, that perfect, inalienable freedom inherent in man, which he had first realized at the first halting place when he was carried away from Moscow, filled Pierre's soul during his convalescence. He was amazed that this inner freedom, which had been independent of all external circumstances, now that he had abundance, even luxury, seemed to remain an external freedom. He was alone in a strange city where he had no acquaintances. No one wanted anything of him, no one forced him to go anywhere against his will. He had everything he wanted. His thoughts about his wife, which had formerly tormented him, had vanished as if she had never existed.

"Ah! How good! How glorious!" he would say to himself when a table with a clean cloth was moved up to him with fragrant bouillon, or when, at night, he lay stretched out on the soft, clean bed, or when he remembered that his wife and the French no longer existed.

"Ah! How good! How glorious!" And out of old habit he would ask himself the questions: "Well, what next? What am I going to do?" And instantly he would answer himself, "Nothing at all! I'm going to live. Oh! How glorious!"

The terrible question that hitherto had torn down all his mental edifices

—the question *Why*—no longer existed for him. Now to that question *Why*, his mind had always ready the simple answer: Because God is, that God without Whose will not a hair falls from the head of a human being.

Pierre had scarcely changed in his outward habits.

At first sight he was just the same as he had been before. Just as before he was absent-minded, and seemed absorbed not in what was before his eyes, but in his own thoughts. The difference between his former and his present self lay in this: hitherto, when he had forgotten what was before him, or paid no attention to what was said to him, he would wrinkle his brows with a martyrlike air, as if striving, but without success, to study something that was far away. He was still oblivious to what was said to him, and to what was before him; but now with a scarcely perceptible smile, which one might almost have thought mocking, he looked at what was before him, he listened to what was said to him, although it was evident that his eyes and his mind were concerned with something entirely different.

Hitherto he had seemed to be a good man, but unhappy; and therefore people could not help being repelled by him. Now a smile, called forth by the mere pleasure of living, constantly played around his mouth, and his eyes were lighted up by a sympathetic interest in people—in the question, *were they as happy as he was?* And people liked to be with him.

Formerly he had talked much, got easily excited when he talked, and was a poor listener; now he was rarely carried away by the heat of an argument, and had become such a good listener that people were glad to tell him the deepest secrets of their hearts.

Princess Catherine, who had never liked Pierre and had cherished a peculiar feeling of animosity against him ever since that time when, after the count's death, she had found herself under obligation to him; after a short stay at Orel, where she came with the intention of showing Pierre that in spite of his "ingratitude" she considered it her duty to take care of him—the princess, greatly to her annoyance and surprise, quickly felt that she was growing fond of him.

Pierre did nothing to win her good graces. He merely studied her with curiosity. Hitherto the princess had felt that only indifference and irony were expressed in view of her, and she shrank into herself before him, just as she did in the presence of other people, and showed only her harsh and disagreeable side. Now, on the contrary, she felt that he had penetrated into the most intimate and secret recesses of her existence; and—at first with distrust, but afterwards with gratitude—she showed him the good side of her character, which she had kept hidden.

The craftiest of men could not have been more skilful in winning the princess' confidence, than was Pierre in eliciting her recollections of the happiest days of her youth, and in expressing his sympathy. But meantime Pierre's entire craft consisted in his own pleasure in evoking kindly feelings in the spiteful, acidulous, and, in her own way, haughty princess.

645

"Yes, he is a very, very good man when he is under the influence of people who are not bad—of people like myself," thought the princess.

The change that had taken place in Pierre was noticed, in their own way, by his servants Terenti and Vaska. They found that he had grown vastly more simple.

Often Terenti, while undressing his master, and while he had his boots and clothes in his hand, and had wished him good night, would hesitate about leaving the room, thinking that his master might like to engage him in conversation. And it was a very common occurrence for Pierre to call Terenti back, noticing that he was in a mood to talk.

"Well, now, tell me—how did you manage to get anything to eat?" he would ask.

And Terenti would begin to talk about the destruction of Moscow, or about the late count, and would stand for a long time with the clothes in his hand, telling stories, or sometimes listening to Pierre's yarns, and then, with a pleasing sense of nearness to his master and of friendliness to him, go into the anteroom.

The doctor who had charge of Pierre's case, and who visited him every day, in spite of the fact that, in accordance with the custom of doctors, he felt it his duty to assume the mien of a man whose time, every minute of it, was precious in the care of suffering humanity, would spend hours with Pierre, relating his favorite stories and making his observations on the peculiarities of the sick in general and the ladies in particular.

"Yes, there is something delightful in talking with such a man—very different from what one finds in our province," he would say.

In Orel there were several French officers who had been taken prisoner, and the doctor brought one of them, a young Italian, to see Pierre. This officer began to be a frequent visitor, and the princess laughed at the sentimental affection that the Italian conceived for Pierre. The Italian was happy only when he could be with Pierre, and talk with him, and tell him about his past, about his home life, about his love affairs; and pour out to Pierre's ears his indignation against the French and particularly against Napoleon.

"If all the Russians are in the least like you," he would say to Pierre, "it is a sacrilege to wage war on a people like yours. Though you have suffered so much from the French, yet you seem to have no ill will against them."

This passionate love of the Italian Pierre had won only because he had brought out in him the best side of his nature, and took pleasure in him.

In practical affairs Pierre now unexpectedly felt that he had a balance that had been lacking before. Hitherto, every question concerning finance, especially demands on him for money, to which he, as a very rich man, was often subjected, aroused in him helpless worry and perplexity.

To give, or not to give? That was the question with him. "I have it, but he needs it. But another one needs it still more. Which needs it the most? But perhaps both are frauds."

And in the past, he found no way out of all these surmises, and was in the habit of giving to all indiscriminately as long as he had anything to give. He used to find himself in precisely the same quandary with every question concerning his estate, when one would say that he must do this, and another would recommend another way.

Now he found, to his amazement, that he was troubled no longer with doubts and perplexities. He seemed to have acquired a sense of judgment, which, by some laws unknown to himself, decided what was necessary and what was unnecessary for him to do. He was no less than before indifferent to pecuniary matters; but now he knew infallibly what he ought to do and what not.

The first time this new sense of justice had to decide a question was in the case of one of the prisoners, a French colonel, who came to him, told him many stories of his great exploits, and finally almost demanded that Pierre should give him four thousand francs to send to his wife and children. Pierre, without the slightest difficulty or effort, refused him, amazed afterwards to find how simple and easy it was to do what had always before seemed to him incredibly difficult.

At the very time, however, that he refused the colonel, he made up his mind, on the eve of his departure from Orel, that it required the utmost shrewdness to induce the Italian officer to take some money, which he evidently needed.

A new proof for Pierre of the greater soundness in his views of practical affairs was his decision in the matter of his wife's debts, and whether his houses in Moscow and his villas should be rebuilt or not.

While he was at Orel his head overseer came to him, and he and Pierre made out a general schedule of his altered income. The conflagration of Moscow had cost Pierre, according to the overseer's reckoning, about two millions. The head overseer, as a measure of relief for his losses, proposed a scheme whereby, notwithstanding the losses, his income would be not only not diminished, but rather increased, and this was that he should refuse to honor the debts left by the late countess, for which he could not be held accountable, and should not rebuild his Moscow houses nor his villa near Moscow, which cost him eighty thousand a year in upkeep and brought him in nothing.

"Yes, yes, that is true," said Pierre, smiling cheerfully. "Yes, yes, I don't need them at all. The fire has made me vastly richer!"

But in January, Savelyitch came from Moscow, told him about the condition of the city, about the estimate the architect had made for rebuilding the Moscow mansion and the suburban villa, and spoke about it as if it were a matter already decided.

At the same time Pierre received letters from Prince Vasili and other acquaintances in Petersburg. These letters mentioned his wife's debts. And Pierre decided that the scheme proposed by his head overseer, which had pleased him so much at first, was not right, and that he must go to Petersburg to wind up his wife's business affairs, and must rebuild his Moscow houses. Why this was necessary he did not know; he only knew beyond doubt that it was necessary. His income, in consequence of this decision, would be reduced to three-fourths; but it was a case of necessity, he felt.

VII

JUST AS IT IS hard to explain why and whither the ants rush from a scattered anthill, some dragging away little fragments, eggs, and dead bodies, others hurrying back to the anthill again; why they jostle one another, push one another, and fight—so would it be hard to explain the causes that compelled the Russian people, after the departure of the French, to throng back to the place that had formerly been called Moscow.

But just as when one looks at the ants crawling in wild confusion around their despoiled abode, notwithstanding the complete destruction of the anthill, one can see by the activity and energy, by the myriads of insects, that everything is utterly destroyed except the something indestructible and mysterious, which constitutes the whole strength of the anthill—so, in Moscow, in the month of October, though there was an absence of authorities, of churches, of priests, of riches, of houses, still it was the same Moscow as it had been in the month of August.

Everything was destroyed except that something, mysterious but potent and indestructible.

Within a week, Moscow had fifteen thousand inhabitants; in a fortnight twenty-five thousand, and so on. Constantly rising and rising, the population, by the autumn of 1813, reached a figure exceeding that of 1812.

The first Russians to enter Moscow, finding it plundered, began also to plunder. They continued the work begun by the French. Peasants brought in carts, to carry back to their villages whatever was to be found abandoned in the houses or streets of ruined Moscow. The Cossacks carried off what they could to their tents. Proprietors of houses took possession of whatever they could lay their hands on in other houses, and carried it home under the pretext that it was their own property.

But the first comers were followed by other plunderers, and they by still others; and the pillage each day, in proportion as the numbers increased, became more and more difficult, and acquired more definite forms.

The longer the pillage conducted by the French continued, the more it diminished the wealth of Moscow and the strength of the pillagers. The pillage conducted by the Russians (and the occupation of the capital by the Russians began with this), the longer it lasted, and the more freely it was shared by the people, the more rapidly it increased the wealth of Moscow and restored the regular life of the city.

Besides the pillagers, the most varied sort of people, attracted some by curiosity, some by their duties in the service, some by interest—householders, clergymen, officials of high and low degree, tradesmen, artisans, peasants from various parts—flowed back into Moscow like blood to the heart.

At the end of a week, peasants who drove in with empty carts in order to carry away things were halted by the authorities and compelled to carry away dead bodies from the city. Other peasants, hearing of the lack of commodities, came in with wheat, oats, hay; by competition with one another reducing prices even lower than they had been before. Master carpenters, hoping for fat jobs, each day flocked to Moscow, and in all directions new houses began to go up and the old burned mansions to be restored. Merchants displayed their wares in booths. Restaurants and taverns were established in charred mansions that had survived the flames. The clergy conducted divine service in many churches that had escaped the conflagration. People contributed ecclesiastical furnishings to replace those stolen. Civil officials spread their tables and set up their bureaus in little rooms. High officials and the police made arrangements for restoring property that had been abandoned by the French. Count Rostopchin wrote his proclamations.

VIII

Toward the beginning of February, Pierre came to Moscow and established himself in a wing of his house, a wing that remained intact. He paid visits to Count Rostopchin and various acquaintances who had returned to Moscow, and he planned to go two days later to Petersburg.

All were enthusiastic over the victory. There was a ferment of life in the ruined and revivified capital. All welcomed Pierre warmly. All were anxious to meet him, and plied him with questions about all he had seen.

Pierre felt drawn by special ties of sympathy and friendship to all he met; but he now treated everyone guardedly, so as not to bind himself to anyone. To all the questions he was asked—whether important or the most trivial— where was he going to live? Was he going to rebuild? When was he going to Petersburg? and would he please take this small box with him?—he would answer "Yes," or "Perhaps so," or "I think so," or the like.

He heard that the Rostofs were in Kostroma, and the thought of Natasha rarely occurred to him. If it came to him, it was only as a pleasant recollection of something long past. He felt himself freed not only from the conditions of life, but also from that sentiment which, as it seemed to him, he had deliberately allowed himself to cherish.

On the third day after his arrival at Moscow, he learned from the Drubetskoys that Princess Maria was in Moscow. Prince Andrei's death, sufferings, and last days had often recurred to Pierre's mind, and now they came back to him with fresh force. When, after dinner, he learned that Princess Maria was in Moscow and in her own house, which had escaped the conflagration, he went that same evening to call upon her.

The Bolkonsky house remained intact. It bore traces of wear and tear, but the character of the house was the same as before. Pierre was met by an old butler with a stern face, who seemed to want it understood that the prince's absence did not affect the strictness of the régime, and who said that the princess had been pleased to retire to her room, and received on Sundays.

"Tell her I am here; perhaps she will receive me," said Pierre.

"I obey," replied the butler. "Please come to the portrait gallery."

In a few moments the butler returned to Pierre with Dessalles. Dessalles, in the name of the princess, informed Pierre that she would be very glad to see him, and begged him, if he would excuse her for the lack of ceremony, to come upstairs to her room.

The princess was sitting in a low-ceilinged room, lighted by a single candle. There was also another person present in a black dress. Pierre remembered that the princess had always with her lady companions, but who and what these lady companions were, Pierre did not know and could not remember.

"That is one of her lady companions," he said to himself, glancing at the lady in the black dress.

The princess rose quickly, came forward to meet him, and shook hands with him.

"Yes," said she, as she looked into his altered face, after he had kissed her hand. "So we meet again at last. He often used to speak about you during the last days of his life," said she, turning her eyes from Pierre to the "companion" with an embarrassment that for an instant struck Pierre. "I was so glad to know of your rescue. That was truly the best piece of news we had received for a long time."

Again the princess looked still more anxiously at the "companion," and wanted to say something, but Pierre did not give her an opportunity.

"You may imagine I knew nothing about it," said he. "I thought he was killed. All that I knew, I knew from others, and that at third hand. All I know is that he fell in with the Rostofs . . . what a strange good fortune!"

Pierre spoke rapidly, with animation. He looked once into the "companion's" face, saw an apparently flattering, inquisitive glance fastened on him, and, as often happens during a conversation, he gathered a general idea that this "companion" in the black dress was a gentle, kindly, good creature, who would not interfere with the sincerity and cordiality of his conversations with Princess Maria.

But when he said the last words about the Rostofs, the embarrassment expressed on the princess' face was even more noticeable than before. She again turned her eyes from Pierre's face to the face of the lady in the black dress, and said:

"But don't you recognize her?"

Pierre once more looked into the companion's pale, delicate face, with the dark eyes and strange mouth. Something near and dear, something long forgotten and more than kind, was looking at him from those attentive eyes.

"But no, it cannot be," he said to himself. "That face, so stern, thin, and pale, and grown so old. That cannot be she! It is only something that reminds me of her!"

But at that instant Princess Maria said, "Natasha!" And the face with the attentive eyes, with difficulty, with an effort—just as a rusty door opens—smiled, and from the opened door there suddenly breathed forth and surrounded Pierre the fragrance of that long-forgotten happiness, of which he rarely thought, especially of late. The fragrance rose, invading his senses, and enveloping him entirely. When she smiled, all doubt ceased; it was Natasha, and he loved her!

At the first moment of recognition, Pierre involuntarily told both her and Princess Maria, and above all, himself, the secret that he long had not confessed even to his own heart. He reddened with delight and anguish. He tried to hide his agitation. But the more he tried to hide it, the more distinctly—more distinctly than in the most definite words—he told himself and her and Princess Maria that he loved her!

"No, of course, it is only from the surprise," said Pierre to himself; but in spite of all his efforts to prolong the conversation that he had started with Princess Maria, he could not help looking again at Natasha, and a still deeper flush suffused his face, and a still deeper agitation of joy and pain clutched his heart. He hesitated in his speech, and stopped short in the midst of what he was saying.

Pierre had not noticed Natasha for the reason that he had not in the least expected to see her there, but the reason he did not recognize her was because of the immense change that had taken place in her since he had seen her last. She had grown thin and pale. But it was not this that had changed her identity; it was impossible that he should have recognized her at the moment of his entrance, because that face, from whose eyes formerly had always gleamed forth the secret joy of living, now when he came in and for the first time glanced at her, had not even the shadow of a smile; they were merely attentive, kindly, and pathetically questioning eyes.

Pierre's confusion did not waken any answering confusion in Natasha, but only a contentment that lighted up her whole face with an almost imperceptible gleam.

"She has come to pay me a visit," said Princess Maria. "The count and countess will be here in a few days. The countess is in a terrible state. But Natasha herself had to consult the doctor. They sent her off with me by main force."

"Yes, is there a family without its own special sorrow?" said Pierre, addressing Natasha. "You know that it happened on the very day that we were set free. I saw him. What a charming boy he was!"

Natasha looked at him, but in answer to his words her eyes dilated and a shadow crept over them.

"What consolation can be given in either thought or word?" exclaimed

Pierre. "None at all! Why should such a glorious young fellow, so full of life, have to die?"

"Yes, indeed, in these days it would be hard to live, if one had not faith . . ." said Princess Maria.

"Yes, yes! That is the real truth," interrupted Pierre, hastily.

"Why?" asked Natasha, gazing attentively into Pierre's eyes.

"How can you ask 'why'?" exclaimed Princess Maria. "The mere thought of what awaits us there . . ."

Natasha, without hearing Princess Maria to the end, again looked at Pierre with questioning eyes.

"Why, because," continued Pierre, "only that man who believes there is a God who directs our ways can endure such a loss as hers—and yours," added Pierre.

Natasha had her lips parted to say something, but suddenly stopped. Pierre quickly turned from her, and again addressed the princess with a question concerning his friend's last days.

Pierre's embarrassment had now almost disappeared, but at the same time he felt that all his former freedom had also disappeared. He felt that his every word and act had now a critic, a judge, who was dearer to him than the opinion of all the people in the world.

When he spoke now, he measured at every breath the impression his words produced on Natasha. He did not purposely say what would have pleased her; but whatever he said he judged from her standpoint.

Princess Maria, reluctantly at first, as is always the case, began to tell him about the state in which Prince Andrei had come to them. But Pierre's questions, his troubled eyes, his face trembling with emotion, gradually induced her to enter into particulars which she would have been afraid to call back to her recollection for her own sake.

"Yes, yes, indeed it is so," said Pierre, leaning forward with his whole body toward Princess Maria, and eagerly listening to her story. "Yes, yes, and so he grew calmer? more gentle? He so earnestly sought with all the powers of his soul for the one thing: to be perfectly good. He could not have feared death. The faults he had, if he had any, came from other sources than himself. And so he grew gentle?" exclaimed Pierre.

"What good fortune that he met you again," he added, turning to Natasha and looking at her, his eyes brimming with tears.

Natasha's face twitched. She frowned, and for an instant dropped her eyes. For a minute she hesitated; should she speak, or not speak?

"Yes, it was good fortune," said she, in a low deep voice. "For me indeed it was a happiness." She became silent. "And he . . . he . . . he said it was the very thing that he was longing for when I went to him . . ." Natasha's voice broke. She clasped her hands together on her knees, and suddenly, evidently making an effort to contain herself, raised her head and began to speak rapidly:

"We knew nothing about it when we left Moscow. I had not dared to ask about him. And suddenly Sonya told me he was with us. I had no idea, I could not imagine, in what a state he was. I wanted only one thing—to see him, to be with him," said she, trembling and choking. And without letting herself be interrupted, she related what she had never before told a living soul: what she had lived through in those three weeks of their journey and their sojourn at Yaroslavl.

Pierre listened to her with open mouth and without taking from her his eyes full of tears. In listening to her he thought not of Prince Andrei or of death, or even of what she was telling him. He heard her, and only pitied her for the suffering she underwent now in telling the story.

The princess, frowning from her effort to keep back her tears, sat beside Natasha and listened for the first time to the story of those last days that her brother had spent with Natasha.

This tale, so full of pain and joy, Natasha was evidently compelled to relate. She mixed the most insignificant details with the intimate secrets of the heart, and it seemed she would never reach an end. Several times she repeated the same things.

Dessalles' voice was heard outside the door, asking if Nikolusha might come and bid them good night.

"And that is the whole story—all . . ." said Natasha.

When Nikolusha came in she quickly sprang up and almost ran to the door; and, hitting her head against the door, which was hidden by a portière, flew from the room with a moan caused partly by pain, partly by grief.

Pierre gazed at the door through which she had disappeared, and could not understand why he seemed suddenly left alone and deserted in the world. Princess Maria aroused him from his fit of abstraction by calling his attention to her nephew, who had come into the room.

Nikolusha's face, which resembled his father's, had such an effect on Pierre, in this moment of deep emotion into which he had sunk, that after he had kissed the lad he quickly arose, and, getting out his handkerchief, went to the window. He wanted to bid Princess Maria good night and leave, but she detained him.

"No, Natasha and I often sit up till three o'clock; please stay a little longer. I will order supper served. Go downstairs, we will follow immediately."

But before Pierre left the room the princess said to him:

"This is the first time she has spoken so of him."

IX

PIERRE WAS conducted into the large, brightly lighted dining room. In a few minutes steps were heard, and the princess and Natasha came into the room. Natasha was now calm, although a grave unsmiling expression remained on her face.

Princess Maria, Natasha and Pierre alike experienced that sense of awkwardness which always follows after a serious and intimate conversation. To pursue the former subject is no longer possible; to talk about trifles does not seem right; and silence is disagreeable because such silence seems hypocritical, especially if one wishes to talk.

They silently came to the table. The footman drew back the chairs and pushed them forward. Pierre unfolded his cold napkin, and, making up his mind to break the silence, looked at Natasha and Princess Maria.

Each of them had evidently at the same time made the same resolve; the eyes of both shone with the satisfaction of life and the avowal that, if sorrow exists, so also joy may abound.

"Will you have vodka, count?" asked Princess Maria, and these words suddenly drove away the shadow of the past.

"Tell us about yourself," said Princess Maria. "We have heard such incredible stories about you."

"Yes?" replied Pierre, with that smile of good-natured irony which was now habitual with him. "I too have been told most marvelous things—things that I have never even dreamed of seeing. Marya Abramovna invited me to her house, and told me all that ever happened to me or was supposed to have happened. Stepan Stepanitch also gave me a lesson in the way I should tell my story. In general, I have observed that it is a very comfortable thing to be an 'interesting person' (I am now an interesting person)! I am invited out and made the subject of all sorts of stories."

Natasha smiled, and started to say something.

"We were told," said Princess Maria, forestalling her, "that you lost two millions here in Moscow. Is that true?"

"But still it made me three times as rich as before," replied Pierre.

Pierre, in spite of his wife's debts and the necessity he felt of rebuilding his houses, which would alter his circumstances, continued to tell people that he had grown three times as rich as before.

"What I have undoubtedly gained," said he, "is this freedom I enjoy"—he had begun seriously, but he hesitated about continuing, observing that the topic of the conversations were too egotistical.

"And you are going to rebuild?"

"Yes; Savelyitch advises it."

"Tell me, you did not know at all about the countess' death when you were in Moscow?" asked Princess Maria, and instantly flushed, noticing that in having put this question immediately after he had spoken of his freedom, she might have given a false sense to his words.

"No," replied Pierre, evidently not discovering anything awkward in Princess Maria's interpretation of his remark about his freedom. "I first heard about it in Orel, and you cannot imagine how it surprised me. We were not a model husband and wife," he quickly added, with a glance at Natasha, and observing in her face a gleam of curiosity as to what he would have to say about his wife, "but her death gave me a terrible shock. When two persons quarrel, always both are at fault. And a person's fault suddenly becomes terribly serious when the other party happens to die. And then such a death! . . . without friends, without consolation! I felt very, very sorry for her," said he, in conclusion, and noticing with a sense of satisfaction a look of joyful approval in Natasha's face.

"Well, and so you are a single man and marriageable again," said Princess Maria.

Pierre's face suddenly grew livid, and for long he tried not to look at Natasha. When at length he had the courage to look at her, her face was cold, stern, and even scornful, as it seemed to him.

"And did you really see Napoleon and talk with him? That's the story they tell us," said Princess Maria.

Pierre laughed.

"Not once, never! It always seems to everyone that to have been a prisoner was to have been Napoleon's guest. I not only never saw him, but did not hear him talked about. I was in far too humble company."

Supper was over, and Pierre, who at first refused to tell about his captivity, was little by little drawn into stories about it.

"But it is true, isn't it, that you remained behind for the purpose of killing Napoleon?" asked Natasha, with a slight smile. "I imagined as much when we met you at the Sukharef Tower—do you remember?"

Pierre acknowledged that this was true; and with this question as a starting point, and gradually led on by Princess Maria's questions, and especially by Natasha's, Pierre was brought to give them a detailed account of his adventures.

At first he told his story with that gentle, ironical expression which he now used toward other people and especially himself; but afterwards, when he came to tell about the horrors and sufferings he had seen, without being himself aware of it, he was carried away, and began to talk with the restrained excitement of a man who was reliving, in his recollections, the most vivid impressions.

Princess Maria, with a gentle smile, looked now at Pierre, now at Natasha. Throughout all this narration, she saw only Pierre and his goodness.

Natasha, leaning her head on her hand, with her face reflecting in its expression all the varying details of the story, gazed at Pierre without once taking her eyes from him, evidently living with him through all the dreadful scenes of which he told. Not only her looks, but her exclamations and the brief questions she asked, showed Pierre that, from his story, she took to heart exactly what he wanted to convey. It was evident that she understood not merely what he told her, but also what he would have wished but was unable to express in words.

Concerning his adventure with the child and the woman whose protection had led to his capture, Pierre spoke in the following manner:

"It was a horrible sight: children deserted, some in the flames—one child was dragged out before my very eyes—women who were robbed of their possessions, their earrings snatched away . . ."

Pierre reddened and stammered.

"Then came the patrol and arrested all who were not engaged in pillage—all the men. And myself!"

"You certainly are not telling the whole story; you certainly did something—" said Natasha, and paused a moment—"something good!"

Pierre went on with his narrative. When he came to tell about the execution he wanted to avoid the horrible details, but Natasha insisted that he should not omit anything.

Pierre began to tell about Karatayef. By this time he had risen from the table and was walking back and forth, Natasha's eyes following him all the time. But he paused.

"No, you cannot understand how I learned from that illiterate man—nearly a half-wit!"

"Yes, yes, go on," cried Natasha. "What became of him?"

"He was shot almost in my very presence."

And Pierre began to tell about the last period of the retreat of the French, Karatayef's illness(his voice constantly trembled), and his death. Pierre, in relating his adventures, put them in an entirely new light.

He now found what seemed to be a new significance in all that he had experienced. Now, while he was telling all this to Natasha, he experienced that rare delight afforded by women—not intellectual women, who, in listening, try either to remember what is said for the sake of enriching their minds, and, on occasion, of giving it out themselves, or to apply what is said to their own cases, and to communicate with all diligence their intellectual remarks elaborated in the petty workshops of their brains—but the delight afforded by genuine women gifted with the capacity of bringing out and assimilating all that is best in the manifestations of a man.

Natasha, without knowing it, was all attention; she did not lose a word or an inflection of his voice, or a glance, or the quivering of a muscle in his face, or a single gesture made by Pierre. She caught on the wing the word as yet unspoken, and took it straight to her generous heart, divining the mysterious meaning of all the spiritual travail through which Pierre had passed.

Princess Maria comprehended his story and sympathized with him, but now she saw something else that absorbed all her attention: she saw the possibility of love and happiness for Pierre and Natasha. And this thought, occurring to her for the first time, filled her heart with joy.

It was three o'clock in the morning. The footmen, with gloomy, stern faces, came to bring fresh candles, but no one heeded them.

Pierre finished his story. Natasha, her eyes gleaming with excitement, continued to look steadily and earnestly at Pierre, as if wishing to read the portions of his story that he had perhaps not told. Pierre, with a shamefaced but joyous sense of embarrassment, occasionally looked at her and

656

wondered what to say next in order to change the conversation to some other topic. Princess Maria was silent. It occurred to none of them that it was three o'clock in the morning and time to go to bed.

"We talk about unhappiness, sufferings," said Pierre. "Yet if now, this minute, I were asked, 'Would you remain what you were before your imprisonment, or go through it all again?' I would say, 'For God's sake, the imprisonment once more and the horseflesh.' We think that when we are driven out of the usual path, everything is over for us; but it is just here that the new and the good begins. As long as there is life there is happiness. There is much, much before us! I tell you so," said he, addressing Natasha.

"Yes, yes," said she, answering something entirely different. "And I wish nothing better than to live my life all over again." Pierre looked at her keenly. "No, I could ask for nothing more."

"You are wrong, you are wrong," cried Pierre. "I am not to blame because I am alive and want to live; and you also."

Suddenly Natasha hid her face in her hands, and burst into tears.

"What is it, Natasha?" asked Princess Maria.

"Nothing, nothing."

She smiled at Pierre through her tears.

"Good-by, it is bedtime."

Pierre got up and took his departure.

Princess Maria and Natasha, as usual, met in their bedroom. They talked over what Pierre had told them. The princess did not express her opinion of Pierre. Neither did Natasha speak of him.

"Well, good night, Marie," said Natasha. "Do you know, I am often afraid that, in not speaking of him—of Prince Andrei—for fear of doing wrong to our feelings, we may forget him?"

Princess Maria drew a deep sigh, and by this sigh admitted the justice of Natasha's words; but when she spoke, her words expressed a different thought.

"How could one forget him?" she asked.

"It was so good for me today to talk it all over; and hard too, and painful, and good, very good," said Natasha. "I was certain that he loved him so. That was why I told him. . . . There was no harm in my telling him, was there?" she asked, suddenly reddening.

"To Pierre? Oh, no! What a lovely man he is!" exclaimed Princess Maria.

"Do you know, Marie," suddenly broke out Natasha, with a roguish smile which Princess Maria had not seen for a long time on her face, "he has grown so clean, neat, fresh, just as if he were out of a bath! Isn't that so?"

"Yes," said Princess Maria. "He has gained very much."

"And his jaunty little coat, and his neatly cropped hair; exactly—yes, just exactly as if he were fresh from his bath! Papa used . . ."

"I remember that he—Prince Andrei—liked no one so well as Pierre," said Princess Maria.

"Yes; and yet they were so different. They say that men are better friends when they are not alike. It must be so. Don't you think that they were very different?"

"Yes, and he's splendid."

"Well, good night," replied Natasha; and the same mischievous smile, as if she had forgotten it, long remained in her face.

X

IT WAS LONG before Pierre went to sleep that night. He strode back and forth through his room, now scowling, now burdening himself with heavy thoughts, then suddenly shrugging his shoulders and starting, and then again smiling.

He was thinking about Prince Andrei, about Natasha, and their love; and sometimes he felt jealous of her for what was past, sometimes he reproached himself for it, sometimes he justified it.

It was six o'clock in the morning, and still he kept pacing through his room.

"Well, what's to be done? Is it still impossible? What is to be done? Of course it must be so," said he to himself, and, hastily undressing, he got into bed, happy and excited, but free from doubt and irresolution. "Yes, strange and impossible as this happiness seems, I must do everything, everything, to make her my wife," he said to himself.

Several days previously Pierre had fixed on Friday for the day of his departure for Petersburg. When he woke up it was Thursday, and Savelyitch came to him for orders in regard to the packing of his things for the journey.

"Petersburg? What about Petersburg? Who is going to Petersburg?" he could not help asking of himself. "Oh, yes, some time ago, before this happened, I had some such thing—I was going to Petersburg for some reason or other," he remembered. "Why was it? Yes, perhaps I shall go as it is. How good and attentive he is! How he remembers everything," he said to himself, as he looked into Savelyitch's old face. "And what a pleasant smile," he thought.

"Aren't you always longing to have your freedom, Savelyitch?" demanded Pierre.

"Why should I wish my freedom, your excellency? While the late count was alive—the kingdom of heaven be his—we lived with him, and now we have nothing to complain of from you."

"Well, but your children?"

"The children will live also, your excellency; one can put up with such masters."

"Yes, but my heirs," suggested Pierre. "I may suddenly marry. . . . You see, that might happen," he added, with an involuntary smile.

"And may I be bold enough to say, a very good thing, too, your excellency!"

"How easy it seems to him," thought Pierre. "He cannot know how terrible, how perilous, a thing it is. Too early or too late . . . terrible!"

"What orders do you please to give? Do you wish to start tomorrow?" asked Savelyitch.

"No, I am going to postpone it for a few days. I will tell you when the time comes. Forgive me for putting you to so much trouble," said Pierre, and, as he saw Savelyitch's smile, he said to himself: "How strange it is that he doesn't know that Petersburg is now nothing to me, and that this matter must be decided before anything! Should I talk with him about it? How will he like it?" wondered Pierre. "No, I will wait a little."

Pierre went that evening to dine at Princess Maria's. As he went along the streets, lined with the blackened ruins of houses, he was amazed at the beauty that he discovered in these ruins. The chimney stacks, the fallen walls, vividly reminding Pierre of the Rhine and the Colosseum, stretched along one behind another, all through the burnt districts. The hack drivers and passers by, the carpenters hewing timbers, merchants and shopkeepers, all with jovial, shining faces, gazed at Pierre, and seemed to say, "Ah, there he goes. Let us see what will come of it."

Before he reached Princess Maria's the doubt occurred to Pierre whether it were true that he had been there the evening before, and had seen Natasha and talked with her.

"Perhaps I was dreaming. Perhaps I will go in and find no one."

But he had no sooner entered the room than, in his whole being, by the instantaneous loss of his freedom, he realized her presence. She wore the same black dress with soft folds, and her hair was done up in the same way as the evening before, but she herself was entirely different. If she had been like that the evening before when he went into the room, he could not for a single instant have failed to recognize her. She was just the same as she had been when almost a child, and afterwards, when she was Prince Andrei's affianced bride. A merry questioning gleam flashed in her eyes; her face had a kindly and strangely roguish expression.

Pierre dined with them and would have spent the whole evening, but Princess Maria was going to vespers, and Pierre accompanied them.

The following day Pierre went early, dined with them, and spent the whole evening.

Although Princess Maria and Natasha were evidently glad of his company, although all the interest of Pierre's life was now concentrated in this house, still, as the evening wore away, they had talked everything out, and the conversation constantly lagged from one trivial subject to another, and often lagged altogether.

Pierre stayed so late that evening that Princess Maria and Natasha exchanged glances, evidently feeling anxious for him to go. Pierre saw it, and yet could not tear himself away. He felt embarrassed and awkward, but still he stayed because he could not get up to go. Princess Maria, not seeing any end to it, was the first to get up, and, pleading a headache as an excuse, started to bid him good night.

"And so you are going to Petersburg tomorrow?" she asked.

"No, I don't expect to go," hastily replied Pierre, with surprise and apparent annoyance. "Yes . . . no . . . oh, to Petersburg? Day after tomorrow, perhaps. Only I won't say good-by now. I will call to see if you have any commissions," said he, standing in front of Princess Maria, with flushed face and embarrassed manner.

Natasha gave him her hand, and left the room. Princess Maria, on the contrary, instead of going, resumed her chair, and, with her luminous, deep eyes, gazed gravely and earnestly at Pierre. The weariness which she had really felt just before had now entirely passed away. She drew a long and deep sigh, as if nerving herself for a long conversation.

All Pierre's confusion and awkwardness instantly disappeared the moment that Natasha left the room, and gave place to an agitated excitement. He swiftly drew his chair close to Princess Maria.

"Yes, I wanted to have a talk with you," said he, responding to her look as if it were spoken words. "Princess! help me! What am I to do? Have I reason to hope? Princess, my friend, listen to me. I know all about it. I know that I am not worthy of her. I know that it is wholly impossible, at the present time, to speak about it. But I wish to be like a brother to her. . . . No, I do not, I cannot wish that; I cannot . . ."

He paused and rubbed his face and his eyes with his hands.

"Now, here!" he pursued, evidently making an effort to command himself to speak coherently. "I don't know when I first began to love her. But she is the only one in all my life that I have loved, and I love her so that I cannot imagine life without her. I cannot make up my mind to ask for her hand now; but the thought that perhaps she might be mine, and that I may have lost this possibility . . . possibility . . . is horrible to me. Tell me, have I reason to hope? Tell me what I must do. Dear princess," said he, after a little silence, and he touched her hand when she did not reply.

"I was thinking of what you have told me," returned Princess Maria. "Now, listen to what I have to say. You are right that to speak to her now of love . . ."

The princess paused. She meant to say, to speak to her of love was impossible now; but she paused because for two days past she had observed, from the change that had taken place in Natasha, that Natasha would not only not be offended if Pierre should confess his love for her, but that this was the very thing that she was longing for him to do.

"To tell her now . . . is impossible," said Princess Maria, nevertheless. "But what am I to do?"

"Leave it all to me," said Princess Maria. "I know . . ."

Pierre looked into Princess Maria's eyes. "Well . . . well . . ." said he.

"I know that she loves you . . . will love you," said Princess Maria, correcting herself.

660

She had scarcely spoken these words before Pierre sprang up, and, with a frightened face, seized Princess Maria's hand.

"What makes you think so? Do you really think that I may hope? Do you think so?"

"Yes, I think so," said Princess Maria, with a smile. "Write to her parents. And trust it all to me. I will tell her when the suitable time comes. I am in favor of it. And my heart tells me that it will be."

"No, it cannot be! How happy I am! . . . But it cannot be!" repeated Pierre, kissing the princess' hand.

"Go to Petersburg; that is best. And I will write to you," said she.

"To Petersburg? Go away? Yes, very good, I will go. But may I come to call tomorrow?"

On the following day Pierre went to say good-by. Natasha was less animated than on the preceding days; but today when Pierre occasionally looked into her eyes he felt that his existence was nothing, that he was not and that she was not, but that one feeling of bliss filled the world.

"Can it be? No! Impossible!" he said to himself at each glance, word, motion of hers, so filling his heart with joy.

When, on saying good-by, he took her delicate, slender hand, he involuntarily held it rather long in his.

"Can it be that this hand, this face, these eyes—all this marvelous treasure of womanly beauty—can it be that it will be mine forever, as familiar to me as I am to myself? No, it is impossible!"

"Good-by, count," she said to him aloud. "I will await your return with impatience," she added in a whisper.

And these simple words, the look and the expression of her face that accompanied them, constituted the basis of inexhaustible recollections, memories, and happy dreams during Pierre's two months' absence.

" 'I will await your return with impatience.' Yes, yes, how did she say it?—Yes, 'I will await your return with impatience.' How happy I am! How can it be that I am so happy?" Pierre kept saying to himself.

XI

FROM THAT EVENING when Natasha, after Pierre had left them, first told Princess Maria with a joyously mischievous smile that he looked as if he just stepped out of his bath, and called attention to his jaunty coat and his closely cropped hair, from that moment something in her heart awoke that had lain dormant, and was unsuspected even by her, but which was irresistible.

Everything about her suddenly underwent a change—her face, her walk, her manner, her voice. Unexpectedly the lure of life and hope of happiness rose to the surface and demanded satisfaction. From that first evening Natasha seemed to have forgotten all that had happened to her. Henceforth she never once complained of her situation or said one single word about the past, and she did not hesitate even to make cheerful plans for the future.

She had little to say about Pierre; but when Princess Maria mentioned him, the long-extinguished gleam was kindled in her eyes, and her lips were curved with a strange smile.

The change that took place in Natasha at first amazed Princess Maria; but when she understood the significance of it she was grieved.

"Can it be that she loved my brother so little that she is so ready to forget him?" mused Princess Maria, when she pondered in solitude over this change that had come over Natasha. But when she was with Natasha she neither felt angry with her nor reproached her. The awakened forces of life that had invaded Natasha were evidently so uncontrollable, so unexpected to Natasha herself, that Princess Maria while in her presence felt that she had no right to reproach her even in her heart.

Natasha gave herself up so completely and with such frank honesty to this new feeling, and made so little pretense to hide it, that now she became glad and merry instead of sad and sorry.

When Princess Maria, after that midnight declaration of Pierre's, returned to her room, Natasha met her on the threshold.

"He has spoken? Yes? He has spoken?" she insisted; and an expression, joyous and at the same time pathetically pleading for forgiveness for her joy, clouded Natasha's face. "I was tempted to listen at the door; but I knew you would tell me."

Thoroughly as the princess understood the look that Natasha gave her, touching as it was, much as she pitied her emotion, still Natasha's words, for an instant, offended Princess Maria. She remembered her brother, his love for Natasha. "But what is to be done? She cannot be otherwise than she is," reasoned Princess Maria, and with a sad and rather stern face she told Natasha all that Pierre had said to her.

When she heard that he was going to Petersburg, Natasha was surprised.

"To Petersburg?" she repeated, apparently not understanding. But when she noticed the sorrowful expression on Princess Maria's face she guessed the reason for her melancholy, and suddenly burst into tears.

"Marie," said she, "tell me, what must I do? I am afraid I am doing wrong. I will do whatever you say; teach me . . ."

"Do you love him?"

"Yes," whispered Natasha.

"What makes you cry, then? I am glad for you," said Princess Maria, already, because of these tears, completely pardoning Natasha's joy.

"It will not be very soon, if ever. Just think what happiness when I am his wife and you marry Nikolai."

"Natasha, I have asked you never to speak about that. We will talk about yourself."

662

Both were silent.

"But why must he go to Petersburg?" suddenly exclaimed Natasha, and made haste to answer her own question. "Well, well, it is best so. . . . Yes, Marie, it is best so."

1813-1820

Peace has come to Europe; once more the Bourbons reign in France, and for a generation no powerful enemy will menace Russia. Napoleon has his hundred days; he has his Waterloo. Tsar Alexander forgets his aspiration to social reform; the serfs remain bound, the nobility pursues its old ignoble course, there is no fear, no friction to deflect it.

Part Sixteenth

NATASHA's marriage to Bezukhof, which took place in 1813, was the last happy event for the older generation of the Rostofs. The same year Count Rostof died, and, as always happens, his death caused the final dissolution of the Rostof family.

The events of the preceding year, the conflagration of Moscow and the family's flight from the city, the death of Prince Andrei and Natasha's despair, Petya's death, the countess' grief, all taken together had fallen as blow upon blow on the old count's head. It seemed as if he could not comprehend, as if he knew he had not the strength to comprehend, the significance of all these events; spiritually he seemed to bow his old head, as if he expected and invited new blows which would finish him. He sometimes seemed frightened and abstracted, sometimes unnaturally excited and alert.

Natasha's marriage, for the time being, gave him something to think about outside of himself. He ordered dinners and suppers and evidently tried to be cheerful; but his gaiety was not contagious as it once had been; on the contrary, it aroused compassion in people who knew and liked him.

After Pierre and his bride had gone, he became very feeble and began to complain of not feeling well. In a few days he grew really ill and took to his bed. From the first days of his illness, in spite of the doctor's encouragement, he felt certain that he would not recover.

The countess, without undressing, spent a fortnight in her armchair by his bedside. Every time she gave him his medicine, he would sob and silently kiss her hand. On the last day he wept and begged the forgiveness of his wife and his absent son for the dissipation of their property, the chief blame for which, he felt, rested on himself.

Having taken the last Communion and final unction, he died peacefully, and on the following day a crowd of acquaintances, who came to pay their duties to the late lamented, filled the Rostofs' lodgings. All these acquaintances, who had so many times dined and danced at his house, who had so many times made sport of him, now, with a unanimous feeling of inward reproach and emotion, said, as if in justification of themselves before someone:

"Yes, whatever may be said, he was, after all, one of the best of men. We don't often find such men these days. . . . And who has not his failings?"

Nikolai was with the Russian troops in Paris when the news of his father's death reached him. He immediately tendered his resignation, and, without waiting for it to be accepted, took a furlough and hastened to Moscow.

The state of the family finances was completely exposed within a month after the count's death, and surprised everyone by the magnitude of the sum of the various little debts, the existence of which no one had even suspected.

The property would cover half the debts. Nikolai's relatives and friends advised him to renounce the inheritance. But Nikolai saw in this suggestion the implication of a reproach to his father's memory, which he held sacred, and he therefore refused to hear anything said about renouncing the inheritance, and accepted it with all the obligations to settle the debts.

The creditors, who had remained silent so long, being kept good-natured during the count's lifetime by the vague but powerful influence of his easygoing generosity, now all suddenly began to clamor to have their debts paid. As always happens, a regular competition sprang up as to who should be paid first; and those very persons, like Mitenka and others, who held promissory notes—gratuities often—now showed themselves as the most pressing of the creditors. Nikolai was given no rest or respite; and those who apparently had had pity on the old man—the cause of their losses, if losses they were—were now pitiless toward the young heir, who was obviously in no way to blame, but had honorably assumed his father's debts.

The real estate was sold by auction, but did not bring half its value, and still half the debts remained unliquidated. Nikolai took thirty thousand rubles offered to him by his brother-in-law, Bezukhof, to pay that portion of the debts which he considered most pressing. And, so that he might not be sent to jail for the remaining obligations, as the other creditors threatened, he again entered government service.

To return to the army, where at the first vacancy he would be promoted to the rank of regimental commander, was impossible because his mother now clung to her only son as her last joy of her life; and therefore, in spite of his disinclination to remain in Moscow among those who had always known him, and notwithstanding his distaste for the civil service, he stayed in Moscow and accepted a position in the civil section, and, giving up the uniform which he so loved, he settled down with his mother and Sonya in a modest apartment on the Sivtsevoi Vrazhek.

Natasha and Pierre were at this time living in Petersburg, and had not a very clear idea of Nikolai's position. Nikolai, who had already had some money from his brother-in-law, strove to hide from him his unhappy situation. His position was rendered particularly difficult because, with his twelve hundred rubles salary, he was not only obliged to support himself, Sonya, and his mother, but he was obliged to live in such a way that his mother would not suspect that they were poor. The countess could not conceive of any existence without those conditions of luxury to which she had been accustomed from childhood; and without any idea that it was hard for her son, she continually requested a carriage, though they had none, to send for a friend, or some rich delicacy for herself or wine for her son, or money to provide some gift or a surprise to Natasha, Sonya, or Nikolai himself.

Sonya had charge of the domestic arrangements, waited on her aunt, read aloud to her, endured her whims and her secret ill will, and aided Nikolai in hiding from the old countess the condition of poverty to which they were reduced.

Nikolai felt that he owed Sonya a heavier debt of gratitude than he could ever repay for all that she had done for his mother; he admired her patience and devotion, but he tried to avoid her. In the depths of his heart, he seemingly reproached her for her very perfection, and because there was nothing for which to reproach her. She had every quality that people prize; but still there was lacking the something which would have compelled him to love her. And he felt that the more he prized her, the less he loved her. He had taken her at her word when she wrote the letter releasing him from his promise, and now he treated her as if all that had taken place between them had been long, long forgotten and could never by any chance return.

Nikolai's financial situation grew worse and worse. The idea of saving something from his salary became a dream with him. Instead of laying by anything, he was driven by his mother's constant demands of him to incur petty debts. There seemed to be no way out of his difficulties.

The idea of making a wealthy marriage, such as had been proposed to him by his relatives, was repugnant to him. The only other escape from his situation, the death of his mother, never occurred to him. He had no wishes, and he had no hope, and in the deepest depths of his heart he experienced a stern and gloomy enjoyment in thus resignedly enduring his situation. He tried to avoid his old acquaintances, their condolence and humiliating offers of assistance; he avoided every sort of amusement and dissipation, and did not even do anything at home except play cards with his mother, or pace in gloomy silence up and down the room, smoking pipe after pipe.

He cherished, as it were, this gloomy state, in which alone he felt himself capable of enduring his position.

I I

EARLY IN THE winter Princess Maria came to Moscow. From the current gossip of the town she learned of the position of the Rostofs, and how "the son was sacrificing himself for his mother," for so it was said in the city.

"I would have expected nothing else from him," said Princess Maria to herself, feeling a joyful confirmation of her love for him.

When she remembered her relations of friendship, almost of kinship, to the whole family, she felt it her duty to go to see them. But when she remembered her relationship to Nikolai at Voronezh, she dreaded to do so. At length, several weeks after her return to the city, she overcame her reluctance and forced herself to visit the Rostofs.

Nikolai was the first to meet her, for the reason that the countess' room could be reached only by passing through his. When he first caught sight of her, instead of showing the joy the princess had expected to see, he assumed a cold, haughty, and unfriendly expression which the princess had never before seen on his face. Nikolai inquired after her health, conducted her to his mother, and, after remaining five minutes, left the room.

When the princess left the countess, Nikolai again met her, and with especial ceremony and reserve ushered her into the anteroom. He did not answer her remark about the countess' health. "What have I to do with you? Leave me in peace," his look seemed to say.

"Now, what makes her come here? What does she want? I can't endure these fine ladies and all their inquisitive ways," he said aloud in Sonya's presence, evidently not able to restrain his annoyance after the princess' carriage had rolled away.

"Oh! how can you say so, Nikolai!" said Sonya, who could scarcely restrain her joy. "She is so good, and mama loves her so."

Nikolai made no answer, and would have preferred not to say anything more about the princess. But from that time forth the old countess kept talking about her a dozen times a day. The countess praised her, insisted that her son return her call, expressed her anxiety to see her more frequently; but at the same time, whenever she spoke of her, she always grew moody.

Nikolai tried to hold his tongue when his mother spoke of the princess. His silence annoyed his mother.

"She is a very good and lovely girl," she would say, "and you must go and call upon her. At all events, you will see somebody. It seems to me it must be tedious for you with us."

"I don't care to see anybody, dear mama!"

"A little while ago you wanted to see people, but now it's 'I don't care to.' Truly, my dear boy, I don't understand you. You have been finding it tedious, but now suddenly you don't wish to see anyone!"

"But I have not said it was tedious to me."

"Did you not just say that you did not want to see her? She is a very fine girl and you always liked her, but now you find some excuse or other. It's all a mystery to me!"

"Why, not at all, dear mama!"

"If I had asked you to do something disagreeable, but no, all I ask of you is to go and return this call! It would seem as if politeness demanded it. . . . I have asked you, and now I won't interfere any more, since you have secrets from your mother."

"But I will go, if you wish it."

"It's all the same to me. I wish it for your sake."

Nikolai sighed, and, gnawing his mustache, proceeded to lay out the cards, trying to divert his mother's attention to something else.

On the next day, on the third, and on the fourth, the same conversation was renewed.

After her call upon the Rostofs and the unexpectedly cool reception which Nikolai had given her, Princess Maria confessed to herself that she had been right in not wishing to go to the Rostofs' first.

"I expected as much," said she to herself, calling her pride to her assistance. "I have nothing to do with him, and I only wanted to see the old lady, who has always been good to me, and who is bound to me by so many ties." But she could not calm her agitation by these arguments; a feeling akin to remorse tormented her when she remembered her visit. Although she had firmly resolved not to go to the Rostofs' again, and to forget all about it, she could not help feeling that she was in a false position. And when she asked herself what it was that tormented her, she had to confess that it was her relation to Rostof.

His cool, formal tone did not really express his feelings, she knew this, and this tone only covered something. She felt that it was necessary for her to discover this something. And until she did, she felt that it was impossible for her to be at peace.

Once in midwinter she was in the schoolroom, attending to her nephew's lessons, when the servant came and announced that Rostof was in the drawing-room. With a firm determination not to betray her secret and not to manifest her confusion, she summoned Mlle. Bourienne and went down with her into the drawing-room.

At her first glance into Nikolai's face she perceived that he had come merely to fulfil the duty of politeness, and she firmly vowed that she would keep to the same tone in which he treated her. They talked about the countess' health, about common acquaintances, and about the latest news of the war, and when the ten minutes demanded by etiquette had passed, at the end of which the caller can take his departure, Nikolai rose to say good-by.

The princess, with Mlle. Bourienne's aid, had sustained the conversation very well; but at the very last moment, just as he rose to his feet, she had grown so weary of talking about things that did not interest her, and the thought that she alone had so little pleasure in life, came over her so powerfully that she fell into a fit of abstraction and sat motionless with her radiant eyes looking straight ahead and not perceiving that he had arisen.

Nikolai glanced at her, and, feigning not to notice her abstraction, spoke a few words to Mlle. Bourienne, and again looked at the princess. She sat as before, motionless, with an expression of pain on her gentle face.

Suddenly he felt a sense of compassion for her, and a dim consciousness that he himself might be the cause of the sorrow that was expressed in her face. He wanted to help her, to say something cheering to her; but he could not think what to say.

"Good-by, princess," said he.

She came to herself, flushed, and drew a long sigh.

"Oh, I beg your pardon," said she, as if aroused from a dream. "Are you going already, count? Well, good-by. . . . Oh, but the pillow for the countess?"

"Wait, I will fetch it for you," said Mlle. Bourienne, and left the room.

Both were silent, though they occasionally looked at each other.

"Yes, princess," said Nikolai at last, with a melancholy smile. "It does not seem very long ago, but how much has happened since you and I met first at Bogucharovo. How unfortunate we all seemed then; but I would give a good deal for that time to return again . . . but what is past is past."

The princess looked steadily into his face with her clear, radiant eyes while he was saying this. She seemed to be striving to discover in his words some secret significance that might interpret his sentiments toward her.

"Yes, yes," said she. "But you have nothing to regret in the past, count. When I think what your life is now, I am sure you will always remember it with pleasure, because the self-sacrifice which at the present time you . . ."

"I cannot accept your words of praise," said he, hastily interrupting her. "On the contrary, I am constantly reproaching myself; but this is not at all an interesting or amusing subject of conversation."

And again his eyes assumed their expression of reserve and coldness. But the princess had once more seen in him the man she had known and loved, and she was now talking only with that man.

"I thought you would permit me to say this to you," said she. "You and I have been brought so near together . . . and your family . . . and I thought you would not consider my sympathy out of place; but I was mistaken," said she. Her voice suddenly trembled. "I do not know why," she continued, correcting herself, "you were so different before, and . . ."

"There are a thousand reasons why"—he laid a special stress on the

669

word *why*. "I thank you, princess," said he, gently. "Sometimes it is hard. . ."

"So that is the reason, then, that is the reason," said a voice in Princess Maria's heart. "No, it was not alone his merry, kind, and open eyes, not alone his handsome exterior, for which I loved him: I suspected his nobility, firmness, and power of self-sacrifice," said she to herself. "Yes, now he is poor, and I am rich. Yes, that, then, was the sole reason. . . . Yes, if it were not for that. . ."

And, as she remembered his former gentleness, and looked now into his kind and melancholy face, she suddenly realized the reason for his coolness.

"Why is it, count, why is it?" she suddenly almost cried, and involuntarily came closer to him. "Why is it? Tell me. You must tell me."

He was silent.

"I don't know, count, what your why is," she went on to say, "but it is hard for me too, for me. I confess it to you. For some reason you wish to deprive me of your old friendship. And this pains me."

The tears were in her eyes and in her voice.

"I have so little happiness in life that every loss is hard for me to bear. Excuse me. . . good-by."

She suddenly burst into tears, and started to leave the room.

"Princess! Wait! for God's sake!" he cried, trying to detain her. "Princess!"

She looked around. For several seconds they looked into each other's eyes, each in silence, and what had been distant and impossible suddenly came near, possible and inevitable.

III

IN THE AUTUMN of the year 1813, Nikolai was married to Princess Maria, and went with his wife, his mother, and Sonya to live at Lisiya Gori.

In the course of four years, without selling any of his wife's property, he settled the last of his debts, and, having inherited a small estate by the death of a cousin, he also paid back what he had borrowed from Pierre. Three years later, by 1820, Nikolai had so managed his affairs that he had purchased a small estate adjoining Lisiya Gori, and was in negotiation for repurchasing Otradnoye, which was one of his favorite dreams.

Having been forced by necessity to manage his own estate, he quickly grew so passionately interested in farming that it came to be his favorite and almost exclusive occupation. From the very first he studied the peasant, striving to comprehend what he wanted, and what he considered good and bad. He only pretended to give orders and lay out work, while in reality he was learning of the peasants, their ways and their words and their judgment as to what was good or bad.

And only when at last he learned to understand the tastes and aspirations of the peasants, learned to speak their speech and comprehend the secret significance of their sayings, when he felt himself one with them, only then did he dare boldly to direct them, that is, to fulfil toward them the duties that were demanded of him. And Nikolai's management brought about the most brilliant results.

Princess Maria was jealous of her husband because of his love for the peasants, and regretted that she could not share in it; but she could not understand the joys and troubles which for him constituted this world, so foreign and apart from her own. She felt that he had a special world of his own, which he passionately loved and which was governed by laws she could not understand.

When, sometimes, in her endeavors to understand him, she would speak to him of the service he was rendering in doing so much good to his dependents, he would lose his temper and reply:

"Not in the least; it never entered my head, and I am not doing anything for their good. That is all poetry and old wives' tales, all this talk about kindness to one's neighbor. What I want is that our children should not become beggars; what I want is to get our property on a satisfactory basis while I am alive: that is all. And to do that, order is necessary, and so is discipline. . . . That's all there is to it," said he, clenching his sanguine fist. "And justice, of course," he added. "Because if the peasant is naked and hungry, and has only one little horse, then he will work neither for himself nor for me."

And, no doubt for the very reason that Nikolai would not think he was doing anything for others as a benefactor, all he did was so abundantly successful that his property rapidly increased; neighboring serfs came to him and begged him to buy them, and, long after he was dead and gone, a devout memory of his régime obtained among the peasantry.

"He was a master. . . . He looked after his peasants' affairs first, and then his own. And he did not show too much indulgence, either. In one word, he was a master."

One thing sometimes troubled Nikolai in relation to his administration of affairs, and this was his quick temper and a propensity, which was a relic of his old life as a hussar, to enforce his will by means of his hands. At first he saw nothing reprehensible in this; but in the second year of his married life his views in regard to this manner of inflicting punishment underwent a sudden change.

Once during the summer the elder of Bogucharovo, the successor of Dron, who was now dead, was summoned over to Lisiya Gori charged with various rascalities and villainies. Nikolai met him on the porch, and at his first reply the sound of cries and blows rang through the vestibule.

On going into the house for breakfast, Nikolai joined his wife, whom he found sitting with her head bent low over her embroidery frame, and began to tell her, as he always did, about all that had occupied him that morning, and, among other things, about the elder of Bogucharovo.

Princess Maria, turning red, then pale, and compressing her lips, sat with her head still bent, and made no reply to her husband's words.

"Such an impertinent scoundrel!" he exclaimed, growing hot at the mere recollection. "If he had only told me that he was drunk . . . I never saw . . . but what is the matter, Marie?" he suddenly asked.

The princess raised her head and tried to say something, but again hastily dropped her head, and compressed her lips.

"What is it? What is the matter, my darling?"

Plain as Princess Maria was, she always grew pretty when tears were in her eyes. She never wept because of pain or annoyance, but always from sorrow and pity. And when she wept, her liquid eyes acquired an irresistible charm.

The moment Nikolai took her by the hand, she could no longer restrain herself, but burst into tears.

"Nikolai, I saw . . . he is at fault, but, oh, Nikolai, why did you?" And she hid her face in her hands.

Nikolai said nothing, turned crimson, and, moving away from her, began to pace up and down the room. He understood what made her weep; but at the same time he could not agree with her in his heart that what he had been used to regarding since childhood as a customary thing was wrong.

"Is it her amiability and female whims, or is she right?" he asked himself. Unable to decide this question for himself, he once more looked into her pained, loving face, and suddenly realized that she was right, and that he had been wrong even in his own eyes for a long time.

"Marie," said he, gently, and he came to her, "this shall never happen again; I give you my word. Never!" he repeated, in a trembling voice like a little boy begging forgiveness.

The tears rolled faster than ever from the princess' eyes. She took her husband's hand and kissed it.

"Nikolai, when did you break your cameo?" she asked, for the purpose of changing the conversation, and examining his hand, on which he wore a ring with a head of Laocoön.

"Today; it's all the same story. Marie, don't speak of it again." He flushed once more. "I give you my word of honor that this won't happen again. And let this always be a reminder to me," he added, pointing to the broken ring.

From that time forth, when he had to enter into explanations with the elder, and the hot blood flew into his face, and he began to clench his fists, Nikolai would turn the broken ring round on his finger and drop his eyes before the man who was angering him. However, once or twice a year he would forget himself, and then, when he came into his wife's presence, he would confess, and again give his promise that it would be the last time.

"Marie, you probably despise me," he would say to her. "I deserve it."

"You should walk away, walk away as fast you can, if you find that you have not the strength of mind to restrain yourself," said Princess Maria in a tender voice, trying to console her husband.

Nikolai was respected but not liked among the gentry of the province. He did not care about the interests of the nobility, and because of this some considered him proud, others stupid.

During the summer he spent all his time in the management of his farms, from the time that the seed was put in until the crops were garnered. During the autumn, he gave himself up to hunting with the same practical seriousness he showed in the care of his estates, and, for a month or even two, would leave on his hunting expeditions. In the winter he rode off to visit his other villages, and occupied himself with reading. His reading consisted, chiefly, of historical works, for the purchase of which he spent a certain amount each year. He was collecting, as he said, a "serious library," and he made it a rule to read through every book he bought. With a grave face, he would shut himself up in his library for this reading, which, at first, he imposed on himself as a duty; but in time it came to be his ordinary occupation, furnishing him with a certain kind of satisfaction, and the consciousness that he was occupied with a serious task.

Except for the time he spent out of doors, in the pursuit of his affairs, during the winter he was mostly in the house, entering into the domestic life of the family and taking an interest in the everyday relations between the mother and children. He grew closer and closer to his wife, each day discovering in her new spiritual treasures.

Sonya, since the time of Nikolai's marriage, had lived in his house. Some time before his marriage, Nikolai, laying all blame on himself, and praising Sonya, had told Princess Maria what had occurred between him and Sonya. He had begged Princess Maria to be kind and good to his cousin. Maria fully realized her husband's fault. She also felt that she was to blame toward Sonya; she understood that her own attitude had influenced Nikolai's choice, and she could not see that Sonya was in any way at fault, and she wanted to love her; but not only did she not love her, but she often found bitter feelings against Sonya arising in her soul, and she could not overcome them.

One time she was talking with her friend Natasha about Sonya and about her own injustice toward the girl.

"Do you know," said Natasha, "you have read the New Testament a great deal; there is one place that refers directly to Sonya."

"What is that?" asked Princess Maria, in amazement.

" 'For unto everyone that hath shall be given, but from him that hath not shall be taken away even that which he hath.' Do you remember? She is the one that hath not. Why, I do not know; possibly she has no selfishness in her. I don't know, but things are taken away from her, everything has been taken away from her. I am terribly sorry for her sometimes; I used to be terribly anxious for Nikolai to marry her, but I always had a sort of presentiment that it would never be. She is a sterile flower; you have seen them in the strawberry patch, haven't you? Sometimes I am sorry for her, but then again I think that she doesn't feel what happens to her as we do."

And although Princess Maria explained to Natasha that these words from the Gospel must have a different meaning, still, as she looked at Sonya, she agreed with Natasha's explanation of them. It really seemed to her that Sonya was not troubled by her uncomfortable position, and was quite reconciled to being a "sterile flower."

It seemed that she did not so much care for any special individual as for the family as a whole. Like a cat, she attached herself not to the people so much as to the house itself. She took care of the old countess, she petted and spoiled the children, she was always ready to render such little services as she could; but all this was accepted unwittingly, without any special sense of gratitude.

The establishment at Lisiya Gori had now been restored to good order, but not on the same footing as during the late prince's lifetime. The new buildings, begun during the hard times, were more than simple. The enormous manor house, erected on the original stone foundations, was of wood, merely plastered on the inside. This great, spacious mansion, with its unpainted deal floors, was furnished with the simplest and coarsest couches and easy-chairs, tables and chairs made from their own lumber by their own carpenter. The house was capacious, with rooms for the domestics and special suites for guests.

The relatives of the Rostofs and Bolkonskys often came to visit at Lisiya Gori, with their families, dozens of servants, and almost a score of horses, and would spend months there. Moreover, three or four times a year, on the saint's-day or birthday festivals of the host and hostess, a hundred guests would be present at once for several days.

The rest of the year life moved in its regular channels with the usual occupations—teas, breakfasts, dinners, suppers, supplied from the resources of the estate.

I V

IT WAS THE eve of St. Nicholas Day—the seventeenth of December, 1820.

That year Natasha with her children and husband had come early in the autumn to visit her brother. Pierre was in Petersburg, where he had gone on private business for three or four weeks, as he said, but where he had already spent seven. They were expecting him at any moment. The Rostofs had as a guest, besides the Bezukhof family, Nikolai's old friend, General Vasili Denisof, who was now on the retired list.

Nikolai knew that on the eighteenth, the day of the festivity for which the guests had assembled, he would have to discard his Tartar blouse, put on his dress coat and tight, pointed shoes, and go to the new church he had just built, and then receive congratulations and offer lunch, and talk about the elections and the crops; but he felt that on the eve of his saint's-day he had the right to spend his time in the usual way.

Just before dinner Nikolai had been verifying the accounts of the bailiff from the Riazan estate of his wife's nephew, had written two business letters, and had made the round of the granaries, the cattle yard, and his stables. Having taken precautions against the general drunkenness which was to be expected on the morrow because of its being an important festival, he came in to dinner, and without having had a chance for a few moments of private conversation with his wife, he took his seat at the long table set with twenty covers for his whole household.

At the table were his mother; old Madame Byelov, an inseparable companion of the countess; his wife, his three children, their governess, their tutor, his nephew with his tutor, Sonya, Denisof, Natasha, her three children, their governess, and little old Mikhail Ivanitch, the old prince's architect, who lived at Lisiya Gori on a pension.

Princess Maria sat at the other end of the table. As soon as her husband took his place she knew, by the gesture with which he took his napkin and quickly pushed away the tumbler and wineglass that were set before him, that he was in a bad humor, as was sometimes the case with him especially before soup, and when he came directly from his work to dinner.

Princess Maria was thoroughly familiar with his mood, and, when she herself was in her usual good spirits, she would calmly wait until he had finished his soup, and not till then would she begin to talk with him and make him acknowledge that his ill temper was groundless. But on this particular day she had quite forgot her previous experience; it hurt her to feel that he was angry with her without cause, and she felt that she was innocent.

She asked him where he had been. He told her.

Then again she asked him if he found everything in good order. He scowled disagreeably at her unnatural tone, and answered hastily.

"So I was not mistaken," thought Princess Maria. "Now, why is he vexed with me?"

By the tone in which he answered her she detected what she thought was ill will toward herself and a wish to cut short the conversation. She realized that her own words had been constrained, but she could not refrain from asking several other questions.

The conversation during dinner, thanks to Denisof, quickly became general and animated, and Princess Maria had no chance to say anything to her husband. When they left the table and went to thank the old countess, Princess Maria, offering her hand, kissed her husband and asked him why he was vexed with her.

"You *always* have such strange ideas! . . . I had no thought of being vexed with you," said he. But this word "always" said with sufficient clearness to Princess Maria: "Yes, I am angry, and I won't tell you."

Nikolai lived so harmoniously with his wife that even Sonya and the old countess, who out of jealousy might have been happy to see some discord between them, could not find any excuse for reproach; but still they had their moments of hostility. Sometimes, especially after their happiest times, they were suddenly assailed by the feeling of repulsion and animosity; this feeling was particularly liable to occur when Princess Maria was pregnant. She was now in this condition.

"Well, ladies and gentlemen," said Nikolai, in a loud and apparently gay tone—it seemed to Princess Maria that it was on purpose to hurt her feelings —"I have been on my feet ever since six o'clock. Tomorrow I have to endure a good deal, and now I'm going to rest." And, without saying anything more to Princess Maria, he went into the little sitting room and lay down on the divan.

"That's the way it always is," thought Princess Maria. "He talks with all the rest, but not with me. I see, I see that I am repulsive to him, especially when I am in this condition."

She looked at her changed figure and caught sight in the mirror of her yellowish-pale, thin face, with her large eyes more prominent than ever. And everything seemed disagreeable to her—Denisof's shouts and laughter, and Natasha's talk, and especially the look that Sonya hastily threw after her. Sonya was always the first pretext Princess Maria found to excuse her irritation.

After sitting down for a while with her guests, and not comprehending a word of what they said, she softly got up and went to the nursery. The children were on chairs, "going to Moscow," and they begged her to join them. She sat down and played with them, but the thought of her husband and his causeless vexation continued to torment her. She got up and went to the little sitting room, painfully trying to walk on her tiptoes.

"Perhaps he is not asleep; I will have a talk with him," said she to herself.

Andryusha, her oldest boy, imitating her, followed her on his tiptoes. Princess Maria did not notice him.

"Marie dear, I think he is asleep; he is so tired," said Sonya, from the large sitting room; it seemed to Princess Maria as if she met her everywhere! "Andryusha might wake him."

Princess Maria looked around, saw Andryusha at her heels, and felt that Sonya was right; this very thing made her angry, and it was evidently with difficulty that she restrained herself from a sharp retort. She said nothing, and, affecting not to have heard her, she made a gesture with her hand to Andryusha not to make a noise but to follow her, and went to the door. Sonya passed through another door.

From the room where Nikolai was sleeping could be heard his measured breathing, so well known to his wife, even to its slightest shadow of change. As she listened to his breathing she could see before her his smooth, handsome brow, his mustache, his whole face, at which so often she had gazed in the silence of the night, while he was asleep.

Nikolai suddenly started and yawned. And at that same instant Andryusha cried from the door:

"Papa, mama dear is there!"

Princess Maria grew pale with fright, and started to make signs to her son. He became still, and for an instant the silence, so terrible to Princess Maria, continued. She knew how Nikolai disliked being awakened.

Suddenly in the room were heard fresh yawns, rustling, and Nikolai's voice said in a tone of annoyance:

"Can't I have a moment's rest! Marie, is it you? What made you bring him here?"

"I only came to see if . . . I did not see him . . . forgive me . . ."

Nikolai coughed, and said nothing more. Princess Maria went away from the door, and led her son to the nursery.

Five minutes later, the little, dark-eyed, three-year-old Natasha, her father's favorite, hearing her brother say that her papa was asleep and her mama was in the sitting room, ran to her father unobserved by her mother. The dark-eyed little girl boldly pushed open the creaking door, ran on her energetic little stumpy legs up to the divan, and, after attentively looking at her father, who was lying with his back turned toward her, raised herself on her tiptoes and kissed his hand, on which his head was resting. Nikolai, with a fond smile, turned over.

"Natasha! Natasha!" Princess Maria was heard saying in a terrified whisper outside the door, "papa wants to get a nap."

"No, mama! He doesn't want a nap," replied the little Natasha, in a tone of settled conviction. "He's laughing."

Nikolai put down his feet, sat up, and took his daughter in his arms. "Come in, Marie dear," said he to his wife.

Princess Maria went in and sat down near her husband.

"I didn't see him tagging behind me," said she, timidly. "That's the way with me."

Nikolai, holding his daughter in one arm, looked at his wife, and, perceiving the apologetic expression in her face, he put his other arm around her and kissed her on the hair.

"May I kiss mama?" he asked Natasha. Natasha smiled shyly.

"Again!" said she, with an imperative gesture designating the spot where Nikolai had kissed his wife.

"I don't know why you should think I am out of sorts," said Nikolai, answering the question he knew was in his wife's heart.

"You can't imagine how unhappy, how lonely, I feel when you are so! It seems to me all the time . . ."

"Marie, stop! What nonsense! Aren't you ashamed of yourself?" he asked gaily.

"It seems to me that you cannot love me, that I am so plain . . . always . . . but now . . . in this con—"

"How absurd you are! Beauty does not make sweetness, but sweetness

677

makes beauty! It is only such women as the Malvinas who are loved for their beauty. Do I love my wife? I don't love her in that way . . . but I can't explain it. Without you . . . or even when we are at odds as we were just now, I feel quite lost and don't know what to do. Now, look, do I love my little finger? I don't love it, but . . . just try it . . . cut it off . . ."

"No, I'm not like that, but I understand you. And so you are not vexed with me?"

"Oh, yes, I am . . . horribly vexed," said he, smiling; then, getting up and smoothing his hair, he began to pace up and down the room. "You know what I was thinking about," he began, now that peace had been made, immediately beginning to think aloud in his wife's hearing. He did not ask if she was ready to listen to him; it was all the same to him. If he had any thoughts, she must have the same. And he told her his intention of inviting Pierre to remain with them till spring.

Princess Maria listened to him, made some observation, and began in her turn to think her thoughts aloud. Her thoughts were about her children.

"How the woman can be seen in her already!" she said in French, alluding to the little Natasha. "You accuse us women of being illogical. Well, she is our logic personified. I say, 'Papa wants to get a nap,' but she says, 'No, he is laughing.' And she is right," said Princess Maria, with a happy smile.

"Yes, yes"—and, taking his daughter by his strong hands, he lifted her up in the air, set her on his shoulder, holding her by the feet, and began to walk up and down the room with her. The faces of father and daughter alike expressed the most absurd happiness.

"But you know you are apt to be partial. You love this one more than the others," whispered Princess Maria in French.

"But how can I help it? . . . I try not to show it."

At this instant sounds of slamming doors and steps were heard in the vestibule and anteroom, as if there was an arrival.

"Someone has come."

"I think it must be Pierre. I'll go and find out," said Princess Maria, and she left the room. During her absence Nikolai gave his little daughter a gallop around the room.

All out of breath, he quickly set down the laughing child and pressed her to his heart. His gambols reminded him of dancing, and, as he gazed into the child's round, radiant face, he thought of the future, when he would be an old gentleman and lead her out and dance the mazurka with her, as his own father had once danced "Daniel Cooper" with his daughter.

"Yes, it is he, it is he, Nikolai," said Princess Maria, returning to the room after a few minutes. "Now our Natasha has got back her spirits. You ought to see how happy she is! And how he caught it for having been away so long! But come quick, let's go and see him, come! Do let him go," said she, looking with a smile at her daughter, who clung to her father.

Nikolai started off, holding the little girl by the hand. Princess Maria remained in the sitting room.

"Never, never, would I believe that I could be so happy," she whispered to herself. Her face was radiant with a smile; but at the same time she sighed, and a gentle sadness showed itself in her deep eyes. It was as if over and above that happiness which she now experienced there was another kind of happiness, unattainable in this life, and she at that moment involuntarily remembered it.

V

NATASHA HAD been married in the early spring of 1813, and in 1820 she had already three daughters and one son—the child she had wanted, and whom she was now nursing.

She had grown plump and broad, so that it would have been difficult to recognize in the strong matron the slender, vivacious Natasha of yore. The features of her face had grown more marked, and bore an expression of sedate gentleness and serenity. Her face had lost all of that ever-flashing light of animation which had formerly constituted her chief charm. Often now you would see only her face and her bodily presence and nothing of the animated soul. All you could see was a healthy, handsome, fruitful female.

Very rarely now did the old fire sparkle. This happened at times when, as now, her husband returned from a journey, or when a sick child was convalescing, or when she and Princess Maria talked over old memories of Prince Andrei (she never talked about him with her husband, imagining that he might be jealous of such memories), and at the very rare times when something happened to make her sing, though, since her marriage, she had entirely abandoned this accomplishment. And at these rare moments when the old fire flashed, with the beauty of her mature development she was even more fascinating than before.

Since the time of her marriage, Natasha and Pierre had lived in Moscow, in Petersburg, and on their estate near Moscow, and with her mother, or rather with Nikolai. The young Countess Bezukhof was seen little in fashionable society, and those who met her were not attracted by her. She was neither amiable nor anxious to please. It was not that Natasha liked solitude—she did not know whether she liked it or not, it even seemed to her that she did not—but while engaged in the bearing and nursing and rearing of children, and sharing each moment of her husband's life, she could not satisfy these demands otherwise than by denying herself society.

All who had known Natasha before her marriage were amazed at the change that had taken place in her, as if it were something extraordinary. Only the old countess knew, from maternal insight, that all Natasha's impulses of enthusiasm had had their origin merely in the need of having a family, of having a husband, as she had cried more in earnest than in jest that winter at Otradnoye. The mother was amazed at the amazement of people who did not understand Natasha, and she insisted that she had always known that Natasha would be a model wife and mother.

"Only she carries her love for her husband and children to extremes," the countess would say, "so that it even seems stupid in her."

Natasha did not follow that golden rule preached by clever men, especially the French, to the effect that when a young lady marries she must not neglect, must not abandon, her talents, must cultivate her personal adornment even more zealously than when she was a girl, must charm her husband as much after as she did before marriage.

Natasha, on the contrary, all at once abandoned all her accomplishments, even the one that was most of an accomplishment—her singing. She abandoned it for the very reason that it was an accomplishment. Natasha took no pains either with her deportment or with the elegance of her language, nor did she try to give herself graces before her husband, or think about her clothes, or dream of not imposing irksome exactions on her husband.

She felt that those witcheries which instinct had taught her to employ before would now be absurd in the eyes of her husband, to whom she had surrendered entirely from the first minute—that is, with her whole soul, not leaving one single corner secret from him.

To shake her curls, to put on billowing dresses, to sing romances in order to attract her husband to her, would have seemed to her as ridiculous as to adorn herself for the purpose of giving herself pleasure. To adorn herself to please others, possibly, might have been pleasing to her—she did not know —but she never did such a thing. The chief reason that she did not indulge in singing or the witcheries of the toilet, or in using elegant language, was that she had absolutely no time to indulge herself in these things.

It is a well-known fact that a man has the capacity of completely immersing himself in any occupation, no matter how insignificant that occupation may be. And it is a well-known fact that any such occupation, however insignificant, through the attention concentrated on it, may expand into infinite proportions. The occupation in which Natasha was absolutely absorbed was her family, that is to say, her husband, whom she had to hold so that he would cling to her and to his home; and her children, who had to be born, nursed, and reared and educated.

Natasha was so neglectful of herself that her dresses, her mode of doing her hair, her carelessly spoken words, her jealousy—she was jealous of Sonya, of the governess, of every woman, whether pretty or plain—were a common subject of amusement for the whole family. The general impression was that Pierre was "under his wife's shoe," as the saying goes, and this was really so.

During the very first days of her married life, Natasha announced her demands. Pierre was greatly amazed at this idea of his wife's, which was so absolutely new to him; she insisted that every minute of his life belonged to her and his children. Pierre, though amazed at his wife's demand, was flattered by it and submitted to it.

Pierre's submission lay in his acceptance of the implied prohibition not merely of paying attentions to other women, but even of talking and laughing with them, of going to the club to dinner or for the purpose of merely passing away the time, of spending his money on whims, or taking long journeys except on business—and in this category his wife included his interest in scientific pursuits, to which she attributed great importance, though she had no understanding of such things.

In return for this, Pierre had a perfect right to dispose of himself and his whole family as he might please—Natasha, in her own home, placed herself on the footing of a slave toward her husband, and the whole house went on tiptoes when he was busy reading or writing in his library. Pierre had only to manifest preference and his wish would be instantly fulfilled.

The whole house was conducted according to Pierre's wishes, which Natasha tried to anticipate. The style, the place of living, their acquaintances, their intercourse with society, Natasha's occupations, the education of their children—not only was everything done in accordance with Pierre's expressed will, but Natasha strove to elicit hints of his ideas when he was talking. And when she actually discovered what constituted the essence of Pierre's desires, and she had done this, she firmly clung to what she had once adopted. When Pierre himself showed signs of changing his mind, she would turn his own weapons against him.

Thus, during the trying time, which Pierre never forgot, after the birth of their first child, which was ailing, and they were obliged three times to change wet nurses, and Natasha fell ill from anxiety, Pierre one time told her of the ideas of Rousseau, with whom he was always in perfect accord, as to the unnaturalness and harmfulness of wet nurses.

When the next child was born, in spite of the opposition of her mother, the doctors, and her husband himself, who revolted against her nursing the child as at that time something unheard of and harmful, Natasha insisted on doing so, and from that time forth she always nursed all her children.

Very often, in moments of irritation, it would happen that husband and wife would argue; but long after the quarrel was forgotten, Pierre would discover, to his joy and amazement, not only in what his wife said but in what she did, his own ideas. And not only would he find his own idea, but he would find it purified of everything superfluous.

After seven years of married life, Pierre felt a joyous, settled consciousness that he was not a bad man, and this consciousness arose from the fact that he saw himself reflected in his wife. In himself he felt that all that was good and bad was mixed together and confused. But in his wife only that which was truly good found expression; all that was not absolutely good was discarded in her. And this reflection was not the result of a logical process of thought, but came from some other mysterious inner source.

VI

PIERRE, TWO MONTHS before, while he was still visiting the Rostofs, received a letter urging him to come to Petersburg to help decide some weighty questions that were agitating the members of a society of which Pierre was one of the most influential members.

On reading this letter—for she always read her husband's letters—hard as it was for her to bear her husband's absence, Natasha herself was the first to urge him to go to Petersburg. She was constantly afraid of being a hindrance to her husband's intellectual, abstract interests. In reply to Pierre's timid, questioning look, on reading this letter, she begged him to go, but to make the time of the return as definite as possible. And leave of absence of a month was given him. When this leave of absence had expired, a fortnight before, Natasha found herself in a state of constant alarm, depression, and irritation.

Denisof, now a general on the retired list, and greatly dissatisfied with the actual state of affairs, had been visiting at the Rostofs' for the past two weeks, and looked upon Natasha in surprise and grief, as on a bad portrait of some once-loved face. Dejected, melancholy glances, haphazard replies, and perpetual talk about the children were all that was left of his former enchantress.

Natasha was depressed and irritable all the time, especially when her mother, her brother, Sonya or Maria tried to excuse Pierre and find reasons for his delay.

"All nonsense, trivial nonsense," Natasha would say; "all these deep thoughts of his, which lead nowhere, and all these foolish societies," she would say, referring to those very matters she actually considered of immense importance. And off she would go to the nursery to nurse her only son, the little Petya.

No one could tell how consoling, how reasonable, this little creature of only three months was when he lay at her breast, and she felt the motion of his mouth and the snuffling of his little nose. This being said to her: "You are jealous, you are angry, you are afraid; but you would like to hurt him; but . . . I am he! Oh, yes, I am he!"

And there was no answer to be made. It was more than the truth! Natasha, during those two weeks of anxiety, went so many times to her baby for consolation, she made such a to-do over him, that she overfed him and he fell ill. She was horror-stricken at his illness, and at the same time it was the very thing she needed. In caring for him, she more easily endured her husband's absence.

She was nursing him when the commotion caused by Pierre's arrival was heard; and the nurse, who knew how much it would delight her mistress, came running in noiselessly but swiftly, with a beaming face.

"Has he come?" asked Natasha, in a hurried whisper, afraid to move lest she wake the sleeping infant.

"He's come, my dear!" whispered the nurse.

The blood rushed into Natasha's face, and her feet made an involuntary movement, but it was impossible to jump up and run. The child again opened his eyes and looked at her. "Are you here?" he seemed to say, and again smacked his lips.

Cautiously withdrawing her breast, Natasha rocked him a little, and then handed him to the nurse and ran swiftly to the door. But at the door she paused, as if her conscience reproached her for having, in her joy, too hastily given up the child, and she looked round. The nurse, with her elbows in the air, was just putting the baby safely into its cradle.

"Yes, go right along, go right along, dearie, have no fears, go right along," whispered the nurse, smiling with the familiarity that always exists between nurse and mistress.

And Natasha with light steps ran to the anteroom.

Denisof, with his pipe, coming from the library into the hall, now for the first time recognized the Natasha of yore. A bright, shining light of joy irradiated her transfigured face.

"He's come!" she called to him, as she flew along, and Denisof felt that he also was delighted by Pierre's arrival, though he had never had any great love for him.

As Natasha came running into the anteroom, she caught sight of the tall form in a big fur coat, untying his scarf.

"Here he is! Here he is! Truly, he is here!" she said to her own heart, and flying up to him, she threw her arms around him, pressed him to herself with her head on his breast, and then, pushing him away, she gazed into Pierre's snow-powdered, ruddy, happy face. "Yes, here he is! Happy and satisfied!"

And suddenly she recalled all the torments of disappointed expectation that she had endured during the last two weeks; the radiance of joy beaming from her face was suddenly clouded; she frowned, and a stream of reproaches and bitter words was poured out upon Pierre.

"Yes, it's very fine for you; you are very glad, very happy! . . . But how is it with me? You've had a great longing for your children! I nurse them, and the milk was spoiled because of you. . . . Petya almost died. And you are very gay . . . yes, you are very gay."

Pierre knew it was not his fault, because it was impossible for him to return sooner; he knew that this explosion of hers was unbecoming, and he knew that within two minutes it would be all over; he knew, most of all, that he himself felt gay and happy. He would have preferred to smile, but he had no time to think about it. He put on a scared, timid face, and stooped down to her.

"By all the powers, I could not help it . . . but how is Petya?"

"He is all right now! Let's go to him. But aren't you ashamed? Didn't you know how I missed you, how I was tormented without you?"

"Are you well?"

"Come, let's go, come," said she, not letting go of his hand. And they went to their rooms.

When Nikolai and his wife came to inquire after Pierre, he was in the nursery, and on the huge palm of his right hand was holding his babe, now awake, and was playing with him. A jolly smile hovered over the infant's broad face with its toothless mouth. The storm had long since passed over, and the bright sun of joy shone in Natasha's eyes as she gazed tenderly at her husband and son.

"And so you talked everything over satisfactorily with Prince Feodor," Natasha was saying.

"Yes, admirably."

"Do you see, he's holding it up!" Natasha meant the baby's head. "Well, how he startled me!"

"And did you see the princess? Is it true that she's in love with that . . ."

"Yes, you can imagine . . ."

At that instant, Nikolai and Maria came in. Pierre, not putting down his little son, stooped down and kissed them, and replied to their questions. But evidently, notwithstanding the many interesting things that they had to talk over, still the baby in its cap, with its vain efforts to hold up its head, absorbed all Pierre's attention.

"How sweet!" exclaimed Princess Maria, looking at the child and beginning to play with it. "There's one thing I can't understand, Nikolai," said she, turning to her husband, "and that is why you can't appreciate the charm of these marvelous little creatures."

"I don't and I can't," said Nikolai, looking at the baby with indifferent eyes. "A lump of flesh. Come, Pierre."

"He really is a most affectionate father," said Princess Maria, apologizing for her husband. "Only at that age, before they are a year old . . ."

"Ah, but Pierre makes a splendid nurse," said Natasha. "He says that his hand was made on purpose for a baby's back. Just look!"

"Well, not for that alone," said Pierre, suddenly, with a laugh, and, seizing the baby, he handed him over to the nurse.

VII

AT THE LISIYA GORI home, as in every genuine family, there lived together several absolutely distinct microcosms, which, while each preserved its own individuality, united into one harmonious whole.

Every event that happened to the household was alike glad or sad—alike important—for all these microcosms; but each one had its own personal, independent reasons for joy or sorrow at any particular event.

Thus, Pierre's coming was one of these happy, important events, and it affected the members of the household in somewhat this way:

The servants (who are always the most reliable judges of their masters, because they judge not by words and the expressions of feelings, but by actions and the manner of life) were glad of Pierre's return, since they knew that, when he was there, the count would cease to make the tour of the estate every day, and would be jollier and kinder, and still more because all would receive rich presents on the holidays.

The children and governesses were delighted at Pierre's return, because there was no one like Pierre to keep up the general life of any occasion. He alone was able to play on the harpsichord that "Ecossaise"—his one piece!—to which they could dance, as he said, all possible dances, and then besides he would probably make them, too, holiday presents.

Nikolusha, who was now a thin, delicate, intellectual lad of fifteen, with curling flaxen hair and handsome eyes, was glad, because "Uncle Pierre," as he called him, was the object of his admiration and passionate love. No one had tried to instill in the lad a special love for Pierre, and he had seen him only a few times. His aunt and guardian, Princess Maria, exerted all her energies to make Nikolusha love her husband as she loved him; and Nikolusha did love his uncle, but his love had an almost perceptible tinge of scorn in it. He worshiped Pierre. He had no desire to be a hussar or a knight of St. George; he preferred to be a learned, good and intellectual man like Pierre. In Pierre's presence, his face always wore a look of radiant delight, and he flushed and choked when Pierre addressed him.

The guests were glad, because Pierre was always a man full of life, and a bond of union in any sort of society.

The adult members of the household, to say nothing of his wife, were glad of a friend who made life easier and smoother.

The old women were glad, because of the presents he brought, and principally because his coming gave Natasha new life.

Pierre felt the effect on himself of these varying views of the varying microcosms, and hastened to give to each what each expected.

Pierre, the most abstracted, the most forgetful, of men, now made a list with his wife's advice, and, without forgetting a single item, executed the commissions of her mother and brother, buying such things as the dress for Madame Byelova and toys for his nephews.

When he was first married, this request of his wife—that he should do all her errands and not forget a single thing he had undertaken to buy—seemed very strange to him; and he was greatly surprised at her grave displeasure when, on his first journey from home, he forgot absolutely everything. But afterwards he became used to running errands. Knowing that Natasha never ordered anything for herself, and ordered for the others only when he himself suggested it, he now took a boyish enjoyment, quite unexpected to himself, in these purchases of gifts for the whole household, and he never forgot anything any more. If he deserved reproaches from Natasha, it was solely because he bought needless and overexpensive gifts. In addition to her slackness and negligence—faults, as they seemed to the majority; qualities, as they seemed in Pierre's eyes—Natasha had also that of excessive frugality.

From the time Pierre began to live on a grand scale—for his new family was expensive to keep—he noticed, much to his surprise, that nevertheless he was spending only half as much as before, and that his affairs, which had been in great confusion of late, especially by reason of his first wife's debts, were beginning to improve. It was cheaper to live because his life was tied down. The most expensive luxury consists in a style of life that can at any minute be changed; Pierre no longer indulged in this extravagance, and no longer had any wish to do so. He felt that his style of life was settled now until death, that to change it was not in his power, and this style of life proved to be cheap.

Pierre, with a jolly, smiling face, unwrapped his purchases.

"How much do you suppose?" he asked, like a shopkeeper, as he unwrapped a roll of cloth.

Natasha was sitting opposite him holding her oldest daughter on her lap, and swiftly turned her shining eyes from her husband to what he was exhibiting.

"Is that for Byelova? Splendid!" She examined the quality of the material. "That cost about a ruble, didn't it?"

Pierre told her the price.

"Too much," said Natasha. "Well, how glad the children and mama will be. . . Only there was no sense in getting that for me," she added, unable to restrain a smile, as she looked at a gold comb set with pearls, which were just then becoming fashionable.

"Adele tried to dissuade me; I didn't know whether to buy it or not."

"When would I wear it?" Natasha took it and put it in her braid. "It will do when little Masha is a debutante; perhaps they'll be wearing them again. Come, let's go in."

All the adult members of the family gathered for tea at the round table, over which Sonya presided. The children, the tutors and the governesses had already finished drinking their tea, and their voices were heard in the adjoining sitting room.

When the elders were at tea, each had his accustomed place to sit. Nikolai near the stove, at the small table, where they handed him his glass. The old borzoi Milka lay on the chair near him, with her completely gray face, from which occasionally bulged forth a pair of great black eyes. Denisof, with his curly hair, his mustaches and side whiskers fast turning gray, sat next to Princess Maria, with his general's coat unbuttoned. Pierre sat between his wife and the old countess. He was relating what, he knew, would greatly interest the old lady and be comprehensible to her. He was telling her of the superficial events of society and about those people who had once formed the circle of the old countess' intimate friends, who, in days

686

gone by, had been an active, lively, distinct "coterie," but who now were, for the most part, scattered here and there, like herself waiting for the final summons, gathering the last gleanings of what they had sowed in life. But these were the very ones, these contemporaries of hers, who seemed to the old countess the only important and actual world.

Natasha knew by Pierre's excitement that his journey had been interesting, that he had much he wanted to talk about but dared not mention in the old countess' presence.

Denisof, who had not been a member of the family long enough to understand the cause of Pierre's reserve, and, moreover, as a "malcontent" was greatly interested in what was going on in Petersburg, kept urging Pierre to tell about the trouble in the Semyonovsky regiment, which had just then broken out, and about Arakcheyef, and about the Bible Society. Pierre was occasionally drawn away and would begin to tell about these things, but Nikolai and Natasha would always bring him back to the health of Prince Ivan or Countess Marya Antonovna.

"Now tell me, what is all this nonsense about Hosner and Tararinof?" asked Denisof. "Is it going to last always?"

"Last always?" shouted Pierre. "It's worse than ever. The Bible Society is in full control of the government."

"What is that, my dear friend?" asked the countess, who had finished drinking her tea, and was now evidently anxious to find some excuse for peevishness after her meal. "What is that you said about the government? I don't understand."

"Yes, you know, mama," put in Nikolai, who knew how to translate what was said into language suitable for his mother's comprehension. "Prince A. N. Galitsin has started a society, and he is now a man of great influence, they say."

"Arakcheyef and Galitsin," said Pierre, incautiously, "are now the real heads of the government. And what a government! They pretend to see plots in everything; they are afraid of their own shadows."

"What! Prince Galitsin in any way blameworthy? He is a very fine man. I met him once at Marya Antonovna's," said the countess, in an offended tone, and she grew still more offended because no one made any further reply. She went on, "Nowadays, they're always criticizing everybody. What harm is there in the Gospel Society?"

And she got up (all the rest also arose), and, with a stern face, sailed into the sitting room, to her own table.

VIII

SHORTLY AFTER THIS the children came in to say good night. The children kissed everyone, the tutors and governesses bowed and left the room. Dessales and his charge alone were left. The tutor whispered to the boy to go downstairs.

"No, Monsieur Dessalles, I will ask my aunt to let me stay," replied Nikolusha Bolkonsky, also in a whisper. "Aunt, let me stay," pleaded Nikolusha, going to his aunt. His face was full of entreaty, excitement, and enthusiasm.

Princess Maria looked at him and turned to Pierre.

"When you are here, he cannot tear himself away," said she.

"Monsieur Dessalles, I will bring him to you very soon; good night," said Pierre, giving the Swiss gentleman his hand; and then, turning with a smile to Nikolusha, he said: "Really, we haven't had a chance to see each other. Marie, how much he is growing to resemble . . ." he added, turning to Princess Maria.

"My father?" asked the boy, flushing crimson, and surveying Pierre from head to foot with enraptured, gleaming eyes. Pierre nodded, and went on with his story, which had been interrupted by the children.

Princess Maria was working on her embroidery; Natasha, without dropping her eyes, gazed at her husband. Nikolai and Denisof had got up, asked for their pipes, and were smoking and getting an occasional cup of tea from Sonya, who sat downcast and in gloomy silence behind the samovar and kept asking questions of Pierre.

The conversation turned to the contemporary gossip about the higher members of the government, in which the majority of people usually find the chief interest in internal politics.

Denisof, who was dissatisfied with the government on account of his lack of success in the service, was rejoiced to learn of the follies which, in his opinion, were being committed at that time at Petersburg, and his comments on Pierre's remarks were made in keen and forcible language.

Nikolai, though he had no wish at all to find fault with everything, as Denisof did, felt that it was a thoroughly dignified and suitable thing to make some criticism of the government, and he felt that the fact that A had been appointed minister in this department, and that B had been appointed governor-general of this city, and that the sovereign had said this or that, and this minister something else, and all such things, were very significant. And he considered it necessary to take an interest in these things, and to ask Pierre questions.

But Natasha, who knew her husband's every habit and thought, saw that Pierre had long been vainly wishing to lead the conversation into another path, so that he might speak his mind and tell why he had gone to Petersburg to consult with his new friend, Prince Feodor, and she tried to help him with a question:

How had his business with Prince Feodor succeeded?

"What is that?" asked Nikolai.

"Oh, it's all one and the same thing," said Pierre, glancing around him. "All see that affairs are so rotten that they cannot be allowed to remain so, and that it is the duty of all honorable men to oppose them to the best of their ability."

"What can honorable men do?" asked Nikolai, slightly contracting his brows. "What can be done?"

"This is what," began Pierre, not sitting down, but striding through the room, occasionally pausing and making rapid gestures while he spoke. "I say, widen the circle of the Society; let the watchword be not merely virtue, but also independence and activity."

Nikolai angrily moved his chair, sat down in it, and while he listened to Pierre involuntarily coughed and scowled still more portentously.

"Yes, but what is to be the object of this activity?" he cried. "And what position do you hold toward the government?"

"What position? The position of helpers. The Society need not remain a secret one if the government would give us its favor. It is not only not hostile to the government, but this society is composed of genuine conservatives. It is a society of gentlemen in the full meaning of the word. We have banded together with the single aim of the general welfare and the general safety."

"Yes, but a secret society must necessarily be harmful and prejudicial— is bound to produce nothing but evil."

"Why so? Did the Tugendbund, which saved Europe"—even then they dared not imagine that it was Russia that saved Europe—"did that produce anything harmful? Tugendbund—that means a society of the virtuous; it was love, mutual aid; it was what Christ promised on the cross."

"Come, now, bwother, this Tugendbund is well enough for the sausage-eaters, but I don't understand it, and I don't say anything against it," cried Denisof, in his loud, decisive tones. "Evewything's wotten, and going to wuin, I admit, but as for your Tugendbund, I know nothing about it, and I don't like it—give us a weal wevolt, that's the talk! I'll be your man."

Pierre smiled, Natasha laughed, but Nikolai still further knitted his brows and tried to prove to Pierre that there was no revolution to be apprehended, and that all the danger of which he spoke existed only in his imagination.

Pierre argued to the contrary; and, as his powers of reasoning were stronger and better trained, Nikolai felt that he was driven into a corner. This still further incensed him, since, in the bottom of his heart, not through any process of reasoning, but by something more potent than logic, he knew the indubitable truth of his opinion.

"Well, this is what I tell you," he cried, rising, and with nervous motions putting his pipe in the corner and finally throwing it down. "I can't prove it to you. You say that everything is all rotten, and that there will be a revolution; I don't see it; but you say that an oath of secrecy is an essential condition, and in reply to this I tell you: You are my best friend—you know it—but if in founding a secret society you should undertake anything against the administration, whatever it was—I know that it would be my duty to obey the adminstration. And if Arakcheyef should order me to go against you with a squadron instantly, and cut you down, I would not hesitate a second, but would start. So, then, decide as you please."

An awkward silence followed these words.

Natasha was the first to speak; she took her husband's side and opposed her brother. Her defense was weak and clumsy, but her object was attained. The discussion was renewed on a different topic, and no longer in that hostile tone with which Nikolai's last words had been spoken.

When all got up to take supper, Nikolusha Bolkonsky went to Pierre with pale face and gleaming, luminous eyes.

"Uncle Pierre . . . you . . . no . . . if my papa were alive . . . he would agree with you, wouldn't he?" he asked.

Pierre suddenly realized what a peculiar, independent, complicated and powerful reasoning must have been operating in this lad's mind during this discussion; and when he recalled what had been said, he felt a sense of annoyance that the lad had listened to them. However, he had to answer him.

"I think so," he said reluctantly, and left the room.

IX

AT SUPPER the talk no longer turned on politics and secret societies, but, on the contrary, proved to be particularly interesting to Nikolai, owing to Denisof's bringing it round to reminiscences of the war of 1812, and here Pierre was particularly genial and diverting. And the relatives parted for the night on the friendliest terms.

After supper Nikolai, having changed his clothes in his library and given orders to his overseer, who was waiting for him, returned in his dressing gown to his bedroom. He found his wife still at her desk; she was writing something.

"What are you writing, Marie?" asked Nikolai.

Princess Maria reddened. She feared that what she was writing would not be understood and approved by her husband. She would have preferred to conceal it from him, but at the same time she was glad he had found her and that she had to tell him.

"It is my diary, Nikolai," said she, showing him a bluish notebook written in a fair, round hand.

"A diary!" exclaimed Nikolai, with just a shade of irony in his tone, and he took the notebook. It was written in French.

Dec. 16. To-day, Andryusha [her oldest son], when he woke up, did not wish to be dressed, and Mlle. Luise sent for me. He was capricious and wilful, and when I tried to threaten him he only grew the more obstinate and angry. Then I took him to my room, left him alone, and began to help the nurse get the rest of the children up, but I told him that I would not love him. He was silent for a long time, as if in amazement; then he jumped up, ran to me in nothing but his little nightshirt, and sobbed so that it was long before I could pacify him. It was evident that he was more grieved because he had troubled me than by anything else! Then, when I put him to bed this evening, and gave him his card, he again wept pitifully, and kissed me. You can do anything with him through his affections.

"What do you mean by 'his card'?" asked Nikolai.

"I have begun to give the older children cards in the evening, when they have been good."

Nikolai glanced into the luminous eyes that gazed at him, and continued to turn the leaves and read. In the diary was written everything concerning the children's lives that seemed important in the mother's eyes as expressing the character of the children, or that suggested thoughts concerning their education. These were, for the most part, the most insignificant trifles, but they did not seem so to the mother, or to the father when now, for the first time, he read this journal about his children.

The entry for the seventeenth of December was:

Mitya played pranks at table; papa would not let pastry be given to him. It was not given to him, but he looked so eagerly and longingly at the others while they were eating! I think that the punishment of not letting him have a taste of the sweets only increases his greediness. Must tell Nikolai.

Nikolai put down the book and looked at his wife. Her radiant eyes looked at him questioningly: Did he approve, or disapprove, of the diary? There could be no doubt of his approval or of his admiration for his wife.

"Perhaps there was no need to do it in such a pedantic manner, perhaps it was not necessary at all," thought Nikolai; but this unwearied, everlasting, sincere effort, the sole end and aim of which was the moral welfare of the children, aroused his admiration. If Nikolai could have analyzed his feelings, he would have discovered that the chief basis of his firm, tender and proud love for his wife was found in his amazement at her cordial sincerity and her spiritual nature, at that lofty moral world in which his wife always lived, but which for him was almost unattainable.

He was proud that she was so intelligent and so good, acknowledging his inferiority to her in the spiritual world, and rejoicing all the more that she in her soul not only belonged to him but formed a part of him.

"I approve, and thoroughly approve, my dear," said he, with a meaning look. And, after a little silence, he added: "I have behaved very badly today. Pierre and I had a discussion, and I lost my temper. Yes, I can't help it. He's such a child. I don't know what would become of him if Natasha did not hold him in leading strings. Can you imagine why he went to Petersburg? They have started there a . . ."

"Yes, I know," interrupted Princess Maria. "Natasha told me about it."

"Well, then, you must know," pursued Nikolai, growing hot at the mere memory of the quarrel, "he wanted to make me believe that it is the duty of every honorable man to go against the government, even though he has taken the oath of allegiance. . . . I am sorry you were not there. But they were all against me—Denisof and Natasha. . . . Natasha is ludicrous. You know how she keeps him under her shoe, but when there is anything to be decided, she can't speak her own mind at all. She simply says what he says," added Nikolai, giving way to that vague tendency which men have to criticize their nearest and best friends. Nikolai forgot that, word for word, what he said about Natasha might be said about him and his wife.

"Do you know, Marie," said he, "Ilya Mitrofanitch"—this was their manager—"came today from our Tambof estate, and told me that they would give eighty thousand for the forest there."

And Nikolai, with animated face, began to speak about the possibilities of very soon being able to buy back Otradnoye. "If only I live ten years longer, I will leave the children . . . in a splendid position."

Princess Maria listened to her husband and understood all that he said to her. She knew that when he thus thought aloud, he sometimes asked her what he had said, and was vexed to find that she had been thinking of something else. But she had to use great effort, for she was not in the least interested in what he said. Princess Maria's soul was always striving toward the Infinite, the Eternal, the Absolute, and therefore she could never rest content. Her face always wore the stern expression of a soul kept in high tension by suffering, and became a burden to the body.

Nikolai gazed at her.

"My God! What would happen to us if she should die, as it sometimes seems must be when her face has that expression?" he said to himself, and, stopping in front of the icons, he began to repeat his evening prayers.

X

NATASHA AND HER husband, left alone, also talked as only wife and husband can talk, namely, with extraordinary clearness and swiftness, recognizing and communicating each other's thoughts, by a method contrary to all logic, without the aid of reasoning, syllogisms, and deductions, but with absolute freedom. Natasha had become so used to talking thus freely with her husband that the surest sign, in her mind, that something was wrong between them was for Pierre to give a logical turn to his arguments with her. When he began to bring proofs and to talk with calm deliberation, and when she, carried away by his example, began to do the same, she knew they were surely on the verge of a quarrel.

From the moment that they were entirely alone, and Natasha with wide, happy eyes went quietly up to him, and, suddenly, with a swift motion, taking his head between both her hands, pressed it to her breast, and said: "Now, you are all mine, mine! You can't go!"—from that moment began the intimate dialogue, contrary to all the laws of logic—contrary simply because the talk ran at one and the same time upon such absolutely different topics. This simultaneous consideration of many things did not prevent their clearly understanding each other; on the contrary, it was the surest sign that they understood each other.

As in a vision everything is illusory, absurd, and incoherent, except the feeling which is the guide of the vision, so in this intercourse, so contrary to all the laws of logic, the phrases uttered were not logical and clear, while the feeling that guided them was.

Natasha told Pierre about her brother's mode of life, how she had suffered and found it impossible to live while he, her husband, was absent, and how she had grown fonder than ever of Marie, and how Marie was in every respect better than she was.

In saying this, Natasha was genuine in her acknowledgment that she saw Marie's superiority, but, at the same time, in saying this she claimed from Pierre that he should still prefer her to Marie and all other women, and now again, especially after he had been seeing many women in Petersburg, that he should assure her of this fact.

Pierre, in answering Natasha's words, told her how unendurable it was for him to go to dinners and parties with ladies.

"I had really forgotten how to talk with the ladies," said he. "It was simply a bore. Especially when I was so busy."

Natasha gazed steadily at him and went on:

"Marie! She is so lovely!" said she. "How well she knows how to treat the children! It seems as if she read their very souls! Last evening, for example, little Mitya began to be contrary . . ."

"But how like his father he is!" interrupted Pierre.

Natasha understood why he made this remark about the likeness between Mitenka and Nikolai: The remembrance of his discussion with his brother-in-law was disagreeable to him, and he wanted to hear her opinion of it.

"Nikolai has the weakness of not accepting anything unless it is received by everyone. But I know you set a special value on this to find a new approach," said she, repeating words once spoken by Pierre.

"No; the main thing is, Nikolai looks on thought and reasoning as amusement, almost as a waste of time," said Pierre. "Now he is collecting a library, and he has made it a rule never to buy a new book until he had read through what he has already bought—Sismondi and Rousseau and Montesquieu," added Pierre, with a smile. "Why, you know him as well as I do." He began to modify his words, but Natasha interrupted him, giving him to understand that this was unnecessary.

"So you think that he considers pure thought trifling."

"Yes, and for me everything else is trifling. All the time I was in Petersburg it seemed to me as if I saw all men in a dream. When I am engaged in thinking, then everything else seems a sheer waste of time."

"Ah! What a pity that I did not see you greet the children!" said Natasha. "Which one do you love most of all? Lisa, I suspect."

"Yes," said Pierre; and he went on with what was engrossing his attention. . . . "Nikolai says we have no business to think. Well, I can't help it. Not to mention that I felt in Petersburg—I can tell *you*—that if it were not for me, everything, all our scheme, would go to pieces; everyone was pulling in his own direction. But I succeeded in uniting all parties, and, besides, my idea is so simple and clear. You see, I don't say that we ought to act in opposition to this one or that one. We may be deceived. But I say: Let those who love what is right join hands, and let our whole watchword be action and virtue. Prince Sergii is a splendid man and very intelligent."

Natasha had no doubt that Pierre's idea was grand, but one thing confused her. This was that he was her husband. "Can it be that a man so important, so necessary to the world, can at the same time be my husband? How did this ever come about?"

She wanted to express this doubt to him. "No matter who should decide this question, he would be so much more intelligent than all of them, wouldn't he?" she asked herself, and in her imagination she reviewed the men who were very important to Pierre. None of these men, judging by his own story, had had such an important effect on him as Platon Karatayef.

"Do you know what I was thinking about?" she asked. . . . "About Platon Karatayef! How about him? Would he approve, now?"

Pierre was not at all surprised at this question. He understood the trend of his wife's thoughts.

"Platon Karatayef?" he repeated, and pondered, apparently honestly endeavoring to realize what Karatayef's opinion would be. "He would not understand, but still I think he would approve. Yes!"

"I love you awfully much!" said Natasha, suddenly. "Awfully! Awfully!"

"No, he would not approve," said Pierre, after a little reconsideration. "What he would approve would be this domestic life of ours. He so liked to see beauty, happiness, repose, in everything, and I would be proud if I could show him ourselves. Now you talk about parting! But you cannot understand what a strange feeling I have for you after being separated from you."

"Why, was it . . ." began Natasha.

"No, not that. I will never stop loving you. It would be impossible to love you more; but this is peculiar. . . . Well, yes!"

But he did not finish, because their eyes met and said the rest.

"What nonsense," suddenly cried Natasha, "to say that the honeymoon and real happiness are only during the first part of the time! On the contrary, now is the best of all. If only you would never go away from me! Do you remember how we quarreled? And I was always the one at fault. Always I. But as to what we quarreled about, I am sure I don't remember!"

694

"Always about one thing," said Pierre, smiling. "Jealo—"

"No, don't mention it, I can't endure it," cried Natasha, and a cold, cruel light flashed into her eyes. "Did you see her?" she added after a little silence.

"No, and if I had seen her I wouldn't have recognized her."

They were both silent.

"Ah! Do you know, when you were talking in the library, I was looking at you," pursued Natasha, evidently trying to drive away the cloud that had suddenly risen. "Well, you and our little boy are as alike as two drops of water." "Our little boy" was what she called her son. "It is time for me to go to him. . . . I'm sorry to have to go!"

They were silent for several seconds. Then suddenly they turned to each other, and each began to make some remark at the same instant.

Pierre began with self-confidence and impulsive warmth, Natasha with a quiet, blissful smile. Their words colliding, they both stopped to give each other the road, so to speak.

"No, what was it? Tell me! Tell me!"

"No, you tell me—what I was going to say was only nonsense," said Natasha.

Pierre went on with what he had begun to say. It was a continuation of his self-congratulatory opinion concerning the success of his visit at Petersburg. It seemed to him at that moment that he was called to give a new direction to all Russian society and to the whole world.

"I was only going to say that all ideas that have portentous consequences are always simple. My whole idea consists in this: That if all vicious men are bound together and constitute a force, then all honorable men ought to do the same. How simple that is!"

"Yes."

"And what were you going to say?"

"Only a bit of nonsense!"

"No, tell me what it was!"

"Oh, nothing, a mere trifle!" said Natasha, beaming with a still more radiant smile. "I was only going to say something about Petya: Today the nurse was going to take him from me. He began to laugh, then scowled a little and clung to me. Evidently he thought he was going to play peek-a-boo . . . awfully cunning. . . . There he is crying! Well, good-by!" and she left the room.

At the same time, below in Nikolusha's apartment, in his bedroom, the night lamp was burning as always—the lad was afraid of the darkness and they could not break him of this fear. Dessalles was sleeping high on his four pillows, and his Roman nose gave forth the measured sounds of snoring.

Nikolusha, who had just awakened from a nap, in a cold perspiration, with wide-open eyes sat up in bed and was looking straight ahead.

A strange dream had awakened him. In his dream he had seen himself and Pierre in helmets such as the men wore in his edition of Plutarch. He and his Uncle Pierre were marching forward at the head of a tremendous army. This army was composed of white, slanting threads, filling the air, like the cobwebs which float in the autumn, and which Dessalles called *le fil de la Vierge*—the Virgin's thread.

Before them was glory, just exactly like these threads, only much stouter. They—he and Pierre—were borne on lightly and joyously, ever nearer and nearer to their goal. Suddenly the threads that moved them began to slacken, to grow confused; it became trying. And his Uncle Nikolai stood in front of them in a stern and threatening posture.

"What have you been doing?" he demanded, pointing to his broken sealing wax and pens. "I loved you, but Arakcheyef has given me the order, and I will kill the first who advances."

Nikolusha looked around for Pierre, but Pierre was no longer there. In place of Pierre was his own father, Prince Andrei, and his father had no shape or form; but there he was, and in looking at him Nikolusha felt the weakness of love: he felt himself without strength, without bones—as it were, liquid. His father petted him and pitied him. But his Uncle Nikolai came ever closer and closer to him. Horror seized Nikolusha and he awoke.

"Father," he thought. "Father!" (Although there were in the house two excellent portraits, Nikolusha had never imagined Prince Andrei as existing in human form.) "My father was with me and caressed me. He approved of me. He approved of Uncle Pierre. Whatever he says I will do. All will know me, all will love me, all will praise me."

And suddenly Nikolusha felt the sobs fill his chest, and he burst into tears.

"Are you ill?" asked Dessalles' voice.

"No," replied Nikolusha, and he lay back on his pillow. "He is good and kind, I love him," he said to himself, of Dessalles; "but Uncle Pierre! Oh, what a wonderful man! But my father! My father! My father! Yes, I will do whatever he would approve."